DisasterLand:

Life's Greatest Adventure

Library of Congress Control Number: 2007928757
ISBN-13/EAN: 978-0-979-64410-8

Cover concept and layout by Seth Mowshowitz: www.misterseth.com
Cover design by Timm Hogerzeil: www.lichtung.tv
Interior design and layout by Conscious Images® LLC: www.consciousimages.com

FIRST INTERNATIONAL EDITION

Life's Greatest DISASTERLAND Adventure

JOHN NIERNBERGER

VisitDisasterLand! an imprint of Conscious Images® LLC
Overland Park, Kansas
2007
www.visitdisasterland.tv

For friends and family,
both mine and yours.

PART ONE. BEFORE.

WEDNESDAY

Elektra hated Terrorist plots. Earthquakes were her favorite, Hurricanes next: her team's mistakes were more easily concealed. They could be chalked up to Mother Nature.

Rest her soul, Elektra thought.

It all came down to one thing: fire. The Hurricane's *Mighty Floods* were but a drop in the bucket and couldn't hold a candle to the Earthquake's thrilling *Roaster*. It was primal, something deeply seated in the animal brain: no matter whether the guests expected it, even demanded it, once confronted with the reality of a raging fire seemingly out of control, all rationality went out the window.

Sure, everyone had their own limits and fears based on personal nature and history, but fires were where Elektra saw guests at their most basic: literally laid bare before family, friends, strangers—and the DisasterLand staff.

It was one of the things she truly loved about her job. That, and the money.

Elektra sighed, gently pulled aside the sheets and padded to the bathroom.

Flooding was somehow less immediate, less threatening, and experience, she felt, had taught her why: it was the physical nature of the death itself. Flooding was peaceful, maternal, a return to the great oneness of the womb whereas fire was a searing alchemical destruction into bare mineral essence. Hardwired over millennia, she suspected, our bodies instinctively knew this.

She sheepishly slipped out of her silk nightshirt, instantly chastising herself for being self-conscious. But it wasn't without reason. Someone, had to be one of the camera guys, had rigged her bathroom last party and one of her directors found her on a voyeur website, showering away. But the real kicker? Even after suing the site she

1

didn't get a dime.

Elektra jumped into the warm shower with a flash, anticipating the fragrant tranquility of her makeshift aromatherapy session. She had sent away for a custom blend of French oils on the recommendation of a girlfriend and as she strategically placed a few drops just above her moistened upper lip, soul levitating on the herbal scent.

She shut her eyes, imagining herself naked in a field of wildflowers. The diffused glass wall of pure sunlight next to her, fogged with charged liquid crystals, obscured the view of the atrium floor twenty-two stories below yet allowed the sun's brilliance to warm her bare skin and complete the illusion—until an army of flashbulbs exploded in her mind, each one aimed penetratingly at her womanhood. Blasted back to reality, she reeled.

Since the video, even her sacred shower had been poisoned.

Elektra was lead producer for DisasterLand, the world's first and only immersive disaster-themed adventure park. Her job was riding this mortal edge without getting caught in the riptide: timing events for optimum emotional impact, yet not, of course, to the point of lasting psychological damage.

DisasterLand exploited what reality TV producers had been pushing since the late 90's—emotional voyeurism—only on an infinitely more extreme level. By adding the spark of genuine danger and mortal fear to the tinderbox of human nature, remarkable personal transformation was possible. But there were, of course, dangers.

In a disaster of two thousand people, the odds were inevitable, even fated: there would be accidents. People would be injured, sometimes seriously. It was going to happen—and that was OK. But one *fatal* accident, on the other hand, and DisasterLand could be finished.

As a result, DisasterLand had ER capabilities matching those of a population one thousand times larger, far exceeding any other single entertainment facility's on the face of the earth. Likewise, an entire staff of psychologists formed a vital part of the production team, on-hand 24/7 to assess the emotional temperature of the house while scanning each guest in real time for signs of difficulty.

If any abnormality was sensed, unconditional treatment was offered, free of charge, for as long as it took to recover. And everyone in treatment did fully recover eventually, just as everyone walked away—sooner or later. Among the staff a contingent existed, albeit a small one, for whom this fact alone proved DisasterLand was blessed, a powerful testament to God's love.

Elektra wouldn't go that far. But she did believe her employment a miracle, and remained eternally grateful that she owned quite a few shares of stock, even if they weren't yet public. They'd come in handy some day.

She lathered up, checking the clock.

With the first season finale kicking off in two days, Elektra felt more unsettled than ever. Maybe it wasn't surprising—there was immense pressure to exceed the hype and end the first season with a triumph. DisasterLand had burst on the scene just twelve months ago, shocking the entertainment world and stunning suburban America. Guests expected the impossible and every show they had delivered. Yet this script, the most ambitious yet, would be the real acid test.

But she knew that wasn't it—she could deal with stage fright. There had been a rhythm to the season and recently it had been shattered, careening her and her entire crew off-balance. The script for next month's season opener was almost two weeks late—and Elektra hadn't even seen *one draft*. Greg, the Creative Director, had suddenly gone MIA on Monday and wasn't expected at today's dress rehearsal. Even though he had ceded the reigns for the show last Friday, he was *always* on the bridge for dress. It all added up to something, but Elektra couldn't imagine what.

Everyone was feeling it. Within the staff, DisasterLand was an emotional echo-chamber, a land-locked island far out in the Nevada desert with only military land for miles around. Without guests to focus on, emotions ricocheted wildly, reinforcing and amplifying each other in times of significant developments.

But she loved every moment of it. Honestly.

Elektra rinsed.

Yet each new terrorist script she produced made her question her life, her priorities, and, inevitably, her choice in mates. And right now the current one was still asleep in bed, snoring. Loudly.

On borrowed time. Only a few more days of good lovin' were coming to him before Elektra gave him the boot after the show's close. This infection would have to be quashed before her vacation.

Vacation. Yes, she needed to get on top of that.

"We can't go M-E on a Terrorist, Jude, you know that. Somebody'd friggin' kill the guy."

An actor's face was displayed on the flat-screen HDTV in front of them: young, shining, and brown.

Elektra was tense. There were routine hints of trouble on the floor judging by the reports flying across her PDA, but nothing directly demanding her attention.

Jude, the lead casting director, seemed distracted, "He's Tibetan, not *Middle Eastern*."

"You don't think some idiot from middle America gives a shit? For all they know, Tibet is *in* the Middle East."

"That's a cheap shot."

"Bullshit. I'm born and bred, you know that. You're fucking Canadian. It's different."

"Half Canadian. And we'll use people's fears against them. He's good, E. Done a couple of Hollyweird movies—bit parts but he steals the scenes. I think you should see him."

Elektra scowled. She took a long draw of her carrot-orange juice picked up in the tiny deli next door. The stakes were huge: casting a movie badly and no one got hurt.

The same couldn't be said for DisasterLand.

They were seated amidst the plush elegance of the spacious twenty-second floor conference room, just a few doors down from her own apartment and a welcome respite from the fray below. Jude had come from the bridge, six stories underground and his tension scented the room. Elektra, in full pre-game mode, was uniquely sensitive.

Show in one month. No script. No idea how many repertory they could use, how many A-list—if any—they'd have to recruit. When she had called Shae on it only minutes ago, he had only whispered, cryptically, "*Chill*."

Her gut said it was another terrorist script, despite their policy of not repeating themes back-to-back. She was beginning to wonder if terrorists were becoming a crutch, if perhaps a bad script had gotten through and they were scrambling.

But why hadn't she *seen it*? Seen *something*? It was unprecedented. And it wasn't cool.

Elektra sank into the warm leather around her, "Look, we're wasting our time. We don't even know what's coming, Jude."

"Someone may grab you, E. It's not a waste. Take advantage and play the field."

"It is. *Totally*. Nothing's going to stick. We're both stressed. It's futile."

She finished the juice, staring at the soothing, opaque window of sunlight. "What's going on with the script Jude?"

"I've got my theories..."

"Which are?"

"I think you're underestimating Greg. It's not a terrorist. I think it's bigger. Something *new*."

"*New*?" Elektra's mind stumbled. Something *new*?

Jude cracked a smile and the room's temperature dropped, "I see the holy trinity dissolving."

Earthquakes. Hurricanes. Terrorists. *That's what they did*. Silence descended as her mind masticated. Something *new*?

Why was she out of the loop?

Elektra flipped on the Feed, now pissed.

The closed-circuit live broadcast was the most relevant raw footage available, nonstop. During the show, it was the production staff's lifeline when away from the bridge. Edited slightly, it was a source of in-room entertainment for VIPs. But now, in the downtime before a major dress, the Feed was free-form.

And irreverent. The space-cadet MTV drop-outs at DTV were conducting man-on-the-street interviews on the floor with handicapped day players working their way through make-up tests for their roles as disaster victims.

Terrorist scripts always gave DisasterLand a circus element that Elektra relished, and she finally cracked a smile.

"Unbelievable."

"What is it?"

Just what they needed—and undoubtedly why Shae allowed the DTV crew out onto the floor in the first place, to relieve a little steam. When the pressure was on, send in the court jesters.

Elektra checked her PDA. The moment a show came together was always an unbeatable rush of single-focused groupthink and she was looking forward to it. If nothing else, this time it was a break from endless conjecture.

Elektra slurped her empty glass. "OK, what the fuck," she said, flipping off the Feed and returning to the actor's smiling face onscreen. "Bring him in. He's cute and maybe he knows a good guru. I need all the help I can get."

"You've got a guru," Jude said, noting her wish.

"I need the Dalai Lama. Nothing short's gonna cut it. Inner peace continues to elude me."

"You need a vacation, kiddo. Why don't you come with us to Greece? It'll be a blast."

"I'm going to lock myself in my apartment and weep."

"Lock yourself on an island and weep." He paused. "Think of the men." His eyebrows raised, "I am."

Her mouth opened in protest, but nothing came out. She tried again with the same result, and Jude laughed.

It really wasn't a bad idea. She desperately needed to get out of the country, even if it did result in her overloading on hotel Europorn.

She caught herself. DisasterLand was doing bad things to her head. What was it? Too many people? Too intense? Jude was right. She needed an *adventure*. A big one.

The irony cracked her up.

"Maybe," she winced.

Jude beamed with satisfaction and Elektra considered hitting him in the mouth. He always got his way, not because Elektra let him, but because he was *that good*.

He'd look better with fat lips, she realized. After the initial inconvenience, and maybe a little bloodshed, he'd appreciate it later.

Elektra's mind was wandering now, sensing a trail. Had she just come up with a natural alternative to injections? She'd rent a small store, charge $50 bucks a swipe, book twenty a day and make a killing. This was big. *Big*. And it just might cross over into the S&M market. She jotted it down in her notebook under 'retirement'. She could see it hitting.

"So you want his number?" Jude asked.

"Sorry?"

"Lhasa? The Tibetan actor? You want his number?"

"I'm writing down another great idea, Jude. A way to revolutionize the world and make it a more beautiful place, naturally."

"Always one for slogans. You should add that under whatever you're writing."

"Just you wait, Jude. The second I falter? *Out of here*. Then I save the world."

"Take me with you."

"I might. I just might. But only because you're gay."

Elektra shut her notebook slowly. It was times like these, she thought.

"Yeah," she sighed, "Gimme his number."

5

The air hissed through the vents of Persistent Media as Steve Beyers stared helplessly out the window at the pouring rain.

It only reminded him of his domesticated office existence, a pet entirely dependent upon its owner. He couldn't open the window to hear the rain, or even just to smell it. As a result, caught in the turbulence of sensorial disconnect on days like this, he couldn't focus.

During particularly weak moments he was forced outside with the handful of smokers to ground himself in his physical existence, acutely aware of the ironic lack of fresh air. The whole thing made him feel ridiculous—and guilty. At least he *had* a window. The thought of his junior creatives in the cube farm, fed artificial light and miserable air-conditioned air, made him weak.

Air-conditioned air. For the third time this summer, he felt a cold coming on. This air was surely worse than an airplane's and the irony was not lost: Persistent was a boutique ad agency, focused exclusively on health and medical clients.

Steve's eyes wandered up to the vents. He imagined innumerable diseases madly copulating inside, a wild orgy of bacterial ecstasy, a mutational fiesta resulting in offspring of The Rock-like constitutions launching out into his office to colonize his helpless body.

It seemed a nearly perfect plan and once realized had caused Steve no end of anxiety. He sneezed.

Looked at in a slightly different way, he had to admit there was a certain allure about the creature's primitive lives. Not about the freedom to conquer, but about the copulating. About the elegant simplicity of a life geared solely towards reproduction. It was downright romantic and Steve envied the near-mystic little creatures.

Steve sighed. It was time for action.

He grabbed the roll of packing tape that he'd stolen from shipping especially for the occasion and slipped over to the guest chair. He cautiously slid it forward, under the vent. *No more conquering*, he thought. *No more satisfaction.*

And no more fun at my expense.

Steve climbed up cautiously, holding on to the chair's back for support, his knees cracking. Unsteadily, he lined up the vent in his sights and felt the first tinges of vertigo.

God, I'm pathetic, he reminded himself.

The sickly stale, cold air blew against his face as he measured the vent and turned away to tear off several long strips. He'd have to do it fast, holding his breath. He bent over and hyper-ventilated to get a good lungful. In a red-faced flurry, he straightened, awkwardly placing the long strips rapidly over the vent.

He finished proudly, his breath exploding as he felt for leaks. None.

Steve turned to dismount and noticed Michael Murphy, Persistent's Chief

Operating Officer, standing in his doorway. He stepped down, slowly.

It always happens like this, doesn't it?

Mike was wearing his overcoat. "Morning, Steve. You know we get discounts over at the gym."

"Morning, Michael. Just closing the vent... my immune system's suffering," Steve replied, tossing the tape back into his desk drawer.

"We had them cleaned a month ago, remember? On your request?"

"Of course... but another cold's coming on. Better safe than sorry, you know, with the amount of jobs coming in."

Michael smiled, eyeing him curiously, "Listen, you available for an early lunch? On the company?"

"Of course, Michael. Love to."

Steve looked up, catching Michael's eye for the first time. He didn't like it.

"I'll meet you there, buddy. We're on the sly."

"Right." Steve felt his sphincter tighten. "Let me hit the bathroom first."

As he entered O.J. HoulaBenebee's, the Midwest's new fast/casual sensation, Steve's discomfort morphed into dread.

Work had been ugly lately, the ugliest he could remember since starting in advertising, somewhat accidentally, fifteen years ago. And now Michael had snuck him to lunch. Something was on the boil.

Despite being in the health care industry—with healthy inflation, an aging population and a rosy future—Persistent wasn't immune from the intensely competitive, ADHD economy. There was a new paranoia, a new *angst*, within the agency. Everyone was watching their back. And everyone had to produce.

It had been Michael's doing. He'd been swept in as the savior to man the guillotine and clean-up the agency, but so far had only succeeded in cutting a few costs and making everyone's life miserable. Persistent had gained no new clients and revenues were stagnant.

For Steve, it had all been particularly clear. As one of a quad of creative VPs, Michael's new org chart meant each team worked as a sort of mini-agency, competing for each job with the other three teams. The ultimate prize was clear: Persistent's long-time Creative Director had been let go two months ago and the desk still sat empty.

Steve's team had fared well in the competition—the best—but his stress level was through the roof and relations with his co-workers had never been worse. *We're focusing the guns*, Michael had said, and he was right. Life at Persistent was now a constant battle.

Permanent insecurity, Steve thought. *No wonder I'm on edge.*

In fact, *insecurity's the new security.*

Steve paused. That's *nice*, he thought. That's *really, really* nice. *That's old-days nice!*

While the sprightly hostess bounced them to their table, Steve got the shiver he associated with a winner. He jotted it down on his notepad, thinking post-9/11 heartburn slogan.

They arrived at the faux-antique wooden booth and Michael excused himself to the restroom. Steve tried to make himself comfortable.

No, the old days were gone. So why was he sticking around? There was the thrill of a new slogan. Obviously. And the satisfaction of seeing his work on TV, during ballgames, at the store. But he'd had enough ego-trips in his career.

Was it because he thought he was making a difference? Thought he was *influencing people*? But what kind of difference was he making? And *how* was he influencing them? Towards health? Or *away from it*?

He just wasn't sure anymore. Maybe that was it too. The older he got, and the wiser, the more warily he treated the whole industry.

Steve leaned back from the table. *Something just isn't right anymore*, he thought. *It just doesn't feel the same.*

With a resigned breath, Steve took out a tiny pharmaceutical bottle from his pocket. *Happinol®*.

Steve had started the anti-depressant a month ago, secretly, without telling anyone, even his family—against the urging of his shrink. She had warned him of possible side effects, including temporary emotional instability and said the only moral thing to do was to prepare his family. But he didn't. Stupidly. He just couldn't.

His doctor had recommended the psychological visit after sensing a general slackening in his mental and physical health, and after one visit Steve was given the prescription. That bothered him. The psychiatrist didn't even *know* him.

Steve had fought taking the pills for a week, finally giving in on one condition: that he would tell no one. If Barb noticed a positive change, he would continue, simply using them to raise the emotional tide. His hope was that eventually this change would be infectious, spreading through the family to the point where eventually he wouldn't need them anymore.

But if he didn't notice a difference in three months, he'd stop and never see the psychiatrist again. He'd try something different. Either way, in his mind it was short term. Regardless of whatever the label said.

Steve dropped one into his hand and eyed the tiny pink pill with loathing. So far, he just felt dull. He had lost his passion, his spark, and become a worse and worse lover.

As Michael approached Steve popped the pill, quickly dropping the bottle back into his pocket. *No signs of weakness.*

Michael took his seat. He cleared his throat and began slowly, building steam, "It's time... at Persistent... for the announcement of a new Creative Director..."

Steve's heart skipped and he solemnly nodded his wholehearted agreement. *Was the end of the Happinol in sight?*

"... but it's not going to be you."

Pete Beyers stood on second base for only the third time this season and surveyed the scene around him. Life looked different from second base, that's for sure. From third? Unthinkable, even at an infinitesimal 60 feet.

The score was 2-2 with one out. It was the bottom of the seventh and last inning, and a win meant a chance at the playoffs. It was a big moment for a hit, and Pete had pulled through.

It had been a fastball, right down the middle and Pete took it cleanly, sending it into left field past the third baseman for a stand-up double. It was remarkable achievement, a virtual statistical impossibility, and one of those things that he knew would stay with him for life. The hit had simply been a miracle.

From the stands, despite the evening's chronic frown, his dad was glowing. All in all, it was a damn fine day to be 14.

"Pitcher pitcher, smell you from here!" Pete called. He took a short lead and drew the thick, August air of Kansas into his nostrils. It meant, at the very least, girls. It had to.

"You should pitch T-ball!"

What Pete lacked, and he lacked it almost completely, was the ability to actually place bat-to-ball. It wasn't physical. He wasn't lacking hand-eye coordination or strength. It was mental. It was fear.

"Yo pitcher! Did you fart or is that your breath?!"

Fear that the rock-hard ball was going to knock him unconscious, or break his nose or his cheek or worst of all, crush his eye socket. He hadn't seen any of it actually happen in person, but he knew it had to, all the time.

Just watching that ball sailing in—particularly from a right-hander—he felt lucky just to be able to hold his bladder let alone connect. Videotape after videotape had captured his face mid-swing: cheeks puffed out and eyes closed. *Closed.*

The blatant show of weakness was not only depressing to him, but to his father as well, which hurt Pete even more. The result was his self-proclaimed retirement from the sport at the end of the season, possibly only two games away at this point and none too soon.

"Heads up, Spikers! Heads up!" his dad's voice boomed, *"Bring 'er home, Spikers!"*

Spike. The nickname had appeared to his dad as a vision, while struggling to witness his son's particularly graphic birth. It had stuck.

Pete had grown into it, now insisting he was named after Spike Lee and cultivating his own subtle inner blackness, manifest in his relentless pursuit of socially-conscious hip-hop as well as the continual amplification of his own street lingo.

He had recently begun to fancy himself dermally camouflaged to hide the black one inside. Stealth. It was an evolutionary advantage, like the way some harmless butterflies are camouflaged to look like poisonous Monarchs.

Spike. The only black kid on the team. *'Cept he was white.*

Pete extended his lead as the pitcher leaned back, contorting his arm desperately, his face following as if in homage. He let loose a vicious ripper.

But the Tiger's super-star was up for it and Davey whacked a liner past the first baseman. The outfielder gave chase.

Pete raced for third, realizing the third base coach and Davey's dad wasn't watching him at all, preferring the drama of his own boy's powerful show of potency.

"'attaboy Davey! Attaboy!" the coach screamed, hands overhead.

Pete was on his own. He turned, instantly gauging the situation. The outfielder was bearing down on the ball. A throw was imminent.

Fuck it, thought Pete. He accelerated, rounding the base, and raced for home. By the time the coach realized what was happening, it was too late. Pete was gone.

The outfielder bare-handed the ball and fired. He'd rushed it and the ball sailed, dragging the catcher hopelessly off the line to the first-base side and leaving Pete a clear shot at the plate. Sensing the increased volume from the stands, Pete slid.

"*SAFE!*"

With the umpire's bellow still ringing in his ears, Pete emerged from the cloud of dirt to strike the pose he had wishfully practiced on video before every game. As his teammates ecstatically spilled off the bench, Pete shut his eyes to drink in the moment, hands outstretched and head thrown back.

Moments later Pete raised his head to realize the Tigers had continued on past him and out to Davey, now held aloft by his beaming father and dropped into the onrushing swarm like so much chum.

Pete was standing on home plate, alone.

"Nice job, kid," the umpire said, removing his mask, "Way to go."

Pete barely heard him. He looked up to the stands to see Davey's mom on her feet, hands clasped desperately to her cheeks and beaming with pride, eyes locked on husband and son leading the celebrations below. She'd spawned a winner and knew it.

Pete missed his own mother. She'd stopped coming weeks ago and he knew why.

"You showed 'em, Spikers!" his dad yelled from behind the fence in front of him, fists clenched overhead, eyes wild.

Parents were now rushing by him to join their kids in the tangled, rolling swarm of gold and black. But Pete wasn't interested.

"Yo, I'm out," he said, to no one, and began the slow walk to his dad's car, alone.

In the back of her dad's hand-me-down millennium Lexus, Sarah Beyers lay snogging as if the world was about to end. And, in a way, it was: she knew she'd never see Rodney again once she left for college, and that was just three short weeks away.

By all accounts this was a good thing—Sarah liked bad boys and Hot Rod, as he was infamously known, was the *worst*.

Currently, however, with his fingers probing inside her body, these were very distant thoughts. She moaned, pulling him on top of her.

Of her close friends, Sarah was the adventurous one. She maintained an absolutely fierce social life and few of her peers—boys included—could keep up with her. Yet through school she easily managed to keep straight A's and was headed to Columbia University to study journalism.

Yet even Sarah had her hands full with Hot Rod.

They'd met under questionable circumstances at the beginning of the summer, escaping arrest at the wildest party she'd ever experienced. A remarkably short time later they were naked in the back of her car and had pretty much stayed there.

Rod was into 'bikes and worked in his brother's chop shop. Twenty, he had never gone to college—no reason. In a couple of years he was going to start his own shop and Sarah knew he could pull it off.

It wasn't the financial prospects that doomed their future, it was the tactile complications. It took him ages to degrease after work, and despite his best efforts, Sarah still felt like she was mating with an eel.

And every girl had her limits.

Yet despite the viscosity, it had easily been the best summer of her life with long sunset bike rides through the prairie between Kansas City and Lawrence, often just for the hell of it. The wind in her hair had become a fix and she couldn't imagine how she was going to live without it.

Speaking of fixes, Rod had also managed a seemingly endless supply of drugs and always had a little something with him. Pot, coke, or once, even Ecstasy and she'd sampled them all. She had found the Ecstasy particularly seductive as her entire being vibrated with love and energy, empathy, and the wonders of life. The other stuff she could mostly do without.

Mostly.

She had a suspicion Rod's brother had a side-gig of putting secret compartments in cars for drug smuggling. There were the odd hours, and they constantly had the best drugs of anyone she knew—and she knew everyone. Even at the tender age of eighteen, she was a fierce networker.

If her parents knew any of this, of course, they'd have locked her in the basement. Yet somehow Sarah managed to pacify their suspicions, while never actually explaining where she spent all of her time.

They knew one side of her life—the journalism, student newspaper editor, straight A's—but didn't manage to learn much about Rod, his bikes, and his drugs.

Rod's fingers found her spot and she slid deeper into the back seat. She pulled up her T-shirt and let Rod have at her chest.

Her phone rang and she jerked.

"Hold on, hold on..." she squirmed. But it only intensified his desire.

She slapped his head, "Hottie! Stop!"

"Come on, you serious?"

"My phone's not key protected! Hold on..."

She managed to delicately extricate the phone from her back pocket. Thankfully it hadn't been answered. She checked the caller ID.

Home.

"Gimme a large vanilla and a super-extreme mega-fudge assault for the game winner here."

Steve smiled proudly while Pete feigned modesty to the cute girl behind the counter at the frozen custard shop, taking care to display his dusty uniform.

After she had rung up the total and disappeared to finish the order, Steve pleaded with Pete not to tell his mother about the treat. Winner or no winner, he didn't want her feeling even more left out.

Steve had phoned Barb from the stadium, amidst the cheering, and she had melancholically began a celebratory casserole for four. Sarah was even going to cut her newspaper editorial meeting short to celebrate Pete's big night. All signs pointed to an old-fashioned evening home together, basking in Pete's redemption.

Steve took the only available picnic table out front, the farthest away, while Pete waited for their order at the counter. In the distance, he noticed a homeless man working his way slowly through the parking lot without success. Steve sensed a nervousness rising around him as the man neared the packed tables and turned away, the evening's glow temporarily dulled.

Pete pulled off his cap and slapped the dirt from his uniform, just loud enough to draw attention. He thought he recognized the girl completing their order as a friend of Sarah's. He imagined their conversation, hoping word would spread: *Hey Sarah, wasn't that your little bro' at the custard shop? Didn't he win the big game? You know he's kind of cute.*

Steve watched his son preening. No doubt about it, he thought, they were going to have their hands full with this one. But after Sarah, who had been remarkably easy, they probably deserved it.

The wind had picked up and a few clouds had begun to roll in, dropping the temperature noticeably. They had plans to go to Barb's parents over the weekend and Steve hoped the weather would hold. Late summer in Kansas could be more than a little unsettled.

"Excuse me..." the gruff voice asked.

Steve turned to face the parking lot, heart sinking.

"You got a Benjamin? I haven't eaten for two days." The man's sour tang slapped Steve senses.

Other patrons were watching the exchange with discomfort, as if an army of homeless lay in wait to begin their assault if Steve broke ranks. But he knew this guy was probably the only homeless man in the entire county, and soon destined to be extradited to the comparatively cutthroat inner city.

"Nothing even close." A pained disappointment descended on the man's face and Steve shook his head, sympathetically. "I'm sorry."

"How about one of them custards?" he nodded in Pete's direction. "Whaddya say guy? Chocolate?"

That was harder to resist. Pete was circling in the distance with their custards, his radiant pride dimmed. Steve waved Pete forward, nodding resignedly. A glimmer finally shone in the homeless man's eye.

"Spike, did you pick up our change?"

Pete glanced at the homeless man, "Sure did, DJ."

"Can you give it to our friend here?"

Pete placed the custards carefully on the table and reached into his pocket. "Here you go bro'," he said, dropping the change in the man's outstretched hand.

"Now that's for a custard," Steve warned. "No drugs or anything."

"That's right. Thanks guy."

He headed for the counter and Pete and Steve dug into their custards. Moments later, though, Steve read the drop in Pete's face and his anger rose.

"Sorry to disturb you again..."

Steve paused, finally turning to sternly face the stranger now licking a chocolate cone, "Yes?"

"I believe this is yours."

The man pulled out a thin, golden DVD case from his pocket and handed it to Steve. Pete gasped, leapt up.

"*DJ!*" he screamed.

Steve hesitated, confused and wary.

"Grab it DJ! *Grab it!*" Pete screamed.

The man's eyes twinkled. Hushed exclamations surged through the crowd as families stared on in shock.

"This isn't..."

"*TAKE IT!*" Pete shrieked.

Steve did, slowly, staring. It was sealed with a golden ribbon.

Pete was bouncing frantically, his face madly contorted, "Open it! *Open it!*"

The stranger smiled, patiently, as Steve cautiously unsealed the box at the continued insistence of his kinetic son.

Inside was a golden disc.

DisasterLand, it said in raised gold lettering, *Life's Greatest Adventure*.

"Is it real *is it real IS IT REAL?*" Pete choked.

"It sure is, my friends. On Friday, *you're going to DisasterLand!*"

Pete, in front of the gawking onlookers and somewhat embarrassingly, fainted dead away.

Steve and Peter's googly-eyed expressions of nirvana betrayed their bliss as they sped past Barb's outstretched hands and on into the house. She had rushed out to meet her heroes, but somehow ended up alone.

Barb yelled something about the game-winning hit but it drew only slightly confused backwards glances as the boys bounded inside the house, front door slamming behind them.

Moments later, a fanfare of tremendous import launched from the Beyers' surround-sound home theater and Steve fumbled for the remote to lower the volume to tolerable levels. It was the DisasterLand theme, undoubtedly heard by the entire neighborhood.

Good, Steve realized on second thought.

He turned it up.

Barb approached the living room cautiously, examining her curious men dwarfed by the wide-screen TV and sonic boom, their faces bathed in the glow of the legendary twin geodesic domes.

These were images very few people on the planet had witnessed, images which brashly proclaimed the family's privilege as the invited few. DisasterLand's secrecy was notorious and any representation of their facilities in the media was strictly prohibited. Yet Google Earth geeks had launched countless speculative websites where artists— some even famous—had mocked-up reconstructions based on these grainy images.

They'd obviously done badly.

The domes revolved like glistening jewels nestled into their secret desert valley. Music exclaimed their infinite potential.

Emerging from its larger brother like a cell dividing, the smaller dome housed a rolling expanse of natural forested park, an alien explosion of green amidst the exterior desert scrub.

The floor of the larger dome was dotted with a brilliant shimmering mosaic of rainbow colors and it gradually became evident that these dots were people. Hundreds and hundreds of people, celebrating. It was a knock-down, full-on, sunrise party.

Barb edged in and Steve shot her a glance. Pete didn't flinch.

The domes continued to spin profoundly, revealing a thin, vertical, mirrored glass extension on the largest dome. The valley's sun-lit mountains were reflected, bubble-like, in the tower's skin.

"What movie's this?" Barb asked, nervously.

"It's not a movie! It's an adventure!" yelled Pete, *"We're going to DisasterLand!"*

"No way!" Sarah appeared moments later, breathless, startled mid-shower by the infamous music. She was draped in a towel, hair still wet, and looking to her mother for confirmation. Barb's face was blank.

"We are too! It's gonna be *dirty!*"

Sarah slid the curtain over the sliding-glass door and tucked in excitedly behind her mom. The Beyers stared, bodies humming, awash in a sea of adrenalin.

"Seriously, Steve. Where did you get this?" Barb's heart was pounding, "If this is a joke I don't get it."

DisasterLand was the new American dream and the waiting list stood at two years and growing for the privilege to drop twenty-five grand a family and have lives changed forever. The Beyers didn't have that kind of time. Or money.

Pete stammered, "A homeless man gave it to us, Superstar! It's the golden disc! It has a secret code!"

The screen went black and their living room exploded with silence.

"A homeless man?"

Cheering shattered the void and a bass-drenched dance groove followed, pounding the helpless family. Sarah squealed.

"As soon as we arrived we knew we were in for the time of our lives," exclaimed a breathless voice with impressive gravity.

Onscreen, a pristine, rushing river. Tanned, trim guests were swimming gracefully in the current. On the surrounding beach, relaxed guests sunbathed while others enjoyed colorful drinks in lawn chairs scattered across the sand.

Barb returned Steve's glance, desperately seeking confirmation.

The groove broke down, and an angelic chord filled the room as a pot-bellied Caribbean man in his 60's appeared, beaming as he strolled along the river's edge. He was dressed only in Bermuda shorts and an intricate, weighty floral lei. Cocktail in hand, his grey dreads swayed with the rhythm of the beat.

"It's MagicD!" Pete yelled. "He's *real!*"

"MagicD?" Barb asked.

"*The DisasterMaster!*" Pete leapt up.

MagicD extended his arms majestically, "Whatevah yah doo, whoevah yah be, DisastahLand is fah you *an' me!*"

The music climaxed and the windows shook. Pete raced an excited circle around the living room and dropped to his knees, hands overhead in triumph. "*This - is - so tight!*" he shrieked.

"Whatevah yah speed ah life, we match it," MagicD called.

Guests were throwing Frisbees on the green. Other families were winding their way through thickly-forested trails while rock climbers scaled a giant cliff face overhead.

"Whatevah yah desire, we offah it."

A picturesque seaside village appeared in the heart of DisasterLand, underneath the vast glass dome. Guests were lounging at bustling street cafés, sharing long lunches while excited shoppers landed at the numerous upscale retailers surrounding them.

"Whomevah yah love, we deepen it."

The music relaxed and the bustle faded as romantic couples strolled next to the river on moonlit walks. Others were enjoying extravagant dinners and tango dancing. Another couple was receiving simultaneous massages in an upscale health spa.

15

Another young couple appeared, soaking in their private candle-lit hot tub. Behind them the sun was setting over the valley through an enormous picture window. Barb gasped.

The woman leaned her head onto her man's well-shaped shoulder and smiled, "It's impossible to do everything... so there's never any pressure!" He kissed her forehead as the image faded.

"It's play time fah dah whole fam'ly. An' daddies, most expenses ah included so dere's nevah anah worries!" MagicD winked.

Enthusiastic teenagers emerged from neon movie theaters, young boys competed intensively in advanced video-game clusters and girls tried on clothes in luxurious dressing rooms.

"I've had more fun in two days than I've had in my whole life! This is *so cool!*" yelled a sweaty kid.

MagicD reappeared, amidst the flashing lights and swaying bodies of a nightclub as a band rocked out in front of the head-nodding masses. Suddenly, the dance-floor lights transformed and a menacing red glow played over MagicD's dark face. Mystery was in his eye.

"An' fah dose of yah needin' ah lit'l action, DisastahLand wi' be a *killah* workout!"

Barb grabbed Sarah as the music exploded, fiercely. Pete went catatonic.

"No contact wit dah outsihde so nah-ting tah worry 'bout... but survihval!"

Pounding rain. Rising water. Stunned guests struggling desperately against the current. A woman swept away by rushing water. A horrified scream echoed as lightning flashed.

Smoke. A wall of fire. Masked guests fleeing. A family trapped in a burning corridor. A singed teddy bear. Screams.

An explosion. Twisted metal. Ghastly, blood-soaked blankets. Half-covered legs. Gunfire.

A building collapsing. Lamp-posts falling, twisting as they hit ground. Families stumbling as debris rained down.

MagicD's voice echoed strong and solid, "Yah fam'ly is yah hope. Nah-ting else. To-gedah."

The DisasterLand logo appeared, powerfully, a bastion of strength.

"Life's Greahtest Adventah!"

Steve, Barb, Peter and Sarah gawked. Sarah took her mom's hand as the music blasted on, relentlessly.

An introspective family of three appeared, the teenage son holding back tears. "Sure I was scared. But I just knew I was going to survive."

His mother hugged him. "I just kept thinking of my son... and how I hoped he'd make it."

Her husband pecked her on the cheek. "We really became a family that week."

MagicD stepped in, wrapped his arms around the beaming family, "Yah safety is gua-ran-teed..." he said, and the music hung, "... excehpt in dah case of anh accident!"

An emergency room, an operation taking place. Over the surgeon's shoulder, giant glass windows looked out onto the atrium. Guests watched the procedure in awe.

The surgeon, a distinguished graying man in his late 50's, paused proudly. "DisasterLand offers the world's best accident-related health care in the world. *On site.* We're so confident about our services, we let you watch."

"Evrah-one's ah survivah... Evrah-one's ah he-ro.... An' evrah fam'ly is dah winnah!"

A family in an examination room, tired but reflective. At peace. The boy's arm was in a cast.

"We had been feeling distant, like we couldn't talk..." the older sister said.

"But now that we've pulled through a disaster together, we know we can conquer anything," her father added.

"I can't imagine our lives without DisasterLand," his wife replied. "Even the simplest day-to-day activities has taken on new meaning!"

The daughter agreed, "We value each other just being around."

The mother leaned in, whispering, "DisasterLand saved our marriage."

Her husband winked, "DisasterLand made me a new man."

The boy smiled, "DisasterLand has prepared me for success in life!"

The family laughed, hugging, as a tear dropped from the mother's eye. "It's heaven on Earth..."

The music swelled sweetly.

MagicD joined them, in a tuxedo. "Ninety pah-cent of guests want tah return wit-tin dah year." He winked. "But dey can't! It's ah once in ah lifetime oppah-tunity!"

He paused, allowing it all to sink in.

"An' it's yah fam'ly's secret for-evah. Yah *can't* tell anahbody else, so yah *don't!* Ah secret for yah fam'ly to *treasure.* Wit *pride.*"

The family faded out, replaced by the velvet desert sky where the DisasterLand logo was waiting.

"Dis is nah accident mah friends, yah are comin' to Disastahland! Dah season finale!"

"The *FINALE!*" screamed Pete. *"Dope!"*

The twin domes reappeared, beckoning all who beheld their majesty.

"Go tah dah website, *visitdisasterland.tv,* wit dis DVD in yah computah. We take care of evrah-ting." He paused. "We evahn pick it bahck up! Tahnight!"

MagicD laughed, heartily, "See yah verah soon!"

DisasterLand's theme recapitulated, softly, fading with the domes...

The family stared at the darkening television in trembling silence. Pete was the first to react, ejecting the DVD and racing into his dad's office.

As emotions continued to settle Steve glanced at the girls, "Yeah," he said. "We're going. *Friday.*"

Sarah ran for her mobile.

Shae Gibbons returned his drink to the bar with a gleeful snicker. It had been a marvelous day and his dry, top shelf martini in the tenth-floor DisasterLand VIP lounge was going down a treat.

The day had been good. So good, in fact, so impossibly good in so many different ways, that Shae was having a very difficult time preventing himself from breaking down and giggling like a child. Continuously, of course, for every so often he had to let one slip, lest he absolutely boil over. It was as if he'd worked his whole life for this one day.

Two drink cap tonight, he warned himself. *There's danger in the air.*

"What's so funny?", the bartender asked, a sweet young mystery who already had him enthralled.

Shae didn't recognize her, but not such a surprise anymore — promotions throughout DisasterLand had been rapid, a result of the constant filtering of employees.

The reverse certainly wasn't true, however. Shae was founder, president and CEO of DisasterLand, Inc., and it was impossible that the bartender didn't know it.

The crowd around them was sparse, yet the room buzzed with the electric afterglow of the show's first full dress rehearsal.

Shae smiled. "That's a good question. Simple, but remarkably penetrating and deceptively difficult to answer."

The bartender stared, "OK... whatever. I'm just asking. You know, *trying to make conversation.*" She smiled coyly, grabbing a handful of lemons to chop. "If you come up with something, I'll be over here."

Shae watched her saunter over to the opposite end of the bar. He giggled.

"I'm just trying to save you embarrassment, you know," she called, overhearing him, "You don't want me calling the cops later 'cause you're all scarin' me." She anticipated a giggle, and as it came she joined in, rolling her eyes.

Shae would have been just as comfortable on late-night television. At this very moment of his young life, he was only 36, Shae was sitting on top of a gusher and riding it to the stratosphere.

The Mouse would soon be crushed, an outdated relic of the twentieth-century. He'd caught them with their pants down. Big time.

Shae giggled at the vision of the famous rodent's pimply ass and grabbed his mobile. Dialed. "Where are you?"

"Coming," Nick replied, "trouble with a band. Seems the lead guitarist was arrested with two transvestites and a bag of smack last night and they're having trouble springing him in time for the gig."

"Some people know how to live, Nick. What's our curse?"

"He may be living but it's gonna break up the band. A gig *here* and the dude blew it for a night of... Jesus, fuck knows what."

Shae's imagination wandered, slightly unpleasantly.

"... Anyway, the rest of the band is pissed. Want to replace him, but their manager fucked up the contracts and they can't do it. It's ugly."

"They should fire *his* ass."

"Someone's going to the lions, it's just not clear who. And when. Anyway, I'll be up in ten."

"Right."

Shae flipped the phone closed... and immediately reopened it. He dialed advertising.

"Amy, gimme Cindy. It's the cheese here."

"Evening, Shae. She's in a media meeting."

Shae checked his watch. Seven.

"Gimme her voicemail... and don't work past nine."

"Thanks for your concern, Shae, that's lovely. Very civilized." He liked her. "Hang on..."

Cindy's voice came on and he waited for the trademarked explosion to begin his message. For Shae, it was all in the little touches.

"Cindy, Shae. Congratulations. Huge success today with the DVDs. I've been watching the Feed." He collected himself, continued. "Listen, what about some kind of campaign... some sort of famous naked rodent campaign... you know, sort of caught Disneyland with their pants down? Can you work with that? Maybe even just internally, you know, for morale? Everyone's working so damned hard this show. Thanks, sweetie. I'm in DmZ."

He hung up and removed his martini to the wall of floor-to-ceiling smoked windows overlooking the million square-foot atrium that was the main center of the DisasterLand experience. Even though Shae was intimately involved with its design and construction, the engineering marvel still stole his breath.

He sipped his martini and felt his senses expand. He was in the zone. The universe was at peace.

Ten stories below, last-minute tweaks were continuing on the village below, inside the maze of tiny, winding streets. The ancient Middle Eastern desert village was exquisitely aged and nestled within a traditional, protective stone wall which itself lay well inside the periphery of the dome. A perfect setting for the upcoming drama.

In the village center, a futuristic three-story sculpted steel fountain rose in contrast, with a reflecting pool and garden radiating out from its base. Shae paused to watch it cycle through it's remarkably advanced hydrological effects—first letting loose a massive tidal wave of water, then presenting several dramatic and profound explosions, then, finally, in precisely timed bursts the shaking of an earthquake. He chuckled.

There had been a few minor technical problems during the dress but nothing serious or out of the ordinary, and the artisans would swiftly work their miracles. All systems would be go for the morning's continued rehearsal.

Previous civilizations were judged by the engineering of their monuments, and the great cultures of the past had built temples to the very foundation of their society—their gods, their pharaohs and their kings. To Shae, DisasterLand was a temple to entertainment and it would live forever in legend like the gardens of Shangri-La.

All this was eloquently proven by the sheer bubble of intellectual property that surrounded the park. As large and imposing a physical presence DisasterLand was, intellectually it was even more so, exemplified by the record-setting number of patents they had pending and the fact that one whole wing of Purgatory, DisasterLand's in-house law firm of more than 100 attorneys, was devoted solely to patent law.

Bit by bit, DisasterLand's radiant glory was slowly being leaked to the public by DL_PR to subtly construct the myth while keeping the park firmly in the headlines. All while remaining acutely aware that a magician simply doesn't give away his tricks.

They were on the edge of a new culture, a new modernity, even a new humanity and everyone felt it from Shae all the way down to the employees in the laundry. DisasterLand had a vibe.

And this show was set to break all the records.

Shae finished his martini and checked his watch. Nick was absolutely killing him. Shae had news, the biggest since he got a verbal agreement on VC in 2001 which formed the company. Nick was going to be the first to know.

"I know a desperate man when I see him," called the bartender. She motioned to a frosty martini on the bar, resting in a glorious halo of light.

Shae giggled. She was good.

"Rockin' the Wonka!" Nick called, entering DmZ and acknowledging the Feed.

The nationwide coverage of the day's DVD giveaways continued, unabated, saturating the popular consciousness in ways far more effective than DL_PR had ever dreamed. Local features were running nonstop and making their way up the food chain, leading to a network feeding-frenzy over the winners now numbering fourteen and rising. Anticipations were growing that this would be the leading story on all four networks' late news.

The dispersal was perfectly timed. It was a publicity coup.

Shae placed his arm around Nick as he plopped down on the next stool. "Mina, this is my buddy, Nick. We went to grade school together. He's our music guy. Double Black, rocks, twist. Nick, Mina. A recent promotion from the floor."

"Hey there," Nick said, as Mina went to work.

"Sorry 'bout that," he continued, turning to Shae, "Been a hell of a day."

"How'd it end?"

"Manager's gone, the band's lawyer is suing the guitarist for breach, they're sampling him and doing without. Smaug arrives Friday morning for the sound check."

"You're joking."

"The competition is fierce, man. You know we get a hundred CDs a *week* now from labels all over the world? Any band invited here's got to cowboy up." Nick paused, noticing Shae's grin. "So you got news, hunh?"

"I can wait another two minutes." Shae sat back. "So who are these cats? Are they really worth it?"

"They're breaking in New York, sort of a hip-hop/grime groove act with a pop-Buddhist sensibility. They're young, spirituality is in and they're just below Viacom's radar. They're perfect."

"You've seen them?"

"Caught a show in 'Billyburg, Brooklyn last week and we're making them the first release for the DisasterLand Live label. Ya dig?"

Shae did. It's what he liked about Nick. "You know I haven't seen a live show in years. I have no idea what's happening out there."

"Come down Saturday, man. All work and no play makes Shae a dull boy."

Mina dropped off Nick's drink to tend to another couple further down the bar.

"Not so, my friend." Shae lowered his voice, "You ready?"

Nick nodded. Shae continued in a whisper, "I'm going to Spain in two weeks."

"You're finally taking a vacation? I don't believe it."

"You're right. I'm going to the Andalusia desert. On business."

Nick's eyes narrowed.

Shae continued, "That's all I can say."

Nick stared, finally accepting Shae's determined silence. He knew from experience there was no point prying. "Well, you'll have to hit Ibiza, you know."

"No time and not my style."

"Not for pleasure—for *work*. You need to be seen there." Shae's ears pricked up as Nick pressed on, "Seriously. It would be great for the new label. You'll make a huge impression on the industry—that we love music, know where to go, where to be seen."

Shae pulled back to scan the growing cliques of cast and crew behind them, settled into the leather couches and taking advantage of the pre-show access to DmZ. Nick was right. It made sense.

"And it'll be great for your head. Get you out of this test-tube and into the real world. I can get you on the list at all the top clubs. The vibe, man... the sound systems! We dropped a chunk on ours, and yeah, it sounds great... but those..." Nick's arms flew out, head thrown back, "It's like they're *injecting* music man!"

"Injecting music? Do I like that?"

"Of course you do. And make sure to drop some of my business cards."

Shae laughed. "Why don't you come with me? Meet me over there?"

"Really? Love to man, *love to*."

"It's done." Shae turned to his friend. "We're going to change the world, Nick. Where religion has failed, politics has failed, culture has failed, science has failed, DisasterLand will succeed."

It worried Nick, statements like these. During particularly insightful moments, he sometimes felt that DisasterLand was becoming a religion and Shae was its prophet.

Or was it *profit*?

Elektra waltzed through security and into the VIP elevator. She was looking forward to the quiet, candle-light dinner Clint was fixing and some good, old-fashioned one-on-one.

Too soon, they'd both be in *the zone*, making it impossible to enjoy anything but a quick meal and an exhausted *good night*.

But for now, she was at peace. The dress had gone spectacularly: the opening's gravity and depth had finally been properly exploited and the elusive tone had finally been found late in the day. The team broke on a high, enthusiastically anticipating running the show's ending tomorrow.

Terrorist scripts were tough, and this one was no exception. But it was a greatest hits of sorts, recapitulating all of the best moments from the entire season as well as the hard lessons learned from a year of trial and error. And they had nailed it.

If this was the way it was going to be from now on, they were all staring at a glorious future. For the first time there was a sense of familiarity with the material, a sense they weren't just bungee-jumping into the void that was welcomed by all but the hardest-core. Now, they'd riff.

But as Elektra stepped off the elevator and into the twenty-second floor hallway, her heart sank. Alcohol-fueled laughter and heightened conversation greeted her, increasing in volume as she approached her suite.

The dinner was clearly unmade.

Elektra quivered. There was a routine involved here, a mellowing-out ritual that she had carefully developed over months. She always went hermit the last two nights to build up strength and energy reserves for the week ahead while methodically reviewing each day's story progression during epic baths.

She had explained that clearly and by the time she stepped into Clint's post-dress cocktail party, she knew the end was imminent.

Elektra laughed, hugged and kissed her way past the throng and quickly poured herself a Scotch to better cope with the situation. The actors present were some of the best DisasterLand had and her go-to people in times of emergency. She needed everything between them straight-up with no second-guessing. Lives were at stake. She had to be cool. She couldn't just order them to leave.

This made the whole situation even more agonizing, alleviated only slightly by everyone's enthusiastic appreciation for offering up her penthouse to the ritual gathering. Friday morning's pre-show security lock-down meant this was their next-to-last chance to visit a suite in the heights and she knew their sentiment was real. But once again, it just proved the lack of awareness within Clint's reptilian brain. What did he think he was doing?

Two hours later, after the alcohol had run dry and the friends lovingly escorted out, Elektra calmly and eloquently condemned Clint to life without her.

Clint whined and pleaded about how last minute it was, how Shae had backed out and there was no other place to keep tradition, about how stressed she was and how Clint would buy dinner to help her relax. But Elektra didn't listen.

While Clint began to gather up his things for the shuttle back to the FunHouse, she went up to the roof to smoke and clear her head. The actor and crew village, tucked out of sight a mile away, was a maelstrom of ego and rumor. He'd be right at home. Once again.

Elektra stepped out into the fresh, crisp evening air and felt only profound relief. The desert heat was radiating up from the parched land and the sun just about to set over the mountains to the west. She unwrapped the rug she kept inside the door for these moments and sat down in half lotus facing the sun. Her timing was perfect.

Clint did have one thing right. She'd order a delivery from the guys downstairs, pull out a damn good bottle of red then hit the bath for a quick visualization of tomorrow's day. The love-making time she'd just saved meant that in the end, time-wise, she was just about even.

They had met several shows ago when Clint auditioned for a leading role as an earthy firefighter. She was smitten, not in the least because he looked pretty damn good carrying babies to safety.

But they'd been drifting apart ever since. At the end of the day, how many babies did she really need carried to safety? Dating an actor had been a failed experiment, broadcasting her weaknesses and compromising her professionalism. It wouldn't happen again.

But who else was out there? A girl had to get laid after all and DisasterLand was like a small mountain village, secluded and dangerous to reach: visitors were rare and everyone knew everyone else's business. In fact, it had already become a little too insular for her comfort.

Soon the tears were falling yet she didn't feel sad. She didn't know what she felt. She just wished she could see the stars. She needed them.

It was always that way, wasn't it? Either men were wonderful in bed but had staggering personality defects, or they were cute and sweet but timid and just not *sexy*. Not *manly*. She didn't want manly in a testosterone-drenched wife-beater way, but in a simple shelter sort of way. Someone to keep the rain out.

She had seen the studies. Most of the time women wanted adventure, a bad-boy, an element of danger. But during ovulation they wanted a softer type, a sweeter type, a fatherly type. Women were genetically schizophrenic about mates, and that's before the topsy-turvy effects of synthetic birth control were accounted for.

Clint... he was the first type. Well trained, she had to admit, but utterly lacking in depth. The whole situation was only made worse because in this case the responsibility for training lay largely with her. And all that work was now down the drain.

No, it was worse. It wasn't just down the drain—someone else (maybe *lots* of someone elses) were destined to benefit from her hours of patient instruction in the ways of women.

Elektra shook her head, correcting herself. No, they would benefit just as she'd benefited herself from the work of others. *We're all in this together,* she silently told her sisters on planet earth, and fought to clear her eyes.

At least the whole thing had gone down sooner rather than later. They were fundamentally incompatible and she had known it from the beginning. Foolishness, she knew, and alcohol were primarily responsible.

Now there was no stress over the vacation, no worries over future plans. Elektra lay back and pulled the fresh air into her lungs, arms behind her head and eyes searching for the faint stars now magically appearing.

There was something to be said for childhood sweethearts. For arranged marriages. For illegal divorce. People made a relationship work—because they *had* to.

Had DisasterLand ruined her prospects for a decent relationship permanently? Maybe she could just have mates shipped in, like they do in zoos? *Was that too much to ask?*

She sighed.

Yes, another one had bit the dust, but theirs wouldn't be the only break-up in DisasterLand next week. Off-season musical beds was about to start. Drop the needle.

Where would he land? Elektra wondered, smiling.

Wherever it was, it sure wouldn't have a view like this.

Shae stuck his mobile on speaker and changed into his robe, finally home and pleased to have his head dry-cleaned by the vodka.

One message. "Shae, Cindy. Got your message. Thanks." He paused, grabbing a French bottled water from the fridge, "It's brilliant. You know, one of our directing understudies is a Cal Arts animator. I'll see if he can pull off something mildly profane during the break for October's welcome back staff meeting." A pause. "And we've got it in our budget."

Shae hung up with a smile and headed to the hot tub to run a bath.

Everyone was hitting stride, everything was falling into place. It was the momentum, the *inertia,* of DisasterLand, and it was now an unstoppable force of its own. In two days, a revolution would shake the world.

He made it a rule never to read the scripts, just to live the experience day-by-day as his crew and guests did, but today it was obvious: this new script was money.

Shae *loved* terrorist plots. They were truly the oldie, the goodie. It was like comin' home in a way, getting back to their roots—they had started terrorist one long year before and never looked back. They represented DisasterLand in all its impossible glory, in its wild, raw beauty, in its faux-savage brilliance.

He double-checked the water purifier, making sure it was on maximum and added his favorite detox bath salts to the steaming output. He wanted to get the alcohol out of his system as soon as possible. The celebratory third martini had been necessary but unwanted.

Shae de-charged the glass wall beside the bath, revealing the ever-darkening spectacle of the village far below, lit by a few glittering work lights as the remaining crew scurried to complete their final tweaks.

Ants, he thought. *And I'm the fucking Queen Bee.*

He turned on the jets and slid out of his robe, lowering himself into the turmoil. His eyes closed.

DisasterLand was born on Long Island, in the $20,000 hand-carved granite bathtub of his Montauk summer home during an intense aromatherapy cleansing which concluded a seven day juice fast in the wake of September 11, 2001, three short years ago.

Living in TriBeCa, Shae had witnessed the attacks and aftermath first-hand, and had spent the first few chaotic hours with neighbors helping to set up tents for the emergency workers.

That evening Shae had taken to the deserted streets, muffled by the inches-thick grey powder that coated the surrounding blocks and still hung in the air, stinging his eyes and throat. Shae quickly drifted away from the tragedy's epicenter and to the periphery of the island, to the growing mass of supporters congregating along the West Side Highway.

As the rescue vehicles raced uptown filled with men the color of stone, Shae lost himself in the overwhelming outpouring of togetherness and support emanating from those surrounding him.

The hours and days to come were worth the sacrifice of his body (like many residents of lower Manhattan, he had lingering respiratory problems to this day) for what it had done to his soul. The personal and social transformations he witnessed in the aftermath had been inspiring, giving him a new appreciation of humanity's compassionate nature. He watched as one person after another used the event to realign themselves towards their own greater good. In a city of relentless self-pursuit watching New Yorkers fiercely competing to serve others was a profound lesson.

Yet it saddened him. Why couldn't the world be like this all the time? Why did it take a tragedy to pull people together?

Retreating to Montauk to escape his growing discomfort with the state of the city's air, Shae embarked on the detox that would change entertainment for ever.

DisasterLand. A place to bring people together, to make them rely on one another, to remember what community is and what being alive was truly about. A place to ground people, a place of healing, a place where that post-September 11 feeling never left; where cultural stereotypes could be broken down and transcended, where bridges could be built.

Each guest would be encouraged to venture into their own darkest forest, to rediscover their deepest, mythical selves, Joseph Campbell-style. It would be a place of initiation, a ritual space for a sacred rite of passage, a modern version of the Greek *mysteries.*

It would be medicine for those who had lost their souls in modernity.

It would be Outward Bound on crack.

It would also be a place of training, a way of creating a new breed of citizen with experience of the worst, taught to make the types of decisions that saved lives in this new, dark world.

It would be a place to change lives. A place where every dad was a policeman, every mother a teacher, every daughter a nurse and every boy a firefighter.

But most importantly, it would be a place to have fun, a hell of a lot of fun, and a place to make Shae, his staff and his investors an obscene amount of money.

The financing for DisasterLand was in place by the end of September 2001: two billion dollars raised almost overnight.

For Shae, the timing was perfect. He had sold his Silicon Alley start-up in the spring of 2000, when expectations were still high and a crash unthinkable. He'd banked a mint and had been scanning new opportunities with increasing desperation.

By the time they broke ground the following June, DisasterLand was the hottest thing Wall Street had ever seen and Shae was the eye of the hurricane, the *zeitgeist wunderkind*. He could have raised another billion if he'd wanted, or five or ten. But he didn't. His team put their heads down and they went to work.

The economy was still in aftershock and many large projects had been put on hold by gun-shy companies. DisasterLand slipped into this hole, working exclusively with many of the top construction firms at cut-rate deals.

As construction progressed, Shae used his experience in building a cutting-edge new media company in the late 90's to build the core creative team. DisasterLand had its pick of Hollywood's top undiscovered talent, left lingering on the fringes of an ossified industry. In the days of reality TV, DisasterLand offered a challenge no theater, no television or movie set could ever hope to compete with: live, real-time character-based acting amidst real people.

Three guaranteed months off a year (January, May and September) didn't hurt, nor did the feel-good socially-conscious vibe. But it was the challenge that kept the best. At every step and for every employee DisasterLand presented tough challenges.

That was the glue which kept the team together.

THURSDAY

Steve stepped out of his car and into Persistent's parking lot, wondering just how he was going to break the news of the surprise vacation in light of Michael's verdict. He hesitated.

He was a few minutes late, yet the lot still seemed oddly quiet. Usually there were a few last-minute stragglers nervously trying to duck in under the radar. Was he later than he thought?

Steve grabbed his briefcase and shut the car door, locking it with a flick of his thumb on the keychain. His car responded with the satisfied chirp that grated terribly on his nerves.

Gingerly, Steve stepped towards the entrance, his head spinning with the remarkable developments of the last 24 hours.

A startling shriek suddenly went up around him as his co-workers jumped out from behind their parked cars, cheering. Steve stumbled as his heart skipped. The receptionists spilled out of the front door, hoisting a banner: *Good Luck Steve!* it said, *You Will Survive!*

A live TV crew stepped out from an unmarked van that Steve now realized had been following him all morning long.

Dick Gentry, Persistent's steely CEO, paused in front of the banner to shake Steve's hand, offering a wave to the rapidly multiplying cameras which now captured their every move. Steve managed an oddly forced grimace.

"It's simple, Steve," Dick said moments later back in his office, hands folded across his expansive desk. "We want in. Get us in."

Before even taking off his jacket, Steve had been escorted to Dick's office and his tension had increased to almost unbearable levels. He shifted in his seat.

"I'll be honest with you, Steve. This is a golden opportunity for the company, one you've probably not even realized."

"No, I..."

"That's understandable. You've got Barb and the kids to worry about and it's all happened so suddenly. Exactly why we need to have this conversation."

"So..."

"Steve, let me put it simply." Dick sat back, eyeing Steve through narrowed eyes. "You've been a real lighthouse at this company. A beacon in the night, so to speak, and now, more than ever, we need you to help illuminate our way."

Steve's stomach turned at the tired metaphors. What was it about management, he wondered, that ate away your brain?

Dick continued, "Illumination, Steve, provided by cash. It's simple: DisasterLand is an enormous untapped market for us. I don't have the facts, no one does, they're real assholes over there, but I know it. *I know it.*" Dick edged closer, "This is your job: look at what they're doing, Steve, and see how we fit in. It's that simple. Pitch them before they eject you and *get us in.*"

"Dick, with all respect, this is a vacation..."

"Bah, don't worry about that, Steve. We'll let you keep your vacation time. I know how much your family means to you. We'll make this a working vacation, so you don't have to worry about a thing."

Steve rubbed his forehead. *A working vacation?*

"Dick..."

"And three percent of whatever business you bring in."

"Three?"

"Five. If that helps." Dick's eyes narrowed once again. "You keep telling me you're not a businessman!"

Steve crunched a few round numbers, quickly. He could easily double his salary this year, if not more... *the exit sign had been illuminated.* "It does, yes. Can we put this in writing?"

"Look at you, busting my balls, big DisasterLand *he-ro,*" Dick called in his secretary on the intercom and continued, slowly, "Steve, I want to be clear here. This could make Persistent. As successful as we are, an account like this could make this company. I want you to understand that. It's money Steve, but it's also prestige. It'll start an avalanche."

"I understand."

"It's either pure dumb luck or the work of the Almighty," Dick leaned back, stretching his arms behind his head, "I can't tell. But don't let any of this interfere with your time with the family."

"No... I..."

"Look, all I'm asking for is to keep an ear open... use your common sense. You'll find a way in, Steve. I know it."

"I'll do my best, Dick."

They shook. Dick leaned forward, conspiratorially, "And Steve, just in case you guys are on TV again, can you wear an Persistent polo? We're fetching a couple for you now. Extra large, right?"

"Oh Barb, that's incredible! You're gonna lose *so much weight!*" Denise couldn't believe her ears. Imagine—Barb Beyers! In *DisasterLand!*

Barb stared. She had begun to worry.

Denise continued breathlessly, "I saw it on Oprah. The average person loses fifteen pounds, some people a lot more! Doctors are recommending it."

"You're joking."

"I'm not! You know people train months for DisasterLand? Gyms offer special packages and everything!"

"You're kidding."

"Humm-umm."

Denise smiled while Barb's stomach churned. *People train for DisasterLand?*

"Don't let it get you down, Barb. You'll make it. You guys are in better shape than most."

They unrolled their matching yoga mats, each conspicuously displaying a new set of tights, confirming themselves as inextricably locked in an escalating suburban tights-race, an ongoing, unspoken battle for class attention.

"Did they say how?"

"No one's allowed to talk about the experience, Barb, you know that. Didn't you sign one of those... nondisclosure agreements?"

"No, I don't think so." Barb cringed, picturing Pete signing away the family's rights with one click of the mouse.

"Well, you *will.* They're strict about that."

"You mean I can't tell you about my vacation?"

"Nope. At least not *legally.*" She winked. "But you know me... I'm not going to rat!"

"I don't believe you. They can't do that! It's *my* vacation!"

"But it's their *script.*"

"I'm not *in* their script. I'm not just some character."

"But you *are.* Just by participating, you are."

Barb froze, remembering MagicD's words: *it's yah secret.* She nervously assumed the lotus position.

The DVD's images had haunted her sleep. She dismissed them, convinced they were all special effects—DisasterLand couldn't be like *that,* those people looked *terrified*—but now she wasn't so sure. Fifteen pounds was *a lot* of exercise for one week.

Barb swallowed. It was scary, DisasterLand, even if she could lose weight.

"Do you think it's safe?"

"Of *course*..." Denise's voice trailed off. "I mean, you know, sometimes people get hurt... but they're probably dumb. You guys'll be fine. Oh Barb, it's *amazing!* You're so *lucky!*"

"People don't die, do they?"

"Don't be ridiculous."

Barb took a deep breath, soothing her fraying nerves as Eagle, their instructor, entered with a new yoga groupie at his side. Barb frowned.

Eagle winked to the couple, "Morning, girls. Looking good! Barb, how's your sadhana?"

Barb broke into an over-enthusiastic smile, thankful for the merciful break from her mounting trepidation, "Oh it's *great...* makes *so much difference!*"

It was a complete lie. She hadn't even begun her daily practice. No yogi could keep it together in a house full of maniacs, she didn't care who they were. Yet with ten days off... she might just have a chance. She needed to stick to the positive.

"And you, Denise?" Eagle asked as he took his place in the front.

"I've missed a couple."

"Then it's not a sadhana."

"I'll be better when the kids are back in school."

Eagle smiled, "Understood. Don't force it. If it stresses you out it's not a sadhana either." He slid out of his T-shirt, revealing his smooth, chiseled stomach.

Barb bent away from Denise in a runner's stretch, discreetly eyeing Eagle as he slipped off his track pants.

It was real, for sure. Her crush. And the feeling that she could pull it off. That she had to pull it off, had to give it a shot. There would be no shame, no second guessing. Her desire was on boil and the end-game was near.

Barb's body electrified as she slowly spread her legs and stretched deeply, her heart accelerating pleasantly. She had been blessed with flexibility all her life, making yoga immediately rewarding. She felt Eagle's gaze.

She would give DisasterLand a chance to work its magic on Steve, but after that she'd take a calculated leap. Everyone has secrets and this one would do her a world of good, a place to channel her generative energy that screamed to be released. It would get her blood flowing again. It would keep her young.

"I see we have a couple of new faces," Eagle smiled to the room of twenty as he let himself down into an easy full lotus, "Welcome. I'm Eagle and I start each class with a rant from the material world, then I end the class with a reading from a master to give you something to meditate on until next class." He settled in, clearing his throat. "Today's rant is on antidepressants."

Barb cringed: a real sore-spot for her. After watching Ritalin sweep through the schools, she was suspicious of anything so powerful—and pervasive. Yet she was sure some people truly needed them. Their lives weren't going well and they needed help. They needed a little extra push.

Barb caught a little smile from Eagle, sure it had been flashed just for her. *I need a push,* she thought, *a strong, athletic little push from his firm anti-depressant.*

Denise was watching out the corner of her eye, wondering if Barb's thoughts could be as lewd as her expression. But Denise wasn't worried.

Whatever was going on, DisasterLand would surely fix it.

Lhasa flew over the mountain pass in his customized '99 Acura Integra, his long brown hair whipping in the breeze.

DisasterLand Valley spread out before him, the twin glass domes glowing in the morning sunlight like vast diamond mushrooms burst forth from the earth.

Fuck me, he thought, *there they are.*

Just two hours earlier Lhasa had received the call he had waited his entire professional life for, the invitation that every actor with U.S. citizenship would do anything to receive: he'd been granted an audition.

"I'm gonna make it," Lhasa yelled as a tidal wave of endorphins washed over him, *"I'm really gonna fucking make it!"*

He pounded the steering wheel in ecstasy, scanning the valley for the legendary FunHouse. Through the actor's rumor mill, he'd heard it was all sex, drugs and the gym at the FunHouse, with media rights for particularly juicy insider stories going for the high six figures.

Instead, he only spotted a dusty road snaking off into the surrounding mountains, the ridges above lined with twisting windmills.

Word was DisasterLand didn't mind these deals at all, in fact seemed to encourage them as another way of rewarding their employees to attract the best. DL_PR had negotiated a clause in the actor's contracts forbidding public disclosure for five years to let the dust settle: just when the excitement might be lagging, the ribald tales would bring another wave of publicity.

That's when I'll know, Lhasa assured himself. *I'll be hangin' in the FunHouse.*

He grabbed his mobile and cringed: no service. He'd been trying to reach his big brother all morning long and it now seemed impossible—Jinpa probably had his phone unplugged after last night's shift. If there was anyone in the world Lhasa needed to connect with at this moment, it was him. Jinpa had been the architect.

Lured from San Francisco three years ago to sous chef a trendy Vegas restaurant far away from the tourist strip, Jinpa watched it all happen, watched DisasterLand supersize the Vegas underground almost overnight as wave after wave of visionary craftspeople gave way to misty-eyed starlets chasing the dream.

After DisasterLand's initial casting sessions in LA, New York, Chicago and Austin, the broken-hearted had flocked to booming Vegas. Everyone in the business knew you made your own luck, and being where lightning *could* strike increased your changes immeasurably.

Agents had followed the scent, an entire deluge of Hollywood agency assistants striking off from LA for the remote desert outpost—now circling DisasterLand Valley like vultures.

Lhasa had been one of the first to arrive in town at Jinpa's insistence, making the leap from LA where he was at the wrong end of bad news game of kick-the-dog.

Screwed out of an LA DisasterLand audition by politics at his agency, he'd been trying to claw his way inside for the past 14 months.

And Jinpa had made it happen. It was inevitable that sooner or later he'd meet members of DisasterLand's notoriously-reclusive staff, but the first was the only one that mattered. Jude had spotted him in the restaurant's kitchen and arranged to have a complimentary word. The conversation quickly broadened past the immediate meal and onto dinner plans for the following weekend.

They'd only dated briefly but Jude still wanted him back. *Obviously*.

Yes, Jinpa had broken down the door, but now it was up to Lhasa to bum rush.

Lhasa's eyes flashed to the sky in thanks. Across the valley, the world's most famous sign, surpassing even *Hollywood* in the latest market research, had been blasted into a cliff face as if to keep watch:

D-i-s-a-s-t-e-r-L-a-n-d®

Lhasa's ego inflated and he snapped a quick photo with his phone. One couldn't just drive here, after all. This was the most heavily patrolled highway in the United States and Lhasa had felt the watchful eye of every dark, unmarked car he had passed. But they had let him through.

He carefully navigated the final hair-pin turn at the base of the mountain and slowed as the road widened out to accommodate the imposing security center. Sign after sign authorized the use of deadly force.

Guards with automatic rifles were waving him into the guest lane as others motioned for him to open his hatch for inspection.

He tugged the release and came to a stop, third in line. Across the median, the employee entrance remained clear, the guards sharing a laugh.

Minutes later, he inched forward next to the guard station and a small spiked barrier rose in front of his tires.

"Easy, kid, unless you want to be towed home," a guard called in front of him. In place of an automatic he was working a sophisticated, handheld PDA.

Lhasa waved thanks as more guards descended to inspect his hatch. He noticed the guards from the employee side eyeing him cautiously.

"How's it goin'?" the guard in front asked, motioning Lhasa out of the car.

"Great, man. Yeah, I'm Lhasa Lapsong. I'm…"

"Right," the guard pressed a few keys and smiled. "Audition, hunh? Might stay for the dress?"

Lhasa knew the numbers. Very, very few were allowed to stay for the dress. "Hopefully."

Another guard approached and carefully patted him down. The first scanned Lhasa's right eye and checked the readout.

"Welcome, Mr. Lapsong. If you need anything, here's my card."

A personalized guest visa emerged from the PDA and the guard passed it over, "This must remain on your person at all times. You must remain in the presence of an employee. The second dress is a closed set and this visa expires at thirteen hundred hours. You stay one minute later and you go to jail for trespassing."

"Wow. OK, got it. Hey, can I keep this?"

"Property of DisasterLand. You keep it and you'll be arrested for theft before you hit the pass."

Lhasa stared, "Yes, sir."

A third guard had found Lhasa's phone. He dropped it into a security bag.

"We'll need to keep that," the guard said.

Lhasa's face dropped. "Can you just snap a quick one of me with the domes in the background? My brother..."

The guard laughed, "Not a chance. And anything you've already got we erase." He slapped Lhasa on the back, "Now you have a wonderful stay, Mr. Lapsong. You're in lot B, spot 12. Hurry up or you'll be late."

His hatch door slammed.

Lhasa climbed in, a bit shaken, ready to embrace his destiny.

"Elektra forwarded your headshot... you were in *One Life to Give?*"

Lhasa smiled, "Yeah... played the Chinese mafia take-out delivery guy."

"*Of course*... loved that."

Julie, DisasterLand's second second AD, had met Lhasa inside the atrium's main security center. Offering the only access between the secure production complex and the closed set of the atrium, the security center was a vital, high-tech nexus. Just outside the glass doors, technicians were swarming the atrium, resetting for the second run-through.

Now only feet from the hallowed ground, Lhasa's perception was on overdrive, relentlessly scanning his surroundings and vividly registering the smallest details. He had glimpsed the promised land. And it was good.

"So you know Ed? Blake? The second AD?"

"Sure. Great guy."

"The best. I've known him for years... we went through the DGA trainee program together."

The colored smoke used to mimic different explosions was still diffusing up and away, through the top of the dome twenty-three stories over their heads. Less than ten minutes earlier the 'all-clear' had been called.

Lhasa had watched the dress from the comfort of DmZ having nailed the audition, safely behind smoked glass. A production assistant had escorted the handful of guests (mostly lucky relatives of trusted A-list staff) to their seats, overlooking the vast stage that was the atrium.

For the next two hours, he sat motionless while others gorged themselves on the complimentary snacks. It had taken the entire force of Lhasa's being not to leap up and rush to join in the fray. To call it a religious experience was only just short of hyperbole. He had found his home.

Behind them, double doors now swung open and a blast of cool air and wildflowers hit before any physical presence could register. With her tight Bruce Lee tank top, low-cuts and weathered DisasterLand cross-trainers it was clear: the chick appearing before them meant *action*. She offered her firm hand.

"Welcome, Lhasa, glad you could stay. I'm Elektra Rogers, lead producer. Sorry I couldn't introduce myself at the audition. We're cruel that way."

Lhasa wiped his clammy palm on his khakis and shook, "Pleasure."

"But I wanted to connect before you go," Elektra checked her watch. "I'll escort you out. Thanks, Julie, I'll take him from here."

The girls hit fists as Lhasa swung around for one last look at the famous atrium. *I'll be back*, he promised himself.

Behind them, Julie flipped on her walkie-talkie and a voice crackled, "... folks. *Forty-five*: Four. Five. Red in forty-five. Red in forty-five."

They whizzed past others waiting at the security checkpoint only, Lhasa knew, because of Elektra's presence. Above their heads, the red light was off, signaling the park was not live.

"Jude seems pretty high on you," Elektra said as they hurried through the nondescript white hallways to the stairs.

"More like high on my brother," Lhasa chuckled.

Elektra froze. Was his brother another of Jude's *shags*?

"It's over but Jude won't give up. Don't tell him though, my brother loves the flowers."

Elektra rubbed her forehead. DisasterLand was downright *claustrophobic*.

She pushed on to business, "You've got the post-disaster glow. We like that. Any thoughts on the rehearsal?"

"Totally, totally mind-blowing. I have to be here."

Elektra bristled, "Please, no sales talk."

"I'm serious. I buy it, you know?"

"Explain."

"Movies are stop and go torture, acting for a box of electronics. Theater's better— live, for people—but there's still no real feedback, no intimate connection. They're in the distance, separated by a wall of light. You can't *touch them*."

Elektra cautioned, "What we do here is easy to romanticize. Some need that separation, that pedestal. They don't want the extreme immediacy of this place."

"They don't want to *risk*. It's a tightrope: it's live, the stakes are high, the ground a long way down. But that's life, right? Living, I mean. Pushing those boundaries. It must be... transcendental."

Elektra laughed, "Maybe."

"I think I approach acting a little differently than most."

"Oh yeah?" Elektra eyed him as they turned a corner.

"I mean, I'm coming at it from a different place."

"Go on."

"Acting is how I strive to perfect myself. The more I play other people, the more

I learn about me." He paused, "What about you? What does DisasterLand teach you?"

Elektra smiled. Ballsy. And it was a good question. Does producing fun-house freights on a massive scale make her a better person? It *must*.

"I guess I'd say I'm beginning to get a solid grasp on the human... animal."

"That must be cool. You'll have to write a self-help book."

Her stride stuttered. *Bank.*

She made a note.

"So you're Tibetan?"

"I was born in San Fran. My parents were both smuggled out as babies in the 50's, just after China took control. They found each other in California."

"Buddhist?"

"I don't know. I think we're all sort of past that. For better or for worse, it's now up to the individual to find his way."

"And your way is acting?"

"Exactly." There was a sparkle in his eye.

Elektra warmed, "I like that idea." Here was a guy she could talk to. Too bad he was so young and, of course, another actor.

"It's what all of us must be doing. Now more than ever. Trying to become better people," Lhasa paused, then pushed the idea home quickly, sensing his time was out as they stepped into the familiar reception area. "Better in the sense of perfecting ourselves to be fair to those things on which we depend. The air, the water, the earth... other animals, plants, spirits... whatever. Not better exactly but *more successful caretakers.*"

For one naked moment Elektra considered inviting him on vacation, "Are you always like this?"

"Is that a trick question?"

"Probably." They stepped out into DisasterLand's reception area and Elektra guided him to a plush leather couch. "Any questions?"

"What's the commitment like?"

"Total, but we get one full month in four off. I'll be honest—almost every day of those other three you'll be working in some capacity. It's very insulated here, very dedicated."

"I like that. Like a monastery."

"Not really." She sat down and Lhasa followed.

"Scripts are released one show in advance for study. Then there's a week of narrative workshopping with your team while the various crews rig effects, whatever— improvisation, of course, is critical, and we're always running scenarios. This afternoon is all scenarios."

It sounded good. *It sounded really good.*

She continued, "So you've got the week of workshopping, then a day off, then a week of rehearsals building from half-speed to where we are now, then another day off, then the show begins in earnest on a Saturday. A show's basically 8 full days of work—very long, very intense days."

"Fine."

"That's the story element. The physical regime is personalized by our trainers depending on character requirements and your build, but you're always training."

"It's the full package. Got it. I'm sure you've got a nice gym."

"Three."

A somber woman entered and Lhasa's eyes reflected the traumatic memory of an earlier legal beat-down. The Purgatory paralegal stepped over, offering copies of his admittance contract, "Your paperwork, sir..."

"These I can keep?"

Elektra laughed, "Proof of your visit, hold on to that for your grandchildren."

"I hope it's not my only one."

Elektra rose, thanking the paralegal, "It might not be. You hit your monologues and the improv was fresh. We like your look and next season has lots of surprises. We might just be in touch."

Elektra felt his hope radiate through her body. She plucked the guest visa from around his neck, "Here, let me sign that."

"Release *form*? Singular?" Steve took a long, astounded sip of his after-work Scotch. The form was the size of a Manhattan phone book.

"Yes, that's Peter's. He's signed it already," confirmed Barb.

"But he's a minor."

"That was their instructions. You co-sign."

Steve set his drink down and began thumbing through the release. "Just the list of places to sign or initial is three pages long!"

"I know... make sure to hit all of them. They say it'll hold up our check-in if we don't."

"So we've got to lug these monsters with us?"

"A courier picks them up in two hours. They have to be processed by the time we depart tomorrow morning or they cancel our plane ticket."

"You're kidding! *Two hours*."

"I guess they've been here since nine. Twelve hours."

"But how are we supposed to..."

"They say it's a standard release."

Steve stared. "It... doesn't look very standard."

"No, it doesn't," Barb sighed.

Steve continued his examination, his expression darkening. "Have you read some of this stuff? Here's a statistical chart of injuries by anatomical location and their relation to previous fitness level!"

Barb looked. "Yes, I saw that. Initial there, at the bottom." She pointed.

Steve bit his tongue, flipping to the end, "Have you seen the last two pages? Pete left his blank..."

"Yes..."

"Phobias. Heights? Enclosed spaces? Crowds?" Steve went on, more quickly, "Can you swim? Do you have nursing experience or lifesaving skills? Any pre-existing conditions? HIV? Previous disaster experience?"

"I know...."

"*Previous disaster experience?* Are they fucking kidding?!"

"Easy, Steve. Here, let me get you another drink," Barb hurried out, fighting a return of tears.

"Look," Steve yelled, "They even want us to appoint a captain of the family!"

"It's you," Barb called.

"Honey..."

"*You.*"

"Fine." Steve picked up his own release and unfolded the papers tucked into the front flap. He gasped. It was his complete medical record, ready to be initialed.

And there it was: the Happinol. *The scarlet letter.*

"What?" Barb reappeared, a Scotch in each hand.

Steve jumped, recovering by slamming the release shut in exaggerated anger. "It's a complete copy of my medical record! Where did they get this?!"

"It makes sense honey. I mean, it saves time if... something... happens."

"If *something happens?* Where in hell are we going? Where are we taking our kids for God's sake!"

Barb's eyes dampened. It was a good question. "It's too late now, honey. I mean, they're coming soon and Pete's at David's dressed in all his stuff. We've already been on TV and everything."

Steve shook his head, flipping the release back open and continuing his examination, "Listen to this, Barb. It's a letter from our HMO. We've got to temporarily sign away our regular health insurance coverage and accept DisasterLand's."

"What does it cover?"

"Everything. One hundred percent."

"Well, that's good news."

"Yeah, I guess... listen to this: 15% of the ticket price goes directly to medical insurance. Can you believe that? God, that's incredible."

Barb took a healthy gulp of scotch, grimacing, "I'm going to fix us some dinner. I can't continue on an empty stomach."

"Great idea. Where did you say Pete is?"

"At David's. He wanted to show him all the new gear."

"What new gear?"

"Oh, God. I keep forgetting. There's a big box in the living room. Cross-trainers, windbreakers, sweatpants, baseball hats..."

"You're kidding."

"It's all specially-designed for DisasterLand. The shoes are waterproof and heatproof. Pete said they're supposed to grip fifty percent better than regular shoes and reduce ankle injuries."

"And they fit?"

"Pete's did. Perfectly."

"How the *hell*..."

"Oh Steve!" Barb was sobbing now, full-force.

He placed his arms around her, shocked to realize he hadn't hugged her all day. And yesterday? He couldn't remember.

"What's wrong, honey?"

"Denise said the average person loses fifteen pounds there. I mean... what do they do to you?!"

"I don't know, sweetie. But people love it. No one at work can believe I'm going. They were all waiting for me to arrive so they could cheer."

"Denise can't believe it either. Pete said his whole school had a special assembly today to send him off."

"See? It'll be just fine honey. Where's this box?"

"The living room." Barb stepped away, wiping her eyes.

Steve pounded his Scotch and disappeared, returning a few moments later with his waterproof DisasterLand baseball hat. He put it on, smiling stupidly, then spun. The back had been monogrammed: *Steve Beyers*.

He grabbed his wife, squeezing, until Barb found herself giggling. "See? It'll be great, honey!"

For the first time in a long time, there was the faint glimmer of a sparkle in Steve's eye, a pale reflection of the kid she fell in love with almost twenty years ago. Barb inched back as Steve kissed her cheek.

"You know we have to wear this stuff."

Steve stared, "Maybe."

"I mean it's in our contracts. Page one."

The blades slowed and gradually the whirlwind ceased. Shae climbed out of DisasterLand's private helicopter and onto the tower's roof, which doubled as the valley's only helipad. He loosened his tie: the sun was setting and the temperature mercifully dropping, but up here it was still pushing the tolerance level.

"Thanks, Swifty. You're the best."

"No sweat, boss. See you next time."

Shae took a methodical lap around the tower's roof to catch his breath before making the descent to the 10th floor to personally OK the preparation of the VIP suites.

Some might call it micro-management, Shae called it attention to detail. Fact was, during a typical show the VIPs were paying upwards of a hundred G's for their stay and their continued support was vital to the business model. If the celebs dried up, so did DisasterLand's future. But this wasn't a typical show.

He took out his phone, scanned the missed calls. Hit redial.

"Hi Shae. Back at base?"

"Just arrived. Where are you, Greg?"

"We're leaving the site now, due in two hours. Unless you want to send back the 'copter."

Shae laughed. "I've booked Del Sol's private room in three. Capitán Vera is taking the night off, but we're in for a treat. Sound good?"

"Sound wonderful."

"We owe them. Let everyone know."

"Big day, Shae."

"Real big.."

Shae flipped his phone shut and took a deep breath. One of the most important decisions of DisasterLand's brief history had taken place hours ago. In short, they were going for it. Balls out.

Shae hit the stairs and his mind returned to the earlier dress: Elektra clearly had what it took to take them to the next level, that was marvelously clear. The writers too were in the zone. The script had come together in new and profoundly satisfying ways with the ending a true wordless ballet—a mystical symphony of explosives, puppeteers and DisasterLand's crack martial arts team. Everyone was hitting and even a potentially serious accident hadn't broken their stride.

It had left him tingling: at this critical time, there was confidence all around.

Shae emerged into the VIP hallway, right on time to meet the tower's manager, Chloe. She handed Shae a sleek, soft rubber mobile phone.

"What do you think?"

"What is it?"

"Depending on how you look at it, it's either a limited-edition collectors' item or a celebrity pacifier."

Shae laughed, heartily. One of toughest part of dealing with the celebs wasn't the inconvenience of multiple layers of invasive biometric security, it was convincing them to surrender their mobile phones.

The break from their agents, managers, accountants, girl- and boyfriends and mistresses—as well as their shrinks and whoever else routinely told them how special they were—sometimes proved too much for their often-fragile personalities to handle.

"Press 'send.'"

Shae did, and put the phone to his ear.

"You're a legend, ba-by... a legend at the top of your game!"

Laughing, he hit it once more.

"I see hardware next year, hardware!"

Again.

"Nothing new's come in, just relax, will ya!"

"Ten sayings at random," Chloe interrupted. "Anytime they get lonely, or need some reassurance, they can get a little shot of support. Also doubles as a doggie toy."

"Fantastic. Can't believe how many four-legged guests we get up here."

"We knew you'd like it."

Shae handed her the phone and wiped the sweat from his brow.

The VIP hallway was lined Hollywood Boulevard-style with hand- and footprints, interspersed with multi-colored glowing panels, all from the celebs who had trod on this sacred ground. It was a who's who of the entertainment world and it still gave Shae the chills.

Graffiti lined the walls, mostly tags and autographs, some wishes for luck and more than a fair amount of raucous profanity from the deranged souls lucky enough to live through a glimpse of the apocalypse.

Their biggest guest so far had been a certain rap mogul, renting out the whole floor to throw one of his infamous birthday parties. Shae had basically sealed it off, largely on the advice of his attorneys, and had allowed the debauchery take its course. The lyricist had reciprocated by giving a shout out to the 'Land in his next album through coded rhymes.

For all paying celebs—CEOs, computer geniuses, rock stars, porn stars and everyone in-between—the private VIP entrance to the floor and complete isolation from the atrium offered maximum security, maximum safety and maximum potential for celebrity mischief. The only access to the atrium was through the second floor security center and there was no way a guest or VIP could transition between spaces without explicit authorization. Most of the time, it was absolutely forbidden.

Later in the week, however, well-behaved VIPs were offered special tours of the floor to slum it with trained guides to see how the other half was living during the darkest moments. These were cautious, supervised affairs and they hadn't yet had a problem—but there had been some close calls. To prevent any possibility of recognition, the VIPs stopped off for complete make-up and wardrobe sessions beforehand to make sure they blended in with the stressed guests. This, of course, was just the type of thing celebrities loved and recently Shae had begun to entertain the idea of a separate charge for the opportunity, with profits going to Disaster-relief charities The marketing department was researching it.

This show, however, was different. Seven of the suites, a third of the total, had gone to the week's performers, as usual. Smaug, a country band called Nest, several DJs and two smaller opening bands had all checked in at the VIP entrance that morning and would complete various sound checks, rehearsals and introductory tours throughout the evening.

But for the first time since the park's opening, DisasterLand's board was set arrive for a brief visit tomorrow, impossible to underestimate in importance. The 10 secretive members representing nearly a trillion in assets and more entertainment and medical experience than most countries was coming to witness DisasterLand's progress firsthand—at least that's what most of DisasterLand's staff believed, those who even knew they were coming at all. But the main reason for the visit, the reason-behind-the-reason known only to a very select few, was to take a serious peek into DisasterLand's future.

Everything had to be right. Everything. There would be no celebrity VIPs at all.

Chloe opened the first suite and Shae stepped right into a Provençal field in the summertime: the lush fragrance of fresh lavender wafted into his lungs and soothed his edge.

A quick sweep revealed the suite in pristine condition: smoked glass perfectly transparent, the lighting understated and elegant, HDTVs tuned to the Feed's VIP edit, Del Sol's exclusive delivery service on speed-dial and the party-sized hot tub primed with hand-made floral salts. Most importantly, the top-shelf bar lay fully-stocked, with back-ups at the ready.

"Chloe, you're a Superstar."

The DisasterLand VIP experience wasn't about chocolates-on-the-pillows niceties, this was about taking a peek into the soul of humanity from a luxurious distance.

And that was a steal at 100 G's.

Later that night, and somewhat shockingly, Elektra found herself holding Clint's clammy hand as he lay sprawled out across her bed.

She'd felt like a ping-pong ball all day but it wasn't until the final improv that she'd been overhead smashed. Clint had fallen from the central fountain during the show's climax. He'd landed badly.

His knee was immobilized, completely wrapped in ice. Elektra grimaced. It didn't look good.

The details were fuzzy and tapes were being examined, but it's possible water had gotten onto the metal wall surrounding the pool and he'd slipped, falling the three feet or so into the garden below. Not a huge distance, but it had been unexpected and awkward. It might have been overconfidence.

When he'd stayed down it was all Elektra could do to stop the rehearsal. As the EMS crew raced to his side, she'd completely lost it. Yet with Greg still unavailable and her understudy not quite match fit, she had no choice. She sucked it up and soldiered on.

Twenty-two minutes later they began right where they left off with Clint's eager understudy, Elektra firmly in control of both her emotions and her dedicated crew. The highest compliment came later via text message from Greg. It said simply:

GR8 WRK

Accidents were remarkably rare, but they did happen. And sometimes they were bad. Fortunately, Clint's MRI indicated a hyperextended knee with no severe ligament damage.

Perhaps it was the joy that came with relief, but Elektra had offered to have him brought to her place instead of spending the night at Good Health, DisasterLand's hospital. If she needed proof that DisasterLand had made her insane, it was that decision.

"You doin' OK, honey?"

"Shit."

"Can I get you anything?"

"More whisky."

An empty fifth stood on her bedside table. It had been at least a third full when he arrived.

"That's all I have."

Clint shrugged.

"Fine." Elektra stood. She'd call down to DmZ, have some sent up. It wasn't a huge pain in the ass, but it was a distraction. And now wasn't the time for distractions.

She needed sleep. It had ended up one of the most exhausting days she could remember and tomorrow wasn't shaping up to be any easier. Fridays were always tough, being transition days, but with the private chaos and still no word on a new script, she felt acutely vulnerable.

She made the call for booze and took the opportunity to unpack and prepare the couch for her script session. When the whisky arrived minutes later, she helped herself to a double and cautiously re-entered the bedroom hoping Clint had passed out. He hadn't.

Clint strained to sit up, grimacing and cursing in pain. He cracked open the bottle and took a long, burning drag and burped his relief.

"Didn't they give you painkillers?" she asked.

"Don't take that shit. Whisky."

"Um..."

"But you could hand me one of those anti-inflammatories."

"Yummy."

He gulped it down and Elektra plopped on the end of the bed next to him, queasily. "You're not thinking of going on, are you?"

Suddenly, unexpectedly, the power structure of their relationship was laid bare. He eyed her carefully.

Elektra clarified, "I'm talking to you as a friend, not as your producer. I'm out of this loop."

"You ever heard the saying 'the show must go on?'"

"Bullshit."

"E, are you out of your mind? This is all of Broadway, all of Hollywood, all wrapped into one. It's the World Cup, the Superbowl and the World Series combined."

"We've got understudies, Clint. That's their job."

"I'm not risking my starting role, E. There's a whole pack back there hungry as fuck trying to steal it from me."

He was right—she'd just met one of them. It was the cold reality. Elektra was pretty good about keeping it together, but today was pushing the envelope. "Just be careful. That's all I'm saying. Or you'll be out for good."

"I'm there dead or alive."

"Don't *fucking* say that!" She was tempted to tear into him, to tell him how angry he made her sometimes, how completely insensitive he was, but for once she held back. At this moment in time, it'd be like kneeing him in the balls. And if she hadn't done that by now, she wasn't going to.

Instead, she squeezed his hand and rose, "I've got work to do."

"Listen, I've got tomorrow to recover. I'll be fine."

"Of course you will."

She grabbed her sleeping bag from the closet.

"Oh, E..."

"Yes?"

"Don't turn on any music or anything. I'll have to wake you to help me piss."

Elektra gritted her teeth.

FRIDAY: A.M.

The sun peeked over the undulating fairy-tale suburbs, painting the hazy sky an ethereal blue. Barb brushed naked past her bedroom window and a stir rustled through the crowd below.

Barb froze. She hit the floor.

"Honey?" she called to her sleeping husband, "Steve? Wake up, there's people outside."

Steve groaned.

"I'm serious, honey."

"Tell them to go away."

"I think they saw my boobs."

"The neighbors?"

"No. KBBQ's *FlameThrower*."

Smokin' 92.5: Fire on the Prairie was Kansas City's sound track, offering nonstop classic rock and blues with two exceptions: Chief's football, and the legendary *Jack's Shack* morning show.

Where there was action, Jack was on the scene—and always in *The FlameThrower*. Half mobile studio and half barbecue pit, *The FlameThrower* was a Chiefs-red monster firetruck of lineman proportions. Where it landed, it tended to stay.

Barb quickly computed the implications of its presence.

"Barb! BARB! *BARB!*" the chant grew, electrifying the neighborhood.

"Mom, what'd you do?" asked Sarah, scrambling into their bedroom on her knees, "They're goin' crazy out there!"

Steve rolled over, slamming a pillow over his head. He hadn't slept a wink. *It was all happening too fast.*

"I'm going to be on one of those voyeur websites," Barb announced. "Naked."

"For real? Mom, *what did you do?*"

"Please... how about shutting the curtains?"

"I'm still in my PJs."

"Steve, can you get up please?"

"*Bey-ers! Bey-ers! Bey-ers!*" arose from their driveway.

Steve bemoaned the tyranny of the clock in a gruff mumble. He wasn't ready to begin the day, especially in front of a bunch of sick exploitationists.

"Hey DJs check out the cool footage I just got!" Pete raced in, head-to-toe in his DisasterLand gear and noticed the open window. "Sweet! I was bein' all secret!" He was shooting again in seconds, "This is *so tight.* I'm gonna put this on MySpace!" Pete pumped his fist and a massive roar went up outside. "Wicked!"

The true proportion of the crowd was brutally revealed and Barb and Sarah exchanged glances. Barb inched to the window for a peek of what had previously been their quiet, leafy block. She gasped.

Media production vans, police cars, corporate Hummers—and *The Flame Thrower*— lined the far side of the street. Hundreds of people surrounded the vehicles, crowding their way onto neighbors' front lawns. T-shirts and breakfast were being hawked by official vendors and dutiful well-wishers were snapping up the schwag.

A creamy black Land Rover with the darkest tinted windows she'd ever seen was parked in their driveway below. Next to it stood Jack, microphone in hand, working the crowd for Pete's camera. *Eye of the Tiger's* famous chorus echoed in the distance and the smell of coffee and hickory smoke wafted in.

Pete flipped off the camera, "Sarah, wanna go be on TV?"

"Yeah, mom, can we? We're all packed..."

Pete shot out the door and Sarah followed before Barb even had a chance to respond. She discreetly tugged the curtain shut and placed her head in her hands. For all of them it had been a night of restless, low-grade fear though none would have admitted it.

Steve flipped on KBBQ, "... BBQ's Jack's Shack Blok-Rok Breakfast Party Live in Leawood to celebrate Kansas City's luckiest family, *The Beyers!* In just over 92.5 minutes, they depart for DisasterLand, *Life's Greatest Adventure!* Who am I with?"

"Nancy. And I just wanted to say me and my husband are big KBBQ fans! We listen to all the Chief's games!"

"Honey, that's Nancy down the street!"

Steve quieted her.

"Let's hope they have a big year. But right now, KC's got the Beyers! What do you think?"

"This whole thing's so awesome! We haven't had a block party since we celebrated the finishing of this subdivision ten years ago! It's so great! All the neighbors are here, we're just so happy for Steve and Barb and the kids... all of us, really. Just so happy for all of us. I'm seeing long-lost neighbors I thought moved away years ago! It's just like a big reunion and DisasterLand made it all happen!"

"Big shout out to DisasterLand!" Jack howled.

A deafening roar tore through the neighborhood and the Beyers' front door flew open, on cue. "Here they are, Kansas City! The Beyers! Kids, over here!"

"Steve, how can they do this?"

"How can they not?"

Barb reeled in the glare of his logic. Steve clawed his way upright, towards his luggage, and pulled out one of the Persistent shirts he'd packed.

"What's that?"

"I promised Dick I'd wear it. For TV."

"What else did you promise? We're supposed to wear our DisasterLand shirts you know."

"Honey, please. My head is throbbing. Let's start out on a positive." Steve turned up the radio's volume, "I'm already wearing the DisasterLand baseball cap and shoes... I'll even wear the rain gear, OK? I'll tattoo my forehead."

"Yo, 'sup Jackie!" It was Pete, on the radio.

"Welcome to KBBQ, You must be Peter!"

"Spike's the handle, DJ!"

"And you're Sarah?"

"Yeah."

"Looks like you take after your mom!"

Outside, the crowd roared their approval as Barb squirmed.

"You guys excited?"

"Oh yeah, dude!"

"What about you, Sarah?"

"It's... just so crazy. Like a dream or something."

"Scared?"

"No way, dude!"

"We'll be cool," Sarah added, "I mean, it's not like we're going to die or anything. We're not stupid."

"We took a poll earlier and KBBQ's listeners voted hurricane. What do you think?"

"I haven't even thought about it," Sarah confessed.

"And you, Spike?"

"That would be cool. But I think an Earthquake would be even cooler. You know, everything falling apart and stuff."

"You're in school, Sarah?"

"This fall I'll be a freshman at Columbia."

"Mizzou? And you're a Kansas girl!"

"No, Columbia University. In New York."

"Oh, I see... you're one of those. Too good for us here in the midwest!" Jack stepped back, playing up the dis as catcalls rained down around them. Pete flipped the crowd the bird.

Jack squeezed Sarah's shoulders, "You excited?"

"It's going to be sad leaving my friends."

"Well don't leave your friends too soon! You guys arrive back from DisasterLand in one piece. We'll be praying for you!"

"Thanks!"

"Kansas City's new favorite family, everyone. The hopes of a city on their shoulders!"

Elektra was on an unexpected brisk early morning walk through the park's shady trails in a desperate effort to calm her frayed nerves. Her Friday morning show ritual, a walking tour of the village streets as they came to life, was a way of grounding herself within the upcoming narrative. Yet today the streets simply hadn't cut it and she bailed, taking an emergency detour towards her favorite respite: the spring.

Here she was, early Friday morning and still fighting to regain her balance. It was looking more and more futile.

Around her the park was alive with groundskeepers applying finishing touches. Lawns were being watered, trails cleared, trees pruned and gardens manicured while the art department was busy spreading downed limbs and other potential props in strategic locations. Camera crews were testing some of the most remote hidden cameras in all of DisasterLand.

She found all of this tremendously reassuring.

It had, after all, been a sleepless night of hell. Clint had been drunk, and angry. He'd awakened her three times, each time insisting she walk him to the bathroom or else he'd piss all over everything. The final time he didn't even bother, preferring to leave a large puddle in the middle of her bed and insisting it was melted ice. She'd had to call security.

After Clint's ejection, she bravely decided against incinerating the defiled sheets. It would have been a shame—high thread-count Egyptian cotton wasted because of his drunken ass. She had them sent downstairs, to be über-washed with the worst of the worst during the show. After the guests were gone, she'd re-wash them at home to get out the chemicals. It somehow seemed symbolic.

The good news was that Clint would be with his doctors all morning long and was receiving the best care possible. The bad news was that the care was almost too good—when his call came tomorrow morning there was a damn good chance he'd be hitting the floor. For Elektra, this show would not be easy.

She'd have to put all that behind her, however, and focus. A quick trip to the spring, then a shower and she'd head down to the security center to observe the guest entrances. There, with Jude, the writers and her production team, they'd do a second casting of the hero families. There, the show would begin.

Tonight, Elektra would contrast her morning impressions of the floor with an evening visit to gauge the guests' moods. Every show was vastly different, just like every audience in a theater, and Elektra had begun to home in on a real sense of how the guests' mood affected the show's trajectory—a mathematical equation of sorts: full floor vibe minus empty floor vibe equals guest vibe. Whatever the result, a floor visit was vital to the work, yet after tonight absolutely impossible to risk.

She checked her phone: forty-five minutes until Shae's routine speech, which this time didn't feel so routine. She quickened her pace.

Perched atop a rise overlooking the river, the spring had been realized by Knut Boettels, DisasterLand's visionary architect, as a creative, rejuvenative space and was well-hidden from everyone but the most die-hard adventurers. Being the source of the park's river—with water bubbling up from DisasterLand's living machine natural bioremediation center directly below—it was incredibly pristine.

The sound of the adjacent waterfall was both soothing and energizing, the gentle mist it produced refreshing and moisturizing. The view too was unique: the spring sat just fifteen feet or so above the river, but because no trees were in the vicinity it offered a commanding view of the river, the wetlands just to the east and further on outside the dome, the external desert stretching to the mountains.

Much of the spring was in perpetual bloom with hand-selected rare breeds of flowers which not only poetically captured the sunlight but whose perfumed essence also worked aromatherapeutically to enhance self-reflection.

Perhaps it was her mood, but to Elektra it seemed particularly divine this morning as she slipped into the cool, refreshing waters, stripped of everything but her underwear.

She closed her eyes.

Unorthodox, but it worked.

Her phone's alarm brought her back to senses, eyes lazily drifting open to the sun's brilliance.

She dried her hands and grabbed the phone, propping the screen open inside her shoe on the ground next to her. She turned on the speakerphone.

Shae's image appeared on the tiny screen, right on schedule.

"Good Morning. First, let me thank each of you for taking time out of your busy day to join me for this announcement," he began. "It's the final show of our first season and we've wildly exceeded everyone's expectations including our own—no mean feat. For that I, and every one of our guests and investors thanks you. None of this could have happened without each one of you."

Elektra stared out through the dome's shining hexagonal frame and onto the desert valley floor, drinking in the moment as the applause continued.

"As we begin this show, I'd like us to remember the roller-coaster we've been on this year, and which will continue to carry us forward. Let's remember the good times and the bad, and let's remember the strength and the sweat it has taken to get us where we are. This show's script is the culmination of that work, yet it is only the starting point for what is to come. This is an ending, but it is only the beginning."

Elektra could feel the entire complex holding its breath.

"In one month, we begin the second season," Shae said, "and apologies are in order. I realize a script hasn't been presented yet and I want to personally apologize for the anxiety it had justifiably produced. It is not an ideal situation. For that I am personally very sorry."

He took a deep breath.

"But I can tell you that one week from Sunday, after this show's close, I will make a major announcement that will explain everything. Our mission is to realize a complete revolution in entertainment and to that end DisasterLand itself is about to transform. We will come out of this larger, stronger, and more mature as a company. Our goal is nothing less than a complete reinvention of ourselves."

The camera zoomed in, and Shae's eyes somberly met it head on. "DisasterLand is primed to explode into legend as the inconceivable becomes commonplace."

A chill shot down Elektra's spine.

"Thank you again, each and every one of you, and best of luck for the biggest show ever!"

Her screen went blank yet cheering from the distant atrium remained.

Security's latest status report followed—over twenty buses were now on the road headed towards DisasterLand, the closest running early and 105 minutes away. Guests would be entering in less than two hours.

Time was running short. Elektra quickly dressed and hit the hidden trail to the atrium, still dripping wet.

The well-dressed dwarf tipped his top-hat to the stunned family.

"You must be the Beyers!"

The family stood, immobilized, confronted by the sea of faces and waving arms crammed into the arrivals terminal of Las Vegas McCarran airport.

Remarkably, *Jack's Shack* had only been a warm-up. They'd been whisked away from the wild-eyed throngs lining their street and deposited almost directly onto their first-class seats via the fortified Land Rover, pre-boarding long before even the most dedicated frequent fliers. Hundreds of star-struck fans had camped out at the airport to celebrate in slack-jawed awe while others were silently leading prayer vigils for the family's safety. Yet none of it had prepared them for this.

"*Bey-ers! Bey-ers! Bey-ers!*"

The dwarf held his ground despite the steady clamor of enthusiastic well-wishers surrounding them, smiling pleasantly. He was, after all, a professional.

Many in the crowd waved signs wishing them good luck, some home-made, others sponsored by local media. The terminal was lit up like a film set and cameras dutifully rolled.

Vegas Welcomes The Beyers to Life's Greatest Adventure!

"Crazy world we live in, no?" the dwarf asked, smiling.

Barb noticed the beauty of his hand-tailored tuxedo and silently pointed it out to Steve. Words continued to elude them.

"I'm Li'l J, and I'll be escorting you to your cabin for the ride to DisasterLand," he continued.

Barb shook his tiny hand, "Nice to meet you Little J." The rest of the family followed. "Does that stand for something?"

"Sure does, ma'am. Stands for Jerome. But you can call me Li'l J."

"I see," Barb had appointed herself spokesperson, in light of Steve's continuing lack of verbal response. "Where do we pick up our luggage?"

"It's all taken care of, Missus Beyers." Li'l J motioned them off with a refined wave of his hand, the sea of bodies parting as if by magic to reveal a red carpet leading out gleaming double doors. "Right this way my friends, your cabin is waiting."

The Beyers took their first tentative steps down the carpet as if re-learning to walk and the volume throughout the terminal increased in response. Barb attempted a few scattered waves as Sarah covered her ears and they pressed on, towards their goal.

There, parked just outside the doors, was the largest stretch tour bus they'd ever seen. Six-foot-high animated wrap-around lettering circled the jet-black surface in rich, vivid colors: *DisasterLand*. As they watched, the letters were engulfed by fire only to rise once again.

"Excuse me, Little J?" Barb asked, yelling over the ecstatic howls.

"Yes, ma'am?"

"Are we special? Or does everyone get this treatment?"

"Everyone, ma'am."

Steve noticed the surrounding cameras closing in, capturing their walk from every angle. He straightened, unzipped his rain gear, and his silence came to a sudden and powerful end.

"Thank you, thank you all! Thanks Vegas, thanks KC! Thanks for your support! *We - will - survive!*"

A thunderous cheer erupted, rocking the terminal.

"Nice one, sir," yelled Li'l J, approaching the double glass doors. "Last cabin on the right. You're the last arrival on this coach, my friends, so you'll be departing shortly."

The doors slid open and they were blasted by the hot, dry air and blinding desert sun.

"Y'all take care now," he said with a bow.

Barb carefully shut the cabin door behind them.

"DJ, you think we're on CNN? Maybe someone from Hollywood will discover us and we'll become famous and rich!"

"Yeah mom, we've already been on TV more this morning than in the whole rest of our lives! We could be on Conan or something when we get out. Wouldn't that be cool?"

Barb was pale. "Kids, this is just like any other vacation."

"Yeah, *right*," Pete rolled his eyes. "What if *The FlameThrower*'s still at our house when we get back?! *Then what?*"

"Then your mother doesn't have to cook dinner," Steve quipped.

"Oh Steve, guess what?" Barb sighed. "We forgot to arrange to have the house looked after."

"We'll call when we get to our room, honey. With the promise of a souvenir, the guys will be falling over themselves to do it. In fact, someone's probably camped out in there already."

"Prolly *lots* of someones DJ!"

Steve shared an unconvincing laugh and turned his attention to the flat-screen TV next to them, featuring a high-school marching band working their way down the terminal sidewalk outside.

He found his stomach condensing into a dark, hard mass.

"You OK honey?" Barb took his elbow.

He winked. But despite the brave face, Steve felt himself slipping away, felt his control over his own destiny, and the destiny of his family, sliding disturbingly out of his control.

It had become asphyxiating: the swarms of people, the fast-pace, the almost assembly-line quality of their morning. They were literally on a conveyor belt to a disaster and they couldn't step off.

Within him a feeling arose, a feeling he had repressed since DisasterLand had burst into their lives. Now firmly in DisasterLand's grasp, Steve had the distinctly uncomfortable feeling their lives were about to change—radically, uncontrollably, and forever.

Steve took a deep breath and focused on the scents of luxury to sooth his overwhelmed mind. They were seated on hand-sewn leather seats, surrounded by dark wood. In place of a window was the widescreen TV, below it a fully stocked bar and refrigerator.

The rich smell of food had confronted them upon entry into the darkened bus, as uptempo jazz and discreetly flashing lights had directed them to their cabin. The other fifteen cabin doors had remained shut.

Maybe that was it too, Steve thought. Maybe a snack would help.

The DisasterLand theme music rang out around them and MagicD's tiny, smiling image suddenly appeared onscreen, arms famously outstretched.

"Next stahp, DisastahLand!"

A cheer went up throughout the bus as it began to pull away.

"Sit bahck, reh-lax an' hehlp yahselves! I'll be bahck, aftah yah big tour!" His image faded.

"Let's see what they've got," Steve said, opening the refrigerator. Surprised, he pulled out a perfectly chilled bottle of California sparkling wine.

"Look, there's an artisan cheese plate too!" exclaimed Barb.

"It stinks!" Pete said, eyeing the cheese plate with disdain.

Sarah pulled out a pint of handmade chocolate ice cream from the tiny freezer.

"Wicked!" Pete grabbed it from her, digging his fingers in. "Ummm..."

"Peter!" Sarah grabbed it back, struggling to carve out the untouched section before it was too late.

Steve held up the bottle for the family to examine. "This is good stuff."

Barb unfolded a small table from the wall to reveal a tiny cabinet, complete with tablecloth, glasses, silverware and ceramic plates. All, of course, emblazoned with the DisasterLand logo.

"Found some crackers," Steve added.

"DJ, can we keep these plates and stuff?"

"No," answered Barb. "And we reserve the right to search you when we leave. *Both of you.*" She eyed Sarah as the sound of popping corks and delightful laughter percolated throughout the bus.

As Steve popped their own cork and poured, Barb read aloud from the card attached to the bottle: "'*Best Wishes for a safe adventure, DisasterLand.*' That's sweet. And look, it's personally signed by DisasterLand's sommelier!"

"You're kidding." Steve took a look. She wasn't.

"It smells like a locker room in here," Pete said, holding his nose. "Hurry up and eat that stuff."

"Should we have a toast?" Steve raised his glass and the family followed. He froze, his mind struggling to find something—anything—appropriate.

Barb headed him off. "To DisasterLand!"

The glasses clinked, and Steve relaxed as the first bubbles tickled his parched throat. Had he been wrong to be so... cynical?

A computer-generated image of the twin domes faded in on the flatscreen and MagicD's voice rang out, "An' now, me turn yah ovah tah yah pehsonal cahncierge. Remembah tah enjoy yahselves!"

The domes spun and faded slightly, replaced by a young, outgoing blonde in a DisasterLand blazer. She smiled, generously.

"Good afternoon, and welcome Steve, Barb, Sarah and Peter!"

"That's us!" Steve wiped the cheese from his upper lip.

"My name's Danielle. I'll be booking your stay. First thing's first."

The woman's image retreated to the top corner of the screen and the domes grew brighter. They spun, revealing the twenty-two story guest tower, and zoomed in. One room, high up, began to glow. "You'll be in room 808, on the nineteenth floor, with one of the finest views available," Danielle stated. "Truly breathtaking."

Steve looked to Barb and the kids, his brow furrowed. "Excuse me, ma'am, maybe I'm missing something, but why is room 808 on the nineteenth floor?"

"Privacy. All our guests' locations are confidential... to prevent inconveniences."

"I..." Steve's mind failed to develop any sort of follow-up.

"Don't worry, Mr. Beyers. You'll understand. Now, it's extremely important that you familiarize yourself with the layout of DisasterLand at your earliest convenience—tonight if possible. Just in case of emergency."

MagicD's voice rang out in laughter. "An' dere will be an' ehmergehncy, mon!"

A map of DisasterLand appeared, highlighting the village, the shops, restaurants, cafés, theaters, clubs and park.

"So what would you like to do first?"

Pete leapt in, unable to hold back the question which had been hounding him , "I heard about a really cool video game but there's nothing on the web."

A devilish smiled crossed Danielle's face, "I might something know about that."

"You *might*?"

"I can only tell you that it does exist. But anything else is classified."

"Really? Pete leapt up, grabbing either side of the thin, flat-screen television. Barb tried to restrain him. "No *foolin'*!?"

"You'll have to qualify."

"How?"

"Play-offs are in the main gaming center, starting at five p.m. First-come first-served."

"That's dope!"

"Wait now, hold on Spike," Steve responded. "This is a family trip. We make decisions together."

"But DJ! It's..."

"If I may, Mister Beyers, there's plenty for the adults to do while the children are away."

Sarah jumped in as Steve retreated, wondering if he had sounded as dumb as he now felt, "What movies are playing tonight?"

"Tonight we have a premiere so tickets are going fast. It's *Gone Forever,* a tragic story of star-crossed young love."

"Blah!" Pete yelled, folding his arms.

Sarah slapped him, "Mind your own business."

"A premiere?" Barb elbowed Steve.

"Every weekend an original DisasterLand independent production is presented in our deluxe movie theater. The hottest talent combines with the latest in technology and stadium seating to offer you the best in modern storytelling."

Steve shook his head, "Honey, we didn't come to DisasterLand to watch movies."

"If you change your mind," Danielle added, "All DisasterLand titles except premieres are available anytime on our HDTV video-on-demand system."

Sarah eyed her parents. "So can I get a ticket?"

"Sure, honey," Barb replied. "Why not?"

"One for *Gone Forever,*" Danielle confirmed, "Nine-thirty or midnight?"

"Midni..."

"Nine-thirty," Steve interrupted.

"Nine-thirty," Sarah repeated, slowly.

"Nine-thirty it is." A tally of the booking appeared next to Danielle's smiling face.

"Honey, that sounds so nice." Barb was refilling the family's champagne flutes.

"What about restaurants?" Steve asked.

"Careful with the little ones, Ms. Beyers. I must remind you the drinking age in

Nevada is twenty-one, just like all other states."

"Of course... sorry." Barb froze, glancing at Steve, who began to discreetly examine the cabin for hidden cameras.

"DisasterLand offers twenty restaurants with the world's best chefs," Danielle announced, "And all deliver."

On-screen, an immense montage of restaurants flashed by, broken down by culinary style.

"Gosh, there's so much to choose from!" The family huddled together to watch.

"This is just amazing!" Barb hugged Steve. "They've got everything. But let's order in, tonight, honey. How about French? Steak frite, delivered! Isn't that just glutinous?" Barb checked the reactions.

No one seemed impressed.

Danielle smiled, broadly, "I've got quite a surprise for you. Seems you're a very lucky family."

"*We are?*" Pete was on the edge of his seat. Again.

"I have a reservation in your name for Del Sol, at seven. How does that sound?"

"*Del Sol?*" Barb wondered.

"The most exclusive restaurant in DisasterLand, featuring one of the few Michelin-starred chefs working in the country."

Barb discreetly whispered to Steve, "Honey, we can't afford that!"

"How'd we get a reservation?" Steve asked.

Danielle smiled, smugly. "Dinner's on your company, Steve. With best wishes for good luck."

"On Persistent?" Steve couldn't believe it.

"Yes, sir. You're a very lucky family. The waiting list for tables is extensive. I don't know quite how they accomplished it, but they did."

"Wow, DJ they must really dig you!"

Steve noticed Barb's scowl, "What, honey?"

"You're not working this week, are you?"

"Of course not..."

"Finally," Danielle continued, as another face appeared on the screen, young and athletic, "Your personal agent will be Maria Mirõn. She'll be at your service around the clock during your stay." Danielle smiled reassuringly, "May I help you in any other way? Reservations for tomorrow? A spa perhaps?"

"I don't believe so. Not yet. I think we'll play it by ear," Steve said.

Barb looked to Steve, disbelieving what she just had heard, "Honey, doesn't that sound good? A spa? What if it fills up?"

"That'll be it Danielle."

"Fine. If I can be of assistance during this journey, just call. Thank you and enjoy your stay. Bye-bye!"

Another mini-fanfare burst forth, and MagicD was now sitting on a bench deep in DisasterLand's park, with the river rushing behind him and a tropical drink in his hand. He winked.

"We be seein' yah *soon*! Now yah'll begin dah fihnal ahpproach!"

DisasterLand's elite were huddled around the underground master security center for their Friday ritual, all bathed in the blue glow of the enormous wall of monitors. Together, they were scanning live feeds from cameras throughout the nation which were following every incoming family's progress.

Elektra surveyed the workspace around her with disgust. After only a couple of hours the cups, cans, bottle wrappers, fruit peels and discarded packaging of all sorts had reached a critical mass. Someone needed to get it under control. She couldn't think straight anymore.

She motioned apologetically to 'Lexi, her understudy, who understood instantly and rose. No one else was free: the four directors were there, along with Colin Knight and his team of assistant directors, including Julie. They were flanked by the heads of both the security and psychological teams, while DisasterLand's head nurse was also on-hand to filter any information from special-needs families to the staff. Shae was hanging silently in the back of the room glued to his Blackberry while DTV's many department heads were constantly popping in for first looks. Only Greg, uniquely, was absent.

"So how many have we tagged?" Elektra asked, returning to the job at hand. There had been a lull and energy levels were dropping fast.

"Six so far," Frankie replied. As the head of security tech, the guest database was his baby. "With two standouts: a family from Louisville and one from Spokane."

"Let's review Spokane. What have we got?"

"A real piece of work," someone said, to chuckles.

Frankie hit a couple of buttons along his massive video mixer and sent the signal to the largest central monitor.

The image of a thirteen-year old Barbie-doll appeared, hovered over by her impeccably-preened family. She was thin, blond, with every curl meticulously sprayed into place.

"That's her leaving this house this morning," Frankie confirmed.

"You'll notice there aren't a whole lot of friends around to see them off," the psychologist added.

"Field crew reported she threw two tantrums before they even got out of the driveway and insisted on the flight being held while she went to Nordstrom's because the dry cleaners had shrunk her entrance dress."

"You're shitting me. I must have missed that part," chuckled Shae.

"They wouldn't of course so they're arriving late."

"Yeah, we'll nail her," Elektra grinned. "What do you guys say?"

She received a unanimous thumbs-up after a brief consultation.

"But ease into it. We're sensing massive underlying instability," the psychologist added.

"No shit. OK, we'll flush the family out into the open first. See how they play."
She added the note to the database.

"So who's this?" Shae was pointing to a monitor on the lower left, opposite side of the room.

"Is that LAX?" Elektra asked.

"Sure is," Frankie confirmed.

"Field is confirming a young couple from L.A."

"And believe it or not," 'Lexi smiled, having returned, "his application lists waiter. Wife's a lawyer, they're newlyweds."

"No kids?" Elektra asked.

"None."

"You guys thinking what I'm thinking?"

"Pretty clear. He's an actor," confirmed Colin.

"And he's found a backdoor. Smart. Have we seen that before?"

"Not so blatantly."

"Starving actors can't afford it!" Julie laughed.

"Let's tag 'em. They could be fun. What kind of law?"

"Fortune 500 corporate. IP. Intellectual property," 'Lexi confirmed.

Elektra leaned back. Friday afternoons were a highlight for all of them... they were molding the week while not actually having to take any sort of real-time responsibility. Mistakes could be corrected. Compared to the fire of the Bridge when live, master security on Fridays was the chill-out room.

The core security team had been monitoring all feeds since early morning to catch first impressions of the family's departures. Screen-grabs and voice-prints were stored within the massive guest database, linked to the original uncut footage to be called up at any time for any reason.

The psychological team was busy cross-linking the families with their background checks and health records, all in an effort to build a comprehensive prediction of the family's future performance. Applications had been scrutinized and any families seen to be crying out for help would be studied particularly intensely.

Likewise, the family's room assignments had been made based on their medical records, and doctors were now assessing whether any last-minute changes needed to be made. This was possible right up to the time the family set foot in the tower.

By now, many families had already landed in Vegas and concrete forecasts were emerging.

The goal for the day was to single out twenty families whom the staff could rely on for action and amusement. All of this information would be at Elektra's fingertips to help head off difficult situations when they'd inevitably arise, or to help construct amusing situations when events were descending into the mundane.

Database contributions would continue to be made throughout the show. Notes, comments and performance reports would join the video and audio, expanding the database minute-by-minute from the moment the first guests departed for DisasterLand until the last ones exited. It then got backed-up, stored, and placed in the vault with the complete video and audio coverage of each show for archiving.

By the end of the week each family had hundreds of gigabytes of information captured about them. It was Shae's hope that at a later date this information could be returned to them, a sort of digital scrapbook of their stay at DisasterLand. But right now the atmosphere was too white hot. Within hours of release, the footage would appear across the internet and that was no good for anyone.

This database was one of the key innovations that made DisasterLand tick. Any of this information could be pulled from the database and sent to any employee's phone, Blackberry or laptop, anywhere in the complex, instantaneously. This allowed almost real-time improvisational power by the actors on the floor, as well as aiding in emergency maneuvers by the ADs to circumvent danger.

It could also be channeled to select staff, via the Feed, for use at any time.

Recently the database had attracted the notice of the CIA and Shae wasn't happy about it, unsure of how they'd gotten wind. In the end he'd talked them into licensing it sight unseen and they'd paid handsomely—built-in punishment for what Shae considered to be corporate espionage.

Yet the most important part of the database still remained top-secret and even the spooks hadn't found it. A hard-core team of social recluses were developing a set of AI algorithms to predict guest's future behavior based solely upon their actions during the entrances. Once fully and successfully developed, the hours of time spent manually flagging heroes could be rendered unnecessary.

"That L.A. actor... you guys think he'd make a good victim?" Elektra wondered out loud.

"It's sort of what he wants isn't it? Attention?" the psychologist confirmed. "But I'm not sure if we should feed it."

"But what if he thinks he's getting just the opposite?" Elektra wondered.

"You mean take him out?" the psychologist asked.

"You're thinking of the vigil, E?" Greg asked. "Kidnapping?"

"Precisely," Elektra smiled.

"That could work," the psychologist added. "Play the fears."

"Lets tag them and note it," Elektra said.

"Done," Frankie confirmed.

"And during their entrance, let's have an actress—how about Angie?—test their marriage. I'm kind of curious about those two," she continued.

There were the good families and the bad, the good Samaritans and the spoiled children. All would be singled out mercilessly, their character tested relentlessly. Those who resisted the most would get hit the hardest.

Elektra's phone buzzed. Clint.

"Shit," Elektra muttered.

Elektra scanned the text message, "They've cleared Clint for tomorrow," she announced. "I guess his tests this morning came out OK. I don't see how."

"He's a strong boy," Shae replied.

"I guess so," Elektra sighed. "Has anyone developed the Eternal Sunshine technology yet? I'll pay."

"Welcahme mah friends! Tah DisastahLand Valleh!"

The flatscreen flipped itself up and away, revealing a tiny porthole.

Peter was the first to see them, down below, his face pressed against the glass. Unable to speak, he simply pointed. *There.*

The domes. From high up on the mountain pass, they looked so small, so fragile, the work of science-fiction gnomes tending a crystal garden. They sparkled magnificently.

A line of dark busses was visible, snaking out from underneath the entrance canopy.

A hush had settled over their bus, all noise evaporating in the gravity of the moment. Steve's uneasiness grew and Barb took his hand.

It was Pete again, grunting. The rest of the family leaned in, over and around him, eventually forcing him aside to wait for his smeared face-print to disappear.

The cliff.

D-i-s-a-s-t-e-r-L-a-n-d®

Steve had been to Mount Rushmore as a kid, but compared to the marvel he now witnessed, Rushmore was easily dismissible as the work of unskilled amateurs.

It wasn't simply the sharply-edged rendition of the enormous letters and mathematically-precise registered trademark symbol. It was the enveloping explosion, perfectly carved to blend seamlessly into the geography of the surrounding mountains, creating the disconcerting illusion that the sign itself was a wondrous, timeless work of nature. As if nature herself had spewn forth the message.

Arms up and actions deliberate, as if he would somehow damage the sign by speech, Pete carefully whispered, *"That is so wicked DJs..."*

Barb longed for her camera, now stuck in her luggage on the request of the Land Rover's driver. But in the end she knew a photograph simply couldn't capture the grandiosity of the monument, the full impact of the statement. It was something that had to be seen, to be *witnessed*, in context. It was a declaration.

The moment glimmered for everyone in the bus as their privilege became wondrously obvious: they were, indeed, the chosen ones. Persuasive and monumental music echoed around them, enhancing, resonating with, and amplifying the moment.

Pete could no longer contain himself and he began bouncing back-and-forth seat-to-seat in the tiny cabin, his family protecting themselves as best they could. *"This is so dope!"*

And for once, the family agreed. It *was* dope.

Steve felt in his back pocket for his pen and paper. They were approaching the front lines of American culture and he was obligated to mine the experience for all it was worth. Already, he felt his imagination recharging. He prayed for a bountiful week.

They watched, eyes transfixed on the near-mythical valley which grew closer with every hair-pin turn of their descent. As they reached the valley floor, the bus slowed, pulling gradually to one side. The security center was approaching.

"They've got big guns!" Pete announced, a little too loudly for the family's comfort.

"Quiet Peter."

The guards smiled, happily brandishing their automatic rifles. They waved, welcoming the bus, waving them all through. Pete waved back, giving them the thumbs-up.

Steve cleared his throat, "Danielle?"

Her voice rang out moments later, "Changed your mind about the Spa?"

"In fact..." Barb was quick to interject.

Steve frowned, "The armed guards..."

Danielle laughed, "There to hold you inside, sir."

Barb gasped and Denise giggled, "Just kidding. Merely a deterrent."

"I mean... DisasterLand has never been targeted by *real*..."

He was cut off by Danielle's pleasantly dismissive reply, "Of course not, sir. You're at the safest place in the world, and that's proven. We own the entire valley and the surrounding mountain range is United States military land. We own the access road as well, sir, so that just about eliminates all options. One thing you'll learn here, sir, safety is our number one priority."

"Thank you."

"Thank *you*, Mr. Beyers."

The bus picked up speed for the home stretch, guards firing in the air behind them for effect.

Steve stared at the approaching domes, assessing his adversary as an awestruck silence overtook the bus.

One hour later, the Beyers' cabin door flung open and the family shot down the chute like a family of prize-winning rodeo bulls.

Tensions had risen with each previous guest entrance and now, jostling out of the bus, they were electrified. As their feet hit the plush red carpet Barb locked hands around the kids, preventing Pete's dive into the frothing maelstrom.

They were immediately swept up into the slipstream and sucked powerfully towards the sparkling glass entrance, through the wild crowd of assembled maniacs.

Flashbulbs popped around them, reflecting in the surrounding glass to create a disorienting, multifaceted jewel of light as afterimages danced in their eyes.

Times Square was a small, dark crevice compared to the phosphorescent magnificence on display here, even in the daylight. Steve fought for a glimpse of tower itself, rocketing above them.

Guest entrances had been playing on their flatscreen, *E!* network-style, since their bus left the security center almost an hour ago. But seeing them on television and experiencing it firsthand were two entirely different beasts.

"This is just like the Academy Awards!" Sarah yelled.

"Except we're not rich, we're not famous, and no one cares!" Steve shot back. The crowd was suffocating him.

Ahead of them, a beautiful couple was being interviewed, their young, wide-eyed daughter between them. The cameras read: DTV.

A roar went up for the Beyers' exit and the Steve turned to catch the little girl watching them. Her mother waved, and Steve waved back.

"What was that all about?" Barb yelled.

"I don't know, I was just being friendly. Come on, sweetie, we're on television."

"Yo! It's MagicD! *Fo'real!*" Pete yelled, pointing. Barb knocked his arm down.

Steve struggled for a deep breath of the dry, desert air amidst the throng but failed. Panic suddenly overtook him and he prepared to flee, until Barb stomped on his foot. Wincing, Steve continued limping down the carpet as his family adjusted to the contorted faces cheering around them. *Who are these people?*, Steve wondered. *Where the hell did they come from?*

The flashbulbs continued firing.

"Ladies and Gentlemen, the Beyers! From Leawood, Kansas!" an omnipotent voice rang out. Unseen fireworks were launched into the air, exploding with profound concussions as the relentless throb of massive dance beats continued their metronomic assault.

The swarming crowd pressed in. The glare of spotlights blinded the family yet they pushed on.

"It's even better than the DVD!" Pete yelled, but no one heard.

A microphone was shoved in Steve's face by a DTV reporter who had elbowed his way to the overwhelmed family.

A terrible thought occurred to Steve as the cameras landed on them—if something happened to them this week, to any of them, something horrific, *this* would be the image released to the media.

Steve put his arm around his wife and waved. He was trying, desperately, to smile, to make his family, his friends, and his company proud. He wasn't sure if he was succeeding.

Barb squeezed her daughter, nervously. Sarah tugged away, under her breath, "Mom, let me *go*."

"Welcome to DisasterLand! Please, introduce yourself."

"You're the first people who haven't known all day!" Steve growled. Barb elbowed him in the ribs.

"I'm Barbara Beyers. We're from Kansas and I'm a teacher. This is Sarah and Peter."

Now it was Pete's turn to elbow his mother. She amended, "But we call him

Spike."

Pete flipped a sign as Barb hugged Sarah. "Sarah's a budding journalist and has had several award-winning stories published in the school paper."

"Welcome! And the little man?"

Steve grabbed Pete, "He's a local baseball hero!"

"In da house!" Pete's fist raised in triumph.

The reporter nodded, impressed. "That should give you guys an advantage." He shot a big, toothy smile to Steve. "And you sir?"

"I'm Steve Beyers. I... I'm in advertising." He opened his jacket to reveal the Persistent logo.

"Oh great, *another* advertising person!" The reporter punched his shoulder, just a little too hard.

"A warm, DisasterLand welcome—for the Beyers! Room 808!" echoed over the immense DisasterLand sound system.

Another roar spread through the crowd and the Beyers waved, their faces blank, searching for context. Steve imagined the line scrolling below their image on the flatscreens of waiting busses: *The Beyers—Leawood, Kansas—Room 808.*

The tractor-beam restarted and they were pulled underneath the massive glass canopy which swept out from the tower like a raindrop, as if the building itself was a biological entity, a future part of nature. Magically suspended inside, a glowing 3-D DisasterLand logo twirled.

Impressive glass columns supported the canopy, fires raging inside some. Inside others, cascades of water rushed by. Ahead of them lay the massive smoked glass double-doors of DisasterLand's official entrance.

The family tried to stop, to admire, but it proved impossible to resist the massive current.

Sarah screamed. *"There he is! Right there!"*

"MagicD! *MagicD!*" Pete was leaping up and down, punching the air. Not for the last time, Barb pitied his teachers this fall.

Only feet ahead, MagicD's grey dreadlocks waved and his fresh lei bounced on his glistening brown potbelly. His trademarked Bermuda shorts were jiggling to the beat which now overtook the family as they rushed ahead to join him.

In a flash he grabbed Sarah's hand and the two of them were dancing chest-to-chest. A massive cheer exploded and the unseen DJ took the beats to the next level.

Pete jumped in, arms around both of them, effervescently.

MagicD smiled, "Yah mon! Dah Beyers be jammin' tah dah DisastahLand beat! Tanks fah joinin' us. Me tinks yah'll hahve ah r-r-r-righteous tihme!"

He pecked Sarah's cheek as Pete gawked, mouth open. Pete leapt into his belly, giving MagicD a giant hug. MagicD sprinkled glittering dust on each in turn, as they passed.

The kids danced on, together, through DisasterLand's remarkable entrance as Barb and Steve laughed after them.

They were inside.

PART TWO. DURING.

FRIDAY: P.M.

The smoked glass doors locked behind them and the Beyers found themselves suddenly and remarkably in a void, lost in a viscous, turbid darkness.

The almost complete sensory deprivation was profoundly shocking, the complete opposite of what had lay just outside the door. A bizarre, almost inverse claustrophobia overtook them and Steve launched himself backwards into the door, groping for a handle.

He found nothing. The rising sound of his desperate, rasping breath grated his family's ears until he spun off, wildly, and thudded into the opposite wall only a few feet away.

"Honey!" Barb screamed.

"Where the hell are we Barb?"

Another thud reverberated through the small space as Steve collided with a third wall, knocking Pete into the fourth.

"Honey, relax!" Barb grabbed desperately for Steve's hand and somehow connected, "You're going to hurt someone!"

Steve slowed, gasping. The family stood, immobile, hearts thudding in ears as they fought to peel back the infinite darkness. The sound of blowing wind tickled their ears, though none was to be felt.

Sarah's voice quivered, "Come on, this is weird. Let's go."

"Go *where*, honey?" Steve asked, acerbically.

"I don't know, dad, anywhere!" Sarah responded, her voice quivering.

As their eyes adjusted, the unbroken outlines of a small box were revealed. They were trapped.

Moments later, and just as their emotional temperatures had become intolerable, an entire glimmering universe flashed on around them as if they were inside a vast chandelier, subtly revealing their tortured faces.

A rustling echoed in the distance, growing wildly, until the entire box began to shake. It seemed to accelerate mightily upwards, as if preparing to leave the atmosphere. The family fought to hide their alarm as they grasped for the walls.

Barb stumbled, choking back nausea.

From the master security center, DisasterLand's staff scrutinized the families' reactions carefully. They liked what they saw.

The rumbling stopped, abruptly, and an unseen door slid open to reveal a clinically white foyer with a solitary door on the opposite wall.

The shaken family stumbled out, cautiously, and the elevator door slid shut behind them. A large black '19' was painted in the center of each wall. Ambient music sonically morphed around them.

"This place is too weird," Pete whispered, while their eyes struggled to adjust amidst the whiteness. Moments later the opposite door slid open, revealing a rush of space and the sound of voices echoing over a vast distance.

Pete took a few tentative steps. "Holy smokes, DJs!" he called, reeling in amazement.

The family followed him out onto a wide glass walkway, suspended nineteen stories above the bustling atrium floor. It bowed out gently to their left, following the seductive curve of the dome.

There, doors to the floor's forty guest rooms trailed off into the distance, while on the opposite side, only a tremendous amount of sunlit, open space lay before them.

"Oh my God," Barb said.

"Good thing we're not scared of heights."

"They asked us about that. What did you put?"

"I can't remember."

Steve followed Pete to the waist-high metal railing. Despite the hype, despite the DVD and impossible expectations, he hadn't been prepared for *this*. None of them had.

The tower swept down and out below them in a gentle pregnant curve which elegantly prevented vertigo, ending almost two hundred feet below and giving the effect of a futuristic layer cake.

A net extended out almost invisibly from each walkway, partially shielding the floor below. It was subtle, yet Steve found its presence menacing.

"You kids ever seen anything like it?" he asked. The girls had joined them at the railing, each lost in their own inspired thoughts.

"Sure. It's like the Death Star, DJ."

"I mean *really*. Have you ever seen anything like it *really*?"

"You mean for real, DJ?"

"Yes. For real." Steve glanced at Barb. "In person."

"Nope," Pete pronounced, firmly.

"Sarah?"

"Hunh-unh."

There was an energy, a joy, they felt radiating up from the floor and directly into their hearts. Their spirits were lifted as the miracle of DisasterLand's very existence impressed upon their consciousness. It was a feeling, an experience, and it set alight their souls. Shae had a nickname for it: *the conversion.*

Nineteen heart-pounding stories below lay the winding cobblestone streets of the ancient, walled village, circling the rustic café tables of an outdoor coffee shop, the elegantly terraced central garden, and finally, in the center of it all, the magnificent hyper-modern fountain.

Early-bird guests were already bustling through the maze-like alleys, shopping bags in hand, furiously hitting the arrival sales.

The village itself was enclosed by the periphery of the dome, with two more floors of neon-lit bars, restaurants, clubs and theaters spreading out from the base of the tower. *If the whole world suddenly went to hell,* Steve thought, *we could live here forever in bliss.*

Opposite them, past the village, they could just make out the Great Lawn at the entrance to the smaller, "twin" dome, which housed the wild green explosion of natural park. Families were lounging together, picnicking, while children lazily tossed Frisbees in the distance.

Pete raised his fists overhead, "Let's go, DJs, right now!"

"Easy, Peter. There'll be plenty of time. We've only been here ten minutes and we've got ten days."

"*YES!*"

Above them, there was one more glass walkway. The twenty-first and twenty-second floors were simply walls of smoked glass.

Yet the most impressive thing of all they somehow noticed last: suspended over the center of the atrium was an enormous video ball nearly fifty feet in diameter: the InfoTron. Scrolling across its vast circumference, the parade of live guest entrances continued. The Beyers watched, entranced, imagining their own magnified entrance appearing only minutes before.

"I just don't believe it," Barb offered.

"Me neither," Steve said.

From nearby, laughter echoed and the Beyers turned. A couple of roughly the same age were down the walkway, smiling at them.

"Sorry, we like to watch!" they smirked. "Don't worry, everyone feels it. We've been here two hours. We *know!*"

Barb and the kids scrunched in behind Steve.

"So you must be the Beyers!"

Barb eyed her skittish kids, protectively.

"How'd you know?" Steve asked.

"We saw your entrance. Your daughter's quite a dancer!"

Sarah's brow furrowed.

"I'm Jim Andrews, and this is my wife Jenny." They approached with hands outstretched. "So what'll you reckon, Beyers? Earthquake? Terrorists?"

"I..."

"Me? I'm hoping for a hurricane. But I'm a water guy."

"It all sounds kind of bad to me," Jenny said, and Barb laughed her agreement, relieved.

"So tell me something, Beyers, if you don't mind, what brings a guy like you here to risk the wife and kids?"

"We won the trip actually."

"Of course! I thought you looked familiar. We saw you on the natioanl news. Saved yourself twenty-five G's! Not bad!"

Steve nodded. *National news?* It was all a bit unsettling.

"Luck brings most people. Some call it destiny," Jenny added.

Steve felt Barb's glance. "What about you?" he asked.

"I guess we're just the kind of people who need to see what all the fuss is about," Jenny said.

Jim nodded. "And we certainly don't shy away from a good adventure. Boy, this otta be something," he laughed. "So you're here on nineteen?"

"Room 808."

"I suppose that's around here somewhere. Those elevators don't lie! We're in 112, just past the central elevators. Fourth one down on the left."

The Beyers turned back to where they had come from. The white door was closed.

"Not over there. You won't have any luck calling that thing," Jim said, "They've got us locked in."

Barb followed his outstretched hand on to two sleek glass elevators set gracefully into the center of the tower, flanked by two all-glass tubes which spiraled down to the atrium floor. Staircases. Lost in the magic of the atrium below, they'd missed this completely.

"She's got dead people in her lips," Sarah whispered to Pete.

Pete recoiled in disgust and Sarah giggled. Barb shot them a dirty look.

"No joke," Sarah whispered, "Some women inject dead people in their lips to make them fat."

Dead people? Pete didn't quite buy it but Sarah was putting on a good act and Jenny's lips were sure fat. Finally, eyeing Jenny carefully, he admitted his defeat. "Whatever," he grunted.

"Well, we better get crackin'," Jim said, sticking out his hand. Steve shook it once again. "We want to do some shopping before the locusts hit. It was good to meet you folks. I'm sure we'll be seeing you around."

"Ten whole days. Good to meet you."

The Andrews ambled off, towards the elevators. The Beyers waited a few moments, and followed.

"That was strange, don't you think? I mean, *destiny?*" Barb shook her head.

"It's a special place, Barb. You can't deny that. They're just a little carried away."

"I don't know if I liked them, Steve. We've got to be careful. This place must draw every freak in the whole country."

"Surely they're priced out, honey."

"Not us, DJ!"

The family slowly made their way down the walkway in confusion, past door after unmarked door, each with a tiny little blank screen next to it. They approached the first set of stairs, pleased to find two charming café patisseries, both subdued and inviting, set next to each landing. *Café Dansant*, the furthest read.

"Look DJs! It's a pati-series... or whatever."

"They make desserts and things honey. It's French."

"Wicked."

Sarah had continued on, past the Andrews waiting for the elevator. Pete hurried to catch up as she peeked into the café.

"Where are we going?" Steve whispered to Barb.

"I don't know, honey."

The kids continued on, jogging now. Ahead of them, one door's small screen began to blink: *808*.

"There it is!"

The door was halfway between the elevators and the opposite end of the tower, a long way from the only exit they knew.

Pete raced ahead, then stopped, short. "Hey, what about a key, DJ?" he yelled.

"Key? They never gave us a key!"

"Well how are we supposed to get in?"

"I don't know, Spike. Barb?"

"Don't ask me."

"There's obviously some mistake. Try your cell."

"It's in my luggage, remember?"

"Where *is* our luggage?"

"I don't know, honey. They told us not to worry about it."

"Oh my God. I don't believe this..."

"Honey, calm down. Let's ask the Andrews." Barb turned back, but they were gone.

"Fuck this. Come on, Spike. Let's go take a look."

Barb couldn't believe Steve was cursing, already. It had taken only minutes.

Steve and Pete approached the door confrontationally. As they neared, it slid open with MagicD's voice ringing out joyfully, "Wel-cahme home! If yah need anah-ting tah-nite, yah jus' call!"

"I thought they said this was high security!" Barb exclaimed as she joined them.

"No shit," whispered Sarah.

"DisasterLand ROCKS!" Pete screamed, at the top of his lungs.

As the yell faded into the background noise of the atrium, Barb and Steve stared at one another, helplessly.

The Beyers entered the suite slowly, their caution laced with mistrust. The front door slid shut behind them and crushed the atrium's white noise, leaving them alone, with the sound of cheering echoing mischievously from another room. Steve frowned.

The entry hall opened up to their left into a utilitarian kitchen which lead to a compact but surprisingly cozy dining area. To the right, down a short hallway, lay another door.

Steve nodded to girls to check the left, while Steve and Pete took the hallway. It led to a small, functional bedroom—Pete and Sarah's—with two twin beds, an end table, dresser and closet. At the far end of the room, a very small round window looked out onto the walkway—another porthole. After a quick once-over, they joined the girls in the dining area.

Steve stopped to admire a small bouquet of flowers on the kitchen table and toyed with the idea of checking the fridge for a minibar. But he knew Barb wouldn't be pleased, and these initial minutes were critical. There would be plenty of time for a cold beer later. Plenty of time for everything.

Ten whole days, Steve joyfully reminded himself.

Past the dining area lay the living room, where Barb and Sarah were seated on a plush sofa, slack-jawed and feet up on a small table across from a gorgeous, widescreen HDTV.

Guest entries were continuing, now with sound, and a female host was commenting on each family's appearance—particularly on any sort of accessories the guests had accentuated the standard-issue DisasterLand gear with. Small ads played in the corner, offering locations of exclusive shops located throughout the atrium.

"What do you think they said about us?" Pete asked.

There was no response.

Pete followed his dad on into the master bedroom where they were confronted by a wall of curtains. The king bed was neatly made with a DisasterLand-branded comforter. Another door, just cracked, was to their right.

Pete raced ahead and pulled back the curtains, not prepared for the result.

"Honey, you've got to see this!" Steve yelled.

The floor-to-ceiling windows majestically surveyed DisasterLand Valley. Mountains ringed the distance, with the sun lingering almost directly overhead as if contemplating its impending descent. The security center was barely visible at the foot of the mountains, with the remarkable DisasterLand logo perched far above and to their right.

Nineteen floors straight down below them, just breaking out of shadow, the line of busses still snaked out from underneath the canopy. The entrance was lit up like a stadium with swirling floodlights, colored disco lights and flashbulbs.

Their window shook to the pounding beats. Fireworks continued to explode powerfully.

"Fresh crib yo!" Pete said, head nodding.

"Peter I want you to start talking like a normal person," Barb said, entering.

"DJ!"

"These are wealthy people here, Peter. They're going to think we didn't raise you right."

"Come on, Mom, lots of kids talk like that," Sarah said.

"I don't care. That's enough, Peter."

"Mom!"

"Enough!"

"You're racist mom," Sarah said.

"I am *not* racist! I just feel, as a teacher, that the English language..."

"Enough... *enough!*" Steve interjected. "Honey, he can talk however he wants as long as we can understand him. *For now.* Please."

Pete smirked triumphantly as Sarah and Steve entered the master bath. A family-sized hot-tub had been built into the wall inches away from the same massive picture window, just like in the DVD.

"I didn't believe it," Steve said, tearing off his shirt.

"Honey! *Wait!*" Barb called, joining them. "Let's wait till after dinner. When there's no pressure." *And the kids are gone*, was her not-so-secret implication.

"Come on... just a short..."

"No," Barb shut off the light.

Reluctantly replacing his shirt, Steve mentally resurveyed their temporary home. It could be worse. Much, much worse. He had to admit a slight air of *replaceability* which he found unnerving, yet the suite still maintained a comfortable, understated elegance.

And better yet, the cleanliness was impressive. This place could surely be the epicenter of natural biotech, a boot camp for epidemics, but in fact it seemed clinical. The kitchen and bathroom were spotless.

Everything was taken care of.

"Let's start a contest to see who can spend the most time in the hot tub!" Pete offered.

"That's not safe, Peter."

"Nothing cool is. Come on!"

Barb threw up her hands.

"Hey, look there's our luggage!" Sarah interrupted. Sure enough, it was neatly tucked away between the bed and the window.

"What's that?" Pete asked. A small compartment was built in the wall above the luggage. The door was open.

"A safe," Barb said, approaching.

"By the way, didn't you read the release? It said not to bring anything of value.

They're not responsible, honey," Steve said, eyeing her diamond necklace.

"I know... but I'm glad I did. You saw those entrances televised for everyone to see. Besides, no one is responsible for anything anymore, honey, you know that. Everything will be fine."

"Look!" Pete grabbed four small fanny packs from the hole, each one shining with a prominent DisasterLand logo, "D-PAKs! For emergencies!"

"Oh God," Barb turned away. "Can't we just enjoy ourselves for five minutes?"

Pete handed one to his dad and Steve dumped the contents on the bed: micro-thin thermal blanket, goggles, a facemask, band-aids and wound-care, tubes of ointment, painkillers, liquid hand sanitizer, a tiny powerhouse LED flashlight and more.

Pete grabbed a small, foil-wrapped package. *DL:PowerStrip*, it read. "Cool! It's an energy bar! I'm starving!"

Barb stopped him as he tried to open it, "Just leave it honey."

"Yeah, you don't want to eat that now Spikers. You might need that later."

"Whatever, DJ. I bet they have truckloads of them. It's all marketing, right?"

Steve chuckled, picking up a thin card, no larger than a credit card, with The Star of Life decorating its white sleekness. He pressed the button at the center of the cross and a voice rang out from the impossibly small speaker, "This is only a test. During a real emergency you will receive up to the minute information which may directly impact your health. Please retain this personal safety kit at all times, failure could result in serious injury."

A security-tone pierced the air and the message began to repeat. Steve shut the tiny radio off.

Barb left the room.

"We better be careful with these, kids," Steve announced. "No telling how much battery power this thing's got."

The children were silent, the implications settling in their minds. Pete shut the door to the safe and it clicked, solidly. A tiny little pad marked the center of the door. Pete pressed his finger against the pad and the door clicked open.

He shut the door and tried it again. Then Steve tried it. Then Sarah. It opened instantly, each and every time.

"Does that mean it's secure, DJ? Or can anyone get in?"

"It might read our fingerprints, I don't know. This place is a real mindf..." Steve caught himself and the kids giggled.

"Hey DJ, how did the front door know it was us?"

"That's a good question, Spike. Let's go see."

Sarah joined Barb in the kitchen as Steve and Pete returned to the front door. It slid open on their approach. Steve ran his hands along the door's edge, looking for a camera, a sensor, anything.

"I don't see any security at all."

Steve stepped away and the door slid shut. With security supposedly paramount, Steve found it all profoundly perplexing. But it did fit the pattern: amazement around every corner.

"I bet it's the dust! Remember, DJ? It's Angel Dust!"

Steve and Pete were seated at the kitchen table while Barb and Sarah took stock of the cabinets and fridge. Steve bit his lower lip, impressed by his son's observation.

"It could be, son. Some sort of magnetic thing."

He checked his arms, wiping one and examining his hand.

"Oh come on, that's outrageous," Barb said.

"It's the only thing it could be. There's nothing else there!"

It really did make some sort of weird sense, Steve knew. But what the hell was that stuff? Wouldn't it wash off? And then how would they get back in?

It sure didn't lend a sense of security. Even if it was secure.

Steve took another long pull of his beer, *DisasterLand's Finest*, one of four furnished as a housewarming gift. Four bottles of enhanced water were also provided, with the rugged DL-branded hiking bottles clearly meant to be reused.

"Next up: Sarah Beyers!" a voice announced from the living room, "Cast your vote for top entrant now by dialing 4-808!"

The family leapt up to catch the replay of Sarah's apparently now-famous dance with MagicD. Entrances complete, awards were now the main attraction.

Disgusted, Barb flipped off the HDTV. Steve chugged the rest of his beer and stepped to the fridge for a refill.

He opened the door. The inside read:

Hydration Works!

Pete went back to examining the DisasterLand phone book. Emergency numbers were prominently featured on the cover but the book was mostly a collection of ads for the atrium's upscale retailers.

Sarah was examining a booklet she'd found on the counter.

"What's that?" Steve asked.

"It's an exercise program," Sarah said, after a moment.

"For what?"

"For the next two days. They say it's going to help."

Barb grabbed the phone. "I'll call about watching the house so we can relax."

"Make it quick," Steve said. "I'm sure the long distance here is a killer."

"Of course."

Barb dialed and put the phone to her ear.

Steve took another long, cold draw of the beer, "Very nice," he said, licking his lips. "Light and hoppy. Wonder what the hell it is?"

"Oh, hello," Barb said, "I'm trying to dial out."

The family looked up as her face dropped.

"Oh..." she said, as the family watched carefully, "Oh really?" she continued, averting her eyes. "Oh, well, thanks. I'll tell them."

Barb put the phone down, her face ashen.

"What's wrong?" Steve asked. "Are they trying to screw us? You need a special calling card?"

"No... It's an internal phone system."

"So how are we supposed to..."

"We're not."

The family exchanged glances.

"So what do we do?" Pete asked.

"Nothing, I guess," Steve answered, shrugging off Barb's glare. He took another quick draw.

"Were you going to tell us something else?" Sarah asked.

"Oh," Barb paused. "Yes. They said they're big fans."

"Fans? Of *us*?" Steve stared.

"Yes."

Barb grabbed a beer from the fridge. She'd never had fans before. And she certainly didn't feel dressed for it.

A gentle knock interrupted their thoughts.

"Who's there?" Steve asked.

"Maria," came the accented reply. "Maria Mirōn. Your runner."

"Our who?"

"Runner. I am the agent for the nineteenth floor."

"Open the door, honey, let her in," Barb urged, taking a seat.

"I don't think we want one."

"Open the door, Steve. Don't be ridiculous."

"What if it's a terrorist?"

"Sarah, will you open the door for your brain-damaged father?"

"Sure mom," Sarah opened it—cautiously—and Maria stepped into their suite with warm, welcoming smile. She was a tiny little knockout, dressed in her trendy DisasterLand runner's uniform: a sleek black-and-white tracksuit with body-hugging neoprene backpack.

"Welcome!" Maria giggled, *"Jou're* here! Do *jou* believe it?"

"Actually not," Steve said. "Does anyone?"

"*Sí*. Soon enough."

Maria stepped to the kitchen table.

"We're the Beyers," Barb said. "I'm Barb and this is Steve, Sarah and Pete."

"Of course. I am very glad *jou* are here. If *jou* need something *dis* week *jou* find me," she said.

"You mean like DVDs and stuff?" Pete asked.

Maria giggled. Her eyes were as big and dark as roasted almonds, *"Jou* have the TV for movies. But if *jou* order anything else, I bring it. If *jou* lose something—or someone—I will help *jou* find it. *¿Comprende?*"

Maria removed her backpack.

"How do we find you?" Barb asked.

Maria pulled out a slick business card, "*Jou* call *dis* number... or search the walkway. I am always here. *Dis* is my floor."

"Thank you. And thank you for stopping by."

"*Jou* are very welcome. Now, I must remind *jou* to always be on the lookout for unattended packages," she said. "*Dis* is very, very important. If *jou* see something suspicious, report it. Immediately."

Maria pulled out a tiny packet of what looked like rubber thimbles from her backpack as the Beyers' eyes narrowed.

"What's that?" Sarah asked.

"A quick blood test."

"*Blood test?*" Steve asked, "As if *our complete medical record* wasn't enough!"

"HIV, *Meester* Beyers. For everyone's safety. *Jou* are first. Give me *jour* finger."

"You know there's a 3 month lagtime don't you?" Sarah asked, "We studied AIDS tests in school."

"*Sí*. If something happens to *jou*, we follow up. Now come on, Mister Beyers, don't be *un niño*. It is only a little sting."

Several families later, Maria stepped out of the elevator and into the runner's staging area, two floors below the atrium.

Descending in the white elevator, now reserved solely for employee use, she had relayed her order via PDA. Now, in the midst of the Friday-night chaos, it was being filled.

Already her night was taking shape and it looked every bit as big as had been predicted. She made her way to the drop-off and slid the receiver behind the counter the first ten blood tests to be forwarded on to Good Health.

"Busy?" the receiver asked.

"A good night," Maria answered.

"Guests OK?"

"*Sí, sí*. So far."

"*Innies?*"

"*Jes*, I think so. Maybe one."

The receiver smiled.

Maria picked up the next ten HIV kits and hurried on to the lounge for a quick glass of water and a snack, followed by a trip to the bathroom. In her few minutes of downtime, she'd upload a brief report on all the families she'd just met. Then, when her orders were ready for pick-up, she'd repeat the cycle all over again.

On and on she'd go, all night, until last call sometime around two a.m. when she'd return to the staging area to file her end-of-night report for the psychologists.

Maria was on the front lines and no one learned more about the families that walked through the hallowed glass doors of DisasterLand than the runners, no one saw more of their bare private lives and struggles. Maria in particular had found each family fascinating, the transitions they underwent almost mystical.

She was a believer.

Tonight she would meet another forty families with their unique dreams and aspirations, their dark fears and their repressed angst. Tonight she would open forty new books.

There were two basic types of guests, she'd been taught, the *outies* and the *innies*. The *innies*, when confronted with the immensity of DisasterLand, the power and the weight not only of the physical presence itself but also the psychology of the situation (the countdown to disaster)—could only respond by cowering inside their suites.

Elaborate techniques existed for flushing these guests out into the open, mostly in the guise of targeted sale offers transmitted directly to their room. Those failing, there were games guests could be recruited for—and the most famous, by far, was *The Hunt*.

Billing itself as one of the most demanding scavenger hunts on Earth, *The Hunt* consisted of sixteen teams of ten progressing head-to-head in five single-elimination rounds until one team was crowned champion, well over eight hours later.

120 of the 160 participants were *innies* (the rest were volunteers recruited on the village's streets) and summoning would begin at midnight tonight, most often by plain-clothed guards demanding surprised families to be on the Great Lawn by eight Saturday morning or else. All showed.

The game not only got *innies* out, but forged important new friendships and introduced participants to the layout of DisasterLand, both of which would be extremely useful in the days ahead. It also provided high-entertainment value to those guests who would watch the show on DTV, either live or during the special Saturday evening highlights show.

The process of selecting recruits had to begin early,—the sooner the psychologists understood each family's true mettle the better.

Maria got to work.

The sun had disappeared behind the tower, immersing the park in ever-deepening shadows. The Beyers stood silently in contemplation on the soft, newly-mown grass of the Great Lawn, just inside the park's magnificent garden border with the atrium.

"I've never seen anything like this," Steve said, piercing the family's reverie. They were dressed head-to-toe in a second set of DisasterLand track suits, with Pete and Steve sporting DL baseball caps. So was almost everyone else.

"I've never *imagined* anything like this," Barb added.

"It's way cooler than the DVD," Pete observed, and it was true. Yet in some obscure way, this too was profoundly troubling. If the beauty had been downplayed, was it possible... other things... might have been as well?

Their heightened senses drank in the lush foliage, joyous laughter and ample evidence of culinary mastery: Del Sol's adobe walls and rustic fenced-in patio were several hundred yards away yet even here the scents portended a remarkable feast.

"I can't believe they took our cameras," Barb said.

"And our phones," Sarah growled.

"And our iPods," Pete hissed.

"But it does sort of make sense," Steve offered.

"It does?" Barb asked, hands on hips.

"I mean, they left my binoculars. At least there's consistency. You know, no recording."

"Did it say anything about that in the releases?" Sarah asked. "I don't see how they can go through our luggage and just steal stuff."

"Honey, there were 500 pages of small print. At *least*," Barb said.

"But there was that fifteen-page summary."

"Look, forget it," Steve said. "We'll call tomorrow morning. I'm sure it's all safe and if not they'll pay. It's simple. Now let's worry about dinner. I'm *starving*."

Enthusiastic crowds were brushing past them, heading across the lawn to the forest trails and eventually, the Beyers knew, to the river. A few smiling families were already returning, many sporting wet hair, beach clothes and flip-flops.

"We could have spent the afternoon at the river," Barb sighed.

"There's plenty of time, sweetie," Steve said. "Plenty of time. We don't want to rush anything. After tonight we've got no plans for the next nine days."

"I'm just lettin' y'all know I'm gonna have a ball here!" Pete announced.

"Besides, mom, it took forever to take showers. Imagine, twenty-five grand and only one shower!" Sarah said, shaking her head.

"Yeah, is that lame or what?" Pete asked. "What if they stuck us in some kind of ghetto or something 'cause it's free? We are really high up you know."

"I doubt that, son," Steve said absentmindedly, but they were basically right. In many ways, it had been a subdued afternoon spent just getting their bearings, as if they were afraid to leave the confines of their secure home.

Finally, a little over one hour ago they had managed to break the spell and the elevator's wide glass doors had opened out onto the crowded atrium floor with a pleasant chime, spilling them—and two dozen other passengers—into the fray.

A cacophony of vibrant street life had greeted them, punctuated with the subdued guitars and saxophones of street musicians. The exterior adobe wall of the tiny village had lay in front of them, much larger than expected and glowing with the neon lights of the bars and restaurants at the dome's periphery. A wide corridor separated the two, which was lined with benches and streetlights.

Behind them, the tower swept up and back dramatically overhead, their own floor disappearing anonymously in the heights. It had been a staggeringly beautiful trip down, and it was a remarkably imposing way up.

To the right of the elevators, the north, was Good Health—the hospital. The large picture windows revealed doctors and nurses chatting and waving to curious guests who had stopped by for a look.

Friendly guards were socializing on the walkway above, out in front of the high-tech security center. On the ground floor opposite the elevators lay Good Food, the gourmet market. Already, it was packed.

"Look at those smart people, honey. No one can eat out all the time here or they'd go bankrupt," Steve said.

"We'll go first thing in the morning and get stuff for breakfast."

"I was thinking we'd put little Maria to the test," Steve said. "How about breakfast in bed?"

"If you're buying!" Barb laughed.

The family skirted the village's crowds and followed the lazy curve of the dome's periphery past the theaters, clubs and restaurants which were filled with guests of every shape and color. Sleek glass stairs dotted the palm tree-lined floor to allow easy access to the walkway above, which offered even more bars and restaurants.

A myriad of delightful smells had wafted their way until they found themselves on the Great Lawn, astounded and hungry. Whatever residual tensions existed from the mornings' travels, and there were plenty, all had quickly dissolved in the sensual overload.

Steve stepped towards Del Sol. "There'll be plenty of time to explore the park after dinner... I don't want to lose our reservation."

Barb caught up with him, locking arms while the kids trailed behind as they made their way towards the fenced patio which extended out into the park.

"Honey, wouldn't it be wonderful to have brunch here outside? With the sun rising over the park?" Barb asked, tickling her husband playfully.

Indeed, the elegantly rustic restaurant seemed transplanted from a small Mediterranean village. Picturesque hand-made picnic tables lined the grass, where delighted cosmopolitan diners were enjoying wine and tapas.

"We'll never be able to afford it."

"Let's splurge!"

"Barb..."

"Come on. When was the last time we did something like this!"

"Yeah, dad," Sarah confirmed. "We saved twenty-five grand on admission, the least you could do is drop a couple of Benjamins for breakfast."

The Beyers entered Del Sol and a hush fell over the restaurant. They looked uneasily around them for an explanation as polite applause ensued.

Barb and Steve embarrassingly removed their baseball hats and realized with horror that the explanation was them.

The Maître d' appeared in a tailored black suit and for a moment Barb felt they were in the presence of a movie star. He bowed.

"Good evening. You must be the Beyers!"

"Yes, sir," Steve answered, still puzzled.

The Maître d' studied their look carefully, "Have you not heard, sir?" he asked with the utmost refinement, his nose just slightly upturned.

"Heard what?" Steve asked, with something approaching despair in his voice.

"Your entry has won third place, sir!"

"Entry for what?" Steve asked, puzzled.

"As in coming in, dad," Sarah clarified.

"You're kidding!" Steve exclaimed, his mind racing, "What does that mean?"

"It means you're the talk of the town. And for us, it means it's an honor to serve you."

"Does it also mean we can get a table for Sunday Brunch?" asked Barb. "On the park?"

The Maître d' smiled, "It does."

He stepped over to his book and crossed out a name. "How about ten?"

"Perfect!" Barb's heart leapt. Steve continued his stare, blankly ahead.

"Right this way, my friends. Again, welcome to Del Sol!"

The kids led happily as the family made their way through the crowded restaurant. Pete raised his arms in victory, his fingers outstretched: #1. Sarah felt all eyes on her and blushed. The conversation returned to hushed whispers, yet the buzz lingered.

"Friday night at DisasterLand," Steve said, bewildered.

"Friday night at Del Sol, sir," the Maître d' corrected.

The Beyers were shown to a quiet back table where a bottle of champagne was sitting on ice, two flutes placed at Steve and Barb's setting. After seating the family, the Maître d' gently raised the bottle, "On the house, sir. Congratulations and thank you. Your wine list is waiting and your server will announce our menu momentarily."

"Thank you, sir."

The Maître d' rested the bottle gently back on ice and effortlessly disappeared. Enormous hand-carved wooden beams crossed the low ceiling. The floor was rubbed a dark brown from thousands of soles.

One entire wall was a massive video image of a permanently setting sun, shining powerfully yet delicately, the hues subtly nuanced. It was stunningly realistic, and appeared almost alive.

Its soft light illuminated most of the restaurant with the shadows filled in by candlelight. The juxtaposition of old and new within the rustic womb was profoundly seductive.

"Kids, this restaurant's not Spanish exactly, more like Latin-fusion," explained Steve as he handed Barb the wine list.

"Whatever," Sarah said. "I'm going to eat something weird."

"I'm going to eat something weirder," announced Pete, "like something raw."

Barb tuned out the children and opened the wine list, her heart skipping. She leaned over to Steve. "Honey, these wines start at $100."

"Get something nice. It's on Persistent, remember?" he winked at the kids.

"Stick it to 'em, DJ! Power to the people! Screw the man!"

"Then I'm getting the most expensive thing on the menu no matter what," Sarah announced. "And no one can stop me."

The next table was examining them with interest. Barb and Steve realized that the other diners were mostly dressed in suits and dresses, not the standard-issue DisasterLand gear that the Beyers were sporting.

The sommelier appeared discreetly, placing his hand on the back of Barb's chair, "Good evening, my friends. Welcome to Del Sol!" He introduced himself, and Barb shot Steve a look: *It's him. The one that signed our bottle.*

In moments the cork had been popped and the champagne tipped, "I'll be with you again shortly, once you've made your final selections for dinner."

The bewildered family toasted their good luck and soon the waiter arrived, announcing the evening's menu as if reading poetry. Steve translated what he was able for the befuddled children, with the waiter filling in when necessary.

It *all* sounded weird to them.

Elektra and Jens were window-shopping luxury goods in the village, camouflaged in DisasterLand track suits and fueled by clandestine margaritas-to-go. But their attempts to match the awestruck visitors' emotional pitch were failing miserably and Elektra was becoming concerned.

Was it the end-of-season vibe? Had the coast-to-coast media hype only energized the other attendees? Whatever it was, Elektra hadn't felt the same collective giddiness since the very first opening night.

"This is some crazy shit, 'Lektra."

"What?"

"All of it. The scene, this stuff. How do people afford it?"

"No one can afford anything anymore, Jens. It's all a house of cards built on credit. Hey," Elektra lowered her voice, "it's good to see you down here, man."

"It's been too long. I'm glad Shae talked me out of my lab."

"I haven't seen you around much lately, period. Lab or not."

"You just haven't looked in the right places," Jens said mischievously. "Let's get out in the open. The village is bugging me."

Jens Fiske, quite simply, was The Man. He was DisasterLand's OFX guy and more than anyone else represented the brave new world that was DisasterLand.

Olfactory effects were where the full realism of DisasterLand was sealed. What the eyes didn't believe and the ears didn't convey, the nose was sure to catch: the smell of a severed body, of fresh nausea, the stench of fear and emptied bowels. It all came out of Jens' lab. All of it, and more.

His job was to capture or create these unspeakable essences, distill and patent them, all while instructing his production team of mad scientists on how and where to broadcast them live, on demand, for maximum effect.

It was a coup. And all a bit of an accident.

Four years earlier, Jens was a 27-year old rising star in the graduate chemistry program at MIT, heading for a promising career off the New Jersey turnpike working on industrial food flavorings.

But at the end of his second year, he freaked and dropped out. It wasn't the courses, or the workload—ever since he was a boy he had been fascinated by the magic of chemistry. It was simply the prospect of spending the rest of his life inside a cold, corporate laboratory, divorced from what he began to consider, more and more, as 'reality.'

He knew there had to be another way and Jens took off on his bicycle to find it. That summer he bicycled all the way up the west coast from Baja California to Alaska, and it was there on the sides of the road that he found his answer. While experimenting with wildflowers Jens discovered an almost savant-like ability to manufacture fresh and incredibly complex olfactory sensations, using nothing more than a basic camp stove and good vodka.

That fall in Eugene he founded a natural hand-crafted parfumerie which quickly built up a mail-order following amongst a certain type of fanatic. Yet eighteen months later his wanderlust was blossoming once again, and at just the right time he received an offer for exclusive worldwide manufacturing rights to his existing scents by a cosmetics multinational.

After the contracts had been signed, Jens was finalizing his plans to bicycle Europe for a summer celebration when an actor friend whispered the first breathless rumors of DisasterLand's emergence. Immediately and powerfully, Jens glimpsed his future.

After an intense week in his kitchen performing almost unmentionable acts, he came up with many of his now legendary trademarked scents and uncorked them in his Vegas hotel room just before Shae arrived for their first meeting. He was hired, though most of the finer points of his contract had been negotiated behind bars, with the two awaiting the arrival of Shae's attorney. Needless to say, Jens had been forced to secure a room in another hotel for the remainder of his stay.

Jens spent the next six months chasing disasters, placing himself and his sommelier's nose in the paths of incoming hurricanes, in the world's worst warzones and nearest the largest and most active seismic faults in the world to discover authentic scents for DisasterLand, fully believing that organic base material would complete the illusion in ways nothing else could.

He had been right.

"Excuse me?"

They turned to see a man in his late 30's, alone—not a typical Friday night sight.

"Yes?" Elektra asked, still scanning the crowd around them. In the distance, she noticed a teenage boy trying to look the other way.

"You two together?"

"No... we're..." Elektra stumbled, suddenly caught off guard as the psychological ground slipped away from under her. *This is what happens when I'm scattered,* she scolded herself. "I mean, we are, but we're just friends."

"So could I talk you into getting a drink later?"

"No, I'm sorry... I..."

"Come on, what's stopping you?"

"Sorry to interject," Jens said, politely, "But her husband just left her..."

Elektra stared at Jens, then put on an appropriate face.

The guest's brow furrowed as he studied their show, but he seemed, after a moment, to buy it, "I'm sorry... I..."

"It's not your fault, sir... they were supposed to come here together, you know... and... well..."

"No, I understand completely. I'm sorry, you just... caught my eye."

"Thanks. But no thanks," Elektra said. "It's just happened. I guess I'm still in shock..."

"Of course. Well, look, if you change your mind, I'm in 1056. For some reason that's on the fifth floor." The man smiled wistfully and turned to catch up with his son. The kid glanced back after a moment.

Elektra stared. It was always tempting, the idea of taking a lucky, starry-eyed pup behind the curtain. But it was suicide.

"Thanks, Jens."

"I guess we don't make a convincing couple."

"He'll ask some other chick in 5 minutes. He's a scammer."

"Happen much?"

"Enough." Elektra took a deep breath and a quick sip of the margarita to settle her nerves.

Venturing onto the floor during a show was always fascinating—to be in the mix, to sense what guests were feeling so intimately, was, for her, both thrilling and frightening. But it was easy to feel like a puppetmaster, with feelings of control, of superiority naturally arising. Guests were, in a very real sense, helpless, and Elektra was responsible for their well-being if not their lives. It could be a real ego rush if she let it.

Shae knew this potential and made sure everyone on the crew fought it. The psychologists not only closely monitored the guests, they often cast a sideways glance at their co-workers. No one wanted any twisted power-trips getting in anyone's head.

The psychological barrier between guest and employee was vital. Which was why, in a few minutes, she'd have to pull the ripcord.

"What are your plans?"

"I need another hour or so down here. I'm trying to work out something to fill the Friday night *olfactory void*. Then I'm meeting my crew at DmZ for a brainstorming session."

"Brainstorming session? Something's happening, Jens. Tell me."

"Sorry, E. Not this time."

Elektra frowned. This was all making her a little uncomfortable. *Why was she the only one out of the loop?*

"Tell you what, Jens, I'm gonna kill this margarita then I'm off. Been a long day." Elektra was thinking she just might land on her roof for a solo nightcap. "But I'd love the company as long as it lasts."

"Then let's take a little stroll towards the theater. My answer may lie there, in popcorn. Care to hold my hand? Keep the creeps away?"

As they strolled, Elektra looked across the joyful faces of the helpless and sensed trouble. The shock of a full-on disaster all at once would be a huge risk. She'd send a quick text to Shae, CC'ing the psychologists for follow-up.

These guests just weren't scared enough.

"Everyone home by midnight, no questions and don't push it for *any* reason or you bleed," Steve dropped the kids $20 each. "Now I don't expect you to spend this. It's for an emergency only."

They giggled.

"Get outta here," Steve said, and the kids bubbled away, jubilantly. Moments later Pete's cries of liberation rang through the park.

Barb turned, "You're sure about this?"

"Honey, this has to be the safest place in the world. There's no way they can get into trouble here."

It sounded like famous last words, but her own biology was calling out and self-interest prevailed: they were alone, at last. And Steve was right: this was DisasterLand.

An older, more sophisticated clientele were now lounging on the Great Lawn, the younger demographic undoubtedly off to experience the unique pleasures of DisasterLand's nightlife.

Barb took Steve's hand and they set off towards the nearest forest trail. Overhead, a blue moon was on the rise and their tensions were already melting away.

Dinner had been a sublime, transformational event, literally lifting their consciousness and placing their awakened selves fully within another, more purely sensuous way of being.

It was a thrilling start that swept even the kids away. Within those hallowed walls, within that cozy space surely realized by long-deceased artisanal craftsmen, the meal had slowly elevated itself to the status of legend, well worth whatever Persistent had paid. And they had paid quite a lot.

They paused at a trailhead near the center of the darkened forest, instinctively questioning the wisdom of entering but soon realized their folly. The forest was eerily mesmerizing, smelling of damp earth and musk, but it wasn't *real*. Surely, there was no threat.

They stepped into the jumbled shadows. The trail gave way softly underfoot and their lungs filled with the fresh exhalations of nighttime foliage. As they pushed on more deeply, they realized the trail was discreetly lit by small solar lamps.

The Beyers continued their languid wander towards the river, encountering more and more smiling strangers along the way. Some just waved pleasantly, others greeted them enthusiastically like long lost friends, yet all seemed amazed, *thrilled*, by the immediate intimacy their shared privilege allowed.

Just like it used to be, Steve realized. *Just like this world used to be.*

Were the people drawn to DisasterLand just these kinds of people or had the knowledge they were about to share something special overtaken their usual feelings of suspicion and aversion?

When had everyone become so suspicious of each other anyway? *Why?*

Discreetly placed wooden benches lined the path and families of all ages were cuddling, whispering, giggling. But as opposed to finding it repulsive, which Barb usually did, she found it romantic in its long-lost innocence. Her heart warmed at their presence.

Barb and Steve continued on, up a small slope which poked them out just above the treetops, leading to a surprisingly satisfying view of the park. With the dark sky overhead, they could almost imagine themselves in the open air.

Straight ahead, to the east, they could just make out the near bank of the glistening river, with distant splashes haunting the air. The trees seemed to end at the river, but it was impossible to tell what lay beyond with the area shrouded in darkness.

Towards the north, their left as they faced the river, a cliff rose up in the distance, way up above the treetops, with rock climbers dangling from it like spiders, their headlamps dancing across the pocked surface. Slightly further to their left, behind them, they again sensed the glistening of water through a break in the trees.

To their right, to the south away from Del Sol, lay a tangle of green all the way to the dome's edge.

"Where to? The river?" Steve wanted to press on. His heart was light and the sense of discovery was energizing him.

"We could save it for tomorrow, for something special. We've got the hot-tub, you know. Think of the stars..."

It *was* a remarkably clear desert night. The view would be spectacular. More couples smiled as they passed.

Steve turned to take in the warm glow of the atrium in the distance. The bustle of the guests had been squelched to a low purr.

"It's so nice here, away from everything. We've got plenty of time for the hot tub later."

"OK, sweetie. But I'm making an appointment for the spa tomorrow, when we get home," Barb announced.

"I could probably use a little something myself," Steve said, turning back towards the river.

Barb leapt up and kissed Steve on the cheek, like she used to do when they first met, improbably, in Africa.

Steve staggered at the raw physical power of the memory's sudden return. In fact, hadn't that sun, that Del Sol sun, reminded him of Africa? Reminded him of their odyssey as a young couple in a foreign land, idealistic youth a generation too late?

Steve shuddered, wiping the lipstick from his cheek.

Barb giggled, squeezing his hand.

He lead Barb gently down the stone steps which comprised the back of the hill, to a fork in the trail. One way, to the left, was labeled *cliffs/pond*, the other way, straight ahead, *river*.

They went straight and deeper into the park, approaching the center of the dome if Steve's glimpses overhead could be trusted.

Soon, they could hear it: the rushing of the river. And with it, Barb sensed the electric anticipation of the upcoming disaster. It too was like a current rushing under the surface, behind every recent exchange. *What was coming? And when?*

But Barb wasn't frightened, at least not yet. In an odd way, she found it tremendously invigorating, and by the recent exchanges knew others did as well.

Several minutes later they rounded the path's final corner and stepped out into a wide, grassy clearing. And there it was! Nearly fifteen feet wide and flowing rapidly, *the river*.

Barb gasped, squeezing Steve's hand. He too was absolutely astonished. It disappeared into the greenery in both directions. It was *huge!*

Couples were picnicking by candlelight, on the opposite bank kids were splashing and one couple was tossing a lighted Frisbee. A few brave couples were even swimming—the river appeared to be five or six feet deep in the middle.

Steve and Barb made their way to an empty place along the bank and stared in. It was *real*. It was *alive*. Plants flourished while mysterious dark shadows darted through the rushing water—*fish?*

Yet there was something human, something *designed* about the river that was palpable to them. It was almost sculpted, the aqueous equivalent of a bonsai tree. It was as if the Mississippi river had been shrunk to fifteen feet. Everything, it seemed, was in miniature.

Barb removed her shoes and sat, dangling her feet into the cold, crisp water. She stretched her hand back to Steve. He took it and dropped down next to her.

They held hands, together, staring up through the trees to the stars overhead. It was indeed a beautifully clear night.

"This is really incredible Steve."

He was looking for the dome up in the distance, to reassure himself, to remind himself that this place existed, to prove where they really were. It was almost invisible and for a moment, he found himself profoundly disoriented.

He realized Barb was waiting for a confirmation. "It is, isn't it? Do you see the dome?"

"No... oh, yes... yes..." There was a long pause as Barb focused on her breathing, in and out, in long, deep breaths. The air was remarkably fresh.

"I just can't believe we're here. And I can't believe it's like *this!*" Barb said.

"Me neither."

Their thoughts faded into the rushing of the river. Barb was the first, again, to speak, "I'm sorry about this week. I just... I just hate your situation sometimes. They push you around. I know you're not happy."

Steve turned to her.

"I..." His brief pause soon grew into a significant silence. Finally, he admitted, "No, I guess I'm not."

"But you keep thinking things are getting better. That's what you keep telling yourself. That you're getting *ahead*."

Steve nodded.

"Now you've got your chance Steve... or we've got ours. What do we want out of this life? It's half over, you know. Maybe more."

"Don't remind me. Jesus, I can't believe it. Every morning I can't believe it. We've got a daughter starting college, you know."

Barb smiled, "Yes, honey, I know."

Steve lay back, hands behind his head. Barb rested her head on Steve's plump stomach.

"Feels like just last year we were in Africa."

"It does."

"You know it was almost twenty..." Barb continued but Steve's own thoughts had outpaced her. Twenty years... from naive kids wanting to save the world to suburbanites nesting not far from home.

Where had it gone? The magic of two kids from Kansas meeting half a world away?

Barb was staring at him, "I was just thinking..." Steve said, "your kiss on the path really took me back. Instantly, I was there. It's odd."

Barb nodded slowly, into his stomach. "Me too. That's why I did it."

Steve ran his hand through her hair, realizing she was crying. Barb swallowed, wiping her eyes. "So where'd it go?"

Steve turned away, anger flashing for blowing the most relaxation he'd known in months, but he immediately swallowed it. He lay back, took a deep breath. "Where does it always go?"

Barb stared. "What *always*?"

Steve turned back to her, away from the stars overhead. "Right."

"Yo? *Fo'real!*"

"Real."

Pete stood at the darkened, unmarked entrance along the dome's periphery, ten-thirty sharp. The door was nondescript, smoked glass draped with a red velvet curtain. Easily mistaken for a private club, it was, in fact, the epicenter of world gaming.

The bouncer scanned his PDA for the results of Pete's fingerprint ID.

Pete's DisasterLand cap was cocked to the side, a silver spike hanging from his neck by a thick chain. His baggy jeans were barely held up by an oversize black leather belt and he was sporting an old-school Wilt Chamberlain Lakers jersey—a gift from his Dad for Wednesday's game-winner.

The bouncer smiled, "Saw your scores bro. Pete Beyers!"

They hit fists.

"Yo, 'njoy yo'self, hear?"

"It's how we doin' it."

The bouncer cleared and pulled the curtain aside. Pete could barely control himself. He puffed out his chest and took a mighty step inside. The bouncer slapped him on the back: "Go get 'em dawg!"

Pete squeezed the spike around his neck.

The kids had hit their room to change after dinner and agreed to abide by the martial law. If something unexpected happened to either, they'd cover, but no one was going to take a fall. Pete was cutting deals with his older sister and it was thrilling: a respect was there, an adulthood that he had never felt before. There was an *equality*.

Now here he was, standing on his own, mission accomplished. He was stepping inside the most secretive video game in the world and his adrenalin was on over-drive.

Qualification had, in fact, been easy. He'd been fighting the urge to bolt for the gaming center since arrival, but kept it confidently under wraps and it worked to his advantage. Kids had started lining up at four, apparently, which meant over a two hour wait. But he arrived just before nine and thirty minutes later he was competing. Fifteen minutes ago, he'd been given the go-ahead.

A tender blonde, barely 16, was waiting for him as the door closed. Her pink girlie-T said in sparkly, cursive script: *Candy*.

"Welcome to *Ghost*," she said. "Follow me."

She led him down the darkened hall with an exaggerated wiggle and Pete drank desperately from her blossoming femininity. He was shown to a tiny little dressing room, with a plush leather dentist's chair the only furniture.

Candy shut the door behind him slowly, a flirtatious smile glancing off her lips, "Good luck!"

Pete sat down on the chair, lost in his own racing thoughts, his heart and hormones pounding.

Artist's representations of DisasterLand's many episodes hung on the walls, crowded atriums with many different villages. But Pete noticed there were tiny little men in the crowded shots, barely visible and completely pale. They looked like futuristic, colorless Ninjas. *Ghosts!*

A terse knock made him jump. The door slid open and a man entered, wrap-around sunglasses shielding his eyes. Pete's heart sped.

The man shut the door firmly and clicked across the floor in polished black shoes which accented his dark gray tailored wool suit.

"Pete Beyers?"

He offered his hand. Pete shook it as hard as he could. The man didn't flinch.

"Yo."

"Call me Falco."

Pete had never met anyone like this guy before. He seemed straight out of a secret agent movie.

84

Pete would have to raise his game.

"You're quite a celebrity this evening, no?" Falco asked.

"Dig."

"And now you're *here. The Core.*"

Pete's heart leapt. *The Core!*

Falco began to pace, increasing Pete's tension.

"So what do you know about *Ghost?*"

"What do I know?"

"What do you... expect?"

Pete stared. *What was this dude on?*

Falco stared back, waiting.

Pete started slowly, "I don't know anything, sir." He added the *sir* at the last moment and it felt right. "I Googled DisasterLand and gaming and stuff but the hits were all lame."

Falco smiled smugly, "Not surprising." He cleared his throat. "Before we go on... *Spike*... we need to come to an agreement."

Pete's mouth dropped. *Spike?*

"OK," was all Pete managed, swallowing hard.

"Anything that happens from now on is *your secret.* It's classified. That means not one word. To anyone." Pete stared as Falco finished, "Not even to your father, Steve."

Pete nodded. "Word."

"Classified knowledge is protected by the laws of the United States of America. You know what that means?"

"Not really..."

"You squeal, you do time. Then you understand the name Spike a bit more clearly. Got it?"

He paused.

Man, this was harsh stuff, thought Pete. He was psyched to be here, but this dude was scaring him. He couldn't back out now, though. And if anything, Pete decided, it just proved that whatever was here was really, really cool.

Pete straightened and Falco continued, "And just so you know, we'll know. You ever heard of Eschalon?"

"Eschalon? What's that? Like *Doom?*"

"It's a global surveillance operation headed by the United States of America and with the cooperation of Australia and the United Kingdom. Internet, e-mail, faxes, voice calls, all monitored in near real-time."

"No way dude."

"It's true. We'll get you." Falco paused.

Pete looked away.

"You got it? *Spike?*" Falco said, stepping towards him.

Pete choked, "Are you *serious* dude?"

Falco pulled out a video camera, the most amazing one Pete had ever seen. It wasn't even a camera, *really,* just the lens itself with a touchscreen wrapped around. It fit Falco's hand perfectly.

Falco turned the business end on Pete. Opposite the lens was a crystal-clear LCD display, which Falco watched, carefully, "Very serious. You still want in?"

Man, it's like the Army or something, Pete thought. He wished his mom was here. Pete swallowed, turning back to meet Falco in the eye.

Falco nodded, "Yes?"

Pete stood up, "Yes."

"Top Secret? Classified? *¿Comprende?*"

"Yes."

"Kick ass," Falco pocketed the camera and offered his hand. Pete gave it a whack, the sound resonating throughout the room.

"You're a feisty one, kiddo. So now we begin. Lay down, relax."

Pete sank into the seat which reclined in response. "First step, I put in a couple of customized lenses."

Pete sat up, "What?"

Falco rested on hand firmly on Pete's shoulder as he continued, "... it's painless. Then you'll be shown to your seat, we'll do a small training run and you'll be *in*."

Falco smiled, broadly. He checked his watch and produced a couple of sterile rubber gloves and a tiny metal jewelry box from his pocket. He opened the box carefully, revealing two tiny plastic fluid-filled bubbles. He popped one and removed the lens from inside. He held it up to the light.

From what Pete could make out there was a barely perceptible wire rim around them. Strange webbing spread out over the rest, making the lenses slightly opaque.

"OK, sit back."

Pete paused a moment as indecision overheated his brain. He had come this far, and if that Eschalon thing was bad for Pete, it had to be bad for Falco too.

Pete took a deep breath, lay back and surrendered.

Falco skillfully pried Pete's eyelid open and dropped a couple of drops of fluid into the eye, then carefully placed the lens over Pete's iris and dropped it in. Pete blinked as his eye teared.

"OK, next one. Don't try to focus yet—it'll just strain your eyes."

Falco deftly repeated the painless procedure and handed Pete a handkerchief.

"We'll remove these before you leave. Don't worry."

Pete stared at him... it was like a grey veil had been placed over his eyes. The colors seemed muted... but were they? He really couldn't tell anymore. What did real colors really look like?

"You're almost in, kid," Falco took the video camera back out, changed a couple of settings, and stretched out his other hand.

"Look at my hand. That's it," Falco passed the camera around Pete's face slowly and then pocketed it. "Good. Now I'll let you change clothes. Give the door a knock when you're ready."

Falco held his palm to a sensor on the wall and a closet opened up, filled with a selection of multi-colored skin-tight suits.

"No way dude!"

Pete stood and shakily made his way to the closet as Falco slipped out of the room. He removed each sleek suit from the closet, finally settling on one, all black, that he instantly knew would fit him.

Gotta get pics in this, he thought as he looked it over. *Come and get it, ladies!*

He stepped out of his clothes and threw them on the seat, making sure his underwear was hidden. Then he slipped on the suit.

His hands and feet were sealed in gloves and boots, with thin wires radiating out from barely-noticeable sensors. The DL logo glowed on the chest. A hood contained tiny speakers of absurd quality. He felt like a leopard, a cheetah. He was ready to pounce.

Pete zipped it up snugly, relishing the sleek, tight warmth on his skin. It felt good. Pete stretched, and carefully made his way to the door, thinking of Candy's reaction when she saw him. He knocked.

As he waited, he realized the suit felt too good. The warmth, the creamy silkiness was having a terrible effect. Catastrophe was imminent.

Pete raced to sit down, but it was too late. Candy opened the door, and Pete froze, bent over awkwardly, hands on his knees.

"Are you OK?" she asked.

"Yeah. Just... umm...."

He knew it was obvious. Candy giggled, desperate to torture him. He had the feeling he wasn't the first.

She stepped towards him, "I didn't introduce myself. Hi, I'm Candy." She extended her hand.

Pete stayed frozen. He looked up at her awkwardly.

"And you?" she asked, innocently.

His face blushed, his soul withered. She stood firm, offering her hand, unable to hide the enormous grin on her face.

Pete straightened, now feeling the rock-hard pressure under the suit. He felt so small, so powerless. He offered his hand, keeping the other one strategically placed. He had no choice.

"Call me Spike."

She giggled.

"How 'bout a good luck hug, Spike?" she asked, leaning in.

Pete stumbled back, falling into the chair. His eyes were on the verge of tearing, he felt the liquid pooling in the corners. But he fought back, hard. The hardest ever.

She pulled away and motioned for him to follow her, "I'm sorry, Spike. Don't worry, I'm just teasing."

After a few moments of awkward paralysis followed by an even more awkward reconfiguration, Pete took a reluctant step towards her and wiped his eyes.

She led him down the same darkened tunnel, flaunting the burgeoning power she was all too aware of. Pete swore her rear was glowing.

And it was: a little gift from the nerds in programming.

At the end of the tunnel, a red stage light hung over a black bomb-proof door. **The Core**, it said. Underneath, the word *LIVE* was unlit.

Candy leaned back as she motioned Pete through the door, thrusting out the buds on her chest just so. Pete averted his eyes and stepped past her, stopping as the door thudded shut behind him.

Hormones surged through his body. His extremities, including one he didn't generally include, were tingling.

Pete checked the door—again, no knob. He had never seen a one-way door before and now, it seemed, he was surrounded by them. There was no going back.

Pete continued into the large round room. A dull throb was pulsing—he was unsure if it was coming from the room itself or the earbuds inside his ears.

The space was dramatically lit by colored lights raking along the outside wall and Pete imagined himself in a space ship. Five tiers dropped down in concentric circles, each one six or seven feet wide, to a central platform twenty feet down where the final two futuristic wrap-around seats were resting.

Six more ringed the top level, one less on each descending circle. Each seat was set apart from the others with spotlights illuminating the few empty ones left. He noticed one blinking below, calling to him, and his pulse quickened.

As he stared, the blinking became more insistent. He couldn't tell if it was an effect of the lenses or the lighting and felt like he was losing touch with the physical world. It scared him.

Pete made his way down to the seat as eyes probed from the darkness. He caught a pair of dull whites, but only for a split second and only to acknowledge their shared secret.

He sat down and the seat's glow dimmed. Moments later another similarly-dressed kid entered the room, then a third. and they too took their seats. Pete could feel the tension in the room rise as the final chair was occupied, the final light extinguished.

The DisasterLand theme rang out around them.

"Gentlemen. Congratulations. You've found *The Core*." It was Falco.

The energy was palpable. A few kids howled. Pete unzipped the suit for a moment, his skin dripping with sweat. He took a deep breath.

"Welcome. This is the third heat. Each of you is a *Ghost*."

Around him, the boy's figures began to glow... and a chill ran down Pete's spine. Their figures shrunk and transformed. Pete's stomach tensed. He felt sick.

"Eliminate the others and you win. You have five minutes to train before competition begins. The last five to survive from all four heats advance to the midnight finals. You can go anywhere. The only restriction is you cannot pass through closed doors, the dome or the walls of the tower. Stomp your feet to disengage at any time."

The space around him began to transform, disturbingly expanding to become the neon-bright DisasterLand atrium. Sounds of the bustling crowds filled his ears. Visitors were talking, walking, laughing around him, obliviously. Yet the *Ghosts'* dull porcelain figures remained in position, circling.

"You're live. *Good luck.*"

Pete's head was filled with a powerful fanfare, this one dark, foreboding. As the tension rose to a new, awful level, Pete blindly zipped up his suit.

The atrium blurred and the *Ghosts* were scattered. Pete landed near the central elevators and the crystal clarity of his vision returned.

Something crashed behind him and instinctively he spun towards it—too quick. The atrium spinning sickenly with him and he gagged.

Heart thumping and growing claustrophobic, he tugged helplessly at the buds in his ears, wanted to scratch out the lenses from his eyes. Panicking, he tried standing from his chair. And fell.

Instantly he was back in *The Core.*

Pete was lying on the floor, his right knee hurting from the awkward fall. Across the room and up a tier another kid was standing slowly, holding his stomach. The warm, caustic smell of puke wafted over and Pete gagged. *The other crash.*

Pete stood up forcefully and sucked it up. He sat back into his chair. *Fuck that moron.*

A voice appeared in his ears, "Restarting Beyers. 3... 2... 1..." And he was back. Instantly.

This time he noticed a faint counter on the periphery of his sight. It was already at three minutes and relentlessly ticking down to zero. It showed '20' and the tiny image of a *Ghost. That's how many are left.*

Guests walked right through him as if he wasn't there. And he wasn't—he couldn't be. But *who were these people?* If they were computer-generated, these were the best he'd seen. If not, it had to be *live.* But *how?*

Pete turned and the atrium turned with him. As he raised his right arm, he began to float up, weightlessly.

A surge of endorphins flooded his brain, liberation coursed through every molecule. His mind had tasted true freedom and he cried out in joy. It felt incredible!

Pete jumped, pushing his feet off the ground—and found himself back in *The Core.* He caught his breath, scolding himself for stomping his feet.

"Restarting Beyers. 3... 2... 1..."

He was back in. A pale figure flashed by and Pete turned. Another *Ghost.* He recognized the face as one of the last kids to enter, ducking into and out of the guests around them.

He had a gun. Pete heard tiny explosions of gunfire and rainbow bullets whizzed around him. His screen flashed red, then white. *He'd been hit.*

Pete was back in *The Core.* Again.

"Restarting Beyers. 3... 2... 1..."

The counter was just above one minute and Pete was dead in the water. He had to learn to move. And *fast.*

Pete focused every bit of attention he had, emergency-style. Seconds later, fueled on instinct and adrenalin, he was rushing through the atrium, darting around guests and turning on a dime. Around him, guests went about their business with no clue of his presence.

Pete shaped his gloved hand into a pistol and a gun appeared in front of him. He fired a few warning shots.

It felt *good*.

As the counter reached '0', a final, almost medieval fanfare rang out. The game had begun.

Pete made his way carefully towards Del Sol and the park, staying to known territory. But the crowd was thin. He felt vulnerable.

On instinct he reversed, ducking into the tiny maze-like streets of the shopping village. He passed wave after wave of shoppers, hurrying from store to store. Overwhelmed, he tried to stay low.

Some guests seemed to sense him. When he approached from behind, they would turn and look right at him. Seeing nothing, they would turn back. To Pete, it was inexplicable. And unnerving.

But he had other things to worry about. He settled into the middle of a crowd of shoppers and waited.

Whizzing, past his right ear. And again. He spun to face the rainbow tracers.

He ducked as another pierced the spot where his head had been moments before. Pete dove around a street corner as a volley of bullets were absorbed by guests' bodies with dull thuds.

They stopped as quickly as they started and Pete leapt out, just managing to catch a glimpse of the *Ghost* as he disappeared into the crowd. Pete opened fire but the bullets were absorbed harmlessly.

He ducked cautiously into the nearest store and froze. Through the window, Pete caught a *Ghost* racing towards him, eyes haunted by desperation and fear.

Suddenly, horrifically, the *Ghost's* face exploded in a mass of gore. *19*, the counter read. Then again, almost instantly, *18*.

In seconds, another *Ghost* raced by and Pete leapt through the window after him, letting loose a torrent of rainbows. One found its target and the *Ghost's* back exploded, staining the walls of the village. *17*.

Pete dropped back inside, stunned, his heart pounding, his lungs gasping for air. Distant cursing reached Pete's ears, back from *The Core*. His mind raced: *would the guy recognize him later?* And if so, *what would he do?*

Whistling raced over Pete's head and he spun, catching a brief flash of white rising over the store.

It was too crowded in the village, too intense. Pete needed to get to the park. He was too vulnerable. He darted out, through the alleys.

And stopped suddenly. Ahead of him, only a few feet away, were his parents.

Barb was hanging on Steve, one hand on his chest. She was whispering something to him, then kissed his ear. Steve struggled to stop her, slightly embarrassed. Pete had never seen the expression that was on her face before—and would have preferred not to.

Holy shit, thought Pete. This must be *live*.

Pete shot several stories into the sky overhead. He had to clear his mind, or he'd be wasted.

Rainbows tore by and Pete saw a *Ghost* below him, following. Pete swerved and fired, ending the *Ghost's* night with one shot. His blood rained down on the village.

Pete darted away, towards the park.

This really was the coolest fucking thing he ever could have possibly imagined.

Steve found himself trapped in front of *Matériel Pornographique*, a boutique sex shop tucked into in a small dead-end alley. It was hopping.

Barb was tugging him inside but Steve desperately resisted. He was distracting himself with the rich black velour exterior, the darkened windows, the glistening bits of what looked like moisture. It was a dazzling storefront, projecting both seductive and luxurious.

"Please honey, I'll meet you upstairs. Surprise me," Steve begged.

He eyed the menacing logo above the door uncomfortably: it was a glowing petroglyphic penis.

They didn't have a shop in Kansas.

"No, no, no. Your choice," Barb pulled harder, more and more theatrically. People had begun to stare. The one thing Steve did not like was providing entertainment for others.

But what was his problem after all? He had a horny wife on his hands, and that was certainly better than the alternative.

Steve gave in with a whimper and allowed her to drag him in, triumphantly. She had publicly broken his resistance.

Once inside, he relaxed slightly. It *was* sort of exciting, wasn't it? He wasn't a Puritan, never had been. Yet sex was something private, something not to be flaunted in public. Or was he just old-fashioned?

Inside, the store's tones had turned a deep, moist pink and Steve found himself pausing to watch the slick, well-produced videos surrounding him from all angles. These weren't some sort of low-budget hackjob, these were beautiful people, some of them gymnasts by the look of it.

How do they get away with this? he wondered.

Naughty smiles abounded as couples browsed the tiny aisles filled with designer silk sheets, expensive lingerie and hand-sewn Italian leather whips. *That's how they did it*, Steve realized, noticing Barb had disappeared. He scanned the front of the store, helplessly and in disbelief.

A display of thongs caught his eye and Steve drew a bit closer as if gauging the threat of a trapped animal. He cautiously eyed one in particular, resembling a pair of interlaced shoelaces.

"Bon soir. May I help you?"

A young French clerk (*too young?*) appeared before him, dressed in a skin-tight leather catsuit. Steve fought hard to maintain his composure under her magnetic gaze.

She smiled, *"D'où vous sont?* Where are you from?"

"Kansas."

"Oui... Dorothy, no? Tornados? *Terrifier?"*

"Not really... better than earthquakes. At least we know they're coming."

Steve wondered for the millionth time what Kansas would be without Dorothy. Something like North Dakota, he imagined.

Dorothy wouldn't be caught dead in a place like this.

"And you?"

"Paris. Have you been?"

"No."

"You must visit. *Incroyable.* You will never forget it. *Je promesse."*

Steve caught himself staring. How did the French do it? How did they produce such stunning women, generation after generation? Women of intense, almost alien, beauty? Was it genetics? The food? The *spirit?* He suddenly felt slighted.

"And this store, it's French?" Steve asked.

"Bien sûr! Of course! All of us, we own it!"

"No!"

"Oui! We are partners!"

"I don't understand."

"Américain nécessité mieux sexe. Very important."

Steve wondered if he was being insulted.

"Make love not war, no?" the clerk offered.

"We invented that slogan!"

"Ah, *oui,* but you don't use it. We want to *help you use it."*

It's because our ladies don't look like yours, Steve thought. *If they did, productivity would plummet, jeopardizing our position as the world's economic superpower.*

In fact, he realized, *this whole store is probably a plot, venture capital provided by French intelligence, her father a foreign minister. A French plot to wreck America from the inside out!*

Sex as the ultimate 21st century weapon!

Steve grabbed his notebook.

"So. *Peux-je vous aider?* May I help you?" she asked, smiling curiously.

"No... my wife..." Steve glanced around the store. Barb was gone. Lost. M.I.A.

"She must be in our tools."

"Tools?"

The clerk rolled her eyes, *"Je suis désolé.* TOYS. In the back of the store, behind those mannequins."

Steve couldn't look, "Oh. I think I'll stay here then."

"You like thongs, no? What size is she?"

When was the last time he'd bought lingerie?

Steve picked up the thong he'd been eyeing earlier, checking the price tag, "135 dollars! For... shoelaces?"

"*Un string, monsieur. Français. Premier dessinateur*. Not available in America. If you like, I will model."

She began to unzip the suit from the neck and Steve grabbed her hand. "No!" he yelled, much too loudly. Dismissing the startled looks of other shoppers, he continued, quietly, "That's OK. Thank you." He let her go. "I appreciate it."

She laughed as Steve retreated, red-faced and nervous. In Kansas, he knew, people got arrested for less.

She turned, displaying her ass, "No lines, see? *Un string*."

Steve looked away.

"*Les Américains sont drôles!* If you want me to display something for you, I will."

"No thank you."

"You know Armani suits?"

Steve nodded.

"This is the same, but different. She feels... like a woman. *Une femme*." She winked, motioning further into the store. "The deeper you go the more rewarding, sir. Remember... enjoy yourself and enjoy *her*."

Steve wanted desperately to flee, unable to come to terms with the idea that Barb had dragged him in then promptly deserted him.

As the clerk moved on, Steve made his way to the back of the store where an intoxicating smell lingered, an intimate, slightly foreign musk. The smell of fresh warm mysteries.

Steve approached the massive wall of toys cautiously, avoiding eye contact with other shoppers. But as the humms and squirms of the test merchandise penetrated his already fragile senses, Steve decided he needed fresh air.

This place *was* threatening, he realized, a threat to the established order. If women realized their power, Steve knew, this world would be different.

He retreated, sweating, and found himself puzzled. There were no checkout counters and only one way out. He was about to find the cat-suited clerk when he realized she was coming towards him.

"*Monsieur* Steve?"

"Yes?" he stammered.

"Your wife would like to see you." She took his clammy hand and lead him to the back of the store, to a discreet, frosted glass door, "Right through there, *ange*. Second door on your left."

Steve entered reluctantly, finding himself in a fur-lined hallway. Lines of candles cast a warm glow. He nervously rapped against the specified door and it opened. Barb reached out and grabbed him, pulling him inside.

She slammed the door shut and spun back against it. Dressed in a tanned suede trench coat, she kicked her leg up on the wall to reveal nothing underneath.

"Come over here..."

"Barb, how much does that coat cost?"

"Like it?"

"How much?"

93

"Five."

"Oh. That's not bad."

"Thousand."

"Honey, get it *off!*"

Barb laughed, "It's OK. Relax."

"*Relax?*"

"Shhh.... she pressed her finger over his lips and locked the door behind him.

"We don't have that kind of..."

Barb clamped his mouth shut, forcing him back against the wall. Steve reeled, disoriented more by his wife's tenacity than by their location.

"Barb, this is a dressing..."

She forced him down, knees buckling, and stepped over him, forcing her primal wetness against his protesting lips. She swayed deeply, painting his face with her scent.

Steve was lost, brain frozen, now operating solely on male instinct—which judging by her guttural moans seemed to be working. Long-lost memories came flooding back...

Steve opened his eyes, saw Barb's forehead pressed against the wall, fingers spread for leverage, breasts bouncing and he wanted to give her everything he had. In one fluid movement, he discreetly liberated himself and slipped out from underneath her.

Before she could react he was inside her, pinning her further against the wall. She yelped with surprise, body shuddering in waves of lust, clenching him inside her.

He pulled her away from the wall and doubled her over, spreading her legs even further as she forced herself back against him. The confined quarters seemed to magnify her moans in an increasingly intense feedback loop.

In what seemed only a matter of moments, she came repeatedly, unstoppably, grasping desperately again for the wall. As they exploded together in animal grunts, Barb's knees buckled and she collapsed heavily.

Steve's senses returned with Barb lying at his feet, and he imagined customers outside gathered around a monitor for the show. Horrified, he checked the walls for a hidden camera, preparing himself for incarceration. Or celebrity.

Thankfully he found nothing but Barb's bag of goodies.

Steve and Barb exited the dressing room minutes later, somewhat sheepishly.

The cat-suited young clerk smirked as they passed. Steve ducked his sweaty head, feigning pre-occupation with the designs on carpet. They were, of course, swirling little phalluses.

"And where do we pay?" Barb held up her bag of items.

"*Oui.* Just leave with what you want, it's tracked. We put it on your bill. Everything you don't want, leave in the dressing room."

"That's incredible. Did you hear that honey?"

"Ummm..." Thankfully, the coat had been jettisoned.

"*C'est bon?* Was everything to your satisfaction?" the clerk asked.

"*God, yes!*" Barb whispered, grabbing the clerk's outstretched hand. Steve's legs trembled and he turned away to face the videos, praying he didn't see an instant replay.

Barb mistook his forced interest.

"Do you sell these?" she asked the clerk.

"We make videos, but we don't rent or sell them. You understand?"

"You *make* them? *Really?*"

Steve edged out of the store as quickly as possible.

"*J'aime l'une timide aussi.* I like the shy ones too," the clerk laughed, continuing. "Would you like us to make one? Five hundred dollars for one hour. We are professionals."

Barb's mischievous side began a relentless assault on her sensibilities. When had she last indulged it?

She bought herself more time, "You mean you would come and film us having sex in our room?"

"Yes, of course. Whatever you like, wherever. Many people do it. We cater to everyone."

"I've seen that," Barb laughed.

The clerk smiled, "You think, *no?* Come back tomorrow!"

"OK. Thank you!"

"*Merci, cher. Juliet.*"

"Barb." They hugged and the clerk gave her a kiss on both cheeks. Barb skipped out, glowing.

Steve was waiting close-by, just down the cobble-stone street. Barb gave him a kiss.

"I need sunglasses," Steve said, wincing.

"Why?"

"Your blinding glow. Post-coital *and* post-shopping."

She slapped him, playfully.

Steve took her hand, "They must make a fortune."

"I hope so. They're practically missionaries, you know."

"So to speak."

Steve led her out of the alley. Barb had zeroed in on the sex-shop with uncanny speed, now it was time to explore.

They wound their way through the tiny, picturesque lanes, through more narrow alleyways and past boutique after boutique.

The illusion of a cozy, thriving village was convincing. They were rapidly able to lose themselves, to forget they were in the States at all—let alone under a twenty-five story glass dome.

Despite the other guests scurrying store to store in every direction, they were able to maintain their blissed-out, leisurely pace knowing the hot tub awaited them, only minutes away.

There was an energy here in the village, seductive and undeniable. Perhaps it was the narrow, winding streets and the confined spaces, but it had the vibrancy, the inertia, of a metropolis many times its size.

"How about some coffee?" interrupted Barb. The hormonal haze was already starting to wear off and she was crashing.

"Sure. I could use a little boost," Steve's own fatigue was wearing on him and he was starting to see the frenzied shoppers as vultures circling the stores in search of fresh carrion.

Barb cuddled up to him. "How about the café by the fountain?"

"You lead the way, adventuress. But let's go somewhere a little out of the way, I'm through with crowds for the evening."

"Let's try it. I want to see the garden."

They slowly wound their way to the center of the village, finding the caliber of the tiny shops only increased. By the time they reached the fountain, the window-shopping alone was beyond their reach. Yet the stores were packed and lines were out the door.

"I always thought we were pretty well off," Barb chuckled.

"For Kansas."

Around them, shoppers were flaunting their designer shopping bags with pride, allowing onlookers to rate their consumptive prowess with a glance.

Barb's bag spoke something slightly different, slightly richer possibly, but Steve was happy to keep it discreetly between them. Fortunately the bag was modest, just a simple matte black with the tiny penis logo in raised black velour. Nonetheless, Steve desperately wanted to get home before the kids.

"I bet it's all the specials, honey. Don't you think we should just take a peek? I feel like we're missing something."

"Nope. Not at all."

They arrived at DarkRoast to find the playfully hell-themed coffee shop bustling but not invasive and quickly found a table next to the flower garden. The steady gurgle of the fountain nearby pleasantly foreshadowed the warm bubbling glory nineteen stories above.

Barb watched the water dance through the air and down across the fountain, while Steve leaned back to take in the majesty surrounding them. The tide had definitely turned and the atrium was thinning out. The glass elevators were busy shuttling people back to their suites.

Steve followed them up, to the smoked glass floors at the top of the tower and beyond, to the center of the dome twenty-five stories above them. Remarkably, he could make out bits of the village reflected above.

"You know it could be raining now?" Steve said.

"It's a desert honey..."

"It rains in a desert. But it could be snowing, it could be anything out there. And in here it's perfect."

The waiter returned with their order and Steve removed his wallet. The waiter waved him off with a smile, "You've already been billed, sir. Come back and see us!"

"Oh we will!" Barb chirped. "Can you believe that honey? This place is really something."

"It's great. No cards, no wallet, no worries. It's so simple."

"But how do they do it?"

"It has to be that dust. Same as our suite."

"The *angel dust?*" Barb giggled, spewing her capuccino's foam over their table.

Steve raised his own and sipped, slowly, relishing the scent of his wife on his fingers.

Barb sat back. "I know we've said it all night, honey, but this is an incredible place. It's literally the most amazing place I've ever been to."

"You've got to be kidding. Better than Kilimanjaro?"

"It's different. People created this. All of this. It's beyond belief. It's..."

"The apex of our culture. The Egyptians had the pyramids, the Inca, Macchu Picchu. We have DisasterLand."

"Maybe Macchu Picchu was an Incan DisasterLand? Bungee jumping, everything?"

Steve laughed. *God, it felt great to be here.*

Barb's gaze returned to the flowers but her smile soon faded. "I wish it would stay like this, always."

"What do you mean?"

"Haven't you thought about it?" Barb paused, then continued. "About the disaster?"

"Oh come on, Barb. You're spoiling the moment."

"Seriously, honey. We really need to appreciate this. It's not going to be here forever. We need to start planning."

"I do," a lady at the next table interjected, "I'm sorry to be listening in, but I think about it all the time. I'm driving my husband crazy."

The husband nodded. "She sure is. Every fifteen minutes."

"It is a little overwhelming, isn't it? When you stop to think..." Barb said.

"That's why you don't think, honey. You enjoy. Which you're entirely incapable of doing." Steve was angry now, angry their perfect evening was being spoiled.

"Is that any way to talk to your wife? I mean, what if that's the last thing you ever say to her? Have you said your last goodbyes?" the wife asked.

"We haven't," replied Barb, checking Steve's reaction. "Not exactly."

"Kids?"

"Two."

"Are they here with you?"

Barb nodded.

"Better tell 'em you love 'em."

"You OK?" Shae asked, standing. He placed his glass of red on the conference room table in front of him.

"Computer brain," Elektra said, stepping in and rubbing her eyes. She had just finished her review of the hero families and as much other raw footage as she could stand. Her thinking was cottony, dulled by the vast amount of data in such a compressed time.

"Well, lookie-here," she continued, eyes landing on Greg. "It's the missing link."

"Hey, E." Greg rose from the table and extended his arms, giving Elektra a much-appreciated hug.

"You're not leaving, are you?"

Greg laughed. "Quite the contrary."

Shae poured another glass and handed it to her. Together, the three stepped over to the vast window overlooking the shadowy, bustling atrium, now bathed in neon. At night, with lights reflecting in the glass dome overhead, it was easy to picture themselves suspended in outer space.

"Good," Elektra said, after taking proper stock of the wine. "The rumors are killing me."

Greg and Shae exchanged a glance.

"Thanks for meeting me here," Elektra continued. "The trip down to DmZ wouldn't have been easy."

"Nor would the conversation," Shae smiled. "No secrets will be revealed tonight, but we don't need any extra ears, if you know what I mean."

"I just appreciate your time. I..."

"Nonsense," interrupted Shae. "We owe you an apology. Keeping you in the dark has been unfair."

"But not without reason," Greg added.

"Two, in fact," said Shae, "One is that we've been up to our eyeballs and we needed someone in control with their feet on the ground. This has been you."

"And you've done a spectacular job, Elektra. Seriously."

"Number two, we didn't want anything to distract you from preparing this show. It's too important."

Elektra nodded, "Only the..."

"Speculation has become a distraction. Of course... that's natural. And we should have approached you. We've just been lost in the details."

Shae took a long sip of his wine and returned to the table. Elektra followed, collapsing into the plush leather.

"I've been in legal meetings all afternoon," Shae said, massaging his temples, "and my head is going to explode."

"So are you guys going to step up or not?"

"In short," Shae said. "No. For the exact two reasons just mentioned. But we do want you to know, from us, that everything is going gang-busters and there's going to be a hell of an announcement next Sunday. You're going to hear it first though, maybe even Saturday night. It's all positive, don't worry. Your job is to have a fucking great show."

"That's it?"

"That's all we can say."

Elektra turned to Greg. He shrugged, helplessly.

"You're kidding me. You've told me absolutely nothing..."

"We're sorry. We want you focused. We also want no leaks. Right now, only one other person knows what's happening. If there's a leak, we know who it is."

"*One other person?!*"

"Relax, Elektra. Need-to-know basis."

Elektra's mind was spinning, due in no small part to the fact that she'd skipped dinner and already downed her wine. Fortunately, the deli down the hall was still open.

Jude.

"How'd VIP check-in go this morning?" Elektra asked, mind already out the door.

"Stellar. You'll have to join us for brunch on Sunday."

"If I'm alive."

Halfway down the hall, she dialed.

"Tell me you bastard," Elektra whispered.

"What are you talking about?"

"You know. You're the one. You weren't guessing."

Jude laughed. "You know these lines are bugged."

"That's a cop out."

"Elektra, come on."

"You knew the whole time! Tell me you bastard!"

"Can't."

"Bastard."

"Elektra..."

"Bastard."

She hung up.

Then redialed.

"No Greece," she said.

And hung up.

"Ready for round two?" Barb whispered.

They were recuperating in the tub's simmering warmth as the vast crystal-clear desert sky blanketed the distant mountains with millions of dancing stars.

Early Coltrane was floating out of the sound system on the DTV:Music channel, and the children were mercifully still away.

Barb slid her hand down Steve's chest, her nipples dancing along his arm.

"Honey..." Steve winced, "You've got to be kidding me!"

Barb leaned in, nibbling gently on his ear, "You're out of shape."

"*We're* out of shape."

"Are *we?*" Barb leaned back, floating to the opposite side of the tub and attempting to convince herself to be happy with what she got. It had, in fact, been the best in years.

But she couldn't. It was like bladder-management during a cross-country road trip: *don't break the seal, you'll start a flood.* She wanted more. She *needed* more.

"I'm sore, baby. I think I might have hurt something."

Barb rolled her eyes.

In the distance, the DisasterLand sign was glowing proudly.

Steve reached over and added more lavender mineral salts, generously provided by the house. He let the crystals dissolve then turned off the jets, drinking in the delicate perfume in silence.

Barb gently hoisted herself up on the rim to face Steve and the desert and slowly spread her legs. She slid a hand down in exploration and delicately peeled herself back to work. She began circling.

Barb's eyes defocused from the vivid scene before her as she increased in speed. She let go of the tub with her other hand and with it began to probe her own rich darkness. Steve still didn't bite.

Her breathing turned heavy and eyes shut as she leaned back, aimed her tail at the desert and rapidly accelerated. Steve watched as her breath stopped and she crescendoed, her body convulsing in wave after wave. She exhaled a fertile moan.

Without opening her eyes, she slid down next to him. He gave her a kiss on the forehead and she relaxed onto his shoulder.

Steve wondered if they had a telescope at the guard station at the foot of the mountains. If not they were crazy—the sky was so clear here, their view would be stunning. And on nights like this, there was a hell of a show going on all over this tower if their little corner was any indication.

Steve wrapped his arm around her. They were pruning. Massages tomorrow, a full-on ninety-minute pummeling followed by a hot tub sweat. Two nights in a row, he'd sleep like a baby.

A tremendous explosion jolted them out of their doze. Barb screamed and Steve nearly lost his bowels into the warmth of the tub.

Panic flashed: *Was it starting? WAS THIS IT? WHERE WERE THE KIDS?*

A second burst was rapidly followed by a third, then a fourth. Outside their window, enormous fireworks were showering the valley in an enormous rainstorm of light, glimmering across the mountains' shadowy face. The entire valley appeared as if it was on fire.

Steve was the first to notice the phone's gentle ring. It was eleven-thirty by the looks of it, time for the kids' pleading calls. Steve leaned over and pressed the 'answer' button, their jazz automatically fading, replaced with the distant pumping rhythm of a club.

"Hello?"

"DJ—turn on the TV!"

"What's up, Spike?"

"I won a video game, dad. I'm in the finals!"

"Hey, that's great, Spikers!"

"But it starts at midnight. I'm gonna be a little late."

"Oh..."

Barb shook her head.

"What's this game?" she asked.

"Turn on the TV!"

"You first. What's this game?"

"I can't talk about it. It's the secret one!"

"No good, Spike," Steve said, sternly.

"It's top secret dad. Seriously. Listen, can you just turn on the television?"

"Honey we're... in the hot tub. We're naked."

"Mom..."

In the VIP lounge of *Ghost*, Pete withered. His new pal elbowed him in the ribs.

"Hold on..." Pete said. "They say there's one in the bathroom. It's right next to the phone."

"They?"

"Just turn it on!"

Steve did.

Pete was onscreen, seated on a deep velour couch, his DisasterLand baseball cap down over his eyes. A traditional Japanese kimono neatly hid his sleek black suit— when he kept his legs together. He flashed a sign.

Sitting next to him, Zander, a black kid around Pete's age, cracked up.

"Yo DJ Mom! DJ Dad! Hope you're not on TV too!"

"Oh f...," Steve gawked, feeling vastly, absurdly naked and infinitely vulnerable. Barb choked back horror.

Pete waved. Zander was pulling faces and bugging out his eyes. His kimono was pink.

"What the hell are you kids wearing?" Steve asked.

"It's a kimono, DJ! All the winners get one!"

"No, that black thing."

"It's top secret. I told you!"

"Fine. Where are you?"

"VIP Lounge with my peeps col' chillin'!" They popped off a high five. "We's rockin' the D-L!" they yelled as flashbulbs fired.

"Spike?"

"Yeah, DJ?"

"You come home right afterwards, OK? No jackin' around."

"OK DJ. Yo I gotta jump."

"Y'all hol' tight!" Zander yelled. "We're out!"

The image dissolved, replaced by DTV's slicked-back evening host, "Be sure to join Pete, Zander, and everyone else here at 12:30 for the awards ceremony. Next, we're going over to the village, where Michelle is at the day's biggest sale. Michelle?"

Standing in the heart of the village and surrounded by hundreds of breathless shoppers waving to the camera, DisasterLand's on-the-ground reporter smiled, "Hi Jake. The biggest sale of the week so far is starting at midnight: all exclusive DisasterLand lines on sale for one hour only so hurry down!"

Steve flipped it off, head shaking, "Did you see all those people?"

"Do you think we're missing something?" Barb asked, suddenly concerned. "Should we go?"

"That sex fried your brain," Steve said, restarting the jets. "You better take it easy, honey."

"Naked dude!"

"They never did that shit before yo," Pete was finishing off his complementary double cheeseburger, fries and Coke.

"Yo, you think they wuz doin' it?"

"No way, dude! They's *too old!*"

Zander cracked up. "Nah, they jus' never been *here* yo! DisasterLand, dude! *Everyone in the house doin' it now!*"

Pete laughed, "'cept us!"

"Who on TV, us or them!"

"*Dawg!*" They hit fists and Pete flashed on the image of his parents outside the sex store, "Yo, man, they *wuz* doin' it. Seriously."

"Yeah, boi!"

Zander kicked back and took a long sip of his Coke, eyeing the scene around them. The four heats had all finished, the top five of each now preparing for the midnight rumble. Zander had finaled at eight and been hanging in the lounge ever since, watching subsequent rounds on special observational monitors showing strategic views of the game's progress. He felt he had a good handle on the competition.

Pete had sat down next to him forty-five minutes earlier because it was the only spot open but they had become fast friends.

"Yo man, I'm full," Pete sat back.

"Yo, you ates too much. You's gonna get smoked. I tolds yah." Zander shook his head, "Dudes is eyein' you. You's fresh meat."

Zander was right. The mind games had begun. But if anything, the massive meal had taken the edge off. Pete's body had been on fire with every nerve tingling, in danger of peaking too early and burning out. But now, he'd be just fine.

Yesterday, Middle School. Today? VIP lounge in *The Core.*

The game had been over flash, thirty minutes in a breath. One moment the opening fanfare, the next DisasterLand froze and slowly faded out like a dream upon first waking. Five lights had faded up in *The Core,* one on Peter.

He felt like he had blown a direct connection between his mind and his *Ghost,* bypassing reality and leaving thought behind in a resonant swirl of phosphor. He had rewired himself from the ground up.

And so had the other winners. He saw it in their eyes.

Zander lowered his voice. "Bro, I gots a deal for you."

"Whatup?"

"You and me, yo. We co-operate."

"Cooperate? Is that legal?"

"It's not *illegal.*"

Pete considered. "Define cooperate."

"We work together until we're the last two left. Then anything goes," Zander paused, letting it sink in. "I'll meet you inside. First thing."

Pete didn't even need to consider it. He trusted this kid, straightaway. "Deal deal dealy-yo," Pete said, and they knocked fists. "Where do we meet?"

"Yo, you know that sex store? Let's go check that shit out."

The bass stormed the dance floor like an angry wind and Sarah and Amir were eyes-shut lost in the groove. The veteran Motor City DJ was on a nostalgia trip, back to the early nineties and the 'E' generation and the crowd was up for it.

Neither Amir nor Sarah were privy to such ancient history, but it didn't bother them. They were just fucking loving it.

Rainbows of light were exploding around them as smiles glistened ethereally over the dance floor. The club was intimate and two hundred sweaty bodies of all ages were going at it full-on, synced in bliss.

To Sarah, the room felt like DisasterLand's battery, powering the machine. Boys and girls, girls and girls, boys and boys dancing as one, the raw sexuality of the dance floor captivating her, surrounding her with a world she had only imagined.

Never having experienced top DJs in a top club, she decided, was something she needed to rectify immediately upon arriving in New York.

Amir leaned over, breaking Sarah out of her reverie, "Water?"

Sarah nodded and they slipped off the dance floor, past the moist bodies lost in the beat. She realized she wasn't really properly dressed but tomorrow afternoon she'd take care of that in the village. And tomorrow night she'd come back, ready for work.

The couple stepped into the plush chill-out room and Sarah peeled away, settling herself into a secluded couch and wiping the sweat from her forehead. Downtempo gems floated through the air and she breathed in the cool, oxygenated air.

Wow, she thought, *all systems are go.*

Earlier, Sarah had remained in her seat after the movie as the credits rolled, dabbing the tears off her cheeks with her sleeve. It was a *real* bummer, and she clearly wasn't the only one who felt that way. It was mass depression in there, and she couldn't figure out why they'd done it. Why had DisasterLand produced such a downer?

A remarkable film showing the transience of life and the timeless power of love was what the poster said, and she'd have to agree. But still. *Everyone* didn't have to die!

Sarah watched as two-by-two the couples stood up and exited, but she remained, alone, contemplating her response card. *They're just opening wounds,* she thought. *Prepping people for what's to come.* It was cruel.

But what *was* to come?

"There's no cheese down that maze."

"Hunh?" Sarah had looked up to see a guy standing over her, slightly nerdy, very Indian. As in India Indian.

"Don't give it too much thought. And throw that card away. They've got plenty. They probably don't even read them."

"You're right. Fuck it," Sarah dropped it under her seat. It *was* making her think too much.

"It's mind control. Liberate your soul. Let's go dancing."

Dancing?

She had no idea what he was really talking about, but with his olive skin and gentle demeanor, she figured whatever it was was worth checking out. Up to now she'd only dated white guys, but now she was starting college and could certainly afford to be a bit more experimental. The United Nations was *in* New York for God sakes and she'd better ramp up.

Amir joined her on the couch with two large bottles of water, handing her one as he scrunched in next to her. *Right* next to her. He laid his arm over her shoulder, "Feel better?"

"Oh, yeah! This is awesome."

"I think it's the impending disaster."

"Really?"

"Sure. If you know you're going to die, you want to make the most of it!"

"But we're not going to die..."

"Same thing!"

Amir leaned in, their lips touched. She liked the way he smelled.

"Great set, hunh?" he asked, scanning the room.

"Yeah. Do you know the DJ?"

"Of course! He's huge—but I never got the chance to hear him spin. Techno isn't really my thing but he's got that great Detroit soul. You go dancing a lot?"

"We don't have clubs in Kansas. Not like this."

"This is world-class, this place. It's so intimate too."

"It's amazing, you feel the bass more than you hear it."

"That's what it's all about. The phat bass. So where at in Kansas? Somewhere I've heard of?"

"KC. What about you?"

"From DC but I go to school in New York. Vassar."

"No shit. I've heard of it."

"Yeah, it's cool."

"You're a freshman?"

"Sophomore."

Sarah laughed, "That's what I meant."

"Are you in school?"

"Going to Columbia next month."

"Columbia, New York?"

Sarah nodded.

"We'll practically be neighbors! Poughkeepsie's only a little over an hour away."

"You're kidding."

"I'm in the city all the time," Amir smiled, running his hand through her hair. He leaned in, softly, and gave her a kiss, gently breaking his tongue through her lips. It went on a bit long for Sarah's tastes and she pulled back, not sure she liked where this was headed. She felt her bladder calling.

She gave him a quick peck and stood, "This water's going straight through me. I'll be right back."

A little too slick, she thought as she wound her way to the bathroom. *And a little too used to getting his way.*

Not this time. No one took *her* acceptance for granted.

"E?"

"Excuse me?"

"E?"

The trendy girl washing her hands next to Sarah was speaking. *To her.*

"E?"

The music from the main floor was pounding, even in the bathroom, and Sarah was still a bit slow on the uptake. The girls' eyes met for a split second.

"Nothing. Sorry," the girl said, and stepped away towards the door.

Sarah checked her hair and was drying her hands when she stopped cold.

E. *Ecstasy.*

Sarah shuddered. Here she was, Sarah Beyers, at a club and being offered drugs. She caught herself in the mirror. She was fully on her own now, fully adult. Unsure of exactly what she was doing, Sarah hurried after the girl.

Catching up to her in the hallway, Sarah took her arm gently, "Excuse me?"

The girl slowed.

"I just heard you."

She stopped, "Heard me what?"

Sarah smiled shyly, "Yes. I mean, yes."

"Fourth stall on the left." The girl twirled back and Sarah took a deep breath. She followed a few seconds behind.

Stepping into the bathroom again, Sarah glimpsed the prescribed stall door close. A few girls were still bustling about, but she preferred blinders on for this stage. She was operating on instinct and on trust—exactly what everyone said not to do.

But this was DisasterLand.

Sarah entered the stall and the girl smiled, "I'm Katie."

"Sarah."

Katie locked the door behind them. The girl was a little older and Sarah suddenly felt like a kid next to her.

"Nice to meet you. Good night, hunh?"

"Yeah," Sarah smiled. *"Amazing..."*

"Thirty each or two for fifty."

"Two please."

Katie pulled a lip-gloss tube out of her pocket and shook out two little white pills. Katie flipped them over to reveal tiny dolphins.

"These are nice. Smooth," Katie offered.

"Cool." Sarah handed her the cash—everything she had, including what her father had given her—and Katie dropped the pills into Sarah's palm.

Sarah Beyers had just bought drugs. In the past, it was always someone else. Hot Rod, whoever. She wasn't ever someone who *owned* drugs. They just appeared.

Her personality quickly began reconfiguring itself, updating itself accordingly. A barrier had been crossed, a line transgressed. She had broken the fucking law. Outright. And still wasn't sure why. Was she proving something to herself?

Sarah noticed Katie staring and awkwardly realized she had nowhere to put the pills. She instinctively brought them to her mouth.

"Wo girl... you by yourself?" Katie took her arm.

"Yes... No... er... yes. I guess so."

"Why don't you wait till you have a friend. No need to rush it, you know? Be safe. Two of these is a lot."

Sarah dropped her eyes... Katie was right.

"Thanks."

Katie fished in her pocket, found another tube. She shook it. Empty.

Sarah dropped her pills inside and stuck it in her pocket.

"Thanks."

"You're welcome. Be safe."
"You too," Sarah answered. "Maybe see you round?"
Katie paused. "Maybe."
Sarah didn't know why she said that.

Pete and Zander exited *The Core* to enthusiastic cheering from the awestruck hordes assembled outside.

DTV was broadcasting live, continuing their coverage from the earlier medal ceremony. To the public, there had been no solid explanation of what the game actually involved—only the hushed insistence of its classified nature—which served to increase its mystique and deify the young winners.

Pete and Zander gave a manic thumbs-up to the cameras, their eyes glowing fiercely. It had been a savage, intense battle and their cooperation had saved them more than once. Zander medaled in third and Pete nabbed fifth. It was a triumph.

Pete did a quick check for family, but didn't see anyone. It didn't bother him. He was still loaded from battle.

As they worked their way through the crowd, Pete felt every tiny movement, jumped at every sound. His senses were on overdrive but he felt like his body was swimming in syrup.

They emerged into the bustle of the late-night atrium to find packs of new friends bar-hopping while bleary-eyed families still swarmed the village's shops and cafès.

"Yo, whatup pimp?" Zander asked.

"Crib, yo."

"Nah, man, we's just startin'."

Zander slapped Pete in the back of the head and raced off, disappearing into the crowd.

"Hey!" Pete yelled, confused. A sense of betrayal welled up, a shattering of the powerful bond they had shared so recently. He felt deserted, alone in the massiveness of DisasterLand.

A shriek echoed through the atrium, temporarily paralyzing nervous guests nearby. But Pete understood. The gauntlet had just been thrown down.

The adrenaline kicked in and they were back, live. *Ghost. For real.* Pete raced off after him, darting in and out of startled guests, fighting to maintain a glimpse of Zander's back. Fire coursed through his veins and a battle cry soared from his lips.

Then he was flat on his back, his face covered in blood with the atrium spinning around him.

A large black gloved hand had appeared in his path, instantly stopping his progress. He was scooped off the ground by its owner and carried off by the scruff of his neck. Zander was ahead of him, dazed, victim of a similar fate.

They were dragged away from the concerned crowd and dropped in a pile around the corner from *The Core*, away from the hubbub and more than a little spooked. They rolled themselves into a seating position.

Pete's nose continued to spill blood and after a long silence he was handed a handkerchief by one of the men in matte black leather.

"You gonna arrest us?" Zander asked.

"There ain't no police here, kid."

"Who are you?"

One of the men unzipped his motorcycle jacket and flashed his DisasterLand Security Badge.

"This is DisasterLand. We kick your ass out," the other guard elaborated.

"No way man." Pete felt sick, his eyes starting to tear. It was *worse*.

The Guards let it sink in. "So what were you guys doing back there?" they asked, finally.

"We was just playin'," Zander offered. "Chase."

"Umm..." The Guards discussed the situation privately. Pete kept his eyes to himself.

"Didn't we just see you at the awards ceremony? For *Ghost*?" a Guard asked.

"No," said Zander.

"Yes," Pete admitted.

Zander gave him a dirty look. A Guard lightly kicked his foot. "Yes or no?"

"Yes," Zander admitted. "You did."

"Thought so. We don't like liars, Zander Bentley."

"You remember your agreement kid?" Pete looked up to find the other Guard staring at him.

"Yes, sir."

"Your agreement includes non-verbal communication too. Anything. And nothing. Got it? Anything which hints at the nature of the game is off limits."

"Are you gonna kick us out?"

The Guards conferred for an unbearable amount of time. Pete almost barfed. Twice.

"No," one finally announced, "You're both warned."

Pete relaxed, finally able to breathe again. He looked over at Zander, who was ashen.

"Now get home. It's late. Your parents are probably wondering where you're at."

"Thank you, sir. Officer. Mister. Guard, sir," Pete said.

"Yeah. Thanks." Zander agreed, standing. "We're cool."

The kids scampered away, stunned, before the guards could change their minds.

"How 'bout that!" Zander said, slapping Pete's back.

"That shit was *close*," Pete removed the handkerchief from his nose.

"Sorry 'bout that bro."

"It's OK. I need to get home anyway. So's your family gonna be psyched? Third place!"

Zander's voice dropped. "It's just me and my dad. My mom died two years ago."

"Shit. Sorry dude."

"That's OK. So you wanna get together tomorrow?"

"Yeah. That'd be a'ight."

"Noon? At the elevators."

"OK."

Zander was staring, "Yo, is you nose OK?"

"I think so. It's already stopped bleeding."

"That'd suck, bro. First night you go and break your nose."

Sarah was walking home with a boy. Not just any boy, but one of the cutest she'd ever seen. He *glowed*, just like a movie star. He was older too. He had to be at least twenty-five.

It was now 4:15 and they were both in the glow of a killer set. Dripping with sweat and vibrating, Sarah, at least, could feel people's stares.

He wasn't Amir. She dropped him when he started to rub his dick against her leg like some sort of dog. She saw him doing it to another girl later who actually seemed to be enjoying it. Good for her, Sarah had thought. *Whatever*.

Sarah felt in her pocket for the lip-gloss. She felt like she had left a part of herself back in that restroom, like she had left little Sarah behind. She still couldn't believe it. E.

Maybe she could do it tomorrow? With him? With *Neil*?

Props to Katie. The night could have ended horribly but instead this beautiful little prince had appeared before her an hour before the end of the set. He was from Williamsburg, Brooklyn and was cooler than anyone she'd ever met.

Around them, the atrium was filled with the haphazard energy of a wild night coming to a close, of parties winding down and people crawling home. Whether it was shoppers crashing post-sales or the drunks spilling out of the bars and yelling at the top of their lungs, it was a mass migration of people to the tower, all in varied altered states of consciousness. Anything could happen.

"You wanna stop somewhere? Let the sheeple clear?"

Sarah giggled, "Sure."

He took her hand, playfully pulling her towards the park.

"I'll show you somewhere I found this afternoon. It's beautiful."

"Um, I think we should stay where people are. You know?"

"Oh, sure. It's just off the trail. You can leave whenever you want and I'll hang out for a while. I want to catch the sunrise."

"Yeah, OK. I should probably be getting back to the 'rents soon. I was supposed to be back over four hours ago."

"Shit, girl. Midnight curfew? In DisasterLand? That's almost criminal."

"Yeah. Child abuse. I'll have to do something about it tomorrow."

"You mean today."

Sarah giggled. He was a bit cryptic, this one. She decided he must be a poet. But poets were poor and didn't wear such cool clothes.

The park was strangely calm, the Great Lawn deserted except for a few tipsy couples necking.

As they entered, Neil paused to slip off his boots and motioned for Sarah to do the same. The park was fresh, alluring, the soft grass moist under her feet. The thought of lying on the grass with this boy was irresistible. But she wasn't stupid: he could be a professional.

"So where're we headed?"

"It's not far."

Neil took her hand, escorting her across the Great Lawn to the furthest trail to their right. Sarah drank in the lush, nighttime scents.

There were just enough people around to reassure Sarah it was safe. After all, this was DisasterLand. *It had to be safe.*

As they entered the trail, squishing through the moist undergrowth, Sarah slowed.

"Don't worry, we'll be right by the river. We can wash off our feet there."

"Oh, OK. So what are you gonna do in the park alone when I'm gone?"

"Write." He pulled a small journal from his jacket pocket with his free hand.

"Are you a poet or something?"

He laughed, "Actually, I'm a singer."

Sarah's heart skipped, "Like in a band?"

"Yeah," he smiled. "Like in a band."

They continued on, silently, Sarah's mind buzzing, through a winding trail and past an elaborate garden. The park was *huge*, Sarah realized, and got a cold chill.

The sound of the rushing river grew, and Neil soon stopped.

"It's through here," he said, pointing into the tangle of woods. "Be careful where you step. It's not a real trail."

Sarah stared. If she was anywhere else, she would think this guy was going to take her into the woods and hack her apart.

Neil sensed her hesitation. "Don't worry, it's safe. If you want to turn around, just say so."

"OK."

He *was* a professional she decided. She could practically feel the lure in her throat. A little tug, then some line. Another tug, a little more line. Before she knew it, she'd be in the boat.

"So how'd you find this place?"

"I went swimming this afternoon. The whole length of the river. I saw this place and walked back."

"Really?" Sarah was impressed. "It's that cool?"

"I think so. And no one would ever find it unless they did what I did."

"That's awesome."

They picked their way though the woods, and a few minutes later they emerged into a little clearing right on the river, just as Neil had described. In the distance to her right, Sarah could just make out a picturesque bridge across the river.

Neil spread his arms out proudly, "This is it! And that," he said, pointing to the bridge, "is the *Bridge of Sighs!*"

"The *what?*"

"I dunno, it's just what I was told."

"This is amazing! It's so... cozy."

"I told you! I figured once you came here, you'd forgive me."

"I do. But don't you try nothin'." She mock-scolded him. He waved his hands in innocence.

She followed him to the riverbank where they sat down, dipping their feet into the crisp water.

"So are you here with your parents?" Sarah asked.

"How old are you?" Neil asked.

"Old enough," Sarah said.

"No, I'm not," he continued. "We're playing here. Tomorrow."

"*Really?*"

"I'll put you on the list. We're recording the first 'Live from DisasterLand' album. At midnight."

"Wow!" Sarah stared, eyes lit up. "Cool! What're you guys called?"

Neil couldn't get over that part: girls' reactions.

"Smaug."

"Nice. Hey, you think my brother could come?"

"How old's he?"

"Fourteen."

"And you are?"

"Twenty," she lied.

Neil frowned, "I don't believe you."

"OK, I'm eighteen. But I'm going to be a freshman at Columbia in three weeks. How old are you?"

"Twenty-six."

"You don't look twenty-six."

"I know... I know..."

Neil lay back, shutting his eyes.

Sarah lay on her side, towards Neil. She liked him. A lot. But he was old. Really old. *Creepy* old. Did people that old do drugs?

"Just listen..." Neil said. "The river's so relaxing. And it's not polluted."

It was Sarah's turn to lie back, to reflect on her evening. First the movie, then Amir, then the club and now this... back to the park, back to where it all began at dinner.

Sarah opened her eyes and Neil was staring.

"I think I saw you on DTV tonight," he said.

"Maybe."

"You're Sarah Beyers."

She nodded, somewhat rattled.

"I'm good at faces. Don't worry." He laughed to himself. "Yeah, I saw your little 'bro. What's his name?"

"Pete. But we call him Spike."

"Right! Yeah... with MagicD. You guys wuz trippin'!"

Sarah checked her watch. It was already a quarter to five and the sun would be coming up soon. She was going to be lynched.

"So the river's great for swimming," Neil asked, cautiously. "I was thinking of taking a little swim. You want to join me?"

"I don't really have anything..."

"There's no one around, Sarah."

She froze, "Oh, well, I don't know..."

"That's cool. I mean, no pressure."

"Yeah, I think I should really be going. I should have been home a long time ago." She sat up.

"OK... so you'll come to the show tomorrow?"

Sarah met his gaze. He was sincere. Never one to leave a party before it was over, she was having second thoughts.

"Yes. I will. *We will.*"

"Good. You know how you got here? Can you get back?"

"Yeah. Don't worry."

"Cool. Keep it a secret? For me?"

Sarah smiled, "Of course."

Neil kissed her cheek. She hugged him and stood up awkwardly. She delayed.

"Goodnight," she said. "Don't drown."

"Goodnight," Neil said. "I won't. *See you tomorrow.*"

As Sarah disappeared into the forest, she turned to see Neil step out of his clothes and leap into the river with a splash.

Why was she leaving again?

Sarah approached 808 in prayer, heart lodged firmly in her throat. As she neared, the door slid open like a gunshot.

She crept breathlessly into the kitchen on her tip-toes and stood, lingering in the darkness. Dim emergency lights in each corner marked the space. From the bedroom, she could hear her dad snoring. Her own heart thudded.

Sarah had just slid into home plate, safe. She carefully opened the refrigerator and pulled out a bottled water, chugging it in one go.

Tip-toeing to her room, she found the door cracked open. Sarah stuck her head in, listening for Pete's breathing. It was there.

She slipped inside and crept carefully to her bed, as silently as she possibly could, hoping she didn't wake him.

"I was worried about you," Pete whispered and Sarah almost leapt out of her skin. "Are you OK?"

She thought she could make out his voice trembling. *Was he trying not to cry?* Sarah sat down on the bed.

"I'm sorry, Pete. I had such a fun night. I met so many people!"

"It's after five."

"Does anyone know?"

"Mom and dad are passed out naked."

"Really?"

"Yeah. I went in with my flashlight after I got home to see if they were OK."

"Are *you* OK? After witnessing *that?*"

Pete snorted—he *had* been crying—and Sarah joined in nervously.

A long pause followed and Sarah wished for a shower. *Maybe she should have stayed...* a swim would have been perfect.

"You know what?" Pete whispered.

"What?"

"I got fifth place in the video game. I was on DTV."

"Really? You think it'll be repeated tomorrow?"

"I think so, DJ. It's a big deal. It's top secret."

"So what kind of video game was it?"

"It was the best thing ever."

"Really? Can I try it?"

"You've got to audition tomorrow night. But I don't think you'd be very good. There was only one girl who got in the finals and she was kinda weird."

Sarah pulled out the lip-gloss tube from her pocket and spun it, listening to the gentle, pregnant rattle. When could she do it? Not tomorrow, not with her brother at the show...

So where would she put it? Sarah tip-toed to the closet and slipped it in her backpack.

"What are you doing?"

"Nothing."

"Where were you?"

"Dancing."

"With a boy?"

"Part of the time."

"Did you do it?"

"Shut up."

Pete snickered. Sarah realized that her ears were hardly ringing, not like some shows she'd been to and this one seemed so much louder. It *was* a great sound system.

"He's in a band," she continued.

"Is he famous?"

"I don't think so. But they're playing tomorrow. He put me on the list."

"You guys did it. Rock stars always do it."

She ignored him, "He said you can come too if you want. If you shut up."

There was a long pause. Sarah made her way back to her bed, wishing again for a shower. There was just no way. No way at all.

Sarah slipped under the covers and out of her clothes, hoping she could have the sheets changed in the morning. It *was* a hotel after all. Wasn't it?

She shut her eyes.

"Are you scared?" Pete asked. It was minutes later, and Sarah had almost fallen asleep.

"Scared? About what?"

"You know, the *disaster?*"

"Don't worry Spikers." Sarah rolled over. "It'll happen when it happens and we'll deal. The important thing is to live moment by moment. Don't let anyone rob you of the present."

Sarah groggily realized that she was pretty much quoting what they had said in *Gone Forever*.

"Besides," she continued, "Neil's gig is tomorrow at midnight. They wouldn't have a disaster before that. It doesn't make any sense."

Pete relaxed slightly. Sarah was right. He gingerly retested his nose. It seemed OK.

And he had a towel down in case it started again.

SATURDAY

Steve opened his eyes and instantly knew the mood had changed. A shadow had descended upon DisasterLand that would only continue to deepen.

In the twisted light of early morning, he lay in bed pondering hair in all its disgusting finality. His mind was floating outside of himself, too big for his shrunken head.

Why? he wondered. *Why hair? Why hair there?*

Steve climbed out of bed, moaning, desperate for fresh air. Barb and the kids were still asleep as Steve cautiously made his way through the living room and out onto the walkway, wearing only his DisasterLand bathrobe and slippers.

The door slid shut behind him and Steve continued out to the glass rail. The sun's virile rise over the park was casting a green tint over the sleeping village below and the distant smell of freshly baking bread and coffee wafted into his nostrils.

Almost instantly, Steve felt his internal darkness dissipate, felt his spirits brightening. Already, he was feeling refreshed. Remarkable, Steve thought. En*light*ening.

He reckoned it was still well before seven.

Steve leaned against the handrail, stretching his back. He had slept well. It was a surprisingly comfortable bed, but he'd still need that massage. He'd call soon, just to make sure they got in. Barb had been right.

He stared down into the village below, eyes tracing last night's walk of shame and eventually gravitating to DarkRoast in the village center. Soon, he realized, the rising sun would strike the fountain and the surrounding garden, bathing them in gold. The garden café, amazingly, was empty.

Steve pictured himself there, the sunlight and caffeine chasing away the last of his morning fog as he enjoyed a warm croissant and latte in solitude. A joyous warmth spread through his soul.

He certainly wouldn't mind stretching his legs, and a latte would be a just reward.

Steve took the first few tentative steps and realized his predicament. He couldn't go down dressed like this. *Could he?*

After only a moment's hesitation, he continued on. He was a big believer in moving forward—once a path was chosen, one accepted one's fate, retreating only in times of danger or desperation.

This was neither. No one was up yet and he wouldn't need his wallet. If he felt awkward, he'd grab the order to go and come straight back up. He didn't imagine that being the case, though, and could think of no more relaxing way to spend a quiet morning.

Besides, it was all fully-branded DisasterLand gear, even if it *was* just a robe and slippers. He'd seen women wearing less last night. *Much* less.

He made his way down the walkway and noticed the twin cafés by the elevators were open, but they simply wouldn't do. If he was going to stretch his legs, to take advantage of having the glorious atrium practically to himself, he was going to have to go all the way.

"Beyers!"

Steve turned back, slowly, painting a smile on his face. Just behind him, a door had opened. The Andrews'.

Jim waved, looking Steve over from head to toe.

Steve felt cold and alone, a complete and utter moron.

"Are you out of your friggin' mind, Beyers?"

Jenny followed him out of their suite, snickering. They were dressed in DisasterLand's best disaster-ready sports gear, and both had D-PAKs cinched tightly around their waists.

"What are you thinking man?" Jim continued.

Steve cleared his throat. "Mornin' Jim. In a word? Coffee." He tried out a little laugh, but it didn't play well. "Mornin', Jenny." He smiled, awkwardly.

"Good morning, Steve."

"Beyers... are you awake? This is DisasterLand, man. It's *Saturday Morning.*"

Steve waited until they caught up, wondering if this was indeed an omen. Maybe the little café up ahead wasn't such a bad idea?

No. He would move forward. The one thing he wasn't was a quitter.

"So where are you folks headed?" he asked as they joined him on the walk to the elevators.

"Stockin' up, Beyers. We're hitting Good Food. It opens at eight. Want to get there before the crowd does."

"*Crowd?*"

"Then if we're lucky we'll hit the sales when the stores open back up at eleven. We missed some good stuff last night," Jenny added.

"*If you're lucky?*"

"Beyers, didn't you watch DTV last night? Almost twenty-five percent of disasters occur on Saturday. Forty-five on Sunday. Over thirty on Monday. We're in *the zone*, man. It could happen," he stared, *"Anytime."*

Jenny observed Steve's reaction, "Jim takes these things very seriously. Don't let it worry you, Steve. You go on and get your coffee."

Steve scratched his head, feeling distinctly belittled.

"I'm telling you, Beyers. *Anytime,"* Jim repeated.

Bullshit, Steve thought. *We just got here.* "No one's even up yet, Jim," he protested, unconvincingly.

Jim laughed, shook his head. "A bunch of yah-hoos if you ask me. They'll get theirs. Spending their time drinking and partying instead of *preparing."*

The elevator arrived and doors opened. Steve decided to juke. Feign the adjacent café, then call the next elevator when they were gone. These people were too... anxious. It was like they *wanted* a disaster or something.

"Remember, Beyers. One-twelve if you need help." Jim gave a hearty laugh as they stepped in, "By the way, have you seen the morning paper?"

"No."

"Um," said Jim, winking at his wife. Jenny snorted.

The doors shut.

Steve slowly counted to twenty and recalled the elevator.

Steve found the young girl behind DarkRoast's counter inexplicably rude and fought vigorously to prevent himself from accosting her.

Eyes shining, cheeks dimpled and barely-restrained smirk playing across her face, she may as well have been pissing in his latte. The morning definitely wasn't going according to plan.

The elevator doors had opened and he'd stepped out onto the atrium floor only to see an enormous crowd assembled in front of Good Food. Somehow, from above, he'd completely missed the hundred or so people in line awaiting its opening. And there, at the end, were the Andrews. Waving.

He'd shot past the group with only a cursory wave, ignoring the murmurs rippling through the line. He felt each of them mocking his audacious bravado.

Fools, he scowled. In the cold light of early morning and dressed Jersey-style in their identical track suits, to him they presented a disgusting mockery of individual freedom and everything else decent in the world. It was small-minded, weak-spined, fear-drenched, middle-American group-think screaming its own inadequacy. It was straight out of the Soviet Union or worse, depression-era America, and Steve found the spectacle revolting.

He had soon reached his place of solace, with the light striking the garden just as he'd imagined, yet even it had failed him. Between Jenny's mystifying snort and this girl's elfin smirk, his morning coffee had been ruined. The moment was lost.

The only thing saving Steve's pride were the murals behind the counter, presenting a comical, perverted hell: Bosch done by Keith Haring. He felt right at home.

Steve silently prayed this girl would get hers.

He believed in instinct, in going with first thoughts—it had treated him well throughout his career. His first thought this morning had not been good, and yet he had wandered off anyway, alone and in a bathrobe. Jim was right: he had let last night's romance go to his head and he was taking foolish chances. But he couldn't turn-tail and run. He couldn't let the bastards win.

He'd lay down the law when he got back: *No one leaves alone, and from now on we move in twos. Nothing will be taken for granted.*

Then they'd hit Good Food, together, after the bourgeoisie had cleared out. And like Jim said, they'd stock up. Whatever that meant.

Steve *was* a little off this morning, that was clear. He'd forgotten to take his Happinol the night before and maybe it was affecting his judgment. He'd double-up when he got home.

Steve reached over the counter towards the offensive barista to collect his order, anything to save a couple of seconds and get him out of here. But as she tried handing Steve the coffee, she lost it completely. Her eyes bugged out and as the laughter spilled, so did the latte, narrowly missing his pristine robe.

Steve's blood boiled and he thrust out his finger in preparation for a devastating verbal attack: there was no way in hell he would stand for this abuse.

A light flashed on over his shoulder, causing his shadow to fall weakly across the counter. Steve spun, directly into the glare of a DTV news camera.

"Mr. Steve Beyers?" asked the reporter in his erudite English accent.

"Yes?" Steve said, stomach free-falling.

"I'm Allan Biggs, *DL:AM Live*. Popped out for a quick coffee, then?" he asked, struggling to hold his excitement in check.

"Yes, sir," Steve said. "And if you wouldn't mind..."

"Have you caught this morning's paper, sir?"

Jenny's snort flashed before Steve's eyes and a cold dark chill raced down his spine. Steve responded slowly, deliberately, aware of the harsh glow of the camera's light, "No, actually, I haven't."

The barista, source of so much of his pain, called out to him, waving a fresh copy. The headline screamed:

4:30 A.M. Love Nest—Sarah Beyers and Smaug's Neil Gallows

A grainy paparazzi shot of Sarah and Neal, holding hands and sneaking through the woods was featured. Across the bottom:

Smaug: Tonight at Midnight

"Careful, there, sir," the reporter said, grabbing Steve's arm to steady him. "Mr. Beyers, I'd like to ask you if you have any comment?"

Steve assessed his bodily functions: heart racing, breathing shallow. He waited a split second to see if either failed. When they didn't, his rage only rose.

The reporter continued, sensing blood, "Care to deny the reports, sir? On behalf of your daughter?"

"No..." Steve said, cocking his fist, "But I'd like to ask *you what your comment is!*" He had pardoned the barista, but this guy was going to get it.

The reporter retreated, hands up, "No sir!" he said, smiling into the camera in a way Steve found profoundly insulting, "No I do not. There you have it DisasterLand, Steve Beyers. One of the few men left with *pride*. I'm Allan Biggs, *DL:AM Live*, the Atrium."

As the light flashed off, Allan spun, giving Steve a strong pat on the back, "Sorry 'bout that, buddy. You've got a good family there. Enjoy yourselves."

Allan and the cameraman hurried away, in the direction of Good Food.

Steve dropped the paper, a wail rising from his core.

"Excuse me, Mister Beyers?"

It was the barista. Steve turned, forcing his wounded eyes upon his tormentor.

"Can I get your autograph?" She was waving a pen. "Please?"

The door slid open and Steve expected to find his family in an uproar. Instead, the suite was mercifully still.

He wondered if Barb had stolen the children in a fit of rage and fled to safety, leaving the police to escort him out.

Or perhaps that was only wishful thinking.

The confrontation had been continuously replayed on the InfoTron and his walk back to the elevators through an even larger queue at Good Food was one of the most miserable experiences of his life. They had cheered, sure, and shown nothing but support. But Steve knew it had been out of mercy, and nothing else. Only a devil would publicly kick a wounded animal.

At the end of the day he was alone, in his bathrobe, his daughter defiled and his ego shattered, all live in front of over two thousand strangers that he would spend the next nine days with.

Steve removed the newspaper from under his arm and hid it above the refrigerator. He had grabbed it off the ground and hurried away, hoping someday it might be something to laugh about. If not, perhaps it could fuel his funeral pyre.

He tiptoed over to the kids' room and nudged open the door. Sarah and Pete were both there, out cold. Which meant Barb probably was too.

He watched Sarah sleeping, wondering if the story was true. He wasn't going to jump to conclusions but he wanted to hear the full story. *Soon.* He'd been completely blindsided. He didn't even know DisasterLand *had* a paper.

Steve sat down at the kitchen table, resting his head in his hands and wishing he hadn't tossed what was left of his coffee at the barista. Fortunately he'd missed, but now he needed it more than ever. All that and he'd come away with nothing.

Setting the DisasterLand phone book in front of him, he pondered the day. Breakfast in bed had never sounded better, followed by hot-tubbing and massages. The theme of the day? *Lay low.*

A few minutes later, the sound of the tub's jets woke Barb up and she joined him with a glass of water. To her bleary eyes, Steve distinctly appeared as if his genitals were being electrocuted.

"Are you OK, sweetie?" She took his cheek in her hand, then gave him a kiss. He didn't open his eyes.

"Yeah. OK," he winced.

"You know, I was thinking we should have stopped by the grocery store last night for breakfast. It's going to cost us a fortune..."

"Breakfast is being delivered, honey, in just under an hour. Our massages follow the recommended two hours later." Steve spoke in soft, desperate gasps.

"A masseuse is coming here?"

"Yeah, I just feel like staying in today, honey. Don't you?"

"The whole day?"

Steve nodded, almost imperceptibly.

"No... not at all."

"Oh. Well, you could always change your mind."

To her, Steve was impenetrable. Barb dropped her nightgown and climbed in.

Steve had decided he wasn't going to break the news. Barb would find out sooner or later and Steve would feign surprise, if possible. He had certainly taken the brunt of the blow and couldn't stomach much more.

Barb stretched a few minutes later, "Do you feel like exercising before breakfast? We could try that plan."

Steve laughed, his eyes remaining shut.

"I'll wait if you'd like," Barb said.

"No, go ahead. It's safer."

"*Safer?*"

Steve rubbed his eyes, "I ran into the Andrews this morning."

"You did?"

"Out on the walkway. He said twenty-five percent of the accidents..."

"I heard that."

"You did?"

"We can't let that affect us, Steve. Is that what's wrong? Sweetie, we've got to live for the moment. That's what we're here for, right? That's what we're here to *learn.*"

Steve formed a reply, but dropped it. "Just take your D-PAK, OK? And after breakfast we only travel in twos."

"OK," she finally agreed. Barb reached over with a towel and wiped the condensation off the window, clarifying the vast landscape outside. DisasterLand's imposing shadow had crept over the red desert valley below.

"Look at that!" Barb gasped as she began to towel herself off. Steve peeked half-heartedly with his closest eye, leaving the other one firmly closed.

Barb shut the door and Steve breathed a sigh of relief. He was absolutely exhausted. What was it with vacations? Why was he always *more tired* during vacations?

He had read somewhere it takes ten days off before the recovery really begins, when the subtle trauma of modern life truly starts to heal. Problem is, if you're American, you're damn lucky if you get that all, let alone all at once.

But here they were. And they *were* damn lucky.

Steve was going to enjoy it. No matter what. This was just a simple setback. He'd learn from it and move on.

The day spread out in his mind, a day of massage and hot tubs, of feasts delivered and mindless comedies relished. He'd choose the movies tonight, and keep the kids around to hold Barb's libido in check.

Something was bugging him though, something serious, nibbling away at the back of his mind.

Where the hell was his Happinol?

Elektra leaned out over the roof's guardrail, face into the rising sun, determined to embrace the full potential of the coming day. Today, she felt, was going to be special.

She took a long, last drag of her hand-rolled cigarette and stepped back from the edge, smashing it out underfoot. It was her second of the morning.

Last night had ended properly, with a long bubble bath and another quick scan of the arrivals, and the result was a morning falling into place.

The goal was staying ahead of the game, and a five a.m. rise had allowed her to do just that. A quick check of the Feed followed, then a trip to the roof for a cool, early-morning meditation to settle her nerves. Next stop had been the deli downstairs to secure a latte and scone and she had returned home to raise the curtain by six.

With a brief prayer murmured for the health and safety of all employees and guests Elektra had ritually de-charged her glass, ceremoniously beginning the show. She still carried residual superstitions from her theater background and this one was the biggie.

Crystal desert sunlight had burst into her suite and Elektra took a deep breath. Two hundred feet below, the cobblestone village was almost completely deserted. She had recognized its beauty immediately upon completion, but in the early morning light with a soothed spirit, it seemed such a shame that it would soon have to be destroyed.

She had returned to the breakfast nook and her laptop for the equivalent of her morning paper: re-scanning the evening's notes and observations, first from the actors, then security, to prepare for the meetings ahead. A quick follow-up on the heroes and back to the Feed to reassure herself, then a return to the roof for another cigarette and a last grab at some private time.

The early morning story meeting would kick off in forty-five, with last night's psychologists' observations front and center. Hero families would be discussed, their files revised as necessary. A brainstorming session would assess their roles, possible directions the story could take and ways to magnify their strengths and weaknesses. Later on at future meetings, as the story progressed, the focus would naturally narrow.

The first daily production meeting would follow, to cement any narrative changes and formally kick the show off amongst DisasterLand's hardest core.

Elektra had a late call on the bridge, four p.m., and would probably work until eight-thirty or nine. Then she'd grab some dinner, hopefully with her best friend Molly, and get a good night's sleep to prepare for the odyssey ahead.

She hacked up the tar-stained phlegm lining her throat and spit, watching it drop the two hundred odd feet to the desert below, drifting with the faint breeze.

Why the hell did she do this to herself?

One immediate reason: Clint's presence still haunted the roof, soiling her sacred territory, and it was pissing her off. God, she hated breakups.

Maybe she was meant to be a nun, or some sort of a monk. Celibate, just meditating all day and taking long walks in the woods to talk to the trees. How bad could that be?

She took another sip of her coffee.

Once she opened her heart to someone, even if she didn't exactly open it up all the way, or didn't even want to in the first place, she became umbilically tied to them somehow. Always. This connection did eventually fade, but it never truly went away. And during the initial separation, when the cord was being stretched, or even bloodily ripped apart, the whole thing was remarkably painful. *Physically* painful, right where it was tied to her, right in the gut.

Two bodies trailing each other, tethered, throughout the rest of their lives. Was it somehow formed by sex? Was it some sort of weird energy thing?

Whatever it was, it was certainly another case for monogamy. Maybe she was just getting old, but more and more, people were just too deranged, their energies too weird, the potential of too many diseases running around to make libidinous experiments worthwhile.

Relationships.

"FUCK!" Elektra screamed, into the wind.

And with it, with the catharsis that followed, Elektra clearly realized what had relentlessly been eating away at her since Clint's injury.

He had drawn a Samaritan part this show and now, with his injury, it multiplied the danger both to himself and to others. Samaritans were the most important people on the floor, the actors who cleared away the guests just before the disaster. They were the first in line if something went wrong. For them, a few seconds mattered.

It wasn't just the fact that Clint had been injured, Elektra was more upset about the potential for the injury of guests.

Surely this had occurred to the doctors? Surely they had taken this into account?

Could she say something? *Should she?*

It certainly wasn't too late. Elektra picked up her phone. Dialed.

"Clint. E."

"Yeah. Hey."

"How're you feeling?"

"Much better. Yeah."

"Good. Where are you?"

"Wardrobe. Early call today, remember?"

"Shit, that's right. I spaced it. So you're not coming to the production meeting?"

"E, I'm on in twenty."

"Oh, I... I was hoping I'd see you."

"You were?"

"Yeah, before you went on. I just wanted to make sure everything's cool, you know? I don't want... just no stress, OK?"

"Everything's cool, E. I mean, it would probably be cooler if you hadn't thrown me out of your apartment but..."

"Clint..."

"... but you know, I'm cool with it. You wigged. Fine."

"Clint you pissed all..."

"I did not, Elektra. Why don't you have the fucking sheets tested? Hunh? Pee sniff the sheets, E."

"Clint, look..."

"No, it's cool."

"Look, I just... listen, you're OK with your part right?"

"What are you saying?"

"I'm just making sure that..."

"Elektra, I underwent fifty thousand fucking tests yesterday morning. The doctors told me I'll be fine. I don't understand why you..."

"OK, Clint. I..."

"... why you want me to fail. You want to get me fired? Is that what you want? Is that how you get your revenge?"

"Jesus, Clint. I was just worried, OK? I was worried about you. You've got a Sam..."

"Well don't be. I'll be fine. I'm a survivor, E. I made it this far, OK?"

"OK, OK. I just want people to be safe. I'm sorry. I'm sorry about everything. I just want things to be cool."

"As long as you don't have me thrown off the floor, everything will be fine."

"Clint, please."

Clint exhaled, heavily, "Look, we're cool. Everything's cool. OK? Don't worry. I gotta run. I'm on my way to make-up."

"OK, Clint. I'm glad we talked."

"Yeah, me too... I mean, we could have a drink or something tonight if you..."

"No, let's not. Big day tomorrow for both of us."

"Right. I tried. OK, I'm out."

Barb was doubled over, sweating. Thighs on fire and heart on strike, her entire body was threatening to disown her. She felt like she had just fled a gangland shooting.

She'd been overconfident. Different fitness levels called for different plans and Barb had overestimated. Beginner's level was up and down five floors, intermediate up and down ten. The record, someone told her, was up and down the tower four times, 80 stories. But now she didn't believe it.

Maniacs had kept passing her, some at great speeds, so she had been keenly aware of the standard. And she had stupidly tried to compete.

After descending nine flights at speed and feeling great, Barb got carried away and thought she'd go for it all. But she hadn't counted on going back up at altitude. They weren't on the plains anymore.

Four more floors down and her legs began to feel like they were being knifed apart. She realized she'd have to turn back. Immediately.

Now, five floors back up with eight more to go, Barb was realizing she'd have to take the elevator up the rest of the way or risk paralysis in the morning.

Then there was the imminent delivery of her breakfast, thoughtfully arranged by her rather odd husband. She didn't want to miss that.

Barb *had* felt the yoga kicking in, though. She had felt powerful, very powerful, up until her body's collapse. A complete and utter collapse.

Barb took the last, long pull of water from her DisasterLand bottle. It was now painfully empty, an entire liter gone in a flash. Strike two. It *was* the damn desert, after all.

There were cafés on every floor, water was easily available. That wasn't the problem. The problem was she wasn't thinking ahead. If there was a disaster on the way, she'd need to pull herself together.

They'd *all* need to pull themselves together. Especially Steve.

Barb collapsed the ingenious bottle into her D-PAK's empty pouch, impressed by the D-PAK's functional design, its refined comfort. It also went well with her choice of clothing: black DisasterLand lycra pants and a tight yoga top. A nice bonus.

She tucked into the landing where the stairs met the eleventh floor, staring at the elevator across the walkway and feeling pathetic. She began to massage her legs, staring at a prominently placed public service announcement at the entrance to the stairwell.

Huge black letters read:

Think Safe!

She chuckled to herself. Barb had noticed one on each floor, each with a different message:

Stay Together!

Know Your Neighbors!

Don't be a hero!

D-PAK!

She turned, preferring to look out through the wide, swirling glass tube and onto the atrium.

The InfoTron was showing interviews with guests in Good Food, which only served to increase Barb's feelings of inadequacy. That should have been the first place they hit. Instead, they'd be lucky if they got there before lunchtime.

Barb tried stretching. Her muscles were already tightening, a very bad sign. She straightened, leaning out against the railing.

The wide stairway allowed for maximum light flow and impact, a stunning work of architecture. To her exhausted mind, she saw the opposing twin staircases as a double-helix, as if enormous DNA had been frozen in glass.

The compelling illusion was of walking on air, or at least not-so-soft clouds—the actual glass stairs had been lightly frosted to assist people scared of heights. But it still worked.

She let her mind wander while carefully massaging her still-throbbing legs. It was funny, actually, how many allusions to life, or at least to nature, were in the building. Forget the park, there was the sweeping entrance, the sleek fountain, and these luxurious staircases.

Sponsored, of all things, by StairSmasher, DisasterLand's own brand of home exercise gear.

The DisasterLand Experience. At home!

The implications were many, but Barb was interrupted before her contemplations ran too deep. Clanging sounded above her, followed by heavy, hearty laughter. Shadows swooped down onto the floor above, combined with the jostling of heavy equipment.

Still attempting deep knee-bends to fight off the stiffness, Barb nearly fell over trying to anticipate their arrival. She saw only boots, then thick canvas pants.

Where they soldiers?

Fear darkened Barb's heart, but as they turned the corner, Barb was relieved to see it was a group of incredibly handsome DL:FireMen. She smiled a welcome and wiped the sweat from her brow.

They continued on, the Captain limping straight towards her. Clint smiled and Barb's heart fluttered.

"Just checking the gate, ma'am."

"I'm sorry!" Barb realized she was standing in his way and removed herself foolishly. He was *cute*.

"Watch yourself," Clint lifted the announcement panel, revealing a touchpad. He pressed it.

A mesh barrier was freed from around the staircase's metal frame, and Clint rapidly swept it across the stairs, blocking entrance or exit. Barb stared as he locked it in place.

Beside them, his three men were examining the emergency lighting. Next to the lights, though Barb couldn't tell, was a tiny ultra-high-resolution video camera. One of the men discreetly cleaned the lens.

"Out getting some exercise?" Clint asked, raising and locking the barrier back in storage.

"Just taking a little break. Seven more to go!" Barb smiled.

"Up or down."

"Up."

"Ouch," Clint winced. He continued playfully, "But it's the most important thing you can do. That's what they say."

He paused, almost conspiratorially. "You might want to take it easy this afternoon. Stay close to home."

"Why's that?"

Clint stepped in, to make sure they weren't overheard. Barb's heart leapt.

"Chatter."

"Chatter?"

"Our instruments are picking up tremors."

Barb gasped. "Really? Tremors? An *earth...*"

Clint placed his hand gently on her shoulder, quieting her, "We're on high alert. We're making sure all of the exits are open, the emergency lighting's on, things are shored up. Solid. *Safe.*"

Barb was stunned. Maybe Steve *was* right. They'd better get to Good Food, *now*.

"Thank you," she whispered. "Do you know... *when?*"

Clint nodded as the men behind him finished with the lighting and continued on down the stairs to the floor below.

"This afternoon," Clint whispered. "Definitely. Our instruments are never wrong."

Barb gasped.

"So you take care, now," he said, turning.

"You too..." Barb called, waving a heartfelt goodbye. She watched as Clint descended gingerly.

"Excuse me!" Barb called.

Clint paused.

"What happened? Your... knee?"

"We had a small electrical fire the other day in the village and a salesgirl's daughter was trapped on the second floor. The floor collapsed as I was carrying her out."

"Oh my God!" Barb grasped her hands. "Was she OK?"

"She's just fine, ma'am. She landed on me! And I'm OK too. Just a little strain."

Barb's heart was fluttering. Now *he* was brave. *And* strong. Steve would have had his entire lower body amputated for less. And now this hunk's humping down twenty flights with gear.

"You be careful, OK?" she said.

Clint returned a thumbs up and rounded the corner.

Barb took a deep breath and stepped up, onto the first stair, grimacing in pain. She was in trouble.

She waited until the firemen were out of sight and stumbled over to the elevators. She could wait a couple of minutes for her water. This wasn't an emergency, for crying out loud.

Not yet.

Perched in the conference room for the show's opening production meeting, Elektra found the conversation nauseating. An electrical fire? The floor collapsing? She knew the script—and that hadn't been in it.

Worse yet, the collected superstars around her were cheering Clint on, enjoying his brief flirtation immensely. But Elektra knew Clint was playing it up just for her. He knew her eyes would be on the Feed, amidst everyone else's, and he'd wanted to make a point. That was pretty clear.

She could feel eyes on her, searching for a reaction. But she remained stone-faced. She would give them nothing.

A few late stragglers were still crowding into the buzzing conference room. The energy was high, as the caffeined-up A-list had arrived to see the end of the season through in style.

Greg checked his watch and lowered the volume on the Feed. Elektra stood.

"Welcome to day one of eight. Our first draft revisions of the show are due in at noon, with minor changes for the day. This morning's story meeting agreed that at 8:12 p.m. we're pulling the rug out from under our guests. Very minor changes to talent scripts, largely DTV, but stand by for your blue pages everyone. Erik's on to direct. Colin?"

The first AD stood, clearing his throat, "Right, E. As you can see, the Ministry of DisInformation is already riffing. Cast-wise we're on cruise control, just getting some face-time in with the guests, see and be seen while sowing the seeds of instability.

Everyone cool on where you stand? Any concerns? E will break down heroes in a minute."

DisasterLand's top actors, minus those already on the floor, dotted the room. These were the hardest of the hard-core, the talent on which the backbone of the story rested. Each department head was also in attendance, from Molly in Hair/Make-up to the reclusive explosives guys to the martial arts trainers, as well as Greg, the four directors and 'Lexi. Clint and other A-list already on the floor would see the recorded meeting after their shift.

There were no concerns and Colin continued, "Crew: we'll meet with Erik right at noon to break down the blue pages for your teams. It won't take long. I was at the story meeting and we've been through this before. It's a rerun, with some nice tweaks."

For most, today's meeting was a nice easing in to the show. In less than 24 hours, the mood would be considerably different.

"Cool. Big respect to DTV who's already causing some trouble. Looking forward to more of that today."

Scattered applause rang out for DTV's on-air producer and Elektra resumed her chairmanship, "Dig. We're going to take a little more time than usual to examine our hero families in detail. We've got 25 this show as you probably caught on the Feed, more than ever but worth it. You might have seen the Beyers this morning, so we'll leave them 'til last."

Elektra flipped off the Feed, and the young L.A. couple appeared in its place, leaving their Silver Lake bungalow in the early morning light to the applause of gathered hipsters.

"This seems to be a first. She's a lawyer, big money. He's a waiter and C-list model, but—guess what—wants to break into acting. Jude's checked and he's unagented."

Her fingers danced along the controller's keys and the couples' DisasterLand entrance appeared. *Dirk Allen and Pam Smith: Los Angeles, California* scrolled across the bottom of the screen. Dirk's eyes were illuminated, as if in dress rehearsal for his stardom. Catcalls were ringing out in the room to everyone's pleasure.

"She's an intellectual property lawyer. Signed the release so everything's kosher, but just keep it in mind. Dirk here is first in line for the Monday night special."

The clip continued, and the everyone edged out onto their seats. They'd seen the clip before. It'd made the Feed's highlights last night.

As they approached the DTV reporter for an interview, a bikini-clad vixen broke through the crowd, leaping at Dirk and planting a giant kiss on his lips before disappearing into the crowd on the opposite side of the aisle. Dirk broke away from his wife, clearly stunned, and searched the crowd for the mysterious nymph. Pam, however, wasn't impressed and had stood motionless. When Dirk came to, ready to resume his walk, Pam refused to hold his hand.

The catcalls continued and Elektra smiled, "Remember everyone, today is the day to see what our guests are made of. Have fun with your toys but don't break 'em!"

Barb entered the suite gaily, swallowing her pain in a failing attempt to reinforce the image of her fitness. But the kitchen was empty.

"Hello!" she yelled, "Where is everyone?"

Steve spun, shocked, his nervous eyes blazing. He was seated on the living room floor in profound psychic distress.

The Happinol was gone.

Barb screamed, involuntarily, at the intensity of his gaze.

They eyed each other carefully, each frozen, two wild animals unexpectedly crossing paths. Fear spread between them like an infection.

Barb didn't know about Sarah. He could tell that. She didn't know about the Happinol. He could tell that too.

Steve was scary. That much was clear to her.

They remained, unwavering, in a long showdown.

"What the hell is going on?" Barb demanded, finally. *"What is your problem?"*

"I've..." Steve took a deep breath, "... just misplaced my... water purification tablets."

"Your *what?*"

Steve plowed on, "I took everything out of my D-PAK. You know, an inventory? And now I can't find the purification tablets."

Barb shook her head. Indecipherable. That's how she'd describe her husband lately: in-de-fucking-cipherable.

He was sitting on their living room floor, the contents of his D-PAK spread around him like a child.

"I'm going to have to get another D-PAK," Steve said.

"I didn't even know we had water purification tablets."

"Hopefully *you* do, because *I* don't. Seriously, Barb. This is a big deal. You better check."

It was the truth and it was the worst possible moment for the additional stress. He *had* taken his D-PAK apart, thinking in a moment of madness he might have stuck his pills inside. And now he'd discovered *this*.

"If they put them in, we need them. That's how business works." Steve wiped his brow.

"I think it'll be OK, honey," Barb said, rolling her eyes. "There's three other sets here."

"We can't just hope Barb. Not here. The stakes are too high."

Barb inched her way awkwardly to their bedroom. "So no breakfast?" she asked, tentatively. "I'm starving."

"No. Not yet. They're late."

"I'm going to take a quick shower. Are the kids up?"

"Probably. After that scream."

Barb passed him silently and paused at the bedroom door. She picked up a small package on the floor, head shaking, and tossed it to Steve. *The tablets.*

Steve wanted to weep. On every front, an absolute worst-case scenario confronted him. He was facing a perfect storm. How would he ever be able to look Sarah in the eye in such a weakened state?

He'd been through every piece of luggage—even Barb's—twice. They weren't in the bedroom, not the bath, nor the kitchen. *The Happinol was gone.*

Either he'd put it in his checked luggage and DisasterLand had removed it—which was unlikely—or he'd simply, stupidly, forgotten it. There was just no other option.

No matter what, it was exactly what you're *not* supposed to do. Start, then stop. He'd read about the alleged suicides on the web.

At least the hospital was just downstairs if he did go mad.

Steve froze: Good Health would have a pharmacy. *Of course.*

"Good Morning," said the familiar soft voice from the door's speaker. "Delivery."

"Good Morning, Maria. Come on in!" Steve stood as she entered.

Maria pushed her sleek aluminum cart inside, dressed in the same trendy tracksuit, this time with the colors reversed. Once again, she was a knockout.

Where did they find these employees? wondered Steve. *It's like a fashion show in here.*

"Smells great!" Steve said and moved to help her unload. The meal was pristinely packaged in covered DL-branded ceramic dishes, sparkling white, with custom silverware and linen napkins.

For a split second Steve considered asking her about the pharmacy, then wisely censored himself—he had to be discreet.

They finished unloading the cart and Maria giggled, "I'm glad you have your clothes on Mister Beyers."

Barb stepped out of the bathroom in her new *Pornographique* top and shorts.

"Excuse me?" she asked, still drying her hair.

Maria smirked, *"Jour* husband? He was..."

Steve pushed her along, towards the door, "That's wonderful, Maria. Here, let me give you a tip."

"Sorry?" Barb repeated, unwavering.

"¡*Mierda*! When *jou* are done, call. I *peek* up," Maria quickly ducked out with her cart. Suburbanites sometimes freaked her out.

"What did she just say, honey?" Barb asked, one more time for confirmation.

"Barb, there's something I need to tell you."

A light bulb went on, something she had never previously imagined: was *he* having an affair? Not with her, not with Maria, but back home? The late hours, the nonexistent interest in sex. He was keeping something from her, that was clear. And now she knew what it was. But it was not the time.

"Look, where the hell are the kids, Steve? It's after ten."

"Well, I, um..." Steve forced a laugh, failing again, "I went down in my bathrobe."

"You went down to the atrium in your bathrobe. To get coffee?"

Steve nodded. "Always moving forward, Barb."

He dug into his fully-loaded plate. Inspiration had led him to order two of everything for breakfast, plus coffee and juice, and there was no way he was letting any of it get cold.

Barb stared at her husband as Pete stumbled into the kitchen from the bathroom, still in his pajamas, wearing his baseball cap pulled low. "Sarah says she doesn't want any," Pete said.

Steve's heart dropped. Pete took his seat awkwardly, head ducked down while Steve passed him the pancakes.

"More for us. Your favorite, Spikers. Pecan!"

"Thanks." Pete took the plate.

"Sarah doesn't want breakfast? I've never heard of that," Barb said. Steve grunted.

"Does she feel OK?" Barb asked.

"I think," said Pete.

"No hats at the table." Barb pulled the cap off Pete's head and he responded with contortion, attempting stop her, the plate twisting precariously in his hands. Frustrated, he gave up and turned away.

"Are you wearing my make-up?" Barb asked, examining her son.

Pete turned away, *"No!* Don't be weird mom. You think I'm gay or something?"

She glanced at Steve but he wanted no part of it. He refilled his coffee mug in denial. *Was her family slowly descending into madness?* Or had they always been this way, and Barb simply too much a part of it to notice?

She refocused on the breakfast spread out before her and took a few exploratory bites, "Ummm... She's missing out. This is fantastic!! We'll have to do this again tomorrow."

"We're brunching at Del Sol," Steve said.

"Of course. If it's still around," said Barb. "You know I just met a fireman—a *captain*—and he said there's chatter. *Tremors.*"

Steve shrugged it off. He couldn't be a part of fear-mongering right now. Firefighters or no firefighters.

"Wow, cool!" Pete said, "I told you guys there'd be an earthquake."

"Listen, Spikers, we'll have to move in twos from now on. And you'll have to help your mom with groceries after breakfast."

"Dad!" Pete whined. "Why? I was gonna..."

"Sorry, Spikers. Rules. Always in twos, and always have your D-PAK," Steve continued, mouth full.

"And water," added Barb.

"Come on, DJ," Pete said, "Always in twos? How can I hang with my peeps?"

"We *are* your peeps, Spike. Your *old skool* peeps. And you're hangin' with us," Steve confirmed.

"How can you even have peeps?" Barb insisted. "You've only been here one night."

"We met at the game. You saw him. Remember?"

"The game. Which is illegal, you said?" Steve asked.

"DJ, come on. Top-secret is top-secret. You don't want the NSA coming to get me, do you?"

"The NSA?"

"You never heard of Eschalon?"

"*Eschalon?*" Barb asked.

Pete suddenly wondered if he'd said too much.

"OK, *stop it people.* You're freaking me out. You're gonna get me busted."

"I've never heard of something so ridiculous."

"Dad, it's just... it's *that cool.* OK? I don't ask you about your work."

Sarah stumbled through the kitchen. "Anyone in the hot tub?" she asked, counting. Clearly there wasn't. She continued on, not waiting for a response. "Sticky," she mumbled. "Sore."

Steve struggled to keep his head out of his hands and somehow managed to succeed. Barb sensed subtext, bizarre, coursing through the conversation and her sense of dread rose accordingly.

"Off you go fearless ones," Steve said, unable to stand it anymore, "I'll hold down the fort with sleeping beauty. Let's go, move!"

"Shouldn't we all go together, honey?"

Steve shook his head.

"And shouldn't we check DTV? For safety?" Pete asked.

"No," replied Steve. "Don't be silly. Now hurry up. *Before it's too late.*"

Barb and Pete floated down in the glass elevator, their eyes locked on the InfoTron suspended over the atrium.

Steve's DL:AM appearance had been supersized.

"No wonder he was so weird at breakfast, DJ. Look at his hair! He looks retarded!"

Pete's eyes bugged while Barb shied away from the other guests who had begun to stare.

"That's not even the best part!" one of the other kids added.

"Yeah, watch this!" his dad said.

"I wish we had our video camera, DJ. This is awesome!"

Barb stood, petrified, as Steve cocked his half-story-high fist at the reporter. "Oh my God," she gasped, recoiling in horror.

Pete leapt in the air, "Sic him, dawg!"

"Peter, that's enough!" Barb yelled ferociously, sending the other guests scurrying into the corners.

"Look, he's got a newspaper!" Pete whispered.

It cut to black. *DL:AM*, it read, *Always a surprise!*

The logo faded out, slowly.

CONDITIONS NORMAL the InfoTron reported.

"You haven't seen the paper?" another guest asked as the elevator doors opened.

"Of course we have, thanks," Barb said, pushing Peter away from the crowd.

"I can't believe your father didn't mention this," Barb said, setting a furious pace towards Good Food.

"I can, DJ!"

Pete was scoping for Zander. He was over an hour early, but with the new martial law he knew if he didn't catch him now they'd never hook up. He wished they had exchanged room numbers.

Good Food was mobbed and Pete fought for a cart at the entrance while Barb stomped over to the check-out to grab a paper.

When her eyes finally landed on the front page, Pete thought she was a gonner. The color drained from her face and she froze, eyes distant and mumbling.

Barb finally slammed the paper down in anger. Whatever it was, Pete knew, it didn't look good.

"What time did your sister get home?" Barb asked, venomously, as she approached.

"I dunno, DJ. I was asleep," Pete said, cowering. "Fo'real."

"What time did *you* get home?"

"Twelve forty-five, DJ. And you guys was naked."

Barb marched past him, scowling, "Come on, let's hurry up, Pete. We need to get home."

"But DJ, what about..."

"Your father can come back," Barb said as she attacked the produce section.

Pete quickly scampered back to catch a glimpse of the front page.

"Sure is packed, DJ," he said as he rejoined his mom, lightheaded and trying to play it cool.

"I think word's gotten out about the tremors," Barb said between clenched teeth. "People are stocking up for the night."

"Yeah, maybe you're right," Pete said, his early morning fear returning. *Was it really coming?*

There was certainly a hurriedness, a determination in the guests' actions that wasn't there last night.

"What do you feel like?" Barb asked.

"Not very good, DJ. Is Sarah in trouble?" Pete replied, unable to look his mom in the eye.

"I'm talking about dinner, Peter."

"Oh, I don't know. Let's have something fun, DJ. Like mac and cheese."

"Something else?"

"Cherry pie!"

"Or?"

"Snickerdoodles!"

"We're eating healthy today, Peter. My legs hurt and I'm in a bad mood. Besides, we want to be properly nourished for the disaster."

"No, DJ!"

Her savage glance shut him up while she grabbed a lot of things he hadn't asked for.

"Come on, let's go to the fish counter."

"Nothing stinky!"

"Salmon would be nice, wouldn't it? I wonder if it's wild."

Somebody bumped Pete, but he ignored it. He continued tailing his mom as she navigated through the packed bulk goods aisle and on to the fish counter.

"Where is everything?"

"This is the last of it, we're almost sold out. Fresh this morning, ma'am."

"How about the Alaskan wild salmon then. That piece? It's for four."

"Wonderful choice. Sushi quality."

"I hope so for that price."

Pete was staring at the bubbling tanks of lobsters wrestling amongst themselves like cockroaches of the sea. To him, they were just big ugly insects. Who cared if they lived in the ocean?

Another bump, harder, this time almost completely knocking him over. He turned to see Zander flip him off and race away. His mom hadn't even noticed.

"I just thought of something, DJ. I'll be right back."

"OK, I'll be in the dairy section. Hurry up," Barb said, absentmindedly.

Pete hurried off after Zander, who was waiting for him in the next aisle.

"Whatup, yo?" Zander asked.

"Coolin' out."

"Yo, I saws ya comin' out of the elevators. Bro, you need to hook me up!"

"Wha?"

"Your sis! She's..."

Pete shoved him back.

"Serious, bro. I need shower pix. No foolin'."

Pete turned away and Zander snickered.

"Yo, how's da nose?"

"A'ight."

"Are yous wearin' make-up bro?"

Pete shook his head.

"You funny, wanksta. So whatup tonight?"

"Martial law, bro. Sayin' there's gonna be an earthquake."

"Bullshit. I'm back in the lounge, chillin'."

"We can go back?"

"Anytime, bro. We's VIPs!"

Zander popped around the corner to scope the scene. He waved to Pete, "Yo, check this shit out. Some dude's scammin' your mom."

Pete joined him, head around the corner. Zander was right. Barb felt their stare and waved Pete over, clearly welcoming the interruption. He motioned for one more minute.

"I gotta jump bro."

"Tonight. In the lounge."

Pete shrugged, "Maybe."

He hurried back. Barb was picking out seasonings.

"Did you find it?"

"What?"

"Whatever you remembered?"

"They didn't have it."

"Have you seen everyone's carts? They're really stocking up. Now I'm a little worried. We'll get some orange juice and muesli for breakfast, just in case our brunch gets canceled. What's your friend's name again?"

"Zander."

"Funny you ran into him. Where are his parents?"

"His mom died and his dad's with a chick he met last night."

"Oh..." Her face dropped.

"Everyone does it, Zander said. His dad's smart. He's a dentist. Drillin' and killin'!"

Barb stared at her alien son.

"*Where is she?!*"

Barb threw open the bedroom door and marched in. The burly man already at work on Steve wasn't impressed.

Steve was naked, lying face down on the massage table. They had just started to get into it, his muscles beginning to relax for the first time in months if not in years. The *gunk* was being loosened and he was devolving into jelly.

But now, in seconds, he was back to square one. "Honey, please, we're paying a lot of money for this and you're ruining it."

"Your daughter has run away and you don't care?"

"She went to get a coffee and some breakfast. Now please, this gentleman is on the clock. He had to come early."

"You let her outside? *Alone*? With *this* on the cover of the paper? Are you some kind of beast?"

She thrust Steve's copy into the hole of the table his face was resting in, found while putting away groceries. The masseuse stepped back, waiting for the storm to blow over.

"Did you tell her?"

"I don't think so..."

"You..." Barb stuttered, "You don't *think so?*" she screamed.

"Honey, relax."

Her arms crossed, "You're a beast, Steve. An animal. That is the most... She... She is your *daughter*, Steve."

Steve wasn't arguing and Barb changed tack, clearly perturbed.

"Well you might be interested to know that your son and I just walked past both cafés," she continued, "and she wasn't there."

"I don't know, sweetie. Maybe she went..."

"She could have been kidnapped, Steve. By some sort of sick-o."

"Doubtful," the masseuse interjected. "Not on a day like this."

Barb wasn't sure what he meant by that and didn't care. Who the fuck was *he* to tell her *anything*?

"There's tremors, Steve, *tremors!*"

"I think you're over-reacting. But if she's not back by the end of my massage, I'll go find her."

"Fine. If anything has happened to her, it's your problem."

She slammed the door.

"Sorry about that," Steve said.

"Perhaps I'd recommend a spa visit next time, sir."

"Understood. In fact, would you mind locking the door?"

"Of course, sir."

The masseuse settled back in and Steve immediately booked himself another fifteen minutes—of Barb's time.

Steve joined Pete on the couch, pink as a newborn baby in his famous robe and slippers. He took a long draw of water, replenishing what had marvelously been squeezed out of him.

Barb was finally well into her massage. Steve had smoothed the ruffled feathers then hit the tub for a detox. The masseuse had brought a suitcase of spa accoutrement and Steve splurged for the trendy best: a Sake detox bath. It hadn't been cheap but it had worked like a charm. Twenty minutes later, Steve felt reborn, and a nap loomed on the horizon.

"What's up, Spikers?"

"There's a whole game channel, DJ! It's awesome!"

Pete was navigating a labyrinthine cave on some uncharted planet.

"What are you looking for?"

"A way out. They were keeping me as a prisoner and I just escaped."

Steve watched. To him it looked like one of those violent games on the news which screwed up kids.

"So is this anything like it? Your secret game?"

Pete considered the question for a long time, wasting a couple of mutants in the process.

"I can't tell you, DJ. I think I've said too much already."

Steve shook his head in disbelief. He watched a few more bloody deaths.

"Where'd you get the gun?"

"Stole it off a dead guard. I had to chew my way through his throat to get it."

Sometimes Steve wondered about their culture. He wasn't some radical nutcase who wanted to ban everything including Bambi, but sometimes he *was* concerned about what sort of a world they were creating. What they were teaching their kids.

Was it good? Especially before a disaster?

Pete paused the game. "You gonna go find Sarah, DJ?" he whispered.

Steve nodded, "I promised your mom. Do you think she's OK?"

Pete went back to his video game. "She's in our room. She's hiding," he continued.

"You're kidding."

"She snuck in when mom was wiggin'. Looked like she was crying."

Steve's heart sank. He *was* a beast, an absolute monster who had set his helpless daughter up for a cruel fall.

Steve stood, "Thanks, Pete."

"DJ, I don't think she feels very good. You know?"

"I know."

Steve took a deep breath before knocking on her door.

Silence.

"Sarah? It's daddy-o."

Sniffles. A long pause. Finally, "Come in."

Steve slipped in, eyes on the ground. She straightened up on the bed.

"Where's mom?" she asked.

"She's getting a massage. You want one?"

"It's expensive."

"I think I owe you."

"For what, dad?"

"For... because I should have told to you. Before you went out."

The tears began again and Steve inched to the edge of her bed, putting a hand on her foot and sitting down. It had been a long time since they'd had a conversation like this. Barb had taken over when the conversations turned to boys, and even those seemed to have faded.

"Nothing happened, dad."

"It doesn't matter, honey."

"It does to me. I'm not like that," she sniffled.

"I'm sorry. I understand."

Steve sat back, next to her, his back against the wall. "I just meant... for me, I wish I hadn't set you up."

"But I... I sort of set *you* up."

"Yeah, I guess you did. Maybe I was just getting you back."

Sarah laughed, wiping her eyes.

"Listen, we just want you to be safe, OK? Whatever you do. For us."

"I am dad. I *am*."

"You broke your curfew, you know. *Big time*."

"It was so much fun, dad. I met this boy at the movie and he took me to the club. It was packed and everyone was dancing and having the best time! I've never seen anything like it. I couldn't leave! But he was a jerk and then I met Neil!"

"The rock star?"

"He's not dad. He's not famous or anything. And he took me to this little place in the park that he found... and then I told him you guys were going to kill me and I had to go."

"You told him that?"

"I did dad, swear."

Steve laughed, "I guess this is sort of a trial period isn't it?"

Sarah cocked her head.

"I'm just saying you'll be on your own soon," Steve continued, "making your own decisions. If you want to stay up all night or sleep with a rock star, you'll be able to. Maybe your mother and I aren't ready for that, I guess."

"Don't worry, dad. I'll be careful."

"We don't want to lose you, you know? There's so many..."

"*Dad*... come on."

They sat in silence for a while, enjoying the company.

"It just bugs me. That people think I'm a slut. Everyone was looking at me really weird just now. Men and stuff."

"People are sick, Sarah. Don't worry about what they think. Just be yourself and be strong. Imagine what they think of me."

Sarah cracked up. Steve hadn't quite anticipated that reaction.

"That was *so funny* dad! They played you on the big ball. I just sat there on the stairs crying and laughing."

"That's probably why they were staring, Sarah."

She continued laughing, leaning into his shoulder.

"Thanks, dad."

"For what."

"For sticking up for me."

He hugged her, realizing they'd probably remember this moment as being something special, some sort of an emotional foci. Sarah was on a cusp, with big changes ahead. The little girl was fading fast.

More and more, Steve found himself impressed with her. In her grasp of the nuances of life, of the relationships between people, in her priorities. He thanked his lucky stars.

"Listen, sweetie, do you think you could do me a favor? I need to run out for a few minutes by myself. For work. Will you cover?"

"I could..." she paused, conspiratorially. "You know, Neil's show is tonight at midnight and...“

"No way, kiddo. No one's going out tonight. Not with a disaster forecast."

"Then I dunno, dad. No one goes out alone. Remember?"

The elevator doors opened and the comparative stillness of the atrium was striking, vastly different than the morning's calm. A slight chill haunted the air.

Steve and Sarah had left Barb in the hands of the masseuse while Pete was forced to angrily restart his battle for freedom. In the end there had been no deal, leaving Steve scrambling to work out how he was going to lose his daughter.

The problem was, Steve had to get to the pharmacy. He had to do it soon, before the disaster hit, and he had to do it alone.

"We've gotta be quick, kiddo. This doesn't look good."

They inched their way forward, taking stock of the situation. With the Pharmacy almost in sight, Dick's last words were ringing in Steve's ears. He wished he could focus on work, on mining the experience the way he had told himself he would, but so far there simply wasn't time. He had other matters to attend to.

"Fine with me," Sarah continued, "But I'm glad we came out. We can't just sit back and wait for this disaster. What if it never comes and we miss out on everything?"

Steve agreed, checking her over. Hair in a pony-tail, Sarah had donned her dinner-plate sized sunglasses and Pete's little league baseball cap to go deep undercover, yet combined with the low-cut jeans and tight top Steve felt it only amplified her conspicuousness. But he understood her fear of reporters, and hoped for her sake that the trick worked.

Not that he looked much better. With hair slicked back and wearing Pete's mirrored wrap-around sunglasses, he looked every bit the part of an aging Italian hit man in his DisasterLand tracksuit.

They were, however, both prepared for the worst: D-PAKS and water were strapped on tight.

"Listen, sweetie," Steve leaned in, whispering, "I don't think we should be together. We're magnets for trouble. For reporters, for confrontation. We'll cancel out each other's disguise like two slightly out of tune frequencies."

Sarah rolled her eyes, "I don't understand why you want to be alone so badly."

"It's not that, kiddo. Not at all. Let's do this, why don't you go surprise that rock star in the park and we'll meet at the elevators in thirty. And tell you what, we'll get an armful of cheeseburgers to take back for lunch."

"But mom bought those groceries."

"Don't worry, they're not going anywhere."

Steve eyed the guests around them, determined in their step, focused on their own individual missions. There was no sense of exploration, of expansion, no sense of the wonderment that filled the previous evening. Where last night had been a warm celebration of community, Steve now sensed families were buttoning down the hatches.

Above their heads, the InfoTron was promoting DTV's all-day survival marathon.

"So I'll meet you right here in thirty minutes. It's almost one."

"You know if there is a disaster, mom's gonna kill us both."

"I know, honey. That's why we've got to hurry."

Sarah didn't think there'd be a disaster today anyway. She didn't care what the DL:FireMen said or what the statistics were. DisasterLand wouldn't make any money and everyone would just be pissed off.

"So what are you doing?"

"Something for work, honey, at Good Health. It'll only take a few minutes."

"Mom said no work."

"Now you understand."

They hugged and Sarah hurried off, deciding that the park was actually a pretty good idea. The faces of the other guests in the atrium were starting to freak her out with suspicion seeming to cloud every exchange. And now that she started looking around, there were a lot of guards, everywhere—it even looked like some people were being searched.

When she arrived at the Great Lawn, bathed in sunlight and joyously green, only a few families were taking advantage and even they seemed preoccupied. As Sarah made her way deeper into the forest, there were fewer and fewer people until she began to wonder if she was completely alone.

She shook off a chill. Maybe her dad was right. Maybe a disaster *was* coming.

For a moment she considered turning back, but decided it would be great to see Neil before his show, especially since it seemed like she'd never be able to get away later.

She hadn't slept with him, that was absolutely true. But she was certainly looking forward to the opportunity if it arose once again.

Unfortunately, though, it wouldn't be this afternoon. When she arrived at the clearing she found it vacant and lonely, and she hurriedly turned around. She didn't like it here, not by herself, not with the whole park so deserted. The river felt menacing, the trees haunted.

It left her with no choice. Her back was against the wall. She'd have to sneak out tonight, KC-style. The only hang-up was that damn sliding door.

And, of course, the impending disaster.

"I'm sorry Mister Beyers, it's a controlled substance," the pharmacist explained, sweetly.

"And?"

"I'll need to speak with your psychologist first." She leaned forward, elbows on the counter, and straightened her glasses, "Before I can refill..."

"It's Saturday afternoon."

"I know, sir... I'm terribly sorry. But I will try her office. Most likely there's an emergency number."

"How long's that going to take?"

"I don't know sir, but I can have the medication delivered to your room if you sign. As long as we have a new prescription, it's no problem. And in the meantime we'll review your medical history."

Steve couldn't believe it. Here he was, a psychological patient without his medication, a potential danger to himself, his family and other guests. With a disaster looming!

This could be the start of a full-on psychological emergency. His behavior today had been odd and he felt it was only getting worse. He could already feel a yawning chasm opening wide beneath him, feel himself slipping down the oily depths into permanent mental disfigurement.

And now he was being forced to slither around in the shadows like some sort of criminal.

"I hate to disturb her... but it is an urgent matter..." he began. "Didn't you see me this morning!"

The pharmacist giggled, "I did, sir... yes. Very good, sir."

"Isn't there any other way? I need it now. Right now. Can't you tell?"

Steve checked his watch. There wasn't any way he could have it delivered... no way at all. Not with the family around.

"Look, there has to be a plan for this," he continued, "We're an entire nation of psychological patients. This must happen a million times a day, at least! I can't believe you don't have the power to do something for me without all this..."

"Alternatively, sir, I can make you an appointment with one of our in-house psychologists."

"No," Steve growled, patting the counter. "No, thanks. I don't have the time. My daughter's waiting. I'll just have to come back later. I sure hope there's no disaster."

"Yes, sir, that's possible. Would you like me to call your room?"

"No... no thanks."

"But if I can't reach her..."

"Then we'll see. I'm sure you can. Please try. It's an emergency."

"You're aware of our emergency helpline?"

"Vaguely."

"If you're in your room, simply call out for help and you'll instantly be connected with a responder. They'll put you in touch with the appropriate department."

"That's incredible. So we don't even use the phone?"

"No sir."

Steve frowned. "Does this mean you're spying on us?"

"Not at all sir. Voice recognition software is constantly scanning for one word and one word only: h-e-l-p."

"Wow."

"Safety is number one, Mr. Beyers. I'm sure you've heard that before."

"I have. Thank you."

"You're very welcome. I will call her right now, and hopefully we'll have your medication for you within the hour. Thanks for coming in."

The pharmacist smiled warmly as Steve turned to leave.

She didn't seem that concerned, Steve thought, *considering. Surely she knew a depressed psychotic when she saw one?*

He turned back, strangely at peace.

"Excuse me, ma'am, sorry to disturb you again, but may I ask who does your in-house advertising?"

"We do."

Sarah wasn't at the elevators. The InfoTron indicated she wasn't due for another few minutes, and Steve decided to cut it close.

Now that he was back out in the atrium and properly disguised, he felt a clarity returning. A tiny bit of his morning lift had crept back into his stride and he wanted to relish every moment.

He thought he'd buy Barb a little present. It could gain him back some valuable points which might make a significant difference down the road, and maybe even take some pressure off.

Steve ducked into the village, relieved to find the streets pleasantly empty. Now was the time for his latte, he realized, when the tiny cafés were actually civilized. He might just grab a quick one to go on the way back.

Die-hard shoppers still trickled from store to store, arms filled with last minute treasures. Signs in every window proclaimed *More Markdowns* and though there was no comparison with last night's orgy, the stores certainly seemed to be doing steady business.

He wound his way into the one he had done so much to avoid the night before, *Matériel Pornographique*, and made a b-line for their world-class selection of marital aids.

There, holding a particularly feisty model, was his daughter Sarah.

Juliet hurried over, dressed in a see-through pink negligé, wrapping her arms over Steve. *"Monsieur Beyers!"* she said. "You are back! Alone, no? You decided to do a video?"

Sarah turned and Steve froze, mid-stride and stammering. The room grew dim.

Juliet turned to Sarah. Indescribable horror had consumed her pale face and Sarah weakly returned the head-turner back to the rack. She nudged her hands into her pockets.

"Oh, Mister Beyers! I am sorry! You two are..."

Steve's body was on hold, conserving energy while his mind searched desperately for an escape route. It found none.

"That's..." he gurgled, but he could get no further. His throat had closed, cutting off his oxygen.

Juliet smiled, sweetly, as Steve fought to remain upright.

"Just..." Steve continued, gasping, "my... da... daughter."

Juliet clasped her hands in excited relief. *"But of course!* From the paper! Monsieur Beyers, I was wrong about you!"

She hurried over to Sarah, squeezing her. "A pleasure to meet you, Sarah! *Oui*, you have very good taste. That one's our best seller."

Sarah finally found the courage to set eyes on her father. "Runs in the family, I guess," she said softly.

Steve managed a long, deep breath, unsure of exactly how to proceed. He cleared his throat and checked his watch. Barb would be furious.

"Two of those, then," he whimpered.

"Ah, yes! Like mother, like daughter. You are a good man, *Monsieur Beyers*. And you, Sarah, you are a very lucky young woman!"

To Steve and Sarah's amplified senses, the tension in the Beyers' suite was immediately palpable.

Barb attacked. "You're not pregnant, are you? Because if you are..."

"Mom!" Sarah shrieked.

Pete almost fell over. One minute Barb had been quiet, happily ordering sundresses from DTV:$hopping, the next minute she was rabid.

Steve inserted himself between the girls, "Barb, use your yoga..."

"What other pictures do they have?" she continued, "Are you going to be on some porn website?"

"Honey, this is an obsession..." Steve was walking her back to the couch, somewhat awkwardly. Barb's reaction had been worse than Steve imagined, and it was not a problem to be tackling with a vibrator down his pants.

"You're just jealous because you never did it with a rock star!" Sarah cried. She dropped the cheeseburgers on the coffee table and marched out of the room, which was exactly where she wanted to be anyway.

Pete grabbed two. "Anyone not want theirs?" he called.

"The triple is *mine!*" yelled Sarah.

"Hunh-unh!" disputed Pete.

"*Enough!*" Steve said, restraining himself. "Sarah risked her well-being for these cheeseburgers and whatever she ordered is hers. The fries are communal. Now," he announced, "I'm using the bathroom."

He scuttled away, relieved. It wasn't an elegant solution but it had worked. They had arrived at their destinations—Sarah her bedroom and Steve the bathroom—without raising suspicions of their exceptional contraband.

It had been a risky plan but they'd been left with few options—the booty had to be concealed for obvious reasons and they couldn't just leave it outside while scoping out the situation in the suite. The reality was, a conspicuous bag of two of the best vibrators money could buy was an irresistible target for thieves and left them no room for error, even if the walkways were mostly deserted.

Outside their door, they were forced to improvise and Steve had rapidly unwrapped the monsters as if they were dead fish. As quickly, privately, and least awkwardly as possible they were safely concealed. Steve tossed the emptied bag and boxes a few doors down, hoping someone else would find a use for it, or at least inspiration from it, while Sarah prayed DTV's cameras were far, far away. She had a strong feeling they weren't.

"These burgers are wicked, DJ! Where'd you get them?"

"Sarah got them."

"Sweet! Can we go get more? I'm *starving!*"

"No," Steve said, re-entering the room and flipping off DTV:$hopping. He began the desperate search for something soothing, settling on the world music station.

"Mom wouldn't let me watch the survival shows, DJ."

"They were making me nervous."

"I agree. It's fear-mongering, son."

"I think it's really important," Pete protested. "They were gonna show evacuation routes and emergency procedures and everything. Lots of tips and stuff."

"Maybe in a few minutes, Pete. Let's all take a little time to relax and digest our food."

"They were sponsored by Good Health."

"OK, OK. In a few minutes."

"So where did the two of you go, Steve?" Despite the reconciliation, the feeling that they had taunted her with their reckless and stupid departure still lingered.

"I went to find Sarah and used the opportunity to do a little errand for Persistent."

"You're kidding!"

"I'm not. Then we stopped by the burger place to make up for everything."

"There's an earthquake forecast and you're *working!*"

"It was my choice, honey. I just thought I'd get it out of the way before..." Steve ground to a halt.

"DJ, can we watch the survival shows? Please? They keep saying it could be difference between..."

"Is anyone going to bring me my cheeseburger?" Sarah called.

"Oh, Lord. I'm sorry honey, come here and eat. I was just worried," Barb called. "It was stupid. Please?"

Sarah peeked around the corner and Barb waved her in. Pete quickly dumped the fries onto a bag on the coffee table and grabbed most of them back before the others could react.

Sarah sat next to her dad, cheeks slightly rosy, "You know mom when I was at *Cheesy Burgers* the guy in front of me said it looked like rain. That's what a guard told him."

"Really?" Barb asked. "Like *rain?*"

Sarah nodded, unwrapping her mammoth grass-fed cheeseburger.

Barb felt her stomach constricting and stood, reflexively. "Drinks?" she asked. "Snag that pop, DJ."

Barb strapped on her D-PAK and made her way to the refrigerator. Soda at home was always against her better instincts, but they were on vacation and Pete had talked her into a two-liter at Good Food. An extra lift couldn't hurt, particularly now, and she was glad she had given in.

Steadying herself as she iced and poured the four glasses, Barb was upset at how strongly the disaster was affecting her. Already. She needed to get a grip.

Why all this stress? They'd be just fine. Of course they would be.

She found herself reflecting back to her childhood in the Flint Hills of Kansas, watching the storms roll in from the distance on the porch with her father. The radio was always on, the windows open, the threat of a tornado never far. And when a storm forced the family into the cellar, Barb's mother would always grab the cat before she grabbed Barb, even when she was a baby. Something Barb's father had never understood but was powerless to do anything about.

And now, here she was, nineteen stories above the warm Nevada desert, a devastating earthquake—or a hurricane—predicted any moment and no cellar for the family, just this little cocoon hundreds of feet in the air. She'd have to focus on the simple things to get herself by: soda was one of those simple things, cheeseburgers another.

Grabbing the family's drinks, Barb smiled to herself. Sarah and Steve had read the mood perfectly.

"After the survival show the chef of *Margarita Mortal* is doing a Tex-Mex cooking show. It's gonna be sweet," Pete was saying.

"They'll have tons of recipes," Barb added as she passed out the drinks. "That's what they said."

"And they make the biggest margarita in the United States," Pete added, slurping down his soda. "A gallon! It comes in a souvenir paint bucket!"

I'll take two please, Steve thought. "Do they deliver?"

"Should we call DJ? Let's order some tacos!"

"No tacos, Peter," Barb said. "We've got plenty of food here. And Steve, stop the imagination."

"Yes, ma'am."

"After that they're doing a tour of DisasterLand Park," Pete continued. "Some big nature guy from Britain is doing it."

"There's also movies," Barb added. "All night on the movie channel. Starting at six."

"That's more like it," Steve said as he sunk back into the plush couch. "Let's hold off on the survival stuff. But everyone's got their D-PAKs, right?"

They did.

"But DJ, if there's a hurricane coming..."

"How was it out there?" Barb asked, interrupting her son.

"Fewer and fewer people all the time," Steve said. "Don't you think Sarah?"

"People seemed scared, mom. You can just tell something's gonna to happen. It's like it's in the air or something. It was kinda spooky."

"How was Good Health?" Barb asked. "I mean, are they preparing for the worst?"

Steve shrugged, "Nothing special... but they're probably used to it."

"DJ..."

"Fine, Pete. Fine," Barb said, tossing him the remote. "We'll watch the survival shows for a few minutes. OK?"

Steve collapsed back into the couch.

"Yeah!" Pete yelled, taking control. Barb soon wished he hadn't.

There was no relief from the onslaught of devastation that assaulted them. There were no lavishly-produced commercials hyping extreme sales at the most opulent atrium boutiques, no teasers promising the world's best food only a phone call away. Just the pure facts on how people had survived the planet's worst fury.

DTV had collected footage from disasters the planet over, combining it with harrowing, exclusive interviews with survivors and expert commentary by DisasterLand's own psychologists to instill the inner strength that was needed to buck overwhelming odds. Research had shown that survivors were made, not born, and DisasterLand's psychologists drove home the point.

A bunker mentality soon descended over the living room, riveting the Beyers to the television and squeezing the life out of their fragile psyches.

The footage was terrifying, the possibility that something like it was about to happen absolutely blood curdling. Their tenuous existence was continually reinforced and Steve had begun to seriously wonder what the hell they were doing. What kind of a father was he after all, completely willing to sacrifice his family's safety in order for... for what?

And what kinds of people were they surrounded by? Who in their right mind would pay for this experience? How sick were they?

The HDTV flicked to the movie channel and the family responded as if oxygen had been administered, shaking off the nightmare they had just witnessed.

"Thanks Barb."

"I don't like that show."

"Was that the way it was earlier?" Steve wondered.

"Nope, DJ. It was all about how to purify water, the dangers of smoke inhalation, how to detect the presence of fire, that kind of stuff."

"Oh... that doesn't sound so bad."

"It wasn't. But now it's over and we don't know squat," Pete huffed. "We missed *everything*."

Shae wound his way through the underground office hallways, six stories below the atrium floor, finding the staff accelerating nicely towards 8:12 p.m. The upcoming gag was merely an apéritif for the guests, but it would give some of the departments a chance to stretch their legs and settle nerves before the big one.

He paused at one of the well-stocked kitchens to grab a glass of water and a quick DL:PowerStrip before heading to Jude's office.

The door was closed. He knocked.

"Yes?"

"Shae."

"Come on in, sir. Just finishing a call."

Shae slipped in, quietly, and seated himself on the couch at the far end of the office. Stopping his movement for the first time in hours, he realized his skin was tingling.

So much so quickly.

Jude hung up the phone, "Evening Shae, sorry about that. Just trying to keep the agents at bay. I've made two phone calls—just routine inquisitive stuff—and the sharks are smelling blood. I don't know how they do it."

Jude rose, making his way across the office and seating himself across from Shae on the accompanying chair.

"How'd your day go?"

"I've got a welt on my ass from pinching myself so much."

"You do look uncomfortable. So give me some advice here. What can I say?"

"Nothing."

Jude leaned back, "I'm not sure how long I can get away with that."

Shae laughed. "What did you find out? With A-list?"

"I completed the one-on-ones this afternoon. Their tails are up but I reassured them. I discreetly surveyed for expertise and we're in very good shape. But there's one or two areas..."

"Change is always tough. And they've had it pretty good."

"I told them we're reassessing their skills in light of new demands—that it's not a big conspiracy. This season is going to present special challenges and once they understood that they seemed cool."

"It may not even happen. There are issues with bringing in new people, particularly here. Can we trust their motives? Where do their loyalties lie? There are security issues as well."

"I think we'll need one or two hard-core specialists this show. Problem is, we've got to audition, clear them, move them and train. All in just a few weeks."

"Remember, think wide-screen because we're almost ready to cross genres. That's what next season is all about."

"Like an earthquake at a ski resort?" Jude laughed.

"I was thinking more of Eskimo terrorists," Shae responded.

"I believe they prefer to be called Inuit."

"Fine. If they've got guns I'll call them whatever they want!" Shae laughed.

Jude considered.

"Agents won't like to hear this. We're talking one or two hires the whole season?"

"Maybe they'll all go back to LA and leave us alone."

"We can always dream. Look, if the writers have a brilliant idea that requires something very, very specialized, we can find that person. Day players wouldn't be a problem."

"No good. If they're critical A-list I need to own them. The family stays tight."

Jude sighed his agreement.

"I can't cast for what I don't know. I need to see these scripts, Shae. Greg and I will have to do first calls Wednesday with call-backs on Friday to present on Saturday. That lets us screen test on Monday morning, just before the break."

"Fine."

"Then I need to be on the phone this Monday at the latest. Actors need to book flights you know."

Shae finished his water.

"You're exactly right, Jude. I've seen all four drafts for the fall, one of which is at 90%, the rest at 70% or 75%. We're on track. By the time we return from vacation, all should be at 95% and we should have one Spring first draft. Stop by my office tomorrow morning and you'll have what you need."

"Am I gonna like it?"

Shae stood. "You're gonna love it."

The name was a shout out to Star Trek, but that's where the similarities ended. DisasterLand's bridge made the original television show look as stone-age as the film it was shot on.

One-hundred and thirty feet below the atrium, one-hundred and fifty feet in diameter and almost ninety-feet high, the cavernous space was the pulse of DisasterLand and the heart and soul of the production team. This was mission control, and only a tiny portion of DisasterLand's employees had clearance. Not one image—video or photo—had ever been shot inside the bridge and that wasn't likely to change anytime soon.

Entered via two magnificent steel double-doors, each bank-vault thick with a giant etched DisasterLand logo spanning their width, the entrance was patrolled by armed guards at all times. Stoplight-colored lights flashed overhead to gauge the moment-by-moment temperature inside, and red *always* meant stop.

A series of five concentric platforms rose up from ground-floor, culminating in Elektra's central rostrum, *the mount*. When she took her place in the pilot's seat, when the ship was under her command, Captain James T. Kirk was a limp-wristed poser in comparison.

She shared her platform with Greg and their staff, the lead audio and video mixers and the current shift's lead director. A few compact leather couches were nestled at one side for meetings, doubling as beds when times got tough.

Enormous HD flatscreen monitors circled the vaulted ceiling in two parallel rings, suspended almost sixty feet in the air, just above the top platform. Under normal circumstances each presented a unique feed from an individual camera, hidden or manned but each ultimately controllable, with each screen visible from all points in the bridge.

The lead video mixer fed these HD monitors live, allowing Elektra's team any set-up they needed, including complete 360° surveillance scans of the park, the stairs, the walkways, or even the atrium at differing levels of magnification, all with one button and all in an instant.

Simultaneously, live sounds gleaned from every inch of the complex washed over the bridge, presented by DJ DL, the audio mixer. Restaurants, bars, shops, conversations, even background noise was all blended to give the current flavor and psychological climate of the floor. If necessary, audio areas could be zoomed in on as well, even particular actors or sometimes even guests could be isolated at a moment's notice.

The audio/video teams were back in DTV's studio, scanning thousands of hidden cameras and microphones for the most relevant material and feeding it through to the lead mixers on the mount.

It was all being recorded, and at any time could be fed back into the atrium, amplified, a powerful tool they used sparingly, and only in the darkest—or lightest—moments.

Under normal circumstances, these live mixes literally made the team omnipotent. When things weren't normal, however, *Ghost*'s technology kicked in and the video mixer could give them anything they wanted, period. Any coordinate in time and space was at their fingertips in times of emergency. And they used it.

Below Elektra's mount, the wide platforms fell away, separated by thin rails with the teams placed around her in proximity of urgency. When the shit hit the fan, everyone was front and center.

Immediately below her sat the assistant directors with their staff and their mountains of technology. Most often during a show the first AD was at the main hot spot itself, with his second ADs spread throughout the floor. The second seconds were in the labyrinth of staff tunnels under the atrium with the actors and support teams, while the production coordinators were glued to these desks at all times.

Below them the department heads spread out around the remaining platforms: lighting, hair/make-up, special effects make-up, wardrobe, pyrotechnics, hydrology and olfactory effects as well as EMS/rescue, security, nutrition and the house managers. Each lead member on the bridge was linked by radio to their team on the floor and in the labyrinth.

The story department, with psychologists and writers, and the DTV studios, which included the radio station, the newspaper, and all of the audio/visual feeds, were both headquartered in separate wings off the main bridge. In many ways each wing was independent, with their own mandates, their own managers, their own crew and even their own entrances. But practically, they were subservient to the greater plan. Greg, Elektra, the writers and the directors controlled that plan.

Right now, the monitors were presenting the mosaic of life within DisasterLand with no special hot areas under close scrutiny.

Elektra adjusted her headset and flipped the switch on her belt pack. Her voice rang out over the radios and all backstage crew areas, "Good evening all you lovely people, and welcome back to show number twelve. It's seven p.m. and first team is up. First team *is up*. Opening cue at 7:50 in the p.m. for an 8:12 launch. Thanks for being with us everyone and have a great show."

Sparse applause broke out on the bridge and Elektra dropped her gaze from the monitors. Below, Greg was entering with a gracious wave. He made his way to the stairs.

On this relatively low-key Saturday evening, most department heads were still out with their crews, making final tweaks as necessary. Empty desks anticipated their imminent arrival.

Erik, the evening director, was settling in at his desk, reveling in the calm before the storm. An expectant buzz was building as the countdown neared. In 12 hours the place would be unrecognizable, but for now the mood was mellow and a few jokes were even being had at the expense of the guests.

The evening's actors was mostly support staff, involving very few A-list. Firemen were on, EMS crews, security guards, as well as some technical workers. A-list with late calls would still be on the floor, fulfilling their roles and getting face-time with the guests, but very few were involved first-hand. The evening's gag was essentially a simply technical exercise that would hopefully pay dividends later on.

"Evening, E," Greg said.

"Almost forgot what it was like to have you around here, stranger," Elektra said.

"Don't get too used to it," Greg said with a laugh. "Good to be back."

"Just cued first team."

Greg plopped down on the leather couch and opened his soda. "How you feeling?"

"Nothing like it is there?"

"Nothing."

Elektra began her slow, methodical pace around the mount, reflecting on the day's events. Quiet, but there had been some truly beautiful moments.

Instinct was telling her the Beyers seemed to have a way of getting into trouble. She liked it.

The TV sizzled off, the refrigerator went dead, and darkness soon suffocated the Beyers.

Disasterland's heart had stopped and distant screams echoed terribly through the atrium below.

"They're being crushed!" Barb yelled.

"I don't feel anything," Pete said. "Shouldn't stuff be moving?"

"They're drowning!"

Nobody bought it.

"What about smoke? Anybody smell smoke?"

Steve leapt up, grabbing his flashlight from the D-PAK. He flipped it on, piercing the menace.

"Wait dad, turn it off," Sarah's voice was trembling. "Something's wrong... really wrong! When I came in here this morning, there was emergency lighting. Now it's totally dark!"

He flipped the light off. She was right.

"OK, everyone, stay put," Steve flipped the light back on and hurried away. He rapidly swept the suite as the family sat, lost in their own thoughts.

"I guess this is it," Barb said. "The quake."

She flipped on her own light.

"It doesn't feel like a quake, does it?" Pete asked once again. "I mean aren't things..."

"I think I smell smoke!" Sarah yelled, standing. "We've got to get out of here!"

Steve hurried in. "Where?!"

The family was sniffing, madly.

"No..." Sarah finally admitted. "Maybe not."

Steve removed the radio from his D-PAK. "Let's not get carried away," Steve said. "We're here and we're safe."

He pressed the button.

Static.

"*What?*" Steve pointed his light at the tiny white card, stunned.

"That's OK," Barb handed him hers, hands shaking.

He flipped it on. Then off, then back on.

Static.

"I don't believe this!"

Sarah tried hers. Pete his.

"*OhmyGod!*" Sarah dropped down on the couch. "What if terrorists have blown up the transmitter?"

"Easy, everyone. Easy. Let's not freak out," Steve looked to Barb in the dim light. Tension dug at her face, aging her by the minute.

Yet the panicked screams in the atrium already seemed to be fading, replaced by lower-grade yelling.

"I'm going to go see what's going on," Steve said, after a moment's hesitation.

"You're not! Steve, are you out of your mind? We're staying right here," Barb insisted. "Where it's safe."

"Come on, Pete. Let's see what we can see."

"No! You're not taking him."

"It's OK mom," Pete said and stood. "We're professionals."

He flipped on his light.

"Listen, everyone, let's be conscious about how much we use our lights," Steve warned. "We don't have spare batteries. If they go down, we're stuck."

Everyone flipped off their lights but Steve, and Pete carefully followed him out of the living room.

"I don't think this is a good idea," Barb repeated.

"Mom, what if something's wrong. We've got to know," Sarah replied, nervously. "What if we've got to escape!"

"Oh, Sarah..." Barb said, realizing her things were spread everywhere. "I'm not packed."

"Me neither, mom."

If they made it out of this, Barb realized, they'd have to consolidate at first opportunity. And not get too comfortable.

Pounding shattered her thoughts and Barb screamed.

"It's OK! It's *OK*! It's us!" Steve called.

"*Why?*"

"The door won't open! We can't get out!" Steve yelled.

"We're *trapped*?" Barb stood. She grabbed Sarah's hand.

"Do you see smoke?" Steve yelled.

Barb swung her light around, Sarah hurried into the bedroom.

"No!"

"Good! We've got to get this open. I mean that. Help us!" Steve's voice had gone dark.

Barb and Sarah hurried to join them. Voices were coming from the walkway just outside the door as footsteps raced by.

"This is bad," Barb proclaimed.

"I know... I know... we're trying," Steve said, sweat dripping.

Sarah wiped her damp eyes, "I can't believe it's happened already," she sniffed. "This is so horrible! Now I'll never see the concert!"

"Come on, honey. Help us get this door open," Steve forced a shoulder against it, painfully.

Pete and Sarah joined him in unison, the three of them flinging themselves at full strength. Uselessly.

"Sweep for smoke, Barb. Can you?"

"Not by myself."

"Sarah, help your mom."

The two of them hurried into the kid's room.

"Can you believe this..."

"A sliding door? Who's idea was *that*?"

"Steve wiped his brow. "We're going to have to break it down."

Barb and Sarah emerged from the bedroom in time to overhear. "You can't do that!"

"We've got to get out! Can't you hear?"

Pete was feeling the walls.

"What are you doing?"

"Feeling for heat."

"Fantastic, Spikers. Great idea. Sarah, help him."

"What's this?" Pete shone his light on the entry way, behind Steve's back.

"Light switch, Spikers."

"No, below, there's a button."

Pete pushed it and a pulley system swung down from a trapdoor in the ceiling.

"Holy shit!"

"*Steve...*"

"Pete, you're a hero!"

"We should have watched the survival programs..." Barb's voice was quivering. "Now it's too late."

"Barb, help Sarah. Come on, Spikers, let's get this thing open."

Pete cranked the wheel and the door opened up, slowly. A deep blue greeted them as the last light faded from the sky. Streaks of light danced across the glass.

"It's dark out there, Spikers. Just a bit more. Wo! That's it, let's leave it there. You ready?"

"Ready, DJ."

Steve sucked in his gut and slipped through. "Come on, son," he called, and Pete followed. They hurried across to the railing.

DisasterLand was cast in otherworldly shadows as yells echoed around them. Worried guests still hurried across the walkways, up and down stairs. Below, masses of people could be seen amidst the dance of flashlight beams. Yet the earlier screams had dissipated, though, as the threat seemed to fade.

Security guards in glowing vests patrolled each floor. DL:FireMen were staged on each landing, keeping the area clear in front of the elevators.

Hundreds of dark figures were snaking their way up the glass tubes in a constant stream.

"People must be stuck inside the elevators," Pete announced.

"You smell anything?" Steve asked.

"No."

"Me neither. I don't see a fire... and it certainly wasn't a quake. Or a hurricane."

They scanned the adjacent floors, as far as their lights would illuminate. Other guests were hanging over the railings, above and below them. There was now no panic, no ominous doom. Only concern—and confusion.

"*Steve? What's going on?*" Barb called.

"We're OK, honey. Everything seems OK. Come out if you want."

"What is it, what's the problem?" Barb asked.

"I don't know. But everything seems OK."

Maybe it had been the survival shows, but to Barb the vast, darkened space of DisasterLand felt like a black hole, swallowing her sanity, her security. She looked over at the InfoTron, so easily silenced. *What was the point?*

"I'm going back in." Barb said. "It's creepy out here."

"I think it's kind of romantic," Sarah said.

"You're just wishing that rock star was here," Pete said.

"You know what's happened? The power's gone out," Steve announced. "That's what it is. The fucking power has gone out."

Fifty-four minutes later, the lights flickered on and the hum of energy resumed coursing around them. DisasterLand, once again, was alive and kicking.

Cheering erupted from the atrium but the Beyers found themselves oddly disappointed. With the power back, tensions had fully dissipated but so too had the coziness. Once again, Barb had been reminded of her childhood and as the memories faded in the electric glow, she was saddened.

The family was hunkered down in the master bedroom, on their second game of cards with a DisasterLand-branded deck thoughtfully placed in a drawer. They'd raided the bathroom for candles and had become remarkably content with the peaceful starlit valley as a backdrop.

Pete had continued his diligent fire-sweeps through their suite and all had come up negative. They felt as confident about their safety as they possibly could and had become determined to make the best of it.

They had been swapping family stories, *freestylin'* as Pete had called it, on a nostalgic field trip into their own fading memories. Within those hazy mists they had indeed found treasure—of friends and family lost by the wayside, of places visited and times shared, of their own mistakes and experiences seen through the lens of greater maturity.

The journeys of the past had begun to feed the future and a renewed vigor was shared as they each sensed a new phase beginning in their lives. Together, they had reached a crux, a rest stop on the highway of their lives, and they relished it.

But that moment, and the togetherness, had quickly been lost.

"I'm glad we got that over with," Barb finally ventured to say, entirely unconvincingly.

"Yeah, that wasn't so bad," Steve agreed.

"It kinda sucked," said Pete.

"It did not," Barb said. "You were scared, I saw you."

"I don't think that was it," Sarah offered. "The disaster, I mean."

"No, you're right I suppose," Barb said, eyeing her family, her voice betraying her emotions.

"Means our food's safe," Steve said.

"Sure is, DJ."

"And so is our reservation for Del Sol."

"In fact, I might have to have a beer," Steve announced.

"Only one left, DJ," Pete reminded him.

"I can't believe you guys didn't buy more," Steve said, shaking his head.

"After brunch," Barb said. "We need to go back anyway."

"Deal," Steve said rising. It meant he'd be able to duck into Good Health to get his Happinol while the family was shopping next door. It would be seamless, and another night without surely wouldn't kill him. In fact, he felt pretty good come to think of it. "Should we continue the game in the living room?"

"Let's see what DTV has to say," Barb sighed.

The family regrouped in front of the HDTV and Steve took a lug of his still-cold beer. Emotions settling, the Beyers were emerging renewed.

"To resilience," Steve toasted. He was proud of his family. They had stuck together marvelously. He passed the beer to Barb as the kids slurped their soda.

Sarah turned up the volume. A somber news anchor was live in the atrium, appearing almost ashamed, "Welcome back. If you're just joining us, power has now been restored to all of DisasterLand after an unprecedented blackout. We sincerely apologize for any inconvenience, and rest assured the source of the problem is being thoroughly investigated."

"Blackout," Barb said. "So it wasn't the disaster."

"I told you," Steve confirmed.

"That means we've still got a quake, or a flood, or a terrorist attack on the way," Sarah said, emotionally exhausted.

The DTV anchor continued, "Please stay tuned for further information. And now, we resume *DisasterLand, Naturally*."

"I don't believe it," Steve said, finishing off his beer. "Imagine if that blackout had happened in the middle of a disaster!"

"Honey, I'm not sure if I trust these people," Barb said.

"Unplug it DJs," Pete said. "Now. You're freakin' me out here."

Sarah flipped off the television and the family agreed to call it a night. They would wait and see, judging DisasterLand afresh in the morning after a good night's sleep, preferably from the front garden at Del Sol.

Pete and Sarah retreated to their room under the guise of being tired from the previous evening's exploits, but planning for the night's escape was about to begin in earnest.

Steve took advantage of the reprieve and fired up the hot tub for his second soak of the day. He slipped in excitedly, thrilled to have a brunch of such potential lying ahead of them, his mind dancing through the delicious permutations.

Barb followed him in moments later, knocking Steve out of his reverie by dropping her robe to reveal a newly-shaved femininity.

"Not again," Steve urged.

"Umm humm..."

"Honey..."

She stepped towards him and Steve retreated defensively to the farthest corner of the tub.

Luckily, he had his secret weapon.

Elektra stepped into DmZ in low-cut pinstripe pants and a tight virginal-T that read, *Hot and Sour*. She was pleased. The blackout had cleansed the air like a light rain.

It had gone completely according to plan, a psychic orgasm simultaneously building and releasing tension in all of DisasterLand, priming guests for the real thing. The outage had lasted under an hour, but the psychological effects would be much, much greater.

DmZ was quiet, with a group of last night's performers huddled on sofas next to the glass, sharing a drink with Nick. Elektra welcomed them with a smile. Molly was waving from the opposite end of the bar, her martini already half empty.

Elektra was enjoying being out for a change. She generally hid under her bed on school nights but was glad she'd made an exception. With Clint still on her mind, a drink in DmZ sure beat sucking dust bunnies.

They hugged.

"How are you?" Molly asked.

"I could use a drink."

"Saturday night jitters?"

Elektra nodded as the bartender appeared with a glass of red, on cue.

"Thanks, Bill. You OK?" Elektra asked.

"Doing great. Beautiful night."

"We try."

"Anything else?"

"More of those killer wasabi peas, Bill," Molly said.

"Right."

Elektra took a long, attentive sip of her Pinot and peeked below, pleased to see the guests returning to the atrium.

"Another success, hunh?"

"By the book," Elektra confirmed. "Where were you?"

"Right here," Molly laughed. "Amazing. We could hear the screaming... flashlights flicking on. Brilliant."

"Fantastic. Yeah, everyone's really happy."

"Maybe it was the martinis, but it was incredible to watch the village illuminated one tiny bit at a time, flashlight by flashlight. I haven't seen that before, always been working."

"Wish I could have seen it live. Maybe someday."

Bill arrived with the replacement peas.

"What's playing?" Elektra asked him.

"Nick's iPod. Band called *Smaug*. I think this track's called *All is One*."

"Name sounds familiar."

"They're playing tonight. They were in earlier. Nice kids."

"I'd love to go," Molly said.

"It's not prohibited," Elektra chimed in.

"It's also not a good idea."

"On a night like tonight? I don't see how anyone would mind."

"I'm talking about our early call tomorrow. I'm too old for that."

"You're not the only one."

Elektra took another sip of her wine, flipping through the text messages on her phone.

"We'll need a bootleg," Molly declared.

"We will," Elektra sighed, returning her phone to the bar. Suddenly she was feeling the weight of the upcoming day, full-force. "Come on, Mol, let's order some food."

Pete and Sarah exited the elevator and high-fived, their escape brilliantly planned and executed. There was no doubt about it: they were liberated, eleven-forty in the p.m.

They rocked off towards the club, surfing on the waves of energy pulsing through the atrium. Packed with thrilled guests, the vibe was impossible to ignore. The blackout had launched a bald devil-may-care celebratory throw-down. DisasterLand had been reborn.

And they were going to be part of it.

Sarah temporarily regretted her hard-won diplomatic victory and considered ditching her brother, seduced by the testosterone fog lingering dangerously in the air. Tonight had an edge to it, Sarah realized, a dark intensity completely opposite to the night before. Where there had been levity there was now gravity. Where there had been celebration, now was oblivion.

The evening had been touch and go, questionable as to whether they'd even be able to risk an escape. But as midnight approached, they got a remarkable break.

Maria had appeared with a delivery and their parents hadn't answered the door. Steve had been sent a small package from Good Health while Barb was getting the dresses she'd ordered earlier. Steve's required his signature, but with the blackout Maria was running behind and agreed to make an exception when Pete offered to forge it. Steve's snores were clearly audible from the kitchen and Maria didn't see why he should be awakened.

Before Maria hurried to her next customer, Sarah asked about the blackout. Maria's response had surprised them: "Scary," she had said, "That never happens."

Spooked, they placed the boxes outside the bedroom door, afraid to witness a repeat of Pete's disturbing vision of the previous morning. Then bolted.

"I ran into dad in the porn store," Sarah said under her breath. Without her mobile phone and friends to download her information, her brain was absolutely exploding. She had to tell someone.

They were standing in line for the show.

"No way, Spanks," Pete stared. "They let you in there?"

"Yep," Sarah whispered. "And dad bought mom a vibrator."

"Yo, you shittin' me!" Pete said, staring at the faces around him.

Sarah shook her head.

"They do it like that?" Pete asked.

Sarah scrunched her shoulders. "Lots of people do."

"Yo, I thought that shit was just for TV."

Sarah shook her head.

The bouncer stepped in front of them, blocking their way.

"Sarah Beyers. I'm a friend of Neil's."

"Yeah, I saw your picture in the paper. You're on the list, plus one. Let me scan your D-PAKs."

Sarah and Pete raised their hands.

"No drinking, OK?" he went on, banding their wrists. "We catch you it's bad news." The bouncer unclasped the rope, "Now you two have a good time."

Inside, the place was pumping. A headphoned DJ was spinning nu-soul warm-ups and the crowd was swayin' to the filthy beats. The elusive tang of marijuana and fleeting glimpses of embers seduced Pete's imagination. Sarah caught Pete's wide eyes as he scanned the crowd, realizing with a great deal of pride this was his first big show. At DisasterLand, and on the lamb!

She knew it had to be more fun than spending it with Zander in some dark lounge, and she was right.

"This is so dope, Spanky!"

Sarah checked her watch. Just about midnight on the nose.

"Yeah, totally..."

The theater went black.

Sarah groped for Pete's hand. It was cold and clammy. He instinctively tried to pull away but she clamped down. They exchanged desperate glances by the dim emergency lighting.

It was here. The disaster. And they were out, in a dark theater, on the floor. Nineteen floors above them, any minute now, their parents would be dying of heart attacks.

The seconds ticked by with the crowd struggling to remain calm, yet growing more and more restless. Flashlights went on, revealing faces on the verge of panic.

In the distance, yelling as the exits filled. Pete and Sarah were jostled as some of the crowd started pushing, desperate to escape. The air was growing rapidly, uncomfortably tense. Sarah felt sick.

"What's going on?" Pete yelled, his voice shaking.

"I don't know, but we've got to get back."

"What if there's a flood or something? Can we get out?"

"Shut up, Peter. Don't say stupid stuff like that. Come on!"

Someone, in the back, was screaming.

Suddenly, deafeningly, an apocalyptic roar tore through the space, shattering the tension into a million bejeweled shards. For a split second, it all seemed over.

Revealed as a guitar chord it continued, echoing, twisting around itself and doubling back to emerge in a reverse loop of feedback and doom.

"*Noise it up!*" commanded an almighty voice.

An unseen turntablist scratched the crowd into an amped, chaotic fury and the bass dropped, blasting all fear from the air.

Neil's voice screamed, "*Hello DisasterLand!*"

Lightning boxes hit, full force, and the room exploded in blinding light. The curtain dropped and the crowd went mental, the panic of only seconds before demolished into nirvana.

"Wha'?"

"DisasterLand!"

"Wha'?"

"*DisasterLand!*

"Peace! Yo!"

"*Here we go!*"

The band broke down into full jam and Sarah's heart soared as did Pete's respect for his big sister.

"Spanky? That's your shag!?" he yelled but she couldn't hear.

"The world's a dark place, let's shine a little light. This one's called *All is One, One is All!*" Neil called.

The crowd was lost, dancing as one.

> "*We want peace, yo,*
> *a real peace.*
> *A new world,*
> *a new beginning*
> *of understanding*
> *cause*
> *all is one*
> *and one is all!*"

> *"Open your eyes, yo,*
> *your heart,*
> *your soul-io.*
> *Everything speaks,*
> *if you listen,*
> *cause*
> *all is one*
> *and one is all!"*

Neil and his opposite MC were furiously trading rhymes from either side of the DJ. The black MC was one of the most handsome young men Sarah'd ever seen, his short dreads bouncing like a pom-pon as he danced.

> *"When you take and take,*
> *what you can't replace,*
> *that's violence,*
> *cause*
> *all is one*
> *and one is all!"*

Behind them the bassist and guitarist battled to hold it together, each tossing off impossible riffs while the drummer was throwing off sweat like a garden sprinkler.

All around Sarah, girls were screaming.

> *"When you be killin',*
> *you be dyin',*
> *cause*
> *all is one*
> *and one is all!"*

Pete and Sarah were leaping up and down with the crowd, arms pumping to the beat.

> *"It's all free,*
> *and we'll fight,*
> *for what can't speak.*
> *We're all free,*
> *and we'll fight,*
> *for what can't be owned,*
> *cause*
> *all is one*
> *and one is all!"*

"*All is one and one is all!*" they echoed, together, Neil and the MC, as the pyrotechnics hit, the lightning boxes roared, and the crowd cheered, ecstatically.

The lights dimmed, the last chords ringing in their ears.

Neil stepped forward, from the shadows, and was hit by a spotlight, "Thank you! This next one goes out to all the girls in the 'Burg, Brooklyn-town," he shouted as the guitar screeched, "It's called, *Your Love Is Toxic Waste (and it's modifying my genes)!*"

Smaug launched into a full-on frontal sonic assault and Pete and Sarah screamed with joy. A togetherness would soon be forged that could never be lost.

Barb flinched as their door slid open and Sarah and Pete recoiled from the light.

"Oh shit," said Sarah.

"Yep," echoed Steve. "Oh shit."

They were sitting at the kitchen table with Barb's sundresses laid out in front of her. Steve was in his bathrobe, his face white as a sheet. Barb had been crying.

"So you're back?" Barb asked.

"Yeah, I guess so." Pete said. "But maybe not. Are you gonna kill us DJs?"

Sarah was holding back tears.

Barb continued, "You're lucky Steve was thirsty. And found my delivery."

"We are?" asked Pete.

"So you went out to see that band?" Barb asked.

To Sarah, Steve appeared distinctly unwell, and there was no sign of his package. She sensed a secret there, somewhere, and if she let him keep it that way, with some luck he'd reciprocate.

"Yeah, we did," Sarah admitted. "And it was really cool, mom. We came straight back home."

"That's right," Pete echoed. "It just got over."

Barb rubbed her forehead then folded the sundresses back into the box.

"How'd you know we were gone?" Pete continued.

Steve took a long sip of water. The truth was, he had wanted some time on his own and was headed for the walkway, thinking the atrium would be quiet. Instead, he found the packages and went in to wake the kids and offer hush money. But when he nudged open their door, they were gone.

Yet they were gone *together*, and he grasped something reassuring in that. He knew Pete and Sarah were at the show, and they weren't the only ones out there. He had actually decided he'd go back to bed and let everything play itself out.

But by the time he returned to the kitchen, Barb was up and opening her package. He managed to conceal his own, but only after sidetracking Barb by the confession that the kids were gone.

"I came out to get some water and found your mom's package. I wanted to ask you guys about it, but..."

"Did you find…"

Sarah cut her brother off, "You didn't go out after us, did you?"

"No. We knew where you were and that you were together. But let's discuss in the morning. It's been a long night. For everyone," Steve said.

"Thanks, dad," Sarah said.

"Yeah, DJs. Don't be angry. We didn't think there'd be a disaster with a band playing and everything."

"OK, Pete. Look, we'll talk about it in the morning."

For Sarah, it was an awkward ending to an awkward ending. When she had tried to let Neil know they were there so Pete could meet him, a roadie had coldly told her there'd be no more girls for the night. Sarah had burst into tears, more in confusion and embarrassment than any real disgust or offense.

"Sorry, Spanks," Pete had whispered. "That sucks but it's cool, you know?"

"He's a big star I guess," Sarah grunted. "He can do whatever he wants."

"No, you're prolly lucky. You're too good for seconds 'n stuff."

"Yeah," Sarah had agreed, sniffling. *Eeeww.*

The Beyers took their hard-won table in the sun, underneath the branches of a maternal oak and bathed in Del Sol's gilded essence. The rustic wooden fence edged the exalted space, enclosing them in a womb of sensuous delight.

Steve had greased the palm of the Maître d' at Barb's insistence, allowing them the prime corner spot deepest within the park. For once, they were treating themselves to splendor.

The Maître d' removed the golden "reserved" sign in the shape of a sun and handed it to Steve as a souvenir while he reveled in his new-found clout.

The family breathed an enormous, collective sigh of pleasure, their sense of anticipation about to reach a sublime finale. Last night's blackout had invigorated them, giving them a sense of second-chance, of a brunch tickled by destiny.

Earlier, Steve had imagined DisasterLand's desperate emergency safety meetings, with strong reservations urged about moving ahead with any sort of dangerous disaster. Surely restraint would win out, for no other reason than legal liability.

If so, the serendipity was remarkable: his family granted ten days of heartwarming recuperation in DisasterLand together, sans Disaster. It was practically a miracle.

Steve chuckled to himself. In fact, they could even complain, demanding compensation for whatever lack of disaster they experienced! *Who cares if they had won the trip?*

Yes, it had been a marvelous morning.

Steve had awoken with the sun licking the distant mountains and Barb trying on her sundresses. After she had decided on a vibrant floral, they'd called Maria for a return pickup and awoken the kids.

They'd descended to the atrium together, with a rejuvenated lightness in their step that had been lacking for years. Barb was stiff, but as they made their way across the atrium her legs had loosened and the unwomanly limp subsided. She was relieved: a disaster with those legs would be absolutely tragic.

Taking their seats, they now contemplated drinks and Barb longed for her camera. With Steve's DisasterLand gear embellished by his favorite cowboy boots, Barb's new sundress, Pete's new Lakers jersey, and Sarah's... Sarah's *nouveau prostitutional* (she'd be in back), with all of them here in the sun on the edge of DisasterLand's celebrated Great Lawn, it was certainly a moment to remember.

"Sarah, are you trying to look like a porn star? Because you're certainly succeeding."

Sarah rolled her eyes, dulled by her past nocturnal exploits, early wake-up call and the hangover from Neil's dis.

"Barb, I don't think that's helpful," Steve interjected.

"Well your daughter needs to get a grip. She's only 18."

Fortunately, their waiter arrived to take the drink order.

"We'll need a pitcher of your best Bloody Marys over here, stat," Steve said. "And some OJs, please, for the kids."

"Bottled water?"

"Please."

"Would you like to make a choice sir? Our bottled water list is on the last page."

Steve flipped to it in disbelief.

"Still at the top, sparking at the bottom, sir," the waiter said, stepping back.

"You have a bottled water list?" Barb asked, in confirmation.

"Yes, of course, ma'am."

"We'll take your best," Steve said, shutting it quickly. "Something in glass."

"And from far away," Pete added.

"Naturally, sir."

"And coffee," Barb added. "Black."

"Two," said Steve.

"Three," said Sarah.

"Excellent. Our specials for today's brunch include a smoked lobster and truffle frittata or piñon bread pudding French toast, both with mesquite-smoked bacon and wild fruit salad or we also have an artisanal cheese and paté platter with a selection of organic homemade breads."

Steve's stomach growled its approval as the waiter departed with a smile. Sometimes, Steve thought somewhat bitterly, Kansas City just didn't cut it.

"Beloved family, listen. I need a nice tension-free brunch. So about last night, and then we're going to enjoy ourselves." He looked over the family. "I'm prepared to cut a deal. If you kids agree to abide the rules from now on, we'll let last night slide."

"OK, we agree. Right Pete?" Sarah offered, quickly. After the way last night's show ended there was nothing to draw her out of the suite anyway.

"Yeah, DJs. Sorry we couldn't resist. We had VIP passes! Sarah hooked us up!"

"Fine. But one more time and you're both in serious trouble. I don't care if you are leaving home, Sarah, we'll RFID you. I mean that."

The waiter arrived with their drinks and Steve's eyes wandered out to the park, meeting the jealous glances of couples strolling in the morning sun.

In the distance, a team of guards seemed to be nervously questioning guests. He frowned and returned his gaze to the Bloody Marys being poured.

"So what piques your interest, ma'am?"

"I'll have one of everything," Steve interjected.

"Sir?"

"I want it all. Barb?"

She stared. "Just the frittata, please."

"French toast for me," said Sarah.

"Me too, my man," Pete added. "With extra bacon."

"You can have some of mine, Pete. I've got two orders coming," Steve said.

"OK. No extra bacon. *Yet.*"

"Two frittatas, three French toasts, one cheese and paté platter?"

"That's right."

"Thank you," the waiter said, departing with a curious backwards glance.

"DJs, can we lose our D-PAKs? Mine's chafing," Pete said, rubbing himself.

Steve looked to Barb. She nodded, "Yes, but put them under your seats where you can get them."

Sarah and Pete hurriedly removed theirs. Barb fought the urge.

"Honey, are you sure you can eat three breakfasts?"

"Completely."

"I don't think that's very healthy. All you've done is eat."

Sarah interrupted, "Hey, look! They had a picnic!"

The family turned. Sarah had spotted four couples of leather-clad hipsters emerging from the forest and slowly making their way through the Great Lawn. The men's cowboy hats were low over their eyes, their sunglasses dark and impenetrable. Scarves were wrapped tightly around the women's necks. Two women carried picnic baskets.

"Now that's the idea," Steve said. "How about lunch? We'll pick up the food just after this?"

"Sounds great. Is that your band, honey?" Barb asked.

"No, I don't think so," Sarah was straining for a closer look. Whoever it was, they sure looked cool.

A glowing couple, bursting with youthful radiance and elegantly dressed for a special day in the park, were being shown to the table next to them. Barb's heart sank as she saw confusion flash across the boy's face.

"Oh honey, we stole those kids' table."

"You snooze you lose."

"Steve..."

The boy whispered something to the Maître d' and he hurried away, apologetically.

The Beyers' eyes returned to the hipsters. They were headed to the village, anxiously chatting amongst themselves and oblivious to the splendid morning. A lush, rainbow feathered boa was draped extravagantly around each picnic basket.

The hipsters reached the village and Barb turned away to find the boy next to them on one knee, the sun cinematically lighting his face. Proposing.

"Oh my God! Look!" she gasped.

The girl blushed as other tables stopped to observe the special moment. She nodded her agreement, slowly, deliberately, and the tears started to fall.

The boy produced a diamond ring which glinted in the bright sunlight. He slipped it on her finger and they slowly embraced with a kiss.

The entire patio broke out in applause and the girl wiped the tears from her eyes, hiding her shy smile.

The Maître d' appeared at their table with a bottle of their best champagne, on ice. To continued applause, he popped the cork and poured two glasses.

"I feel terrible," Barb whispered. "Absolutely terrible."

"That's bad Karma dad," Sarah announced.

But it didn't matter. If anything, it put the couple more in the spotlight. All of the patio was smiling goofily and a shared toast spread across every table.

"Have you kids heard the story of our own..."

"Yes, mom," the kids sighed heavily. "Only a million times."

"Steve, what was that?"

"It sounded like fireworks."

"Why would there be fireworks *inside*?!"

"Clear! Everyone *CLEAR OUT!*" a voice bellowed.

In seconds, panic had seared the atrium as a wave of screams crashed around them.

"This is it!"

Bursts of gunfire were ringing through the airy vastness in discordant melodies. The atrium superheated and devolution was rapid.

"Come on, let's go people! Out! OUT!"

Guests were now desperately fleeing the village, eyes haunted. A piercing tone blasted through DisasterLand, momentarily displacing the human suffering.

The InfoTron flashed: *TAKE COVER.*

"I can't breathe!" someone screamed in the distance, their body crumbling beneath them.

"My husband's been shot!" cried a blood-stained woman, her hands upraised.

"My God help me! *Help me!*"

"HELP!"

A vicious torrent of gunfire erupted from the village entrance and fleeing bodies dropped to the floor in mid-stride, sickeningly, their chests exploding in gore before they even had a chance to scream.

Barb heaved.

A figure raced out of the walled village, automatic weapon raised. The Beyers recognized him instantly. A hipster.

"Soon you will understand!" he screamed, letting loose an emphatic burst of punctuation. "You will all understand!"

For a split second, a perverse, mind-warped second, with his flashing gun, dark sunglasses and cigarette stubbornly dangling out of his mouth daring to defy gravity, his dark potency was excruciatingly seductive.

"The picnickers!" Sarah screamed. "The picnickers!" She leapt up, pointing. Steve grabbed her, yanked her down. She landed, hard, on her seat, eyes tearing.

Another hipster appeared in the distance, firing non-stop. Store windows on the atrium's periphery were shattering, bodies exploding in red tangles of glistening flesh.

Sirens were ringing.

"*Stop! Oh God Stop!*"

"No! Help us!"

"*NO!*"

Guards were spilling out of the security center in full body armor, exchanging gunfire with the dark menace as the hipsters darted through the fleeing crowds.

The closest hipster continued racing towards Del Sol, leaping over the broken bodies, firing back into the center of the atrium in mighty barrages. Guards fell.

Steve grabbed their table, flinging it towards the fence and forcing the family behind it as glassware shattered around them. Sarah and Pete were sobbing now.

"Get down!" Steve yelled. "*Get down!*" he repeated to the young couple next to them.

But it was too late. The hipster had turned on them.

The couple's chests exploded in a slow-motion red mist, their lifeless bodies falling back and collapsing upon themselves in a mass of blood and mangled tissue.

Barb vomited, uncontrollably, as Steve gripped her back. Pete and Sarah had curled into a tiny, sobbing ball.

Gunfire was all around them now, a flurry of whistling danger. The hipster was struck, the side of his face exploding. His body fell, face down, in a crumpled mass.

Then a flash and a massive concussion, pounding chests and shocking eardrums. DisasterLand itself seemed to sway, sickeningly, as debris began raining down.

"Masks! Masks!" Steve yelled, choking, as he fumbled for the kids' D-PAKS in the hazy wreckage. Locating them, he pulled out the tiny masks, thrusting them out to the numb children.

He grabbed the thermal blanket from his own D-PAK, spreading it over them and ducking inside. Their ears rang, their lungs filled with stinging smoke. The tang of urine assaulted their noses, accented by fire and the fetor of burned bodies. Together, the family sobbed.

A second explosion and the whole of DisasterLand was sent rippling by its tremendous force. The floor rang beneath them and as debris rained down Barb pictured the dome's shattering glass slicing them to pieces. The first explosion had only been a warm-up.

The Beyers cowered. The minutes passed, devastatingly slowly, in silence. The atrium settled.

Steve stayed down over his family, fighting to breathe. Tears blurred his vision and burned his cheeks.

In the distance, a child howled, punctuated by continuing bursts of gunfire and shrieks as the cool-headed terrorists continued their deadly mission.

"No! *Please! No!*"

"*The staircase!*"

"*GET AWAY!*"

A symphony of exploding glass overwhelmed the atrium, followed by the rain of a million shards striking the atrium's cool tile, muffled only by bodies unlucky enough to be in the way.

The sound faded and the atrium stilled.

As quickly as it began, it was over.

There was before and there was after.

"I peed my pants," Pete repeated, over and over and over, in the most miserable, despairing voice any of them had ever heard.

All sound rushed back at once and the atrium filled with the wailing of the injured and the sobbing of those luckier.

Steve raised his head from the blanket, cautiously, and removed his mask. As the smoke cleared, the extent of the devastation was revealed. It had been almost complete.

The atrium was in ruins, the air smelling of explosives, feces and the ghastly stench of ruined flesh.

Barb rolled over, violently heaving.

Sarah pulled away from Pete, her stomach soaked in urine.

The young couple's bodies lay in a pool of glistening blood, their hands still clasped, their chests torn open.

Steve collapsed.

"You OK man?"

Steve awoke to a hand, shaking him.

"You alright?" It was an EMS worker.

"The couple..." Steve mumbled.

"They're gone."

"No, I saw them..."

"I mean we couldn't help."

"I don't understand."

"None of us do, sir. None of us do."

The paramedic helped Steve into a sitting position. Barb was already leaning against the fence, head in hands. The kids were next to her, their eyes vacant.

"You guys got it pretty bad. You sure you're OK?"

"Yeah. I guess. I mean, I don't know."

"Come on, let me help you over to your wife."

Steve inched through the pools of vomit to collapse against the fence. A few feet away, the couples' bodies had been covered by Steve's thermal blanket.

"You wait here a while, OK? We'll be back."

Steve nodded, taking Barb's hand.

The EMS worker hurried away to another table, closer to the blast, where his partner was already at work.

Flashing lights and sirens blanketed the atrium, eviscerating the continued cries from the shocked and injured victims.

"Can you tell me what you saw?"

The Beyers traded emotionless glances.

"We need you to help us," the DTV reporter urged. "Please. While the memories are fresh."

Nothing.

"Did you see anything suspicious?"

Finally, Sarah nodded. The reporter offered a bottle of water and she took a long sip.

"Eight people. With picnic baskets. In the park."

"Where?"

She pointed, with difficulty, to the forest trail. The reporter motioned to the cameraman, who zoomed in.

"They did it," Barb confirmed.

"You're sure?" the reporter asked.

"Positive," Steve said, unable to look the reporter in the eye.

"Now it all seems so..." Barb struggled to find the words. "Like we knew the moment we saw them something was wrong. Sarah saw them first."

"I just turned around," Sarah said, "and they were *right there*."

"From then on we were just waiting..." Barb said as the tears began to fall. "Just waiting..."

"The dead one shot the couple next to us," Steve finished. "We saw him."

169

Barb was sobbing now, "They just got engaged and..."

"He shot them dead," Steve finished.

"Their chests exploded," said Pete. "Like in the movies. It was like a war."

The cameraman lowered the camera, flipped off the light. The reporter put his hand on Barb's shoulder. The bodies had been removed, but the image remained, singed into her soul.

"You sure you're OK?"

"Why did you do this?" Barb asked.

"Sorry?"

"You did this horrible thing. Why?"

"We didn't do anything Ms. Beyers. We're trying to get to the bottom of it."

The crew stood, faces long, and hurried past the blood-stained table to other shattered families.

"What the hell did that mean?" Steve mumbled.

"It's all a show, honey. We've just got to remember that. They're all... in character," Barb said, eyes distant. Quietly, she continued, "That could have been us, Steve. That was our table."

For a split second Steve allowed himself to believe it and the implications came tumbling down, picking up speed. *Something had gone wrong. Terribly, terribly, wrong.*

He felt the abyss opening up beneath him once again, a yawning black hole in his consciousness, and he fought to pull himself back. He wouldn't let himself believe that. He *couldn't.*

"That's right, honey, they're professionals," Steve said, and reached down to his D-PAK, hands shaking. He grabbed the tiny radio and flipped it on.

"... still on the loose. Please exercise extreme caution in returning home. Elevators are temporarily unavailable. Both North and South stairs are damaged and undergoing repairs," the announcer reported. "If you're on the floor, please be patient. Help is on its way. Repeating. Eight terrorists..."

Steve threw the radio against Del Sol's stone exterior. It shattered.

"I think we should go home," Barb announced, her voice cracking. "Now."

"Barb..." Steve cut himself off. If anything, the experience was just starting. And that, realistically, was the best case scenario.

"I don't like this place. I'm taking the kids and we're going home. To Kansas."

"I just don't think that's an option, honey."

Whatever happened, they weren't going to be allowed to leave just like that. They were trapped. But he wasn't going to say it.

Steve hoisted himself up to the fence, pulling the kids up after him. They stood, looking out to the village for the first time. The space had been radically transformed.

In the distance, three lonely buildings rose from the heart of the village, insides gutted by fires which were still smoldering. DL:FireMen were dousing the ruins with water pumped from the fountain.

The buildings were now merely shells, but they had survived. The rest of the village had been completely leveled.

The shops, the expensive merchandise, the beautiful streets and cafés, the encircling wall—all of it had been instantly reduced to rubble. Several enormous craters lay gaping where it all once stood, twisted metal projecting menacingly skyward.

Somehow, though it was crippled, the fountain alone had been spared the worst.

Aid workers were frantically digging through what remained of the village with rescue dogs. Firehoses and stretchers were strewn across the debris, cutting across trails of blood.

The body of the man who had shot the couple lay at the edge of the park, ringed by DL security guards. Photos were being taken while a gloved firearms expert examined the weapon that only minutes earlier was used to such awful effect.

"I don't understand, DJ."

"I don't either, Pete. I really don't." Steve hugged his son.

"Is everything OK dad?" Sarah asked.

"I told you, honey, I don't know. OK?"

Sarah turned away, fighting off tears.

Across the atrium, another riot team raced out of the second floor security center and down the nearest stairs. Soon, they had disappeared into the rubble and out of sight.

Shouting could be heard from beneath the tower, but the family's view was blocked by what remained of the village.

Steve let his glance drift up to the tower, past walkway after glass walkway. Each was filled with motionless guests, stunned into silence yet lucky enough to have been spared the worst.

Steve envied their innocence.

The InfoTron downgraded the warning to yellow and the migration slowly began. Steve helped his family over the fence and hand in hand they made their way out of the park, joining the steady stream of refugees cautiously advancing to the tower.

They had watched the repairs progress, and at any other time they would have been awed by the delicacy of the operation and the swiftness with which it had been accomplished. As it was, the Beyers could only look on with disengaged emptiness.

Repair workers had descended from the top of the tower like mountaineers, rigging enormous drapes of Kevlar webbing across the staircase frames to seal the gaping holes left by the shattered glass, several stories high. In the days to come, this webbing would serve as a constant reminder of the terrible event.

"DJ, can we go look at the dead terrorist?" Pete asked as they passed. "We can see if he's real."

The twisted body still lay where it had fallen, a blood-stained hand clearly visible from behind the wall of security guards and detectives. Pete tried to weave closer, but Barb grabbed him forcefully.

"Were do you think you're going?" she roared, and Pete froze, haunted by the tone of her voice. Barb hadn't witnessed the male animal in many years, since Steve had survived his mid-twenties. She felt like she had just finally recovered, yet already she was being confronted by his offspring. A metallic taste spread through her mouth.

They ventured into the atrium, wading through the piles of rubble, the pools of blood and gore, and nothing had prepared them for the reality of the devastation which now surrounded them. One horrific vision after another, one horrible smell after another, left the family fighting nausea with every step. The floor was an hallucinatory ecosystem of emotional microclimates with pieces of flesh, blood and wreckage littered throughout in a gruesome stew.

Bloody victims were still crying for mercy, some cradling mangled body parts, other staring at their own detached limbs strewn by the blast in shock. A small child picked up a still-warm finger and gave it to her screaming mother.

EMS workers bravely plied through the waste with thick rubber boots to reach the victims, but they were clearly understaffed and already fatigue seemed to be setting in as the scale of the operation became clear. Rescue lights flashed in the red, white and blue colors of the American flag and black-suited forensics experts dotted the landscape.

Broken families huddled around shattered bodies and the true fragility of the human body, the human existence, was made starkly clear.

Barb desperately wanted to help. But what could she do? She stared into the eyes of the nearby rescue workers and they told her all she needed to know.

"Don't look, kids," Steve mumbled, eyeing his wife. "But keep watch," he hastened, cryptically.

Barb stared.

"We're not home yet and more always go off when rescue workers come," he finished.

In the hazy distance, firefighters were working to stabilize the village's three remaining structures. The smoldering fires were now completely under control. Twenty-five stories above them, the dome's enormous vents had opened and the air was rapidly clearing.

As they stumbled through tragedy, a nauseating artifact lay before them.

It was the burnt handle of a picnic basket.

The Beyers approached the staircases knowing something was wrong.

It wasn't the sea of blood being cautiously sanitized at the foot of the staircases by teams of space-suited emergency workers, the result of the falling glass blades surgically slicing those trapped below.

It was Good Food. The enormous windows had been shattered and guests were leaping out of the ransacked store, their arms filled with bounty.

Good Food was being looted. And the guards were doing nothing to stop them.

The riot police dispatched earlier were standing shoulder-to-shoulder in front of the store, merely preventing others from entering. They seemed genuinely surprised— and clearly understaffed.

When Steve realized what was happening, he grabbed Peter and raced towards the store. Barb shrieked after them.

Steve approached a guard, furiously, "What the hell is going on here? *What are you doing!*"

"It's not safe here, sir, take the boy and move away."

Steve stared into the guard's flaring eyes and saw the transparent fear lying shallowly beneath. Spooked, he froze.

Then pulled Pete on to the windows.

The store had been emptied. Completely. Inside, pathetic fights were breaking out over petty scraps as the last of the strongest were escaping with their hoard, viciously protecting their armloads from others.

Steve stood, frozen, with Peter at his side, shaken by the savage display of human nature lying just below the surface. Nothing was indeed sacred. No one was truly civilized. These weren't just kids.

An empty stomach knows no laws.

"DJ, they got all the food!"

"No, Peter. No way. This is another part of this stupid show. These are rich assholes making fools out of themselves."

"We don't have much upstairs."

"Shut up, Peter."

Weren't they all in this together? This disaster thing? Surely DisasterLand wouldn't deprive people of food?

"Come on, Peter. Let's get back to the girls. This is making me sick."

They returned to find Barb sobbing.

"I can't do it, Steve. I can't walk up nineteen flights. I can't…"

"Take it easy, honey. What's wrong?"

"The elevators are staying closed," Sarah explained. "Bomb threats."

"What if it happens again? What if they attack the stairs? Look at that blood… we'll be killed, Steve."

"Remember, Barb: this is a show. It's like a movie but we're in it." He looked to the kids. "Everything will be fine, honey. We'll help you. We're all here, together."

Hand-in-hand, the Beyers placed themselves in line, waiting patiently for the last of the sanitation crews to finish mopping up.

Steve attempted to look at it positively: it was for their own health. DisasterLand clearly wanted the worst left in the atrium, not tracked into the individual rooms.

Sarah turned to Peter, whispered, "What's going on?"

"It's all gone. All the food is gone."

Sarah looked over in disbelief. The guards had chased away the last of the looters and crews were already replacing the windows with plywood.

"I don't like this place," Sarah whispered.

"Yeah, it's kind of weird," Pete replied. "Like bad weird."

Moments later, the guards stepped away from the foot of the stairs and a murmur of relief swept through the numbed crowd. Finally, they were free to begin the long ascent.

The Beyers took their first steps as sparse, hesitant applause was breaking out above. Shockingly it grew, in intensity and in scope.

Steve's stomach turned. "They obviously weren't here," Steve spit. "Or they'd shut up."

"Monsters," someone added, ahead of them.

"Barbarians," Barb agreed. "Disgusting neolithic babyeaters."

But the applause was spreading rapidly now, all across the walkways. It was building to a deafening roar. Guests were rushing out of their suites to join in.

"No, DJ! Look!"

Below them, a hundred thumbs were raised in thanks as the EMS crews acknowledged the crowd. A guard fired his gun in the air, shocking the weary souls back to life. Through all of it, one lone EMS cart appeared from the wreckage, whisking an injured fireman to the safety of Good Health.

Tears were being shed from those above, falling down the tower like rain as ecstatic cheering filled the atrium.

Then, from above, a deafening chant:

"U-S-A! U-S-A! U-S-A!"

The line of guests bearing a thousand nightmares proceeded steadily up the spiraling staircase, covered in dust, sweat, blood and worse. Much worse.

Inside the glass tubes, the air was polluted with fear. Guards were placed at each floor's landing, watching the procession intently with weapons drawn. Their eyes were scanning each guest relentlessly with nothing escaping their gaze. No one was being allowed down.

The stench at any other time would have been unbearable. But now, in the shadow of the morning's events, it was a minor inconvenience that a long, hot shower would easily fix.

Surrounding guests were yelling encouragement to the ascending survivors and the emotional rush from the overwhelming show of sympathy had helped Barb up the first ten floors. But now she was hitting the wall and as her legs gradually gave out, dark visions of an attack on the crowded staircase were relentlessly forcing themselves upon her. She felt the glass steps being blast out from beneath her, and the fall, ten stories or more, to her death.

The tears were falling, she was hyperventilating, and Barb swallowed a cry every time she took a step, even with Pete and Steve's assistance.

Reaching the twelfth floor and fresh air from the Kevlar webbing, Steve pulled the family off the staircase and onto the walkway behind a sympathetic guard.

Other families continued to pass, many wishing her good luck and some even offering them hospitality on nearby floors. Flattered, Barb declined. She wanted to press on. She wanted to be *home*.

Barb couldn't get the vision of Good Food out of her mind. Less than twenty-four hours earlier, those shelves had been full and she was chatting at the fish counter. Now, it simply didn't exist. She had made a terrible, terrible mistake.

And for what reason? *Vanity?*

While Barb rested, Steve and Pete edged to the walkway to look out onto the atrium below. The craters had been barricaded. The injured had been removed, and those remaining, emotionally paralyzed by the events, were receiving counseling. The macabre piles of glass, blood and tissue were being carted away by specially rigged sanitation carts.

An eerie, muffled calm was descending upon the atrium as guests retreated to the safety of their individual suites.

Steve examined the twelfth floor around him, noticing one door down the walkway had a large cross mounted on it. He watched as one traumatized family knocked and were given entry.

A makeshift sanctuary, Steve realized.

The family gently rested Barb in their entryway and collapsed around her in a rancid heap. They sat silently for many minutes, each battling the dark quicksand of their minds. All track of time was lost.

They knew what they had seen, what they had experienced, felt the biological reality that had been all around them. Yet their minds fought to deny it.

Outside, it was now completely silent except for the sporadic clang of heavy machinery. They had been one of the last families to leave the atrium.

"We smell," said Barb, finally. "Horrible."

The family silently agreed. They looked pretty bad too. Steve's swollen feet, finally released from his cowboy boots, were unspeakably raw.

"Could be worse," Sarah said softly as her eyes teared. "We could be dead, like..."

"Sarah, stop it!" yelled Barb. Her own mind had been circling the thought like a raptor who'd spotted prey. She didn't need to hear it from anyone else.

"They're not dead. They can't be," Steve said, forcing himself to spit out the words.

Sarah was sobbing. "But..."

"I know what you saw honey. I saw it too and..." he paused. "These people are professionals," he went on and stopped. He glanced to Barb. Her head was down.

Steve collected himself, putting on a brave face for his family. "This is DisasterLand, folks, and that was a disaster. Got it? That's the point of this place. This is what they *do*. Now it's over. Now we heal."

They weren't convinced. Steve tried to push on, stumbled, and tried again. He failed.

"Look, I don't know," he finally admitted. "I just don't know. But DisasterLand doesn't go around murdering people. It's bad for business," Steve huffed.

"You're just in denial. We were the closest in the whole place, dad. We're the only ones who know the truth," Sarah sobbed. *"We saw it."*

Steve had no reply. Soon, Barb couldn't bear it any longer.

"OK, everyone. Clothes off. Now. No shame. In a pile for Maria. We're keeping this place clinical."

"Honey, our laundry's... embarrassing," Steve replied.

"That's their *job*, Steve. I'm sure they've seen worse."

Yeah, maybe, Steve thought, *but those stories made the rounds at the Christmas party.*

She read his face. "Are you volunteering?"

No, he wasn't. And she wasn't either. As far as she was concerned, each pile was a tiny Superfund site, better off burned.

Her dress definitely needed professional attention. In fact, if they couldn't get it back to new she'd demand a new one. And get it.

Barb was right, Steve realized. DisasterLand's laundry would inevitably have the world's most advanced facilities, techniques and detergents, specially formulated for clothes just like this. They'd *have to*. The military has Area 51. Laundries have DisasterLand. He could already see the commercials. He made a mental note.

Everyone stripped down to their underwear as ordered and Steve helped Barb to the bathroom while Sarah and Pete stuffed the rank garments into a garbage bag.

"Are there new towels?" Sarah called as they sealed the bag.

"Yes," Barb called back.

Thank God.

Barb turned on the shower and let the fresh, warm water rain down on her head. She gathered her strength, and began to lather the soap all along her body, massaging her grainy, throbbing legs and releasing the soothing aroma. Slowly, very, very slowly, the rank, multi-layered stench finally began to dissipate.

As Barb relaxed, the faces of the couple appeared in front of her, frozen in shock as their chests exploded.

Barb cried long deep sobs, as they all would do in the end.

Champagne was flowing, spirits were high and Shae's penthouse suite was bathed in the adrenalin-drenched afterglow of another successful disaster. Giddy laughter was tickling the rarefied air, punctuated by self-congratulatory boasting and the enthusiastic slapping of backs.

Times were good. But it hadn't always been so.

One hour earlier, DisasterLand's elite board of directors had watched the Feed's countdown anxiously, nibbling on hors d'oeuvres to calm their increasingly raw nerves. Shae was putting on a brave face, but inside his stomach was a cold, hard mass. Today's gag was one of the most complex they'd attempted, and the stakes were unmatched since their virgin flight.

Shae had pointed out the picnickers casually making their way across the park, tiny little dots from their twenty-second floor vantage point, signaling the start of the countdown. As the eight approached the atrium, DisasterLand's invisible machinery effortlessly slid into place behind the scenes. With the help of Shae's experienced eye, a few more firefighters than usual were seen appearing in the village, while guards seamlessly slipped onto their marks.

The picnickers stepped onto the atrium floor and the Feed zeroed in on them exclusively. DisasterLand's security level went from yellow to red and Elektra's voice rang out emotionlessly through the speakers as the final fifteen-minute countdown began.

The board members edged closer to the glass while down in the atrium all other activity proceeded normally. The village's shops would not open for another hour, but families crowded the small cafés for brunch and bargain-conscious window-shoppers were already mapping out plans of attack in the winding, cobblestone streets.

The eight entered the village and separated with friendly goodbyes, each calmly proceeding to their drop. The Feed split-screened the action.

"Five," Elektra called. "Five minutes. This is final and Panic aborts. Here we go, cowboys, let's show 'em how it's done."

Fifty unseen actors had settled in throughout the atrium, their ears filled with Elektra's play by play, while another hundred were in the labyrinth below awaiting their cue.

Three minutes later, one picnic basket was casually dropped at the far end of the village, under a bench on the corner of two busy streets. "Drop One," Elektra announced, "One-Twenty and counting. One, Two, Zero. Cue Alpha Team! *Alpha Team!*"

The four paired off, each team making their way down a separate street. "Hey!" a man yelled. "Hey! What are you doing! Police! *POLICE!*"

Gunfire flashed and the man dropped, his legs cut out from under him. He lay on the bloody pavement, wailing in agony. The horrified screams of witnesses filled the air, presaging what would soon become an unstoppable tidal wave. Guards rushed to the scene but the hipsters were long gone.

Simultaneously, the second team of four was exiting a crowded café, coffees in hand, on the exact opposite side of the village.

"Drop Two," Elektra announced. "Bravo Team! *Bravo Team!* Ninety seconds! We are ninety away. Nine! Zero! Final countdown in sixty."

The deadly team was casually strolling out into the street when an employee appeared, basket in hand.

"You forgot your picnic basket!" he yelled after them.

"Go ahead, keep it," one of the terrorists laughed as they disappeared into the crowd.

"*It's a bomb!*" someone else screamed and suddenly the café was in chaos, tables and chairs tipping as guests fought towards their families. Guards were arriving to help but the terrorists had positioned themselves for an assault and began cleanly picking them off one by one, splattering the fleeing guests in blood.

The panic turned desperate as families were separated in the chaos. Fear consumed the village and guests were racing to claw their way out of the doom.

"Get out! Let's go, *GET OUT!*"

Guards and firemen were swarming, frantically clearing the lost and confused.

"*HELP US!*"

The siren's wail blasted the atrium and the symphony of violence escalated rapidly. The terrorists' gunfire shredded the flesh of those who stood in their way of escape. They surged into the atrium with guards impotently laying chase, leaving a blood-soaked path of devastation in their wake.

The board looked on in reverent silence, somewhat ashamed of their giddy titillation. But not really.

The terrorists quickly fanned out to all corners of the atrium, continuing to cut wide swaths of death on their way. Frantic Samaritans nearest the bombs hurriedly mopped up the inevitable families stranded behind, paralyzed with fear, urging them further and further away in the desperate race against time.

"*GET OUT! EVERYONE OUT! OUT!*"

"Thirty!" Elektra yelled, "Twenty-nine! Twenty-eight!"

One terrorist fell, shot by guards as he fled. The others pocketed their weapons and ripped off their outer layer of bloody clothing to reveal DisasterLand tracksuits, blending in with the stunned victims. Instantly, and effortlessly, they disappeared. Guards frantically continued pursuit nonetheless.

"Sixteen! Fifteen! Fourteen!" Elektra cried. "*Drop one clear!*"

"*OUT! OUT! OUT! OUT! OUT!*"

"*TEN! Nine! Eight!*"

The board held their breath.

"THREE!" Elektra called, "TWO! *ONE!*"

The first of the twin bowel-cleansing blasts rocked the atrium, filling the village with smoke. Guards and guests alike dove for cover while the glass of Shae's suite rattled.

A deadly silence suffocated all thought.

Elektra's voice appeared as if at the end of a long, dark tunnel, "*DROP TWO CLEAR! DROP TWO CLEAR! And TEN! NINE! EIGHT!*"

The cataclysm reached its zenith with the second spirit-crushing detonation. The floor of the penthouse shook and one board member fainted, while others hurried to his side. Shae stared on, eyes focused only the rising smoke.

"Roll Charlie Team! *Charlie Team is UP!*"

The billowing black smoke had blocked all sight and the board turned desperately to the Feed. Images of the periphery of the atrium were flashing by, featuring masses of crumpled guests debilitated by terror. Guards with heat-sensing goggles could be seen clearing the space under the stairs as smoke billowed up around them, eventually obscuring all view.

"*Charlie Team clear!* Here we go! Five! *Four!*" Elektra continued.

Directly below the board the stairs began to shatter, one floor below the next in visceral succession: fourteen, thirteen and finally twelve. For a few terrible seconds, the air was filled with a jeweled rain followed by the grisly sprinkle of the glass landing below, piercing the atrium's fragile silence.

"Delta Team! *Delta Team's up!*" Elektra paused, breathlessly. "Cue the vents! Let's open 'er up!"

A longer pause. "Check-ins! Check-ins! Alpha team, let's hear from you Alpha team!"

And Elektra's voice ceased.

Vents open, the smoke began rushing out of the top of the dome.

Seconds later, the Feed revealed the first smoky images from the village, portraying almost complete devastation. Soul-shattering wails arose from the apocalypse below.

"Alpha team, report!"

Nothing.

Shae gagged as the hot, sour taste of bile filled his throat. He grabbed his water. For the first time in his career, he was worried. *Had something gone wrong?*

He checked his PDA for emergency messages. There were none. He fought the urge to call the bridge as the seconds continued to tick by.

What was happening?

He felt worried eyes scouring him and focused his own on the billowing smoke below. Painfully slowly, the atrium's scars were becoming visible. It was clear. The village was gone.

"*Good Food! Team Good Food in!*" Elektra cried.

Bodies and debris were scattered throughout the village remains, pools of blood growing vast and awful.

Sirens replaced the screams as EMS crews began arriving below, their flashing lights dancing across the dome's glass.

"*ALPHA TEAM!*" Elektra shrieked. "*REPORT!*"

Shae turned to his board for the first time, sensing they needed something and felt their relief as he cracked a small smile. Two other members hurried out of the room, the pressure simply too great.

The first DTV crews were arriving on the scene. Body parts were strewn over what remained of the blood-drenched streets.

Shae steadied himself against the wall, pager still silent. Las Vegas hospitals were on stand-by on big days, just in case. And in one way, today they were lucky: with the board visiting they had two private helicopters waiting on the roof in addition to the usual Life Flight.

He squeezed his phone. When reality was the goal, and their strive to achieve it so absolute, all but the inner sanctum were standing on quicksand. This was his first show off the bridge, and the disconnect was killing him.

Was it all over? Everything he had worked for? *Was he a murderer?*

"Cueing security response!"

Guards raced down from the second floor security center, on their way to Good Food below. The Feed's character was changing as DTV reporters had begun to wade through the carnage.

"*All teams clear,*" Elektra sighed, clearly relieved. "All teams accounted for. Awaiting EMS confirmation. Stand by."

Shae's head dropped. Their actors were OK. He tested the anxious eyes of the board, and gave them a heart-felt thumbs up. *But something had happened to Alpha Team.*

Slowly, very slowly, with the images of the rescue workers filling the Feed adventurous sips of champagne resumed. Everything was under control. The response had been swift and appropriate. Help had arrived.

Fifteen minutes later, slightly later than usual, lingering tensions were swept away in spontaneous hugs as Elektra gave the final all-clear. There had been no significant injuries.

From the penthouse, it had been the performance of a lifetime and the board had received a priceless view from the emperor's box. The atrium's drama had filtered through the windows intact, injecting those inside with a strong dose of intoxicating supremacy. It was Sunday at the Coliseum circa 200 AD.

Each was lost in personal reflection, processing the significance of what they had just witnessed. Shae was the first to speak as he surveyed the destruction below like a proud father.

"That..." he said, softly. "Was really fucking something."

The other witnesses softly concurred.

Visible below them, repair crews had begun their inspirational work on the stairs and the board looked on with wondrous fascination.

The intensity of the experience had caught them all by surprise. They thought they knew what was coming, thought they knew what to expect, yet the degree of realism had sent them spinning. They weren't prepared for it. And no one could be.

That was the miracle. That was the g-spot. That was *bank*.

At the base level of craftsmanship, it was flawless. It was the Armani, the Prada of stage shows, and it had been worth the secret trip under the cover of darkness for the board to experience it. There was nothing else like it on the entire planet.

DTV was surveying the gruesome scene at the foot of the stairs as crews worked to clean up the blood, bodies and glass. Soiled families were cowering nearby, miserably awaiting return to their suites. A sea of humanity, a universe of stories. Intercut with these scenes were live interviews with vacant-eyed witnesses and selected slow-motion replays of the attack.

As the DL:FireMen, sanitation and construction crews worked feverishly to clean and stabilize the village over two hundred feet below, Shae and the board retreated to the hand-carved mahogany table for the culmination of a glorious morning—and one of the most important strategic sessions in DisasterLand's remarkable history.

Champagne was again flowing and dollar signs seemed to pirouette over the dark wood as the board took their seats.

They were watching dailies from the biggest Hollywood blockbuster of all time—and then some.

This wasn't staged for the cameras over months of production. This was live. In real time, with real danger. And guests were paying to star.

This was revolution.

And they liked it.

For DisasterLand's board, it was nothing less than an evolutionary moment. It was bifurcation. It was mitosis. Worldwide.

Soon, DisasterLand would rocket forward in a blitzkrieg of corporate manifest destiny.

Elektra was sprawled, semi-conscious and reeling, across her favorite leather sofa atop the mount, iced peppermint tea in hand. Dressed to maim in tight black leather pants and a hand-made punk T-shirt featuring a collage from the 60's Japanese film *Tokyo Drifter* to celebrate the occasion, she had deliberately saved the killin' for later.

She was glad she did. She had needed it.

Only now, thirty minutes after calling the morning's *all clear*, was the bridge finally returning to any semblance of normalcy. It had been a tough one. And for her, an unwelcome validation: her ominous feeling had only intensified the closer they came to the countdown.

The morning's meetings had done little to assuage her growing feeling of unease and Elektra had hurried straight to the bridge, desperate to confront the source of her discomfort. Her female intuition was speaking loud and clear: it wasn't the usual case of gameday nerves. It was something deeper, and something infinitely more worrying.

It was Clint. There was nothing she could do, however, nothing practical, and that was possibly the worst part. Yet right on time she cheerfully greeted the first team with her usual élan and prepared the crew to launch the most spectacular attack in DisasterLand's history with an artful little ditty.

Yet almost ninety minutes later when she called "Action!" to send the picnickers on their way, it was with a dark feeling of foreboding she had never experienced before. The thrill of the moment, the surge of unconquerable confidence, was submerged beneath a dull haze of trepidation. And it scared the hell out of her.

Knowing thoughts can affect reality, she did everything in her power, used every cell of her being, to wipe the negativity from her mind and heart. And she had succeeded... until Clint didn't report to his AD for the Alpha-team *all clear*. Then she had been racked by all-consuming dread.

On the surface, there wasn't anything unusual about a slight delay. Sometimes things happened. But once they'd hit the sixty-second mark and Bravo-team had all weighed in with still no sign of Clint, the bridge hit emergency mode.

The video mixer was on it, and *Ghost's* unmatched network of parallel computers and high-definition optical sensors was called into operation. Chatter filled the AD's radio channels and for the first time ever, Elektra felt she might need to step down.

With the disaster continuing to rage around them, the bridge was completely silent. Soon the mixer had pinpointed the first blast in time and space and began visually sweeping around it, backtracking in time as the entire bridge held their breath.

He'd found Clint, dropping heavily into a safety trapdoor, ten feet from the blast. *But why hadn't he responded?*

The mixer continued back in time. Clint rolled out of the trapdoor, and limped back. *His knee.* The mixer rewound to the beginning of the sequence, spun to a new and better vantage point, and progressed the scene.

A family of three had wandered, panicked and disoriented, back into the danger zone after the 'drop one clear' had been reported. Clint had succeeded in turning them around but his knee had given out with the force. Only seconds before the blast he knew he was in trouble and he'd only just managed to roll into the trap before the bomb went off.

So where was he?

Following up moments later, the ADs had their confirmation: he was in the labyrinth, having exited the trapdoor into the staff tunnels. His radio had been smashed in the fall.

Shout out to the designers, Elektra thought, heart pounding. *You've saved another one.*

While Elektra continued to call the disaster's resolution, Karen, the lead writer, joined her and Monica, the shift's director, in a quick conference on the mount. 'Lexi plugged in Shae, Greg, and the ADs via radio.

"Let's get him back in," Karen insisted.

"*In?*" Elektra asked.

"We'll turn tragedy into opportunity," Karen smiled, "It's perfect. Help him back in, we'll have EMS take him to Good Health. We'll interview the family and guests will love it. It's a great story."

The ADs agreed, alerting EMS. Clint was located and the plan shared with him.

Elektra silently objected, but only for personal reasons. She had a bad feeling Clint was in the mood to stir up trouble. She'd have to pay him a visit later to take his temperature.

It was highly unusual for injured cast to stay public for treatment, but Clint was high-profile and the writers obviously recognized his potential immediately.

The footage was truly remarkable, Elektra had to admit, and absolutely something for her reel if she ever needed it. True, it wasn't planned, but in the face of danger, Clint's determination, his fire, was clearly on display as he battled the family to safety. DTV was going to have a field day.

"Pink pages coming," Elektra announced. "Stay tuned for pink pages."

Clint *was* giant fucking chick-magnet, Elektra knew, and there was no denying it. Therein lay the problem—she just wasn't the kind of girl that followed the crowd.

"E?"

Elektra clawed herself up from the couch. "Hey Greg."

"You doing alright?"

He took a seat on the armrest next to her.

"Yeah, nothing a heart transplant won't fix."

"I'll donate."

"You're such a sweetie. But it would never fit."

Elektra's first stop was the staff canteen for a good hot meal with the troops. Sixty minutes after the all-clear it was packed with ravished day players of all ages and persuasions, each devouring their lunch before the afternoon debriefing.

These were the disaster's victims, and they looked the part. What at first sight appeared to be the film set of a hospital special-effects thriller was, in fact, a real-life chronicle of the human condition that offered mesmerizing proof of the miracle that was DisasterLand.

A surreal mélange of disabilities both real and manufactured, it was hard to tell where the show stopped and reality began. The B-list had been through a quick post-disaster clean-up but they still looked like refugees from a warzone. Some had bits of fake flesh still attached, some still sported red-stained skin where the stage blood had sat a few minutes too long. It would all disappear in the end, but if a stranger had walked in unknowingly their lunch would have been less than satisfying.

The mood was wonderfully celebratory, however, with the air of a surreal post-game locker room. The mission had come off, and now it was time for some serious chow.

Lines snaked their way through the cafeteria's service area, each counter constructed to aid a particular actor's disability. Those in wheelchairs were in one line, actors missing arms in another. Actors on crutches made up the third, and those who could move unaided were making a show of team support by assisting their friends who couldn't.

Elektra shot straight for the line at one bipedal counter where hearty Southern fried chicken, mashed potatoes and roasted veggies were on offer. It wasn't usually her thing, but after the morning's disaster it somehow felt right. This was All-American comfort food and she needed it.

She patiently listened to the tales being swapped while the line progressed.

"Where were you again?"

"By the theater. You should have seen it. *Classic!*" The one-legged teenager cracked up, adjusted himself on his crutch. "I was soaked in blood, right? Somehow they rigged this thing that made it look like my guts were falling out when I walked..."

"Yeah, I've had that. That's a *good-'un*. So what happened?"

"This family right—they were all bling—so I stumbled towards them, screaming for help. Just dropping organs left and right, heaving, all of this foam oozing out of my mouth. They didn't know what to do. Just froze. So I reached out to grab them and spilled my intestines all over their designer shoes."

"Dude."

"Extreme!"

"So what happened?"

"Bro, you don't even want to know. But it smelled terrible! They may need professional help!"

"Them, what about *you!*"

Laughter echoed and the line inched forward. Further over, Elektra caught Shae patiently working the lines, chatting to the actors and congratulating those who had caught his eye on the Feed.

It was true: the B-team's genius had been unquestionable. These were everyday heroes and the respect was mutual. Shae's response from the actors was gracious and genuine.

During the apex of the smoke's infiltration they had appeared invisibly from trapdoors all over the floor to take their blood-drenched positions of misery or death. When the smoke had cleared, they were on stage.

Nothing epitomized Shae's attitude toward business more than the dozens of disabled actors now surrounding him in the cafeteria. The thing was, and it was beautiful really, DisasterLand was the largest employee of the disabled actors in all of America *and* they received massive government checks to subsidize it.

After all, the Disaster 'victims' had to come from somewhere, and why waste lots of time and money on prosthetics when there were plenty of ideally-suited actors who weren't getting a break otherwise?

Giving back, creatively and with a heart. Eliminate what would be expensive and wasteful and replace it with something nontraditional, something which lifted people who otherwise weren't being given the chance. That was Shae.

Noticing Elektra, he briefly excused himself.

"Great job this morning, General. Your finest hour. How are you holding up?"

"Be better after a good meal. How's the board?"

"Thrilled. We're taking a break. Big things are happening, Elektra. On all fronts."

"Keep me in the loop."

"*Of course*, E, you know I always do what I can."

He returned to the actors with a wink.

After a brief stop at the dessert bar for apple pie and some good old-fashioned sweet tea, Elektra worked her way out into the dining area.

"Tuck! My man!"

"Elektra!"

"This seat taken?"

"'Course not!"

Elektra joined him at the corner two-top with a quick hug.

"You ever done this before?" he asked.

"Sometimes," Elektra smiled. "When I need it."

She tore into the meal, her first real one of the day. After losing her breakfast to a nervous stomach, a not uncommon occurrence on such a big day, nourishment had to wait. Until the *all clear*, she had only managed to down a few plain crackers to keep herself upright.

Tuck glanced around them. The smiling faces, wet hair and healthy complexions belied the fact that ninety minutes ago many of them were screaming in agony.

"Yo, man, this is pretty fucked up. Even for me."

Tuck, one of DisasterLand's more mercurial heroes, was the wardrobe designer behind DisasterLand's startling collection of apocalypse couture. Yet his personal visits were restricted almost exclusively to big show days, when he was on hand to supervise the instillation and execution of his elaborate designs by hand-picked staff. Best known for obsessively watching the Feed's replays to understand both the functioning of his garments under pressure as well as the ways in which the actors' bodies responded when inside, he worked reclusively from a studio loft in Vegas.

He also traveled extensively, visiting the most advanced fabric factories in the world to catch all of their newest technological developments before they hit the market. This allowed him to exploit the bleeding edge of what was physically possible in a garment: threads of impossible tensile strength which let him create designs almost exclusively out of nothing at all, fabrics which were so temperature sensitive that even tiny increases would cause them to melt away and designs incorporating wafer-thin heat barriers which provided an extra margin of error in difficult situations.

More and more often, Tuck was participating in the conception and creation of the fabrics themselves, giving DisasterLand one more source of licensing revenue if they ever chose to capitalize on it.

Yet with only this technological savvy, he'd be just another geeked-out twenty-something. The secret to Tuck's success was his almost super-human ability to design garments which simultaneously seduced and repulsed, creating a tremendous emotional tension in those who came into contact with them. Within his designs the two polarities intertwined like snakes to such a fine degree that guests were often left incapacitated, frozen in place as their brains tried to work their way out of the perverse conundrum they had been trapped within.

He somehow showed way too much and way too little, grotesquely revealing bits which should be kept covered and uncovering the bits far better left unexposed. The combinations were often bizarre and horrific and, needless to say, wildly successful.

Working closely with the special effects guys as well as the writers, he was able to custom-integrate remotely triggered blood-filled squibs directly into his designs as well as other, much more revolutionary effects that each specific script, and even each specific part, demanded.

He was a cool dude and shared an exalted position among Shae's collection of deviant savants.

Elektra dug him too.

At the next table, an actress in a wheelchair took a bite of her burger as the others roared with laughter. A bandanna kept her blonde hair off her bloodied face. Mid-twenties, she was missing both of her legs.

"I've got a better story..." she began.

"I don't believe it," said the actor next to her.

"Let her talk!" insisted the one-armed man in his 50's across from her.

"They gave me these fake legs," she continued, giggling now, "It's not funny... I mean, actually it is... but..."

"Yes?" the table insisted.

"Well, they planted them in the glass a few feet away—I was under the stairs— just the feet sticking out with a smear of blood between us, and I just kept screaming, over and over, how much my legs hurt. And whenever someone would come over to help me, I had this little button I'd press and blood would squirt up at them from my waist... People were so *freaked out*."

"More than usual?"

"Well," she said, "Not really."

The table broke down into near-hysterical laughter.

"Yeah, that's nice," Tuck said. "That's really nice."

"Gotta hand it to them, they enjoy what they do," Elektra said. "As much or more than we do."

"Are they sane?"

"As sane as can be expected. They're all rigorously tested by our psychologists just to make sure. There's a definite line they're trained not to cross... we don't want any lingering damage. At least, no more than we plan for."

They shared a smile.

"Besides, they have a reason to stay in line. We watch the show carefully when it's over, and the best are promoted. There's a strict hierarchy there."

"Guess that makes sense."

"They're absolutely critical. If their performances aren't real, if they don't register as genuine for any reason, the whole thing is blown."

"I gotta hang out with these cats more often," Tuck said, taking a long swig of his sweet tea. "I could learn a thing or two."

The soap disappeared down the drain and Steve was emotionally molting. Layer after layer of psychological accumulation had been rinsed away with the filth, cleansing his battered soul.

It was over. The worst was behind them.

The attack had cost them what could have been the greatest brunch of their lives, but maybe—just maybe—it had been worth it. If anyone in the park had the front row seat, it was them. That, at the very least, was bragging rights.

Besides, Del Sol hadn't been significantly damaged, Steve knew. In a few days it would surely reopen and they'd be offered their table back. It was that simple.

Steve stepped out of the shower, one of the most necessary, and satisfying, of his life by any method of accounting. As he toweled off, he felt he had intimately glimpsed DisasterLand's genius.

He felt good, somehow, damn good. It had been horrible, what they'd witnessed, but they'd come through it stronger as people. Steve was sure of it. It was like a purge. And despite the lingering questions, there was simply no way it had been anything other than planned.

This was what DisasterLand did.

The good news was, he was starving. Steve stood in front of the mirror, reflecting on the extreme discomfort he felt by skipping just one meal. It was pathetic.

But having his appetite back so soon had to be a good sign. He dressed quickly and strapped on what remained of his D-PAK, having discarded the blanket in the atrium and rinsed off the mask. Steve checked the strap carefully, and with relief. It wasn't anywhere near the end. He had several inches yet.

No, he wasn't obese, far from it. But he was... soft. That was it, wasn't it? He was mushy, undisciplined. Weak. An edge had disappeared some time ago, so gradually that it was impossible to pinpoint. He had become something he had told himself he wouldn't.

Hadn't he?

It wasn't just his girth—it was the sensation it created. Like he was always swimming in fluid, with resistance everywhere. Or like he was caught, perpetually, in some sort of permanent personal tractor-beam. It irritated him.

No. It *scared* him actually. How quickly one's life can get out of control... working more, exercising less. The weight begins to slip, the body starts to crave only calories, not nourishing food. Then it's a rapidly tightening vicious circle—weight is put on, exercising becomes more difficult, more unpleasant, the body feels worse... and on and on and on.

Next thing you know, Steve thought, *you're forty-four and you look like every other suburban dad. Which you swore you wouldn't.*

That's it. Here he was, doing something he swore he'd never do, being someone he swore he'd never be.

It was undeniable. Here he was, a full-on suburban plumper.

Steve stepped into the kitchen. The rest of the family was sitting gloomily around the kitchen table. He sensed trouble.

"Phone's dead," Sarah said.

"Bullshit," Steve replied.

"*Honey,*" Barb said, her head in her hands. "Please..."

Steve marched over to the phone and picked it up. The family held their breath.

"No, it works," Steve said, handing it to Sarah.

She smiled, "Oh, good. That's weird."

Steve let out a deep breath, "You guys had me scared there for a second."

He dialed, leaving Maria a quick message that their laundry was ready for pick up.

"This place scares me," Barb finally admitted. "Nothing works right around here.

I'm not... secure. I don't feel confident."

"There's got to be an explanation," Steve said. "For everything."

"I don't like it sweetie. It's a recipe for disaster."

It had been a half-hearted joke but it wasn't funny. Not even for Barb.

Steve opened the fridge, carefully assessing its potential.

"Easy, Steve. Go easy. We need to conserve."

"I know..."

"So what are you doing?"

"I'm fixing the biggest breakfast you've ever seen, honey. And it's going to be better than yesterday."

"I don't think... I mean, I didn't get much. I thought we'd be eating out this morning. Please don't fix it all. Save *something*."

"I'm sure Good Food will reopen tonight. Come on, I'm absolutely starving."

"I am too mom," said Pete.

Barb shot him an icy look.

"OK," Steve said. "I'll save a little bit."

Steve turned on DTV:Music, selected the classical music station, and rolled up his sleeves. The family sat uneasily at the table in silence while Steve cooked.

"The looting was just a shallow, disgusting plan to make us eat out and spend money," Steve finally announced. "But we're not giving in."

"They were guests, honey. Guests looted that place."

"They looked like guests. But they weren't. It was all controlled."

"How do you know?"

Steve turned from the stove, arms folded, a scowl etched deeply across his face. "Because they didn't go up the stairs. They ran away. Into the atrium."

"The stairs were closed, Steve. They would have been lynched. Everything would have been stolen back from them."

"Everything they stole would have been stolen? I don't believe it, Barb. *They were actors.*"

For the Beyers, the morning disappeared in a post-adrenalin crash and resulting semi-detached lethargic haze. Very gradually, the turmoil had receded and a sort of stoic reflection emerged.

"I think we should complain," was Barb's opinion after they had finished cleaning up breakfast.

Steve had fixed all they'd had—the salmon, with potaroes and buttered spinach as well as other odds and ends—and it had been a supremely satisfying meal, perhaps not as extravagant as Steve had imagined, but doing much to calm their uneasy stomachs as well as their minds. More importantly, it managed to keep them out of the living room and the presence of DTV.

"Barb..."

"Or at least go ask the Andrews. See what they think. Where they were. If they think it's normal. The power going out, the elevators not working, the phones screwed up."

"I can take care of my own family, Barb."

Men, Barb thought. *Men and pride.* "Then call and complain!"

"Honey, this is DisasterLand. It's not supposed to be perfect and we're supposed to enjoy it. Don't you see? It's part of the experience."

Barb decided she'd spend the rest of the afternoon in bed. She could barely stand up anyway, she might as well go with the flow. She'd hit the hot tub, then bed. She was over this whole disaster thing. Already.

"I'm going out to the walkway, to collect my thoughts," Steve announced.

"Do whatever you want. But follow your rules or you're setting a bad example for your children."

"Bah!" Steve made a quick detour to the bedroom and then left the suite in a humph, the door sliding shut behind him.

Steve walked out to the end of the walkway and sat down in front of the handrail, dangling his legs through the rail's brushed steel slits like a little boy. Just this one simple act lightened his heart.

Ahead of him, the InfoTron had begun to feature grainy clips of the terrorists with a giant red question mark.

Who are they?

He removed his binoculars from the case. If DisasterLand didn't take them, he was going to use them. Big time.

He began examining the clean-up below and gradually, very gradually, he was reassured. The rescue dogs had gone home. There was no panic, no obvious signs of trouble. Even the guards seemed to be joking amongst themselves.

Yes. Barb was over-reacting.

Steve dropped the binoculars and stretched. There was something right about being in the atrium now, something correct in seeing the site for himself, observing the hurried, but not chaotic, clean-up in person.

It's all meant to be, he knew. *It's all part of the experience.*

Indeed, the longer he sat the more the initial shock faded, replaced by intense feelings of admiration, of respect, for everyone involved. They had been part of something very, very special, firsthand. How many people could say that?

Distant sounds of sobbing caught his ear and Steve held his breath to listen. He couldn't place it.

Steve lay back, legs still dangling over the atrium, and looked up. Above him was the last walkway, then the two floors of smoked glass, then finally the dome, arcing up over the tower.

Who was in there?, Steve wondered. *In those two floors? And what were they doing?*

They were surely corporate boxes, he realized, just like at a football stadium.

Corporate boxes for the rich, paying to watch the peons suffer.

Get us in, Dick had said. *Get us in!* And that was a pretty good place to start.

The door opened behind him and footsteps approached.

"You OK?" Pete asked, quizzically.

Steve sat up. "I'm fine."

"Mom sent me out here to make sure you hadn't jumped."

"Not yet."

Steve handed Pete the binoculars and he sat down next to him. Pete looked out, over the atrium, lost in thought. Steve let his own thoughts drift.

"What's Sarah up to?" Steve asked.

"There's another show on survival she's watching."

"How can she even..."

"Mom's making her. I guess she feels bad about yesterday."

"Are they showing highlights?"

"You mean the dead people? Not yet."

"They're not dead, Spikers."

"I *know* dad."

Below them, the gore had been almost entirely removed, the tile restored to its previous sterile luster by crews driving large water-based vacuum-cleaners like Zambonis.

Pete dropped the binoculars. "Yo, dat shit wuz da bomb," he said simply.

Steve slapped him on the top of the head.

"They planned it, DJ. I know it," Pete said.

Steve nodded. "Me too, kiddo. I just got scared. That's how good they are."

"They no foolin' 'round, yo."

"Sho 'nuff," Steve replied. They cracked up.

Pete sometimes thought his dad was a hopeless goofball, but he did appreciate the effort.

"DTV's showing *DL:Heroes* in a few minutes. Wanna join us?"

Steve stared at the scene below him. "I don't think so."

"It's gonna be cool. It's all the interviews they've been playing. With EMS people, guests, everyone, all together. We're probably on it, DJ!" Pete raised his fists, looking out over the atrium. "I wish my friends could see it."

"I'm sure they will... at some point."

"What do you mean?"

"Well, all this is being recorded, right? At some point we'll probably be able to buy it."

Pete's eyes sparkled.

They looked out, over the remarkable scene. Beyond the devastation lay the park's entrance, almost untouched. And over the treetops, past the far dome, lay the mountains, barely visible in the hazy dusk.

DisasterLand deserved every piece of recognition they got, Steve decided.

He turned to Pete. "So Spike, why *do* you talk like a black kid?"

Pete rolled his eyes.

"All I'm saying is you better not fail your English SAT's."

"'Cuz it's real dad, hip-hop's the real thing."

"What do you mean?"

"It's life, it's death. It's love and hate. It's hungry wolf style. You know?"

"You mean all those guys on MTV, with the girls, the SUVs, the drugs and money. That's real?"

"That ain't hip-hop dad. That's been stolen. Packaged. Hip-hop comes from the street. The heart. It's honest. It's real life."

This made some sense to Steve. He knew about fake—it was his job. Never mind the reality, give us the gloss. Make us feel, but not too much. Advertising.

Steve patted his son on the back. "I'm proud of you, Spikers. You've got a good head... you're gonna hit some rocky times soon if you're like most of us. But you'll do OK. I know you will."

Pete's head dropped. "Thanks for bringin' us, dad. Whatever happens, we'll remember this, you know?"

"Yeah," Steve replied. "I know."

Pete stood up. "You coming back in?"

"In a few minutes."

Pete left Steve staring down below, imagining the days stretching out ahead of them, like ripples from the morning's attack. Would they rebuild the village? Completely?

He chuckled. Wouldn't that be perfect? The stores back, just in time for going away sales? It just didn't seem possible though. The devastation was almost complete... all of that work, those products, those people down there... *Juliet!*

His thoughts had drifted back to the morning, the crystal-clear images branded into his consciousness. His heart sped to keep pace with the increasingly-disturbing flashbacks.

The strange sense of inevitability in seeing the picnic baskets... how clear it now seemed, every movement significant, the way the group exited the park, the way they never looked to anyone else, never took in the beautiful, clear morning that surrounded them.

The screams, then the gunfire. And then it was a blur... the couple... the couple... the couple.

"Amazing, isn't it Beyers?" Jim Andrews called, causing Steve to bang his knee on the steel bars.

He turned to see them waving from the handrail a few yards down. *How long had they been there?*, Steve wondered, uncomfortably. He gave them the thumbs up.

They were a little creepy, he decided. Barb was crazy to ask them anything.

"It is," Steve called back.

"You guys OK? We saw DTV. You were *right there*."

"We're OK." Steve said. He repeated it, mostly for himself, "Yeah, we're OK. Thanks. Where were you?"

"At home, expecting the worst. You *are* a Superstar DJ, Beyers. You are! Brunch *outside* on a Sunday morning!" Jim laughed, "How much did they pay you for that table?"

Jim put his arm around Jenny and they started back to their suite.

He turned, "Hey, you coming to the vigil?"

"Vigil?"

"Are you a Commie or what, Beyers? You with them? With the terroristas?" He laughed heartily. "Just kidding, buddy. Vigil at 7, around the fountain. It's some sort of tradition, they just had it on DTV. See you folks there?"

Steve nodded. *Yes. Yes, they would.* It would be good to get out. Otherwise they risked becoming prisoners in their own home.

"Who's it for?" Steve asked, hesitantly.

"Us," Jim replied. "The survivors."

Four hours later, with his family waiting outside on the walkway, Steve was locked in the bathroom and unable to flush the Happinol. He was stuck on how much his insurance company had paid for it—two bills—and only for the week's supply.

$25 a day. It was robbery.

But he knew the score. He oversaw the company's advertising and he knew what Persistent charged *them*. And they paid it. Happily. Probably because they were all Happinol-ed out of their minds, Steve chuckled.

The thing was, Steve and Barb also owned a few shares and the stock was rising nicely. Losing it on one side but gaining it on the other. That's life.

It wasn't just the money though... of course not. It was his health, his *sanity*, and the consequences could be serious. As serious as they got.

Right now, he felt OK. But tomorrow? And the next day? He still had a week to go and he'd only been off it two days. Yet if he was going to restart, he needed to do it as soon as possible.

A terse note from the prescribing DisasterLand psychologist had reminded him of the danger. *Potentially dangerous* was how he had worded it, and a follow-up appointment had been scheduled for Tuesday.

But now, in the disaster's fresh afterglow, Steve's desperation had somehow faded and he had a growing sense that this was a golden opportunity to prove his own self-reliance, his own inner strength and focus of mind.

Mind over mind. Commit to your commitment.

Yet once back home, would this desire still be manifest? Or would he slip easily back into old habits... it might be easy with a disaster, but what about real-life?

Steve dangled the opened bottle over the toilet.

To take or not to take. *That* was the question.

The question of the 21st century.

This wasn't his only problem: Happinol was also a controlled substance. If he "lost" this bottle, the second one in three days, at the very least it was cause for a great deal of suspicion. And he did have that follow-up coming.

No, he'd have to hold on to it, but that upped the stakes. It'd take that much more willpower to refuse. It would take a sustained effort, not one rash moment.

Fuck you Happinol, Steve thought, *I'm up for it.*

Steve turned and leaned into the mirror, staring into his own eyes. He was unsure of what he saw.

The good news was Maria had been by in the afternoon to pick up their laundry. Steve had asked about getting some beer and amazingly she said she could score him a six-pack before the end of the night. But it had cost him: $50 cash.

The laundry was already going to run $10 per person, delivered in 72 hours, paid up front. They were talking $90 for beer and laundry, plus a $15 tip.

That didn't include food and Maria had refused to say when—even if—Good Food would be reopening. Barb had pleaded for her to find something for them but Steve had only brought $200 in cash total, and now he'd spent almost three-quarters of it counting last night. After the vigil he'd have to hit an ATM and until he did, they'd have to rough it on food.

He didn't want to worry anyone.

As for the $50 beer, he'd get reimbursed by Persistent. If he could pull some business out of the week, or at least get a conference call scheduled, nothing would come out of his pocket at all. He'd be able to drink all the $50 beer he wanted.

Even without a deal, he might be saving Persistent money in the long run. If DisasterLand did what it claimed, if it renewed him, then the lower stress meant increased productivity. Soccer players have their feet, tennis players their serve. He had his mind and he had to protect it. The beer was essential to this end.

The Happinol, on the other hand, was an unknown. It might even be a danger.

Regardless, Maria's six pack would buy him some breathing room and get him through the night. Tomorrow was a new day and they'd hit Good Food when it reopened to replenish supplies—at more reasonable rates.

Steve caught himself with a laugh. That's where DisasterLand snared you. Take you to the brink, then let you go. Catch and release.

He dropped the Happinol back into his toiletries bag. Just to the brink.

Besides, if things got bad financially, Steve realized, really bad, the pills had to be worth *something*. A week's supply of *the* anti-depressant for those in-the-know?

Survival did funny things to people, Steve admitted to himself as he zipped up the bag. He flushed the toilet for effect and stepped out.

It was already well after eight.

Steve exited the suite to quite literally a breath of fresh air, confronted by one of the most inspirational sights ever to grace his being. A tiny galaxy spread out below him ringing the ruined village below.

Voices soared up, in unison, from the hundreds of guests assembled throughout the atrium,

> *"This little light of mine...*
> *I'm gonna let it shine... let it shine... let it shine..."*

Up and down the walkways and throughout the atrium floor, each figure had a tiny candle, a flickering light of hope illuminating the dangerous, dusky evening.

Steve joined the rest of his beaming family at the railing with a hug. DTV wasn't showing *any of this*!

"I *love* this song!" Barb whispered, taking Steve's hand. He squeezed.

Steve took a long, deep breath, willing the tension from his body. They'd tuned back in to DTV after Maria's visit, catching the tail end of *DL:Heroes*. It had wrapped up with the remarkable story of a brave DL:FireMan, a Captain, who had saved a disoriented family seconds before the first bomb only to disappear beneath the rubble. As the shocked family relived the riveting story in voice over, rescue crews were shown scouring the debris with their dogs, racing against the clock in their search for signs of life. Multiple digs moved forward in promising locations, predicted by close scrutiny of the surveillance footage. Expert interviews explained this.

A roar had spread throughout the crew as Clint was pulled from of the rubble, dazed and kept alive by his oxygen tank. It had been nothing short of a miracle.

He had been quickly evacuated to Good Health and a rapid recovery was now underway. An invitation was extended for guests to visit him—and all of the *Heroes* they'd seen on DTV—to personally wish those who had lost the most a speedy recovery, to *Make a Difference*.

Barb vowed they would.

But as the sun continued to set, the stoic positivity of *DL:Heroes* had given way to the dark menace of constantly evolving updates revealing more and more of the latest on the terrorist threat. Most, after all, were still at large.

Ridiculously, Steve now realized, they had bought it, awaiting each new piece of information from the investigation on the edge of their seat. It became an evening of non-stop psychological rubber-necking, and it had taken its toll.

They had gradually slipped into despair, too slowly to notice like a suicide victim bleeding to death in a warm bath. They had grown more and more tense, feeling more and more trapped, until they had practically been cowering in front of the HDTV. It had taken a Herculean effort just to open their front door and step out.

Steve now felt ashamed. There was a lesson in there, somewhere, and he wondered how many families were still trapped inside the tower, held to their couches by chains of light.

Simultaneously, awe-inspiring footage revealing the true scope of the disaster had gradually been trickled out, yet none of the disaster's victims were ever shown. As a result the uncertainly which had plagued the Beyers throughout the day only intensified. DisasterLand's tricky editing had left the undeniable impression that something had purposefully been left out—because it had been.

And the Beyers knew it. They had been there, they had seen it all—the wounds, the carnage, the broken lives—and it had all been edited out. Something was not being told.

This worried them, all of them, profoundly.

The one man they did show, over and over, was in fact the terrorist and his corpse was leading the guards to their first clues. DTV zoomed into the Kentucky driver's license found on his person, his dark image filled with inner turmoil and millennial madness.

Barb's eyes filled with tears. "He's a baby!" she sniffed.

"Mom, he's older than we are," Sarah pointed out.

"I ain't no baby, yo," Pete clarified.

Steve tried to calm her. "Honey, it doesn't matter... it's a..."

"But he's so young!"

"Mom, he's an actor. It's not like he's really dead or something. Or even really a terrorist."

"He looked dead."

"Of course he looked dead. That's his job!"

The argument had woken them from the nightmare and they were shocked to find it was already after eight. A split second of bravery and they were free.

Now, out on the walkway, Steve began to focus on the handmade signs raised over the crowd below:

Detroit for Peace

Panora, Iowa loves our Heroes

Goddess Bless America

Hit 'Em Where It Hurts

With a cold chill, Steve realized it was the perfect time for another attack. He checked his own walkway nervously and returned a woman's tense glance. Just contemplating an attack's effects on crowd of this size would be enough to send them rushing back into their suite.

"Honey, let's go," Barb was playfully pushing him towards the elevator.

Steve stuttered. There were several security guards at the elevator, scanning the guests' D-PAKs for ID. Below, armed guards were stationed in front of Good Food, extending all the way across the elevators to Good Health and beyond. Security guards were literally ringing the atrium.

He wasn't sure which he disliked more: the threat of the terrorists or the overwhelming presence of the guards around them. In any case, he didn't feel particularly reassured.

And, to make matters worse, it didn't look like Good Food was reopening any time soon.

To Steve, the whole thing seemed slightly odd. They were crowded into the elevator with other expectant families, an armed guard along for the ride.

His children silently eyed the man's weapon and Steve wondered: *wasn't this just a bit too much?*

What if the gun was loaded? And what if something went wrong?

Or was it indoctrination, preparing America for a 21st century police state? Hadn't Pete spoken—seriously—of an NSA-sponsored video game?

But as the doors opened and guests flooded out into the candle-lit atrium, Steve's reservations melted away into the human warmth.

Someone handed them candles and the fire was passed from guest to guest as the family wound their way through the crowd.

> *"Oh, I'm gonna let it shine, let it shine...*
> *Let It Shine... LET IT SHINE!"*

Introspective silence followed the applause, and the Beyers continued on, picking their way towards the ruins for the first time. As dark as the morning had been, the evening was bright and many faces were already damp with tears. Steve squeezed the family closer to the makeshift stage near the fountain, the atrium's center, interrupting Sarah and Pete's candle fight with a stern frown.

From somewhere in the distance, a lonely trio of voices rang out, slowly building.

> *"O beautiful, for spacious skies..."*

The tune spread almost instantly, magnificently,

> *"... for amber waves of grain..."*

Thirty-six hours earlier, this very spot had been the scene of Steve's embarrassment at the hands of DTV. Less than twelve hours earlier, it had been a horrific scene of remarkable devastation. Now, it was the epicenter of a heart-warming scene of emotional reconstruction.

A nearby security guard nodded to him: *Everything's under control, sir.* Steve nodded back.

The massive craters remained closely guarded, but little else of the devastation was off-limits. It was a miracle. Paths had been plowed through the waist-high piles of rubble, many following the original cobblestone streets which still remained intact.

Temporary flooring had been placed around the garden and the café, replacing what had been damaged and allowing guests unhindered access to the fountain and stage. The fountain, almost directly in the middle of the two massive craters, was working again at a trickle.

Barb pointed out that many of the children around them were wearing tiny little dove pins, obviously acquired from somewhere and for a price. Steve felt sure he'd know the specifics soon enough.

One sign said simply, *The Jones Against Terror*, held by a somewhat bookish family of three near the front.

> *"... and crown thy good with brotherhood...*
> *from sea to shi-ning sea!"*

More applause, now stronger. It faded to a natural stillness. Someone produced a guitar and a couple of chords were strummed, hesitantly.

A woman's voice rang out, pregnant with emotion and strong,

> *"Amazing grace...*
> *how sweet the sound..."*

She paused, letting the words dissipate into the farthest reaches of the atrium. DisasterLand was absolutely silent, the soft reverberation of her voice fading out gently. Tears fell as the rest of those present joined in,

> *"That saved a wretch like me...*
> *I once was lost, but now I'm found,*
> *was blind but now I see..."*

Steve caught the security guard singing along and the two of them shared a laugh.

> *"'Twas grace that taught my heart to fear...*
> *and grace that fear relieved.*
> *How precious did that grace appear...*
> *the hour I first believed..."*

The song continued with the entire atrium singing as one until the final refrain faded out. Another lone voice immediately took the baton, remarkable for its poignancy,

> *"I can see clearly now the rain is gone...*
> *I can see all obstacles in my way..."*

Sarah peeked up at the stage on her tiptoes and her eyes confirmed what her ears had heard. Neil flashed a smile to the crowd and continued on, effortlessly, stoically,

Smaug's guitarist now joining in with the drummer. Sarah's heart skipped.

With the chorus, the atrium again joined in. More and more guests were emerging from their suites and lining the walkways, admiring the atrium lit by the healing warmth of togetherness.

Steve and Barb were eyeing the crowd, feeling, for the first time in a long time, really part of something, something bigger than themselves, feeling the fragility of life itself and yes, the gift of being alive. They could tell others were feeling it as well. It shown in their eyes, a pure, warm-hearted healing.

DisasterLand's gravity had surely spared no one.

Across the vigil, a couple caught Steve's eye and they traded smiles. It was the honeymooners from Friday's entrance. He was behind her, arms around her in a bear hug. Tears were running down their cheeks.

Continuing to examine the flushed faces around him, Steve suddenly felt uncomfortable. It was all just a bit too... easy, wasn't it? People were almost too open, too enthusiastic. It seemed forced.

But he felt better than he'd felt in months, if not years. He truly did. Undeniably. A weight was off his shoulders, very literally. The massage yesterday had loosened him up, and this morning's trauma had awoken him from of his slumber.

The effect of the attack was still with him, the after-effects still lingering in his system. He felt alive. Perceptive. He felt human.

Why couldn't he just go with it?

He thought back to those moments, not even twelve hours ago, right here. How crystal his thinking, how definitive his instincts. When had he felt that way before? He knew the answer and it gnawed at the pit of his stomach: Africa.

And now he was another American sleepwalker. Another guy who goes to his job to feed his kids and pay his mortgage and get his family educated.

Steve breathed deeply, took in the fresh mountain air seasoned by the desert. It was so clear to him, now, but he hadn't noticed it before. He took another deep breath, squeezed his wife. She kissed him and shut her eyes.

Steve understood. It was a giant release. It was a rebirth. Since 9/11, the terrorism threat had been drilled into their heads so relentlessly, so effectively, that they were scared. Everyone was. Without even really knowing it.

And after years of this constant build-up—with no release—they were all on the verge of emotionally exploding. But they didn't even know it, nor where the exact source of this stress came from. But this morning, in a flash, it was gone.

The attack was the equivalent of an underground nuclear test... it was a controlled explosion. And it worked marvelously. He wished everyone on the planet could join him here. Together.

A lightness in the guests' spirits was palpable around him. There was an openness, a weightlessness. People sang out. Their eyes told the story: the cream was rising to the top.

> *"I think I can make it now the pain is gone...*
> *All of the bad feelings have disappeared..."*

The chorus returned, marvelously, as the song played out then soon faded, with guests lost in the rich, contemplative silence.

"Johnny Nash..." Neil whispered as a woman was being helped up onto the makeshift stage. From somewhere, a microphone appeared.

"In this morning's attack, my daughter broke her leg," she said, gathering strength. "She's an All-State Volleyball player, and she just had started the first practices of her senior year. We're scared... that..." she paused, pulling herself together, "... but we'll see it through. I'm here to ask you for a thought, or a prayer, or a visit to Good Health. Her name's Stephanie Hale."

The announcement hit the guests like a kidney punch. Steve had fooled himself into romanticizing the experience. DisasterLand, suddenly, was all-too-real. And they couldn't let themselves be tricked into complacency. Steve nodded to the family, to rally them, "That's why we stick together, kids."

She was helped down, replaced by a young man in his mid-20's. "My dad's in Good Health too... he had a heart-attack on the stairs climbing up. Turns out he has a rare heart condition his doctors never found... but here they did." The tears were falling down his cheeks. *"DisasterLand did! And because of that, he's recovering from the surgery that saved his life! I just want to say... God Bless DisasterLand!"*

An ear-splitting siren echoed throughout the atrium, interrupting the heart-wrenching stories and shattering the warm ocean of empathic tranquility.

Guests dropped, terrified, cowering under the sonic pressure.

The InfoTron flashed: **SECURITY RAID IMMINENT.**

Massive floodlights lit up the floor like a movie set, every shining detail revealed in HD clarity as the guests huddled, eyes fixed to the InfoTron. Fiercely, it blinked red.

Please clear the atrium for your safety:
Security raids commence in 15 minutes.

"Raids? Are they kidding?" Steve screamed. "What the hell did they have to do that for?"

"Come on, let's get upstairs," Barb took his hand, standing. "Come on kids."

Steve's voice only grew in volume. "No! Here we are, having a very nice moment, some genuine healing time and solace with our fellow guests, and now they're screwing with us again! *Why don't you just set off another bomb, assholes!*"

"*Steve, shhh!*"

Sarah and Peter joined the other nearby guests to stare at their father in awe. Above them, the message repeated, and a countdown soon began, *14:59, 14:58, 14:57...*

Families throughout the atrium were scampering prudently for the elevators but Steve was resolute. He was pissed. His family stood in front of him, mystified.

"I'm sorry honey. I... just don't get it. I mean, what are they raiding?"

"Let's just get home, OK?"

Uniformed guards were descending on the atrium like locusts, locking down the ruined village and leaving only one escape route open for the fleeing crowd: to the stairs and elevators. Barb and the kids dragged Steve away.

From the second floor security center, an officer was shouting orders through a bullhorn. "Code red! Elevators on express! First five stories walk! No elevator service one through five! Let's move it people! *MOVE!*"

The Beyers were hurriedly threaded through a channel of armed guards and into position at the end of the nervous line for the elevators. Steve checked his watch: impossibly, it was just after nine-thirty. It had been the longest day of his life.

Steve imagined a long soak in the hot tub to try to regain the mood of the vigil before it was lost for good. The morning shower had been ideal, but now he needed more. He needed therapy, on the cheap. Today had been difficult but Steve had a terrible feeling that tomorrow wasn't going to be any easier.

He examined the sealed plywood windows of Good Food in the distance and wondered what was happening inside. *They better be putting some food in there*, he thought, *or there's going to be trouble.*

His eyes soared to the pandemonium above as the clock continued its relentless countdown—*8:32.* In the midst of guests scuttling into the safety of their suites, Steve thought he glimpsed a trio of dark figures duck into one of the suites. But he couldn't be sure.

Sarah and Pete were mooing like cattle. Behind them, others took up the chorus.

Steve straightened. "Look, I'm sorry. I was wrong," he told his weary family. "No sense in getting carried away. It takes energy which we don't have. We've got to look ahead."

Barb hugged him as the kids continued mooing.

Rumor was spreading through the crowd that security had solid leads. They knew who the terrorists were and where they were hiding. Suites were about to be raided, and it could quickly get messy. Steve didn't like the sound of it.

Packing into the elevator, the family kept their eyes down for the vulnerable ascent to the heights. They were immensely relieved when the doors finally opened, depositing them on the nineteenth floor just as the InfoTron was launching into the final minute's countdown.

The Beyers hurried to their front door, which opened on cue, but Pete went the other direction. He placed himself at the railing, looking out over the evacuated atrium.

Another tone rang out, this time a short series of bursts.

"They're starting, DJs!" Pete yelled as the lights over DisasterLand cut out. It was black, pitch black, and Steve hurried to his son.

"Peter, get in here!" Barb screamed.

"DJ, can we watch?"

"On TV."

"Come on!"

Steve grabbed Pete's shoulder.

The InfoTron was blinking—*00:00*.

SWAT teams burst onto every floor from the single white doors at the end of the each walkway. They were armed to the teeth, efficient beyond compare. Light beams shown from the tips of their rifles as they raced down the walkways in formation, mere shadows.

Separate units fanned out below, through the atrium and into the park, visible only because of the very tiny, but very precise light beams which preceded them.

Gunfire rang out.

Barb screamed.

And the family dove inside, breathlessly.

Elektra checked the timecode on the monitors: *on the money*.

Thirty minutes after the raids had launched, her shift was drawing to a close, right on page. Another day flawlessly executed, even with Clint's high-profile accident.

Elektra radioed Colin on the floor—'The Center of the Universe' as he called it—and received his approval almost instantly.

Nicole, the overnight director, was waiting patiently with her understudy on the couches and they rose in unison to take the reigns from Monica. Elektra took one final look around the circle of monitors overhead then formally signaled to the waiting masses on the radio, "That's it, boys and girls, that's a day-two first team wrap. *That's a wrap.* First team call tomorrow is one p.m. One p.m. See you then. Second team is up, *second team.*"

Nicole chimed in to greet her team and a wave of levity swept through the bridge as department heads were relieved by their assistants in a cascade of personnel.

A fourteen hour day, a tough one, but not brutal and that made for an enjoyable, if intense, time. Elektra hung her headset on her desk and high-fived 'Lexi who was off to prepare tomorrow's dailies with her compatriots in DTV. She then settled into the couch next to Greg for a much-needed drink.

They were allowed to leave the bridge instantly after the *all clear* and Elektra sometimes did. But on big days Elektra liked to linger for an hour or so to have a drink and decompress. Going straight back to a quiet home, particularly considering Clint's newly-imposed absence, was just too much of a shock to the system. A girl could get the bends.

There was also the chance with a script like this that the low-level action happening for the next few hours could trigger some sort of larger incident. After a few drinks and a meal, they'd all have a much better idea of how the night might flow.

"Who's joining us for Thai?" Elektra called out to the bridge and the usual suspects returned their requests. By this point she could predict the order to within a Pad See-Eu or two, but it was always her policy to check.

At DisasterLand, rituals and superstitions weren't only for Elektra—the whole park was full of them. Perhaps it was the knife's edge intensity or the impossibly high stakes, but the staff clung, almost absurdly, to routine—and one of the most enjoyable was imminent.

"You're going to need this," Shae said, joining Elektra and Greg on the mount. He presented them with a single-malt Scotch of impossible pedigree: a 1974 bottle of Isle of Nesse.

"That's exactly right," Elektra laughed, "We are."

Glasses were retrieved as the pace of arriving department heads picked up to join in the toast.

Elektra was the first to receive the libation in salute. She sipped, cautiously, then hastily swallowed the ball of fire which detonated in her stomach and filled her with warmth. Her head tingled.

"Nice, hunh?" Shae asked with a proud smile.

"Yep," Elektra rasped. "Peaty."

As the glasses emptied, Elektra picked up the phone and ordered from the Thai restaurant on the floor, now seemingly abandoned. After this order, Elektra knew, they'd shut down until the weekend.

Molly ducked through the crowd and onto the couch next to Elektra. They hugged.

"I saw you ordering."

Elektra nodded. "You're covered. Every minute counts you know."

They had instigated the tradition together, on opening night almost one year ago, based solely on necessity. As the first night drew to a close, they were starving, buzzing and lonely. It had rapidly grown into an institution.

"I need a beer," Molly said. "Long day. Make-up call at seven this morning."

"How's the labyrinth?"

"Hopping. The mood is brilliant. Gonna be a big night in the FunHouse. What are you drinking?"

"Scotch." Elektra pointed to the bottle. "Greg says it's four hundred a bottle or something."

"You're kidding."

"No. 1974 limited run. Isle of Nesse."

"Hit me."

Elektra poured a glass while Molly settled in to hold court. "Speak to Clint?"

"Only to tell him I'm dropping off his sides."

"Watch it."

"Come on, Mol, of course I will."

Elektra handed her the Scotch.

"To vacation!" Molly laughed.

"Speaking of which," Elektra whispered, "what are your plans?"

"I haven't decided. But right now I have a strong desire to feel sunlight on my titties."

"And..." Elektra laughed. "...when do you not?"

Molly acknowledged the point with a hard-won smile, "You?"

"No idea."

"Let's Thelma & Louise."

It was one thing partying in the bubble-world of DisasterLand, quite another in the big bad world-at-large. They were best friends here, but they'd never even shared a drink outside.

Elektra took another long sip of Scotch. Yes, that needed to be rectified. They'd probably get in a fair amount of trouble, but the odds were strongly that it'd be worth it.

"Deal," Elektra agreed, and they clinked glasses. It was just what they needed to cement their relationship and Elektra could surely score some beauty tips on the sly from a pro. That alone was well worth whatever jail-time they might incur.

Elektra stuck her head into the shiny white room with revulsion. She hated hospitals.

The tell-tale moans of softcore flipped off as Elektra stepped in to the rustling of sheets.

"You can't watch that Clint. What if I was a guest?" Elektra shut the door behind her. And, on instinct, locked it.

"It's late-night cable, E. What do you expect?" Clint put out his arms and Elektra gave him a reserved hug and kiss on the cheek. An enormous ice pack was strapped to his knee.

Her face scrunched, "You OK?"

"Been better. Drinking Scotch?"

"A little."

"Bullshit. You're tanked."

Elektra placed the flowers she'd brought on the nightstand to calm herself, adding to the ever-growing display which had spread to every corner of his room.

It was Elektra's habit to visit Good Health a few times a show, undercover, not just to see her own cast and crew but guests as well. She always brought flowers for all, doing her part to *Make A Difference*. The trip was another thing she could always draw on to check her head.

She flopped into the chair across the room, Clint's last words reminding her why they no longer shared a bed.

"So what's the diagnosis?"

"Fucked it up."

"And?"

"They're going to do more tests tomorrow. Might have to have arthroscopic surgery after the show."

She was finding the whole thing more difficult than she had expected, and as hormones swirled she wished she'd had the clarity not to come. *Thanks, alcohol.*

"Why don't you sit over here, E. I can barely fucking see you over there."

"Your eyes fucked up too? I don't trust you."

"You don't trust me what?"

Elektra shook her head, let the moment settle, "I wish you hadn't gone on. It was stupid."

Clint moaned. "Please."

Elektra stared.

"E, you don't get it, do you? Now I've got the opportunity of a lifetime! I'm starring! It's better than ever. You got my sides, right?"

Elektra nodded. She couldn't deny it.

After her lunch with Tuck in the canteen, Elektra had joined the writer's meeting in DmZ, the location chosen for the increased intimacy with the floor. She quickly found herself torn.

Clint's role would be diminished in many ways practically, but realistically he was being promoted almost to the center of attention.

His role as mythic hero, defending the innocents from the forces of evil, once born would now be carefully cultivated in the coming days. The end result wasn't yet entirely clear but Elektra had a cynical hunch girls would be involved.

The good news was a more compelling sub-plot couldn't have been created, and it was opening up another vista of narrative experimentation that had previously been hidden.

It could be a keeper.

"I would have thought you'd have been proud of me," Clint continued.

"I am, Clint. I am. You deserve it. But..." Elektra shook her head. "... Just don't do anything stupid. Please."

"What are you saying?"

"We're counting on you, that's all. You're right. You've got more responsibility than you've ever had. Use it wisely."

She stood, fidgeting, and crossed to the door, "That's all."

"Please don't go."

Elektra stopped, a terrible sense of foreboding growing in her chest, another quite different feeling rising in her loins.

"Come on, E, spend ten minutes with me. All I've had all evening are visits from mothers who want to hook me up with their daughters."

"You're lying."

"I'm not."

"You are."

"I'm *not!*"

Elektra moved to straighten the flower display. Someone had been here, that was for sure, lots of someones, and attack or no attack they saw fit to buy flowers in the shop next to reception.

Elektra picked through the cards in disgust, finding several phone numbers inside.

"Was DTV here?"

"All rock star all day. Kids lining up for autographs, permagrin, the whole nine."

"That's good." Elektra sighed and put the cards down.

"How 'bout you?" Clint asked. "How are you?"

"It was tough. Seeing the video," Elektra turned to him.

"See? You still love me." Clint smiled.

"Clint, I'm not sure I ever loved you. But you were a decent shag and we had some good times together. But seeing you almost blown to bits was tough. OK?"

"Sorry. I understand."

"Gee, when did you learn to apologize? Did those mothers teach you something?"

"Fuck off."

"Look, I've got to go."

"Been a long day for both of us."

Elektra grabbed Clint's sides out of her backpack.

Clint took them hungrily, flipping through the script. "Not many scenes."

"That's just tomorrow's. We're doing some polling in the morning. You're gunning for spokesman... *if* you're back on your feet by the end of the week."

"You're joking."

"No. They're prepared to rewrite."

"Yes!" Clint clenched his arms overhead, then witnessed Elektra's hesitation. "What, afraid rabid nymphomaniacs are going to break down my door?"

Elektra wasn't the jealous type, but in moments of weakness everything was up for grabs. It was all too fresh, and... *look, maybe she did have a soft spot for him, OK?*

"Come here," Clint said.

Elektra approached his bedside, warily taking his hand. He reached up, took her neck, and brought her lips down to his.

They shared a kiss, and Elektra rested her head on his chest. She took in his scent.

Moments later, as she straddled his face with panties lying across the room, she was glad she had locked the door.

Shae scuttled across the deserted atrium floor, his guard's uniform blending into the dark night. Soon, he was safely lost amidst the reconstruction crews.

Across the walkways above, a delicate ballet of lights played off the glass as SWAT teams continued their work. The raids deftly formed a psychological barrier between the guests and the floor, allowing the crew below to work in much-needed peace.

Shae slowed as he neared the focus of his attention: an intense young man in a garish, reflective vest leaning against a pile of rubble and smoking a cigarette. The DisasterLand symbol was prominently fixed to his hardhat, a flak jacket lay unashamedly beneath his workman's uniform.

"Alex."

The man turned, eyes squinting. He broke into a smile. "Evenin' boss."

"How you doing, sir? Just thought I'd check in."

DisasterLand's Art Director laughed, "Doing well. Crew is on schedule and happy to be doing some fine work."

"Yes, I can see..."

Gunfire interrupted him, ringing out from the tower above.

Shae took in the space around him. With the village almost completely reduced to rubble, the fish-eye vastness of the atrium was viscerally palpable.

"Everything OK?" Alex asked.

"More than OK. I'm just out to catch a breather. Got time for a walk?"

"Sure."

They picked their way along the shadows of rubble-strewn walls until they reached a newly-recovered ruined cobblestone street. It lead deeper into the village's center.

The clanging of the small construction crews echoed eerily through the cavernous space. Shae breathed in the crystalline air. Twenty-five stories above, the vents still lay open to fully vent the day's pollution.

"You really get a sense of the desert here at night, hunh? Just incredible."

"It's empty."

"Physically yes. But you can *feel* them, no? The guests? They're still here. They're still at the vigil."

Alex smiled and they slowed. This was what Shae had come for.

"If you listen," Shae continued, whispering, "this place speaks."

After the day's journey of trauma and healing, the stillness was almost occult in nature. Outside, the mountains were just visible, while behind them the park glowed blue from the nearly-full summer moon. DisasterLand's nature—amorphous, mercurial—impregnated the night.

Shae's mind wandered. All of the action, the stories, the intense emotions of those who have graced this space... they *did* charge it with an energy. And now, with those people gone, only this energy remained. It wasn't so different from some theories of ghosts, Shae knew.

Bottom line: the atrium had power. No one, not even the most skeptical, could deny it. If only there was a way of harnessing it, of gently nurturing guests safely into the space to witness its magic...

The writers had been at work on the idea for months, but hadn't yet come up with anything satisfactory. In truth, the timing couldn't be worse—inevitably it ran against the grain of the story.

Shae returned his focus to Alex's crew. Around him, they were diligently making sure the village was safe for the days ahead, while assuring it still looked like a ruined village. Subtly shifting what needed to be shifted, rebuilding what needed to be rebuilt, all while meticulously maintaining—even accentuating—the site's compelling authenticity.

In the distance, a welder was scarring a new piece of flooring, deliberately damaging it as reminder of the morning's tragedy. No stone would be left unturned in pursuit of psychological effect.

Alex's radio crackled to life to request his presence and Shae bid him a quick farewell with a friendly, military-style salute. Alex was soon lost amidst the piles of rubble.

Shae would have give anything to bring his board here, but it was, again, too much of a gamble. In a few hours they'd be gone their business accomplished. They too were about to leave DisasterLand, transformed.

Shae cautiously meandered back to the tower's base. He paused in front of the windows of Good Health, still wide open and true to their policy.

It seemed bizarre to some, but Good Health was the heart and soul of DisasterLand, literally, the life-giving force. It was the foundation, the safety net. It reassured guests in difficult times to know help was close-by, to know injured loved-ones were close. To know they were in good hands.

Good Health was the glue which bound them all together—cast, crew and guests. If this trust broke, DisasterLand would crumble. Overnight.

Shae offered a respectful wave to the staff and patients inside, who returned an appreciative response.

It was time to bid the board goodbye.

Elektra had landed in DmZ for a quiet nightcap before heading home, needing to put the day in perspective.

That wouldn't happen again. In fact, she'd stay away from Clint for the rest of the show. What better excuse to move on?

She settled in at the bar, next to the elusive chemist responsible for DisasterLand's lifelike biomatter. Blood, brains, arms, legs and more, Martin Elinwood made it happen. The son of one of Hollywood's most famous alchemists, Martin had declined to follow in his dad's footsteps when he bought Shae's pitch of the uncompromising world of immersive live production completely.

He was a natural. His blood looked like blood, felt like blood, smelled like blood and, perhaps most importantly, it even tasted like blood. But it wasn't blood. Not... exactly. Only he, DisasterLand's attorneys and the United States of America patent office knew just what created its mysterious authenticity, making this one of the hottest topics of debate amongst bored staff.

The miracle was, it was completely safe. A few insane crew members had even concocted special Bloody Marys at the Christmas party with his blessing, and were no worse off for it.

His body parts were a whole other thing entirely.

"What brings a nice boy like you to a place like this?" Elektra asked, saddling up to him.

Martin was wasted.

"I should ask you the same question."

"I'm not a boy."

Elektra took off her track top and threw it down next to her bag, offering proof. Martin agreed, eyes lingering on her T-shirt.

It was all too easy, she felt, like a sport fisherman heading out to battle a swordfish and realizing when he got to the open sea the fish was waiting on a floating grill, already having committed a bloody suicide by filleting its own body. All the guy needed to do was add some fire.

What was she doing anyway? Boosting her confidence?

Elektra scanned DmZ. A few crew members were quietly sharing subdued drinks at the tables behind them. Nick was there again, with two other bands Elektra didn't recognize. *Smaug?*

Martin filled the silence, perhaps sensing the moment's evaporation, "So tell me about the film on your shirt."

"*Tokyo Drifter.* Seijin Suzuki," Elektra replied. "It's a ridiculously cool 60's Yakuza noir. You know *Branded to Kill?* About a boxer with a rice fetish?"

Martin shook his head.

"You like Japanese cinema?"

He shrugged.

"Chinese? You know Hou Hsiao-hsien? Taiwanese? Tsai Ming-Liang?"

"I don't really watch that kind of stuff. I'm more mainstream, you know? More of a *Planet of the Apes* guy."

"Yeah, well, they're sort of, you know, poetic realism," Elektra took a sip of her drink and felt Martin's gaze on the back of her neck. She pictured a tidal wave of semen rushing towards her, threatening to drown her. She quashed the image in her mind.

She needed a beach.

Elektra turned, "So you ever make dicks?"

Martin stared.

"Or just focus on arms, legs, pieces of brain... that kind of thing?"

Martin finished his whisky, motioned for a refill, "Is this business or personal?"

Elektra was shocked to find herself blushing.

"Bit of both maybe," she lied.

"Are you asking me if I'm able or do you have a request?"

Elektra laughed. "No... I mean, I know you *can*, of course you *can*... I don't know why I'm asking this. *Do you?* I'm just wondering."

"I don't. I don't need the work. But a buddy of mine does. You know, guys buying their girlfriend's wedding presents, birthdays, that sort of thing. Makes a mint."

"You're telling me some dude clones his thing so his woman's never without?"

"Not some, lots."

Elektra wondered if she'd keep Clint's if he gave it to her. You know, *just to remember him by.* Maybe she could start collecting them, in her closet, like an Amazonian headhunter. All her old boyfriends' shrunken members in a trophy case? Who wouldn't love that?

"Does he do famous people?"

Martin shrugged. "He's a Hollywood effects guy. Probably."

"You think he could score me one? Just for a trophy? Someone... big?"

Martin stuttered, "I..."

Elektra laughed, "Sorry. Not big *big*, you know. I mean, not necessarily. Big *famous.* It's just for..."

"Sure. I might, but usually the molds are broken to prevent it. Part of the contract."

"I'd pay."

"I'll ask."

Elektra downed her Scotch in one go and stood. "Yeah. I think I'd like that." She really had to get home.

It was nearly two in the morning and Pete was up on sentinel duty, nibbling the DL:PowerStrip from his D-PAK and nervously riveted to the television. He was alone in the living room, skin crawling, his family sound asleep.

With the sound down and DTV's phosphors dancing across the opposite wall, Pete felt like he was camping in a remote and terrifying wilderness of the future, where the prehistorical crackling fire was replaced by the frames-per-second flickering of the HDTV.

The television gave no literal warmth, nor mysterious spirit, no calling of the primal. But Pete couldn't turn it off. In a very real way, even though it terrorized him, it also comforted him. And he needed it.

Chaos still lay just beyond the periphery of the "fire", and the thought of terrorists nearby—maybe even next door—had long ago became too much for him to handle. The sound of boots pounding the walkway had echoed all night long and his head ached.

The night had begun with a cascading series of dramatic, multi-floor raids which had kept the family riveted to the television. These had accelerated, rapidly growing in intensity, in ferocity, until the gunfire had become almost constant.

Then, as quickly as they had begun, the raids had ended. It was as if DisasterLand's security had reached a dead end. But the raids had yielded fruit.

Based on follow-ups on information retrieved from the dead terrorist's body and a diligent surveillance analysis of his movements since Friday, guards had raided one suite down on seven which, though empty, had revealed important clues, leading to other raids throughout the night. Finally, they had struck gold: a terrorist was discovered in hiding on the fifteenth floor, actually in the act of making a bomb when security arrived!

That was Pete's favorite part: the *bust*. It had been magnificently captured on DTV and the replays still excited him. The fearsome firefight had resulted in the injury of two security guards who would be taking visitors on Tuesday. It was clear from the brief images of the suite that this was a big one. It was some sort of terrorist nexus, some sort of *lair*. Consecutive replays through the night offered new details, more pieces of the puzzle.

The first live terrorist had been taken into custody, and she was reported to be talking. In a few hours, DL:AM was expecting to make a big announcement.

Graceful images now filled the screen, beautiful images of last night's vigil, the thousand shining lights illuminating the atrium. *If you lose hope*, Pete was reminded, *you have nothing*.

It already seemed like days ago. After the vigil, Steve had retreated to the hot tub, but it hadn't achieved the desired effect. With the gunfire just outside their door, it was never quite as relaxing as he had imagined. To everyone's dismay he emerged angrier than he went in.

After Steve's effort, the family had taken turns in the hot tub, two people in the living room on DTV duty and a relay stationed in the bedroom in case of emergency.

For a few minutes each, they were able to forget where they were, lost at sea against the backdrop of stars, memories of the vigil still warming their hearts.

In the end, Good Food hadn't reopened and Maria hadn't delivered Steve's beer, which only added to the family's tension. There had been discussion on whether to eat dinner, but with only one full meal remaining and appetites in chaos, the decision was made to wait. They would eat it as a late brunch in the morning and hope that Good Food reopened soon.

Just after midnight the rest of his spent family had retired, leaving Pete on guard until two. Replays of the earlier events became more and more common, and the day's massive expenditures of energy had finally forced them under. Their exhaustion was complete.

Pete finished the DL:PowerStrip and hid the wrapper under the couch's cushion. *Be Alert!* a promo silently screamed at him, warning him that more devastating attacks could be coming.

Grainy live surveillance images, *Cops*-style, continued to flash over the screen but the evening seemed to be winding down. Guards had finally re-secured the complex.

Pete continued to watch the seconds tick by on DTV. It was ten 'til two, the end of his shift. Sarah was on duty until four, then Steve would supervise the sunrise. Pete would give her another couple of minutes. He was still very much awake, his stomach still growling, and he was feeling restless.

The energy bar hadn't gone down well and he wanted to walk it off. He thought about turning off the TV, but his dad had already woken up twice and wanted updates.

Pete got up, making his way through the dark kitchen and on to the front door. Leaning against it, he heard nothing.

Exhaling, he pushed the button and the door slid open with a *whoosh*. He'd only be out for a minute.

Pete stood at the railing and stared down at the atrium, now mostly darkened.

Words eluded him. It was *doper than dope, wickeder than wicked*. It was one of the most amazing things he'd ever seen, and no one—*no one*—would believe him. He was dying for a video camera.

The work lights, still on, created a dim, shadowy scene of destruction that his tired mind only intensified. He told himself it was all a fake, but it wasn't convincing. He could almost sense the ghosts of those who had been lost.

Further on, in the distance, in the presence of the dark, wild park, his imagination wandered.

A door slid open behind him and Pete spun, his heart almost bursting through his chest. Sarah was there, anxious.

She saw him, relief spreading across her face. "There you are."

"Is dad up?" Pete asked, nervously.

"No. What are you doing?"

"Creepin' while you sleepin'."

Sarah stared.

"And thinkin'," Pete added.

"About what?"

"Stuff."

Sarah ducked out, joining him at the rail.

"Wow... it's beautiful."

"If dad catches us we smelt smoke," Pete whispered.

She smiled, "That's cool."

Pete was happy she liked the idea. He pointed, "They've fixed the holes."

"I can't believe all those shops are gone."

"Yeah, it's weird."

They sat together, in silence.

"Sarah, can I have your room? At home?"

"Pete..."

"What?"

"So that's what you've been thinking about?"

"We could swap," he continued. "Yours is so much bigger, Spanks. You won't even be using it."

"Let me think about it."

Pete aped their mom's often-heard teary-eyed voice, "Our little girl... in college. I don't believe it!"

Sarah slapped him.

They watched as the last few workmen below shared a smoke, their distant laughter echoing through the atrium.

"Are you going to see Neil again?" Pete asked.

Sarah nodded. "I hope so."

"Really?"

"Yeah. That wasn't his fault."

"I liked them. Smaug's a cool name."

"He's gonna give me a CD of the show last night. DisasterLand's going to release it."

"Where's he live?"

"Brooklyn."

"No shit? Y'alls is gonna be neighbors."

Sarah smiled, "It's..."

Pete grabbed her shoulder. Below, on thirteen, two men in blue coveralls stepped out of the elevator, determinedly. They headed away from the kids, towards the white elevator.

They each carried duffle bags and one even seemed to be talking to himself... or even *on a headset*!

The kids watched silently as they stopped in front of a suite and knocked. The door slid open and the men stepped inside. A dark figure stepped out to check if the men had been followed.

As his gaze rose to the walkways above, Sarah squealed and Pete froze. They'd been spotted. A rifle was leveled at them.

Pete and Sarah slowly raised their hands.

"Back inside! It's not safe!" the man yelled from below.

They tried to move, but both were frozen stiff in fear. They didn't want to respond, didn't want to wake their dad. A tear dropped down Sarah's cheek.

The man let off a burst of fire which echoed through the atrium as holes exploded into the walls behind their heads.

Sarah swallowed a scream. Like two startled rats, the kids scurried inside.

MONDAY

It was just before six and Steve was in the kitchen, nervously anticipating DL:AM's morning briefing. The scent of brewing coffee filled the air.

Considering the night's swirling drama and his own troubled sleep, Steve felt remarkably calm. With the chance discovery of fresh coffee in the freezer, the day suddenly held promise and his mood had rebounded. Good Food was bound to reopen and by evening their current lack of food would be a long-forgotten joke. And this time, they wouldn't make the same mistake twice: they'd stock up no matter what.

His thoughts trailed off to the previous morning, how innocently it too had began, how little they had anticipated the devastation. Would they be surprised again?

No, surely not. With no village, nothing worse was even *possible*.

Regroup and stick it out, he thought. *This is where we come together, where bonds are forged that will last the rest of our lives.*

Steve yawned, scratching his head, then leaned over the counter and rubbed his puffy eyes. It wasn't a bad night, exactly, and in some ways it had even been fun. Like watching an all-night action movie.

Three down, six more to go.

Perhaps the night had reminded him of the summer nights back home spent watching storm updates, maybe it was the smell of brewing coffee, but suddenly and powerfully Steve was overwhelmed by the relief of not being stuck in Monday morning rush-hour traffic.

Right now, he knew, trucks, vans and SUVs were jockeying for position as they made use of their power and size, all racing ahead at well over the speed limits. Drivers were darting in and out of traffic while eating breakfast (*breakfast...*), putting on makeup and chatting obliviously on their cell phones, sacrificing lives just to arrive at their destination a couple of minutes earlier.

Steve wished he could prescribe DisasterLand for all of them. America *needed* DisasterLand. It was psychological nourishment. It truly was. And he was already stronger for it.

Yes. With a beautiful family, a killer view and a hot tub from which to appreciate it all, the coming week was certainly destined to render his Happinol unnecessary. Despite having no food, despite having no beer, despite exposing his children to the most horrific thing he had ever witnessed, these facts, in the end, would make it all worthwhile.

What else had been weighing him down? How many other things did he accept as being "facts of life" and not tried to change or avoid? He was going to figure that out. That was his *real* mission this week and he would see it through. Fear feeds on fear, unhappiness creates unhappiness, a snake eating its tail.

The brewing had gurgled to a stop and Steve rose to pour a cup. He sniffed. *Wow.* And sipped. *Yes.*

At least we have good coffee, Steve thought. Fair trade *and* organic. *Fuck you, terrorists!* He kicked the air, wincing in pain. Steve sat down heavily at the kitchen table, rubbing his hamstring.

With the disaster behind them, it was time for Steve to focus, to GET US IN as Dick had said. Another recon at the pharmacy was probably in order, as well as a little chat with his psychologist tomorrow. These were both good places to start. His thinking clear, he would pounce.

Steve made his way to the couch, relishing the tiny crack of sunlight on the carpet underneath the closed bedroom door. Again, the sun's mere presence forced all of the night's insecurities back into the cracks from whence they came.

Steve flicked on the HDTV just the DL:AM title sequence began. He turned up the sound.

The Long, Dark Night, DTV announced, *Anatomy of Terror*.

Steve chuckled.

Pete emerged moments later, rubbing his sleep-swollen eyes.

"You're up early," Steve said, making way for his son on the couch.

"Has it started DJ?" Pete asked, yawning.

"You're just in time."

Pete plopped down heavily as DTV's logo spun with gravity, morphing as the music peaked definitively.

DTV: The Truth.

Clint's image appeared, soft-focus and bright in the halls of Good Health. He hobbled forward, on crutches, with a restrained smile, "I'm Clint Lewis, FireMan here at DisasterLand."

The image cut to grainy action footage of Clint selflessly clearing guests in the midst of chaos just before the bomb. Then, suddenly, he drops in pain.

The living room speakers roared with sub-bass as Clint inched across the cobblestone street to safety, determination in his eye, bravely dragging his injured leg uselessly behind him.

"Those of us injured in the line of duty are unlucky," he continued, "but those injured by accident are the ones who need your help. Take some time out of your schedule to visit those less fortunate, those just a little less lucky than you."

Returning to Good Health and tighter now, Clint's face appeared gentle but committed. "When you can, visit Good Health. *You'll make a difference.*"

He pointed towards the camera as it nudged in to catch his wink. The lens poetically caught a flare.

"Please... *make a difference,*" Clint urged again with a tender smile.

The music roared back, exploding in finale.

DTV: Making A Difference.

"Son, don't let your mom hear about that. You'll never leave."

"Right, DJ."

DL:AM faded up in muted, hushed tones. A surveillance image materialized, eight figures and two picnic baskets, striding darkly across the park's sun-drenched Great Lawn, singly-focused on their gruesome mission. The pregnant juxtaposition sent shivers down Pete's spine.

"We were right there!" he whispered.

The eight reached the atrium and the image froze mid-stride. One by one six figures darkened, the word *WANTED* splashing across each in red.

Two were left and the image lingered. The next figure, a male, disappeared completely. *DISPATCHED,* DTV announced powerfully in green as the music drove home the point. The final figure, a woman carrying one of the baskets, resumed her walk, alone. *ARRESTED* scrolled across the bottom of the picture in yellow as the image closed in on her.

The host appeared, somberly, "Good Morning, DisasterLand. Dillon Becks here. After a long night of raids, I am pleased to announce much progress has been made. One terrorist has been captured, one has been killed. But six remain at large."

Steve shifted in his seat.

"Wow, DJ, should I wake the girls?" Pete asked, leaping from the couch, overcome by the power of the broadcast.

Steve shook his head. "No, they'll see it. Don't worry. It'll be replayed, trust me."

The lone woman's image dissolved, replaced by surveillance footage from minutes later inside the café: she drops her basket casually behind a trash bin and the four terrorists slip out the front door. Seconds later, a staff member notices the basket and hurries after them. Chaos erupts as the threat is realized and guests are frantically cleared out of the doomed space by the café's staff. Only seconds after the final guest is hurried to safety, a flash.

Then nothing.

DL:AM began working backwards through time, rapidly constructing an intricate timeline of the terrorist's movements before the massacre. Selected images of the tragedy itself were interspersed with the earlier surveillance footage, terrible reminders of the horror DisasterLand had witnessed and images which would become iconic in the coming days. Once again, however, they had been oddly sanitized, leaving Steve with an uneasy feeling in his stomach.

Pete, however, had stumbled upon DisasterLand's secret: with *Ghost's* technology the guards had something else to use, something infinitely better than these lame, low-res surveillance shots. If they wanted to find them, he knew, they could. *So why weren't they trying? Why weren't they using Ghost?*

It was solid proof that this was all fake—a show.

Pete rolled his eyes.

The sequence culminated in the terrorists' Friday night DisasterLand entrances, shown for the very first time. Their faces, obscured behind sunglasses, were frozen in close-up, carefree and glowing like eight Hollywood brats as they strode disdainfully down the red carpet in pairs.

"Ladies and gentlemen," Dillon Becks announced gravely, "DL:AM presents the faces of death. These are the faces of the killers at large. *Watch, learn, and act.*"

DL:AM's music peaked powerfully. At it climaxed, computer-enhanced images of the terrorist's faces were revealed, their sunglasses digitally removed. The images cycled slowly, imprinting themselves on the public's consciousness.

"Amongst the first suites raided last night were the four assigned to these couples. Remarkably, each one was completely unused."

The empty suites were shown, questions left unanswered.

"Investigators are struggling to learn how. And why," Dillon said, turning as the camera angle changed to a close-up, "Now, it's time to reveal something so shocking that an attempt has been made to bury it. I'm sorry to say, but it took the threat of a news strike to bring you the following report. Again, if you feel you might be adversely affected, please turn off now."

Steve and Pete hung on the edge of the couch as the now-familiar images of *the bust* were shown. The images were hand-held, shaky, and attempts at digital stabilization had only been partially successful.

It happened fast.

Guards stormed the terrorist's lair, interrupting her despicable work. She rose from the kitchen table, armed and firing. Two guards fell, writhing on the ground in pain. A flood of guards entered the suite, with the images rapidly progressing past the familiar. For the first time, footage of the raid's finale was being released, images that illustrated the making of what could have been a tragedy beyond comprehension.

The terrorist had been tackled, yet she persisted in her struggle for freedom, lashing out at her subduers. A guard produced a syringe and her struggle ended as she lost consciousness.

Impenetrable silence followed as the camera swept across the disturbing scene. The two wounded guards fought to raise themselves up. EMS crews were already arriving.

"Holy sh**!" one screamed, "This place is rigged!"

The camera swung, sickeningly.

"Where!" another guard screamed.

"There!" a downed guard pointed, to the underside of the kitchen table.

Two bomb specialists attacked the unmarked box only to find a broken tripwire had activated the timer. The guards stationed behind them urgently radioed to clear the neighboring suites.

"It's with mixed emotions that I admit," Dillon continued, "that in another twelve seconds, this bomb would have cost innumerable innocent lives, lives of guests and guards in several surrounding suites who never would have known what hit them. Many, many more would have been injured."

A computer-generated dramatization of the bomb's effects was shown, a terrible gaping hole in the tower's midsection.

The captured video returned, the specialists managing to freeze the countdown and dislodge the box. They raced out, through the front door, under a full armed escort.

"Animals," Steve sneered.

Evidence of the tripwire's placement was shown, an awful glimpse into the terrorist's twisted, diabolical thinking. It was clear: she had wanted to die and take as many as possible with her.

"Again," Dillon repeated, "I urge you: *Watch, learn, and act!*"

The repulsive suite was searched, methodically, for evidence which lay hidden in the clutter.

"Fortunately," the host continued, "this story has a happy ending. But for many families, including the Jacobs', whose suite this used to be, it was not without price."

There, bound and gagged in the hot tub, was a family of five, still conscious but pale and hungry.

"This evening, we will interview the family, together," Dillon Becks promised, "once they have put the past 24 hours of hell behind them. They are in Good Health recovering, but tomorrow morning they will be relocated to one of the empty suites. For their safety, the exact location will remain a secret."

"They look horrible, DJ." Pete said.

"Actors," Steve confirmed.

"You sure?" Pete asked. "They don't look like actors."

"Of course they don't."

The six wanted faces cycled by once again and the host resumed, deliberately.

"Friends, on behalf of DisasterLand, I encourage you, in fact I urge you, to visit this appalling lair of evil. The suite will be opened to the public at noon, on the fifteenth floor, after a complete forensic examination has been completed. We urge you to come and understand what we all face in this struggle, in the hopes that we all may remain free and do what is necessary to divert tragedy in the future. You will never forget it."

"DJ, we gotta go!"

"OK," Steve said absentmindedly, "Maybe this afternoon."

Something still didn't seem right to him.

"And be sure to catch today's paper," Dillon said, holding up the collector's edition for the cameras, "for all the current leads, exclusive terrorist biographies and a detailed timeline of the attacks as well as twelve pages of eyewitness photos and accounts."

He dropped the paper and the camera switched angles. He turned, smiling, while the music lightened.

"For the remainder of the hour," he continued, slickly changing tone, "we're going to focus on the remarkable scenes of resilience already blossoming throughout DisasterLand. Allan?"

Allan Biggs was back in the atrium, surrounded by a pack of smiling families. The unexpected flashback cost Steve his tranquility as he fought to restrain his emotions. In the background, armed guards still ringed the atrium.

"That's right, Dillon. I'm here at *Margarita Mortal*, which is set to reopen with many other restaurants at 11 and already a line is starting to form. Your name please?"

Pete nearly leapt out of his skin, "Did you hear that? There's food!"

Steve had. Perhaps the morning's optimism was warranted after all! Already the community seemed to be pulling together and maybe things really would be back to normal soon. Good Food couldn't be far behind.

"I'm Cindy Johnson, from Tallahassee."

"And why're you here, Cindy?"

"Our lifestyle is not negotiable. At eleven this morning, me and my husband are gonna to be sittin' right 'n there, downing two buckets of margaritas and a trough of nachos."

"Sounds good to me," Allan confirmed.

"Me to!" her son chipped in. "That'll teach 'em!"

"Well good luck, friends. Dillon, earlier I talked with some of the folks waiting in line at Good Food. They told a slightly different story, but no less remarkable for their firm defiance."

The sun was flirting with the mountains in the distance and Barb was down dog in their bedroom yogically acknowledging its arrival with a basic set of sun salutations.

Her legs felt better but that was only because the rest of her body felt worse—much worse. She had awkwardly fallen asleep on the couch hooked on the raids and despite eventually making it back to bed, her neck was screaming. Idiotic was too tame a word and she vowed it wouldn't happen again.

Steve cracked the door, "I didn't know you bought coffee honey!"

"I couldn't take any more chances with you," Barb said, gingerly rotating her hanging neck. "No more public incidents."

Steve entered the bedroom with his third cup of steaming coffee. He took a loud, thankful sip, "How'd you sleep?"

Barb followed through to up dog, exhaling heavily. She had started out with her D-PAK still on, but it was simply impossible. It now lay just in front of her nose. Steve eyed it with interest.

"Terrible." She worked her way back to down dog. "I kept seeing that couple, just when I'd finally get to sleep. You know, proposing. Then blown apart."

Steve stared, brow furrowed.

"What about you?" she asked.

"I was dreaming there'd be another attack."

"Thank God there wasn't."

"Yeah," Steve reflected. Amazing how absolutely inevitable it had felt in his darkest moments, leading to him awakening at even the littlest noises throughout the night.

Steve stepped past Barb and on towards the window, captivated once again by the valley's remarkable beauty. Yet now he was struck by an overwhelming sense of loneliness.

Barb brought herself into half-lotus. "I don't like it, Steve. I don't like the kids seeing things like that. People gunned down. Blown up. It's not positive. It's not healthy."

"I'm sure it's OK, honey. Somebody must have done tests." He scanned the horizon, now suspicious. Of what he didn't know.

"In fact," he continued, "I think it's absolutely necessary for this place to have any effect. It's the whole reason we're here. To be traumatized. Only then will we find our deepest selves."

"Are you out of your mind?" Barb stared at him.

Steve slurped, then turned back to face her.

"We have to embrace it, honey. Seriously. We've got to see *more*, not less." He went on. "We're all too conditioned by the constant violence surrounding us in our ordinary lives. I mean, it's relentless. We're a violent culture of extremists."

Barb watched him carefully.

"Besides," Steve continued. "It's over and done with." He smiled broadly.

Barb snorted. "You really think this is over?"

"I do," Steve announced, proudly. He sipped with extra force, as if to prove it.

"Well, I still don't like seeing it. Even if it is fake. Deep-down, where it counts, our minds didn't know it's not real. I don't care what anybody says. It felt real to me. I mean, look at us. Case in point."

Steve had to admit: they hadn't slept a wink and looked it.

Barb shut her eyes. "So we've got to protect ourselves. Just the way we wouldn't expose ourselves to any other virus or pathogen or whatever, I don't want to be exposed to these things and I don't want my children to either. We will not live in fear."

"Honey, that's my point! That's why we're *here*! *To live in fear!*"

"That's not why I'm here, Steve. I'm on vacation. And I'm not watching people getting blown up on my vacation."

"It's a little late now, Barb."

"I'm staying in."

"You're going to spend all week in this room?"

"As much as possible. I don't trust them."

Steve took another long, suspicious sip of his coffee and reflected on his wife's now-meditating figure.

However she came up with this one, Steve thought, she did have a point. But she was taking it way too far.

The attack *had* shaken her up pretty seriously, he knew. It had shaken all of them up. *But come on.*

Steve cleared his throat, "I was just about to take Pete out for a scout."

"You're not." Barb opened her eyes.

"Security's yellow. Restaurants are opening at eleven. I'm getting a caged-animal feeling."

"Finally! A moment of self-realization," she sneered. "How many cups of coffee have you had?"

Steve pouted.

"You're not going down. If you have to get out, go on the walkway. And don't take Pete."

Pete jumped in the room, "She's escaped! The terrorist! And she's heading this way!"

"Oh God!" gasped Barb. Steve eyed his son.

Pete cracked up, "Just kidding."

His parents frowned.

"Come on, DJs. You guys need to chill."

"And no more DTV. It stays off," Barb announced, firmly.

"Honey..."

"No more."

Steve walked over, gently took Pete's shoulder, and escorted him out of the room.

"What's wrong with mom, DJ? She's wiggin'!"

"Quiet, Spikers," Steve said shutting the door, "Your mother's attaining enlightenment."

Steve stared at the large pool of fresh blood on the walkway just outside their door. It trailed off mysteriously into the distance, towards the elevators, and begged many questions—all of which Steve felt were better left unanswered.

He had exited the suite slowly, with great care, covered by Peter who followed him out moments later. Pete had continued on around, cautiously, and now stood at the railing.

Steve remained staring at the pool, reminded that blood and glass did not mix. And this wasn't just a couple of drops. It was ounces. Many ounces. Ounces that someone, somewhere, was surely missing.

Steve looked past the glistening pool and down, through the walkway and onto the floor below, then further on to the floor below that. As far as he could see, they were spotless. He checked above him. Crystal clear.

Typical.

Steve was wondering if he shouldn't try to clean it up when Pete noticed the gears turning, "No way Superstar, that's disgusting!"

"We can't have a pool of blood in front of our door. People are going to track it everywhere. Your mother won't like it."

"That's *their* job, DJ. There could be weird diseases in it and stuff. I bet terrorists are really dirty."

"I'll call Maria."

Steve turned to head back into the suite and noticed the bullet holes above the door. Remembering the early morning warning, Pete slipped away to the railing and Steve found himself joining his son with a long, resigned breath.

"Some place, isn't it kid?"

"You said it."

Despite the unsettling reminders of the night's battle, with the sun rising ahead of them and the atrium once again bathed in the park's green glow, Steve's found his spirits lifted. *Yes, the worst was surely behind them.*

Something deep in him relaxed, as if for the first time.

"Heads up, Spikers."

"Right DJ."

Pete and Steve leaned out cautiously from the railing, examining the lines forming at restaurants around the atrium's periphery. They'd need to move fast if they wanted a place for lunch.

Directly below, a few construction workers were still at work in the village. Security guards were posted around the atrium, many determinedly fixed around the fountain, but their numbers were greatly reduced compared to last night's army.

Yes, Steve thought, *the wounds are healing.* The craters had been filled, the barricades removed, much of the rubble had been cleared and most of the floor had been completely re-opened—with the exception of the immediate area around the three hulking steel skeletons.

We're moving on, Steve told himself. *Moving forward. This is the togetherness part.*

"Raze or rebuild?" he asked his son. "Are they going to rebuild those buildings or tear them down?"

"Tear 'em down. For sure."

Steve didn't agree. Structurally, they looked to be in pretty good shape. And retail space was now at a premium.

"Money, Spikers. They rebuild, quickly. To have shops ready by the time we leave."

"Really?"

Steve chuckled. "I bet they do. It's part of the lesson, you know, moving on. Getting back to our cherished ways of life."

"Yeah, you're prolly right DJ."

Both wordlessly scanned the tower for the raids' aftermath, Steve with his binoculars.

"What time did the raids end?"

"After two, DJ."

"People were up late last night, hunh?"

"Yeah. That's prolly why it's so empty."

"How'd you like staying up late?"

"It was a'ight... Hey, look, DJ! There it is!"

Steve focused his binoculars farther down and across the walkway, to the opposite side of the elevators on the fifteenth floor. Pete was right. *The Lair*.

The door had been removed. Guards stood firmly at either side of the entrance, their automatic weapons at-the-ready, gently cradled in their arms. A die-hard crowd was already forming outside.

Steve monitored the suite, fascinated by these constant, profound reminders of the impermanence of life lying all around them, of how quickly it could all go.

Pete's memory was shimmering. After hours of DTV, nothing about the suite below seemed familiar. He started sliding up the walkway, trying to get a better view.

Neon caught his eye, reflecting off the glass.

"Wow, DJ, look! The café's open!" Pete pointed.

Steve followed Pete's outstretched arm to the elevators. Shockingly, his son was right. And it was almost empty!

"Buy you breakfast!" Steve called.

"Dope!" Pete took off. "Race you!"

Steve tried to catch up but it was useless—Pete won by a mile even though he let up at the end.

"Dad, they've got hot muffins!" Pete yelled as Steve slowed up with a grimace. "Three!"

"Get 'em all. With four fresh OJs," Steve was bent over, heaving. "And a water."

"You've got water!" Pete pointed to Steve's D-PAK.

"Right..." Steve said, huffing. He pulled out his bottle and inched inside.

"That'll be $42.50," the clerk repeated, slower, for the third time and with a completely straight face. Steve was sure he had misunderstood.

"Last muffins on the floor, sir, if not all of DisasterLand," he reiterated.

"Yeah, I guess we're pretty surprised you've got any at all."

"The most important thing sir, is a speedy return to our normal routines. That's what they say."

Pete offered to let his dad out of the deal, but Steve floated it with his remaining cash to anti-oxidize and soothe their frayed nerves. But now he now needed that ATM worse than ever.

"Can I get a receipt?" Steve asked.

"Sure." The clerk hit the button and tore off the receipt, handing it to Steve. He disappeared into the back room with the empty muffin tray.

Steve was glad. He jiggled the tip jar to fake his contribution and followed his son to a table.

Pete had grabbed the day's newspaper and they sat down in the front, alone, next to the large windows as the sun streamed in. A few other families were sitting further inside. Steve sensed uneasiness amongst the faces buried in the papers, lives desperate for normalcy.

The blueberry muffins turned out to be fresh, still warm, and damn good. Had they been any other way, Steve imagined, he would have gone ballistic. Confronting raw market forces in times of scarcity wasn't pretty.

An elderly couple had watched Steve and Pete with interest. "You don't mind sitting by the window?" asked the tanned gentleman finally. "You think that's smart?"

"Sorry?" Steve asked.

"Don't listen to him," his partner chimed in without removing her sunglasses. "He's always looking on the dark side."

"Always criticizing." The man folded his arms and huffed. "You folks were the lucky ones, I see," he added.

"Looks like it," Steve said, flashing a smile flecked by muffin. He wondered how their night was. He couldn't even imagine visiting DisasterLand at their age. Come to think of it, *what the hell were they doing here?*

"Those could be the last muffins in the whole place," the man continued.

"Yes," Steve agreed reluctantly. "That's what the kid said."

"I mean for the whole week, son."

Steve frowned.

"You don't think so?" the man asked.

"I guess I don't."

Pete nodded his agreement. "No *way* dude!"

"I hope you're right. But we'll be here at 4:30 tomorrow morning to get in line. Just in case."

"4:30?"

"No guarantees you know."

"No..."

Gunfire sounded disturbingly from the atrium. The elderly couple barely noticed. Steve wondered if they were partially deaf.

"Keep an eye, Spikers," he whispered.

"Just like the bread lines," the elderly man said, almost under his breath.

"Excuse me?" Steve asked, through gulps of orange juice.

"The bread lines. In the 30's. You ever heard of the depression, boy?"

Steve said he had.

"Well, I'm 78 and Mildred here is a sprightly 76."

Sprightly? If Mildred hadn't spoken Steve would have insisted she was stuffed.

"It's the tennis," she added and Steve choked back a laugh.

Arizona? Florida? They originated from warmth, from somewhere which facilitated a properly sun-inspired lifestyle and the careful cultivation of pastel spring sweaters.

"If you like muffins like we do, I'd get here early," the gentleman said with an air of resignation.

"And if you get here before us, let us in line," Mildred said without a smile.

Her husband nodded, "It'd only be fair, son."

"The bread lines?" Steve asked, to clarify.

"Just like 'em. You wait."

"I was kind of wondering that. Our fridge is almost empty..."

"You fucked up, son."

Steve straightened, avoiding Pete's look. Mildred nodded her agreement.

"You sure you're doing OK?" the gentleman asked.

Steve's temper was rising.

"We recognize you, you know," Mildred said.

"We saw you folks on the tee-vee. You were pretty lucky. All four of you," the gentleman added. "You got the worst of it."

"Yeah, I guess we were," Steve said. "But we're fine. Thanks."

He noticed others staring and joined Pete in examining the paper's front page. It was the captured hipster, a surveillance image gleaned from just before the bomb went off. Black leather, blonde hair with pink highlights, enormous white sunglasses concealing chiseled features, her image was gritty, deeply unnerving. A terrorist.

A red question mark was superimposed over her face, her eyes staring out with menace.

The headline screamed: *Terrorist Mute.*

Steve relaxed slightly with a satisfied smirk, glimpsing the familiar, reassuring narrative trajectory lying ahead: titillating investigation—dramatic captures—swift convictions.

A guard stepped into the café, scanning the tables slowly, eyeing the customers with a wary interest. "Those your bags?" he asked one family. They nodded and the guard slipped out.

"They don't know nothin'," said the same elderly gentleman, spitting.

Steve didn't respond.

"And insecurity's not good for muffins, if you catch my drift."

"May I ask you two a question?" Steve asked.

Mildred deferred. The gentleman finally grunted.

"What are you two doing here? I don't think you're exactly the... target demographic."

"Vacation."

"You had nothing better to do?"

"We're retired sociologists. We like observing people. So we thought we'd come here," Mildred said, her face emotionless.

Her husband leaned in. "You heard about the bomb, son?"

"Bomb?" Steve glanced at Pete, who shrugged.

"There was a bomb. At the vigil."

"There was?" Steve checked in with Pete. Pete shook his head subtly, his brow furrowed.

"That's why they cleared the floor."

"No, they cleared the floor for the raids."

"That's what they *said*. But we talked to a guard. At five this morning. While we were waiting for muffins."

"And?"

"He was there. They barely got it diffused in time. It would have been worse than the morning's attack."

The café had gone silent.

"If people hadn't been cleared," Mildred added, "it would have been a catastrophe. He said the whole floor would have gone up. Hundreds injured. Or dead."

"I don't understand..."

"It was in a backpack. A kid's butterfly-shaped backpack. That's what he said. And you know what else?

"What?"

"It wasn't them terrorists." The man was pointing at Pete's paper. Other guests were watching now, discreetly, peering over the tops of their papers.

"Come on," Steve laughed, nervously.

"Look, son, we're just telling you what we heard. I don't think no guard's gonna to be goin' around lying. He seemed scared. He wanted to do the right thing."

"But they wouldn't let him," Mildred added. "He told us not to tell anyone. But we're telling you."

"'Cause you got the kids."

"But why wouldn't that be on DTV?"

"You think they want to scare people, son? People paid a lot of money to come here."

Steve eyed his son. Pete's face was emotionless.

"Come on, son," Steve finally said. "We've got to get this muffin back to the girls."

Pete jumped up, "Yeah, DJ, let's roll!"

"Some gentleman you are. You only saved one muffin for two ladies?" Mildred was shocked.

Steve stood, "Thanks for the tip. Maybe we'll see you tomorrow morning?"

"Maybe. You take care now son, and keep those kids safe."

Pete and Steve hurried out with a wave.

"Old people are weird, DJ," Pete said.

Steve took a deep breath. He was happy to be moving again.

"A lot of them are, Spikers. But give 'em a break. They've seen a lot. The world isn't always a nice place."

"Never said it was."

"Did they say anything in that paper about Good Food?"

"Nope..."

"So how're we gonna get your mom down to the restaurants?"

Only a few steps later the InfoTron's piercing tone of danger rang out and gunfire erupted from walkways all around.

TAKE COVER, the InfoTron roared.

Bullets whizzed over their heads as warning shots were fired to clear the walkways.

Steve threw Pete to the ground and dove after him.

"Go!" Steve yelled and Pete obeyed.

The two pushed on, slithering down the glass walkway. Ten more doors, then nine. Steve's arms ached. Pete was extending his lead. "Hurry up dad!"

Steve was trying. He'd landed awkwardly and his left knee was giving him trouble. His vision blurred.

"Come on, dad! Hurry!"

Pete was nearly to the door.

"Get in! Get in!" Steve yelled.

The gunfire stopped. Screaming echoed in the distance.

Their door slid open and Pete rolled inside. Steve clawed his way to his feet, then followed, landing inside in a pile. Sweat was pouring down his face. He grabbed his knee.

The door slid shut.

Sarah stood in the entryway, shocked. Barb had raced out of the bedroom, her concern rapidly giving way to fury.

"That was pretty stupid, Steve. You saw what they said about heroes. And after I specifically..."

"What?"

"Don't you pay attention to anything?"

Pete handed his mom the juices and muffin. "We brought you breakfast," he said quietly. "We split one too."

"They're starting the raids again," Barb continued. "With new information."

Steve's thoughts were distant, his dreams for a long, satisfying lunch harshly fading so soon after conception. *And what about the Floridians?*

He stood, painfully making his way to the phone.

"Who are you calling?" Barb asked, as she finished her half of the muffin.

"Maria," he said. "There's blood on our doorstep."

"Lots," Pete added. This, he found, was unwelcome.

"And I want my beer. *Now.*"

While Steve and Pete were outside, Sarah had locked herself in her room and Barb had retreated, once again, to the hot tub.

Sarah had stood at the porthole, looking out over the atrium and imagining herself at sea. She might as well have been—it was impossible for her to see the village's ruins, but she imagined they were as empty as her view. If she had to spend a whole week inside this room, it might get ugly.

She plopped down on her bed, head in hands. No phone, no iPod, no e-mail. The overwhelming experiences of past few days were piling up against the locked dam of her desert island existence, and the pressure was finally beginning to affect her. She imagined herself going mad and starting a cult.

Relief from the onslaught of rapidly fermenting thoughts was desperately needed, and she was profoundly unsure of how to achieve it. How the hell was she going to download all this stuff? *Where?* And *to who?*

Certainly, not her family, not Neil... and all their communications devices were locked away somewhere to torture them. Sarah tried to remember when she'd last been away from her computer this long and with the stakes this high.

Never. Absolutely never.

She'd been slacking on her blog lately, but it was summer and there really wasn't much she could publicly write about without blowing her cover. The juicy action and saucy musings on the players and dynamics at her high school, both students and faculty, had earned her anonymous blog more than a little notice, drawing twice the hits of the school newspaper on a bad day.

Now here she was, with pages and pages of earth-shattering bits, and absolutely nowhere to put them. First off, she needed to clear her head.

Sarah grabbed her backpack from beneath the bed, zipping open the main compartment. She peeked in at her father's gift, reminding herself that it really existed, that it wasn't the result of some sort of bizarre dream in poor taste. It wasn't.

Someday, maybe, *hopefully*, she'd be able to disengage the silicone phenom from the thought of her father, but for right now there was no way that thing was going anywhere near her. That was just *too weird*.

Instead, she pulled out her journal and fingered it hesitantly. It was a last minute addition to the backpack, for emergency use only, but these were desperate times. It had been a sixteenth birthday present from her mother and still hadn't even been opened, but now seemed to be the time. She had no other choice.

Sarah grabbed a pen and shoved the backpack underneath her bed. She leaned back, happy at least to be in silence, happy to be alone and happy to be comfortable.

DisasterLand, August 2005. Head to explode. Data overload.

She rested the journal on her lap, letting her hand rest. She wondered if DisasterLand sold postcards.

Terrorists attacking, family insane, dad bought wigglers for the ladies, she wrote.

It was strange, the anonymity she had so expertly forged online was completely lost here. She realized that if her nosy brother, or her nosy mom, or anyone nosy at all found this journal, there'd be no excuses.

She'd have to be discreet.

But if she was discreet, then what was the point? The point was, she needed to vent. *Big time.* And this was adult stuff!

Neil. A sweet, radiant god of a poet, and I, too slow on the draw, too weak in the knees.

The tip of the pen against her lip, she added quickly, *Diseased?*

Her life was about to change, radically. Act Two was about to begin. New York City. The not-as-mean streets of Manhattan. And he would be there, across the river, waiting.

Longing to taste his nectar, she wrote.

She was angry with herself, angry that she had let him slip. Had he left? Last night? After anonymous sex with groupies?

She thought better of the last line, and started to scratch it out. Then stopped, and inserted *was* at the beginning. *Was longing...*

"Argh!" she said, too loudly. There was no reaction.

That was the whole damn point. Was she or wasn't she? Should she or shouldn't she? That's what she needed to find out. She needed help!

A tinge of jealousy shot through her. She wondered what the groupie was like. Probably dumb. Sarah was more to him than that, she knew. But now he was probably gone. And she didn't even know his last name.

She imagined the phone call to his record label. *Hi, I'm Sarah Beyers, I'm trying to get in touch with Neil from Smaug. I know he's a rock star, but I met him in the woods at DisasterLand. We didn't do it, but now I've changed my mind.*

Sarah closed her eyes. How was she going to last another day, let alone a whole week?

Surely Neil had more women than he knew what to do with... but in New York City who knew what was crawling around inside them? Why was she even bothering?

Sarah gagged. She'd already got the big city lecture from her gynecologist. Think of it as a Petri dish, she'd said. But they survived on *Sex and The City,* and so would she.

Love and death, she wrote. And repeated it: *Love and death.*

That's why they made condoms. No way he was ever scoring a blowjob from her. *No way.* She didn't suck rubber.

Sarah realized that she hadn't seen the morning's paper. That was her next step. That would tell her a lot.

She pulled out the backpack and found the one condom she had brought. She hadn't really imagined it ever being used, had only brought it to convince herself of her full adult potential. Having it along was practice in thinking ahead, in imagining the unimaginable. In positive thinking.

But not actual product testing.

Smaug. She wrote. *Pollution. Tolkien. The little black boy who wasn't so little.*

He had been cute... Wasn't the MC more exciting? Wasn't that the adventurous move?

She crossed her legs and squeezed as her thoughts drifted to the MC. Maybe he was the one she should go after? Maybe what she needed wasn't to write all this stupid stuff down, maybe what she needed was a good old-fashioned rebound. This was all just stupid.

Jungle fever in the desert, she added, laughing.

Sarah dropped the backpack, removing an imaginary phone. She pretended to dial.

A soliloquy. It was her only hope. If it was good enough for Hamlet, it was good enough for her.

"There I was," she began, "under a table and doused in my brother's urine..."

Gunfire.

Sarah hurried to the porthole just in time to catch her dad diving through their front door.

Hot set!

Upon waking, Elektra had three thoughts in vigorous succession.

One: she had gymnastically fucked Clint, her *ex-boyfriend*, on a noisy, unstable hospital bed in Good Health while the floor was technically live.

Two: the whole thing was quite likely sitting on a surveillance hard-drive somewhere which would have to be erased. *Immediately*. She could not allow those images to be leaked under any circumstances.

Three: she'd clearly been out of her mind. It had to have been the Scotch.

First order of business was to rock down to the security center in person for a diplomatically-worded plea to erase the evidence, with the possibility of bribes very real. No chances could be taken with a phone call. A few curious clicks of the mouse and things could get ugly fast.

Yet it was already possible that someone had seen the footage and word—and *image*—was rapidly spreading. Needless to say, Elektra was uniquely sensitive.

She rolled over to take in the Feed and turned up the sound. The morning raids had already begun and DTV's live images were being used almost exclusively. A few seconds in, Elektra was confident: on the surface at least, everything was under control. She relaxed, slightly.

Today would be DTV's day in the sun, with most of the daytime action choreographed specifically for television. Monika, DisasterLand's daytime director, was supervising micro-production while Elektra took boiler duty, ready to stoke or suffocate the social fires as necessary to hit the desired house temperature and build to phase two.

The day's script was a continuation of the night raids, giving families more of a chance to bond, both within and amongst themselves, for the increasingly difficult times ahead. All was proceeding according to script. Informal guest surveys were reporting the DL:AM show had been extremely effective.

The stage was being set.

Elektra turned down the sound and hurried out of bed. This was another, unforeseen positive to Clint's absence: viewing the Feed without hassle. One thing she certainly wasn't going to miss was Clint whining about the Feed.

Bottom line: she wasn't missing a plot point just because of him—or anyone else.

No matter what they were doing.

On impulse she grabbed her phone and rang the employee spa, booking an emergency pedicure in forty-five. Regardless of the outcome of her visit to the security center, she'd need it.

Racing out the door minutes later, Elektra had a breakthrough: *the pedicure as spiritual practice*.

During her vacation she would pen the bestseller.

"Elektra! This is a surprise—never seen you during a show before."

"Never had a reason, I guess."

Elektra stepped in, discreetly closing the office door while trying to hide the most unladylike sweat gushing out of her. Judging by the warm, if slightly surprised, response Elektra received, she wasn't world famous. Yet.

"Something tells me you've got a reason now," Carlos Rodriguez smiled. "Go ahead, shoot."

"What's the surveillance story on Good Health? Are we covering it?"

"Always."

"All of it?"

"Mostly. All public spaces are surveilled completely. No exceptions..."

"But the private rooms..."

"If a DisasterLand employee is in attendance, it triggers our cameras automatically. But otherwise, no. Privacy is preserved unless there is a specific request or legitimate reason to override those concerns."

Elektra's heart dropped. "So... room 153..."

Carlos brought up the log on his computer. "Clint's room."

"Yes..."

"He's an employee so the space is live 24/7."

Elektra felt her throat constricting. "Carlos..." she coughed.

"You OK?"

She heaved, "I'm going to need a favor."

"Anything, Elektra."

"No questions asked?"

Carlos stared. "As few as possible."

Elektra turned away, feigning a coughing attack to gather strength and clear the air. She'd have to play it lightly, not to raise concern. If she was worried, he would be too. She couldn't show fear.

Carlos had been around the block as the head of security in many of the country's highest-profile public spaces. He'd know the drill.

She'd be cool.

"Sorry... something caught in my throat. Look, Carlos, can we just lose some of that room's footage from last night? From say, 22:30 until 23:30? Just have an... *an 18 minute gap*, you know?"

Carlos laughed. "Oh boy."

"I don't... I mean... this is just... nothing really..."

"Relax, Elektra. I'm getting the picture. Things happen... and things..."

"So you think that'd be a problem?"

"The problem is we've got two systems running in parallel. Traditional surveillance and then the *Ghost* system. Unfortunately, we'd need to lose the footage twice. I'm not saying it can't be done..."

"It's just more work."

"It's two separate divisions."

Elektra shook her head. *Was she stupid or what?*

"But I'm more worried about the ethical problems. I mean, we have that footage for a reason..."

"Of course..."

"I'd need to get a clearance from Shae..."

"I'd rather not... you know, this is... sensitive..."

Carlos' head tilted, "Are you here in a professional or private capacity?"

She stared, reading his eyes for a split-second.

"Professional," Elektra blurted out. "I've been notified that Clint has engaged in conduct his agent would rather..."

"Oh, OK," Carlos smiled. "I see... he doesn't want it archived..."

"Or reviewed at all. That's the impression I was given. He doesn't want to risk it ever being made public."

Did Carlos not know about them? Was the security department *that isolated*? *What the hell did these people do with their lives?*

"I see..." Carlos said, rubbing his chin.

"Has anyone seen this footage?"

"Chances are, no. We generally only monitor hot areas live. Hot areas meaning..."

"I know, go on." Elektra felt herself blushing and coughed.

"So there would have been no reason to check out that room at that time..."

"I'm sure that's a relief."

"Look, Elektra. What I suggest is this. I can have one of my guys go into *Ghost*'s database and we'll lose that. That's what you really need to worry about. It's fully resolution-scalable, which means the footage could end up anywhere from any angle at HD quality. Artificial camera moves, everything."

Elektra could no longer conceal her horror. "Of course. I think I remember something about that."

"We'll also go in and lose the visuals on the traditional end. But I can't get rid of the audio. I just can't—my first duty is to the park. We'll time/date stamp all of it continuously and I'm going to have to notate that it's all been done on Clint's request."

Elektra gulped. "Fine. Yes, that's fine. On Clint's request."

After all, he had more to lose than she did. It was his face up there, his career as an actor at stake. He'd never work again once the public had caught sight of the size of his...

"My guys are professionals, Elektra. In fact, I'd almost encourage you to leave well-enough alone. But the *Ghost* footage is a concern, I'll admit that. You don't want to have that lying around for someone with a grudge against him to find later."

"Of course not."

"Look, why don't you have Clint phone me and formally request what we just spoke about himself and we'll keep his agent out of it. I'll add the phone call to the database and we'll get rid of the visuals on his request."

"Yes, that makes sense. Very good."

Did it? Was it?

"You can always trust a surveillance professional to be discreet. We've seen it all. But don't make us angry."

"Thanks, Carlos. I knew you'd be able to help."

"We'll take care of it. But you understand someone will have to view the traditional footage once to make these edits..."

Elektra stared.

"... Obviously, in this case, that'll have to be me."

A gentle knock landed on the Beyers' front door and Steve placed himself just around the corner in the kitchen, strategically clutching his chair.

Peter had pinned the morning paper's centerfold on their kitchen wall, which featured easily-recognizable computer-enhanced images of the terrorists. Steve committed the dark faces to memory.

"What are you doing?" Barb demanded.

He frowned, nodding to the front door. "Terrorists," he mouthed silently.

He wasn't in a good mood. Steve had been monitoring the patrols outside their suite from the kids' porthole, watching the blood outside their door being tracked across the walkway by guards, watching it dry from a glistening freshness to a thick, dull paste and on, finally, to a solid maroon mass. Soon, Steve knew, it wouldn't matter anymore. It would be pounded to a fine dust, ending up inside their suite, on their carpet, and stuck to their bare feet. *A stranger's blood!*

No, he wasn't in a good mood at all.

"Dad's right, mom, I bet someone smelled our food! They're here to get it!" Sarah said. "Or not!" she laughed.

"Sarah, *please!*" Barb scolded.

The family had been somberly contemplating the realization that their refrigerator was empty. They had nothing. Absolutely nothing.

Worse yet, both *The Lair* and the restaurants had been closed for the morning raids, with the faithful angrily being held under armed guard in the park until minutes ago when it was announced the restaurants would remain closed.

It was Monday, just after one, and many full days lay ahead. With one DL:PowerStrip each to their name, a speedy reopening of Good Food was a necessity. Surely they weren't the only family in this position?

And surely DisasterLand wouldn't let them go hungry? After all, it was their negligence that resulted in the looting in the first place! They had a responsibility to their guests. It was as simple as that.

Another more urgent knock echoed, then a woman's muffled voice. Steve picked up the chair and turned the corner, legs out towards the door, and squatted. The door slid open and a girl stepped in. Steve lunged. Barb screamed. Maria reeled back, terrified and shrieking, slipping on the dried blood.

Steve continued his lunge, now horrified, just managing to drop the chair and catch her hand before she fell. He pulled Maria inside, avoiding her eyes.

Barb stood, hands on hips, dumbfounded.

"Maria, where's your uniform?" Steve asked.

She was dressed as a tourist, in a DisasterLand sweatshirt, baseball cap, and jeans.

"No good. Too dangerous."

"*Dangerous?*"

"One of us was kidnapped. For food."

Maria stepped into the kitchen, tracking the dried blood across the hallway while Barb looked on in horror. Maria undid her backpack and placed it on the kitchen table.

"Do not be angry. I have your beer, *Meester Beyers*. I am very sorry I am late. The raids just ended."

"Maria, you were supposed to be here *yesterday!*"

"Bad things happen yesterday," Maria said, cryptically. "Bad things *Meester Beyers.*"

Maria unzipped a large padded coozie, revealing two bottles. Steve took one skeptically. The small, handwritten label simply said: *Beer.*

Steve's cheeks reddened and Barb hurriedly took a wet towel to the soiled carpet, sensing conflict. Maria dropped the empty coozie back inside her backpack and zipped it up.

"*What the fuck is this?*" Steve roared.

"Beer." Maria said. "See? It say."

"It's moonshine!"

"I think *jou* should taste. It is a microbrewed wheat ale, *señor*. ¡Que rico! Good for summer."

Steve stared. He twisted off the top and angrily sipped.

"Holy cow!" he exclaimed. He took another pull. "This is good stuff!"

Maria smiled. "Not easy to get. The raids. *Dis* is why it took so long."

"That's OK, Maria. It was worth it!" Steve hugged her. He passed the beer on to Barb and she licked her lips with delight. "So where's the other four?"

"But I am sorry, *Meester Beyers*. Only two."

"Oh, well... so what, $15?"

"No, still $50. Very hard to get."

"$50 for two beers?!"

"No beer. Restaurants no sell."

"No *beer?*"

Maria shrugged her shoulders. "I do not think maybe not."

Steve stared as Maria fidgeted.

Huffing, he finally grabbed the beer back from Barb and finished it in one long gulp.

"Did you see this at Good Food?" he asked Barb. She shook her head.

"*Especial, Meester Beyers.*"

"I want a six-pack. I'll pay $100. Not a dime more. I've only got one beer left now."

"Honey..." Barb said, concerned. "We need food. Not beer."

"I do not think so. But I try," Maria answered. "For *jou*. Tomorrow. I bring it here, OK?"

Steve frowned. "Where else would you bring it?"

"In case something happen, I bring here. *Jou* wait."

Steve eyed Barb and Maria giggled, "It's OK, *don't be worry*. Just in case."

Steve wasn't buying it.

"So $100 please," Maria said.

Steve left the kitchen for his wallet and Barb asked, quietly, "Do you have food or just beer?"

"Some food. I have a list of emergency supplies," Maria opened up a pouch and handed Barb a small, hand-written list.

"Mom, if dad is spending a buck on beer, can we at least get some food?" Pete asked, rubbing his stomach. "I'm startin' to go all Ethiopian 'n stuff."

Barb smiled at Maria, embarrassed. She leaned in, whispering confidentially, "We made a mistake. We don't have much food left. I think your little list here isn't enough for us. When will Good Food reopen? "

"I do not know ma'am. I think it *depend.*"

"Depends? On what?"

Maria shrugged and Pete flopped heavily against the wall.

"Everything OK?" Steve called from the bedroom, having heard the thump.

"Yes," Barb called, eyeing the list. Her eyebrows raised.

"What do they have, mom?" Sarah asked.

"Herb-encrusted free-range turkey breast."

"Thirty-five dollars a pound," Maria nodded.

"Let's get a lot!" Sarah said, and Barb scowled.

"Hand-milled Oaxacan corn tortillas?"

"From a secluded Indian mountain village. Fifteen dollars for six."

"Do you have bread?"

"Rustic whole-grain baguettes from organic Dakota wheat. Fifteen dollars. With fresh hand-made wild currant jam, twenty."

"Ooh... and heirloom apples?"

"From an ancient native-American spring-fed mountain grove on an island off Washington state. Twenty-two dollars a pound."

"Mom let's get it all!"

Barb stared, in shock.

Steve entered. "Twenty-two dollars a pound for what?"

"Apples."

"*Apples*? Fuck that. That's a rip off, Maria."

"They sound special," Barb suggested.

"I don't care if they're the apples Eve gave to Adam to cause all the hubbub, they're not twenty-two dollars a pound. Fuck that! That's *insane!*"

Steve approached Maria, almost in a whisper, "Look, Maria, I've only got $12.50. Will that do? For a deposit? I will pay you everything upon..."

"Maybe, *Meester Beyers*. I can try."

"OK," Steve said, through clenched teeth, "Please do."

He handed her everything he had.

Maria placed the bills in her pocket slowly, eyeing him carefully. She didn't move.

"Honey, I think she wants her tip," Barb suggested.

"*Another tip?*" asked Steve. "*Now?*"

Maria shrugged her shoulders and giggled uncomfortably. "It is how I make money."

"How many customers do you have?"

"I can *no say*."

Steve's mind raced. She was pulling mad bank. He saw it in her eyes.

He turned to Barb. "Barb, could you..."

"OK, honey, *hold on*," Barb left to get her purse.

"I just don't want to spend everything," Steve called. "You know?"

He scowled at Maria.

Barb returned and Steve grabbed a twenty, one of only three she had. "There you go, Maria, twenty dollars. Why not? I'm on an account."

"What account?" Barb demanded. "I'm..."

"Then let's *get food!*" the kids yelled in unison.

Maria smiled thankfully, and waved. She winked at Barb, turning to Steve, "Are *jou* going tonight? To the vigil?"

"Another one?"

"Just announced. Because last night was short."

"And it's safe?"

"Who knows?" Maria answered, "But who ever knows?"

"We might, yes," Steve announced, after letting her words sink in. Maria made her way to the door.

"We're not surviving on beer. I'm buying food," Barb said, putting her foot down. "I want some turkey."

"And apples," Sarah said.

"And those wa-hockey tortillas!" Pete added.

"Look... we're not *all* getting mugged. I've got a plan," Steve insisted. "Just the beer," he said, practically pushing Maria out the door, "Thanks! See you tomorrow!"

Barb wondered if it was moonshine and had already somehow damaged his brain, "Honey, do you think that was smart?"

"Don't worry, sweetie. I've decided this whole trip's on Persistent. We'll see what happens this afternoon with the restaurants. If worse comes to worse, I'll find an ATM after the vigil, or just charge it, and we'll call in whatever we want from Maria tonight. We'll pay her extra for a night delivery." Steve reached for the other beer. "Don't you see how this works honey? Artificial scarcity?"

He popped off the top and took a long draw. "It's all about money."

Relive the Magic!

Promos had begun to appear on DTV for the evening's vigil, featuring last night's atrium awash in radiant candlelight.

Peter yawned. The thought of another vigil seemed lame. Not even two hours had passed since lunch, and already he was hungry and his DL:PowerStrip was long gone. There was still no word on the restaurants reopening, despite the brief lull which had washed Maria up on their shores. Guests escorted into the park by guards during the raids had safely been led home, but they had received nothing for their troubles.

Sarah was seated on the couch next to him, fidgeting, tired of DTV's unfulfilled promises of terrorist revelations. The raids had been in response to a bomb threat, DTV said, yet the comprehensive searches had revealed nothing. Absolutely nothing.

Barb and Steve had decided to cautiously embrace the freedom and spirit of vacation, and were attempting to spend the afternoon in bed, trying to catch up on sleep.

"I'm starving, Spanks. Let's go score some calories, yo."

"We can't leave. Mom and dad would kill us. Besides, where would we go?"

"Whatever. They're already killing us, trying to starve us to death 'n shit. *Child abuse*. Come on, we got no food. What if we die here on this couch?"

"That's stupid."

"What if we have to go all cannibal and shit? Would you do it?"

"You're retarded."

"I'm going down to *The Core*'s VIP lounge and get food."

"They're not open."

"It's a VIP lounge. And I'm a VIP. They have huge cheeseburgers."

"They *had* huge cheeseburgers. What if mom and dad wake up and you're gone?"

DTV cycled the only existing footage of the captured terrorist in her cell once again: grubby, eyes blackened, her designer T-shirt bloodied from a blow to her face. She turned to the camera and spit, hitting the lens dead on. The image froze.

The host regurgitated a canned statement about the continuing failure to elicit intelligence, optimistically reiterating that all legal tactics were being pursued and a breakthrough could happen at any time.

"Whatever. Then let's go check out the terrorist lair. I bet I can get in. I'm a VIP."

"Dad said he wanted to go."

"But mom doesn't."

The truth was, a promo that had played a few minutes earlier was starting to bug him and he needed a change of scenery. It was of a backpack, hidden in a corner, out of the way. *Watch*, it said simply: *Watch, Learn and Act.*

Had the old people been telling the truth?

Pete stood. "You want some coffee?"

"You don't drink coffee."

"I'm *starvin' here!*"

His dad seemed to think the old people were crazy and he did too. But the whole thing was starting to freak him out a little—unless the old people saw the same promo last night and got confused. Old people got confused all the time, he knew.

Actually, it all seemed kind of stupid. Pretending to be under attack. Getting scared. This whole game was becoming so silly he almost felt embarrassed for them. It wasn't nearly as cool as he thought it would be.

All he really wanted to do was eat, then find Zander and hang. He wondered if there were more places for VIPs to go, maybe closer.

The body count ticker continued, unchanged: *1 DISPATCHED, 1 CAPTURED, 6 AT LARGE.*

"This is so lame, Spanks, I can hardly stand it. All we're doing is sitting on a couch and watching TV. We don't need to be on vacation for that. I do it all the time."

"Remember how scared you were Friday night? You were crying."

"Was not."

"Was too."

"Besides, that's before I found out how lame it was. I thought it was really gonna to be like the DVD."

"It wasn't?"

"I dunno. But now what?"

"How should I know?"

"You think that rock star is gonna be at the vigil?"

"No, I think they went home. Before it got bad."

"You gonna do it again if he didn't?"

"Shut up."

"You think the terrorists are gonna to attack again?"

"There's only six of them left."

"So? One's all it takes."

"No. I don't. *OK?* I think they already did."

"Do you like it here?"

"Why all the questions?"

"Do you?"

"Kind of. It's kinda neat."

"I think it's stupid, everyone pretending to be under attack."

"You were scared."

"Yeah, for a little while. But not anymore. I'm going to make coffee."

Pete stood, interrupted by music ricocheting through their suite. The announcer proclaimed, *"DTV:NEWSFLASH!"*

He somberly sat back down and crossed his arms.

It was Dillon again, his face alive with fresh revelations, "Welcome. Tremendous progress has been made today and it's my pleasure to share this breaking news with you. At the end of this report, we will have a very important special request. You may wish to gather your family together for this information. First up, more on the captured terrorist. Bobby?"

The frozen image of the terrorist reappeared, bloody and grimacing in her prison cell.

"That's right, Dillon. Investigators have established she was a fashion model, an American living in Tokyo. Her name is still being withheld while relatives are notified."

DTV cut back to the reporter, Bobby Davis, from within the second-floor security center, "It has also been established that the terrorist killed in the attack was her boyfriend, also a fashion model. Both had hit on hard times recently. Their connection to the other six is still being investigated but it is believed this was nothing more than a deranged attempt for revenge on an uncaring public."

"So the two were definitely a couple?"

"I think that's definite, yes."

"Had they really intended to kill? Or was it simply a publicity stunt gone wrong?"

"It's hard to imagine this was anything other than deliberate, cold-blooded murder. With DisasterLand's high profile, they wanted to go out with a bang, Dillon, their young careers over long ago. They had no other skills and they had become desperate, hooked on fame and easy money."

"Both had run out."

"Definitely."

"Amazing. And the latest from *The Lair*?"

"One puzzled investigator I spoke to was blunt, 'They've left us with nothing,' he told me, 'there was no note, no manifesto, just a relentless pursuit of the cool.'"

"You mean their dress, their demeanor?"

"And the contents of *The Lair*."

"Bobby, many of us want to know—is there a connection between the bombing and the looting of Good Food?"

Sarah turned to Pete. He yawned.

"Privately the authorities believe there is, yes. But they have yet to make a statement as investigations are still underway."

"We've gotten word that the raids have picked up again this afternoon. Can you elaborate?"

Images again, *Cops*-style, of the aftermath of Sunday's gory blasts.

"Security will only say that extensive measures are being undertaken to completely secure the atrium for the evening's vigil. No surprises, Dillon."

"No surprises Bobby."

"The authorities are singly focused on one message: the terrorists will be brought to justice."

"You know this is all a lie, right?" Pete interrupted. "They could find them if they wanted to. Easily. They just don't want to."

"Why do you say that?"

"Trust me, I know. I'm a VIP."

Behind the closed door, Barb was lying in bed uncomfortably, her mind filled with dark, competing scenarios of the future as the newscast's audio reverberated through her drifting consciousness. She was having a difficult time pinpointing what was happening, really happening, and she felt herself succumbing to a downward mental spiral.

She prided herself on always been able to read the way forward, to separate the wheat from the chaff, yet their situation seemed to be growing more and more obscured every hour. When was Good Food going to reopen? What about the restaurants? Why had Maria ripped her husband off so blatantly? Why wasn't Maria in uniform? More *raids*? And that weird blackout...

She had a terrible feeling this whole thing was not even close to being over, that more—maybe many more—unpleasant surprises lay ahead.

The idea of a vigil was becoming more and more tempting. Barb had to get out, had to be around other people despite her morning promises to Steve. Besides, once out they might find food.

But if not, like Steve said, they could always make a quick call to Maria to secure a late dinner no matter what the cost. They always had credit cards after all.

A loud bump startled Barb out of her thoughts. She turned to Steve, his eyes opening groggily. While Barb fretted, he had spent an odd, dream-soaked afternoon dozing off the beers.

"What's going on, honey?" Steve asked. "I was asleep."

"It wasn't you?"

"What?"

"That bump?"

It had sounded like it had come from inches above their heads, right next to them.

"No."

"It seemed like it was inside the wall," Barb mumbled. "Must be the neighbors."

Steve rose and gingerly stepped to the window. The afternoon light was growing in intensity as the sun began its descent and Steve scanned the distant, reddening landscape.

What made the mountains' presence so welcome, so profoundly comforting?

Now, emerging from sleep, it was easy for him to see their religious significance in simpler times.

"Mom? Dad?" Pete stuck his head into the bedroom, eyes closed. He didn't want any more surprises.

"What is it son?" Steve whispered. "You can open your eyes."

"DisasterLand wants every family to call the switchboard," Pete said squinting. "I think something's wrong."

Securely wrapped in her bathrobe with lights turned down, Elektra was glued to the Feed, monitoring the rising house temperature from the comfort of her bed. Next to her, the laptop was scanning hero families in real-time.

With a four p.m. call, these were her last predictable moments of sanity and she was using the time to brainstorm possible hero narratives. Two of the families had been no-shows even after being recruited for *The Hunt*, but others were showing definite promise. After tonight, the go-to list would be whittled down to a handful and one way or another those families would find themselves the center of the action.

For better or for worse.

The work was a nice mental escape to fight off the butterflies, and the chamomile tea on her bedside table was doing its part to calm her nerves and stomach. Both the earlier story and production meetings had gone flawlessly, with what to her seemed just the right mix of anticipation, exhilaration and fear to properly combust and achieve flight.

Yet there was always the ominous unknown, an unknown that hadn't been so kind to them the first time around. The evening ahead of them was big, as big in many ways as yesterday morning, and the potential for trouble was ever-present.

A knock came to her door and Elektra jumped, cursing the invasion of her mental space. 2:40? No deliveries were scheduled and Clint was still bed-ridden downstairs... with no logical explanation she was determined to play evasive.

Another knock.

"Fuck off," Elektra huffed under her breath. "Go away."

A text message across her phone. Jude.

U?

Elektra lowered the screen on her laptop, truly mystified. *Surely the events were related?* It was all too weird.

She rose and hurried to the door, managing to catch Jude waiting nervously at the elevator. He quickly slipped back into her apartment.

"What's up?" Elektra asked. "You OK? Want a tea?"

"Sorry for the surprise visit. I had to talk to someone and you're the only choice. Glad I caught you."

He was rocking back and forth on his feet, excitedly. Still frozen, Elektra was awaiting a verdict on the tea.

"Sorry, yes, tea. Yes. Iced."

Jude strolled over to her majestic window, surveying the atrium's deceptive calm. He spun to her in the kitchen.

"Are we being recorded?"

"*What?*"

"Here. Now. You recording anything?"

"No!" she shouted. "*Who do you think...*"

"Elektra, I've seen them. All morning I've been in Shae's office. I've seen the scripts for the fall season. And I've seen more... much more."

Elektra stared. Jude was beaming, eyes alight.

"I mean it. All of it. Elektra, you have no idea... I had no idea. No one has any idea. They're... it's... just... it's crazy. It's just fucking crazy, man."

Goosebumps had erupted on her arms and a chill shot down her back. Elektra poured two iced green teas from the pitcher in her fridge. She bruised a stalk of mint, split it, and dropped half in each glass.

The couple took a seat in Elektra's breakfast nook, their voices dropping to whispers. For both, the clandestine meeting suddenly felt hatched from a spy thriller.

"Like what?"

"I'm not even going to give you specifics. I can't. It's not fair. It's too big. All I can say is that..."

"You show up at my door and you can't say?"

"All I can say..."

"Yes?"

"Is that..."

"*Yes?*"

"All I can say is that we are not alone."

"*We are not alone?*"

"Right."

"What the fuck are you talking about, *we are not alone?* Is Shae an alien or something? Are you an alien? You're freaking me out here."

Jude held up hand, as if taking an oath. Gradually, one by one, fingers dropped—the thumb, the pinkie, the ring—until all that remained was a peace sign.

Two.

"Open Up! Security!" roared a voice from the hallway.

"*Who!?*" Steve yelled.

"OPEN UP!"

"One minute!" Steve called. "Hey, maybe it's food, honey."

"Wouldn't Maria be bringing it?"

"I don't know... could be emergency relief or something."

Steve hurried to the door, checking the peephole to reveal two massive security guards. Before he could react, the door slid open and the guards burst past Steve with a two-man DTV crew in tow.

"Hi," Steve said, "Can..."

"Just following up on your phone call, sir. Mind if we have a quick look around?"

"Of course not..."

A third guard took up a defensive position just outside the door as the guards hurried into the living room. They eyed the three Beyers remaining on the couch with interest.

"Ain't no terrorists here dude," Pete said.

"Glad to hear it, kid."

The guards disappeared into the master bedroom, then the bathroom, then out for another look around the kitchen. As they disappeared into the kid's bedroom, Sarah broke out in a cold sweat.

Seconds later, they reappeared holding her bag. She fought against the roaring darkness that now threatened to consume her. With her new vibrator and the Ecstasy inside, jail was surely minutes away. *God, what had she become?*

"Who's bag?"

"It's my sister's. You want to search it?" Pete asked.

"No, that's OK," the guard said, handing it back to Sarah who avoided his eyes. The blood surged back to her head and her consciousness wobbled. DTV silently captured the exchange.

"Are you guys just lookin' for butterfly backpacks?"

"Why do you say that kid?"

"Well these old people told us about one last night at the vigil. They said it had a bomb in it."

Barb stared at her son as the DTV camera crew edged in. She glanced at Steve, who shrugged.

"They lied to you, kid," the guard said, his eyes focusing intensely. "Got it?"

Pete cowered. "Yes... sir."

"OK, we're gonna need some prints."

He produced a digital fingerprint scanner and confirmed the Beyers' names and suite number. One-by-one the family was authenticated with the flashing of a satisfying green light.

"Thanks, y'all," he said.

"You folks take care," the other added as they turned to leave. "We'll see you down at the vigil."

"Can you tell us what you're doing?" Barb asked.

"Manhunt. Every suite."

"You're kidding! There's probably 700 suites here!"

"That's why we're out of here."

The door slid shut and the Beyers refocused on DTV, slightly dazed from the whirlwind exchange.

"That seems a little... extreme. Doesn't it?" Steve finally said. "I mean, you know, all this for... a show?"

"It's just part of the realism, honey," Barb replied.

Gunfire erupted in the atrium.

1 DISPATCHED, 3 CAPTURED, 4 AT LARGE

Less than an hour later, with the sun superheating the suite with its evening descent, the Beyers could relax. DisasterLand's understated counterattack had worked like a sublime poem. Yet not without a price.

The ticker had proudly been updated minutes after the Beyers heard the shots— but the truth was only now finally coming out.

Security had pinpointed several suspicious suites during the morning's raids and had been keeping them under particularly close scrutiny. As soon as DisasterLand's request was made for calls in to the switchboard, the terrorists had felt the squeeze. And they had made their move.

Surveillance footage revealed the two terrorists exiting a suite adjacent to the stairs, on seven, as the raids began. They hurried down to the atrium's floor, where they were stopped by undercover agents at the foot of the stairs. When the agents attempted to scan their D-PAKs, the terrorists fired.

One agent was injured and both terrorists wounded in a brief but fierce firefight later replayed from several impressive angles on DTV. Unseen snipers had taken the terrorists down but not out in a powerful show of omnipotent restraint.

Once in custody, it was clear the terrorists had aged themselves with stage make-up. Their D-PAKs and fingerprints were scanned. Of course, they didn't match.

Meanwhile guards had broken into the suite and found another hungry family tied to the master bed.

Terrorists are amongst us, DTV now warned. *Watch, Learn and Act.* Four terrorists remained stubbornly at large and the most comprehensive security yet would guard the evening's vigil.

Yet the cell had surely taken a body-blow.

The evening's episode of *DL:Heroes* would focus on the agents who had been injured today in the line of duty as well as the family who had suffered at their hands.

"The phone calls worked," Steve said.

"What did they say, anyway?" Barb asked. "When you called?"

"Said they just wanted to make sure we're OK. What else were they going to say?"

"Did you tell them we didn't have any food?"

"I did."

"And?"

"They made a note of it."

"*Made a note of it?*"

"Yeah, they sort of apologized for the inconvenience and told me everything would reopen shortly."

"That's good news."

"I thought so."

"But how'd they know it was really you dad?" Sarah asked.

"They asked me a question about our application."

"Really?"

"Yep. They were pretty serious about it. I didn't want to worry you... but now I understand."

"Why would we be worried?"

"Well, like Pete said... this couple told us there were real terrorists here, on the loose, and..."

"Come on," Barb hissed.

"That's why we didn't tell you, honey."

"Look, there's still four left," Pete observed. "Don't be all gettin' all confident 'n stuff."

From their doorway, Barb could hear the subdued buzz of people amassing for the vigil below. In the far distance, a gentle chorus of voices picked up and Barb's heart warmed. Yes, this was *good*. This was *positive*, this was *healthy*.

> "*Here Comes The Sun,*
> *Here Comes The Sun...*"

George Harrison.

Barb would draw on these people, as they would draw from her, to expunge the dark energy of fear and focus instead on the light. She smiled. *River would be proud.*

It hadn't been easy to accept this. In fact, she hadn't at all until now. Until hearing *the people*.

But suddenly it all felt right.

What the terrorists had tried to stop, they had only postponed.

The family stepped out onto the walkway, almost two hundred feet over the growing crowd below them as brave guests gathered in the midst of destruction to seek understanding, to gain strength.

On fifteen, the line for *The Lair* was growing longer by the minute but they were in no hurry. Arm in arm, the Beyers set off to join them.

> *"Little darling, it's been a long, cold lonely winter,*
> *Little darling, it feels like years since it's been here..."*

Groups were touring *The Lair* in eights and the Beyers waited patiently, chatting with the other guests, sharing stories of the long, solitary night as the line slowly shrank.

Finally a masked guard took one hand off his automatic rifle to motion the Beyers inside. The time had come.

They stepped inside, hearts pounding, and Steve's arms tightened around his family's shoulders. The first thing they noticed was the smell.

"Stinks in here," Pete said, his empty stomach churning.

The distinctive smell seemed a blend of cigarettes, stale red wine, artisan *au de toilette*—and body odor.

"Europeans," whispered Barb. "I knew it."

They entered the kitchen, stunned to find Jim and Jenny there, stone-faced, still examining the macabre artifacts.

The Andrews hurried over. "Thank God, a friendly face! Terrible, isn't it?"

"It is," Steve agreed. "Where'd you come from? We didn't see you go in."

"We've been here over an hour. Just taking it all in. You ever seen anything like it?"

"No." Steve answered. "Never. The guards let you stay?"

"Sure did," Jim whispered. "I slipped them a bribe. I'll show you sometime. Check it out."

There, on the kitchen table, lay a remarkably small puzzle of destruction, now under armed guard.

"This could have been bad, Beyers. Really bad. You know the story?" Jim asked.

Pete jumped in, "This is where she was sitting. The guards burst in and she got two of them before she was overpowered. But it was lucky 'cause they saw the bomb under the table. And somehow they got it disarmed."

"That's right, kiddo."

"I don't get that part," Steve offered. "Isn't that hard to do? Doesn't it take a long time?"

"I don't get it either, Beyers." Jim's voice dropped, "That's what I've been wondering. I guess it's what you'd call a *hole in the plot!*"

Jim winked, nudging his wife, "Well look, enough of this. We're going to get downstairs. We'll see you down at the vigil, OK?"

Jim patted Steve on the back and took Jenny's hand. The guard thanked them on the way out.

Pete pushed further in, back to the bedroom, and the rest of the family followed. More empty bottles of red wine stood on the nightstand, filled with cigarette butts.

"I thought the rooms were no smoking," Barb said, sighing.

Under an improvised glass display, detailed scraps of paper plotted out the location of each bomb, while rough calculations detailed how each had been chosen for maximum destruction.

Maps of the suite showed where these notes had been found.

Pages torn from fashion magazines featuring half-naked models and impossibly priced clothing still remained strewn across the bed. Items were circled in marker— boots here, a sweater there, a hat, a purse, jeans. A program for the last Paris Fashion Week lay discarded in tatters.

"Dreamers," Steve pronounced. "Wannabes."

The closet was completely empty. Two small duffle bags were crumbled below the lonely coat hangers.

"That's all they brought?" Barb asked. "That should have been the first clue. That wouldn't have lasted them a week."

Pete stepped into the bathroom, the rest of the family cautiously joining him. On the mirror someone had written, in lipstick:

Forever in Style

"What the hell does that mean?" Steve wondered out loud.

"It's not supposed to mean anything," Barb said. "It's just the nonsense of a deranged mind. Come on kids, let's get downstairs."

"I think it's kinda cool," Pete said.

"Me too," Sarah agreed. *"Forever in style.* That's *so cool."*

"DJs, I'm starving!"

"Quiet, Peter. It'll do you good."

"Yeah *right!*"

"Look, why don't you go to the park, rub your face in mud and go sit by the elevators. Maybe someone, in the kindness of their heart, will take pity on such a sad and pathetic boy."

Barb, quite simply, was sick of it.

Peter thought it was a pretty good idea. "Join me Spanks?"

"VIPs don't lay around with muddy faces," she replied tartly. "Don't you know anything?"

"VIPs can do anything they want. That's what it *means*, stupid."

The Beyers had just stepped onto the floor and were patiently progressing through the last security checkpoint. Steve felt the noose tightening on those at large.

They had been scanned once above, on nineteen before descending, but it was a small price to pay. Soon, they were through.

Steve led them away from the elevators and on, towards the music in the heart of the ruins.

"OK, peepers open everyone. You saw the promos."

"Yeah, watch for backpacks," Pete said.

Steve frowned. He had re-sworn Pete to secrecy about the butterfly backpack—no sense in worrying Barb unnecessarily based only on a rumor disproved by the guards. He took Barb's hand.

A lone guitarist was standing on the rim of the fountain, the intimate crowd swaying around her on the rebuilt floor. From every direction, armed security guards stood at the ready.

Tonight's crowd was only a few hundred, in comparison to the thousand-plus of the night before, but to the Beyers this was a relief. The odds of nefarious agendas transpiring behind-the-scenes was remote in such an intimate gathering.

As the Beyers made their way to the fountain, conversations brushed their ears... recalling the suffocating bad vibes inside *The Lair*, the shocking unconcern for anything other than the terrorists' own personal appearance. Indeed, *The Lair* had been an overpowering insight into the human animal to many of those assembled.

Here and there, restrained smiles were shared with vaguely recognized faces. The size, the scope of DisasterLand was narrowing, the bond was being strengthened between guests.

Through adversity, they were becoming a community.

Love and Vigil-ance! the InfoTron screamed, the words swirling endlessly around the circumference of the enormous ball.

An adventurous spirit overtook them and the Beyers wandered on past the fountain, entering the eerie silence of what now remained of the far side of the village. Picking their way carefully through the rubble they followed the deserted streets, passing stores' gaping foundations one-by-one in the dim, makeshift light.

What before was a complex and wonderful maze of shops, life and joy, now seemed a barren, scorched wasteland. The family approached the charred remains slowly, hand in hand, in reverence. Now barricaded off, they remained a monument to what had been stolen.

All along the cracked, winding streets lay tiny little store memorials, having sprung up where once the stores themselves had once stood. Composed of shopping bags, labels and receipts for treasured purchases, together they became a scene of wrenching loss.

The pungent smell of drowned fire and charred remains still lingered, blending with the unmistakable scent of burned flesh. Their stomachs revolted.

The fact that no one had been killed was simply a miracle.

A few guests were milling about silently, emotionlessly dazed. Others were crying.

Had it really been less than 36 hours ago?

Barb couldn't wrap her mind around it. Just two days before these stores were filled with diamonds, jewelry, leather and fashions worth hundreds of thousands of dollars.

Now? *Gone.*

"Look, DJs, look—a real film crew!"

"Hey! Over here!" he shouted.

With horror, Barb realized it was Juliet, leading a *Matériel Pornographique* crew into the wreckage. The object of their cameras' gaze wasn't immediately apparent, but there was every reason to believe it wasn't family friendly.

Barb smacked her hand over Pete's mouth as Steve barred their way, but it was too late.

Juliet saw the family and waved, her smile broadening as she stepped daintily away from the unseen action. "Mister and Missus Beyers! *Bonsoir!*"

"You're OK!" Barb called. "I was worried."

"*Oui, oui!* Beautiful night, no? What do you think? Time for a shoot? On location?" she called.

"No thanks!" Barb yelled back, taming her embarrassment.

"Come on," Pete pleaded. "Let's do it!"

Juliet smiled. "'allo Sarah!"

Sarah blushed, meekly, and Barb froze. Steve instigated an immediate and radical detour.

"*A bientout!*" Juliet called.

Barb waved a confused goodbye and the family continued on, deeper into the ruins yet avoiding the side nearest Del Sol for fear of reliving their own dramatic experiences of the previous morning. Soon, they found themselves in the presence of several simultaneous sub-vigils, small congregations of religious practitioners, each spreading positivity and togetherness in their own way. The combination created a tapestry of healing that was marvelously inspirational, much different and yet equally as powerful as anything they had witnessed the night before.

The Beyers lingered, yet soon found themselves longing for the comfort of the mainstream. They gradually migrated back to the atrium's center where a group of reality-show connoisseurs was softly debating the best moments of the last 24 hours. Expectant waves of titillating energy surged through the group at the thought of more impending arrests, more arresting television. In their midst, heightened muffled gossip raged.

Closing in on the fountain, two figures stood waving at them. Sarah realized it was Neil and Katie, while next to them the black MC was checking her out. Sarah squeaked and did a double-take.

Katie? With Neil?

No.

Her heart soared, "Mom, dad, can I go hang?"

To Barb, they looked just like the hipster terrorists but Steve gave his consent if she stayed close. Sarah hurried over to join them and Neil and Katie both gave her a surprised hug as Steve and Barb watched.

A round of applause rang out for the previous singer who made a heart-felt peace sign and jumped down off the fountain. Another ascended, a blonde woman in her early thirties also with a guitar who was joined by a bongo drummer. The rumor quickly spread that she was the leader of *Nest*, the country band that had played on Friday night.

Fans edged in around the fountain as if it were an autumn campfire. Barb smiled, hips swaying to the comforting, folksy Americana.

Steve discreetly scanned around him, attempting to conceal his eyeing of Sarah and her friends. Barb elbowed his stomach.

"Nosy," she whispered.

Steve continued scanning, up to the walkways far above him, to the lines of guards posted at the stairs and elevators. There were hundreds of guards present, he realized, with fifteen or twenty on each floor, plus the hundred or more, surely more, in the atrium...

It was incredible. And kind of creepy.

Steve checked the faces of the guests around him, noting amongst those gathered a degree of mistrust absent the previous evening. Steve watched as younger guests, in their mid-20's, were being singled out for particularly serious scrutiny.

"Yo P!"

Pete spun. "Yo Z!" he yelled. "No way dude!"

Zander and his dad were standing farther back, a lady on his dad's arm.

"DJs, that's Zander, remember? From the TV?"

Pete waved. They all waved back.

"Can I go hang too, DJs?"

Steve checked in with Barb, who resignedly shrugged her shoulders. Compared to Steve and Barb, Zander's dad was well-dressed with a sport coat, jeans and loafers. Latisha, as Pete soon learned, was wearing an elegant dress that Barb recognized from the shopping channel.

"Don't move from that spot without our permission," Steve said.

"Rock on!" Pete yelled, spinning off and joining Zander. They slammed their chests together.

"What a world," Steve whispered to Barb, finding themselves more or less alone for the first time since Friday night.

"What do you mean? Our kids?"

"Yeah, here's Zander, some upper middle-class black kid from the 'burbs who's dad's a dentist, and there's Pete, some upper middle-class white kid from the 'burbs and they're both into street music and sympathy with the oppressed."

"So?"

"Why? I mean, what's speaking to them there?"

"Why don't you ask your son?"

"I did."

"What did he say?" Barb asked, genuinely interested now.

"He said because it's real."

"Maybe we live in a gangster world and like all of middle America we just don't know it yet because no one's come out and told us."

Barb was drifting back to her notion that everything had gone insane. As she continued to monitor the walkways, each scan seemed to find ever more menace in the shadows.

One suicide bomber and...

She shivered under the growing sense they were on borrowed time. Barb was beginning to rethink her decision to leave their suite. Sure, guards were placed throughout the atrium, but in the end they were only human. Four terrorists were still at large, and they could strike at any moment. And when was better than during a public event?

She shook her head. The perversity of the drama they were engaged in bordered on the absurd. None of this, of course, was even real. Not *really real*. But still, she was scared. Because people were really getting hurt.

She wanted to go back upstairs. Very definitively. Her body was telling her something wasn't right. That was clear.

Barb considered calling her children back. But, when she looked on to Sarah, then Peter, they were laughing, happy to be with their new friends, and probably, equally happy to be away from their stifling parents. They needed a break.

The singer sang on, a poetic elucidation of the joys of seeing your man on his tractor with the sun setting behind him, bathed in the scent of the harvest. Barb sighed, longing for simpler times.

Her thoughts broke as a scuffle flared above and expectant eyes were raised to the tower.

Screaming erupted from the tower's lower floors, where guests were already rushing for the safety of their suites.

Gunfire.

"*You're kidding me!*" Steve yelled, impotently. His eyes landed on three guards on the fifth floor, setting up a military-style tripod. *Guards?* Two more stood behind, securing the trio with automatic weapons drawn. Five total.

Five?

Barb fought towards the kids, screaming.

Guards were charging from adjacent floors and a firestorm erupted as those in the offensive position took aim at the onrush. Weapons flashed in a furious call-and-response.

One impostor grabbed his leg, screaming. Even from the floor, Steve could see the blood splattered across the walkway. Yet he stood, reloaded, and fired off another metallic barrage.

The onrushers too were taking casualties while guards from throughout DisasterLand were respositioning to head off the threat.

A small explosion. A streak of light.

"MORTAR!" someone screamed.

Shrieking filled the atrium as horrified guests ran for cover. The whistling grew louder.

"Incoming!" a terrified voice screamed.

An explosion detonated above the crowd and a thick cloud of smoke quickly engulfed the helpless guests. Blind and disoriented, chaos reigned.

The InfoTron roared red in the suffocating air.

Bursts of gunfire continued.

The tone rang out deafeningly over the atrium.

Another blast. Whistling. More gunfire. And an explosion. Panic tore through the atrium, spreading like desert wildfire.

When Steve turned back towards the hazy fountain, Barb and the kids were gone.

He rushed desperately towards the stage, eyes tearing and caught in the crush for cover. Guests were falling around him and Steve felt the nauseating sensation of the floor—or whatever it was—giving way underneath his feet.

A third distant blast and the whistling grew closer, blending with the shrieks of panic from the desperate souls surrounding him. Steve dropped as an explosion detonated overhead. Smoke filled his vision.

The darkness was complete but for the devilish cast from the InfoTron above.

Steve pulled himself up into the dissipating haze by the fountain and cautiously drew the light out of his D-PAK. Gunfire continued around him.

He flipped it on.

Nearby, a guard lay on the ground writhing, his leg a bloody stump.

Steve reeled backwards and ripped off his mask for air. Instead, he choked on the acrid stench of detonated explosives.

Something was wrong. Were... they loosing control?

But to whom?

"Dad!"

Steve's heart leapt and he spun.

"Sarah! Where's mom!"

She was crying, "I don't know... I just ran..."

"Peter?"

Sarah shook her head, collapsing at his feet.

"Come on, Sarah, let's get out of here. These assholes are libel to kill someone!"

She was immobile, sobbing. On instinct, Steve dragged her towards the park, towards the calm, clear air and away from the lost, flailing masses. Flashlights danced across the atrium's glass as the gunfire continued.

Rage ignited his body, blood catching like lighter fuel. He had never felt as bare as he found himself at that moment, completely manipulated from bottom up. They'd been sucker-punched.

"Why are they doing this to us?" Steve howled.

Ten feet in front of them, a guard's stomach exploded in a thick, red mist. Guts spilling out, he fell.

Sarah screamed and Steve dropped on top of her limp body. No sense in trying to run anymore.

Where were they, anyway?

He peeked up to the fifth floor, witness to the ongoing ballet of death. Quick bursts of gunfire twinkled overhead.

The guards seemed unable to reach the terrorists. A vicious core of resistance had coalesced, entrenched behind a makeshift fortress of broken furniture.

Another distant burst and whistle... Steve hunched over his daughter's fetal body as the inevitable explosion rang out, smoke once again descending over them.

Steve choked, pulling his shirt over his face. Sarah was as limp as a rag, hands over her ears. She ducked into his chest.

All went strangely quiet.

I can't believe they'd do this, Steve spat. *Dogs!*

An impenetrable blast of gunfire erupted around them, reverberating harshly off the atrium's glass. Frantic voices rang out and unspeakable scenes assaulted his imagination.

A massacre, Steve growled. *A fucking massacre.*

"Doctor! I've been hit!"

"We need *a doctor!*"

Steve picked up his head. The surreal darkness only made the scenes around him more terrible, simultaneously more dreamlike and more real, drilling them into his subconscious and smothering his spirit.

A team of guards had set up behind a nearby EMS cart, guns blazing towards the tower. Bursts of gunfire ricocheted off the floor in front of them then stopped. As the guards rose to return fire one was hit by another burst, his arm instantly severed. He dropped, writhing, the bloody arm now lying uselessly on the cold atrium floor.

A woman in front of Steve stumbled, gasping for air. She vomited, violently.

Tear gas.

Steve gagged, spit, ducking back down as the molten pops of lead landed around them, continuing to haunt the space with their dark and brutal statement.

Moments later, shouting arose from above. Reinforcement guards were racing across all walkways now, simultaneously attacking from all sides. They were giving it everything they had. They were storming the fifth floor encampment.

Two more blasts above, and the walkway filled with smoke. Guards pulled back, lost in the smoke screen, as the terrorists mounted their escape.

All eyes remained on the fifth floor as a desperate last-ditch stand-off roared in the slowly clearing air. Guns were blazing.

A figure emerged, standing on the fifth-floor railing. He ripped off his guard's uniform to reveal a giant butterfly tattoo on his biceps.

He shot a line, Spider-Man style, at the InfoTron. Once secured, he swiftly launched himself over the rail, swinging over the atrium to unrestrained gasps.

"Nel-ly!" he roared, "We will sacrifice ourselves for understanding! We will not let you go without a fight! Save the Pimpernel, lest you rot on earth heathens!"

He let go, above the fountain's pool.

And instantly realized he'd misjudged.

Then, horrifically, he was falling, flailing as if in slow motion. Screaming, he dropped, hitting the cracked cobblestones with a sickening thud which echoed as a thick, disgusting silence melted over the atrium. Time froze.

He'd *missed*.

One lone scream rang out, desperate in its ferocity and heartfelt pain. All heads spun to the crowd, away from the fallen terrorist and towards the park.

But it was lost as floodlights flashed on, illuminating the destruction lying around them. Sirens rang out from all corners of the atrium as EMS crews raced towards the injured.

Steve lay back, next to his daughter, who peeked out for the very first time over the swirling scenes of destruction.

Eyes focused on the distant, dim glass dome above, he saw only the falling body, frantically grasping for anything, flaying, destined to confront the inevitable.

And he heard only the long, stomach-churning splat.

The terrorist's body was loaded onto an EMS cart and whisked across the secured atrium to Good Health under full armed guard. Just before entering the double-doors, the terrorist raised his fist in triumph.

"Dad, he's OK!" Sarah yelled. She was on her feet now. "He's OK!"

Sparse applause rang out throughout the atrium in appreciation, as if supporting the fallen opposition hero injured on the game's final play.

Sirens continued to wail and Steve pulled himself up, sitting with arms around his shins. He didn't get it.

He didn't get it at all.

DTV crews were swarming the floor, prying for interviews, but Steve angrily waved all of them away. He looked up to the fifth floor, where guards were rummaging through the remnants of the terrorists' position. One door behind them had been smashed, and guards were swarming the suite.

Steve shook his head.

He stretched his hand out to his daughter, who took it warmly. He pulled her gently down next to him.

"We've got to find food, Sarah."

"Maybe this is the end."

"It's only Monday night. It's not over. We leave on Sunday."

"Yeah, I guess."

"Mom's not going to be in very good shape. I'm sure Pete's with her and I'm sure they're OK. But you and I are going to stay down here until we get some food for them. OK?"

"Are you sure? I mean..."

"*OK?*"

She stared into his eyes. They were ice cold.

"I dragged you guys down here and I've got to make it right. If we return empty handed, you'll have a new stepfather soon."

Sarah nodded.

"I don't trust these people, Sarah. I don't trust them at all. They'll do anything. We've got to take matters into our own hands."

A chill ran down her spine. "OK, dad. Sure. But what if mom's already ordered food?"

"Fine. That means we have more for tomorrow."

Sarah nodded. "OK."

Around them, stunned guests continued to disperse, some heading into the park, others approaching the glass elevators. Steve stood, gingerly, wiping his hands on his sweat-stained shirt. "What's our best bet?"

"I dunno."

"Should we try Good Food?"

"It's still boarded up."

"We'll see what's happening."

They took their first few steps and Sarah pointed, "Dad look! Something's wrong!"

Steve followed her finger, realizing Sarah had singled out a woman in her early 30's, crumpled on the atrium floor. She was gasping for air through deep, convulsive sobs, her chest heaving uncontrollably. Face utterly distorted by pain, Steve nonetheless recognized her from Friday night's entrance. The bright, shining girl he remembered was now gone.

An EMS crew was around her, their faces unreadable, almost mechanical, yet they told Steve the truth. Sarah had been right. Something was wrong. *Desperately, desperately wrong.*

A guard stood just over the woman's shoulder, automatic at the ready.

Steve put his arm around his daughter, guiding them closer to a crowd that was rapidly gathering around the fallen young woman.

"*He's gone!*" she was weeping, "They *got him!* Oh God, *my husband's gone!*"

The paramedic was shaking her.

"My husband!" she screamed, "*He's been taken!*"

The crew quickly helped her up and over to a waiting cart. Seconds later, it raced away, sirens screaming, towards Good Health.

In her hands, Steve realized, was a sealed envelope.

The packed glass elevator ascended the atrium and Barb scanned the retreating landscape of flashing lights, spilled blood and devastation.

For the first time, their true predicament had sunk in. They were trapped. They could minimize their exposure, but they couldn't eliminate it. They were along for the ride.

Barb struggled to remain upright, one arm around Zander's dad's shoulder, the other around Pete. Pete was straining. Limp, his mom weighed a ton.

They'd found her passed out, halfway to the stairs.

"I'm so sorry about this," Barb whispered. A tear slid down her cheek.

"Don't you worry. We'll have you home in no time. We're just glad we found you."

Barb shut her eyes. She had no strength for anything else.

"I just... panicked..."

"You'll be alright Missus Beyers. My dad's a dentist," Zander said.

"Did you see your dad, Peter? Or Sarah?" Barb asked.

"No DJ..."

"I'm sure they're just fine, Missus Beyers. Don't you worry about them. So where're we headed?"

"Nineteen," Pete said.

"Cool!" Zander replied.

"Yeah, it's pretty neat. 'Cept we ain't got no food."

"You don't?"

"Nada, yo. We've only had a muffin since yesterday afternoon."

"*Peter*... Some people don't even get that you know."

"That's their problem."

"I see," interrupted Zander's father. "Well, maybe we can help out. What do you think Zander... we don't have much..."

Zander's face fell, "Yeah, maybe dad."

"We'll find you guys something."

"*Really?*" Pete almost shot through the roof. "Fresh!"

"Thank you..." Barb looked up at her companions for the first time. "I hate this place," she continued, her eyes flaring. "This place is sick. And I'm not playing anymore."

"DJ, you can't do that!" said Pete.

"Watch me!" Barb hissed. "There were families down there, Peter. Little kids. These devils are playing with us, like ripping the wings off a moth. It's..." she fought for words, "It's just *disgusting*."

Steve was squatting at the rim of the fountain while Sarah washed her feet, shoes and all. At one particularly gruesome moment in their quest, Sarah had accidentally waded through a thick puddle of vomit and now sought relief in the comparatively clean waters.

As the rank scent dissipated to semi-tolerable levels, she looked over to her dad. He was undergoing a transformation.

They had been watching the replays of the terrorist's five-story fall on the InfoTron above them, and as yet another angle of the slow-motion fall appeared, Steve turned to his daughter, eyes alight. Steve was beginning to buy it. His mind was shifting, the tide was turning. A broad smile broke out over his face and Sarah wondered if he had finally lost it.

"You OK, dad?"

"It's incredible, honey. I mean, it looks *so real.*"

Above them, what had to be the new iconic shot of the week appeared in dramatic super-slow-motion: the grainy close-up of the terrorist's fist being raised. In only a few frames of video it portrayed loss, sacrifice and the unknown while simultaneously representing hope and struggle.

Simple and compelling, it clarified the essence of the human condition.

Suddenly, radically, the image spun, 360 degrees around the fist, Matrix-like, and a roar went up throughout the atrium. The image faded to black.

"Amazing."

"Yeah."

"I think I get it now... I think I really get it. I've stepped back and I'm appreciating it for what it is, you know? These are the most talented entertainers on the planet."

Sarah sloshed back to her dad. From the center of the knee-deep pool, she looked out over the emptying atrium, scattered blood gleaming under makeshift worklights.

"I guess..."

"I was just taking it too seriously..." Steve stood. "They're geniuses. I really mean it. *Geniuses.* Sarah, we are in the presence of..."

Words failed him and he helped Sarah over the fountain's edge and onto the floor. In that one shot, the remarkable ability of DisasterLand's craftspeople had become blindingly apparent.

"Honey, if they can pull that off, they can pull off *anything.*"

"I don't know why they have to be so gross..."

"It's like I was telling your mom," Steve was growing excited now, his hands animated, "just this morning in fact—they *have to be gross.* It's the only way it works! And *they know it!*"

"Yeah, I guess I can see that."

"So what d'you think?"

"It does look cool."

"*So cool*, Sarah. I'm just wondering how they did it. Minutes earlier we walked across those same cobblestones—and they were solid. Like rocks. Remember?"

"Yeah. I remember."

"Thirty minutes later he splatted. Big time. You heard it. *I* heard it. *And he lived.*"

"How do you know he lived?"

"We're not going through that again. *Conspiracy theories.*"

"I mean it, dad."

"Sarah, please. He raised his God-damned fist! You saw it! All beautifully choreographed for the cameras! Am I right?"

Sarah shrugged.

"We're in the presence of genius, honey. Someday you'll look back on this, and you'll tell your kids, you'll say, 'Yeah, I was there. *First year.*' It's *history*, Sarah."

"Maybe."

The ashen face of a DTV announcer appeared on the InfoTron above them.

"The floor must be some sort of weird material," Steve said, finally. "It's the only thing I can think of. Really high-tech stuff. Feels solid. But under high-pressure *gives*. Think about that."

"OK..."

"I mean, think about your physics. Water, right, it's the *opposite*. It's soft, but if you hit it wrong from five stories, you're going to be in trouble. It's... it's *awesome*, Sarah. It's *just fucking awesome!*"

Sarah giggled.

Barb was in the hot tub again. She had gone full stop, throwing in the rest of the aromatherapy bath salts—everything they had. First thing in the morning, she told herself, she'd hunt down the head of this place and demand more food and more bath salts. And get both.

Zander and Peter were on the couch, waiting for Steve and Sarah.

"So why ain'ts ya got no food?"

"Just never bought none yo."

"Y'all's doin' it *the hard way*, bro."

Pete shrugged.

DTV was replaying the terrorist's fall in slow-motion, arms and legs flailing, insanely, desperately attempting flight until his destiny was met.

A long, poignant dissolve followed, to the man's triumphant raised fist.

"Yo, that shit is *ri-dica-lous!*" Zander whispered.

"So wicked yo..."

The images were remarkable. Crystal-clear, cinema-quality widescreen HDTV, captured live. And not even a single camera jitter.

"Being a stuntman..." Zander said, whistling.

"Bro..."

"Bet he's doin' two chicks at once right now."

"Prolly."

Zander checked his watch. "Yo, I gotta jump. You 'member a'ight, if your dad don't come back you hit our crib. Yous is stayin' wit us t'night."

"A'ight."

They hit fists.

Zander skipped out and Pete picked up the food his dad had left. Cans of corn, potato chips, and something called collard greens. Whatever those were. They looked gross and he wondered if he should hide them.

DTV: BREAKING NEWS flashed across the screen, amplified by the powerful theme tune, and Pete sat up. He called back to Zander but he was already gone.

Onscreen, the shaken face of a DTV reporter appeared.

"Ladies and gentlemen..." he began somberly, "I'm on location in Good Health..."

Pete heard the voice echoing through the atrium. The broadcast was live on the InfoTron!

"... I need your attention. Please stop what you're doing. This is quite possibly the most important announcement you've ever heard in your life. And your life might very well depend on it."

"Mom!" Pete called.

"Quiet!" she yelled back.

"Mom it's important!"

"I don't care!"

Pete turned up the volume as the tear-stained, desperate face of a young wife appeared from her hospital bed. She wiped her eyes, trying to focus on the piece of paper in her hands.

DTV panned back to the reporter, who took a deep breath. "Ladies and gentlemen, minutes ago on the atrium floor this woman's husband was kidnapped. At gunpoint."

"Whoa!" Pete yelled.

"This is not... us," he said. "This is not the work of DisasterLand. This is... something else."

The reporter paused to compose himself, "I need to make this very clear. *We are not responsible.*"

DisasterLand was silent now, except for the surreal echo of the reporter's voice through the vast atrium.

"She was given a message to read on-air. In this request, and only in this request, will we indulge the terrorists."

He turned to the woman, placing his hand firmly on her shoulder. "Are you ready?"

With all of her strength, she nodded and raised the letter.

"Nelly is dying," she began weakly, "and soon, the Indonesian Giant Pimpernel will be no more. These are dangerous times."

She choked back tears and continued slowly, her voice gaining in strength, "We will use every means at our disposal to wake up the world. We have no choice. *We must save our winged brethren.*"

She looked at the camera, her young face torn apart by pain, "If the last Pimpernel is murdered, his spirit will return to earth in three days to unleash a wrath upon the planet that will consume it in fire.

"A Pimpernel has not been spotted among dedicated followers for 329 days and we fear the end is neigh. We will do what is necessary to make you understand. We are prepared to sacrifice ourselves in service of Nelly."

She sniffed, "The Pimpernel represents nothing less than the secret to human transformation. Like the caterpillar who becomes a magnificently liberated butterfly, we too must arise to meet our true nature as pure spirit. Only the Pimpernel holds the key.

"If the final Pimpernel is murdered, humanity is destined to be confined to the prison of the flesh for eternity."

She was crying now, and the reporter patted her back gently, "Free Our Winged Brethren," she finished. "Martyrs for liberated love. Signed, Monarch."

The reporter hugged her as she cried, silently, resting the paper on her lap.

"*What the fuck?*" Pete whispered.

The image cut back to the studio, to another grim-faced anchor. "Thanks, Chip. Ladies and gentlemen, DisasterLand is under attack."

"No shit Sherlock!" Pete yelled.

"Quiet!" Barb retorted, from the bathroom. "No cursing!"

The announcer continued, "Over the last several hours, it has become clear that terrorists have infiltrated DisasterLand. We are all in danger, this is not a joke. Please return to your suites and remain calm. Wait for further instructions. An important interview will follow."

Just before the image cut, the anchor broke down, his eyes filling with tears. Screaming echoed from the atrium.

The words of the elderly couple came flashing back to Peter and goose bumps prickled his skin.

The butterfly backpack.

The DTV anchor articulated each pregnant syllable with staggering gravity: "*The Indonesian Giant Pimpernel.*"

An image appeared, a digitally-enhanced zoom into the terrorist's tattoo as he stood on the rail. It was large butterfly, showing remarkable similarities to *anagallis arvensis*, the famed flower. The Scarlet Pimpernel.

"As the grave nature of what we all face came to light," the anchor stated, "we managed to contact one of the world's most distinguished lepidopterists in the jungles of Malaysia for confirmation. This interview was conducted moments ago and we play it now in its entirety."

The image of Dr. Renny Arlesberg appeared, sunburned and somber, surrounded by the immense green of the rainforest. His head nodded, and he began to speak. "Yes. Well, without a doubt Nelly's the most rare and elusive butterfly on the planet. And, until very recently, the stuff of legend... somewhat like a mermaid or a unicorn. In fact, until now very few people even knew of its existence. I suppose you could call it a bit of a professional secret."

"I've been told you've seen one sir?" the female DTV reporter asked, from the studio. Her eyes were piercing, worried.

The lepidopterist's eyes softened in misty remembrance, a wistful smile spreading across his face. "Yes. Once. And only for a moment."

"You're positive, sir?"

"Of course. It was the greatest moment of my life. I will never forget it."

"Then perhaps you can understand the motives of these men, even in some small way?"

Arlesberg was stern. "Never. This is a disgraceful, barbaric act entirely inconsistent with any true spiritual principals."

There was a long pause and his face relaxed. "But Nelly's primary habitat *is* threatened. I've seen that personally. And the situation could indeed be grave."

"You mean the species could be on the edge of extinction?"

The moment was pregnant. The doctor nodded, gravely. "Almost certainly is. Yes."

The reporter shook her head in understanding, then pushed on, "Doctor Arlesberg, earlier you referred to the Pimpernel as 'Nelly', can you please elaborate?"

"The species was named, and nicknamed, by its discoverer Sir Reginald Browne, who immediately recognized the uncanny resemblance to the fabled flower."

"It is astonishing."

"Quite."

"As one of the world's most celebrated experts on the butterfly, would you perhaps have a few words for those that are perpetrating this ghastly tragedy?"

"Yes, well, I can try. Please, I share your sense of outrage at the possible loss of one of the world's most beautiful creatures... and I do agree that everything must be done to preserve its habitat so that not only Nelly but all of the forest's inhabitants may be allowed to live in peace. But if your goal was attention to this matter, you have achieved it. You must now free these innocents. You must stop this madness lest it get out of hand."

"Thank you, Dr. Arlesberg."

"Thank you. My heart goes out to you all—every one of you—and I pray for your safe release."

His image faded.

DisasterLand hung, breathlessly.

The anchor returned, eyes filled with tears, "Ladies and gentlemen, wherever you are, again, please immediately return to your suites and wait for further instructions. Your safety can no longer be guaranteed.

"We will broadcast as long as we are able."

"Mom, we're under attack! For real!" Pete was pounding on the bathroom door.

"*Stop it!*" Barb yelled, shaken from her peaceful semi-slumber, "No more. I'm finished. I told you. I'm seceding from the union."

"No, for real. DTV just showed all those fashionistas, all eight of them, even the dead one! And they've laid down their arms! They *all* said it's real! We're under attack!"

"Peter, why don't you go get your suit and come and join me."

"Shouldn't we find dad? And Sarah? *What if the terrorists got them?*"

"They're fine."

Pete stared at the glossy paint of the closed door. Images of his mother, wrists slit and slowly dying in the warm bubbling water flashed through his mind. "Mom, are you OK?"

"Just go get your suit."

"Mom, I'm not even kidding. The announcer was crying!"

"Of course he was, honey. I'd be crying too if I made that much money. Now go get your suit. I'll turn the jets back on."

Minutes later, Pete tentatively climbed in the hot lavender water. Outside the window, the desert night was crisp and clear.

"Mom, don't you think one of us needs to guard the front door? What if a terrorist broke in and tied us up?"

"Peter, this is the last time. I mean it. Nothing is going to happen to us. Your father and sister are fine and these people are a bunch of sick evil lying bastards."

They looked out, over the desert, to the tranquil security center and beyond to the darkened mountains.

Maybe his mom had a point, Pete finally realized. It sure was nicer in here. Pete sat back, trying to relax. But he couldn't.

"Mom?"

"Yes, Peter."

"I'm worried about you."

Barb smiled, opening her eyes. She rubbed his head, gently.

"I'm fine, honey. Really. I just don't like seeing dead people—or people playing dead people. And I don't like seeing splattered brains and severed limbs. I do not like smelling what I've smelled. I would rather sit here in this hot tub and admire the beauty of the natural landscape."

"Yeah, that sounds a'ight."

The warm water frothed around them.

"Smells good in here, DJ."

"Ummm..."

"Think about when we came in. Remember how stressed we were? How do you feel now mom?" Pete asked.

Barb had to admit: her everyday cares felt a million miles away. In fact, she hadn't thought about her classroom once. And she did feel good. Hungry... exhausted... But as empty as she was physically, she was full emotionally. Cleansed, in a strange way.

Barb smiled. "You're right, Peter. I have to agree."

"Yeah. Whenever it's gotten bad I've just thought of being home and it gets me through."

Barb stared.

"You know what I mean," Pete added, awkwardly. "I'm just glad that we're not really under attack. I got kind of scared there."

"From now on, Pete, we're leaving DTV off. OK?"

"OK, mom."

For one heart-stopping moment, the brilliance of the massive explosion turned the entire valley to daylight, rattling the thick glass windows only feet away from Barb and Peter's previously relaxed bodies.

"Holy cow!" Pete screamed, leaping up, launching a tidal wave of water over the bathroom floor.

Barb grabbed her son and sloshed to the far end of the hot tub, cowering. Their startled faces glowed with a hellish flicker as the ground beneath them shook.

The security center at the foot of the mountains was now gone, obliterated in one terrible instant. An enormous fireball was ascending into the darkness, obscuring the clear night sky.

Barb flipped off the jets. As the water around them settled, they were overtaken by absolute silence. DisasterLand was holding its breath.

"DJ..." Pete whispered.

"Quiet, Peter... Please..."

Moments later, two black SUVs burst through the raging fire. One spun and blocked the road while the other continued on, roaring straight towards DisasterLand.

"Peter," Barb said staring, "tell me what they said on DTV."

"They're butterfly terrorists," Pete said. "They want to save this Pimpernel thing. They said if the last butterfly is killed the world will be consumed in fire."

"Oh, Lord."

"Yeah, it seemed kinda weird. I wasn't sure if it was real..." Pete paused. "But..."

"But what?"

"Well, dad said not to tell you, but we met these old people this morning when we were getting muffins. And they said last night a bomb was found at the vigil in a butterfly backpack. They said that's why the floor was cleared."

"How did they know?"

"They said a guard told them. They said he was worried."

"Oh my God."

"Mom we've got to find dad and Sarah."

"I know, honey. Get your clothes on."

Far below, a masked figure leaned out of the approaching SUV to hoist a flag. *A butterfly*.

Barb was nervously pacing the walkway with Steve's binoculars, scouring the deserted atrium below for signs of her husband and daughter. Pete was perched atop the rail for a better view of the elevators.

They were still wet, having raced out hoping to see Steve and Sarah emerge from the elevators unharmed. But the panicked exodus had slowed to a trickle and there was still no sign of them.

A firm, powerful voice repeated, blasting out from the InfoTron, "For your own safety, please immediately return to your suite and await further instructions. Again, please immediately return to your suite."

Guards had sealed off the fifth floor beneath them and were patrolling the floodlit stairs to build confidence in those returning home. Elevators were on express and the lines below had all but disappeared, and with them many of the expectant families lining the rails of every floor to await family members. Amongst those still peering out from the walkways, a stifling sense of dread was rising.

The InfoTron was strangely low-key, reading simply:

Please return to your suites.

For several minutes, Barb and Peter hadn't shared a word. But now, near tears, Barb had to break the silence.

"I don't understand it, Peter. Where are they?"

"There was lots of people down there, mom. Don't worry. It just takes time."

"Should we call Good Health? What if something's happened?"

"OK, mom. I'll stay right here."

Barb handed Pete the binoculars and hurried back into their suite. Peter continued to scan the atrium. Guards were still flooding out of the security center.

As Pete sat alone, the truth of what they faced began to take shape and his thoughts slipped into the unthinkable: what if his dad and sister *were* gone? What if

DisasterLand *was* under attack?

There had been a comforting undercurrent to his earlier fears, stemming from *Ghost*-hyped feelings of superiority. Deep down, he knew for sure it was all a game, that nothing serious was ever going to happen.

There was fear, fear of the unknown maybe, or of an accident, but ultimately he knew they would be safe. But now, if all this was true, than nothing could be guaranteed.

Barb hurried out, in tears, "I can't get through."

"Maybe they've been kidnapped?"

"Jesus, Peter. I..."

A fierce, sustained rumble rocked the building and the atrium suddenly went black.

"Peter?"

"Yeah mom?" he called, his voice an octave higher to crest over the rising screams.

"You OK?"

"Yeah."

"Get your flashlight."

"Got it."

"Turn it on."

Barb was grabbing the rail for support. She took the light from him, shined it down the walkways in both directions.

"It's another blackout."

An immense spotlight began to sweep each floor, shooting out from somewhere near the park. The light soon hit their faces, transporting them to the inside of a sun. Then it passed.

A distant voice called out, this time from a megaphone, "Please! Return to your suites! *Return to your suites!*"

Their vision cleared and Barb looked up to see guards rushing towards her, motioning them inside.

"Come on, let's go Peter. We'll never see them now anyway."

On the floor of the swaying elevator, Sarah and Steve's eyes met for one timeless second. They were suspended in darkness, seventeen stories above the atrium floor. Alone.

Moments earlier, the elevator had instantly and violently froze with a deafening screech, knocking them both to the floor. The lights had dimmed, recovered, and finally went out altogether as the elevator bounced to a stop.

A horrible and deadly silence overtook them. Disasterland's heart had stopped.

A slow and painful wail grew inside Sarah as Steve clung to her, fighting to calm his own overwhelming nausea. "Easy," he whispered, "Easy honey. We're fine... we're just fine... just breathe. Breathe."

Gathering strength, Steve inched carefully towards the glass doors to look down onto the dark, crippled atrium.

"They've hit the power. There no lights. Anywhere. Unless that spotlight found us."

Steve rested his hand on Sarah's back. Once again, he had failed, putting not only his own, but also his daughter's life in danger. *They should have taken the stairs.*

"Dad, I'm scared."

"Me too, honey, but we're fine. We're going to wait a moment for help. If no one comes, we're going to climb out of here. We're not far from home."

Lost in the crush of guests following the InfoTron's release of images from the devastated security center, Steve's only thought was to redouble their efforts to find food and return home as soon as possible.

They had frantically continued their search while keeping an eye out for Barb and Peter but in the end had come up empty on all counts. Most guests already having fled and guards desperate to clear the atrium, they had hurried into an elevator without a second thought, not realizing that they were gambling.

Now they were trapped.

Steve stood, cautiously, and the elevator trembled. He felt like he was surfing.

"Dad... *don't!*" Sarah shrieked.

"It's OK, honey. It's OK," he gave her his hand and gently pulled her up. They steadied themselves.

"What do we do?"

Steve was examining the elevator. He pointed to the ceiling, "See—there's a hatch. I'm going to hoist myself up. Then I'll pull you up after."

"Are you sure we shouldn't just wait?"

"Honey, I think DisasterLand has bigger things to worry about. We're on our own here and it's up to us. OK?"

He squeezed her tightly. "We're going to be just fine, honey. Just fine. It's less than two floors. I love you honey, more than anything."

"I love you too, daddy..."

Steve looked out, past his daughter and towards the black void of the dome. Not a soul seemed to be moving. His blood froze.

"Dad, I'll go." Sarah pulled back. "You hoist me up. I'm smaller."

"But you can't pull me up. It's OK, honey, just get on your hands and knees. I'm going to step on your back."

Sarah carefully bent down onto all fours. The elevator swayed, creaking.

"OK, honey, here I go. Ready?"

"Ready dad."

Steve stepped gently onto her back, and flipped the hatch's handle just in front of his nose. It turned easily and Steve flung it open.

"OK, honey, it's open. I'm going up."

"Be careful!"

"I will."

As he considered the task before him, Steve vowed, once and for all, to get in shape. There would be no more excuses after this. No more.

Sarah grunted as he sprung up off her back. Sweating, he clawed his way up and out, onto the roof of the elevator.

Cautiously, resting on all fours, he looked back down inside.

"You OK, honey?"

"Yeah," she said, rubbing her back.

Steve turned away to contemplate the scene over his head, carefully avoiding another glimpse of the atrium. His stomach was free-falling.

"What's it like, dad?"

"We're in good shape, honey. Real good shape. There's a ladder right here. I'm going to pull you up and we'll climb to the next floor. We're almost to eighteen and we'll break the glass. It's a piece of cake."

"OK, dad."

"Ready?"

Steve wiped his hands on his thighs and leaned over, down onto his stomach, carefully, legs extending out towards the silent atrium.

For one split second, he allowed himself to appreciate the delicacy of what was happening. Then, quickly, he forced it out of his mind.

Sarah extended her hands and Steve met them halfway, locking onto her wrists. With all his might and with a spring from her legs, he was just able to pull her arms clear, where she was able to brace herself against top of the elevator on her own.

She struggled up and out and froze, allowing the elevator to regain its equilibrium.

Their labored breathing filled the shaft.

"OK, honey, that was the toughest part. We've got only eight feet or so up, then we'll break the glass."

"How?"

"With a shoe or something."

"OK."

"You ready?"

"Yeah, let's get out of here."

"I'll go first."

Steve cautiously slid over to the ladder and stabilized himself against the rungs. His whole body was doing the Elvis and he fought to steady himself.

Failing, he took the first few uneasy steps to preserve momentum.

"When I'm clear, you climb up, honey."

Come on, Sarah, cowgirl up, she told herself. "Coming up now."

Steve felt her weight on the ladder, and soon, her hand on his calf.

"That's me, daddy. I'm OK."

"Let's go up, sweetie."

"Climbing up."

Another screech rippled through the shaft, continuing and growing in volume.

"What's happening, honey?" Steve yelled.

"I don't know!"

It was soon unbearable. Hands occupied, they couldn't shut their ears.

Then, suddenly, it stopped. And with a swoosh, the wind hit.

The elevator was dropping out from under them, seventeen stories straight down. Long seconds passed, measured in thudding heartbeats.

It hit with a massive crash, splinters of glass ricocheting in every direction.

Steve fought back molten tears.

"Sarah?"

She touched his ankle and he managed to exhale.

"What happened?"

"I don't know. When I stepped off... it... the whole thing fell... it's so far down, daddy."

"Don't look. Nothing has changed. We're just going up these couple of feet and we're breaking the glass, OK?"

"OK..." She was hyperventilating.

"Sarah, everything's OK, just be strong and relax, OK?"

Steve peeked down, trying to see her, and found himself staring into the dark abyss instead. He swallowed.

"I'm climbing up, Sarah. Follow me up. I'm just going a few feet, then I'm breaking the glass on eighteen. Just a couple more feet."

He inched his way up the ladder. His hands were sweaty, shaking, his grip tenuous and weak.

Sarah groaned.

"What is it, honey?"

"My shoes are still wet. They're slippery. All the water's squishing out of my socks..." Her breathing grew more and more rapid, her voice more hysterical, "They're really slick, daddy. I'm scared... I'm scared I'm going to fall!"

Her desperate words were magnified by the empty shaft.

"It's OK... just... relax... take a deep breath. Come up slowly."

Knocking echoed. From overhead.

"Sarah! Firefighters! They're right above me! They're waving—they're going to cut the glass on eighteen! Just hang on!"

"Daddy I'm scared... my shoes..."

Suddenly the shaft was filled with fresh air.

"They've got it honey! Come on, take it easy, easy... slowly..."

"*DADDY!*" Sarah shrieked, and for a split second he caught a flash of her blonde hair, then nothing... only the long, soul-shattering scream fading below.

Steve waited, paralyzed, for the inevitable crushing sound of her impact. It never came.

His strength was failing as desperate wails racked his body. He was fighting with all his strength just to hang on but all he really wanted was release.

His hands weakened and he prepared himself to fall, to join her, unable to face another second without her, unable to face Barb, unable to live with this terrible knowledge.

Instead, he felt the grasp of the firefighters as they took hold of him.

"*Whooo—hoooo!*"

"SARAH?!"

"Daddy! I'm OK! I'M OK! *I landed on this big airbag thing!*"

An all-encompassing, effervescent joy like he had never known arose from the depths of his soul and Steve looked up to his rescuers through teary eyes.

"You just relax, sir," one said, "We'll take care of everything."

Sarah hit the bag and an ecstatic cheer swept through the bridge. Yet the rush of relief washing over the crew barely mitigated the evening's crushing sense of loss.

Half-hearted high-fives were being shared as the footage of Sarah's fall was replayed, the action swirling above them like a tornado.

It had been brilliant, the timing extraordinarily fortuitous. When Elektra had realized they had a hero family trapped in the elevators, they went for broke. She dropped the elevator and fired the bags. Then prayed.

Maybe it was cruel, maybe a little rash—and maybe they had even endangered lives unnecessarily. But they'd pushed the Beyers for all they were worth and it had paid off.

Elektra knew the crew needed a boost, needed something to celebrate at the end of the darkest evening they'd shared. When she'd glanced at Shae before pulling the trigger, his eyes had told her to go for it.

She slipped her headphones down around her neck and rubbed her swollen eyes.

As soon as Jimmy'd hit, she'd known. They all had, and a terrible hush had fallen over the bridge. Elektra had never experienced anything like it and hoped she never would again.

But she had pushed on, immediately.

"We're on red here! Crew on red!" she screamed into her headset. "A5, quadrant A5! Let's get him up! Get him up! *ADs, we need guest repellent!*"

EMS crews were already responding and Good Health reported the 'copter was scrambling. EMS expected to have him stabilized and on the helipad in 12.

"Colin?" Elektra cried.

"Guards are flyin' in," he said, "I'm on the second cart. You've got my second second confirmed on that flight to Vegas if you need her."

"Get on the roof, honey."

"Flyin' up," her voice crackled.

"Secure phone?" Elektra asked.

"Already on its way," the production coordinator responded.

"Beautiful."

Elektra felt nauseous, her head spinning. The sudden chaos of the atrium on the screens above was too much. She abandoned herself to the single-shot Feed, surrendering herself solely to her director's eyes. She needed the nonessential pre-sorted for her own critical survival. She had to focus on one thing at a time and it would be the shot of his choosing.

Guests closest to the fall scattered by gunfire. Jimmy's motionless body. Guards cordoning it off, faking his arrest. The EMS arrival. The remaining terrorists fleeing the walkway. Guards retaking the atrium.

Elektra stood speechless, petrified she'd muddy the psychological waters with nervous chatter. But as Elektra relaxed, as her mind settled, a growing sense of helplessness rapidly overwhelmed her. Staring at the Feed, peeking at the screens above her, for the first time in her career she felt absolutely powerless. She choked back a claustrophobic scream.

Those on the floor were in the moment and nothing she could say or do would matter. It all boiled down to their training. For once, Elektra was a spectator. She could only watch.

And then it all turned once more. Abandoning herself of ego, she was soon able to fully appreciate the magic in what was taking place. The actors' skill was blossoming into fruition, unmistakable to all. Their instincts, their complete presence of mind, had been carefully honed, exquisitely cultivated by DisasterLand's experts. Their training had worked wonders and the show was indeed going on. Seamlessly.

By the time Jimmy's cart had disappeared into Good Health, his fist raised in triumph, her despair had turned to pride.. For a split second, all hearts on the bridge fluttered with hope.

Seconds later, however, it again turned to crushing loss. Colin reported back from Good Health in hushed tones on a secure channel to the bridge: Jimmy was gone.

Colin had sculpted Jimmy's motionless fist like a puppetmaster, raising the elbow unseen by the cameras. It had been a gut reaction based on years of producing world-class drama. It was one last tribute.

And it alone sold the fall.

"Under the nose!" Shae screamed, interrupting the icy stillness that had consumed the bridge. Someone tossed him a headset.

"Shae, here. Thanks everyone. I need to say that what's happened is tragic but we must not lose focus. We must move forward. And if you want something hidden, you hide it where it's most conspicuous. You hide it under everyone's nose," he paused to let it sink in.

"We don't suppress this. We don't censor it. In fact, it's all we show on DTV from now until we lose power. I want it on the InfoTron immediately—bigger than life!"

It was the Word Of God, but was greeted with puzzled silence. *Could he be serious?*

DTV's lead producer responded seconds later, "Preparing the packages now, Shae. Jimmy the hero."

"Exactly. And he is. We must make sure everyone here knows it even if he was on the wrong team. Karen—we need a miracle!"

"Gotta let the dust settle, Shae. We're no help here. But we're with you: Jimmy's staying in the show."

One long and desperate hour later, Barb and Peter were seated in darkness, listening only to the dry rasping of their breath as it broke the dark, thick silence punctuated only by screams.

Pete stared through the open bedroom door and out at the moon floating in the lonely nighttime sky, sensing the cries of the injured structure around him.

The horrific sound of distant, shattering glass had splintered the night air earlier, but neither had the courage to investigate. Reverberations were still being felt.

Barb was curled up next to him, eyes frozen ahead, unblinking, as she traced the evening's progression from bad to worse.

Guards had forced their door open, allowing them to slip back inside the suite, but they had nothing. Absolutely nothing. Ten minutes before, their last candle had gone out, and with it any hope of continuous light. Barb had used all the candles for hot-tubbing, and now, when they really needed them, they were gone. It was unforgivable.

How many more mistakes had they made?

She was going through a mental checklist in her mind, trying to recall what Sarah had told her about surviving. One week without food, she remembered, but two days without water.

Barb opened her D-PAK and grabbed her light. She flicked it on.

"Where are you going mom?"

"I just had a thought."

"Good thought or bad thought?"

Barb didn't answer. She hurried into the kitchen, to the taps. Holding her breath she turned them—and found nothing.

They had no water.

Barb flicked off the light, grabbing her head in her hands. She fought for strength, fought for survival. Her son needed her.

"Mom, you OK?"

"Yes..." she called, after a long moment. "I'm coming."

"Everything OK?"

"No," Barb laughed. "Not really."

No water.

There was Good Health. And maybe—just maybe—Good Food. Del Sol had that bottled water list...

But was there enough for over two thousand people?

And for how long?

They had their purification tablets which would produce enough clean water to last each person two days—if they had a source.

There was the fountain. And there was the river. But both were nineteen stories down in the pitch black chaos.

"How much water do you have, Peter?" Barb asked, returning to the couch.

"My bottle's almost full."

"OK, me too."

"Why?"

"No water."

Pete stared and she flipped off her light to fend off his gaze.

"Are we gonna go find dad?"

"I don't think so, honey. We're just going to have to wait for now. The elevators won't be working so it'll take time."

"OK..."

"They'll be back. In the meantime, let's turn everything off. The TV, the lights, turn it all off. Come on."

As they were finishing their tasks, footsteps halted outside their door. Pete hurried over, his mom in tow.

"Shh..." she whispered, heart racing.

Words were being exchanged outside in low voices, and Barb grew concerned. Pete flipped on his light, but Barb placed her hand angrily over it. He flipped it off.

The door started to wedge open. As the moonlight grew to flood the entryway, Barb retreated, dragging Pete with her towards the bedroom.

With a scrape, the door slid open, wider, the light almost blinding compared to the simmering darkness they had been submersed within.

"Barb? Peter?"

"*DAD?*" Pete yelled.

"*MOM?*" Sarah cried.

"We're here, honey!" Barb called, racing back into the hallway where they met in teary-eyed hugs.

"Y'all take care now. Get this door shut, y'hear?" said a silhouetted guard.

"Right away, sir," Steve said. "Thanks."

"You had an escort?" Barb asked.

"Sort of," Steve said. "Yeah, I guess so."

"We got stuck in the elevator, mom. And we had to be rescued," Sarah replied, quietly.

"Oh my God. Are you OK?"

"We're fine," Sarah said, "just fine." But before she could stop herself, the tears were flowing and she buried her face in her mom's stomach.

"You sure?"

"Just a little fright, Barb. Nothing more," Steve said.

"How long were you in there?"

"I don't know, honey. Too long. We're just happy to be home."

"Oh God, Steve. I was so scared. We've got no food, no power and no water."

"No *water?*"

"None."

"Mom, we've got a little food," Pete offered.

"You're right. Zander's dad gave us some snacks."

"There's some good news," Steve said. "OK, first thing's first. We've got to get this door shut before we get in trouble. Then we get packed. It's going to be a long night."

Minutes after the night's *all clear*, DisasterLand's department heads were gathered for a tense emergency meeting on the mount.

Shae broke the news to all: Jimmy had been pronounced dead on arrival in Vegas. Resuscitation efforts had continued throughout his journey but they had been unsuccessful. After this meeting, he would personally alert the family.

"This may sound cruel," Shae said after allowing the news to settle. "But we need a replacement. Immediately."

"We're covering-up?" Elektra asked.

"In wartime truth is so precious that she should always be attended by a bodyguard of lies," Shae quoted.

"Churchill," Karen answered.

Shae nodded. "We've got no choice. We cover up or we lose everything. Trust seals the illusion and by being honest in this case we destroy it and us. We investigate what happened and we report it to the board, honestly. *Brutally* if necessary. After I notify Jimmy's family I'm personally speaking to each of the board. Thank God they weren't still here for this. Then we shut up and we move on."

"Problem is," Elektra said, clearing her throat, "All of our Asian actors are on the floor. We don't have any A-list Asian understudies. People will know."

"Not from that far away," Shae offered. "No one saw anything."

"But DTV," Jude said, still clearly shaken. "They're playing close-ups. And his *character* is Asian Shae."

Karen concurred.

"Then we need someone who can *play* Asian. This is sensitive. *Highly fucking sensitive.* I need someone we have a relationship with. Someone *here*. Not from outside. What about B-list?"

"No..." Jude said, his head shaking. "I'm sorry. We don't. It'd be too big of a gamble."

Elektra took another restrained sip of water, dying to down a double of Scotch in one right now. Her eyes met Jude's.

"We've got someone, Shae. An actor we saw last week. He's Tibetan. Jude knows his brother so there's at least a degree of trust. And I liked him."

"He doesn't know the script."

"He watched the first dress with Julie. On Thursday."

"And he can play Asian?"

"He *is* Asian Shae."

"Right. Look, this doesn't happen again. We've fucked up. Messenger him a script and let's get him here by sunrise."

"Done," Jude leapt up, flipping open his phone.

"Colin, I need an AD at the rewrites tonight to represent production. Your call."

"Of course," Colin backed away, flicking on his radio.

Shae's thinking deepened, his eyes slowly closed.

"Where do we stand, practically?" he finally asked Greg.

"Writers are assembling next door and espressos are being brewed. We'll have yellow pages by five a.m."

"So are we set?"

"We are set, sir."

"What about Clint?" Elektra asked. "I've got to tell him."

"Let Colin worry about that, E. I need you to go up, have a very strong drink and get a good night's sleep. There's nothing you could have done and we need you fresh for tomorrow. Don't worry about the rewrites, don't worry about anything. Greg has it covered. If you've got questions tomorrow morning, we'll deal with them first thing at the story meeting."

Elektra nodded. Shae was right. As always.

"Do we make a public statement?" Greg asked, "Or do department heads notify their crews?"

For the first time, Shae's head went in his hands, his fingers massaging his temples.

"I'll make a statement on the Feed," Shae finally replied. "Let's get this over with. We all need to get some sleep. Are DTV's studios free?"

"Of course," DTV's producer confirmed.

"I've got to calm nerves. This dude was an Olympic gymnast, guys. Not sure you knew that. We're going to get to the bottom of this to make sure it doesn't happen again. Meanwhile, everything is above-board. Rumors are not going to be allowed to catch and all attempts at honesty will be made. But the truth does not leave these domes."

"Lhasa's in," Jude said, returning to the meeting. "Car's picking him up at three-thirty. Script will be waiting in the back seat, he'll read it coming up. I'm faxing the contracts to his agent now."

"Karen, can you have something in the car by one-thirty?" Shae asked.

"Something, even if it's just an outline."

"Fine. He's OK with this Jude?"

"Shae, are you kidding man? He's freakin' *wetting himself*!"

Thirty minutes later, DTV's producers had assembled a tribute reel of Jimmy's enlightened stunt work and all eyes amongst DisasterLand's cast and crew were now locked on the Feed. There wasn't a dry eye in the house.

The five minute reel faded out to a standing ovation amongst those on the bridge and Shae's image took its place. Slowly pacing an empty studio, he somehow radiated strength.

"Jimmy Ono was pronounced dead on arrival tonight in Las Vegas..." he began. "In the midst of the darkness, I feel it's important to remember the light: why we're here, why we do what we do despite the risks, why what we do is important."

He paused, taking a long sip of water as the camera slowly closed in.

"We've all got work to do in the coming days. The script is about to catch fire. But I wanted to take a moment to share my appreciation both for Jimmy Ono and for each one of you. I really do believe this will be the most successful show ever—we're well on our way—and there's no greater tribute to Jimmy and his work that we can give. I mean that.

"We exist to immerse our guests in an environment where positive personal transformation is facilitated. That is our goal, our mission. We're catalysts in that sense.

"We are in the personal liberation business, specifically personal liberation through danger, through fear. We are a factory for the transformation of people and we are all about the universal need for togetherness, about fighting the corruption and alienation of families worldwide. Our work often produces transcendental moments, one of the reasons people of faith are drawn so powerfully here. We dissolve boundaries between philosophies and religions.

"*We are not in the exploitation business.* There's no cynicism here. We're the good guys and our continuing ability to perform this public service is priority number one. Our survival, our mission, gets more important, more *necessary*, each and every day as the world darkens. Enormous amounts of fear and tension exist in the population, and all of it must be released or it will do damage. We will all pay the price.

"DisasterLand offers catharsis. We're an analgesic for modernity. Our guests spread their knowledge, their lessons, their more in-tune, more enlightened ways of being when they leave, lightening the loads of those around them. We bring people together and we make the world a better place. I know you all believe this. You see it every day.

"That said, I feel it's important to lay out our response to this incident and why we did what we did and why we're continuing. Some of you may feel—and I'm only guessing here—that we're somehow diminishing his memory or his work by continuing our show or that we even glorified his passing tonight. Nothing could be further from the truth. It's honestly the only choice we have.

"If we let this get out—and by the way our leak policy is always in full effect—it endangers our very existence. I've said it a million times but our business is trust. This is our currency. The guests trust us and we trust them even when we intentionally ensure the exact opposite. If this trust is broken, we have nothing. It makes all of us less stable and in fact endangers lives even more. And it will end horribly—either in personal tragedy or in the failure of our business—neither of which will I let happen. We must all keep Jimmy close, in our hearts and souls and memories. But we must leave him there. This does not go public. Under any circumstances. Elektra?"

The camera panned and Elektra walked on to join him, a last minute addition. Clearly exhausted, her appearance only garnered sympathy.

"Thanks, Shae. That's sort of hard to hear, I'll be the first to say. If any of you need to talk to anyone at any time or for any reason, please call or visit our psychologists. They're up all night tonight and every night and they can help. Maybe even more importantly, check in on your friends. Talk. But I have to remind you—not a word on the floor. We're listening. Don't even think about it."

Elektra smiled faintly, then continued.

"There's no real easy way to do this, but I sincerely want to welcome Lhasa Lapsong as the newest member of our team. He's of Tibetan ancestry and will be taking over Jimmy's character. Some of you may have met him when he was in on Thursday's dress."

Lhasa's face appeared, the headshot photo.

"His exact roll is being decided as we speak, but we're confident that he's going to make an amazing addition. Please introduce yourselves to him if you get the chance and help him feel welcome under these difficult circumstances. He is now a full member of our team. Nothing less.

"Our psychologists have decided it best to keep him in the dark about Jimmy's fate. He's been told that Jimmy's only been injured and was rushed to Vegas for surgery. I hope you all understand the point of this little white lie, and help us to maintain it at least until the end of this show. I think you'll agree it's absolutely vital. Please be discreet. Thank you."

The shot widened to welcome Shae once again, "Yes, thank you all, for your courage and your bravery and for your continuing commitment to the success of our mission. Do what you have to do to perform and don't hesitate to let your department heads know if you need something. Anything at all."

Shae took a deep breath, his face softening to reflect the weight of the evening's developments.

"We will now observe a minute's silence."

And for the first time ever during a show, the Feed cut to black.

A barely perceptible lightening in the desert sky lured Steve from his entryway post. The walkways had been quiet—too quiet—and Steve's festering thoughts desperately needed a turn to the new day.

He surveyed his sleeping family, fully dressed and spread out before him on the living room floor, one giant mass of bodies and cloth with D-PAKs strapped vitally around their waists and luggage within reach.

Steve tiptoed silently over them and on into the bedroom, relishing the outline of the mountains slowly emerging from the dark infinity. *Morning was coming.*

He placed his hands against the picture window, cool from the night, and shut his eyes in appeal for sanity.

It had been a long, soul-searching night haunted by mental phantasms. He had turned his family's predicament over and over in his mind repeatedly, attempting to comprehend the night's glaring silence, a silence entirely opposite of the night before. There had been no indication of activity in the dark atrium. None whatsoever.

Where were the raids? The shoot-outs? If they really were under attack, where was the help? The aid?

Where was the... *action?*

Instead, there had been nothing. Nothing at all.

Fear had oxidized his courage until it dissolved painfully into the night. Bizarre roller-coasters of thought led to fun-house mirrors which mocked his life's decisions and left him, by the sun's recent arrival, a hollow shell.

The butterfly backpack and the mysterious elderly couple, the lack of water, food, power and cash.

They would soon need help, for soon, they would be helpless.

By far the most disturbing revelation of the night had been biological in nature and its effects were already being felt. Soon, perhaps more than any other.

Their toilet, of course, was no longer functional.

The Happinol, Steve thought. *If he had only taken the Happinol, that ground would have been there. But now, he was left only with indecision, fear and pain.*

Why had he been so stupid? For the thousandth time that night, he chastised his lack of courage. *Why the secrecy? Why the shame?* It was only a drug. *Why couldn't he just talk to Barb?*

This would never have happened if he would have been brave, if he would have been honest with those he loved. He had abandoned his family, leaving them defenseless at the very point of their greatest vulnerability, when they most needed him to be strong. And now they were all in very serious trouble.

Steve opened his eyes. Once again, not for the first time and hopefully not for the last, he greeted the sun's arrival with something approaching profound thanks. The clichés held true, it was like seeing an old friend. And it gave him courage.

Steve stepped back to the door and flipped the light switch. Nothing. Slipping into the bathroom with dread, he flushed the toilet without lifting the seat.

Again, unbelievably, nothing.

He retreated to the bare bed, source of so much comfort in the previous evenings, now stripped of bedding to provide some sense of comfort to his sleeping family in the living room. He sat down, back against the wall.

A few minutes later, Barb kissed his cheek, startling him awake.

They looked out, together, at the devastated security center, now really only a charred shell. Directly in the center of the seared pit sat a black SUV, still parked across the road and blocking all access to DisasterLand.

Steve grabbed his binoculars from the bedside table, sure he could see two dark figures behind the tinted windows. A banner draped from the side featured the Earth, proclaiming:

One World Under Nelly

Barb squeezed his waist. "You OK?"

He gave her a silent, considered nod and finally dropped the binoculars. They were no use. It was just too far.

Barb slid the window open the maximum few inches and drank in the crisp air, like a diver preparing to submerge.

"You need some fresh air, honey. I think you've got no oxygen. You're brain's shutting off. You're on reduced capacity or something," she said.

Reduced capacity? "Are you calling me a dumbshit?" Steve asked, anger flashing.

"No, but you're all worked up. You need to crawl out of that dark corner."

Fresh desert air slowly leavened the suite and Steve realized Barb was right. It was impossibly stuffy in the enclosed space, after a night of no climate control.

That too would only get worse.

Steve took a deep breath, eyes shut, and let the fresh dawn air wash over him. Barb stared, fretting at the deep shadows under his eyes.

Eventually they popped open and Steve returned the stare, puzzled. Barb seemed alien in her odd calm. Was her capacity for denial greater than he ever could have imagined? The juxtaposition of his dark night and her determined nonchalance sent his head reeling.

"What's wrong with you?" he finally asked.

"Nothing, honey. Really."

"Aren't you worried?"

"Of course I am."

"No you're not."

"You're right, I'm not. Not anymore."

"You're not?"

"We agreed to be attacked by terrorists and now we are. I don't see the benefits of complaining."

"Are you *out of your mind?!*"

Barb turned away, motioning for silence. To her, Steve looked genuinely ill. She couldn't reinforce it.

"Look, I better get back to my position," Steve said, finally.

"OK..."

"We'll need to do a recon, honey, before the rest of the floor wakes up," he continued, at the door. "I need to know what happened last night. Or what *didn't* happen."

"Fine. But don't take the kids."

"We'll all go."

"No. Honey, please..."

"I need everyone's opinion, including yours. We'll be fast. This could be life and death. I'm sorry you don't get it, but you will."

Steve turned purposefully and strode into the living room, braced against the sour air which confronted him.

Barb returned her gaze to the desert valley dawn.

Returning to the entryway, Steve noticed a handwritten note slipped under the door. Had it come during the night? Had he fallen asleep?

He flipped on his flashlight.

Stay calm. You won't be hurt.
This isn't about you.

Steve ducked out into the silent, muted tones of the wounded atrium and edged along the wall towards the elevator to see if he drew fire. The rest of his family remained tucked inside the door, spotting him with frantic prairie-dogging. To them he appeared crippled, disfigured by exceptional efforts to protect his D-PAK.

Steve spit the bitter dregs of his chewed coffee beans onto the walkway.

So far so good, Steve told himself, and a chill shot down his spine like a thunderbolt, energizing him. Suddenly he was raising the stakes. He was pushing it, risking something. He was going to get answers.

Pete followed, Sarah next. Barb reluctantly brought up the rear, hurrying to the rail. They would inch down the walkway slowly, as far as the elevators. They would keep their wide-open front door within sight, allowing cross-ventilation to work its much-needed magic, then return as quickly as possible.

Armed guards were posted in pairs at every critical target on the atrium floor, and an impenetrable ring stood facing out from the fountain, weapons at-the-ready. Thick firehoses snaked out from the fountain towards the tower, limp, their presence holding menace. The terrorists' fifth-floor bulwark been disassembled but there were no other outward signs of response to last evening's attack.

"Oh my God!" Barb's screamed, one hand covering her mouth, the other pointing below.

"What?" Steve asked, following her hand.

"The elevator!" Barb whispered.

Below, the crumpled mass of steel lay motionless with shattered glass still littering the atrium floor, a terrible reminder to Steve and Sarah of how close they had been to the edge.

Sarah reeled away from the rail, gagging into her sleeve. Steve stared, covering for her, amazed there had been no effort to remove the gaping evidence of DisasterLand's colossal failure.

Why not?

He needed to change the topic quickly and it wasn't difficult. He let out a yell and raced to the landing.

Barb and Peter followed, allowing Sarah time to regroup. Additional teams of guards had been posted to each floor's landing and the closest were scrutinizing the Beyers' movements carefully. Steve realized he should have brought a white flag.

The glass windows of both cafés were shattered and water was still dripping inside the gutted spaces. The stench of fire was thick in the air.

The cafés had been torched and they were now in ruins. It had been recent.

Graffiti was splashed across the ruined walls.

FREE RED ADMIRAL!

LONG LIVE NELLY!

MONARCH RULES!

One guard stepped forward, pointing his weapon at a sign taped to the stairs. It was a hand-sketched copy of the terrorist's tattoo: The Pimpernel. *Watch, Learn and Act!* had been written in thick, block letters.

"You've still got him?" Steve asked.

Another guard reluctantly nodded, "Surgery."

"Goes by Red Admiral," another confirmed.

"DJ! Look!" Pete had found the final insult, spray-painted on the walkway above. Sarah maintained an uneasy distance while Barb pushed in for a closer look.

It was a giant floating butterfly, rendered in the distinct style of an anime character. Its body was a marvelous peachy color, the face distinctly human, reflecting infinite purity and loving kindness like a miniature Bodhisattva.

It was meditating.

The Beyers stared.

"So that's it?" whispered Pete, after many moments. "That's Nelly?"

"I doubt that's it *exactly*..." Steve said eventually, eyeing his son. Barb put her hands on Pete's shoulders.

A small, yellow halo ringed its two nubby antennae.

"DJ?"

"What son?"

"I think Nelly looks cool. Does that make me a terrorist?"

Steve lowered his voice as Barb smiled stupidly to the guards on behalf of her son. They glared.

"No, son, terrorism isn't a belief, it's a practice," Steve whispered. "If you blow us up because we think Nelly sucks, or to warn others what'll happen if they think that too, *then* you're a terrorist. Terrorists use the technique of fear to advance an agenda."

Pete thought about this. "Why are all terrorists brown people?"

Barb jumped in, "Honey, not now. And they're not. That's on TV. There've been terrorists in Northern Ireland for years and they're not brown."

"What are they?"

"They're Irish, honey, they're as pale as people get."

"I can't believe the cafés are gone," Sarah said, creeping in closer. The tears were flowing down her cheeks. *"I hate it here,"* she sniffed.

Her voice faded out and the family lingered, their thoughts ricocheting wildly across the fields of human emotion.

Steve's own emotions were succumbing to gravity as the night's mysteries portended worse to come. Barb, however, was finding Nelly's image oddly invigorating, her emotions enhanced as if her consciousness was being raised. Somehow, she felt, she understood.

Nelly was cute. And *meditating*.

The terrorists couldn't be *all bad. Could they?*

Barb stepped back to take in the walkway sweeping out around them and it all began to coalesce. Seeing the same destruction wrought on many other floors, it was too good. It was too perfect. DisasterLand looked like a movie set—not like the work of real terrorists.

Despite the sickly-sweet stench of burnt destruction around her, Barb realized that no matter what happened, she was glad they had come. No matter what, she felt secure. This was all meant to be and they would do what they felt was right. There would be no regrets.

"Time to go. We've been here too long already," Steve said.

The Beyers took one final look at Nelly's image and scurried back to their suite.

Sarah disappeared into her bedroom, desperate to lose herself in the abyss of deep sleep during the comparative safety of day.

In the kitchen, Barb opened their canned breakfast with a sigh and shake of her head. By popular demand, she divvied up the corn and potato chips and placed the last can—the collard greens—on top of the fridge, off-limits.

Steve offered to take Sarah her meal since she wasn't feeling well.

"Just put it on the dresser," Sarah moaned after he had stuck his head inside. "My head hurts."

She was on her side facing the wall, head smashed under a pillow.

Steve tiptoed in, shutting the door carefully. He put his hand on her shoulder and she yelped.

"You OK?"

"Yeah, my shoulder just hurts."

"You want to go back to Good Health?"

"No, I think I'm OK. I slept like 5 minutes all night."

"Look, I just want to say that I'm sorry. I..."

"It's OK, dad, it's not your fault. Please."

"But..." Steve paused and Sarah peeked an eye out from under the pillow. Tears were welling up in his eyes.

"*Dad... it's OK. Really...*" A long silence followed, until Sarah continued, almost pleading, "Please, just leave me alone, OK? I'm fine..."

Steve collected himself, nodding, "OK. If you need anything..."

"*Please?* I just want to go to sleep."

"OK, sweetie."

Steve returned to inquisitive stares at the table.

"We had a little incident last night..." Steve explained. "It scared her. I just wanted to check in."

"Getting stuck in the elevator?"

Steve nodded, "It was far up, honey... the whole place went black you know."

Pete was staring at his dad.

"This doesn't have anything to do with the elevator smashed on the floor, does it?" Barb asked.

"Of course not," Steve lied. "I just wanted to make sure she was OK," Steve insisted. "And she is."

Barb nodded, "So I propose a Beyers family summit. Right now."

"OK," Steve said.

"We need a definitive plan of action."

"Agreed. But first, we need context. We can't create a plan of action if we don't know what we're acting *against*."

"We've got very little food. Our drinking water will be gone soon. We have no power and by tomorrow our toilet is going to be..."

"A bad scene," Steve finished.

Barb nodded. Pete bit his lip.

"Maria is probably not coming any more," Steve continued, "which means no food, no water and no help. The question is, are we under attack?" He sat back.

"Of course, DJ," Pete said. "Duh!"

"You think so?" Steve asked.

Pete nodded.

"Why?"

Pete looked down at his empty plate, never close to full anyway, head cocked to one side. "The other night, when I couldn't sleep I went outside on the walkway."

Barb put down her fork.

"'Cause I thought I smelled smoke," Pete added quickly and looked up. His parents were watching him carefully. "And I was sitting there, just thinkin' about stuff. You know?"

His face dropped once again, "And while I was lookin' around I saw these two weird guys wearing work clothes, like repair guys, get out of the elevators. And one of them had one of those Bluetooth things in his ear."

"He was talking on the phone?"

"Yeah. I swear. And they went to this door, down on thirteen. And they knocked and it opened right up and they stepped in and the door shut right away. But while it was open, I saw two guards. Big ones, with guns, right inside the door."

Barb and Steve traded glances.

"And I watched for a little while... but no one ever came out."

"Well..." Steve said, "I don't necessarily think that means..."

"I think it could mean something," Barb said.

"Yes, it *could*... but..."

Pete smiled, happy his observation was getting some attention and seemed to be making up for his transgression.

"Do you remember which door it was?"

"Of course, DJ, and you know what? I haven't seen anyone go in or out since."

"Well, that doesn't mean anything..." Steve crossed his arms. "Necessarily."

"Look, Steve, I'm not going to freak out or anything, but I think we need to talk to people. I think you need to go have a talk with the Andrews. They're so close and they seemed prepared for anything."

Steve nodded. "OK, honey, I will."

"DJ?"

"What, Peter?"

"Why are we eatin' someone else's canned food for breakfast? Why ain'ts we eatin' herb-encrusted turkey and heirloom apples again?"

Steve stared at Peter as the seconds thudded by.

"Because, son," he finally said, eyeing Barb for effect, "Maria's list was a wish-list, not a menu. You see me drowning in beer kid?"

Pete shook his head.

"Right. She was just screwing with us."

Few souls in DisasterLand slept that night, Shae and Elektra least of all.

Elektra took the last long draw from her cigarette and extinguished it in the overflowing ashtray by her side. She was seated on her kitchen table, knees to her chest, staring out at the atrium. The dog-eared yellow pages of the new, revised script lay at her feet.

She'd dreaded the morning after the loss of an actor with such obsessional fervor that she was now worried she'd actually manifested it in some horrific way. Yet having imagined herself emotionally crippled, lying in bed and quivering, she was at least somewhat relieved to find that now, once in the midst of the dark reality, she felt only a peculiar vacancy.

In some ways, she was even proud.

Under the strain, the team had come together in ways gloriously richer than she'd ever felt possible and last night, she knew, DisasterLand had truly been born. Despite everything they'd been through over the last twelve-plus months, they'd awoke yesterday morning green rookies and went to sleep battle-hardened vets. The effects had been immediate. Even in the night crew's shift reports there was a renewed sense of purpose, a strengthening of the team's resolution, of their belief in the delicate and profound nature of their mission.

In the heart of the sleepless night and with the help of the Feed, she had analyzed the A-team's live performance almost second-by second. It had been so natural on so many levels that some of the on-duty guards had even been fooled into thinking it was all part of a last-minute script change.

If there was a light in the midst of the darkness, this was surely it. They had arrived.

Yet something was bothering her and she knew just what it was: Sarah Beyers' fall. Elektra had gambled needlessly with lives, and even though Shae had implicitly authorized it, that was no excuse. She had lost her center. It wasn't cool.

And it could never happen again. They'd been lucky.

Elektra resurfaced with the ringing of her phone. She reached over to the counter and grabbed it, thankful for the interruption.

"E, Shae. How are you?"

"Been better."

"I'm on the upswing. Just met Lhasa. Love him."

"Really?"

"A gem. I just spoke to Jude to thank him and I have to do the same with you."

"Good, I'm glad to hear it. Maybe there's a silver lining after all."

"You're on your way to welcome him?"

"I..." Elektra hesitated, suddenly embarrassed by her inaction. "Yes. of course, Shae, I am. I'll meet him in Good Health, in thirty or so. Before the script meeting."

"He'll be happy to hear that. He's just starting make-up now, so your timing should be perfect."

"Great."

"Details for the Sunday evening memorial are already coming together. I've got a team at work. Jimmy's parents have agreed to come in and we're discussing scattering his ashes through the valley by crop duster. We're going to do it right."

She had no reply. Despite everything, it still didn't feel real.

Shae continued, "So I'll see you in a few?"

"See you there."

Elektra hung up the phone and pulled the hero database up on her laptop for the third time.

Then made a b-line for the roof.

Elektra smiled. "Told you we might be in touch."

"Mornin', Elektra," Lhasa mumbled from beneath several layers of gauze. He stuck out a bandaged hand as she leaned in to hear. "Pleasure."

"I see you've met our make-up team. And hair it looks like. Sorry about that."

Chunks of Lhasa's long brown locks lay on the floor around the hospital bed and his barely-visible eyes narrowed with a smile. Yes, he had indeed. Arriving just after five, he'd met Shae and Jude for an intense contractual shake-down to culminate the night's ongoing negotiations. Amazingly, Lhasa's own joy had been paled by his ecstatic agent's during the teleconference.

By six-fifteen, Lhasa was in make-up, and now, one hour later, sprawled out over a hospital bed in a remote operating room of Good Health off-limits to the public, he was still thirty minutes or so away from being ready for his call despite being covered head-to-toe in bandages. Tomorrow, the ADs had been assured, it would be one hour tops—if he was ever allowed out of make-up at all.

"I just wanted to welcome you and say how thankful we are that you can join us. It seems almost meant to be. You're doing us a huge favor."

Lhasa took a long sip of his Perrier through a straw. "Unbelievable," he mumbled. "Dream come true."

"I'm thrilled. So you've read the script?"

Lhasa nodded.

"It may not be very glamorous, but there are some absolutely critical moments in there. Each of the next three days is huge for us but we'll ease you in, don't worry.

Thursday will be your big moment, a truly beautiful scene. Shae's told you what you're doing here?"

"Injured actor."

"Exactly. So you'll be playing his character, basically, since he's in surgery down in Vegas. You got the character's bio?"

"Very interesting."

"Fantastic. Our lead writer is on her way down now. Her name's Karen, she's the best there is. She'll lay out some background for you and answer all your questions. We've also got a highlights reel of Jimmy's work this week to give you a solid idea of his physical characterization."

"I'll watch anything you've got."

"If you want more let Karen know. Don't be afraid to speak to any of us—Jude, Karen, myself. Even Colin, our AD... has he..."

"He was the first one in with make-up."

"Fantastic. Any of us, Jude. At any time. These are special circumstances. Otherwise, you know how it works. We try to model ourselves on a feature production and sometimes do a pretty good job of it."

Lhasa nodded.

"Keep in mind there will be script revisions to come. At this stage of the game things are always in flux. Just go with the flow, use your Buddhism. There's another script meeting happening in a few minutes, but most likely no more pages will come out of it. It's more of a brainstorming session for future scenarios. The ADs will keep you in the know. If they don't, have the guards call me."

Elektra had received the revisions, slipped under her door, sometime before six. To her they seemed natural, which was perhaps the highest compliment. The writers hadn't missed a beat.

"At one this afternoon we've got our dailies meeting. We'll be examining yesterday's work and looking ahead to any revisions that are in play for tomorrow. Ordinarily, as a member of the A-list, you'd be in attendance. A couple of special circumstances are preventing that today and probably for the rest of the show, mainly the necessity of you remaining in your hospital room. But we'll do what we can to integrate you and make you feel part of the team."

Lhasa nodded, "Thanks."

"As you've seen, you'll have an armed guard posted outside your door at all times. What we'll probably do is keep your door shut and teleconference you in for those sessions so you can get a feel for everyone and how it all comes together."

"I'd love that."

"We'll make that happen then. It'll start tomorrow." Elektra checked her watch. "Right. So a bit later you'll meet Clint, another of our lead actors who you'll have your first scene with later this morning. He was injured earlier as well, on Sunday. He's getting released from Good Health today, just after your scene."

"Jumping right in."

"No better way." Elektra reached for his bandaged hand. "I'd tell you to break a leg sweetie, but looks like you already have."

The Beyers' front door flew into their hallway and splintered into pieces on the floor. Steve was the first to land behind the couch, confirming his own worst fear.

There, heart stopped and breathing shallow, he shamefully realized once and for all that he simply didn't have what it took. For the last thirty-five years he had managed to persuade himself that the battles lost and fled in the schoolyards of his youth were an abnormality, that deep down he was a brave and capable fighter—if he was pushed.

All that was clearly out the window now. For good.

Four armed security guards marched in and Barb and Pete dove under the kitchen table.

"Steve Beyers!" the first of the guards roared, gruffly.

There was no response. Pete checked his mother's reaction, her face devastatingly confused. A DisasterLand force of four had come to bear on her husband and the largest now separated them, his automatic rifle drawn.

Another was preventing exit from the front door. The remaining two had planted themselves firmly on either end of the couch.

A two-person DTV crew had followed, cameras rolling.

Sarah cracked open her bedroom door and peered out.

"That your foot behind the couch, sir?"

The foot was immediately yanked out of sight. The couch jumped.

Staring out from between the legs of the closest guard, Barb felt something awaken deeply within in her, a clarity arrive as soft-focus sharpened: *the root of all injustice in the world*.

The DTV cameras were scanning the suite, their gaze eventually landing under the table. Barb scowled, but her hard edge had softened slightly: whatever was happening, she felt, DTV's presence was certainly reassuring. Things would eventually be put right. *The whole world was watching.*

The closest guard suddenly spun, ducking down to meet Barb and Peter face to face.

"Sorry ma'am, we'll have to take him."

"Why? What did he do?" Barb said, her voice cracking.

"He's been linked to the terrorists."

"*What?*"

The nearest of the two guards kicked the couch, "You can either make it easy or you can make it hard, sir."

For as long as Steve could remember, during times of intense stress he pictured himself before an intelligent and sympathetic interviewer on a darkened set, before a wise and engaged studio audience hungry for his innermost thoughts. This, he found, often helped.

There I was, he now told this audience, *boot to the neck. But I didn't give up. I couldn't give up. I had my pride.*

They'd have to take me... if they could.

"On the count of three, sir, we're going to pick you up and escort you out. If you choose to fight, you'll be drugged for your own safety."

"What are you doing?" Barb screamed.

"One..."

Barb broke down. Pete took her hand.

"Two..."

"Bullshit!" Steve grunted, muffled and not very convincing by any account.

"I don't understand! He's no terrorist! He's my husband!" Barb yelled.

"Three."

The guards bent down and swiftly pulled the couch away. Steve lay on his side, hands over head, in a fetal position. DTV cameras captured every movement.

Steve was whisked up powerfully, one guard under each arm. They stood him up. He cautiously opened his eyes to examine his surroundings. Then he noticed it: the cameras.

Invigorated by his own obvious humiliation, Steve suddenly struggled to resist, his face twisting into an absurd grimace.

"I'm an innocent man!"

Within seconds, and with complete professionalism, Steve was hooded and cuffed.

"This is *staged!*" Steve yelled, muffled. "I'm innocent! Barb! Tell them!" he continued as he was dragged out of the room, camera in tow and gasping for breath.

Barb chased after. "He's not aiding the terrorists! He doesn't even like butterflies! I mean, no more than anyone else!"

"We've got proof," the last guard growled as he brushed her aside to join the team down the walkway. "And sorry about your front door."

"I want a lawyer!" Barb screamed, defiantly.

A guard mocked her in falsetto, "I want a lawyer!" he teased. *"I want a lawyer!"*

One armed guard was on every side of Steve, rifles drawn. They laughed.

"This is DisasterLand, lady! And your husband's a sympathizer!"

One cameraman spun back to Barb, catching her gutted reaction. Pete raced out from the suite and muscled in front of his mom.

"Leave my dad alone! I'll take you down! *I'll take you all down!*" Pete yelled, fists shaking.

The other cameraman captured Pete's menacing stance.

"You're going down too, dude!" Pete leapt at him. The cameraman continued shooting as he retreated.

From down the walkway, his son's voice reverberated in Steve's ears. Whatever sense of shame had manifested from his own sorry reaction, the sense of pride in his son now overwhelmed it.

"It's a good family you've got there, sir," one of the guards whispered in confirmation.

Steve grunted, confused and still hooded, sucking in his own morning breath.

The guards began their long descent of the stairs and Barb knew they were headed for the security center below. Steve had been *arrested*.

Pete dropped the stance as they disappeared out of sight. The cameramen were still shooting, telephoto, as tears rolled down Barb's cheeks.

Gone!

"Screw you assholes!" Barb screamed. "I hate this whole God-damned park! You're a bunch of lying, manipulative thieves! *KISS MY ASS DISASTERLAND!*"

Pete stared at his mother, who now seemed near collapse.

Sarah had watched quietly, peeking out from the doorway, reeling from her own exhausted disorientation.

Peter gently helped his mother inside and the family stood, silently, over what remained of their front door. A giant footprint was planted right in the center, cracks radiating outward all around. Chips of laminate were scattered throughout the entryway.

"Cheap-ass shit yo. Look DJ!" Pete pointed.

Barb's mind, a thundering maelstrom, barely registered his observation.

Pete and Sarah propped up the door as best they could but they all knew: they'd been violated by those who were meant to be protecting them. Now, they could trust no one.

And if word of this got out, they themselves wouldn't be trusted.

They were all alone.

Steve sat in the corner of a dark concrete cell, the air impregnated with the suffocating acidic tang of stale urine.

The burlap hood remained, hands still cuffed firmly behind his back, legs tied in front of him. He was completely immobile.

There I was, he told the audience, *accused of conspiring with terrorists. Fuck them and their sickness. What did they want from me?*

The minutes ticked by, dropping into a limitless void impossible to track. Steve's emotions darkened as the tenuous nature of his desperate situation was gradually revealed. He faced the unmistakable dread of a profound unknown, alone.

In the distance, a man's agonizing screams filled his cell.

With every passing second, Steve's bladder continued to impose its needs with ever greater force.

Through tears of shame, he finally had to let go.

The steel door creaked open. Steve jumped, his heart skipping.

A man's firm footsteps echoed off the hard cement as he found his leather seat. The cell door slammed shut.

Dark expanses of time passed until Steve heard the flash of flame as a match was lit.

Cigar smoke soon drifted to Steve's nostrils, exciting them, welcomingly replacing the stench he had become accustomed to.

Steve finally allowed himself a full breath. *That was some cigar*, he realized.

As the minutes passed, Steve's tension lessened, if only from sheer exhaustion.

Half the cigar later, he simply couldn't take it anymore.

"What's your fucking problem?" Steve screamed.

There was a slight pause and the *tap-tap-tap* ashing of the cigar on the tray. Within the cell, cameras rolled.

"It's about time, Mister Beyers. You think we've got all day?"

The man's voice was disconcerting: intellectual and an octave too high, the exact opposite of what Steve had expected.

Steve heard the creaking of the chair as the man leaned back. The wheels in Steve's mind spun, aimlessly.

"Excuse me?" Steve asked.

"Is it patience or fear?" the man asked.

"What?"

"Your silence."

"It's anger you asshole! Anger, shock and frustration!"

"Ummm... yes..."

Silence descended once again.

"Who... the hell... are you!" Steve demanded.

"The questions flow in one direction, Mr. Beyers, at least at this time."

Steve growled. With the sudden rush of emotion, sweat was pouring off him. Or was the room being heated?

"I've done nothing. *Nothing!* You've endangered the lives of my family and I want answers!"

"Of course..."

Silence.

"Mr. Beyers, do you know why you are here?"

"I am an innocent man!" Steve roared.

After another extended period of fruitless silence, Steve's voice softened, "At least tell me where I am."

In the next room, his heart-rate was being monitored. At the mention of his family, it had skyrocketed.

"Mr. Beyers, we've got information..."

"I am not a sympathizer!"

"... information which leads us to question your sanity, sir."

"My *sanity?*"

"We've brought you here for your own safety. We believe there is a chance that you might act in a way which may harm you or your family."

"*What!?* Are you questioning my love for..." his mind sputtered to a halt as his heart cracked.

Last night. *Sarah's fall?*

"I..." he grunted, "You..."

Steve slid forward, away from the cement wall, scraping his arm along the rough surface. He was defeated now, a broken man.

"It was a terrible accident..." Steve whispered. "That's all. I've talked to my daughter and..." He faded, collecting himself, fighting a breakdown under the hood. "I thought I lost her."

"Are there any factors which could have contributed to this... accident... Mister Beyers?"

"We were tired... scared. My wife and son were missing and we had no food... we wanted to get home."

"Anything else?"

"*What are you saying?*"

"I'm just asking, sir."

"*No!* No, I'd never..."

The *Happinol.*

Steve felt like he'd been kicked. His mind raced, grappling with the implications, but he didn't get far. Somewhere along the line, a key neural pathway seemed to have gone down.

Who was this guy?

"I've been... on an anti-depressant," Steve volunteered, "Only for a month. And I'd forgotten to bring it. I was given a refill here... but..."

"But you never took it."

"No... I..."

"So instead you put your family at risk."

"That had nothing to do with it! I didn't think I needed it anymore. I think it's... situational."

"What is?"

"My depression."

"Do you think you're depressed?"

"My psychologist does."

"Do *you?*"

"I think I have been."

"But not anymore?"

"I just... I feel better. Since I came here I feel better. I didn't think I needed them. Maybe I do... I don't know... Now I don't know..."

Steve's exhausted soul longed for silence, for solitude, for endless sleep.

"I see."

"I mean... I feel like myself. My old self."

"Your love life is good?"

Steve recoiled. "It's better now."

"Are you sure?"

"Look, I don't know who the hell..."

"You can't hide it, sir, her disappointment."

Steve struggled to stand like an overturned turtle, his blood boiling. The man was forced to look away in embarrassment.

"Do you think your depression is involved in your severely reduced libido, Mr. Beyers?"

Steve fell back against the wall in a crumpled pile. He whimpered. "Yes. It's a symptom. I know."

"Symptom? Of what?"

"Of depression."

"But you're not taking your pills."

"I'm *done* with the pills, Goddamn it! *I'm done with them!*"

"Fine. That's all we needed to know. As long as you're clear."

The man stood from his leather chair, walked over to Steve and removed the blindfold.

On the mahogany desk before them, a camera sat, pointed straight at Steve. Next to it, a candle was burning, the only light in the room.

"Don't worry about the camera, Mister Beyers. No power," the man lied. "Obviously. But we push on."

Steve shook his head. "Who are you?"

"Dr. Theodore Benedict, DisasterLand psychologist."

Steve stared.

"You don't remember? We had an appointment. Come on, let's get you home. It's too dangerous up there to waste any more time."

Steve sat, dazed, as the psychologist removed the cuffs.

Massaging his tender wrists, Steve suddenly knew he *did* have what it took. And he was going to make sure the world knew it!

"Listen, Mister Beyers, I hope you understand. In all of this chaos, we had to make sure you're OK. And we had to do it discreetly. For everyone's safety. It's a sensitive time now, during negotiations."

"Negotiations? So it's real?"

Dr. Benedict's head dropped as he nodded slowly, "I don't want to scare you, but you do need to be careful. You must stay vigilant. Guests are disappearing."

Steve's brow furrowed in resolve.

Dr. Benedict continued, "Just be careful, OK? Stay out of trouble and keep that beautiful family of yours safe. Soon all this will all be over."

"Yes, sir."

"Let's hope, anyway. Now let's see what we can do about those pants of yours."

Lhasa lay alone in his hospital room, pondering the realization that it was going to be a long four days. Since his arrival just over an hour ago a constant stream of injured guests and family had stuck their head past the armed guards outside his door to creatively insult him.

It had taken all of his training to maintain his grim, tortured character at those puzzling moments. His background wasn't Stanislavsky, but with such a Baptism method-acting was rapidly becoming the path of lease resistance. Fortunately he'd been briefed to expect this treatment.

He checked the clock on his bedside table for the second time in ten minutes and sighed. It wasn't exactly the breakthrough part he had hoped for—not yet anyway—but then again, he couldn't really complain.

Shae's words to him about Jimmy, about his fall and the critical injuries Jimmy'd sustained on the job were haunting him. It didn't seem right, taking over another guy's part like this, kicking the dude when he's down. But then again, that was life, wasn't it? That was the nature of the biz. To offset any negative karma, Lhasa was occupying himself by sending Jimmy some very positive vibes.

He had moved to Vegas, along with every other actor, to be in the shadow of DisasterLand. To put himself in the line of fire. To get himself closer to the battlefield. And it had worked. Lightning had struck. The dream had come true. He was *inside*.

The whole thing just might pay off and not a moment too soon. Vegas was killing him.

Lhasa jiggled his ass. With both legs and one arm in traction, he was still trying to find a comfortable position. The draft script called for him being here most of the duration of the show, with key public appearances possible depending on how the days played out.

The latex effects make-up across his eyes was smothering his skin under the bandages. Luckily, only two and a half hours to go before his union lunch.

Yes, it was going to be a long few days.

But this was the *Big Time*.

Two long hours after Steve's abduction, the Beyers' water was running out and the inevitable loomed for each of them: *number two*. The individual events lay unavoidably on the horizon and with each calling, their collective situation would grow indescribably more grim.

A decision was made: Barb and Pete would venture out for water, and with any luck void themselves on the way. To stick around and wait until their water supplies were gone was surely to court disaster—or at least a very unpleasant future.

It was also possible that they'd get answers—somehow, from somewhere—as to the details of Steve's abduction and the specifics of the threat against them.

Sarah would remain behind, awaiting her father's return, armed with nothing but kitchen chairs and the remaining 11 oz. can of collard greens. She downed the rest of her water in preparation, handing over her empty bottle. In reality, she was deeply thankful for the time alone, even if the threats against her were real. She was already more than a little pissed off and convinced she could handle whatever nasties would come her way.

Barb and Pete would bring all the containers they could carry to ensure as much water as possible was on-hand in the suite. Wherever they were headed, it wasn't a trip to be making a few times a day, not by any stretch of the imagination. Yet even with the most stringent of rationing it seemed impossible that they could make it through tomorrow without a repeat.

No one could argue the practical necessity of Barb's decision, but her real reason for expediting the trip was simple—she needed out. And she needed understanding.

Steve's abduction had been the final straw in an increasingly more chaotic and absurd experience and Barb was determined to ascertain what was happening first-hand—and the sooner the better. She was getting nervous.

Irrational fear was one thing, rational fear quite another. To sit at home and emotionally suffocate was simply not an option. The best defense was a good offense.

Rules of engagement were carefully negotiated for Sarah considering their lack of a front door: one intruder's foot inside meant a strong verbal warning to prevent inquisitive and possibly helpful guests from receiving a can to the face. But one additional step inside the suite meant just that.

"You gonna be all right, sweetie?" Barb asked, hand shaking on Sarah's cheek.

"I need a shower," Sarah said.

Barb nodded. They all did.

They shared a nervous goodbye and Barb and Peter stepped out onto the walkway. Together, they replaced the front door.

Sarah took up her position at the end of the entryway. Can in her lap and wrapped in a blanket, Sarah's mind was stuck on Saturday afternoon—on Steve's mysterious errand and his brief disappearance into the hospital.

What was that all about, anyway?

"You're sure about this, DJ?"

Barb and Pete stood nervously on the nineteenth floor landing, eyeing Nelly's image above with questions flooding their minds. Armed guards stood silently behind them, noting their reactions.

Pete had put on his Chamberlain jersey for good luck, but as they stared at the tattoo drawing posted to the stairs Barb realized what a fortunate move it had been—Pete's biceps were out in the open. After the reality of Steve's detention any acts to reduce ambiguity were vital.

Barb too had dressed wisely, for comfort and for patriotism, decked head-to-toe once again in her DisasterLand tracksuit. No one could possibly question their loyalties.

Nineteen long floors below them, DisasterLand simmered as the full afternoon sun beat down on the defenseless greenhouse atrium. The disquieting stillness below was punctuated only by the clicking of boots as security guards marched in formation in a show of force.

The InfoTron was dark, of course, and their moods gradually followed in the shadow of DisasterLand's official silence. Throughout the tower, there had been no effort to eradicate any of the terrorists' rude defilements.

Watching the guards below, Barb, somewhat surprisingly, found herself threatened by the militaristic qualities the atrium had taken on, wondering whether this increased her feelings of safety—or decreased them.

Was this show of force for the terrorists? *Or the guests?* If it was the latter, it was for naught. There were few guests to be seen.

Barb turned to her son. "We need water, Peter. And food if we can get it. I'm not waiting until we've got nothing to do something about it. We could be in trouble here. I'm serious."

"Then let's bounce, Superstar."

Upon seeing their empty bottles, the guards manning the nineteenth floor checkpoint silently parted to allow the couple passage.

Drenched in sweat and acutely aware of the fact they'd have to ascend the same stairs fully-loaded at the end of their foray, Barb and Peter stepped heavily out onto the atrium floor.

It had been an eye-opening descent, each floor having been damaged in unique and often offensive ways. Something had indeed gone down last night, something which Barb couldn't even begin to understand. She inhaled a deep, cleansing breath while Pete stared out at the floor's subtly transformed landscape.

"I'm glad we're out of there," Barb said, patting her son on the back. Perhaps it was the sun, but to Pete, his mother's eyes had regained a lost sparkle.

"Me too, DJ. It smells funny."

"Like what?"

"Rotten us."

The sour smell of fear, thought Barb.

She looked up to their suite, easily recognizable by their splintered door resting cockeyed against the frame. Also visible, as she had hoped, was her small red top tucked into the crack. It meant everything was OK.

"You think Sarah's gonna be alright?" Barb asked. "I don't know if we made the right decision."

"Yeah, she's cool, DJ. Sarah's tough."

"Let's not make her wait longer than we have to."

"So where to?"

Behind them, armed guards in riot gear stood against the plywood façade of Good Food, watching out over a small crowd of angry guests which stood defiantly in front of them. Even now, and surprisingly aggressively, determined guests were continuing to demand a reopening.

Barb's eyes migrated to the middle-aged, track-suited suburbanites comprising the group. *The DisasterLand Mall Walking Team*, Barb spat.

Talk about futile, she told herself. *We certainly won't count on Good Food reopening any longer*.

Ahead of them in a small ceremony at the fountain, guards were being relieved of their duty and replaced by another team, equally intent, it seemed, on protecting it at all costs.

"Good Health," Barb said. "Where else is there?"

Nearing the darkened hospital, Barb and Pete were confronted by an extensive, living memorial to those injured, which had carefully been assembled across Good Health's vast picture windows.

Judging by the majority of crisp, digital prints taken from the beds inside, it dated back long before last night's attack and in some cases even prior to the original attack on Sunday morning. In fact, since last night, it seemed, there were fewer guests injured—not more.

Please, Make a Difference, the display begged, and Barb responded with embarrassment. *How in the world had they missed this?*

Yet their ignorance may have been a blessing in disguise. The increasing emotional burden was already beginning to take its toll.

"Mom, you OK?"

"I'm fine, honey, let's go in."

"Not long, right?"

"Right."

They entered Good Health's chaotic candle-lit lobby and were shocked by its immediacy. Stretchers crowded the cramped space, and the faces of the injured turned to stare out in pain.

Armed guards nodded a somber greeting.

All the comfort-inducing signs—the soft mood lighting, the friendly Good Health welcome display, the soothing classical music—were all absent and shadows had arisen in their place. Barb staggered forward.

"I'm sorry, we're on emergency power," a frazzled nurse called as she hurried through the lobby. "May I help you?"

Barb stepped forward, with Pete dragging behind. The place was creeping him out.

"Good afternoon. Yes, we... we don't have any water. We need to refill our bottles."

"I'm sorry, we've barely got enough for our own patients, let alone ourselves. We're on severe emergency rations."

"Oh..." Barb stared. "Well, what about..."

"No food either," the nurse said.

"Bathr..."

"Sorry."

"So what are we supposed to do?"

The nurse shrugged, "I'm afraid there's only one thing you can do for water, ma'am. There's the river."

"The *river?*"

"You've got your purification tablets?"

"Yes..."

"Good. If you have any sort of reaction, you come right here. OK?"

Barb stared.

"Yo, can we see the terrorist lady?"

"Peter!"

"He's off-limits. Recovering from surgery, I'm afraid," the nurse said.

"He's really here?!"

"I wish he wasn't. It's a security nightmare." The nurse checked around her and leaned in, lowering her voice, "But we're forced to keep him. For *collateral.*"

Barb stared.

"I think it's crazy," the nurse finished. *"It's dangerous.* When he gets out of surgery they're gonna want him back!"

Clint limped by on crutches, down the hallway running perpendicular to the entryway, babying his bad knee. He paused, mid-way, "Hanging in there Kelly?"

"Hi Mister Lewis," the nurse flashed a resigned smile.

"DJ look! It's your famous injured firefighter guy!"

"Clint?"

He hobbled closer to the couple, curious, "Oh, hi there! Looks like your exercise is paying off. You doing OK? Tell me nothing's wrong."

"No... other than my husband's been ab..."

"Glad to hear it. Are you here to *Make A Difference?*"

Pete's heart sank.

"We're here to get some water," Barb said.

"Wish we had some extra, I'd give it to you. That's the biggest problem everyone's facing. Don't worry, they'll get something figured out soon. What's your name, little dude?"

"Pete. But you can call me Spike."

"So you want to be a firefighter when you grow up?"

"No way, dude!"

Barb cringed.

"Why not?"

"You see me running into burning buildings and shit? That's whack! Look at you and your crutches!"

Barb tried to change the topic. "The river... it just seems so far away... and... *unsafe*."

"It's simple, ma'am. There's nowhere else. The fountain's polluted after the attacks and more importantly, it's our only source of water for the tower... if anything happens, we need it to fight fires."

"Oh my God."

"Hopefully, of course, we won't." Clint shrugged. "But if so, we've got the hand-crank pumps ready to go."

"Do you really think..."

"I sure hope not." Clint hobbled over to the reception desk. "Since you're here, did you know we sell flowers? You can take them to any of the patients here, your choice. They're grown in the park and all the money goes to scholarships to bring underprivileged children and their families to DisasterLand. I guess this sounds kind of stupid, but we're way down on visitors this morning. I know some of the patients would like to see you. It'll get everyone's mind off what's going on."

"That does sound nice."

"No, DJ, we don't have time!"

"Is that young lady here, the one on TV whose husband was kidnapped?"

"She sure is."

"I'd like to take her flowers."

A stretcher whisked by down the hall, in the company of two doctors in starched white lab coats and several armed guards. Clint spun.

The figure on the stretcher lay helpless, draped in bandages.

"Oh my God!" Barb said, "Is he OK?"

"Hey!" Clint yelled. "Hey!"

"It's the terrorist!" Pete whispered, in awe.

DTV cameras chased after the gurney.

"*HEY!*" Clint screamed and everything froze. Clint muscled through the guards, wielding one crutch as a vicious pry.

"Hey Commie!" he growled, reaching the helpless, bandaged soul cowering within the bleached sheets. Cameras zoomed. Breathing stopped. Flashbulbs popped.

"Listen up, bro. We lose a guest, they lose you. You pass that on. *Got it?*"

"Got it," came the muffled reply.

Barb put an arm over her son's shoulders and together they approached the fountain's makeshift security center to the clicking of safeties being released. A chill slithered down Barb's spine.

"Help you ma'am?" asked the nearest guard.

Barb slowed, taking her son's hand as he tucked in behind her. "What are those photos?"

The guards took a step to the side, lowering their weapons just slightly. Pete stared at the barrels, mesmerized.

"The disappeared, ma'am."

"Oh my God."

A few beat-up, wallet-sized photos of guests, clearly old family photos, had been taped to an American flag and flown from the top of the fountain.

"Take a look and remember the faces. Alert us if you notice anything out of the ordinary. But most importantly, just focus on your family—and stay in your suite. You don't want your picture on this fountain, I can tell you that."

"Are they OK? The *disappeared?*"

Barb counted thirteen photos. *Thirteen and counting.*

The guard passed her a hand-written piece of paper, crudely depicting the location of each abduction. Amazingly, some were abducted in their own suites, including one whole family. Three had happened in the park. *If you have information on any of these guests,* a large sign read, *please report it to a guard, immediately. Beware of impostors: look for the holographic DisasterLand insignia on their badge.*

Barb examined the guards' chests.

"We can't say, ma'am. Don't want to compromise our intelligence-gathering techniques. You folks on your way to the river?"

Barb nodded, displaying her empty containers.

"Only place there is, hunh?" she asked.

The guards nodded.

"But I'd be quick about it. We're hearing chatter."

In crossing the remains of the village, ghosts of the ruined shells had called out to them. But they resisted.

Barb had left the fountain, much to Peter's disbelief, with an offer to help however she could. In a way she couldn't explain, Barb felt she had something to share with the terrorists, perhaps an understanding of their passion for life, for nature, for the sacredness of being. They'd never said any of this of course, but to her knowledge there had been no loss of life thus far and she respected that. She recognized it as a conscious decision.

Making a Difference had left her in a reflective mood, secure in knowing guests were unified against the threat they faced. It had been remarkably uplifting to spend time with the injured, to bring them flowers and to hear their stories.

In every case, entire families had moved down to Good Health to be with their loved ones and the support each had shown were tremendously buoying. Barb had walked away feeling like she had a ward of new friends and had enthusiastically promised a return.

These were dark times, Barb reminded herself, *yet dark times had the greatest potential for light.*

It was a time to be strong, to be supportive, and to come together. It was also a time to stay put.

The threat was now clear, the danger of being out in the open undeniable. They were sitting ducks. They would get in and get out.

Barb stole a glance across the atrium, all the way up to nineteen. The red cloth was still there.

The sound of chanting reached their ears, and they slowed for a glimpse into the ruins. In the heart of twisted metal, illegally inside DisasterLand's barricades, a very small group was gathered.

To Barb's surprise, she realized it must be roughly where *Matériel Pornographique* had been. They inched a bit closer and the smell of frankincense and myrrh filled their nostrils. Barb realized it was a tiny group of worshippers, holding crosses. They were chanting and praying softly, and walking in a circle.

"Look mom! Hairy Christians!"

"That's Hare Krishnas. And they aren't, Peter. They're Evangelicals I think. Come on, let's get this over with."

They hurried away, with the blessings, the chanting, the thankful prayers of ridding the space of the devil's work fading into the distance behind them.

The fragrant foliage welcomed Barb and Peter into the park and they found themselves spontaneously relaxing.

"OK, Pete, we've got to hurry. We're out of touch with your sister now. And we've been down here way too long already."

She turned to check their door one last time. So far above, so fragile. But it was holding.

"Word."

"Word? What's that mean?"

"It's verification of communication, DJ. You and me, we's hookin' it up."

"Word?"

"*Word.*"

The Great Lawn was eerily deserted as they scurried across the soft green, in stark contrast to the last time Barb had visited on opening night. Yet the smell of damp grass again nourished her soul and Barb fought the urge to slip off her shoes.

Hurrying towards the familiar, the wall of the forest and the trailhead nearest Del Sol, Barb realized, shamefully, that Peter had never even been inside the forest at all and she herself had seen only a tiny fraction. It was an embarrassment. A complete embarrassment.

After pausing to take a deep, appreciative breath, they entered the forest for the last stretch.

"Wow, DJ, this is wicked!"

Barb was reassured by one fact: the park hadn't been attacked. And, more importantly, these terrorists were fighting to preserve natural spaces so why would they want to blow one up?

Equally as likely though, there'd be no better place for them to call home. *Is that why they hadn't been found? They were hiding in the park?*

After all, Barb and Peter had yet to see one guard.

"Keep your eyes open, Pete. There could be guerrillas."

"You're crazy, there ain't no gorillas in here! It's a park! Gorillas is in Africa!"

They pushed on towards the river and the light dimmed from the overgrown canopy above. Barb's thoughts trailed off.

The gradually narrowing trail weaved through the trees and their feet fell ever-more softly on the pliant earth. The benches, which had been so full of lovers on Friday, now looked lonely.

Pete led the way up the hill. There, from the top and looking out over the entire expanse of park, they heard voices in the distance. Reassured, Barb shut her eyes to the sun, to the fresh, oxygenated air.

"Life is breath, Peter. The yogis call it prana. Life-force. We must remember to breathe."

Pete laughed, "Right-o, DJ." He rolled his eyes.

"Seriously. We must breathe consciously. We must use breath to find our strength and light."

"You sound like one of those Hairy Christians!"

"Just for that, you're coming to class with me next week."

"MOM!"

"I'm serious. *And* Sarah. If I knew what I know now when I was your age..."

"That's if we ever get out of here."

"We will, Pete. Don't say that. *Don't even think that.* Whatever's going on here, we'll get out of it."

"Yeah, I know mom. I'm sorry."

Barb hurried down the stone steps and Pete followed. Minutes later the trail began to widen slightly, signaling the approaching river.

More quickly than she had remembered, the first sounds of the rushing water appeared, accompanied by flickers of light through the green. They hurried on, seeking the river's damp vibrancy.

The light grew more intense and the clearing suddenly opened out in front of them. Several families were gathered at the water's edge, filling anything and everything they could with fresh water—milk bottles, used cans, pots and pans, anything. No one even looked up. Pete cheered.

But Barb was shamed. Once again, a ridiculous lack of foresight on their part. But a mistake that, tomorrow, wouldn't be repeated. They'd all come and bring everything they could posibly carry.

But Pete didn't care. He stood on the riverbank, consumed by the wetlands on the far shore. "This is so cool mom, I can't believe we haven't been here!"

"I'm sorry, honey. We'll be back, I promise. And we'll bring Sarah and your dad."

"Do you think we could find some food down here?"

"I don't know, Peter. But we should try. We certainly need it."

Eyeing the length of the bank, Barb was pleased to find two guards seated under a large tree at the edge of the clearing. They were practically invisible.

Pete bent down to the rushing river, dipped in his hands and brought the cool water to his face. A few of the families looked at him with disgust.

It didn't matter though, Barb knew, there had been swimmers here only a few days ago. Hopefully the tablets would work, that's all they could hope for.

Barb handed Pete the bottles one by one, and soon they were sealed and ready to go. Pete stood, clearly unhappy.

"Shouldn't we drink some now, DJ? So we can take more?"

"We've only got a limited number of tablets, Peter. And I'm worried about Sarah. I just want to get back."

Pete shook his head. An entire raging river and not a drop to drink. Each stashed a bottle in their D-PAK, relieving the burden only slightly. Their hands remained full.

Barb felt a tap on her shoulder and she turned, startled. It was an African-American woman, roughly her age. Another guest.

"Sorry, I couldn't help but overhear. Could you and your son use some fried chicken? It's cold, but..."

"*Really?*"

The plump woman opened a giant basket. Barb peered in.

"*You're joking!*"

"It's real homemade Southern fried chicken. We're from Georgia. We make it for special occasions, guaranteed to brighten your mood. We made enough for the week but it won't last much longer without electricity. So we're giving it away."

"DJ, we ain't got no bread," Pete interrupted.

"Well, yes," Barb replied. "Actually my son is right. We've run out of cash. You mean give it away for free?"

"Of course, ma'am. Help yourselves. But that's not good. Not good a'tall"

"That's what I say," Pete said.

"Yes, we're working on it," Barb said as she dug in, removing four giant pieces. "Thank you! Oh, this is a miracle!"

"You're very welcome."

"I'm sorry," Barb paused, "we shouldn't take the biggest ones..."

"If you can finish 'em you can have 'em. I saw the look on your face and I just wanted to help."

"We've got two others upstairs who'll be just as thankful," Barb smiled. "You are truly an angel."

Pete was grabbing and Barb stepped discreetly on his foot.

The woman patted Barb's shoulder and hurried on to another family with two small children.

"I do not believe that," Barb said.

"Maybe that yoga stuff works, DJ. You know, positive thinking and all that?"

"Maybe so, Peter. We need to keep it up. OK?"

"Word."

"Excuse me," Barb called.

"Yes?" the woman answered, turning around.

"What room are you in?"

"315, on the eighth floor."

"We'll remember that! We're in 808, on nineteen. Thank you again. This is a real blessing."

"Y'all be safe now."

After a moment of indecision, Barb awkwardly pocketed the chicken in the only free place she had—her track top.

"Let's go back a different way, OK?" Pete asked.

"Peter..."

"Don't you want to see something new while we're out?"

She did. "We can't, honey. We might get lost."

"We won't... come on."

"No, Peter. Think of your sister. She's probably worried sick."

"But we're gonna waste all this good luck and stuff."

Barb shook her head and Pete sighed, looking to the sky forlornly. Above them, the dome was now, remarkably, only a few stories overhead.

It's a good thing he didn't jump into the river, Barb thought, *because I would have followed.*

Some families had finished filling their bottles and decided to rest in the sunshine before the long trip back. For a split second, Barb wished they hadn't tried to *Make A Difference*, so they could have made a difference here, with themselves. But it was too late for that. Tomorrow, she vowed. *Tomorrow.*

After all, they would need more water. They'd have to come back.

"Come on, let's go."

Barb put her arm around her son and they turned away from the river.

"You understand, don't you?"

Peter was silent as they re-entered the forest, with Barb giving a cursory wave to the guards on duty. One flashed a thumbs-up.

Thrust and release. Repeat. Faster.

It was the rhythm of love and drama and DisasterLand had mastered it with tremendous success.

The biggest push of another big day was about to begin, rivaling both Sunday morning and Monday night for intensity, though now it was building to a new sustained level of tension, a higher plateau. This was a one-two technical/human punch and as Elektra wound her way through the green rooms of labyrinth below the atrium it was clear: the old buzz was back.

Elektra was decked out in a luscious purple velour tracksuit, vintage Expos ball cap and foot-hugging hiking sandals, the last to give maximum exposure to yesterday's labor: her toenails were black with the painted faces of Kiss airbrushed on. Gene, of course, was on the big ones.

Wardrobe assistants, hair and make-up assistants, effects make-up assistants as well as a few select special effects guys were hovering around the assembled actors. These were the elite members of DisasterLand's B-list and each had been carefully dressed in trendy office attire that Tuck's team had discreetly soiled and disfigured in creatively revolting ways.

Fresh scars and dark circles under the eyes were being touched up. The props department was busy handing out makeshift crutches and casts. Several especially prominent actors were having their legs wrapped in blood-stained pieces of cloth to complete the illusion of hastily-treated bullet wounds and the effects guys were placing slow-release squibs inside to keep the blood fresh and spreading. Other injuries were being prepared for as-needed responses to the story's development.

Make-up kits, scripts, shoes and other bits of wardrobe were scattered over the rooms' couches and actors were jostling in front of the full-length mirrors.

In the midst of it all Shae was circling silently, giving the actors an encouraging smile here, a firm grasp of the shoulder there. This generally wasn't his style and any other day he preferred to be less of a distraction, but under these difficult circumstances he wanted to be in personal touch with the actors, to make sure they knew management was behind them one hundred percent.

Most of them had either been victims or played intimate roles in Sunday's attack, and many had also played crucial roles in last night's as well. With two more big days to go, this was the hump day and their energy had to be maintained.

To that degree, nutritionists were busy handing out DL:PowerStrips, to be hidden for discreet consumption in the hours and days to come.

"We're twenty away here, twenty away," Colin's voice crackled over the radio. He was hidden in the tower with the safety and effects team, supervising the upcoming gag which would launch the afternoon into play.

"Final positions everyone, final positions. Twenty away, *final positions...*" Elektra echoed, now from Shae's side.

She wiped her forehead. In five minutes, she'd race down to the bridge for the call, but here Elektra liked what she saw. Game faces were on, conversation at an absolute minimum. It was all about concentration.

Detailed images of the atrium and tower were being surveyed on monitors placed throughout the green rooms, all selected live by the production mixer on the bridge. Hero guests were being surveilled for their current movements and the actors were constantly being briefed on context by Karen and her team of writers. As fully as possible, the actors were being brought into the floor's current emotional fold.

One of the most challenging sequences DisasterLand would attempt was only an hour or so away and selling it was absolutely critical to the script's success. This was a test of endurance unlike any other, an acting challenge almost unique in the profession. The fifty select B-list would be required to maintain character for up to 48 hours—or even longer in a worst-case scenario.

Under these difficult and demanding physical conditions, they would have to maintain unbroken levels of concentration. If an actor failed, if character broke, lives could literally be at stake.

The success of the vision rested on each actor's shoulders and they knew it. Their character's personal histories had been memorized, elaborated and finally tested in extensive improvisations during the previous week.

A specific resolution was impossible to predict, though a current flow-chart of possibilities had been presented to the actors at the morning briefing and updates would be strategically disseminated as appropriate. Yet success would be truly up to them.

In thirty minutes the actors would share a final snack and bathroom break, then last looks from wardrobe and hair/make-up. Finally they'd be escorted up to the staging area just behind the security center in preparation for their entrance.

Timing was indeed everything, absolutely crucial to emotional impact and the timeline was infinitely flexible. If necessary, they were prepared to go on now. Or they could take their places in two hours or twenty-four.

Elektra withdrew silently into the hallway and checked the massive digital clock on the wall.

The tunnel was in sight. Soon, the real world would fade away, all outside concerns would disappear and DisasterLand's staff would find themselves living in the expansive and mystical moment with lives the only thing that mattered.

The screws were about to be turned.

Stepping from the forest and out onto the Great Lawn, Pete and Barb both smelled it immediately. *Fire.*

For a split second, their view ahead obscured by the thick haze of smoke filling the atrium, Barb had considered running back to warn the others at the river. But it simply wasn't possible. Nineteen stories above them, the state of their suite was impossible to deduce. Sarah was in serious danger.

They had to get home.

Terrible images were assaulting Barb's mind, images of the entire tower in flames, of burning bodies leaping for their lives and cracking on the atrium's floor.

What had they done, leaving their daughter vulnerable to terrorists?

Cursing *Making a Difference*, Barb grabbed Pete's hand and raced into the murky chaos, filled with the dreadful sense that the membrane of civility had been permanently ruptured.

In the distance DL:FireMen stood inside the ring of armed guards at the fountain, feverishly working a battery of hand pumps to ensure the flow of water to the tower. Their headlamps created a surreal light show dancing within the fog.

Massive firehoses again snaked across the atrium floor towards the tower, this time protected by two walls of armed guards. The couple raced forward along this line, other guests disturbingly absent, desperately scanning the tower above.

Step by step faces began to emerge from the haze, until it became hauntingly clear that the tower's walkways were lined with masked figures as far as they could see.

Tormented voices crystallized as they neared the tower. An angry mob of guests had formed at the foot of the stairs, desperate for access. Armed guards in riot gear were actively preventing the crush and tempers were boiling over.

Inside the cordon, EMS crews hovered, awaiting orders.

Barb faded back with Peter, afraid of the fury percolating through the mob, her eyes focused upwards. The smoked glass of the tenth floor had been scalded and a gap in the chaos of the walkway below revealed several ninth floor suites had been damaged. Guards had cleared the vicinity and guests were in stark absence. DL:FireMen were bustling outside the suites.

The minutes passed and the haze continued to disperse, painfully slowly, until Barb could just make out their own suite far above.

The red cloth was gone.

Barb took her son's hand and together, they took their first shaky steps up the exposed staircase. With each step, they were intimately reminded of their profound vulnerability.

The tower had been stabilized and hoses patiently withdrawn, wound at the foot of the stairs and placed under armed guard. Guests stranded on the atrium floor were slowly being allowed to return to their undamaged suites floor-by-floor, with the highest floors receiving priority. Above, guards had cordoned off the blackened suite.

By the time Barb and Peter reached the ninth floor, the red cloth had returned above and Barb, relieved, stopped to demand answers.

They forced their way out of the ascending masses and down the walkway, quickly losing themselves in the throng of guests now swarming outside the damaged suite. The smoke's still-fresh sweetness assaulted their lungs and turned their stomachs, yet there was something more lingering in the air, something foreign, bitter and vile.

They pushed on, choking, edging through the ripe, sweaty bodies blocking their path and to the front of the huddled crowd.

Though the suite's front door had been removed, the view inside was blocked by a thick fire blanket stretched between two enormous, well-armed security guards.

Barb and Pete had reached the limits of their progress, several feet away.

"What's going on here?" Barb yelled.

"Keep back, ma'am!"

"I demand to know what's happening!"

Others angrily echoed her calls.

Rumors swirled in the heart of the mob and tempers were growing by the minute. Frustrated, Peter dove down and squirreled ahead until he was peering into the suite through a small gap below the blanket.

The suite's interior was caked in foam.

Seeing him, a guard nudged him back with his boot.

"Ain't nothin' to see here kid!"

Barb pulled Pete clear before trouble erupted and fought the forward surge back towards fresher air.

On the crowd's periphery, DTV crews had materialized for interviews.

"What did you see?" Barb asked her son, quietly.

"Foam, DJ. All over. What's it for?"

"Another way of fighting a fire. More portable I guess..."

Barb stared down at the DL:FireMen still posted at the fountain. *Were they expecting more trouble?*

"The suite was empty. That's the thing..." one guest telling DTV. "We're two doors down. Their son was injured on Sunday's attack and they're down in Good Health."

"Are you sure?"

"Absolutely. There was no one there. We went to check on them earlier this afternoon."

"Did you hear anything sir?" the reporter asked.

"Nothing."

"It was a bomb!" yelled another. "I saw the *hole!*"

DTV pushed forward, to a middle-aged woman, lines of exhaustion etching her face. A smoke-stained handkerchief was nervously crumpled in her hand.

"I was here when the DL:FireMen put out the flames," she insisted, "And I saw it. I saw the damage. I saw the *hole*. It was a bomb!"

"But there was no explosion!" yelled another.

"That's right! Definitely no explosion! Just gobs of smoke pouring out!" yelled a third.

Another woman agreed. "I was walking by when I smelled the smoke. I'm the one who called the FireMen. There was no explosion," she told DTV.

"But it was them terrorists!" someone yelled.

"It's a warning!"

Barb froze. The floor around them had broken out in chaos and guests were being forced aside by yet another team of armed guards.

The adjacent suites soon opened and two families emerged with armed escort. The crowd parted and they were slowly led down the walkway with their suitcases. One woman was attached to an oxygen tank.

Gasps spread through the guests as DTV crews zoomed in to capture the scene.

"Oh my God!"

Barb caught one mother's eye, and for an instant stared deep into her uncertain heart. Barb's sweat turned cold.

"Peter, they've lost their homes!"

It was clear now, all so terribly clear, the reality of their predicament made undeniable by the brutality which confronted them. In the harsh light of day, yesterday's *Lair* now seemed a perverse insult, a crude theme park attraction simply manufactured to titillate.

Now, only 24 hours later they were staring at the real thing.

Someone tapped Barb on the shoulder and she spun, gasping.

A third team in chemical suits were forcing their way down the same path, through the guests and on into the charred suite.

"I knew it!" a guest yelled, spitting. "You smell that?"

"*Poison gas*," shouted another. "Low concentration!"

"We're lucky to be alive!" choked a third.

"A warning!" the first confirmed.

"Let's get out of here," Barb said, frantically tugging her son away.

Automatic gunfire burst up from the floor, piercing the fragile calm which had been preciously nourished inside the tower. Shrieks filled the air as those still remaining in the atrium dove for safety among the debris. Guards scurried behind the fountain to take up positions and all along the tower guests hit the floor, peering over and through the walkways for some understanding of the fresh threat they faced.

A masked man brandishing the mighty weapon was firing single-handedly into the air, leaving a trail of spent shells smoking behind him. One-by-one, a seemingly endless line of grim figures emerged from the security center in tow, blindfolded, arms tied uselessly together behind their backs. Heads down, they limped down the stairs and out onto the floor.

All sound from the atrium died away except for the awful rhythmic pulsation of the weapon. After the last of the hostages exited, a second masked man stepped onto the floor with an identical weapon. He too raised it and fired, producing an awful chorus, an almost constant wall of threat.

With the image of the shattering stairs fresh in their minds, Barb and Pete joined others in taking the stairs as quickly as they could, sweat pouring off them, water sloshing in their bottles and arms hugging into their sides to protect their precious stash.

They paused at the seventeenth floor landing to catch their breath for the final break, momentarily tucking back into the entryway of another gutted café with more jittery guests.

"Barb!" came a distant shout, and Barb's heart leapt. She lifted her head to catch Steve's waving hand from down the nineteenth floor walkway, binoculars pressed to his eyes. Sarah was squeezed in next to him.

"Come on, Peter. Hurry!" Barb yelled and she was running again, legs on fire and lungs searing.

Peter was trailing up the stairs after her, amazed at his mom's pace. They reached the floor together and sprinted to their suite, past the cowering wall of onlookers frozen along the railing. There, the Beyers shared a teary-eyed group hug.

Safely reunited, their attention returned below where the hostages were being marched around the fountain's edge. When the circle was complete, the two masked men came together and the firing stopped.

Silence filled the atrium. One by one at gunpoint, the remaining guards were forced to drop their weapons into the fountain's waters.

The hostages were helped down into seated positions by the impotent guards, who sat down next to them, all along the fountain's edge. One masked man quickly made his way around the circle, blindfolding and tying up the guards without protest.

The masked men then continued pacing the circle in opposite directions, weapons drawn and aimed inwards at the helpless hostages.

"This atrium's closed!" one of them screamed.

And guests raced for their suites.

Constantly reminded of the deteriorating climate outside, the Beyers struggled to consume the last of their gifts of food. After this—the collard greens and the cold fried chicken—once again they had nothing.

The master bedroom door was open and as the sun fell, so too did their spirits.

"Employees," Steve announced, breaking the stifling silence and giving voice to the family's darkest thoughts.

"You sure?" Barb asked.

"Positive," he confirmed. "They still had on their security badges."

The truth landed heavily.

"Some had been beaten," Steve finished. "It was pretty clear."

"Yeah," Sarah confirmed. "We didn't need binoculars to tell that."

Barb gagged down her final bite of chicken and dropped the bones, shoving the shared plate away. She felt sick.

"They say it was a bomb," she said, softly. "Down on nine."

"And poison gas," Pete said.

"*Poison gas?*" Steve gasped.

Barb's eyes dropped. "Maybe. Just a little bit. A warning or something."

"It didn't smell right down there, DJ."

"No!" Steve choked. "Even a little bit of poison gas isn't a good thing."

"I know, honey, I know. But it was too late…"

"You… sure you guys are OK?"

Pete nodded, "Just fine, DJ."

Steve eyed them carefully.

Barb's mind was swirling again, the questions relentless and brutal: *How could she have exposed her teenage son to poison gas? How could she have pushed on, into that air? Was there a dumber mother on the whole planet?*

Barb's eyes raised, scanning her husband's dark unshaven face, his own eyes sunken and dull.

"What happened to you Steve?" Barb asked.

"Mistaken identity," he said, softly.

"*Mistaken identity?* They called you by your full name!"

"You know what I'm saying, honey. They had the wrong guy."

"Well we could have used you Steve. If you two would have come we…" Barb was crying now, in quiet, tortured sobs. "None of this would have happened!"

Steve rose and stepped around to her, bending over to take her in his arms. Somehow disguised by the family's earlier relief, it was now obvious the DisasterLand track pants he was wearing were at least two sizes too small.

"They wanted…" Steve took a deep breath. "They wanted to make sure we were OK. Honestly. They may be doing it to everyone."

"I don't see everyone's front door in pieces," Barb sobbed.

"Dad what happened to your pants?" Sarah asked. "You know the butt just split and I can see your boxers."

Barb wiped her eyes.

"They had me strip down and something must have happened. I guess they brought back the wrong pair," Steve said.

Barb pulled away. "They wanted to check up on us but it was mistaken identity. They had you strip down but gave you back someone else's clothes. And the whole time you didn't say anything?"

Steve shrugged.

"Let's just be thankful they didn't sodomize him, mom. Cops do it all the time."

"Peter!"

"If dad was a brotha' he'd be…"

"*ENOUGH,*" Barb howled.

Steve returned to his seat. Silence resettled over the table and Sarah excused herself.

"So the trip for water was OK? Sarah said it took a long time."

"We had to *Make a Difference*, DJ."

Pete pointed to the button on Barb's top. It all seemed so silly now.

"We stopped by Good Health, thinking they might have some water," Barb clarified.

"They didn't?"

"Only for patients. They've got whole families living down there."

"Then how'd you make a difference?"

"We took some of the people flowers," Pete said. "And talked to them. Remember that commercial?"

"Bathrooms?"

"Wouldn't let us in," Barb admitted.

Steve shook his head. The good news was that now the family was back together, there was at least a break in the low-grade relentless worry that had marked the day's separation. The threat, though constant, now seemed somehow more distant. With nourishment, surely, their strength would grow.

"So where'd you get the water?" Steve asked.

"The river."

"You're kidding!"

Sarah emerged, pale, from the bedroom.

"What's wrong, honey?" Barb asked.

"There's still no water," she said. "And I just took a *huge* dump."

"Sarah!"

"I don't even know how. I haven't eaten in..."

"Deal with it!" Barb angrily flung a water bottle at her and Sarah just managed to catch it.

Who raised these animals?

"I'm sorry mom. There's no good way to say it," Sarah said and disappeared.

"It's bad news, alright," Steve agreed as he began to clear the table. They had eaten like primitives, all sharing one plate to reduce water usage. "We're going to have to go back down soon."

Barb groaned.

"Before things get any worse," Steve continued. "We've got a day of water here, tops," he pointed out. "And tablets for an additional day. Maybe two if we're very careful."

Barb and Peter's tablets had purified half the water they'd brought back and already almost half of that was gone.

"Not today, DJ. No way. I'm beat."

"First light. And we use every container we have. *Everything.* We get as much water as we can carry."

"DJ, let's fill the hot tub!"

Steve nodded. "Good idea, Spikers. Don't know if we can do it, but let's make it our goal. A reservoir."

Steve returned to his seat at the table. "Then there's the little matter of food... luckily we've got our bars. We're good for another couple of days in an emergency."

Pete's head dropped.

"Spikers, you didn't."

Pete remained silent.

"You ate your bar?"

"When I was on duty the other night. I got hungry, DJ. I couldn't stand it!"

"Seriously, Spike. This is for real here."

"I didn't know..."

"Beyers!" a gruff voice yelled into the afternoon haze.

"Oh no!" Pete yelled, leaping up, "Not again!"

Their front door crashed to the floor and two burly guards once again burst into their suite. Steve panicked, caught in the eddies of a terrible flashback, his past humiliation, his present fear and his eternal inadequacies swirling relentlessly through his mind.

"Yes?" he stammered, shaking.

A dog barked and Steve nearly leapt out of his skin.

"Easy Pooch..." a third guard said as he entered. Pooch followed, sniffing the edges of the Beyers' hallway as the family looked on, numb. The Labrador was wearing a tiny headlamp.

The two guards stood firm in the entryway as the third made his rounds through their living room with Pooch.

"Who's he?" Pete asked.

"Pooch. The bomb-sniffer," a guard responded.

"Bomb-sniffer!" Barb and Steve exchanged glances.

Pooch and the guard entered the master bedroom, then the bathroom. Sarah cringed.

"Yo Pooch! Hey Buddy!" called Pete. Neither the dog nor the guard was in any way distracted from their business as they trotted back through the living room and into Sarah and Pete's room.

"Everyone here?" the other guard asked. "You folks doing alright?"

"Depends," Steve muttered. "What's going on out there?"

"Stand-off," the guard said. "But we're pushing forward."

"You sure that's safe?" Barb asked. "What if..."

"Don't worry, ma'am, we're covered. Can't tell you how, but if they try anything they'll be in trouble real quick."

Pooch emerged from the bedroom and exited the suite with two of the guards. All business.

"Here you go, folks. For your safety."

The remaining guard handed them a hand-written card on his way out:

Please, remain in your suite.
Don't let the terrorists win.

311

Maria was tucked next to a hidden safe just off of Café Dansant's kitchen. Low-profile once again in a guest tracksuit, she was double-checking her backpack's inventory and carefully matching it with her list of deliveries.

It was going to be a busy evening. Demand amongst her hardcore clients had only increased, predictably, while her deliverable hours had begun their dramatic decrease. Without power and with the growing threat in the atrium, it would take her much longer to locate some of the scarcer products now available only on adjacent floors. To her, lost time meant lost cash.

Now that shadows were consuming the atrium and the walkways remained clear, she was awaiting her cue to begin deliveries. Too many curious guests meant hassles. It meant more desperate requests from clients who couldn't afford her services, requests that she simply didn't have the resources—or the sympathy—to handle.

Out of sight, out of mind.

Her first delivery happened to be an expensive bottle of Bordeaux, the sixth in two days for a preferred customer at the far southern end of the walkway by the external elevator. From there, she'd slip down to sixteen to trade another runner for the last bottle of 25-year single malt left above fifteen. She'd been lucky there. And she'd make a killing.

The radio in her backpack crackled to life, "You're clear, Maria. Nineteen is clear," stated the dispatcher.

Maria checked her watch. *"Gracias,"* she whispered. "I am out."

A quick prayer for safety and prosperity and Maria ducked away, tapping the safe's keypad for good luck.

The familiar gentleman answered the door in his bathrobe, hair slicked back. His splashed-on cologne assaulted her senses.

"¡Hola Maria! ¿Es tarde, no?"

"Lo siento. ¡Rehenes, Dios mío! Safety is first."

"Por supuesto, mi angelito."

The man laughed, welcoming her inside. He was drunk.

"Where's *jour* wife?" Maria asked as she moved into the kitchen. She removed the bottle from her backpack.

"She went to a neighbor's to socialize. Someone she met Friday night."

"Jou did not want to go?"

"I'm sure she'll tell me all about it. I prefer to enjoy myself here."

"That sounds very nice. One-fifty, please," Maria set the bottle down and the man passed her two hundreds. She quickly verified them as authentic and dug for change, but he waved her off.

He picked up the bottle, appreciatively, "Would you like to join me?"

Drinking with clients was discouraged but wasn't technically prohibited—Maria was free to use her own judgment—and facing the long evening ahead, her sense of adventure got the best of her.

"*Una copita, por favor,*" she said, laughing. "*No mas.*"

She'd have just half a glass. It *was* a very nice wine after all.

"*Naturalmente,*" he smiled, and opened the cabinet to remove the corkscrew and two glasses, which he placed out of her sight.

With great ceremony he popped the cork and turned away to pour. Maria grew suspicious. *Was this really the oldest trick in the book?*

He passed her a glass and toasted, "To you, Maria, for making this stay so pleasant."

"*Gracias.*"

They clinked glasses and Maria smiled, catching his eye. She put the glass to her lips, but didn't drink.

"Um..." she licked her lips, "*Rico.*"

"*¡Sí, un gran vino!*"

The man winked. He was attractive and despite his age, radiating bravado. Maria remained on guard.

"*Español, no?*"

"*¡Sí, sí!*" the man said, turning to grab the bottle.

Maria deftly switched the glasses.

"Rioja," he continued, "My favorite. Have you been? To Spain?"

He passed her the bottle.

"*No...*"

"Where are you from?"

"*Guatemala.* A little town. In the mountains."

"I see. Beautiful?"

"Oh *jes...*"

He stepped forward, deliberately. For a split second, she recognized the look of a predator.

She fondled her necklace seductively, then took a long, luscious sip of the wine. He followed.

"*Sí,* very nice," Maria continued, "It is going to be a long night for me. So many deliveries!"

"Then you must stay for a full glass."

"We finish this one first."

"Of course!"

Ten minutes later he was out cold, naked and tied spread-eagle to the couch. Head down, his bare ass protruded menacingly towards the front door.

His wife would undoubtedly be surprised. But unfortunately for him, that was only where his trouble would begin.

The plain-clothed DisasterLand special forces team made the final tugs on the knots while Maria emptied his wallet. The investigative team packed away his wine glass and a blood sample for testing.

Maria counted the bills, pleased, then reset her security necklace. She had considered writing his wife a little note sealed with a kiss, something to roll up and stick where it would be most obvious.

But Maria resisted. She was, above all, a professional.

Besides, it just meant her family would be receiving a little bonus installment this month.

"Guests of DisasterLand, your attention please!" a distant voice announced.

Inside the Beyers' dark suite, nervous glances were shared. They had each drifted into an uneasy doze on the couch and their racing hearts now struggled to regain equilibrium.

Steve flipped on his light and they waited.

"Guests of DisasterLand, please. I have an announcement!" the voice repeated.

"That sounded like Clint!" Barb said.

"I'm going out," Steve said.

"*Steve...*"

"Who's coming with me?"

"I'll come," Sarah said, digging for her light. She flipped it on.

"Let's roll, sweetie."

"We'll all go," Barb said. "Come on, Peter."

The family ducked out onto the walkway, just after eight. Darkness had blanketed the atrium and Barb and Pete carefully reset the door behind them before joining Steve and Sarah at the rail.

All down the tower, guests were cautiously spilling out of their suites. Dozens of armed guards lined each of the walkways.

Below, in the shadows of the atrium floor, the two masked men continued to pace slow, methodical circles around the ring of hostages. In the center of the fountain, the DL:FireMen's hoses and pumps sat abandoned and exposed.

The tower's very safety now truly lay in the hands of the terrorists.

Resting deep inside no man's land, between the tower and the fountain, a Good Health gurney was illuminated by the battery-powered lights of DTV's hovering cameramen. Its back was raised to allow the patient a glimpse of the guests lining the dark tower above.

"Ladies and Gentlemen, Guests of DisasterLand," Clint repeated, stalling for the late-comers.

Steve doubled back into the suite for his binoculars.

"Ladies and Gentlemen, I'm Clint Lewis."

He limped out from behind the gurney on crutches, wearing jeans with one leg cut off to allow for his brace and a matching DL:FireMan T-shirt and baseball cap. He was speaking through a megaphone.

"And this," Clint scowled, "is Red Admiral."

Lhasa raised his fist, mimicking Jimmy's final action, and a respectful yet hesitant ovation arose from the still-swelling crowds filling the walkways.

Steve raised his binoculars to examine each floor one-by-one, and froze. Teams of guards had been placed outside certain individual suites all the way up the tower.

What were they guarding?

Were all those suites empty?

Had all those families left for Good Health?

Were they injured? Or *kidnapped?*

To Steve's darkening sensibilities, the tower had become a very dangerous place indeed, with everyone's motives suspect.

"This is not an act," Clint continued. "I am speaking to you not as Clint Lewis the FireMan, but as Clint Flibbermester the actor. Extraordinarily complex negotiations are taking place as we speak—negotiations which could affect the health and safety of each and every one of us. Negotiations which are much larger than the staff here, or the few deranged cowards within our midst. This is a problem of world-wide proportions and must be dealt with as such. However, negotiators are aware of the deteriorating conditions here and are working around the clock to see that a resolution is achieved quickly."

A few isolated cheers echoed through the vast space.

"It is of the utmost importance that nothing interfere with their progress."

"We want out!" someone yelled.

"*Release us!*" screamed another.

Clint hobbled a few steps closer to the tower and continued, "Please, I am begging you. It is urgent that each one of us does what we can to ensure the negotiations' swift conclusion, for the good of all. That means to stay calm, remain in your suite, and monitor the changing conditions.

"We all share the problems of sanitation, of the lack of fresh water and food. Together, we must be strong. *United we stand!*"

Cheers rang out.

He passed the megaphone to Lhasa and a hush again fell over the tower, "Guests of DisasterLand, I must apologize. You came for a vacation and have been caught up in something much larger and perhaps much more threatening than anything you have ever known. But you must understand the gravity of what we all face. For Nelly belongs to us all."

The guests lining the tower jeered. Steve passed his binoculars to Barb.

"For your own good," Lhasa said, "please do not force us into a position which we do not want to be in. Please do not back us into a corner. You will all regret it. I assure you."

He rested the megaphone on his chest and seemed to scan the tower with derision, before once again raising the megaphone to his lips. A rain of hisses descended from above.

"We are peace-loving people, but we will not compromise in the defense of Nelly. I must inform you that three of the hostages behind me are wearing timed explosives," he said, a hush falling over the crowd above. "Every fifteen minutes they must be reset or they will blow. And only two people in DisasterLand know the codes."

Behind him, bursts of gunfire flashed from the masked men.

"If anything happens to them, it will happen to all of us too. That is a guarantee."

He returned the megaphone to Clint, who withstood the cries of horror with a determined stoicism.

"We at DisasterLand are your friends, not your enemies," Clint began, with increased fervor. "We are the solution, not the problem. We are doing what we can to help you. But we must be allowed."

Sobbing now punctuated the dramatic silence left by the fading horror.

"It is urgent that each of you remain vigilant, that you report anything out of the ordinary and you remain in your suite except in the case of an emergency. Fresh water is available at the river during daylight hours only."

"Those of you protesting at Good Food, those of you questioning our motives, please. We are doing what we can. We are giving you what we have. Things may get even more difficult. But by confronting us, by interfering in our operations, you are only doing the work of the terrorists. The guards you see around you have had little sleep and little food. Their friends have been assaulted and one is in critical condition. Treat them with respect. They are on your side."

He cleared his throat. "Ladies and gentlemen, we are under threat from barbaric thugs who envy us, who do not understand the meaning of life and liberty, who only wish us and our families harm. It is urgent that we give them no cause to push forward their apocalyptic plans."

Restrained applause broke out but the Beyers couldn't partake. Steve found the speech profoundly unsettling and reeking of desperation. Barb passed the binoculars to Peter.

Clint gained speed with his conclusion, "We're stronger than they are, we're smarter, wealthier and we're better looking. But we will not fight. Conflict is not the answer. We will wait, patiently, for diplomacy to take its course, and soon this terrible experience will be behind us. *God bless you all!*"

Clint raised his arms overhead, then turned to Lhasa and dropped the megaphone. They embraced, an act which spurned the assembled guests to a reluctant ovation.

Together, they waved one final time and Clint limped around the back of the gurney, to slowly and dramatically begin wheeling it back towards Good Health as scores of families solemnly retreated back to their suites.

"I'm..." Sarah began but was unable to finish. A woman's heart-wrenching screams pierced the air and all eyes turned to the opposite end of their floor.

Just in from the external elevator, an elegant woman was hanging onto the handrail, red-faced and heaving, illuminated by the flashlights of guards racing from their posts at the stairs.

"Let me out of here," Barb said, hurrying inside with Pete in tow.

Steve realized Jim and Jenny Andrews were seated at a table in front of their suite, anxiously monitoring the developments nearby. A crowd had been gathered around them.

Guards were entering the woman's open suite while others stayed to tend to her.

"Nothing we can do," Steve said. "Let's go pay the Andrews a visit."

Below, Clint's words of cooperation had done nothing to quell the fury of protest in front of Good Food. It had grown in both size and venom since the afternoon and an additional team of guards had been dispatched to quarantine. They now ringed in the protestors, preventing entrance or exit. Shouting echoed up from below as conflict simmered.

"Good idea, dad. This is all gettin' kinda weird."

"Dad the guards look really freaked out," Sarah whispered as they passed a patrol.

"I noticed that."

"Does it worry you?"

"Does it worry *you?*"

"Yes."

"Me too."

"Excuse me..." Steve said, to the passing guards.

"Back inside, sir. You heard the guy."

The guards slid around and continued marching, head down, without acknowledgement.

Steve put his arm around his daughter. "Just a quick chat with the Andrews. It'll help calm your mother."

Jim and Jenny flashed a huge smile as Steve and Sarah neared. The Andrews had moved their bedside table outside their front door and were sitting on two kitchen chairs as if the entire walkway was their front porch.

A nervous crowd was assembled, darting to and from the table like fish being fed. Steve noticed guards monitoring the table from a distance.

The Andrews waved them in, making room to proudly show them their spread. Tiny little Jesuses on the cross had been laid across the table, delicately handwoven out of stalks of wheat. Steve and Sarah eyed the figurines with awe.

"They're amazing!" Sarah said.

"Crafted with love for difficult times," Jenny said somberly.

"Guaranteed to increase the power of prayer," Jim added and other guests agreed.

"How'd you do that!?" Sarah asked.

"A lot of patience, honey."

"How much do you want?"

"Two hundred."

"No!" Steve laughed.

Jim leaned in, confrontationally. "You don't think they're worth it? Everyone needs strength in times of adversity, Beyers."

Other guests frowned at Steve as they forked over the cash. Steve realized Jim's pockets were already bulging.

Steve laughed awkwardly, "No, I know... I do... it's just..."

"Takes a while to do that, Beyers. You know?"

"I'm sure it does."

"And they're preserved. So they'll never rot. But you can't tell."

"They're artisanal quality," Jenny chimed in.

"They sure are," Steve agreed, re-examining one.

"Want one?"

"No thanks..."

"You're not going to take one of these back to Kansas?" he asked.

Sarah felt sorry for her dad.

"I don't think so," Steve said. For the first, and probably the last time, he was glad he had no cash.

"He who has ears, let him hear," Jenny added.

"Selling a lot?" Steve asked as more and more guests crowded around the table.

"We'll sell out. Only brought thirty," Jim announced, loud enough for all to hear.

"Thirty!"

"We don't weave them all ourselves. We've got a couple of friends who share our passion. We have weaving parties of living prayer," Jenny explained as a young couple listened with interest.

Sarah had tuned the whole thing out for self-preservation. She stepped out of the increasingly rabid crowd, unable to deal with the growing fervor as supplies dwindled. She thought of her cell phone, of her friends back home. She tried to imagine herself back on her bed, on the phone or the computer, sharing the sickest internet sites she could find with her friend Emily.

Suddenly the most boring night ever seemed like the best.

Jim took Steve's arm and left the table to his wife, joining Sarah in relative privacy a few feet away.

"You know anything about this fire, Beyers?" Jim asked quietly, unexpectedly.

"We were coming to ask you," Steve whispered.

Sarah leaned in, "My mom was there. Right after. With Spike. I mean, Pete."

"You're kidding. What'd she say?"

"The eyewitnesses said there was a hole. In the suite. It could have been *a bomb*."

"A *hole*?"

Steve nodded.

"That's the other weird thing," Sarah added, "The family was already gone. It was an empty suite. They'd gone down to Good Health yesterday to join an injured relative. It's like the terrorists *knew that*."

Jim frowned, "What did security say?"

Sarah shrugged. "Nothing."

Down the walkway, a stretcher was carried out from the open suite by an EMS crew with guards accompanying it. A handsome man was laid out, his motionless body covered with a sheet, his face exposed with an oxygen mask covering his mouth.

His wife rose with help, and joined the grim procession as they made their way to the stairs.

"Heart attack I'll bet," said Steve. "But his eyes are open. He'll probably make it."

"They're gonna carry him 19 stories down?" Sarah asked.

"What else are they going to do?"

Jim leaned in further, and even Sarah had to strain to hear. "Let me ask you something, Beyers," Jim whispered, "you think this terrorist thing, you think this is real?"

"I don't know."

"You ever thought they're a bunch of sickos? Like those Japanese freaks—those Aum-Shin-Reekios or whatever?"

"You mean like them threatening to poison us? Just release a big cloud of something? Right down there?"

Jim nodded and Steve's stomach was free-falling as Barb's words came roaring back to him. *Poison Gas.*

Steve saw his daughter's reaction and his wished Jim had been more discreet. It was almost cruel. Steve's mind, even in his darkest moments in the middle of the night, the cold sweat moments, the crawling stomach moments, even in those moments he'd never thought of *this*.

"Dad," Sarah choked, "tell him about what Pete saw."

Steve nodded, relieved she didn't take it the whole way. "Yeah, listen to this Jim. My son was out on the walkway, Sunday night. Late."

"Must have been around two. Or even later," Sarah added.

"And he said he saw these two guys, maintenance guys, with duffle bags down on thirteen. Big guys. *On the phone.*"

Jim's brow furrowed.

Steve continued, "And Pete watched the guys enter a suite down there. They were let inside by armed guards!"

"And we... he... never saw anyone come out," Sarah added.

"Peter said that?"

"Yeah."

"Beyers, I've seen the same thing."

"No!"

"The exact same thing. Guys with bags, guards inside. Except it was on twenty. Right over there." He pointed.

Steve and Sarah looked on nervously.

"Early this morning," Jim said, "I had to stretch my legs. My head wasn't right, this whole thing was getting to me. So I came out here, real silently, and I watched them come up the stairs and go right to that suite. Just like you..."

Below, a yell. And a single shot.

Then a terrible silence.

Screams spread over the tower's length as lingering families scattered for cover. Steve ducked behind the railing with Jim, his daughter behind. Steve raised his binoculars.

There, in the heart of the atrium below, in the center of the Guard's powerful flashlights, a body lay motionless. Hands still tied, leg bandaged and eyes blindfolded, a pool of dark red was spreading from the woman's back.

She had tried to escape.

Steve passed Jim the binoculars.

"Those bastards!" Jim cried.

"Back inside!" the guards nearest them cried. "Let's go folks, party is over! *Back inside!*"

Sarah was tugging her dad's shirt.

"Jesus, Jim. I got a real bad feeling about this," Steve said. "Real bad feeling."

Jim's face shrunk into a grimace, "Only one way to tell what's going on, Beyers. Are you with me?"

"You mean go down there? To thirteen? I don't think so Jim..." Steve said. "This is the real deal here."

"That's crazy," Sarah said, "You heard the guards!"

"No..." Jim decided. "No, you're right. Not there. Too dangerous. We'll hit twenty." Once again, Jim pointed to the nondescript door.

"I dunno..." Steve said, voice fading. His eyes met Sarah's, silently pleading.

"Look, Beyers, I'm going," Jim decided, his eyes hardening. "No terrorist is gonna bullshit me and no actor is going to tell me what's best for my family."

Steve couldn't figure out exactly where Jim was coming from, but he wasn't about to be shown up. He turned to Sarah. "You'll be OK?"

Sarah panicked, "Dad *you can't!*"

"Jim's right, honey. We've got to confront this thing sooner or later, and now's the time." He took her hand. "We may never have this much energy again. Go tell your mom."

Sarah nodded, silently, her eyes filling with tears as she raced back down the walkway. Steve watched while Sarah pounded the front door and darted inside.

Jim hurried over to explain the plan to Jenny while Steve wondered what the hell he was doing.

"Let's move Beyers," Jim finally called.

Jim gave Jenny a peck on the cheek and the men headed for the stairs. Steve looked back.

Jenny looked as worried as he felt.

"So you're Catholic? Or Christian?" Steve asked as they made a break for the stairs, brushing off the attempts of the harried guards to step them.

"Capitalist."

Steve stared.

"Disposable income, Beyers. Just like those swordfighters and more willing to spend it. The more they spend, the stronger their belief."

"Swordfighters?"

"Jousters."

Steve shrugged, "I'm lost."

"Jesus, Beyers, what do they feed you in Kansas? *Ho-mo-sex-uals*. But we don't sell to them. It'd ruin our reputation within the church community. We make religious artifacts to augment personal worship. *Exclusively*."

"So you're entrepreneurs."

"That's the name of the game. Indians make those in South America for $3.75 each and they're happy as clams. Jenny just delivered that prayer circle line because of the crowd. They love it. I bet Jenny's sold out by now. You know, we'll make almost six grand this evening. I told her we could have waited until tomorrow and got more, but she wanted to take the money and run."

Steve shook his head.

"Exactly."

Rounding the stairs to reach the landing above, they found a simple message which affirmed the necessity of their quest.

Giant block letters were smeared across the terrorist's prior defamations with a mysterious and threatening substance:

Help Us

Spurned on by the validity of their essential crusade, Jim and Steve quickened their step. Guards were now in pursuit.

Jim turned to Steve and Steve mentally immunized himself.

"You know how much you could get for one of these in Kansas Beyers? A wheat Jesus?"

Steve feigned disinterest, but Jim saw his mind working. Jim continued, "You want to distribute? If we make it out of here, we'll wholesale them to you for $75. You keep whatever you can sell them for above that, square. Give you Kansas and Missouri, maybe Colorado... You could send your girl to college with wheat Jesuses."

Steve did the math. Could he get $300 each back home? If he bought ten at $75, he'd pull down $2250 for his trouble. That'd furnish Sarah's dorm. *And* pay for the trip out.

"I'll have to think about it, Jim," he said, yet unable to hide his growing interest.

Jim nodded. "No pressure, Beyers. But not a word. To anyone. 'Cept Barb, of course. She's a real *beaut* Beyers, you did well."

Steve straightened, "Going on twenty years."

"Well don't fuck it up, guy. She must get approached every day. Live bait, Beyers."

They were running now, guards closing in.

"Hey, Beyers what happened to your front door?"

Steve eyed him carefully. It finally dawned on him, flat out, that he didn't trust this guy. No one bit.

But it might not matter. In the face of terrorists and lies, they had a higher calling, a shared purpose.

"Security got mixed up. Mistaken identity."

"You're kidding?"

"That's what they said."

"Damn. I spoke to another guy. Same thing happened to his wife. Down on six."

Steve's mind spun.

"I don't like this at all, Beyers. We've got to stick together. Me and you." Jim said as they arrived at their destination.

Jim patted Steve on the back. "You ready?"

"One—*Two*—THREE!"

Adrenalin surged through their veins like molten lead, fueling their bravado as Steve and Jim rode the liberation of the pure moment. They burst through the door together, full-force, and it splintered around them with a crash.

"*Argh!*" Jim yelled, grabbing his shoulder and slowing.

Steve stuttered. "You OK?"

A muffled yell echoed from inside.

"Yeah! Go!" Jim grimaced and Steve resumed his advance, alone.

"Holy shit!" Steve howled as he stepped into the living room.

"No!" Jim screamed, seconds later, "*No!*"

Jenny, Barb, Sarah and Peter were anxiously monitoring the suite above from the rail across from the Andrews' door. They were beginning to fear the worst.

Only seconds after the break-in, armed guards had followed the men inside. Now, almost twenty-five minutes later, more and more had flooded in but there was still no sign of their men. Two guards now stood posted in front of a fire blanket, restraining the throng of nose-holding curiosity seekers. DTV cameras roamed the scene and interviews were already being conducted.

The Jesuses had been sold and the table and chairs were stashed out of the harm's way. But Jenny's financial gains offered no solace.

"I can't believe they did that," Jenny said.

"I can't either. You know it was Jim's idea."

"I know. He gets carried away sometimes. I'm so sorry..."

Jenny was thankful for the company but Barb was wondering if she needed to approach the suite for herself. She needed answers and she sure wasn't going to find them here. Inaction was eating her alive.

Jenny chirped with horror and Barb refocused on the scene above. An unidentified man, covered in a DisasterLand fire blanket, was being carried out of the suite on a stretcher, motionless. They waited in horror, but a second body never appeared.

Worse yet, another DTV crew was headed down the walkway. Towards *them*.

For the second time in his life and the second time in less than 12 hours, Steve found himself threatened with arrest.

He sat handcuffed, lost and barely able to breathe, stewing in the fetid suite surrounded by rotting pools of human excrement. His body writhed beyond his control. Caustic sweat poured down his brow, stinging his eyes.

Jim, sitting next to him, had wretched twice, vomiting the indescribable.

Had this been a rescue?

Or had they made a mistake?

Had they failed or had they succeeded?

One thing were for sure: they had broken into a puzzling scene of terrible human suffering and had learned things they now wished they hadn't.

They had rescued the young woman's kidnapped husband.

But now there was no going back.

A blood-curdling scream ignited Steve's nerves and he awoke with a start. It was dark. He was in his entryway, guarding his family's suite.

He must have passed out. *Cold.*

Heart thudding, he prepared for a terrible reprise that never came. The atrium remained deadly silent.

The living room behind him was still, his family's breathing regular and comforting in its innocence. They were ignorant, in bliss. He hadn't told them a thing.

After his release two hours ago, Barb had greeted him with a simple, exhausted hug, gently shrugging off all explanation until morning.

Yet now he was suffering in silence, alone, and it would continue indefinitely. Jim and Steve had personally been sworn to secrecy by the captain of DisasterLand's security force with terrible consequences if they failed. It was their price for freedom.

"You're only going to hurt us all," the captain had warned. "This is exactly what we don't need."

Steve's eyes burned, his bloated head throbbed, inflated by the danger lurking all around them. Nausea rippled through him in waves.

A hole, seared into his consciousness like a ghastly afterimage. A hole. *Of terror.*

Shafts behind every wall of their suite. Spaces. A vast, dark matrix surrounding them.

And terrorists living *within*, like vermin.

The rescue had looped before him, relentlessly, oppressively, each time with a far greater intensity and inspiring ever more profound fear.

Chained to the wall, blindfolded, amidst spray-painted tributes to Nelly and taunts to DisasterLand's authority, the young male victim had been stewing in his own excrement since early Monday evening. And it was him. The husband of the woman who had read the letter.

Others had obviously been there long before.

"Careful!" he had screamed, his face ashen, his breath sour. "The whole place is rigged to blow!"

There, next to him, a gaping hole in the wall leading to the vast industrial innards of DisasterLand. Plastic explosives lined the periphery, rigged to his handcuffs. If he moved even an inch, let alone attempt escape, the entire tower would go.

A second razor-edged scream brought Steve painfully back to reality. Dazed, he clawed his way past the damaged front door and stuck his head cautiously outside.

Below him, on seventeen, a young woman lay crumbled outside her suite. Otherwise attractive in her luxurious satin bathrobe, her hair was up for the night.

Guards were rushing to her side.

"My husband!" she wailed, "He's been taken! *From our own bed!*"

Steve alone knew the implications and his heart froze. But he turned away, cutting off his own interest. It wasn't worth the energy. He was powerless.

Steve collapsed against the walkway. His heart raced, his mind swirled through the depths and detritus of his soul.

A kidnapping. In a guest's own suite. *The holes.*

And security was impotent. *Impotent.*

Suddenly, uncontrollably, hot tears blurred his vision as the true significance of the last night's vision kicked him in the teeth.

This was real, he realized, *really real. No one, not even DisasterLand, would put someone through that.*

And no one knows any of it.

No one could *know it. But us.*

In the dark vastness of the atrium, Steve finally broke down and cried. The studio audience hung on his words: *That's when I realized: we won't be leaving on Sunday.*

We might not ever leave at all.

We could die here.

Elektra was sitting at her kitchen table, the tower spilling below her like an open wound. Wrapped in her silk robe, she was nursing a chamomile tea and an unshakable case of insomnia.

Her post-shift trip to the gym and hot shower had done little to abate the onslaught of nervous energy. Fearing a sleepless night ahead, she was growing increasingly desperate.

They were well into the terminal phase of the script, slightly ahead of schedule. These were the most dense, dangerous, unpredictable and potentially overwhelming times and she needed her wits about her. Tomorrow, and then for as long as it took, she needed to be *on*.

They were walking a tightrope.

Elektra had to get to sleep and she was wondering if the herbal tea was going to cut it. Alcohol was out of the question—she needed to be sharp. Drugs—even prescription—would be insane.

Once again, her nighttime thoughts returned to Clint—though not Clint specifically, rather the idea of Clint. A kind of meta-Clint, that possessed all of the physical attributes but lacked his specific personality.

She hadn't spoken to him since Monday and certainly didn't *really* miss him. It was *someone* she was missing right now, actually *anyone*. It was the feel of getting into a warm bed after a long night's work, the gentle welcoming kiss. It was an exhausting lovemaking session and falling asleep in someone's arms. That's what she needed.

And she wasn't going to get it.

Incoming shift reports were flashing across her laptop's screen but she hadn't found much new. She'd carried the first team all the way up until just after one and had been monitoring the Feed ever since. There wouldn't be many surprises.

At least, probably not.

She muted the Feed and took another long sip of tea. She closed her eyes, slowed her breathing.

Vacation.

Three undeniable components had manifested during the week thus far—beach, mountains and *life*—and now, clear-headed, she felt no need to compromise. With three weeks off, she would do them all and she would do them balls-out. Molly would surely join her.

First up would be the beach, a transitional environment to ease relaxation. She would detox, decompress and emerge renewed for her mountain retreat.

Mornings spent with beachfront meditation and breakfasts of exotic fresh fruit. Long, sun-drenched afternoons spent with chilled red wine and the warm Caribbean as it lapped against the shore, meshing with the calling of seabirds; snorkeling amongst the etherial beauty of the tropical fish, perhaps even a lucky communion with a dolphin. Evenings would be spent getting quietly drunk, nights as an instrument awaiting her maestro.

Then an extravagant trip to the Caribbean's most remote Ashram where she would arrange a week-long silent meditation to cleanse her mind and spirit.

A trip to the Dominican Republic's mountainous jungle would give her the two last requirements, plus a reprise of the first. There were other islands to choose from, of course, but she was thinking DR. She was thinking *Latin*. She was thinking *energía*. *Vida*.

She'd speak to her travel agent in the morning.

Elektra stood and gathered her things, carefully placing her sleeping laptop in its case. She'd make a quick trip to the bedroom, packing an overnight bag to take with her to the bridge.

She knew where she stood: she wouldn't be getting any more sleep this show and she may as well be where she could act.

After another quick shower, she'd hit the bridge. For good.

Steve heard a rustle and flipped on his flashlight to find a flyer under his door.

Please stay in your room except in case of emergency.
You are not hostages. Thank you for your cooperation.
In solidarity,
DisasterLand.

He turned it over.

HUMANITARIAN AID: Emergency Water Available in River.
Faith-based escorts depart even floors every 30 minutes
during daylight hours for your safety.

Steve flipped off the light, the darkness blinding him. He dropped the flyer. *So this is what it's come to. If we're not hostages, then why are they reassuring us?*

With dwindling strength, Steve forced the door a foot or so to the side and squeezed through. In the distance, the sky above had just begun to lighten.

He slid out onto the walkway on his stomach. His raw breath bounced off the glass and slapped him painfully in the face.

Anxiety percolated around him, up from the atrium floor below. Across the walkways, teams of guards continued their night-time patrols, undistracted by the growing unrest below. They had dropped the flyer.

Fools, Steve cursed. *The terrorists are* inside! *Who are you trying to stop?*

Steve froze. *Who were they trying to stop?*

He stared as they marched away into the distance.

Them?

Or *us!*

Steve cautiously edged himself to the rail. The Good Food protest had only continued to grow in ferocity after Clint's plea and now, even before sunrise, it was an angry, throbbing mass.

Their chants echoed clearly, almost twenty stories overhead: *O-PEN O-PEN O-PEN O-PEN O-PEN...*

It couldn't last. Steve planted himself at the rail, sensing trouble. In the heart of the atrium, the masked men remained in front of their captives, huddled together in conversation.

The body had been removed but the pool of blood remained, a terrible reminder of the life lost, a terrible reminder of the continuing threat.

Distant flickers of light caught his attention, and he raised his eyes to the dim park.

He gasped.

There, a ring of torches provided medieval lighting for the shadows that circulated behind an enormous, well-fortified mesh fence which now enclosed the far half of the Great Lawn.

Inside lay an enormous white tent. Splashed across its roof above The Star of Life:

DL:HumanAid

A refugee camp! Erected while guests were sleeping!

"Back inside!"

Steve turned, confronted by the boot of a security guard. It nudged his shoulder again.

"Let's go, guy! *Back inside!*"

Steve picked himself up and scurried back through his door with every ounce of strength he had left. He didn't look back.

Behind him, he knew, the tension was about to boil over.

Dangerous and uncertain times lay ahead, and Steve feared he would soon be called to act on the terrible knowledge he shared.

Barb rested her hands on Steve's shoulders, sending him leaping out of his skin. Her hand flashed over his mouth muting his yell but he ducked away, spinning for a weapon. Steve's eyes were full of wild, animal fear and Barb recoiled.

Finally seeing his wife clearly in the dim light, Steve relaxed, letting his head drop in shame.

Barb closed in gradually, joining him on the floor. She could hear his heart pounding and breathed in his spoiled musk.

"Honey, what's wrong? What was that horrible noise?"

Behind them, the kids remained asleep. Through the door's cracks, the sky outside continued to lighten.

"Riot guards stormed the protest at Good Food," Steve continued, wiping his eyes to catch her reaction. It wasn't flattering.

"They've built a refugee camp," he finished.

"Oh my God."

"They used tear gas, Barb. To force them in."

"*Tear gas?* That's..."

"I went out—twice—until guards chased me back at gunpoint." He passed her the flyer. "Here. This came a little while ago."

She examined it and he continued, "The protest was gaining strength. They were threatening violence. Riot cops went in to stop it before more guests woke up. Before people could see what was really happening..."

He was desperate, shaken, and witnessing his pain Barb felt as if her own heart was being squeezed.

Something was terribly wrong.

Barb collapsed next to him, "Steve, what happened to you last night?"

"We've got nothing, Barb. Nothing. Do you know that?"

"We'll be OK." Barb said. "We..."

He cut her off, viciously. "We *might* be OK. We *might* be. Don't you understand?"

She didn't.

"Honey, this is *real. REAL.*"

A grotesque smile spread across his face, revolting her.

"How do you know..." she stammered.

"I KNOW!" he hissed. "Trust me."

His eyes were fierce, yet distant, watching something. Something terrible.

He continued, "There are no guarantees, honey. Of anything anymore."

Sweat was dripping from his brow. Barb tried to slide away, but he leaned in, cornering her. She averted her eyes.

"We're not leaving on Sunday, honey. *We're not leaving.* Don't you see? We could be here a week. A month. Or more. We could *die* here, honey!"

"Steve! You need to get a hold of yourself."

"Don't you see? I'm trying to take care of my family, Barb. I'm taking responsibility!"

"*We'll* take responsibility. *Together.* And I think you're overreacting. This is a place where people go to have these things happen."

"To have a security center blown up? To have holes in our walls?"

"Have you lost your mind?"

Steve was sobbing, openly now. "What if I'm not *over-reacting*? *We've got absolutely nothing*... nothing!"

He tried to catch his breath. "No food. Soon, no fresh water. And practically no cash. The sanitary situation in another day or two will be dangerous."

Barb's face dropped. She couldn't argue. Barb looked up to find Sarah and Pete in the hallway, staring. She shoed them away. Steve hadn't noticed.

He dropped his head in his hands. "Honey, we put our faith in these people and they've let us down," he whimpered. "They've *fucked* us! We've got *nothing*!"

Steve gathered his strength for one final statement, "They'll lock me up for telling you this... but there are gaps between these suites. Gaps big enough for rope ladders. The terrorists are *inside.* All around us. *Real terrorists.* And DisasterLand won't go in to find them. Won't confront them. Because they *can't.* So DisasterLand is controlling *us.* And they can't even do that anymore!"

Barb felt like he had kicked her in the gut. She bent over. "Oh, honey..."

"This whole tower is rigged to blow."

Barb froze.

"This could be worse than Waco. The hole you heard about downstairs wasn't a bomb, it was an *access point into their network of death!*"

The Beyers were restlessly scattered about their living room, acutely aware their supply of food had been exhausted. All they had now was DL:Powerstrips, three total.

Ethereal dawn light trickled in from the bedroom and stomachs growled.

"This is not subject to debate," Steve said, finally breaking the thick silence. "We've got a week, maximum, from tomorrow." He leaned back, "We've got eight days to live."

"DJ, there's a whole river of water down there."

"Spike, it's contaminated. If we drink it without purification, we get sick and we die."

"Don't you think that's kind of harsh?" Sarah felt like she had swallowed gasoline. She looked at her mother, whose head was now in her hands.

"We need to get a grip here," Sarah continued. "I mean, has anyone stepped back to think about this? A butterfly that no one's ever heard of that also happens to be salvation of mankind? *And* its extinction will destroy the whole planet? Isn't that... kind of *far-fetched?*"

"Sarah..." Barb was pale.

"I think she's right. *Butterfly terrorists?* It's so... dumb." Pete said. "What do butterflies *do* anyway?"

Steve sat up, angrily, "They're fanatics, that's all it proves! They're out of their minds. Half the planet is filled with these people. *Over* half! There's billions of them out there, just waiting to strike."

The after-effects of Steve's verbal blow still stung Barb. *Waco? Had Steve really said that?*

"Look," Steve continued, "if you were a terrorist, where would you hit for maximum effect?"

The family stared.

"Exactly." Steve rested his case. "After the twin towers, there is no other target. *The twin domes,* get it?"

"Honey, don't you think DisasterLand would be prepared for something like this?" Barb cried. "That *proves* this isn't real. Because here, it could never really happen!"

"Don't be stupid!," Steve barked. "Obviously they weren't prepared because it's just happened!"

"Has anyone thought about the fact that no one's really seen one of the terrorists lately?" Sarah asked.

"Other than the men guarding the hostages? That proves nothing," Stave said cautiously. "Look, if you were a terrorist would you want to make a spectacle of yourself?"

Sarah shrugged, "Guess not."

"Go ahead, Steve, tell them."

"Barb..."

"They're your children, Steve. And if what you say is true they need to know."

Steve nodded slowly as he considered the consequences. Finally, he slid to the edge of the couch, and he told them everything. In all of its terrible detail, in all of its heart-stopping intensity, Steve shared the night's awful revelations.

"You sure you're OK dad?" Sarah finally asked.

"Yeah, you don't look too good, DJ."

Steve rubbed his eyes.

"Why don't you take a nap, honey? We'll keep guard."

"We've got to get water. Before things get any worse."

"We'll go to the river, DJ!" Pete said. "Mom and I know just where it is."

"Yeah, dad, why not?" Sarah asked. "All three of us could go. It'll be good for us and three people can carry a lot."

"You're not going without me. I need to take a good look at this refugee camp."

"Hold on," Barb interjected, "You're in no position to go anywhere, Steve. You were up all night two nights in a row. You look terrible. We can make it."

Steve looked to the kids. He hadn't had a glimpse of himself since the power had gone but judging by the others' reactions, he knew it couldn't be too good. If he looked anything like he felt, it was a miracle they hadn't caged him.

"OK," Steve sighed. "I'll rig the door so if someone breaks in it'll wake me."

"We'll help you," Barb said.

"Don't worry, dad, there are people out there. People who can help us."

Steve snapped, "You've got to change that mindset, Sarah. *Immediately*. You're looking out for number one now. And number one is you. Number one is us. We're a family and we're all number one."

Pete raised his fists in triumph. *"We're number one! We're..."*

Steve shot Pete a look of annihilation and pushed on, "Everyone else is competition. Bottom line. Why is anyone going to help us? It's not in their interest."

"Because it's the right thing to do," Barb said. "It's called sharing and every child learns it and every adult has forgotten."

"It's fine, dad. The Andrews will help us. They're loaded with cash, right? We know that." Sarah smiled to her mom, "If we need to buy things we could pay them back when we get out."

Steve shook his head, "Sarah, what the hell is there to buy? No one here has any power, any food, any water, *anything*! Don't you get it?"

"Some people do," Barb said. "They have to. You should have seen their carts!"

"Then the answer isn't buying it from them, the answer is finding a decent weapon and taking what's ours."

"Oh, God."

"This is the type of mindset we have to have," Steve said. "If we're going to survive."

"Let's find Maria," Barb said.

"You really think she's still around?" Steve spat.

"She better be."

"Well I'll be here if she comes back."

Barb, Sarah and Peter stepped tentatively onto the walkway in DisasterLand tracksuits, each uniquely telling the week's story through accumulated stains. Behind them, Steve was already rigging the door closed.

In Barb's mind the first light of day was producing a surreal depth to the atrium below, making it appear endless, infinite, almost galactic in nature; alien, yet ancient, as if from the depths of time—like they were on another planet somewhere, or had always been here and always will.

Strange.

She wondered if the hunger was beginning to affect her perceptions. That could help explain a lot about Steve's mindset too, she realized. They needed food and she'd do what she could.

Distorted thinking or not, as they descended the stairs it was immediately obvious that a profound shift had occurred during the night.

Seated on piles of rubble, the two masked men had taken up positions at either end of the fountain, opposite the tower and park. One was checking his watch.

In front of them, the hostages remained blindfolded, leaning against the fountain, many of them nodding into and out of consciousness, others holding injured body parts, obviously in pain. Muffled cries could sometimes be heard, with some nervously rocking figures obviously keeping those around them awake.

The farthest masked man rose, casually strolling over to one of the guests. Barb removed Steve's binoculars from the case and brought them to her eyes.

While she watched, the masked man raised the back of the guest's shirt, revealing a bulky dark vest with several colorful wires attached.

Words were shared as he worked at the back of the vest, finally dropping the man's shirt and moving on to another guest, halfway around the circle.

Bitterness bubbled up from the pit of Barb's stomach, and she gripped the handrail.

Around them the floor was ghostly silent, the front of Good Food absolutely clear. For the first time, the immense atrium was almost entirely devoid of people.

In the distance the swollen refugee camp was slowly awakening. Barb shifted her gaze. With Steve's binoculars, many of those lining the fence looked strangely familiar.

Below them Good Health was dark.

Dark?

"Where're you headed, ma'am?"

Reaching eighteen, they found their way blocked by a makeshift coalition of religious figures, supported by a particularly well-armed guard. A few grimy guests were already anxiously awaiting departure.

"We're going to the river. We need water," Barb announced, confused.

"We leave in ten minutes."

"No, *we* leave now."

"Didn't you get the flyer?" someone called, "We go in groups."

"Yes, but..."

"The crossing's too dangerous," another guest interjected. "The guards have pulled back to the park. The atrium's a no-man's land."

"That's ri..."

"Snipers," a priest stated, flatly.

"It's better this way," said a rabbi, nodding.

The kids were looking to Barb for answers and she decided she would do the right thing. They were not going to give in to fear, to desperation. They were not going to *look out for number one*. They would do what they were told, for the good of all. She acquiesced.

"Look kids, your dad is feeling a lot of pressure," Barb whispered on the way down, partly to reassure herself. "He thinks he let us down. He needs us, so let's show him we can be there for him... but not that we don't need him."

"How'd he let us down?" Sarah asked.

Barb considered her response. "He doesn't like the idea that we don't have any food."

"But that's not his fault mom, it's yours," Pete said.

Sarah quickly changed the topic, "That Andrews guy is freaky mom. I think he scared dad."

"I think so too."

"Do you think they really saw a..."

Barb hushed her. "I do, honey. And, please, don't mention that."

"I was just..."

"*Sarah*," Barb hissed, fiercely. "Quiet."

Silence was maintained for the rest of the descent, while the group picked up several more guests on every other floor. Soon, they were a group of nearly thirty ragged, odorous individuals, all weak and ravenous for information.

Barb and the kids remained separate, not giving in to rumor and not wanting to fuel the fires of dissent. For the full extent of the journey, they would mind their own business.

"Who's park?"

"*Our park!*"

"Who's park?"

"Our park!"

The group stepped onto the newly-shrunken Great Lawn with relief, yet the smells that Barb desperately longed for were late in arriving.

The true magnitude of the refugee camp had become startlingly clear. Twelve foot-high fencing stretched from the park's edge almost the entire way to the forest, taking up half of the Great Lawn's width. Inside, a series of interconnected tents towered over most of the enclosed space, creating the illusion of one enormous, all-encompassing tent.

Barb was shocked to find the camp more like a prison than a hospital or humanitarian aid station. The tent's population, as surprisingly large as it was, still had plenty of room to grow.

A dark portent of events to come?

Guards were posted at critical intervals along the fence's periphery. From within the open-air gap between the tents and the fence, angry protestors were shouting at the approaching group, their chants growing more furious with each approaching step. The residents clearly weren't happy.

Some were minding their own business near the forest, some of the injured and early arrivals had even secured cots deep within the tents. But the rest, led by the Good Food protestors, weren't hard to pick out. They confronted those on their way for water with a barrage of chants and immediate demands to be freed.

It was profoundly disturbing to all and the group hurried on into the forest, with the promise of water and relief now imminent. The trip had been cautious, even methodical, but as they reached the trail leading to the river the pace picked up considerably.

Minutes later, the air had freshened and the rushing river could be heard. Moments after that, they'd finally reached the clearing. For those who had never seen it, the river's presence was nothing less than an epiphany.

But Barb's eyes only saw the river in comparison to what she'd seen in the days before and it was not favorable. Barb had feared this would be the case but she simply hadn't prepared herself for the brutal reality.

Armed guards now lined the river on both sides of the clearing. The sweet green grass, the sparkling pure water, the glimmer of life-giving sunshine—all had been despoiled by the artifacts of war.

"Tip ma'am?"

One of the priests was approaching her, his hand out, while the family waited in line for access to the river.

"I'm spiritual, not religious," said Barb. "I give to everyone and to no one."

"Doesn't matter," he said, matter-of-factly, hand still out. A wad of cash bulged from the pocket of his robe.

"You can't charge for the river! It's humanitarian aid!"

"We're not charging for the water, it's for the escort. We're risking our lives for you, to get you and your loved ones safely back to your suite in once piece. Surely that's worth something."

"You're a bunch of sick opportunists preying on the weak. And DisasterLand's too scared to stop you."

"Mom..." Sarah said, under her breath.

"Just pay it!" someone yelled from behind them in line, obviously frustrated, "You've got no choice lady!"

"It's a fundraiser, ma'am, to build an interfaith church here at DisasterLand. The money don't go to us. It goes to The Lord," a larger man said, approaching.

"I don't care if it goes to a bunch of Nelly-lovers, I said *no*. We were prepared to come down alone and you stopped us."

The larger man stood, dumbfounded, finally able to choke out one sentence in disbelief, "Look lady, you tryin' to cheat *The Lord?*"

Bad taste still lingering in Barb's mouth, the family took up their positions at the end of the departing line.

Blackmail was one thing, the inability to pay was another. With neither side willing to back down, Barb and the kids had been blackballed by the others as unpatriotic atheists. And that meant last ones in line.

It also meant the last ones to leave the river clearing, and as the line snaked away into the distance, Barb urged a few more precious seconds alone within the sunny, green expanse of life.

"Come on, mom, let's go!" Sarah urged.

"Don't worry, honey, we'll catch up. Isn't this nice?"

With the group's departure, the guards posted to the river had begun to relax slightly, and friendly words were being shared. Barb gave them a thumbs up, which was promptly returned.

"OK, sweetie. Let's go."

Hearts heavy, the family awkwardly picked up their filled containers and stepped into the forest, maintaining a slow, methodical pace to extend their time alone.

Hearing voices ahead, they assumed the group had stopped to wait for the stragglers and Barb slowed their progress even further in protest.

"Let 'em wait," Barb whispered.

"No mom, look!"

Sarah was pointing into the forest, where a flash of color streaked by. Moments later a couple raced out of the woods, dripping wet, and crossed the trail behind the three stunned onlookers. They disappeared into the forest on the opposite side in a whirl of energy, without even noticing Barb and the kids.

Stopped cold, Pete watched as they disappeared, then began to examine the forest they'd just left.

"DJ, you think they're terrorists?"

"They didn't look like terrorists."

"Not at all, mom," Sarah agreed. "They seemed really happy."

Pete inched forward, motioning the girls to join him. "Look! A secret path!"

It was indeed. An unmarked trail, barely noticeable.

"Let's go!" Pete begged.

"Peter..."

"Come on, mom!"

Before she could stop him, Pete had adventurously ducked in and Sarah was quick to follow.

"Peter!" Barb screamed furiously, but her naughty side quickly got the best of her. If groups departed every thirty minutes, it meant another one was due soon. She'd spend a few minutes exploring with the kids, then join the guards in the clearing to wait for the next group. With any luck, they'd be led by more charitable souls. A delay would also give Steve more time to rest.

Smiling, she stowed her containers out of sight in the forest next to the kids' and hurried ahead to join them.

Actually, *it was just what they needed.*

Emerging into the humid spray of the ten-foot waterfall, all thoughts disappeared in the glistening bliss of sunshine and hearts soared.

It had been too easy, almost like it was meant to be.

The barely-worn, subtle path had led off towards the North-East corner of the park and the river's source. Peter, Sarah and Barb had ducked through the woods with undergrowth pulling at their feet. Gradually, the trees had thinned and sunlight had pierced the canopy. Then, almost instantly, the trees had fallen away completely and the air had suddenly freshened.

The waterfall.

A giant swimming hole lay at its roaring base, surrounded by sandy beach—a real beach!—with a few swimmers nervously enjoying the pool's tempestuous currents. Several dwarf palm trees lined the beach where other families were gathered.

Barb could only stare until Pete had leapt ahead and tore off his shirt. He had raced forward to the river's edge and quickly stripped to his tighty-whiteys. Howling, he cannonballed in.

Sarah rapidly assessed the situation around her, deciding if she would follow. Other women were there, stripped down to their underwear, some even topless. Without a look back to her mother, Sarah had pulled off her tracksuit and followed her brother in.

Barb's mind had been a raging torrent of conflicting emotions and disparate realities. In front of her, a refreshing paradise she hadn't dare dream of. But behind her, their obligations lay with the Steve, in hell.

She delayed.

They now stood at the extreme end of the small dome which curved dramatically over them, wrapping them up inside a futuristic tropical fantasy. Through the glass, the desert mountains were as clear as they'd ever been, the widescreen desert tantalizingly close.

The river continued on to the south, disappearing around a sharp bend on its way to the clearing. On the opposite bank the trail picked back up, leading into what seemed like wetlands. A few guards were spaced evenly along the river, relaxing under shade trees, weapons draped across their laps. *Was the threat clearing?*

"Come on, DJ! It's perfect!" Pete called, splashing joyfully.

"Yeah, mom, it's totally amazing!"

Those better be some tablets, Barb thought, imagining the water they'd just bottled up. But how could she resist?

She couldn't. She'd be a fool. If nothing else, it was a much-needed bath. *Damn those downstream!*

Seconds later Barb was leaping into the crisp, cool water, tracksuit discarded onshore. She landed lightly on the sandy bottom and bounded up out of the water, splashing her kids.

"Aren't you glad we found this Superstar?" Pete asked, splashing her back.

"I am, kiddo. This is wonderful. I feel so much better. We need to bring your dad!"

"Yeah! DJ, maybe we could even *live* here!"

Why not?, Barb realized. *If the tower really was rigged to blow... there would be no safer place.*

Pete had already turned his thoughts to the next thing, a small ledge part way up the waterfall. He swam away, towards the opposite bank where the trail wound around to the cliff and Sarah followed.

Pete's comment had wedged itself into Barb's mind. *Why couldn't they stay here? Why the hell were they staying in a dark and nasty room when they could be here, enjoying the fresh, clear air and all the water they could purify?*

"Five minutes, Pete," Barb called. "Seriously. We really have to go. I'm not kidding."

"OK, OK! Whatever. Alls I gotta say is do your business here, DJ, cause it's gonna get real ugly in the crib."

"Don't you dare."

"Already did."

"You are not my son."

Barb retreated, head shaking, and rested her back against the river bank. She peered through the remarkably clear water to the sandy bottom below where a few scattered plants were thriving. As she stared, she realized tiny minnows were darting around her feet, nibbling at her toes.

Barb drank in the moist spirited air and closed her eyes to the sun. The waterfall's white noise soon drowned out all cares.

Finally, five days in, Barb was naked and on vacation like it was all supposed to be.

"Look what I found!" Sarah cried. "Mom!"

Barb forced her eyes open, groggily. *Had she fallen asleep against the riverbank?*

Nearby, Sarah was discreetly flashing an object.

No. *No...*

Barb rubbed her eyes.

Yes. It was a bar of soap.

Somewhere in the mindless experience of sunlight, Barb had understood she should embrace positivity at all costs. Instead of succumbing to the worry, to the paranoia and the despair, she would radiate joy. The human saga playing out in and around them had rekindled her belief in compassion. She would pray for the salvation of all beings—including the terrorists—and by so doing would honor the eternal resilience and beauty of the human spirit.

Already, she was being rewarded. Already, the circle was being made whole.

"Is that legal, DJ?" Pete asked, swimming over.

"Who cares," Sarah whispered. "But we'll have to be discreet."

"Isn't it kind of *rude?*" Pete asked.

"Honey, there is *a lot* of water here," Barb said. "Besides, in an awful lot of countries this is how it's done. This is what people drink."

Pete gagged, "That's why they're so scrawny and ugly and we invented hip-hop."

"That's a horrible thing to say, Peter. And not true."

Pete's chest thrust out, "You're saying we didn't invent hip-hop?"

Barb rolled her eyes.

Together, the family swam slowly away, downstream, until they were lost around the bend in a covering of trees.

The resulting makeshift bath kicked Barb into a new sensual gear, completely reinvigorating her like nothing else possibly could. She lingered afterward, floating on her back as Sarah, then Pete, discreetly washed onshore.

The waterfall was indeed an ideal world... it felt somehow wild, but safe. Sanitized. No snake was going to bite them, not even a mosquito or tick would steal their blood. Indeed, only tiny dragonflies fluttered around them.

Under these conditions, Barb just couldn't take it seriously, *this whole terrorist thing.* The idea they were under attack. She couldn't. *She wouldn't.*

We came here to be attacked and now we're attacked.

It was as simple as that.

Though she did have to admit... if she was a terrorist she'd want to hit DisasterLand. That was true. That part made sense.

But she wouldn't give in to the fear, no matter what—at least, not yet. Not until the waterfall was gone. When this peace had been destroyed, when the falls had been violated, then she'd worry. When she had nowhere to turn for grounding, then she'd believe.

Barb shut her eyes, allowing the crisp water to flow around her, soaking up the scents of the tranquil oasis.

She just couldn't imagine why more people weren't here. Yes, it was hard to find, but it certainly wasn't *impossible*. And compared to the tower, it was heaven.

How had it remained so isolated?

Perhaps the peace of the waterfall lay in *perception of threat*, Barb imagined. With little clothing, a terrorist's tattoo would be quickly spotted let alone a gun or even plastic explosives. There was nowhere to hide. They were terrorist-free, guaranteed, unlike everywhere else.

But it couldn't be that simple. The park's magic also had to be a reflection of the pervasiveness of fear in DisasterLand, and maybe in the country in general. Even if everyone knew about these falls, which she doubted, few were willing to explore, to venture off the beaten path, to abandon themselves to the unknown, to isolate themselves where anything—including magic—could happen.

It was the new American way, wasn't it?, she realized. *A country of pioneers turned into a country of followers. The shepherds becoming the herd.*

Yes, it was all clear now. After the bath they'd return for Steve. They'd bring all they could carry in one trip, and stay here as long as possible... until the bitter end.

"Let's roll, DJ." Pete called. He had finished and was swimming away, "Before we get done in by the bath fuzz."

Together, they lazily swam back against the current to the main swimming hole.

"Yo, P!" came a voice.

Pete spun. "Big Z!"

Dripping wet, Zander stood at the wetlands trail in his underwear, throwing signs.

"Look mom! It's Zander!" Pete yelled and his mom waved a surprised greeting.

Pete swam over and climbed out. With both in their underwear, an awkward moment was spent negotiating the bumping of chests.

"Yo, I thought that wuz you. Where'd y'all go?" Zander checked out the girls. "This place is mad yo!"

"Hells yeah! You just get here?"

"I've been here for two days, bro. One of the kids in *Ghost* told me 'bout this place when we wuz VIPs. He must have seen it. I thought he wuz lyin'."

Zander cradled his balls as he spied a topless nymphet in the distance. "Whoa! Look at that, bro! Imagine rag-dollin' *that*!"

"You *done it*?"

"Left 'n right, bro. They lines up for Mister Z."

Sarah had expressed a longing of such heartbreaking profundity that Barb nearly wept: *laundry*.

After Pete and Zander had disappeared up the trail to scout, Sarah and Barb grabbed the family's clothes and secretly retreated back into the darkest depths of the river.

Soon though, the initial adrenalin rush of paradise had given way to plain exhaustion—hand washing their water-logged clothes was a major undertaking. Energy levels were plummeting and the current didn't help matters.

Barb sighed heavily as the weight of their predicament intruded. They had their DL:PowerStrips back in their D-PAKS on the shore, but to eat them now would be stupid. Steve was right: they needed food. *Real food*.

They also needed Steve. A solid plan was forming in her mind: they would return to their suite to pack all of their valuables into the kid's duffle bags. They would travel light so as not to raise suspicions, and they would return to the park for good. Along the way, they would stop at the Andrews', inviting them—and their food—to join them for the journey.

It would solve all their problems.

Barb rang out her top. She would remain downstairs while Steve and the kids packed. Steve had been right about that too—she didn't want to expend any more energy than necessary. Skepticism was one thing, foolishness another.

Once back here, she would get a good sense of where his head was at. Appearing in public in his state of mind wasn't something to encourage, but she had no doubt the waterfall would work its magic soon enough. So too would the presence of friends.

Through almost twenty years of marriage she had never known him to be unstable. But now, it was undeniable: he had lost it.

Sarah interrupted her thoughts. "Mom, I was just thinking, can I be on my own too? Just for a few minutes?"

"Honey," Barb frowned. "We've got to get back."

"I'll just make one quick loop of the trail."

"I don't know..."

"But Pete's..."

"He's with Zander, scouting. I can hear them."

"I can scout too. Maybe there's other places like this. Other people."

Barb hung their clothes on a limb in the sun. Come to think of it, she could stand some time alone as well, just to get some personal space. Collect her thoughts before retrieving Steve. *God, when had she last been alone?*

"Tell you what," Barb offered. "I'll walk you to the love nest and maybe leave you there to walk back separately. Then we go. Deal?"

"Mom, nothing happened!"

Barb laughed. "I believe you, honey. But it's probably a good idea to see more of the park and that sounds like a perfect place to start."

"Hey, you're not supposed to be here!" Katie yelled, surprised, as Barb and Sarah emerged into the tiny clearing across the park. The band stopped their rehearsal and Katie's video camera turned to capture the intrusion.

All eyes fell on Sarah. Every word she had said to her mother, despite being the truth, now seemed to be revealed as a desperate lie by the stares.

"Hi Sarah," Neil stammered. "Everyone this is Sarah—and her mom, looks like."

"Barb," she said.

"We'll go," Sarah quickly added. "I'm sorry. I was just showing my mom around."

Neil laughed, "No, that's cool. Barb, we're Smaug. Welcome to our hideout!"

"What are you guys doing here anyway? I thought you went home," Sarah said.

"We wish," Katie laughed. "We're trapped too. It's kinda weird here isn't it? Kinda scary. That's why we wanted to play again."

"Wow."

"Yeah, we were just sitting around and freaking out," the drummer said, laying down his congo. "Why not do something?"

"We're doing a special acoustic show for the refugees in a few minutes," Neil said. "It's a surprise. We're just doin' what we can, you know?"

"That's really wonderful!" Barb said.

"Yeah, I guess some of them aren't very happy about being in there, so..."

Sarah and Barb exchanged glances.

"So we're just trying to make the best of the whole thing," the drummer finished.

"Hey, we're just warming up. Why don't you guys hang for a while..." Neil added. Katie's video camera had landed back on the band.

"I don't think so," Sarah said.

Barb eyed her daughter, "Go ahead, honey, stay for a few minutes. I'll be back at the waterfall. We'll go as soon as you're back."

"Really? *Thanks...*"

"Just don't stay too long. Ten minutes tops."

Barb hurried out of the clearing and Sarah found herself completely alone for the first time since Sunday morning. She glanced back, where her mom was waiting to give a final wave.

Neil stood to stretch his legs while the band launched into a quiet, reflective track, sounding completely different unplugged than they had on stage Saturday night.

Sarah found a comfortable spot by the river and lay back, admiring the dance of the afternoon sun across the water, the wetlands before her and the *Bridge of Sighs* off in the distance. She longed to cross the river, to find the edge of DisasterLand, to see what was there. It wouldn't happen now, but it would later. She would make sure.

Smaug jammed on and Sarah found herself captivated. They weren't just standing behind computers, they were *doing things. Playing things.*

They were real musicians, *professionals*, completely altering the space around them with vibration. Earlier, this had been a beautiful clearing but it took Smaug to infuse it with... soul.

She snuck a glance at Neil, lost in the rhythm, and she realized there was nothing in the world like a sexy musician making love to his instrument. She thought she'd wanted him before, but now it was sealed. How could she have let him get away on Friday? *Sometimes, she was so retarded.*

Sarah was startled back as the last chords faded out. The band was staring at her and Sarah realized she must have had a stupid grin on her face.

"Sorry, that was really cool," she said. "Are you gonna play more?"

"How're we doing on time?" Neil asked Katie.

"Unfortunately, badly. Sorry, Sarah. But you can come hear the show if you want."

"No, that's cool. I kinda like it here. The refugee camp is kind of creepy."

Neil joined Sarah on the river's bank while the band packed up their instruments.

"Hey, good to see you again."

"Thanks," she blushed, "yeah, I'm so happy I found you guys. That was amazing."

"Glad you dug it."

"So... you think you'll be back here? Later?"

"Maybe," Neil said. "It sort of depends on the guards. They didn't want to let us in here in the first place. In fact there's a couple of them in the woods right now to protect us."

"You're kidding," Sarah laughed.

"No, I'm serious."

"Really?"

"Sure."

"Oh," Sarah's face dropped. "Well maybe I'll check back anyway."

"I'll try, OK? But no promises."

Katie finished putting away her camera and joined them. "Neil, do you mind if I hang here for a while? There's nothing for me to shoot for twenty minutes or so while you guys set up. I've got to watch my battery levels."

"Sure."

"Cool. Send the guards back in twenty. See you soon. Be careful."

Neil gave Sarah a quick hug and followed the band out while Katie took off her shoes and rolled up her jeans. Sarah followed suit, dipping her toes in the river.

She tried to imagine the length of the river, starting at the waterfall and flowing all the way here, to where they sat. They weren't even at the edge and it had been a good fifteen minute walk... the park must be *huge*. She longed to see it all.

Katie turned, "So's your family OK? You're pretty lucky to be down here, don't you think?"

"We're OK. My dad's back in our suite. He's kind of freaking out."

Katie grimaced and Sarah froze, "You think it's bad?"

"I don't know. I'm just telling you what happened to us."

"Maybe I should get back after all..."

Katie took her arm, "Sorry, didn't mean to scare you. I'm sure it's OK. There's nothing we can do about this whole thing anyway, you know?"

"I guess..."

"Sure. We're all in this, whatever *this* is."

Suddenly, Sarah felt exhausted. She lay back on the grass and took a few deep breaths. She didn't want to talk about anything related to this place any more.

"So where do you live?" she asked Katie.

"With Neil."

Sarah rose up on her elbows and winced, pain racing through her shoulder.

"What's wrong?" Katie asked.

"You don't even want to know..." Sarah rolled her eyes and plowed on, "You live with Neil?"

Katie smiled, "Don't worry... we're like a little artists' collective. We've got a loft in Williamsburg and five of us share it. We're just friends."

"Wow, that's cool," Sarah said, looking out over the wetlands. That's how she wanted to live, once she got out of the dorms. "How far's that from Columbia?"

"University? At least forty-five, less if you're lucky."

"Oh..."

The pain in her shoulder had caught Sarah by surprise and she tried stretching it. It hadn't been bothering her at all... she wished she could remember how she'd landed, but it was all such a blur. She couldn't even think about it.

Katie scooted over, placing her hands on Sarah's ailing shoulder, "I'm good at backrubs. Where's it hurt?"

"Really? Sweet!" Sarah pulled herself up, touched the offending spot.

Katie rubbed her hands together, warming them up. She placed them together, on Sarah's shoulder, and rubbed gently. Katie's hands were warm, the pressure felt good. Sarah relaxed and Katie pushed a little harder.

"Ooh, careful," Sarah breathed in, "Yeah it's sore. Right there."

"Have you been to Good Health?"

"When it happened. I think maybe I slept funny last night."

"When what happened?"

Sarah shook her head, "Nothing... please."

"OK..."

Katie gently but firmly worked her hands up Sarah's neck and Sarah dropped her head forwards.

"Yeah, you're really tight."

Katie swung Sarah around in front of her, and widened out to work both shoulders, tickling goose bumps onto Sarah's tingling skin.

"That feels so good. I think I did sleep wrong."

Katie continued to knead more deeply. Suddenly the tension released, sending an explosive chill rocketing through Sarah's body. Katie jumped back, laughing.

"Mind if I put my hands under your shirt?" Katie asked, "It'll be a lot warmer."

"No, that's cool," Sarah said.

Katie's smooth hands made their way slowly up Sarah's back and she readjusted the T-shirt to make it easier. To Sarah, Katie's hands seemed to be on fire as they landed on her bare shoulder. Katie held them still as the heat soaked in.

"Ummm... that feels good." Sarah said.

"You were swimming earlier, right? Did it hurt?"

"No, it's just when I sat up, I think I did something to it."

Katie edged in. She rubbed the shoulder slowly, gently, and Sarah, eyes closed, felt her pulse quicken as Katie extended her strokes along both shoulders, then down her back.

Katie carefully undid her bra, and Sarah again bent forward as Katie worked the bottom of her neck, gently, vertebrae by vertebrae. Katie worked her way out, over to the shoulders, then gently down to the small of her back.

Very, very slowly, Katie continued expanding, working her way up Sarah's back, to the shoulders, and back around, to her sides and finally her stomach. Sarah's nipples stiffened and she realized what was happening.

Katie raised her hands, gently cupping Sarah's breasts, her warm breath tickling Sarah's ear. Katie handled them with a profound tenderness that Sarah had never felt in the feverish gropings of boys. Katie's thumbs dancing over her nipples, Sarah rested her head back against Katie's shoulder.

Katie kissed her cheek, flicking her tongue.

Sarah giggled. *It felt so good.*

Katie began to nibble deliciously on Sarah's ear, squeezing Sarah in to her, one hand dropping to Sarah's warm stomach. Sarah moaned.

She turned her head to meet the kiss, their hot mouths locking.

Katie slipped her hand down, down inside Sarah's trackpants to cup her warmth. Katie squeezed and Sarah moaned, louder now, her legs spreading.

Sarah gasped, ravenously, her back arching and her arm locking powerfully around Katie's neck as Katie found her goal.

Floating, eyes closed and alone, Barb was once again drifting gently downstream with the current. She had allowed her mind to completely free itself as her hungry skin drank in the sunlight filtering through the trees.

She had lost track of time, drifting and gently returning to the swimming hole to check on the boys, then drifting and gently returning to check for Sarah. She'd reached a wonderfully meditative rhythm and felt her body recharging with each passing moment. She was working out the kinks.

Pulling up in the forest's mottled darkness well past their bathing spot, Barb realized there was someone resting against the river's bank. Her heart stopped and she choked back a scream.

"I'm sorry," the young man said, smiling. "I didn't want to scare you."

"No..." Barb said, laughing awkwardly with relief, "I mean... you did. But..."

She looked around, nervously, realizing they were alone. The boy effortlessly slipped underwater and she lost sight of him. Her pulse quickened.

Seconds later he appeared, rising out of the water a few feet away. She stared, too stunned to move. His handsome eyes were shining, mischievously.

Barb glanced around them again. Entirely alone.

Body shimmering, Barb quickly processed the implications, "Did you follow me here?"

The boy's smile broadened.

"Don't you think I'm a little old for you?"

"I think you're just right," he whispered, edging closer, "and I'm never wrong."

"I doubt my husband agrees."

"Then we won't ask him."

He reached in, gently brushed the hair back from her face. Barb put a hand against his chest, about to push him away. But didn't.

Eyes resting below his chest, Barb froze. He was naked.

A gentle hand under her chin tipped her head back up and she caught a flash of his electric eyes, then his warm, full lips were against hers. Slowly, her lips parted and their breath met.

Every cell in her body tingled as he slipped his arms around her, locking her into him. For one last time, she thought of pushing him away, but his rigidity brushed against her stomach and her blood turned to fire.

Her hands cupped his ass, pulling him to her, forcing her chest into his. His hands landed behind her head, now offering no opportunity for escape.

She moaned and he squeezed, the cool water flowing around them. She forced his mouth down to her chest and took one final look around. They were still alone. She took him in her hands.

As his teeth gently teased her with pain, she leapt explosively onto him, devouring him, her legs wrapped powerfully around his back and swallowing his length into her depths.

Her hands slammed his face into her chest as she danced on him, his hands clutching her waist powerfully. She lost herself to him, dammed emotion released a raging flood which surged through her.

Opening her eyes she realized they were at the river's bank. He pulled out and she gasped, clutching for the lush, fragrant grass of the moist bank. She sank her fingers in, and spread.

He was back in, easing her momentary longing and thrusting her face-first into the dark earth. She was growling, growling into the rich soil as she came, more and more powerfully in ever-expanding waves until his own powerful blast detonated inside her, sending her soaring on one final oxygen-starved flight.

He collapsed against her, desperately clutching her back for support.

Minutes later, still panting, she crawled up onto the bank and collapsed on the small patch of grass.

He reached up, took her head in his hands and gently planted one last kiss on her cheek, then slipped back into the water and disappeared upstream.

For a few stunned moments, Barb fought to rematerialize. Then, alone, body and soul wrenched open, she wept.

Sarah was still basking in her own luminous glow, the subtle refreshment of energy synergistically enhanced by the rush of a profoundly new and surprising experience.

She stood on the riverbank and scanned for her mom, thoughts racing at warp speed.

Kinda fun, she had to admit. *All the good feelings with no danger of ruining your life. Yes,* she decided. *Talk about safe sex!*

Her mom's damp clothes were on a limb near Pete's, and she could hear her brother's howls from somewhere near the falls. But there was no Barb.

Sarah was growing worried and decided to find Pete to see what he knew. She hurried towards the river, noticing a cute hunk returning upstream with the biggest, sexiest grin she'd ever seen plastered on his young face. Something clicked.

No, she thought. *No way.*

She retreated back to their clothes, where she sat down to take stock of her new self. She felt like she was floating. Sarah watched as the hunk emerged from the river to gather his clothes nearby and quickly disappear into the forest.

Minutes later, with Sarah still spinning, confused, and really starting to worry, Barb emerged from downstream, her face flushed and glowing.

Sarah froze. With Katie's intimacy still perfuming her lips, her own body was on high sensual alert and the truth seemed instantly revealed.

By the time Barb joined Sarah, Barb's complexion was going supernova despite her futile effort to hide it.

"Hi honey... you look happy. Just get back?" Barb said, awkwardly slipping into her tracksuit.

Sarah struggled for words, fumbling like her whole body had been novocained. "Yeah, just a second ago. I was about to go find Pete."

"Where is he?" Barb asked, suddenly worried.

Sarah's stomach dropped, "He's up there mom. Above the waterfall."

"Oh. *Still...* OK. I thought..." her words faded as she sat down next to her daughter.

Sarah was struggling to remain material, to not float away. Barb put her arm around her and Sarah turned to catch Barb's smile glistening in the sunlight.

Sarah realized, with an ever-larger degree of discomfort, that it had been ages since she's seen her mom this happy. Subtle nausea welled up from deep within her, poisoning her joy.

"How's the band? They looked like nice kids."

"Yeah..." Sarah said, "They are. They're from New York you know."

"Really?"

"Yeah. I got the girl's number."

"Oh, honey, that's *great*! That was *meant to be*."

"Yeah... I guess..."

Sarah tried desperately to take stock of the situation, but found it impossible. She was spinning, spinning, spinning... scared she was breaking apart, only to lose herself forever.

Sarah glanced at her mom, so radiant, so *beautiful*...

The tears instantly fell in torrents and Sarah buried her face on her mom's shoulder.

Barb held her tightly, thanking her lucky stars that she had just got it all out of her own system. But despite that, she too was starting to feel a little queasy.

Pete landed in front of the girls, breathless, pointing above the waterfall.

"Hey DJs! There's a whole spring up there! It's crystal clear with flowers and stuff! Come and see!"

After the emotional purge, Barb and Sarah longed to find themselves deeper in paradise and they were gone in a flash.

"Five minutes," Barb reminded them. "No more. This is getting ridiculous."

Pete led them across the swimming hole to the dirt trail which briefly cut through the wetlands before doubling back towards the river and up, to the backside of the falls.

They approached the top to find Zander resting inside the large deep spring, head back, enjoying the afternoon sun amidst the pure water and abundant flora.

They dropped their tracksuits next to his, keeping their shirts and underwear on.

"Hi Zander," Barb said as they slipped in. "This is quite a spot! Thanks again for helping me on Monday."

"That's OK Missus Beyers."

"This is Sarah, Pete's sister."

"Hi."

"Hi."

"Where's your dad?" Barb asked, scanning the beach below.

"I dunno."

"You... don't know?"

"Hunh-unh."

"And you're not worried? You don't think terrorists..."

"Mom, remember he was with that woman? He prolly ran off with her."

"Really?"

Zander nodded, "I think so. He went to visit her and never came back."

"Oh my God... but he could be..."

"That's OK, Missus Beyers. He... kind of told me this might happen."

Barb attempted to conceal her amazed distaste, "Do you know where she lives?"

"No."

"Mom the guards told him it happens all the time. They took his name and stuff and if his dad is found they'll find him."

"That's right Missus Beyers. Don't worry, I'm good. This place is *tight*."

"Well if you get... if you need a place to stay, sweetie..."

"Mom we're staying *here* tonight, remember?" Pete interrupted, "He don't need to go nowheres! And neither do we! *We in our crib now!*"

"That's so dope yo. You guys is cool."

Pete leaned back to join Zander, arms outstretched, surveying the magnificent views in every direction.

Barb had started to protest, but it was ridiculous. Of course they were coming back! She settled in across the spring from the boys, next to Sarah.

"You OK, honey?" Barb whispered.

"Yeah..."

"You want to talk about it?"

"Not really."

"OK..." Barb squeezed Sarah's knee, "Isn't this beautiful? Aren't you glad we're not upstairs with your dad making him nervous?"

"Yeah," Sarah said, emotionally nose-diving, "You look really happy mom."

"Really?" Barb jumped, momentarily uncomfortable. "Thanks."

"We should probably go get him soon, hunh?"

"Yeah. We will, honey," Barb exhaled, heavily, "So you like that boy? What's his name?"

Sarah lowered her gaze.

"Neil? Sort of."

"I've never been able to figure you out."

"What do you mean?"

"Your *type*."

Sarah couldn't believe her mom was changing the topic to *boys*. Her cover was blown. Guilty as charged.

"I don't have a type."

"What do you mean?"

Well, you know, mom, I do anything that moves these days. "I just... you know, like experimenting," Sarah mumbled.

"I did too when I was your age. I certainly did too. It's a learning process, like anything else." Her mother flashed a bright smile.

Barb hated to admit it, but in a way she envied Sarah and her whole generation schooled by the web—a far cry from the sex ed of her own youth. Maybe it was over the top, maybe the pendulum had swung too far, maybe sex was too far removed from love and commitment. But there was something to be admired in the simple belief that sex was something to be enjoyed, and perhaps even broadcast, by all, as much as possible.

Then again, the dangers were so much greater now too.

Barb's smile dimmed, "It's just such a different time," she continued, "It's easy for us to worry. You're so pretty. And there's so much... danger out there."

Barb's face froze as she realized her own reckless behavior, but she recovered quickly and slapped Sarah playfully on the head. "Just play safe," Barb said, "That's all I'm saying, honey."

"Mom I do."

"You know how much you mean to us."

Sarah nodded. She wanted to tell her mom about the fall, about how close she had been. The time seemed right and, to her, the sooner the better. With each passing moment, Sarah only felt the weight growing. But she couldn't. She just couldn't.

She imagined her dad, alone, in the suite, still feeling guilty.

It just wasn't right. *They had to get home.*

Not surprisingly, it had caved with one good solid kick.

Steve stood before his bare living room wall, dust rising from the roughly foot-sized hole in the cheap wallboard. The couch sat behind him in the middle of the suite.

Steve stuck his head into the hole, relishing the burn from the dust filling his lungs.

There, in the darkened space, his mind reeled. It was undeniable: *cigarette smoke!*

Steve cracked his head against the wall as he exited, dust dropping down his collar, itching his back. With determined ferocity, he widened the hole with his foot. Sweat poured off him, fixing the particles to his skin.

I knew we were surrounded, he told the audience. *I had to fight fire with fire.*

Steve's eyes were wild as he ducked in and flipped on his flashlight, illuminating the wonderland inside. Gradually, as the air cleared, he was given his first real glimpse of the omnipotent threat.

He choked back a yell.

It was a worst-case scenario. It was a terrorist's dream.

The guts of DisasterLand lay spread out before him, a vast maze of heating vents, water pipes and electrical bundles peeking out of the darkness and running the length and breadth of his suite. And attached to those vents, those pipes and those bundles were several sets of vertical cables rigged only a few feet apart: rock climbing gear, offering simple access to every level of the entire tower. *A professional job.*

To Steve, it all suddenly made sense. Rock climbers, adventurers, Nelly Lovers. *Of course!*

Worse yet, one of the cables less than five feet away was still moving... as if someone had escaped only moments before.

Bring 'em on!, Steve told the audience.

He forced his head in farther and reached his free hand out to the opposite wall roughly three feet away. Plenty of space there for a person, no doubt. He leaned in, his toes just barely on the floor, shining the light below his own suite.

There was no doubt about it: a crawl space, for terrorists, between floors. A place to sleep, a place to relax, a place from which to unleash devastation. And lying on it as if to taunt him, a discarded organic granola bar wrapper.

Below that the darkness dropped infinitely and his heart told him it continued straight down to the atrium floor, nineteen stories below. No place for amateurs.

Steve pushed himself back onto the floor and turned his attention horizontally along the length of his suite.

I'd have to check the opposite wall as well, he continued. *There was no guarantee we were safe. A bomb? An arms cache? They could be that close.*

The scope of the terrorist's creativity had been revealed in all its naked depravity. He'd assumed they'd entered with other guests, last weekend. But they could have been waiting for days, for weeks, for *months* before this show, preparing for this very moment. Everything they'd need for support could be stowed away inside these walls.

Was that DisasterLand's problem? They didn't even know who they were dealing with? *Was it that basic?*

A cold chill ran down his spine but the hot sweat continued to drip. His worst nightmares were true. Steve shut off his light. *This was the real deal.*

He'd have to see Jim. Right away.

A knock came at his front door and Steve spun, wiping the sweat from his face. He lunged for a chair.

I would defend my freedom at all costs. If they took me in, the lies were guaranteed to continue. Failure is not an option!

"*Meester* Beyers!" a gentle voice called, "Is anyone in there?"

It was Maria. *Maria!*

"Coming!" Steve yelled. He shoved the couch back against the wall, barely covering the hole. On impulse, he took one of the cushions and crudely shoved it inside.

He hated to seal it, though. The light was a clear invitation to the terrorists.

Come on in dickless slugs!

"It's Maria. I have many things for *jou*. Can I come in please?"

Many things! Steve hurried down the hall, breathlessly, sweat dripping off his brow. His head pounded.

Steadying himself with one hand, he dismantled the makeshift alarm he had rigged and carefully pulled aside the door.

Maria stood, her shining face silhouetted in the early afternoon light. Joy filled his heart. An angel, *bearing gifts!*

Steve squinted. *Where were the gifts?*

She quickly stepped past him, into the hallway. *"Meester* Beyers *jou* look terrible. Where is *jour* family?"

"Getting water."

"At the river?"

Steve nodded.

Maria whistled. "Very good."

"We're almost out of tablets, you know."

"Oh no."

"Oh no?"

"Me too."

"You're out of tablets?"

"Of everything, *Meester* Beyers. That is why I am here."

"You don't have *anything?"*

Maria shook her head, helplessly. *"Nada.* No beer, no food, no water tablets. We cannot get below. It is sealed off."

"But you said you have *many things* for me," Steve said, his voice approaching a whine.

She shirked into the doorway, self-consciously.

"I must tell *jou* this in person. It is our contract."

Steve stared.

"I am sorry *Meester Beyers."*

"Maria we have no food."

"No one has food, *Meester Beyers."*

"I have no beer."

"I tried, *Meester Beyers.* Like crazy."

Steve stepped away for a few breaths and Maria let loose a rapid torrent of Spanish that sounded vaguely sympathetic.

Steve turned. "Maria," he asked deliberately, "Are we in trouble?"

Her face dropped. "Trouble?"

Steve nodded, "Danger. *Peligro."*

"I cannot say, *Meester Beyers,"* she shrugged. "I am only to make sure *jou* are safe."

Steve found himself utterly devoid of a response. Choking on his breath, his voice continued but his mind was incapable of keeping pace. The unappealing result was a forceful collection of incoherent, unrelated syllables.

"Meester Beyers..." Maria fell against the wall heavily.

Seeing the fear in his eyes, the desperation and the shame, her heart overflowed. "I am sorry, *Meester Beyers.* I will help you."

"You will?"

"For free."

"Really?"

Maria nodded.

"Do not worry, *Meester* Beyers. *Jour* family will be safe. I will help *jou*."

"You have to, Maria. You *have to*." Steve clapped with the release of an enormous weight lifted. He felt good now, bathing in the rush of victory. The future looked bright, if only temporarily.

Steve, spurned on, approached her with little tact, "Tell me, Maria. Are we under attack?"

Maria fidgeted, nervously, avoiding his eyes.

Steve stepped in aggressively, "I want to know, Maria. Now. Are we hostages?" He was losing his temper, "Are *we under attack?*"

"*Meester* Beyers. Please. *Jou* are scaring me."

"And you are scaring *ME*! Are we under attack *or not!?*"

Steve stepped in, further, and Maria grasped her security necklace. She gnawed her upper lip. And then nodded, recoiling.

Steve's eyes bulged and he stumbled back.

"I have to go," Maria whispered. "If *jou* tell anyone I will not be here to help *jou*. I maybe lose my job."

As she watched his face, she felt genuinely sorry for him and for some reason missed her dog, Chuki, back home with her parents in Guatemala.

Maria hugged him, cautiously. "Do not be scared."

She took his hand, nodding sweetly, "You will be OK, *Meester* Beyers. *Jou* are a good man with a good family."

She opened her backpack and for Steve, everything suddenly went slow-motion. She magically pulled out one icy cold beer, complete with condensation dripping down its side, just like in a commercial. She proudly presented it to him.

Steve grabbed her, squeezing her tightly. She giggled, shrieking with joy.

"You are a goddess, Maria. A *goddess!* And worth every penny!"

She twisted off the cap and handed the bottle to Steve, now near aneurism, with a genuine, priceless smile.

He received the frosty bottle and chugged, mightily.

It tasted good. Really, really good.

Steve passed out only seconds later, unable even to reach his living room.

Barb was pacing the foot of the stairs, alone and emotionally lost at sea.

Around her, the atrium was taking on an increasingly dark and desperate tone in the stifling heat. Faith-based escorts were operating with much less frequency and, aside from the armed men and hostages, she was the only soul left in the entire, oppressive space. The angry chants of those confined to the refugee camp were ringing out unsettlingly in the distance.

She had persuaded the skeptical escorts to leave her behind and continue on with her children only after letting loose a storm of profanity the likes of which they'd probably never heard, being pious men. How exactly her family would return to the river, together and with their belongings, remained to be seen. Yet with her below they simply had no choice. She had forced the issue.

But now she was having second thoughts.

In front of her, on the plywood covering Good Food's shattered windows, someone had scrawled *Fuck Nelly*, complete with a grotesque illustration. Further on, *Tree-Hugging Commies Suck Ass!* was scripted in large, unmistakable letters.

Shouts were being exchanged behind her, at the fountain, the hostages obscured by the village remains. Earlier, she had seen one of the masked men pacing furiously, his automatic weapon raised. The other had remained hidden.

Barb remained emotionless. Amazingly, and somewhat fortunately, Barb was almost entirely oblivious to everything but her own inner turmoil.

Coming down from the endorphin bath following her *liaison*, she still couldn't believe it had happened. Couldn't understand how it *had* happened.

Barb glanced up at their suite, so far above. The kids had entered several minutes ago and she longed for their return.

Yet the fact was, it had left her physically satisfied in ways she couldn't have dreamt of. The boy had hit spots she had forgotten she had, that hadn't been worked in well over a decade. The experience had stretched and cleansed her body and mind while launching her nervous system on a stellar display of fireworks. She felt internally rearranged, massaged, and wondered whether she had somehow become semi-petrified with routine.

Regardless, whether physical or psychological, the coupling had liberated her sexuality from chains she hadn't known existed. Where Steve had softened, the boy had been firm, like an arrow, piercing her into awareness and loosening something in her, something deep and profound. It had brought her powerfully back in touch with the mysterious danger of young men, high on testosterone and flesh.

Truly amazing how completely the hunger fades, slowly, and without a trace...

It had also loosened the beast called shame, and Barb was harshly reminded of a primary law in physics: the equal reaction to her opposite action was now hitting her hard in the gut as she waited for the first glimpse of her husband.

Her *husband*...

As her family's reappearance was delayed more and more, a lingering suspicion was reasserting itself, demanding to be acknowledged. *Did Sarah know?*

She had seemed strange when Barb returned, but it could have been Barb's own soaring emotions, or maybe even a tryst of her own. *But what were those tears about?*

Barb had definitely noticed a look Sarah had given her, as if assessing her in a new light, as if reevaluating her. At the time, high as a kite, Barb hadn't thought much of it.

How long had Sarah been sitting there? Had she seen him?

What if Sarah had told Steve—and they'd gone to the guards?

What if they were refusing to come down?

This boy was no threat after all, it wasn't an affair, it was a chance act of nature. He wasn't River, her yoga teacher, and there would be no possibility of a repeat. The whole experiment was thankfully now safely behind her. She was the dedicated wife she'd always been, this freak experience only clarifying her satisfaction with her mate.

She just prayed there wouldn't be ramifications... health or, God forbid, *otherwise*. She'd have to get tested for STDs at the first opportunity and somehow evade sex with Steve until it happened. Though judging by their recent record at home, that wouldn't be the hardest thing she'd ever done.

Another warm drip eased down between her legs, dampening her panties with a reminder of his potency. She was also desperately looking forward to a washing of clothes when they arrived back at the falls.

"Come on," she growled nervously, "What's the problem!"

Barb squatted, stretching her lower back. Her feet were killing her and the weight of stress on her shoulders was crushing her spine.

She was desperate for the falls, for the beauty and isolation—for the ignorance. She was done with all this destruction and death. They would scout a spot and drift off to sleep with the knowledge there would be no more stairs and everything she needed was within arms reach.

Including her husband.

Steve awoke from the void of empty, black sleep. Someone was over him. Yelling.

High voices. Small people. *Children.*

His children?

"DJ!"

Steve fought off the suffocating grayness. *Donkey Juice*, he thought.

Girl. Crying. *Sarah.*

Daughter. Yes, screaming.

Light.

Pete and Sarah had stepped into the dark suite with trepidation, sensing that something was terribly wrong.

When their light fell on Steve's downed body lying motionless on the kitchen floor, they had assumed the worst. And panicked.

Steve desperately jerked an arm with overwhelming effort.

"Superstar? What's wrong?" Pete squatted, shining his flashlight over Steve's body. "Did they get you?"

"I'm going to the guards!" Sarah screamed, "To get help!"

Steve made a ferocious effort and rolled over, loudly. He looked up, his face scrunched and pasty-white in Pete's light. Sarah recoiled.

"Head..." Steve groaned. "Beer..."

Pete shown his light carefully around the suite as Sarah stood over her father, crying, fearing the vicious attack had left him permanently brain-damaged.

On the counter, an empty bottle and a note.

"DJ scored some hooch and went arctic," Pete whispered.

He grabbed the note. It was a receipt.

One beer: $35.

Their dad was in the red, $22.50.

One beer had laid out their dad. *One beer.*

That's where they were at.

Pete and Sarah helped Steve to the couch where he sat, dazed.

"DJ, let's roll! Mom's waiting! We're going to a waterfall! We've got to pack our stuff."

Being back in the squalid conditions of the suite were too much for the kids to handle. The longer they stayed, the more the conspicuous pungency of the rotting toilet was abusing their senses. They had to get out.

"No."

"*What?* Come on dad, let's go! There's a waterfall down there!"

Steve shook his head, "Maria's coming to help us."

"What? *How?*"

"She's bringing food. *Secretly.* Just for us."

Sarah and Peter exchanged skeptical glances.

"But mom's waiting down below, at the stairs! She's *alone!*"

"Then *I'll* go. I want to scout this river place anyway. I don't trust it. It seems too good to be true. You kids will have to hold down the fort."

"But dad, there's not much time to get back before the sun starts setting!"

Steve stood, shakily, and made his way to the bedroom.

"It won't be long," he called, "Maria should be here soon."

Sarah collapsed on the couch in despair, "Pete, dad's lost his mind."

"I think so too. Should we go anyway?"

"Maria's not coming back."

"No way, Spanks. It was hit and run. What's that pillow doing up there?"

Sarah turned and pulled it from the wall, revealing the hole.

"*Oh my God!*"

Pete spun, "DJ, were the terrorists here?"

Steve emerged, sweating, back in his too-small DisasterLand tracksuit with the pants split open. Sarah averted her eyes while Pete gawked, goofily.

"DJ, you *can't!*"

"I need to see Jim first," Steve said, cinching his D-PAK. "Then I'll meet your mother. If you get food before I return, meet us at the waterfall with our valuables. Don't stay here a moment longer than you have to. It's not safe."

"Wait dad, you've got your tablets?" Sarah dug in her D-PAK for the precious purifiers. "Mom and Peter used theirs yesterday, remember? We'll use mine."

She held them up, and after a moment Steve produced his.

"Good thinking, sweetie."

He patted her head lovingly. And then, like that, he was gone.

The resulting silence was too terrible to contemplate and they quickly set about their business: purifying the small amount of water they'd carried back (intended just for the brief return), re-rigging the front door and sealing off the bedroom with sheets to cut off the smell.

Sarah then began examining the hole with her light.

"Do you see anything? Bombs or stuff?"

"No."

"Terrorists?"

"No. But there's ropes," she called.

"What do you think they're for?"

Sarah pulled her head out, waving him inside. "I don't know. What do we do?"

Pete pulled out. "We cover it the hell back up to make damn sure ain't no terrorists is comin' out."

It sounded good to her. They stuffed in all the pillows they could, then Sarah's blanket to make sure no light at all could escape. They finally pushed the useless HDTV away into a corner and spun the couch to face the hole so it could easily be monitored.

They sat down, sweating, and chugged all the water they had.

"Spanks, you think dad's a secret agent?"

"What the fuck are you talking about?"

"Well, you know, yesterday he gets kidnapped then he goes commando, and now there's a big hole in our wall like someone's after him..."

"Dad is not a secret agent."

"I am."

"You are not."

"I am too, but that's all I can say."

"Whatever."

Steve descended the stairs slowly at first, testing his feeble legs.

The Andrews weren't in, deepening Steve's sense of menace. They'd been taken, he knew, in a warning to him. Jim had shared intelligence and DisasterLand had nabbed him in retaliation.

Criminals, thought Steve. *Arresting guests while letting the terrorists have free reign!*

Steve regretted leaving the kids on their own but surely Maria wouldn't be long. They'd be able to take care of themselves in the interim. For sure.

Once Maria had made her delivery, one way or another they'd make a final break from the suite, fully stocked, away from the rigged tower to sequester themselves in the forest until... the end.

Steve's thinking was now clear, his desk wiped clean and he was taking action. *Had he been drugged? Had the terrorists poisoned his beer?*

The implications of the afternoon's findings were undeniable, overshadowing any concerns of Barb's convenience. They were hostages. *Hostages.*

"Easy there!" the religious leaders called as he approached eighteen, "Where are you going?"

"Down!" Steve yelled.

"You've got to go with us, sir! We're your escorts!"

"Fuck you and your complicity!" Steve yelled and hurried past them, seeing Barb below. He waved and she returned it, shocked.

I knew my captor's ways, he told the audience. *I had their number.*

And knowledge is power.

He would let DisasterLand do things their way. And he would do them his.

Perhaps there were negotiations, perhaps diplomacy *would* work. But it hadn't yet, that was for sure. *And in Indonesia, Nelly wasn't getting any safer.*

Steve's mind raced, matching his ever-increasing rate of descent. He was in a unique position and he had to use it.

Probe. Seek weakness. Then counterattack.

It wouldn't be easy, but it was time to act. Things would only get worse, only get more difficult the more time passed. We would only get weaker and weaker, more and more dependent, more and more desperate. We had to hit back. Now.

Steve had hit play on the documentary in his head and the opening credits were rolling: *Dark Days in August: The Rescue of America's Pride.*

This was the opportunity of a lifetime. And he would take it.

The overwhelming odds against such a prospect—of a legitimate terrorist attack against the fortress that was DisasterLand—simply had to be disregarded. It was a *fact.* It was *happening.*

Nothing was sacred anymore. It truly was a brave new world. A war without end.

Steve stepped off the stairs.

"There you are!" Barb yelled, hurrying to him, eyes filled with concern. "Where are the kids?"

"They're waiting for Maria. She's bringing food."

"You're kidding!"

"She's helping us, Barb. She's on our side."

Barb landed in his arms then quickly pulled away, horrified, suddenly realizing she might smell like *the boy.*

Things hadn't started off well. Steve looked even worse than she had remembered.

Her discomfort had only increased Steve's own growing unease and he eyed her suspiciously. She felt herself starting to shake. She fought to keep eye contact.

But Steve's own darting eyes had moved on, assessing the atrium.

He now knew the solution. Simple, elegant. They wouldn't hide at some cheesy waterfall like a bunch of frightened sissies.

They'd show the hole.

Already, he longed to be back in the suite. They'd go wide, quickly. A blitzkrieg. Before DisasterLand could react.

Steve marched off rapidly, into the ruins. Even if a return was imminent, they'd need to recover the water containers the kids had hidden at the falls. And the sooner the better.

Barb hurried after him, frantically. She felt she was failing—terribly—just to be herself. And who the hell was *he*?

I longed for ignorance, Steve told the studio audience. *But I couldn't turn my back. I had to move forward. Responsibility had fallen on my shoulders. And I would rise to the occasion.*

The masked men had stopped pacing to watch the couple's crossing with interest.

"Kiss my ass!" Steve screamed.

"Resistance, Barb. It's alive. I can smell it."

To Barb, Steve's brain had bid farewell to reality and she found herself on a mental precipice, mired in deep resonances she hadn't anticipated.

They'd entered the park, continuing Steve's relentless drive to the clearing. Steve had saluted—*literally saluted*—those in the refugee camp, who looked out at the two guests with dazed longing and the irresistible animal urge to be free.

Barb had found the whole exchange profoundly disturbing, a symptom of the distressing demise in predictable behavior—rationality—that she equated with war. The stakes had been raised and they were descending into instinct.

These were Steve's first words to her since crossing the atrium, and it didn't leave Barb confident in his leadership. She simply couldn't understand what was now going through his mind.

Leaving the kids vulnerable... for what? For *imaginary food?* For *empty promises? And why this haste?*

Steve marched them on, all the way into the clearing and paused, eyeing the line of security guards assembled along the river with distaste.

Punks, Steve scowled. *I could take any of you.* To him they seemed frightened and weak as their eyes nervously scanned the group of guests hurriedly gathering water at the river's edge.

Steve was probing for a reaction, daring a response. He felt taught, stretched, but in an exceedingly positive way. Whatever had softened inside of him throughout the years was beginning to firm up, and the feeling was thrilling.

He was not going to be fucked with. By *anyone*.

It was personal responsibility, just as he had explained to the kids. They were in a dangerous situation, and he'd do what he had to do to get his family out of it. It was that simple. If he happened to save a few thousand others in the process—well, that was a nice bonus. After Maria's candid admission there simply was no more *if*.

We were under attack, Steve explained, *and there they stood, the "security guards", just a bunch of third-rate actors, unable to hide one fact: they were scared shitless and in way over their heads.*

"Suck my big one!" Steve yelled at the nearest, and Barb withered. "Heroes my ass!"

"Honey!" Barb grabbed his chest, desperately. "Let me show you the..."

Steve tore away.

"... *waterfall*," Barb pleaded.

It was their only chance. Steve might be better off in custody but she would give the waterfall one shot. She summoned her strength.

And had a terrible thought: *could the boy still be there?* The thought of Steve encountering the boy in this state of mind terrified her and a unique image of dismemberment appeared.

But it didn't matter. Steve was scaring her and they needed to be alone, away from others, away from danger. For everyone's sake.

If she faced the boy she faced the boy.

She grabbed Steve's hand and turned to find a man blocking their way. A big man, dressed in leather with a tiny blond wife beside him, cigarette dangling from the corner of her mouth. Despite the state of DisasterLand, her hair was immobile and stood at an impressive height.

"Are you with us or against us?" the man asked. Steve stared.

The man shifted. "You don't support our troops guy?"

Goatee, tan, American flag do-rag and muscles, Steve knew his type. They didn't often cross paths.

Steve's eyes burned, the man's veins throbbed. The woman stamped her cigarette out on the grass and exhaled on Barb.

"Do you or do you not support our troops?" the man repeated, slower. His eyes flicked to Barb.

She felt Steve tighten and she answered, "Of course we do, don't we honey?"

As the silence resettled, Barb felt absolutely alone, and found herself fighting for air.

Steve needed help. *Real help.* It was time to stop fooling around—someone was going to get hurt.

"What troops?" Steve asked. He stepped in, nose-to-nose. "All I see are *actors*," he grimaced. "*Bad ones.*"

A stunned whisper spread through the small crowd of water-seekers who stood at the river nearby. Two guards approached the men.

"All you see is my fist in your face, guy, now answer the question."

One guard dropped his rifle between the two figures and leveraged them apart.

359

"Come on, Steve," Barb pleaded, "Let's go."

"I know things that would make you cry like a girl," Steve said edging back around the rifle.

"I bet you do you sick fuck."

"Out of here or we'll take you both in!" the guard yelled through clenched teeth.

"Will you feed us? I'm game for that. Let's go Barb, the old joke is true."

Steve presented his hands for cuffing.

"You show these gentlemen some respect or I'll crush you, you lazy fuck!"

"Not unless they earn it," Steve spat.

Barb eyed the guards, who seemed to be considering letting the pit bull of a man loose on her husband.

"I bet you're not even an American. You're one of them Canadians, ain't you? Hunh? How'd you even get in here? This is the greatest damn country on the face of the earth, guy, and you don't even know it!"

"You ever been anywhere else?" Steve asked, his eyes narrow.

"Don't need to!"

Steve nodded, slowly.

Then deliberately extended his hand. The man frowned, but after a long, tense moment, took it and squeezed. Steve hid a grimace.

"We're on the same side, man. We're on the same side," Steve said, then turned. "We only want what's best for our families."

He marched away, back down the trail and away from the river, the surrounding guests' applause fading out behind him. Barb was nipping at his heels, head spinning, caught in his psychological undertow.

She wasn't going back to the tower. Not with this man, not with these bad vibes. Something dark was percolating under the surface up there, something violent, and she was going to remove herself and her kids from the equation. She would chose another way.

She would choose the waterfall—without Steve if she had to.

"Good afternoon, everyone. General Elektra here and I hope you're all ready for the ride tonight. Strap yourselves in and break out the Ritalin, kids, 'cause here we go. First team is up, folks, *first team is up* and we're thirty away, *thirty away*. First cue at 15:27. One. Five. Two. Seven."

Elektra slipped the headphones down around her neck and exhaled. She had just returned from her suite, where she had taken a long relaxing bath to focus and prepare for the evening ahead.

It was going to be something. It always was.

She'd be spending another sleepless night on the bridge, along with the security elites and first team leaders who were now on until the script's final resolution, in case things got ugly. Or *when* things got ugly, Elektra chuckled.

Yet as she stood and surveyed the bridge around her, empty seats outnumbered bodies for the first time. And despite the energy of the evening coming alive, there was a palpable emptiness at its edge. From here on out, they would rely less and less on DisasterLand's own staff—though more and more on a vital, hard core.

Lucky Bastards, Elektra huffed, turning her back to the empty seats.

Karen was stationed with Greg and Shae and Elektra gravitated towards them, stretching her sea legs.

They were staring at a flowchart on the temporary widescreen monitor set up in front of them, a real-time color-coded assessment of the evening's possibilities and dangers, shared with the team of writers still stationed in the psychological wing and in permanent, live communication with Karen.

It was by no means complete, there was no way it could be, but it damn close. From here on out, the linear structure of a traditional script would be left firmly behind and the writers' job was to surf the ever-changing waves of potential with flair. Elektra would act more as a wrangler than a traditional director or producer, ensuring the disparate actions taking place throughout the atrium matched the needs of the script in tone and timing. Her go-to first-team on the floor would carry out her commands.

She took a seat on one arm of the largest couch and smiled to herself. She knew she'd look back at this moment after the show's finale, remember herself sitting here imagining herself there, and it would feel as though a week had passed, as if, by some sort of magic, she'd managed to steal a bit more out of life than traditional physics allowed. And during this time, amazingly, perceptibly—inevitably—she would somehow have changed. Always.

Hundreds if not thousands of decisions were about to take place over the next ten, twelve, even fourteen hours, all of them impossible to foresee in advance and many of them vitally important. They were embarking on a journey that no one could predict—even though they firmly knew where they were going, it was just impossible to understand how exactly they would get there. They were entering the unknown with only the dim LCDs of the writers' laptops and their guests' passion as their guide.

"So what's the word?" Elektra asked.

"Wonderful stuff, embryonic but lovely," Karen replied. "Don't you think"?

"I do," Elektra replied. "Couldn't ask for a better set-up, if you ask me."

"Gonna be a real old-fashioned throw-down," smiled Shae.

With the firm discovery of the holes last night, word had begun to spread throughout the morning and by now very real actions were being taken by those in the tower. The script, at last, was taking on a momentum all its own. This evening, Elektra and her skeleton crew would simply nudge it along until liftoff.

All teams were now at-the-ready. The MoDi was kicking in again, their goal full-frontal destabilization by all means necessary. Provocateurs were on stand-by, ready to accomplish what the guests couldn't or wouldn't by themselves.

Security was finalizing preparations for their most sustained, most vital responsibilities of the week. With few notable exceptions, thus far the guards' role had largely been ceremonial, but that would soon change dramatically.

They were up to the task—like the DL:FireMen, all guards either had real police or military backgrounds or had received extensive professional law enforcement training in order to fulfill their roles.

The earlier post-dailies security meeting had reconfirmed and updated the rules of engagement to take into account the specifics of this show. Time would condense and everyone had to be prepared for vital seconds, seconds which quite literally could save lives.

For the other A-list actors, Lhasa's energy and confidence had electrified the battle-hardened vets. In the end he hadn't been wired in to join them for dailies for fear of breaking the guests' illusion. But after last night's performance, all the top actors had stopped by today to privately welcome him into the fold and they'd each left with a renewed sense of purpose.

Other pieces of the dramatic puzzle were being put in place as well: Spokane had been released and escorted with her parents to the refugee camp to begin re-socialization. L.A. had also been released with his wife back to their suite. Emotionally drained, he had nonetheless clearly been pleased to have DTV's cameras in tow.

These were the times the staff had arduously prepared for over the previous weeks and months. These were the moments for which they'd scanned the guest database, read and re-read the shift reports and constantly been glued to the Feed during waking hours. Their knowledge of these guests was now as complete as it ever would be. The long and perilous home stretch had arrived. They had entered the tunnel. The final push would begin.

DisasterLand's actors had brought them this far, but now it was up to the heroes—discovered or undiscovered—to bring the script home.

Elektra stood and replaced her headset.

Now was the time for the heroes to shine.

"Yes. This will do. As long as the actors stay away."

Steve spit. He was mercilessly pacing the beach.

This will do? The mood at the waterfall had changed, Barb knew, but *this will do?*

She had dragged Steve through the forest, literally, along the secret trail that led to the falls. But when he had caught the first glimpse of the rush of the falls, she had detected a change in him. Slight, but it was significant. His mood, momentarily, had lifted. It showed promise.

Already, however, it had faded.

Nervous tension now impregnated the waterfall's humid air and a growing collection of misfits seemed to be arriving all the time, most seeming to be in it for the long haul. She sensed a window of opportunity closing and longed for her children and belongings so they could stake out their own choice territory before nightfall.

Until then, she wouldn't be able to relax.

"Honey, the guards are here to help us," Barb replied, chasing after him.

Barb's bubble of peace had already been punctured, her sanctuary violated. The swimmers were gone. This was no longer a retreat, it was shelter. It was survival. The falls had rapidly been reduced to the base level, along with everything else. How had it happened so quickly? Where did all these people *come from*?

Despite her disappointment, at some level she had expected it, had known the magic couldn't last forever. She forced her thoughts to the positive. Though paradise had fallen, the boy was gone. *The boy was gone*, she repeated to herself.

Steve froze, aimed a finger downstream towards the clearing, "The guards are under orders to control *us*, Barb, not the terrorists. Can't you see it? Open your eyes."

"Why don't you get in, honey, and clean off," Barb suggested cautiously, "I hid some soap down the river. Wash off, wash your clothes. You'll feel a thousand times better. You're all covered in white dust you know."

Steve didn't respond. His eyes were scanning the dome overhead, the desert beyond, scrutinizing every person, every piece of sand, every tree.

"OK," he said, finally. "OK... I'm so tired, Barb. So tired."

Barb nodded her agreement. She couldn't remember being this drained in all of her life. She was beyond hunger, beyond thirst. She existed outside of herself, running only on the fumes her body could create out of nothing.

Steve was right, Barb knew, about one thing: if they had no water they had nothing. And soon, they would confront that reality.

She was about to purify all the water she had with the tablets Steve had just given her. Then they would be gone.

After sharing the location of her stash, she bid him luck. She wouldn't join him. Not for the second time today, and certainly not at *that spot*. The memories were too fresh, too fragile, and Barb wanted time to properly segregate them. Her heart would hold them in a beautiful bejeweled compartment forever. Her mind, though, had already set about purging them.

Barb retreated to a choice tree, relieved to count several guards still present. She sat back against the trunk slowly, heavily, with the arthritic movements of the elderly.

Relaxing for the first time since they'd left hours ago, she noticed her hands were clenched. She forced them open and an immense pain was lifted. A pain she had grown unaware of, or perhaps even enjoyed.

She tried to calm herself, to breathe her way into liberation, but it only brought about a crash from the day's massive emotional expenditure.

She collapsed onto the soft grass, focusing on the leaves of the tree overhead. She shut her eyes. More than anything, she wanted sleep. But it was impossible.

She heard a splash and turned to see Steve swimming awkwardly downstream, still fully clothed.

Crucially, her children were a world away, hundreds of feet in the air—and all for some stupid reason she didn't understand. She wanted to run to them, to get them, to carry them here if she had to. But she knew she couldn't. Not yet. Thirty-eight stories up and down again, two more crosses of atrium... no. Not yet at least.

What fools they were. All of them.

Barb forced herself back up into a sitting position and pulled off her shoes and socks. She needed to dangle her legs, needed the cool, flowing water to calm her hot, dry blood, to lubricate the cells scraping through her blood like sandpaper.

She needed to keep moving.

Barb crawled forward ridiculously, braving other guests' stares to make her way down to the river's edge. Dipping her feet into the rushing water, she found the sensation overwhelming, almost painful.

She exhaled.

Barb longed for another wash of her panties, now heavy and stiff and funky, but she just couldn't see how it would happen. She just didn't have the energy for the river.

Love, Barb thought.

Love and Death. Creation and Destruction. Sex and War. Life and Death. Shiva and Shakti.

Love.

She straightened, ears at attention. From the distance, back towards the atrium, distant yelling.

Barb checked around her. Others had noticed it too. A hush had fallen over those at the falls.

And there it was again, louder.

She checked the river for Steve, but he had disappeared downstream.

Behind her, guests were running towards the forest. Spinning, she now saw the haze.

No, Barb told herself. *Surely not. It's only someone barbecuing.*

The guards had disappeared.

"Steve!" she yelled. "*Steve!*"

A sweat-drenched guest raced out of the forest. "Fire!" he called, "Forest... *on fire!*"

Could it be? The *forest?*

That would be it—the surest sign of the terrorists' authenticity. The willful destruction of those most innocent, those least able to defend themselves. The immobile ones. *The trees.*

It was the perfect message to their captives, the perfect attention-getter for the world stage. It proved the threat, proved their potency, without significant human loss of life. It was disgusting.

Blindly, Barb leapt into the river, gasping at the cold. She found Steve around the bend, swimming towards her, choking against the rushing current. His face was stone, both in color and expression.

The haze now consumed the river and was rapidly increasing in density.

"The masks Barb!"

Helped out of the river by guests they crawled, half-drowned, towards their D-PAKS. Soaked, with no way of drying themselves off, they put on their masks with shaking hands. Barb couldn't tell if she was crying but she thought so. She had to be. She certainly wanted to and thought Steve might be as well.

"Everyone to the wetlands!" someone screamed.

Steve floundered, paralyzed. His mind was racing as fast as his exhausted body was staying still.

Steve thought of breaking the glass and fleeing now, before things got any worse. When the reality spread, when word finally got out, when everyone truly understood their predicament, the true extent of the terrorist's infiltration and power, things would turn ugly. Very, very ugly. And *fast*

It was important to *get out now*.

DisasterLand, or the terrorists, or *whoever,* would never have enough people to stop him if they headed out into the desert. *Never.* And if others went—if they fanned out? Surely freedom would bless some.

Wasn't it important to try? Rather than to sit back and wait for death?

Steve didn't know the surrounding geography, of course, and they wouldn't last long in the desert with no water. But they wouldn't last long *here* without water. How long it would take to be rescued?

He'd need a flasher. For planes. *A shard of glass from the shattered dome.*

The time was right. They'd have to break out. *Now.*

But what about the kids?

"Come on, Steve! *What are you standing around for?"* Barb grabbed him, dragging him the opposite way, towards the forest, towards the atrium. *Towards the fire!*

Steve tried to hold back but she was pulling him viciously, relentlessly onwards, forcing their way through the ever-increasingly onrush of panicked families headed the opposite direction, families hurrying towards the river and into the wetlands, intent on using the river as a barrier against fire. They seemed to be carrying everything they had.

Those are the smart ones, Barb cursed, *and if I had my children we'd be leading the way.*

Pete and Sarah woke frantically, with smoke searing their lungs.

Pete leapt up from the couch, disoriented and suffocating, and grabbed his light from the D-PAK. He flashed it on.

Their television, only a few feet away, was a vague outline. Pete gasped instinctively and began choking fiercely, his eyes filling with tears.

Sarah was already fumbling with her mask and motioned for him to get his. Pete glimpsed her wide eyes, panicked and irritated by the smoke. Illuminated by the flashlight, he found them alien and profoundly unsettling, and he panicked. Caught in a vicious cycle, hyper-ventilating and hacking, he began to fade. He was in trouble.

Sarah grabbed him as he collapsed, opening his D-PAK and attaching the mask. She had seen *Survival.* She knew what to do.

She raced into the bedroom, carefully avoiding the bed and their parent's suitcases, to the huge picture window. She slid it open as wide as it would go—only six inches or so—but wide enough.

Pete arrived moments later and he ripped off his mask.

Together, they staggered their heads out of the gap in the window and hacked the sweet acid soot from their lungs through the narrow opening, to the anger of many of those guests below who were unlucky enough to experience their wrath.

The setting sun was blazing into the windows, heating the metal frames and scalding their faces. To everyone hanging precariously out of the windows, tens to hundreds of feet above the red desert with smoke wafting over them, it felt like the hellish end of the world.

All along the tower, disembodied heads were shouting updates, desperate for information about the nature of the threat they all faced. There were very few answers.

For Sarah, the shock of the transition from sleep to danger had unleashed a tempest of emotions. She imagined herself having to jump, squeezing through the tiny space, the fire nipping at her ass, singeing her feet and catching her hair as she went, risking everything not to be burned alive. Then she was back falling, falling through the elevator shaft, waiting for the inevitable crush of her bones as she hit the ground, her last moment on the planet one of all-encompassing pain.

"You OK?" screamed Pete.

Sarah nodded, gagging.

Pete replaced his mask.

"I'm going out front!" he yelled. And before Sarah could protest he was gone.

Sarah shut her eyes, fighting to collect herself, and gently pulled her head back in through the window. With her last breath of fresh air, she replaced her mask and flung off her shoes to make her way barefoot along the outside perimeter of the suite, *Survival*-style, as quickly as she could, heart thudding, feeling for heat.

In the kitchen she grabbed a chair and, with it, made another round stretched to the ceiling. They were all cool. Literally.

Pete returned as she finished, his breathing heavy, distorted. "I can't see anything. *It's filled up. The whole atrium!*"

Sarah's fury overshadowed the desperation in his voice. "I can't believe you ran off like that! What if something happened?"

But Pete pushed on, "There's no one out there Sarah, it's bad. *Really bad!*"

"We're OK. The fire isn't by us. We'll stay in the bedroom."

Pete shone his flashlight around the suite, watching the stagnant smoke continue to accumulate despite the open window.

Barb and Steve burst out onto the Great Lawn and found themselves lost in a murky crush of foul-smelling humanity, eerily anonymous in their emergency masks.

They had made it through the forest.

"The whole tower's going up!"

"What about the forest?"

"Fire's in the tower!"

Terribly, the fatalistic wails were impossible to prove or deny—the atrium was clouded with thick, black smoke, and visibility was nil.

The guests' frantic, smoke-inflamed eyes were emphasized by their masks, creating a rich, haunting sense of apocalypse.

"Our babies are suffocating!" Barb screamed, spurning Steve on towards the atrium.

She clung to him as he clawed his way through the crowd, the thick smoke only growing heavier as they progressed. Ahead, Steve thought he could make out a line of flashing emergency lights in the distance, perhaps from guards ringing the periphery of the park.

Barb was revolted by herself, by her own intolerable conduct. She had vowed never to leave the suite and now here she was in the park, her children trapped helplessly alone as far away as they could possibly be. It was shameful and she deserved whatever she got. *But they didn't.*

"They've got the window!" Steve yelled back. "And Sarah's watched *Survival!*"

The colored lights of EMS carts could now be seen flashing dimly ahead, marking the atrium.

"They're burning alive!"

They continued on, forcing their way through. Angry guests struck back. Tension throughout the park was rapidly increasing to unbearable levels.

"We're such fools, Barb!" Steve yelled, "So self-indulgent! We've left them defenseless!"

"*You! You* left them defenseless... why did *you...*"

Steve flashed around, shoving her away violently. Barb cried out as she fell into a tangle of legs. Guests grabbed Steve, tackling him to the ground and someone clocked him hard in the jaw. He was forced up, hands restrained behind his back.

He tasted blood. But it only energized him.

Barb too had been helped to her feet and she stared at him, lost, while others supported her limp body. Several men stood between the two.

"Let me go, barbarians!" Steve yelled. "We're going to nineteen!"

"Good luck wifebeater!" someone yelled.

"You ain't gettin' anywhere man, we're quarantined!" howled another.

"Quarantined?" Barb asked, voice breaking. "But our kids are upstairs!"

"It's martial law. The park's sealed!"

Proof, Steve realized, spitting blood, *that DisasterLand was losing control.*

It was time to step into the void.

"We're going to die in here!" someone screamed.

"I'm suffocating!"

"Calm down!" another guest shrieked.

"Fresh air!"

"My wife's fainted! Help us!"

"I can't take it!" Barb howled, "My babies are suffocating!"

Steve forced his way back to her, taking her hand. The men watched, cautiously, their own families scattered defensively behind them.

"Come on, Barb, we're going to nineteen."

Steve strode ahead, and Barb stumbled forward in his wake, semiconscious... *She'd lost them...*

Visibility was becoming worse by the minute. Even the forest behind them was now completely lost in the haze.

Continuing on, forcing their way through the angry masses growing more dense by the foot, they approached the figures in riot gear obscured by the smoke.

Worn out and aching, they attempted one final push for freedom but soon realized the true extent of their predicament. Rapid-deploy Kevlar fencing had been installed in front of the guards, all along the park's periphery as far as they could see. The quarantine was no joke. They were trapped.

Fury welled up in Steve with a roar while Barb hid her eyes. It had become too much for her. It had crossed the line. She couldn't take it, couldn't go on. She desperately wanted it to be over, whatever *it* was. *Now.*

The guards' guns were drawn. Behind their masks, their riot gear and through the depths of the haze, they now seemed invincible.

"My kids!" Steve screamed to the closest.

"You gotta wait buddy," he yelled back, muffled.

"*Wait for what?*"

"The *all clear*!"

"Our children have no water!"

The guard gave a shake of the head, signaling the end of the conversation.

Steve's temper flared, "Don't you understand? It's never going to *be safe*! They're inside! The terrorists are *inside*!" Heads were turning. "Inside the walls of the tower!"

Barb was eyeing him, carefully, and felt the ladder of civility quaking beneath their feet. Steve was seething, his eyes sparking with menace. He turned from the guard, heaving, gasping for one clear breath of fresh air.

"They've lost control!" Steve yelled, to no one in particular. "DisasterLand's leaders are helpless or murdered! We're trapped! On our own! We must free ourselves!"

"You're a fool!" someone yelled.

"DisasterLand only wants to control us! To prevent us from engaging the terrorists directly, to keep us from fighting our own battles! *They will not succeed! We will not be imprisoned! We will not die here!*"

"He's right!"

"It's now or never!"

"We've got no food!"

"No water!"

"Let's march!"

"We must not give in!" Steve yelled. "We're making a break! Who's with us?"

Am isolated group of enthusiastic cheers greeted him. Above their heads, in the distance, tiny beams of light were probing the haze.

"Sir?!" a gruff voice shouted.

Guards began to step forward, one by one out of the retreating crowd to surround them. Barb cowered while Steve faced the guard who had spoken.

"I'd suggest you let that little idea go. You're not going anywhere," the guard said, a Taser aimed squarely at Steve's ribs.

Retreating back towards the forest for safety, Steve confessed in hushed whispers the existence of the exploratory hole he had made to test the terrorists' penetration.

Unwittingly, he had mainlined the terrorists into their children's lives and now they could only sit back and watch, helplessly quarantined.

Silently, Barb wept.

The kids exited their suite, hitting the hard glass of the walkway face first. Ahead of them, mysteriously, three hugely powerful beams of light hung in mid-air over the dim, smoke-drenched atrium. The beams' powerful glare had lured the kids out, away from the window and the fresh air.

Nothing else was visible around them. The railing itself, only inches away, was nearly lost in the haze.

They lay in the disorienting smoke, restricting their breathing as much as possible, watching the three beams slowly ascending the void. Finally, way above them, the beams seemed to pause in space and then come together like three tiny UFOs mating in the nighttime sky.

Suddenly and without warning, a massive rush of fresh air blasted by the kids' prone bodies and the smoke began to clear. Soon it was obvious—the smoke was rushing out the top of the dome. The vents had been opened!

Pete and Sarah watched, stunned, as the first faint outlines of the walkways stretching above and below them appeared, revealing hundreds of masked guests anxiously watching the proceedings.

Three Day-Glo figures were soon visible behind the beams of light, rigged into tiny harnesses and hanging twenty-five stories over the center of the atrium. Their lights remained, but with the dissipation of smoke, the beams soon faded.

A tremendous roar erupted from those assembled, led by the hundreds of guests interred in the refugee camp. Undoubtedly they'd been hit the hardest, with no fresh air available to them at all.

"You know what this means, Pete?"

"What?"

"There's no power. Really. Because if there was, they would have opened that hatch automatically. Like they did after the first attack."

Pete nodded slowly, his thoughts elsewhere. Across the atrium, the rest of the park was emerging from the haze. And it didn't look good.

Security teams with oxygen tanks were busy constructing a massive extension to the refugee camp which now spanned almost three-quarters the Great Lawn's width. Inside, the refugees were cowering under the overflowing tents where oxygen was being administered to the worst off under armed guard. All taunts had long-ago ceased.

Extending along the remaining expanse of the park's periphery was a smaller fence, yet the message was just as clear. Guards had taken up defensive positions to prevent the exit of a massive throng of guests which were pushing out from the forest. The park was a sea of people. And they weren't leaving.

Below, the ruined atrium lay empty. The only signs of life were exhausted DL:FireMen assessing their equipment.

The kids did a simultaneous double-take.

The ruined atrium *lay empty*.

Another enormous cheer was spreading across the walkways.

Empty! The masked men... the hostages. *Gone*!

Sarah raced in to grab her dad's binoculars.

There, under armed guard at the refugee camp's entrance, were the weak, newly-rescued employees and their SWAT team rescuers. EMS crews were hurriedly providing treatment to the neediest.

The explosives were gone, the threat had somehow been defused. *Yet where were the terrorists?*

Throughout the tower, relief mixed with the elation of a successful, perfectly-timed rescue. For the first time in hours, spirits were lifted. The volume of cheering only grew as the realization spread.

No shots had been fired and there seemed to be no casualties. Though there was no sign of the masked men, the terrorists had clearly been dealt two serious blows.

Peter and Sarah's eyes met. *But where were their parents?*

And what were they going to do now?

As the last of the smoke cleared the tower's base, the true extent of the damage was revealed for the first time and joy quickly turned to awe. Huge, open gashes lashed across the tower, festering wounds of brutality opened by the heartless aggressors.

At the sight, something profound inside Sarah turned over, the first glimmer of a panic she realized her dad must have felt earlier that morning. She tried to force it out of her mind.

"Four suites, I think," Pete reported, sliding over for a better view. "Or maybe five."

The damaged suites were spread radically throughout the tower, all at opposite ends and widely different floors, the attack clearly engineered for maximum damage and maximum difficulty for the DL:FireMen.

DTV crews were scurrying amidst the damage like insects.

From two suites, eleven and fourteen, the last remnants of smoke were escaping the hot, smoldering ruins still drenched in foam. Others further down had been extinguished with water and crews were hurriedly cleaning up the damage. Way below, on two, one of the restaurants had gone up. Yet for every suite ruined by fire, there were two or three adjacent suites that had sustained enough damage to make them uninhabitable.

The fires had been synchronized. It had been a coordinated attack. And there was nothing to prevent a repeat.

DL:FireMen were sprawled over the damaged floors, masks off and exhausted. EMS crews were tending to their needs with bottles of water and DL:PowerStrips. They had clearly been stretched to their limits by the sheer number of simultaneous events.

The effect on guests had also been profound. Many had been hit and hit hard. The first refugees were already beginning to gather at the tower's landings, those who perhaps had lost everything. Below, at the tower's base, guards had mobilized to form an impenetrable barricade. Preparations were clearly underway for an emergency atrium crossing to the refugee camp but this left individual walkways, for the most part, completely void of protection.

Other guests, more fortunate, those whose suites escaped the most serious damage, were already beginning to reconstruct their lives with the help of neighbors.

The kids lay alone on their walkway watching the smoldering fallout below and Sarah finally allowed herself to believe that they really might be in trouble. It was just all too real.

"What do we do, Spanks?"

"We wait here. That fence in the park is temporary, just to let them get control of everything."

"You really think so?"

"Of course. They don't want people coming back when everything is such a mess. Mom and dad will be back soon."

"Why don't we go to the park?"

"You think they'll let us?"

The first groups of refugees were already departing for the camp—at gunpoint. This time, it seemed, it was against their will.

Worse yet, it was clear that the fountain's emergency reservoir was gone. More fires like this could be unstoppable.

Had that been the point?

By the time Sarah saw two shadows at the door and grabbed Pete, she had just about given up hope. The early evening sun had dropped behind the tower and the first hints of the coming darkness were overtaking the walkways. Her heart soared.

"Mom? Dad?" she called, rising from the couch, her voice cracking. *"Maria?"*

The kids had taken the kitchen table and wedged it into the entrance hallway, its top cockeyed towards the door for maximum camouflage of themselves and maximum disorientation for visitors.

There was no reply as the figures stepped inside. Sarah nervously tried to glimpse the nature of the feet behind the table.

Pete's mind snapped out of his speechless disgust and he searched desperately for a weapon. He had just returned from the bathroom which had been almost intolerable, even in the smoke-dulled air. They were already running low on water and things would only get worse. If something wasn't done soon, he imagined, the UN would have to send in bioweapons scientists to oversee its dismantling.

Sarah stepped warily towards the door, leaning in to get a better view. "Hello?"

Her eyes flashed to Peter. With a terrible crash, the table dropped harmlessly to the floor and Sarah shuddered.

Two uniformed men were revealed, stepping over the table and into their kitchen. Their guns were drawn. Guards.

Two more men entered behind them, dressed in Hawaiian shirts, Bermuda shorts and hiking sandals. Sarah and Pete retreated, back into the living room.

"Is everything OK?" Sarah asked, meekly. Her heart was about to break. She knew. Her parents hadn't made it.

The guards had stopped at the end of the entryway, cleanly blocking the exit. The beach bums continued on to meet Pete and Sarah face to face.

They eyed the pillows stuffed into the wall curiously.

One pulled out a tiny hand-held computer. It chirped as he shot a photo of the two stunned kids.

"Pete Beyers?" he asked.

Pete shook his head. "We're just kids dude. Squatters."

"Your name isn't Pete Beyers?"

"I'm Zander. Zander Bentley."

Sarah smiled, agreeing.

"Who's this?" they asked.

"My girlfriend," Pete answered. "Have you seen *Natural Born Killers?*"

The guard showed Pete his PDA: on it, a surveillance still of Pete in the VIP lounge Friday night, decked out in his Kimono. His name was captioned below.

Pete's mind rewound to those good ol' days.

"Says *here* you're Pete Beyers. And we know you're not Zander." He paused as Pete's heart throbbed. "We've already got him."

Pete tensed. Sarah scanned him for any sort of reaction, anything at all. *Was he in trouble?*

"Who are you?" Sarah asked, trembling.

"We're from *Ghost*. Pete, you're G-5, our highest ranking. And you're coming with us."

"*Ghost!*" Pete's eyes bugged.

They nodded slowly.

"No way dude!" Pete leapt up. "Prove it."

"Remember Candy?"

"DUDE!" His jaw dropped. "But wait... there's no power! How..."

A hand went up and Pete was silenced. He understood.

Top Secret.

"Pete!" Sarah yelled, her mind reeling. "You can't go! Mom and dad will kill you! *I'll* kill you! You'll be grounded for a *year!*"

Pete's hands rested on his hips, "She's not my friend she's my sister. And she's coming with me."

A guard stepped over, took Pete's shoulder, and silently shoved him towards the door.

Sarah sniffled. Pete turned away.

"Sorry, honey, classified," the guard said. "But we'll have him back as soon as we can. You'll be OK. We'll make sure."

"How?" she sobbed.

"How will we make sure? We just will. Come on, kid, you got your D-PAK?"

Seconds later, he was gone.

Sarah stood, immobile, alone in her living room, the sounds of DisasterLand around her melting into sinister poison. She stumbled to the front door, fighting to replace the table with her useless arms. She did the best she could and collapsed, edging against the wall.

She was alone. Truly alone. In the darkening tower.

She leaned over and heaved, but nothing came up.

So hungry...

Sarah felt her D-PAK for the bar. It was there. No matter what, she had that.

Should she go? To the waterfall? *Alone?*

Could she?

She couldn't stay here. Not anymore. Not with the open door, not in the dark, not with her parents in the park.

Pete and Sarah had packed the family's valuables, but surely there was no way Sarah could carry them all by herself without becoming a target.

Besides, would the guards still ringing the tower's base ever let her pass? It seemed like a full military lockdown. And she certainly didn't want to end up in the refugee camp.

No. She'd have to stay.

After all, Pete was coming back. They said so. And then they'd go find their parents. Together.

Maybe her brother *was* a secret agent after all.

"You've been called here because your family, your friends and your country need you," Falco said, entering *The Core* and hurrying down through the darkened space. "And you're the best we've got."

Rowdy howls greeted him from the dawgs of *The Core*.

This time there were no fancy lights, no ambient music priming them for combat. It was bare-bones, clandestine war-style and for those breathlessly assembled it was even more invigorating.

This was the real deal.

Earlier, they had been given up-to-the-minute classified sketches of the terrorists-at-large, to be memorized by candlelight. Pete had surreptitiously stashed his into his sock, undetected.

He knew his dad would be interested.

Falco reached the lowest level and froze. He flicked on a lighter, its flame dancing across his face. "This information, once again, does not leave this room."

The lighter flicked off.

He began pacing, head down, speaking in quick, precise words, his figure only a shadow in the sea of darkness. "We obtained intelligence at roughly 18:43 local time concerning the probability of a terrorist device being planted somewhere in DisasterLand. We have reason to believe that this device... that its effects... will be devastating. The only hope of preventing it, we realized, is *you*."

He stopped, flicking on the lighter. "Minutes later we had corroborated the facts and the search immediately went out for all of you. We were unable to find four."

The four empty seats had been glaringly obvious for everyone entering in *The Core*, even in the dark. "Which means you'll only have to work harder."

Falco resumed circling, the flame flickering nervously.

"Our intelligence confirms the terrorists are about to strike. We have less than thirty minutes of backup power available for *The Core*. You must find it, whatever *it* is. A suspicious bag, purse, box, whatever. No lead is too small. The same restrictions are in place: no closed doors, no walls in the tower. Use your gut. If you find something, alert us. Yell."

Falco stopped, cold. "*GOT IT!*" he screamed at the top of his lungs.

Pete nearly stained his suit.

Falco eyed his recruits and continued, softly. "The hero will not be disappointed. Good luck. And Godspeed."

The lighter cut.

And then, just like that, they were *back in*.

Pete was in the atrium, by the fountain, facing Good Health. *28:38* was on his clock, and counting.

Night was falling on the scarred atrium and the deepening shadows only strengthened Pete's resolve.

He looked up to nineteen, an impossible distance above. There, in the midst of the darkening ruins of the tower lay their suite, the door resting awkwardly across the doorway.

Pete set off towards it, scanning the afternoon's widespread damage on floor after floor as he passed. But he stopped himself. He was being stupid.

He knew Sarah would be in the suite, worried. And what good would it do him to witness it? Sarah wasn't a terrorist, and there wasn't a bomb in his place.

Was there?

Pete slowed. He was being selfish, stupid. He had twenty-seven minutes to find this thing and he'd have to gamble.

He imagined Candy handing him his trophy and whispering an invitation to a secret spot in the park. Minutes earlier, she had kissed him good luck and her perfume still lingered, subtly working its magic. He was a caged animal. He'd do whatever it took.

Then he remembered: *the hole...*

His dad had even said—*the tower was rigged!*

Pete rocketed up the remaining stories in the blink of an eye. He slipped past the open front door and there she was, on the couch, flashlight in hand. Sarah was waiting. Just waiting.

Waiting for him to be a hero.

Pete flashed past her and darted inside the hole. Suddenly, amazingly, he was *inside*.

A dim glow surrounded him, illuminating a couple of feet in every direction. Pete eyed the clock: *25:21.*

Another world away he felt the sweat dripping off his forehead and dampening his back. And he realized the problem. Though he could navigate the spaces, it was going to take much longer than twenty-five minutes to search every inch of the tower. He couldn't just zip through every passage—the pipes, the vents, it all had to be navigated. Examined.

As the true extent of the job dawned on him, his heart began to race. He was being crushed. He wanted to scream, *help me!*

But why give away the secret. This was it, he knew. The answer. *But where?*

Twenty!

The hostage!

Pete deliberately ascended the few feet to the ceiling of nineteen. Then crawlspace by crawlspace he made his way towards the goal, his breathing shallow and quick.

Detritus was strewn throughout. A sleeping bag here, discarded flashlight batteries there. Cigarette butts, markers and spray paint.

His dad was right. *Terrorists! Everywhere! Surrounding them!*

Then, as he neared the suite, he saw it. Just above. The soft illumination signaling *the hole.*

18:49

He approached slowly, cautiously, the words *GOT IT* choking his breath. Back in

The Core, he leaned forward, ready to pounce.

He rose and darted inside. The walls were defiled with predatory graffiti but the floors had been cleaned. All of the furniture had been stacked in one corner. The bombs had clearly been dismantled. It was empty.

He raced into the master bedroom and bathroom, then doubled back through the kitchen to the second bedroom.

Nothing. *Nothing!*

10:04.

"GOT IT!" a kid screamed and Pete's heart stopped.

What?! Where?!

Pete sat back and his character began drifting, gradually, sucked back towards the hole. Like a feather.

Falco's voice rang out, far away and desperate. "Keep going! Might be a false alarm! Keep going! *We need intelligence!*"

But Pete felt lost. He was tired and his head was hurting, his stomach protesting in anger. He had hoped for another visit to the VIP lounge, for a miracle burger.

The winner will not be disappointed, Falco had said.

But that was all gone now and Pete's heart dropped. *Fuck this*, he thought. But he knew he had to at least pretend to search until Falco called it off. He couldn't just *stop*.

He drifted on, watching the clock tick down past eight. He thought of his sister, alone down below, and his parents, at the waterfall.

His parents!

This was the perfect way to locate them. When he got back he could grab Sarah and they could go straight there!

Pete shot through the blanket covering the suite's front door, past the guards on duty and straight out over the railing. Floating over two hundred feet above the atrium, Pete kicked in the turbos and in a matter of seconds he was barnstorming the refugee camp and on into the forest. He caught the gauze flashes of other *Ghosts* as they zipped by.

The renewed sense of urgency propelled Pete on, straight over the heart of the forest and on, to the river.

He had entered the opposite end of the park, the South end, towards Sarah's clearing and the bridge. *He hadn't seen any of this!*

06:16

Pete dove swiftly and skimmed the length of river on his way to the falls. The view was incredible and all heaviness had once again left him. A crackling rush of energy propelled him on.

He stopped. Suddenly. Something was there, hidden in the forest. Just next to the river!

He spun.

There, in front of him, a naked young man was leaned against a tree, resting on a pile of clothes, his hand caressing a woman's long brown hair. She was bent over him, head bobbing, exposed rear gaping towards Peter.

He froze.

He tried to retreat, only to pull back in, closer. And closer.

Pete's hormones were on overdrive and he painfully adjusted himself, squirming in his seat. He was losing control, flooding, his senses overwhelmed. He longed for release.

Pete edged in, closer and closer, until he was almost on top of her delicate muff of fur, hanging down so mysteriously, guarding its secret so magnificently.

Then, with a physical smack of shame, Pete realized his stupidity. Here he was, one of sixteen people selected to save the whole stinkin' place, and he was watching naked people doin' it. Something he could see online any time he wanted.

His stomach dropped and his eyes teared. He pictured Falco in the control room, watching Pete's feed with disgust. He'd grab Pete's parents from the park and tell them flat-out: *Peter had a chance. He had an opportunity to be someone but he fucked it up. He wanted to watch naked people instead of doing his job. He failed us all.*

Pete suddenly felt worse than he'd ever felt in his life, hollow, ashamed and worthless. He'd let down everyone.

02:11

Pete recklessly shot out to the river again, trying to hold back the torrent of emotion. He wanted to find his parents. He *had* to find his parents. Before Falco. And he'd explain everything.

He just wanted one glimpse now. One glimpse to tell him they were OK.

Arriving at the falls he ascended to get a better view. Families were huddled together on the beach, difficult to separate in the growing crowd. But there was no sign of his parents. Pete wiped his eyes, careful with the contacts.

He continued on towards at the spring, scanning backwards at the wetlands that he'd only previously glimpsed. They too were filling up with families longing for safety, for isolation.

A man was hurrying up the deserted dirt trail towards the spring. But no Steve. No Barb. No *anyone*.

Only a man. With a backpack.

A man who looked just like...

"GOT IT!" Pete screamed. "*GOT IT!*"

"Beyers! Beyers you in here?!"

Jim Andrews tucked his head past the splintered front door, his eyes resting on the kitchen table lying upside down in the hallway.

"Oh no!"

Jim tossed the door aside and stepped in, carefully. Jenny followed, taking a defensive observational position just inside the entrance. They were sporting their matching DisasterLand track suits and sneakers.

At the first sound, Sarah had grabbed her duffle bags and scurried silently into her parents bedroom and under the bed.

"Beyers! Anyone?" Jim stepped inside. *"Oh God..."*

His voice faded.

"What's wrong?" Jenny called, from security detail.

"They got 'em," Jim called.

His wife slipped in, stepping across the overturned table.

"NO!"

Jim Andrews tore away the pillow and aimed his light inside the hole, examining it from a cautious distance with profound, deep respect. He stepped closer, carefully.

Then attacked. Bravely, arms first. Jenny stared, hands on cheeks. There, for the second time, Jim admired the extensive web of death the terrorists had constructed.

"They're gone, Jenny. Gone."

Jim pulled out, "The Beyers have paid a high price for their knowledge. They've been kidnapped inside their own suite!"

"With no witnesses."

Sarah listened, every utterance chilling her to her core. She didn't know what to do. She wanted to run out and tell him everything. But after what Jim had done to her dad, she really didn't want anything to do with him. She didn's trust him. Not in her present, fragile, state of mind at least.

She'd keep her ears open for their disappearance and split at the first opportunity. She'd flee the suite with her family's belongings. And leave a note for Pete.

"DisasterLand must have rescued the boy."

Jim waved Jenny over to take a look inside but she declined.

Sarah realized they'd seen Pete's kidnapping. *No!* she wanted to scream, *you've got it all wrong!* But she didn't. She couldn't. She just wanted them to leave.

But... not really, or at least not entirely. There was an immense security with them being there. A security she had yearned for since Pete had gone.

Jim stepped into the bedroom and grunted. "No indications of struggle, honey." He stepped in further and got a whiff of the bathroom. He retreated.

The Andrews stood silently in the darkness as Sarah strained to hear. She wondered if they could hear her heart pounding. She was sure it had to be echoing off the walls.

"Here. Watch this..." Jim said, stepping over to the kitchen and grabbing a serrated knife from the drawer.

He fired up his flashlight and ducked into the hole. Grabbing the nearest rope, he began sawing. Soon, he had it well over halfway. He stopped, sweating, and pulled out of the hole to eye his work.

"Pretty dull, but it did the trick."

Jenny nodded, gravely, and together they collapsed onto the couch.

Jim and Jenny had brought jerky, enough for both families. They unwrapped one each, pocketing the others with disappointment. They pondered their future, speaking through nervous chews.

"You know, honey," Jenny said, "it really doesn't look like they were kidnapped. I mean, it's too... clean. Things should be all messed up."

"Like what, like they were having a pajama party? No, it's obvious, honey. Look at the table. The stinkin' terrorists have stole 'em. We're on our own."

Jim put his hands over his eyes and leaned back, his blood turning to venom. "I bet DisasterLand *let* the terrorists get 'em. Practically *fed* the Beyers to 'em. He was a thorn in their side you know. Just like me."

"Honey, I just..."

Jim cut her off. "Beyers is a good guy, honey. I'm sure they were packed and ready to go in an emergency. Efficient, not shit lying everywhere."

Jenny scowled at the jab, "Come on, Jim. I'm sick of it. I need things where I can see them."

Sarah quashed a giggle and found her heart warming to Jim, though infinitesimally. She would tell her dad what he said.

The main thing was, it sounded like they were *eating*. Shouldn't she just show herself? Maybe they'd share. And besides, the longer she remained under the bed the more difficult her exit was becoming. She was trapped in the thickening fluid of inertia.

"You think you're next?" Jenny asked, nervously catching his eye.

"Maybe, honey. Yes. Maybe. God, I hope they're OK."

The couple retreated to their own thoughts. Jenny stared at her husband, his chiseled face edged by moonlight.

In the bedroom, Sarah's mind was reeling. *Were they staying? Or had they gone?* Her bladder didn't like the idea of them staying, nor did her nose. A breeze was already kicking up the bathroom's caustic air and Sarah feared she would soon lose consciousness.

Jim knew his wife's point, heard the fear in her voice. Yet the day had been productive. Despite their pledge, Jim had managed to liaise with neighboring floors and form watches. This, at least, would help guarantee everyone's safety while also allowing them to pinpoint other potential terrorist enclaves.

Networks were being formed. The groundwork was being laid. Surely it wouldn't be long now.

Jenny took a long sip of her bottled water. She had bought three cases at Good Food on Friday night, especially for the occasion. That had been their first stop. They had been in line, waiting for it to open.

Jim shot up from the couch.

"Only one answer, honey, we stay here."

In the bedroom, Sarah squirmed.

"What do you mean?"

"We're going public. It's time for show and tell, honey."

"What do you mean?"

"Jen, we're showing the hole."

Steve hadn't previously found himself at the business end of a loaded weapon and the effect on his afternoon had been profound. A million plots had hatched and re-hatched in his mind, each more refined, more elegant and more elaborate than the last.

He uniquely understood their true predicament and was acutely aware of his duty to share it. They were trapped in a desperate situation that could only worsen.

Regardless of any external developments, the basic truth remained: the longer they went without food, the weaker they would become. They could not delay. They would never be as strong as they were right now.

Without food, there could be no resistance. Without food, there was no chance of escape. Without food, they would soon be helpless.

All of their tablets were now gone which meant all of their fresh water. They were facing a darkening horizon, a ticking clock, and action was their only hope. Action in the form of education.

They would educate the guests about the true extent of the terrorist's penetration, about the terrible, forbidden knowledge that the tower was rigged to blow.

This knowledge alone would build him a team to secure food. There was strength in numbers.

And then they'd break the glass.

Steve and Barb had retreated to the wetlands—away from the violence stewing in the Great Lawn largely as a result of Steve's own incitements, threats and counter-threats—to regroup, prioritize and plan.

We'll wait for our break he told the imaginary audience around him. *It won't be long now.*

With her husband tackling the big picture, Barb remained firmly grounded in the pragmatic as she paced the river's rapidly-darkening bank. In her mind the children's rescue had to be paramount despite the quarantine, and Barb had decided she would go it alone if she had to.

Depending on Maria's return had been insane... and proof of their ever-worsening mental state. When Barb had realized the children had been left alone, she should have acted. *How could she have been so stupid?*

Yet how could she have known about the hole, a hole which only intensified the threat? Had she known about that—had Steve been forthcoming, had she asked questions about his appearance—none of this would have happened.

Their negligence bordered on the criminal. If their children were gone Steve could never be forgiven. It was practically *murder.*

Taking a seat along the riverbank, Barb rested her head in her hands. All she wanted was a sign, just some sort of sign from them saying everything was OK, saying they would be on their way once the guards had things under control.

Now, here, she had nothing.

She unzipped her D-PAK and drew out the small radio. Taking a deep breath, she flipped it on.

Static.

She tossed it into the river.

Collecting herself, she looked over to her husband.

Alone on the side of the river, he had ripped the legs off his tight track pants, creating shorts. While Barb watched, he found two medium-sized rocks and rested them in each of his two front pants pockets.

He squatted, experimentally. And smiled.

It was clear: to him they felt good, felt right. Like a spare set of *cojones*.

There, above the rushing waters, Steve's confidence had blossomed into fertile clarity.

Barb's head hit her hands once again.

A terrorist. Poisoning the river.

The match had been lit, the militia had practically formed itself.

The deviant was being led across the beach in handcuffs by a DisasterLand SWAT team, his T-shirt ripped open to reveal the menacing image on his biceps. The backpack followed him under armed guard—and on it, a large, hand-sewn decal.

A butterfly.

"WHITE ADMIRAL DOWN!" he cried, "*WHITE ADMIRAL DOWN!*"

Despite guards clearing the way through the fading light and heaving crowd, he was rocked by malicious shoves and drenched in virulent taunts.

"*Long Live Nelly!*" he shouted to the innocents as restraint was urged by the guards. "Death to the agents of destruction, the forces of evil, the assassins of spirit!"

The scene was threatening to boil over and he was hurried up the trail. As they entered the forest, access was efficiently sealed off behind them by yet another team of guards but one final, triumphant howl echoed over the beach.

"*Save our winged brethren!*"

The guests responded with a venom that rekindled Steve's passion. He was standing with Barb on the opposite shore, observing the arrest with a sardonic joy he couldn't explain.

He had seen everything. And initially, the incident seemed to favor the case for DisasterLand still being in control, for surveillance to still be occurring. But now Steve didn't buy it. He detected the stench of an inside job and his jaw clenched.

It was a covert action campaign, designed to reassure a devastated populace, to boost the guest's confidence in DisasterLand's abilities to maintain security under ever-worsening conditions. The guards stationed at the falls had never moved—rather the SWAT team had raced for the spring from the forest *like they knew he was there*. And they had instantly made the arrest.

Reinforcing Steve's instincts was the suspiciously rapid spread of the story behind the attempt from the guards: White Admiral had been living in the woods, alone, waiting for the signal to strike. His only job was to retrieve the pack, hidden in the forest treetops, and release the small glass test tube of powder contained inside.

If it was true, DisasterLand had been seconds from unimaginable tragedy. And how many more terrorists could be lurking in the forest unseen?

A wave of helplessness was crashing over those at the falls and panic was spreading. Guests were reeling in a frothing swarm, angry wasps whose nest had just been destroyed.

Barb and Steve remained distant, across the river in the wetlands while Steve's mind tore through the implications.

Moments later, Steve jiggled his *cojones*, signaling a decision had been made. Barb cowed, sensing the crossing of a threshold from which there could be no return.

Steve stepped to the river's bank. His voice was fierce.

"We're taking the river!" he yelled. *"Who's with me?!"*

A roar erupted all along the swimming hole in reply.

They would rely on DisasterLand no longer, not for anything. The people were in control now.

"From this moment on, the river and wetlands are a free autonomous zone! DisasterLand has no power here! We do not recognize their authority!"

Steve was pacing in front of the growing crowd, filling the emotional void left in the wake of White Admiral's arrest. He felt the guests' hunger, he sensed their desperation. And it strengthened him.

"We take responsibility for ourselves, by ourselves!" Steve roared, his voice dry and cracking. Someone handed him a half-empty bottle of water.

The guests at the falls responded with enthusiastic cheers of support. The sky above was glowing a furious hue and there, under the desert glass dome it felt like a science fiction end-of-the-world. Other guests from around the park, from the clearing to the Great Lawn, were streaming in as word spread.

Steve's voice reduced to a rumble and the crowd strained to hear. "We're under attack, folks. Have you realized that? *We are under attack!* DisasterLand has failed in their most basic responsibility—*to keep us safe!*"

Steve painfully screamed the last sentence at the top of his lungs, pausing for the weight to sink in. He scanned the crowd, their faces tight, their eyes narrow, "Remember the power outage? So long ago?"

Families were huddled together. Children were crying.

"Proof of incompetence!" he continued, recovering his failing voice. "It's no surprise something like this happened! In fact I *knew* something bad was going to happen! *I had a feeling!*"

"That doesn't tell us anything, Beyers! This is DisasterLand!" one of the men pronounced calmly. "We *all* had that feeling!"

A snicker spread through the masses and Steve bristled, "I've been to the piss-stained bowels of this beast and I guarantee they're torture chambers!" he screamed.

The man sank invisibly back into the crowd. Steve stood tall, sneering at those closest to him. DisasterLand had failed to castrate him, failed to keep him down. And for every one of their failures, he only grew stronger.

"And yet DisasterLand does nothing... nothing except try to *control us*! Lock us up here, in the park! An *open-air jail*! *For our own good*, they say!"

He was pacing the length of the beach with guards looking on, tense.

"Today's fires were blatant, transparent acts of desperation, meant to control us by fear! To intimidate us! The fires prove the terrorists' weakness just as the refugee camps and martial law proves DisasterLand's weakness! DisasterLand *has* to scare us. The fires were probably *allowed to burn*. *Why?*"

Steve paused, pushing on as the crowd yelled their support, "Because DisasterLand has lost control! Because they're *afraid of us*!"

Hushed whispers broke out. Word was still spreading and more and more wild-eyed guests were arriving every moment, desperate for a glimpse of their champion, *their savior*.

"Why?!?" Steve hissed.

"Because we'll want our money back!" someone yelled, and Steve shot the imbecile a filthy glance.

"Liability folks, liability. They're protecting the terrorists while they assault us— *to keep us down*. If we rise up, their failures cannot be ignored! Think of the publicity! So they keep us down, keep us quarantined, shut us up! The less food we have, the less water, the quieter we'll be! They want us weak! *We have to fend for ourselves!*"

Steve paused.

"We've got nothing. Nothing! Only this river and whatever food we have left, which I can tell you is not much! Am I right?"

"*Right!*" they echoed.

"Storm the restaurants!" someone yelled and others applauded, cheering wildly.

"Yes! That's it!" Steve acknowledged excitedly, but dropped his voice. "But good luck getting out of this park." Steve spat. "We're trapped here like caged animals. And they will not let us out willingly."

"Storm the refugee camp!" the man yelled once more and Steve shook his head.

"We begin where we stand. First, we give up any hope of DisasterLand stopping the terrorists. *Why?!*" he yelled.

There were no takers.

"Because the terrorists are *inside*," Steve pushed on, "There are spaces, between our rooms. And that's where the terrorists are operating from. Yet DisasterLand keeps the guards *out here*. To deal with *us*! While *the whole tower is rigged to blow!*"

Silence exploded over the guests.

"How do you know?" someone eventually dared to ask.

Steve laughed, darkly, as his face soured. "You don't even want to know."

Nervous glances drifted through the crowd. Hands were squeezed.

"I don't know how to say this folks... but we could be here a while. Everything I've seen tells me something very, very dangerous is happening here. Something bigger than any of us. And from now on, we must live each moment as if it is our last! Because folks, *we may never get out!*"

Stunned gasps shook the crowd. Steve let the full weight of the statement descend.

"Even if you don't agree, it's critical we take action! Critical that we tell DisasterLand, 'If you won't take care of us, we will!'"

Steve cleared his throat. His eyes shone.

"There's no power. Which is why the vents didn't open. Which is why there's no decent communication. Which is why we're on our own. This arrest was staged, I'm convinced. We must empower ourselves! We must secure our own food, our own water! *And we must stay clear of the tower at all costs!*"

"How!" someone screamed.

"We need two groups. Group one will search and secure every square inch of these wetlands and as much of the park as we safely can."

Cheers rang out.

"Group two will line the river end to end, each in sight of the next. We protect our fresh water at all costs. Because it is literally life itself."

Steve's revolutionary sermon reached a fevered pitch, "Then, tonight, we plan our attack. *And at dawn we strike!*"

Cheering broke out as the massive pressure of the days' events was simultaneously released.

"*Folks...* We control our own destiny. We are one! *All for one and one for all!*"

Cheering.

"If you have food, share it! If you have water, share it! No one will go hungry unless we all go hungry! There will be no attacks, no fires, no murders while we're on duty! DisasterLand has no power here! They are not welcome here!"

The cheering only grew.

"Divided we fall. But *united we stand!*"

Fanatical cheers enveloped him. Families were hugging, greeting their equally overjoyed neighbors for the very first time since the tragedy's beginning.

His soldiers had been galvanized.

Barb breathed in deeply through her nose, eyes shut. "Let's call our cosmic consciousness, our infinite selves, with the ancient mantra 'Ong Namo Guru Dev Namo.'"

A small group of mostly women were seated cross-legged in front of her at the spring's edge. A small bonfire had been lit, casting a flickering warmth over their shadowy bodies. "And we're not going to let the terrorists stop us."

Barb opened one eye, checking the reaction. The guests were nodding with determination.

Barb sniffed in one last breath of air, "Ong..." she began.

The class followed.

Their yoga meditation wasn't a high-brow, academic show of restraint, nor a Ghandi-esque denunciation of violence. It was simply the result of an overwhelming stabbing of fear in Barb's gut. And yoga, she thought, was the only way to release it.

Barb wasn't going to rise-up, she wasn't going to take up arms, she wasn't going to overthrow anyone. She would do a little yoga and lead a nice long meditation to soothe the nerves. Anyone else was welcome to join her, for whatever reason.

They would use this opportunity to forward their own spiritual evolution. And, to that effect, the class had shared a pen and some paper and put down one thing about themselves they most wanted to change. Each having done this, they tossed the pieces in the fire and watched as they burned.

That would be their first meditation, their second a prayer for the safety and health of their family and friends at DisasterLand. With her own children still missing, their safety unknown, every little bit would help.

Giving in to the growing helplessness would only serve to increase the magnitude of their collective fear.

Barb would not give in to her base self. It would have been easy to do, as would assuming yoga was a ridiculous waste of energy at a time like this.

But, like always, when Barb could least afford it, that's when she needed it the most.

"Hi I'm Spike and you're at DisasterLand!"

"Gimme one more!"

"Yo, this is Spike and you're chillin' at DisasterLand!"

"One more!"

"Spike here and yo, you's hangin' at the big D-L!"

"And *cut*... Perfect!" the director screamed, "Right on, kid."

The DTV crew scurried out the door and Falco slapped Pete on the back, "Thanks Spike. Just in case we all make it out of here, you know?"

Pete nodded, delirious with the rush caused by comparatively vast quantities of food and drink in such a compressed period of time, all garnished with his newfound celebrity.

In reality the meal was meager, but in comparison to what he'd had the past two days, it was a king's dinner and all in his honor.

And Falco didn't even seem bummed about the naked people!

They were somewhere beneath *The Core*, in a dark, luxurious room at the foot of a spiral staircase.

Pete longed for his dad to see him now, for his whole family to join him at the head of the candle-lit mahogany table piled high with enough food for twenty.

He suddenly pushed back from the table, chock full. He didn't want to hurl. Not here. Besides, he had more for later. He'd stuffed a couple of choice selections in his pockets for his family.

Pete reached down, discreetly checking to make sure nothing was squashed. Or leaking. That could get ugly.

"Two minutes," Falco said as he checked his watch. Pete pondered another fire-roasted steak.

Instead, he fingered the shining gold medal around his neck, tugging it once again to make sure it was real. The hurried feast had followed an abrupt but magnificent ceremony, with the awarding of the solid gold medal to Pete for preventing the attack. His name had already been engraved on the back.

Peter Beyers, Hero

Zander was scowling from across the table, vibing Pete hard with jealousy. *Whatevs*, Pete thought. *Now I'm throwin' game.*

Falco stood behind Pete and rested his hands on Pete's shoulders.

"Let me thank each and every one of you once again for the supreme commitment you've shown. Each one of you, not just our hero here, have sacrificed and each of you have saved lives. I know that for a fact."

He paused, letting the statement fully sink in before continuing. "And it's possible you may save still more. The situation, I'm sorry to say, remains far from under control.

"Your mission does not end here. You must be vigilant every minute of each day until this horrible situation has come to an end.

"Furthermore, you must not speak a word of this to anyone. *The Core* does not exist. This meal did not exist. The terrorists must not find us. We are DisasterLand's last hope.

"Please stay well, stay where we can find you. We might need you again. Consider yourselves on call. Thank you."

Falco motioned through the only door and several elite guards in black appeared. Blindfolds were placed over each kid and they were marched out through a long, disorienting labyrinth of tunnels and stairs, to the security center way above.

The armed guards escorting Peter back up to his suite forced him to a stop midway up the twisting glass stairs and he was glad. He was crashing from the feast, big time.

Pete sensed unrest in the dark, menacing shell of the scarred tower above and gaping holes of moonlit darkness warned them away. But that wasn't why they had stopped. The guards' radios had crackled to life and they were focusing their attention to the dark, desolate atrium below.

Pete had been hoofin' it up the stairs like a homey, shoulders hunched, hands in pockets to conceal his stash, and he now slumped awkwardly against the rail in the same position. He desperately wanted to sit down but knew he'd squish everything and blow his cover. He'd have to pull himself together.

Falco had made him surrender his medal, promising to return it after his safe exit. He'd said it was for Pete's own safety and at the time Pete hadn't believed them. But now, he was glad. It would have made him an obvious target. And he had more important things to worry about.

A clamor had broken out in the overflowing park, disrupting the atrium's unsettling silence. The medieval torches had returned, erected on poles throughout the Great Lawn to provide safety illumination to those who had been quarantined. In the depths of the lights' flickering shadows, teams of guards were working to part the crowd. They were meeting resistance.

Above, cowering guests began edging out onto the tower's walkways to witness the source of the growing furor. They were soon rewarded as a small group emerged out of the forest depths, greeted by howls of fury from those held against their will around them. Guards battled to maintain clear passage.

Other guards at the fence were working to open an exit while still more were arriving from the refugee camp to provide backup support and more significant illumination. The entire length of fence was soon illuminated by small, handheld solar lamps.

"Who's that, yo?"

"White Admiral."

"A *terrorist?*"

Suddenly, Pete realized he was watching real-life fallout from his rescue. It was *him!*

Pete wanted to scream but he knew he was a hero and heroes didn't do that. Besides, there could be other terrorists around who would want nothing more than to see him gone. *Tit for tat.*

As the small group arrived at the fence, the terrorist was seamlessly handed off to still more well-armed guards for the rapid crossing to the security center. All support lighting across the length of the fence was instantly refocused on the elite group, creating a traveling pool of light in the inky blackness.

The man continued his defiant struggle against his captors, his vibrant butterfly tattoo now unmistakable for all to see.

"WHITE ADMIRAL DOWN!" he cried, once again, "*WHITE ADMIRAL DOWN!* This is a warning! A warning to you all! A very dangerous time is approaching and your government is not cooperating!"

Another struggle broke out as attempts were made to silence him, yet his voice soon resumed, stronger than ever, ringing out through the desolate shadows of the atrium, "You must make your voice heard, before it is silenced forever by the forces of darkness! Your lives are at stake! You must stand up! Stand up for freedom! And for Nelly!"

A crack rang out and he fell forward, silenced by the stock of a gun. His limp body was carried the remaining distance to the second floor security center.

A chill shook Peter's spine. Minutes earlier and Pete could have met his nemesis.

"Let's go, kid. Things are heating up. We gotta move."

"Word."

They began the second half of their journey and Pete turned his attention away from his pounding legs, his bloated stomach and his throbbing head and on to whatever it was that was happening above. Flashlights were flickering across a huge crowd. Angry voices could be heard.

The guards were whispering amongst themselves.

"Is you guys real cops yo?"

"Ex-Army, son. Part of DisasterLand's secret anti-terrorist team."

"*Army?*"

"Special Forces."

Pete gulped. "I'm glad I'm on your side. Wouldn't want to be those ugly terrorists now!"

Moments later they had hit seventeen and the source of the unrest was finally clear. Above, outside his own door two floors up, Pete saw the riotous crowd and nearly lost everything he'd eaten.

"What's goin' on yo?" Pete asked, stopping. "That's my crib!"

It didn't look good. The guards had pulled up, with one placing his hand over his earpiece to listen.

"Everything's fine," a guard said.

"It don't look *fine*, dude."

"Look, we've got to leave you here. We're needed elsewhere," the first said. Emergency."

"No way man!"

"Sorry, kid."

"But *shite*, I mean, that's what the other guys told my sister and now look, dude."

"You're a smart kid," the other said. "You'll make it."

Pete shared a reluctant high-five and the guards raced back down the stairs, tossing him a bottle of water for the road. Pete turned to face the crowd, still awkwardly trying to protect his pockets.

He inched up the stairs. The crowd was right outside his door! It didn't look fine *at all*.

And with the atrium still under martial law and transit passes required for passage, the odds of making it to the park with his sister seemed slim. But what was the alternative?

It was too dangerous to stay in the tower, that was for sure.

Besides, it wasn't like he hadn't just saved the whole place or anything. Someone owed him something for that, surely. Something besides a medal, which he didn't have anyway, and a meal and a water. Something *big*. Like a new black Escalade with mad thumpin' bass. And a free trip to the falls.

There'd be no more waiting in the queue for this dawg, Pete told himself. *It's strictly red carpet now.*

The nourishment was finally reaching his depleted cells.

He'd grab his sister and split. *Pronto.*

"They got 'em. *Inciting violence.*"

"The Beyers? You sure?" another asked.

"Dead sure. They're gone. Both of 'em. Led away in 'cuffs."

"He's right," said another, "I saw it too."

Pete was standing on the periphery of the immense crowd, the breath knocked out of him.

Both of 'em? *His mom and dad?*

But why hadn't the guards told him?

It meant he was alone. *Completely alone.*

In the center of the scrum an angry man in a stained DisasterLand tracksuit was ranting to the group gathered tightly around him. All were eyeing the guards stationed outside Pete's front door with open contempt.

While Pete stared the man continued, "*Classified information* they claimed. Imagine!"

"They're patriots the Beyers!"

"*They showed the hole!*"

"*The holes are real!*"

"Terrorists! Inside! Like *roaches*!"

"I've seen it!"

"Storm the atrium!"

Unable to take it anymore, Pete dove into the rank, sweaty crowd while trying to protect his pockets. The guests must have sniffed something, because all wanted a piece of him but Pete fought off the offenders with well-placed punches to sensitive areas.

It was an ugly scene and turning worse.

An elbow landed above his ear and a crack echoed inside his head. He winced and tears came to his eyes but he pushed on, even harder now, and with irrepressible determination he reached the front to find his doorway blanketed.

"I'm Pete Beyers, dude. I *live* here!" he screamed at the guards.

"Crime scene, kid. Away."

"*Crime scene?* You don't get it. I'm a hero. I've got a medal and everything. Where's my sister?"

"Out of here kid or you're under arrest!"

"Sarah!" Pete screamed. "Sa-*rah!*"

Still under her parent's bed, Sarah felt sure she heard Pete's calls. She had reached the culmination of her terrible, debilitating inertia with the escalating shocks of the last hour. She was now plastered to the floor, trembling.

Murmurs were ricocheting through the crowd, acknowledging Pete's presence. The crowd was pushing in, sensing the tide had turned. The guards stationed outside the door were being forced back and called for reinforcements.

Pete was trapped in the crush.

With a surge of anger Pete tore through to the guards, darting through their legs like a jackrabbit and ripping through the blanket. In the chaos, the crowd of guests rushed to follow him in.

"*The hole!*"

Inside, two workmen were busy re-sealing the wall. The master bedroom door was shut, the family's duffle bags presumably gone. Easily eluding the guards who now had their hands full with other onrushing guests, Pete raced into his own bedroom and locked the door.

He breathlessly grabbed Sarah's backpack and emptied his own pockets inside. He scoured the room for any valuables they might have missed when packing the first time.

Moments later the door came down, splintering as it hit the floor.

"Out of here kid."

"Where's my sister, yo?"

"You don't get it do you?"

"Where do you want me to go?"

"You're on your own, kid. This suite is being sealed."

Pete stood at the top of the stairs, eyeing his suite in exhausted disbelief. He just wanted to be home. Wanted this whole stupid thing to end. He was *out*.

His actions had sparked a small but threatening insurrection and DisasterLand had responded by hauling the most vocal to the refugee camp. The remaining guests had received the message loud and clear but most had voluntarily returned to their families in silence.

Yet the word had gotten out.

After their dispersal, Pete had been escorted from the suite and dropped at the top of the stairs, left to his own devices. There, he had monitored the walkways for any sign of his sister while he watched the doorway to his suite being sealed tight.

In the end, Pete knew, he had to take action. Sarah was gone, his parents were arrested and he was all alone.

He would head for the falls. There was nothing else to do, nowhere else to go.

Pete cinched the backpack tight and hit the stairs for the fifth time that day, slowly descending into the moonlit atrium to find someone. Anyone. Even Zander.

Feeling for the top secret paper in his sock, he discreetly slipped it out and stuck it inside his underwear, between his legs. No way that was leaving his person. Not while he was still alive.

Scanning the park below with longing, Pete was able to pick out what seemed like reflections of fires in the very tip of the small dome bordering the desert—the wetlands. An almost unimaginable psychological distance away.

If there was any hope, it was that Sarah had made it there. To the falls.

Stationed on the bank of the moonlit wetlands just above the river's cold rushing water, Steve received the flash of light from his right. With a respect and gravity appropriate to the situation, he flashed his own light to his comrade on the left who repeated the action. They were in position.

It was like doing the wave but with infinitely higher stakes. If the light returned, the river was secure.

Steve squeezed his tree limb powerfully. The entire length of river would soon be under full observation. They were succeeding. No matter what else happened, they would have water.

Group one had begun collecting downed limbs for weapons and firewood while hunting for terrorists' hidden arsenals. They had already awarded the largest to Steve, which he now handled somewhat clumsily with his reduced strength, relieved that no one would notice in the dark.

A small subgroup of teenagers, nicknamed *The Monkeys*, had ascended the forest trees, climbing limb to limb by flashlight in search of further agents of destruction. The forest across from Steve continued to twinkle as if illuminated by giant fireflies.

Experimental fires were being tended in the wetlands' comparative openness behind him and vessels for boiling water were being secured from anyone who had been wise enough to bring pots and pans. With tablets scarce, the necessity for more and larger pots had only strengthened the group's resolve to raid the restaurants at dawn.

Barb was a hundred feet away, tucked onto a little patch of dry land with a newfound yoga friend, a professor from Oregon whose husband was just down from Steve in the river team. Together, the girls would try to get some sleep.

Steve had convinced Barb of what he knew to be true: the kids were OK, and they were undoubtedly headed to the only safe place they knew—the park. He had enough faith in them that the morning's warning would convince them of the danger in remaining in the tower. Their best option was to stay put.

With the cold water rushing past and the sun having set hours ago, Steve began to prepare himself for the long night ahead. Relief was coming in three hours, when the next shift would take over. Then all thoughts would turn to the future—and the sunrise revolt. So far his plan had worked perfectly and now Steve had the silence, the tranquility, to organize the next step. The offensive.

It was clear. We'd have to turn up the volume in a few short hours. A day of insurgency, beginning with daybreak raids on the restaurants. By securing food and pots to boil water, we would also secure our future.

With any luck, we'd be well into the desert by noon.

A chill shot down Steve's spine as a cold wave sloshed across his feet. *War isn't pretty*, he thought, and slid further back from the river's edge.

A flash from his left interrupted his embryonic scheming. Heart swelling, he artfully flicked his light to the man on his right who undoubtedly, Steve knew, received it with pride.

That's it. *Done. Full circle.*

Steve let out a cheer which spread down the river.

With a smile, Steve opened his D-PAK to toss his light inside then thought better of it, chiding himself for his lingering naiveté. He'd need to stay on top of things. A threat to their safety could come at any moment and he'd have to be ready. He was surely the most wanted man in DisasterLand, next to the terrorists.

In the distance he could just make out the shadows of both men surrounding him. He gave each of them an exaggerated thumbs-up to compensate for the darkness. They returned it with what seemed to be broad smiles. *Teamwork.*

I need my lieutenant, Steve thought bitterly. *And Andrews has been taken. Brothers in arms, he must be freed.*

He had been wrong about Andrews, completely wrong. And after Steve's team had secured the closest restaurants, buttressing their food and water supplies, they'd mount a rescue. Jim's leadership would prove invaluable in the desert when Steve began to tire. But first they needed intelligence: *where was Andrews being held?*

Steve knew the current situation would be vastly different if Andrews was free, if his attempts to share what only they had seen had been allowed to continue. If Jim hadn't been imprisoned, they would be standing side by side along the river right now.

Even so, perhaps Jim's efforts had planted seeds which were germinating even now. Perhaps meetings just like their own were happening all over the tower and preparations to go inside and root out the terrorists were being developed.

If so, the tower must surely be close to revolt, Steve realized. After all, they were in the most dangerous position of all—their very lives depended on it.

Steve raised his eyes to the stars overhead. For a split second, he felt he could sense this revolutionary energy, the guest's determination to take responsibility for their own lives throughout all of DisasterLand. It thrilled him.

And yet if they did that, Steve suddenly realized, *the tower too would be targeting the same restaurants and for exactly the same reasons.*

In fact, if Jim had indeed told them everything—had told them the tower was rigged to blow and they somehow confirmed it—there would be a massive exodus, an influx which DisasterLand wouldn't be able to stop and his men wouldn't be able to handle.

An influx which would overpopulate the park.

And it could be coming at any moment.

Steve stretched back, placing the limb carefully behind him on the bank. It was too heavy to hold for three hours, and he couldn't risk losing it.

Another darker threat had suddenly been illuminated, a threat which Steve had overlooked: *other guests*. They were in four groups now: those within the autonomous zone, those inside the park, those in the refugee camp and those stuck in the tower. DisasterLand had managed to quarantine each group, effectively, with one exception.

Steve's group already controlled the one vital resource which all others would need very, very soon. And after daybreak, Steve's group would control the rest.

There were two options: either they begin trading water for other resources which they lacked, like food, or they would be forced to defend the river at all costs from their fellow guests. And they could find themselves overwhelmed in a hurry.

What could be traded? *Intelligence?*

Steve needed those within the tower to go *inside*. Maybe this was even what Andrews had been urging? Maybe this was what caused his arrest?

A noise in the bushes across the river brought Steve plunging back into reality. He was quick to react, swiping his light across the opposite bank ahead of him, towards the atrium.

"You got somethin'?" his neighbor called, shooting his light to meet Steve's.

"Thought I heard some rustlin'."

"I don't see nuthin'."

"Nah, me neither."

Their lights flashed off.

DisasterLand's assassins could be anywhere.

Steve took a swig of water to wet his raw throat. He'd have to keep words to a minimum the next couple of hours, until his voice was really needed.

He shook the bottle. Not much left. He'd need more before the planning session, hopefully the attempts to boil water were succeeding.

The problem, Steve realized, was if the tower went for the restaurants as well. Because then they were direct competition and his men would already be stretched thin. There were many times as many people in the tower as he had here. Many, many times.

Trades were possible, but would be difficult to leverage with their shortage in manpower. Bottom line: *they needed to get out as soon as possible.*

Raids at daybreak. Not a minute later. Had they already waited too long?

Never again, Steve thought. *Never again will I abandon responsibility for my safety so completely.*

He took another long, satisfying sip of water, finishing his bottle.

In the meantime, he told himself, *until the tower fell, resistance was resistance and it was to be applauded.* DisasterLand, and the terrorists, had to understand that lives were at stake, that guests were not going to lie down easily.

Answers would have to be forthcoming.

Steve imagined himself being led into the bowels of DisasterLand, through dark, fetid hallways filled with bound, withering employees. They would radiate a sliver of hope when Steve passed, on his way to a high-level summit with the terrorist leaders and DisasterLand's own inept management team.

He'd give the employees some sort of a sign, perhaps just a slight flick of the head. Something to show he was on his game, that the terrorists didn't have much time left.

Steve smiled. He felt good. Sharp. Tight.

He itched his cheek, his shadow long ago having turned into beard. It felt right. He imagined his new gruff self, a sort of sexy hero to the downtrodden here in the wilds of revolution. He tightened his stomach muscles, sure the tire around his waist had shrunk. Definitely.

The Revolutionary's Weight-Loss Program by Steve Beyers he told the expectant audience. *Look for it this spring.*

Swimming in nausea, Sarah had nervously crept out of the bathroom and on into the living room. As her light had fallen across the abandoned furniture and the memories flooded back, her sickness had thawed into an overwhelming sadness.

She had collapsed on the couch, sobbing.

Now, an indeterminate time later, Sarah was finally able to pick herself up and properly examine the state of both the suite and her own existence. The hole in the living room wall had been sealed by the same sort of futuristic netting they used to fix the stairs and when she arrived at her front door she found it was the same. She pushed against it with all her might but it didn't budge.

She was sealed in.

A quick recon to her bedroom revealed that her backpack had been stolen. The vibrator, the Ecstasy—her survival kit—was gone.

But under her parents' bed, she still had the family's valuables, crammed into the two large duffle bags. They wouldn't do her any good though, not unless she could get water and food.

She was trapped, her suite now a prison. Her heart was thudding. She was all alone.

Returning to the picture window, Sarah stuck her head out to help herself think. *Help Me!*, she wanted to scream, but fought the urge.

With the stars glowing, the massive glass tower rocketing beneath her and the air faintly scented with pine, her head began to clear almost instantly. In reality, the situation was far from desperate. At any moment she could open another hole into the wall and escape via the terrorist infrastructure—the duffle bags would probably be safe until she could return. Or, she could even stash them somewhere within the tower. Surely the terrorists had better things to worry about.

The problem really was, *why? Why had she been abandoned? Why had she been sealed inside?*

Then she knew. They had found the Ecstasy. It was all over and this time she was going to jail. Sarah Beyers, a drug criminal. She had been sealed in until this was all over, until the real police could come.

A cascade of thoughts buried her. She'd lose her student aid and probably flat-out have her admittance revoked—druggies didn't attend Columbia. The felony would haunt her working life as would a degree from a second-rate school, ruining her future and committing her to a life of boring friends and jobs in call centers.

A massive panic attack struck and Sarah took desperate action with superhuman strength. The next thing she knew, she was hurtling full bore at the front door, behind the battering-ram couch on its side.

The netting split open with a thunderous crack and she was free.

She stepped out into the silent atrium, tears and sweat drenching her shirt. The smell of smoke lingered in the oppressive evening air.

"Come and get me!" she screamed.

"This is sick. Don't you see how sick this is?"

"Um, kind of."

Sarah wondered, after all she'd just been through, how in the world she'd ended up sitting next to this freak.

The good news was that she was sitting next to someone and she would have thought anyone would have been just fine. But she wasn't so sure anymore.

Sarah had grabbed the duffle bags and struggled to wedge the couch into the suite's doorway on its end, a somewhat pathetic deterrent to entry. There were still no guards in sight.

Hurrying towards the stairs—she was making a final break for the falls—Sarah realized with shock that the cafés had been reopened. Amazed, desperate for company and wondering if Pete could even be waiting inside, she stepped into what days ago had been Café Dansant.

Guests had broken the charred gates and filled the burned-out space with spare furniture scavenged from ruined suites. It had rapidly filled to capacity and more guests had set to work on the second café next door. Part of a lightning renaissance of unity, she'd heard, these underground social centers were springing up all throughout the tower. Guards seemed helpless—or unwilling—to respond.

Across the peeling wall, the terrorists had spray painted:

No Nelly = No Peace

But it was crossed out, in its place:

No Nelly = No Cry

Sarah had been handed a bottle of water with vitamin powder and she chugged it, now realizing she had been dying of thirst. In the corner closest to the entrance a few guests were singing softly, recapitulating inspirational songs from past vigils and giving comfort to all. The men were gathered in the farthest corner, gesticulating passionately, faces frozen in dramatic focus.

The worried families surrounding her on the charred floor, in their filthy track suits and huddled together beneath blankets salvaged from their suites, seemed desperate for conversation, for news, for meaningful contact with others. All were yearning for an understanding of their situation yet she found their presence profoundly reassuring. Though this couldn't last, they each were not alone.

Her pulse slowed as the adrenalin dissolved. She was free.

This kid had approached her, put his arm around her, asked her if she was OK. But now, sinking onto her makeshift seat of duffle bags, she was finding him kind of weird.

"No, you don't," he continued. "You don't understand how sick this is. The wealthiest people of the wealthiest country in the world paying a fortune—more than a McDonald's worker makes in a year or enough to keep a couple thousand people alive in the global south for a year—just to experience fear, threat and scarcity? What the poor and oppressed experience every day?"

Sarah hadn't thought about it in exactly that way, but...

"Not everyone here is rich," she replied, "Some people have scholarships."

"How many? One percent? Bah..."

"OK, I mean, that sounds bad, but DisasterLand helps people. Don't you think it helps people? The people that need help the most?"

"Do you think so?"

Sarah paused, nodded. "Yes. I do. It's helped me. Already."

The kid forced a laugh. "How? Other than forcing you to go without a shower and making you stinky."

"I've learned a lot. Not about the poor or anything, but about me. Stuff I needed to know. Stuff I'll be better knowing."

"This is the sickest thing in the world this place."

"So why are you here?"

"My family made me."

"Bullshit." She stared him down. He crumbled.

"OK, I admit it. I wanted to come. To see what it was like. Who wouldn't?"

"But instead of experiencing it and abandoning yourself to it, you sit here being all pissy and not having a good time. That's just dumb."

In the resulting silence, Sarah finished her water. She couldn't believe she was having this conversation with such a freak when her whole family was missing.

The good news was, though, that she didn't seem to be under arrest. Where had her backpack gone?

"So your family has money?" Sarah asked.

He nodded. "And yours does too. We don't even know our own power."

"We won our trip from a homeless guy."

"Oh God..." he reacted as if he'd been struck. "Look, doesn't matter. I can tell by looking at you. We're the ones who have to change the world, Sarah."

"How?"

"By each following our heart. In life, in love, and in action."

That sounded pretty good to her. There was something a little scary about this guy, she realized, but at the same time it was captivating and attractive. Not dangerous scary, like Rod, but intellectually scary. This guy seemed to live on another planet and she found it fascinating, like discovering a lost tribe of natives deep in the jungle.

"So what do you propose, Chairman Mao?"

"We must move towards a cooperative worldview. Nature is not competitive. That's a myth. Nonviolence, with the exception of self-defense, is the only way forward. And I mean self-defense broadly. Very broadly."

She eyed him skeptically.

"The majority of violence is against the poor and the defenseless. Whether it's state violence, physical or emotional violence, or whatever. Seriously, Sarah."

"So you're another unibomber or something? You live in a little log shack in the mountains and eat roots?"

"You don't get it. We're on a bullet train headed off the cliff and our noses are stuck in the dining car menu."

He stared at her. She stared back.

"It's no time for complacency."

Sarah eyed an older couple, against the far wall, in matching pastel sweaters and sunglasses. They were holding hands quietly, if not stoically, and smiled at her politely. She realized she had seen almost all of these people before, somewhere, at some time during the week. She was relieved by the presence of all of them. And wished three could play.

"So you think this is a conspiracy or something, right? You don't think we're really under attack?"

"No. Of course not."

"Good." Sarah relaxed. "Good. I think so too. I need help. My dad's freaking out. What can I tell him?"

"Tell him America is an empty culture of death without joy or celebration."

"Thanks, just what he needs. You're an asshole."

"And you're stuck in a river in Egypt. *De-Nile.*"

"And you need some new jokes."

"Sarah, the American Dream is built on the backs of the slaves and the poor, of nature, of the conquered and the dead the world over. This is why we're so depressed, so medicated. Because we know this."

He paused and Sarah stared. He patted his heart. "Deep down, we know this. And we know by simply participating in this system, we're just as guilty as those who actively exploit it."

Sarah put out her hand. Enough. But he pushed on.

"This way of life, Sarah, it's going to end. Soon. It has to. Our society is collapsing in slow-motion." He paused dramatically. "If you listen carefully, you can hear it."

He stood. And with remarkable nonchalance he made his way to the exit, threading through the exhausted families who watched him with suspicion.

Good riddance, Sarah thought, but soon found herself feeling nakedly alone despite all those around her. She again examined the faces of the shell-shocked families, realizing how terribly she missed her own.

THURSDAY

Pete elbowed his way through the throng of gaping refugees and into the shadow of the medical tent's narrow entryway. He was in the center of the refugee camp, its heart and soul.

The center of the cyclone.

All across the camp rumors swirled, typhoons of breathless speculation, their effects felt as far away as the river as information spread then rapidly soured to venom.

But Pete wanted the truth.

Flitting around the guards posted at either side, Pete could make out cot after cot trailing off before him into the depths of the tent. On them, the freed hostages lay dazed, with eyes staring blankly into space, residual trauma slurring their repeated mumblings. Frayed nurses were nervously circulating.

Nearby, with two nurses at his side, lay one of the three employees who had been strapped with explosives. Pete instantly recognized his bloody shirt, the staff pass dangling from his neck.

His face was etched with tension, the obvious effect of living each minute of the last 36 hours as an infinity, on the edge. Over and over, he was endlessly repeating something but it was impossible for Pete to make out.

All along the remainder of the tent, Good Health evacuees were lying in various states of discomfort, prioritized by the degree of severity of their injuries. Families were huddled around the worst off, tending to them in ways the strained nurses never could.

Earlier, Pete had learned there had been a bomb scare last night and everyone in Good Health had been evacuated for safety. Now, it seemed, the staff could only make do with what little primitive equipment they had.

"Is anyone alive down there?" the hostage suddenly shrieked. *"Anyone at all?"*

He leapt from his cot flailing madly, the sweat pouring off him. Nurses were struggling to control him and guards rushed to their aid. While the guards restrained him, the nurses produced a syringe.

"Back, kid!"

"I ain't no stinkin' refugee dude, I'm a hero!"

"I don't care if you're Superman. Keep back!"

The guards manning the doorway closed ranks and Pete and the others surrounding him were pushed back. Reinforcements stepped in, their message clear.

The refugees scattered to spread the news but to Peter it was unnecessary: he'd heard the terrible confirmation he'd been led to expect.

He hurried away from heart of the camp and towards the forest. It was time to get serious.

Earlier, Pete's luck had run out at the base of the tower. Detained and prevented from crossing the atrium alone, he had been escorted at gunpoint to the refugee camp for admission.

Abandoning himself to hope, Pete had scoured the vast camp for Sarah, Zander or even his parents. But he had found no one, and every refugee he asked failed to recognize the descriptions.

In the end, exhausted and frustrated, he had settled at the fence's forest edge where he could glimpse bits of the Great Lawn through the gaps. Fingers tasting freedom through the Kevlar mesh, the rhymes of a thousand hip-hop lyricists cascaded through his mind, blossoming sympathies with a million injustices. A howl of rage boiled from within.

Horrific rumors were circulating furiously throughout the camp, tales portraying the employees' desperate plight below, reinforcing a dark reality that could no longer be ignored.

In an attempt to glean the truth, Pete had gone to the heart of the matter.

And once again, he'd come away the winner.

Pete again neared the fence and all around him chants were rising, the refugees growing more and more frustrated with the primitive conditions and their own helplessness.

Knowledge had spread, impossible for the guards to conceal: the river had been taken by a militia and declared an independent, autonomous zone.

Now, the refugees wanted to follow.

In the face of the very real threat they all faced, there was simply no way the guards would be able to hold them back.

Soon, the refugees inside were pushing, sympathetic guests outside pulling, and all were chanting in time with the rocking fence.

"Down—Down—Down!"

With every cycle, the arc grew wider, the fence coming ever-closer to the ground. The refugees tasted a freedom that only grew more sweet.

Seconds after the clock struck midnight, a unified cry of liberation arose from the entire Great Lawn. The interior fence had fallen: DisasterLand's Iron Curtain had come down.

The refugees were free!

Pete cinched up his backpack.

One of the first over, he kicked an upended post for good luck before leaping past the triumphant revelers and disappearing into the ecstatic crowd now rushing towards the river.

"Our defense has been firmly established. Now it's time for offense. We escalate! *Escalate the resistance!*" Steve yelled, to thunderous applause.

He was briefing his commandos, nervously assembled around a roaring bonfire deep in the heart of the wetlands. Updates of the park's worsening security situation were being relayed from distant outposts at the forest edge of the Great Lawn. Reinforcements had already been preemptively dispatched to hold the river.

"We cannot allow DisasterLand to become an extermination camp. We must break out and take our chances in the desert. But to do that we need health. We need food and water. At daybreak, we must secure the restaurants for our own use!"

"How do we know that employees haven't already raided them?" one commando asked. "Or the terrorists!"

"If we've got it bad," Steve growled, "be assured the employees have it worse. I can guarantee you, those left are locked up—or dead! And that's why there's been no official response. It's as simple as that. They're incapacitated."

Skepticism lingered and Steve raised his voice, "Don't you understand? What better place to attack than a place where the guests thought they'd be under attack? Don't you see the genius? The terrorists counted on cooperation, on placidity. On us sitting back and enjoying it!

"DisasterLand is a symbol of America," he continued, "Of capitalism, of the freedom of entertainment. It's the hottest thing going on this back-assward planet and the terrorists are out to get it!

"Bottom line: you're either with us or against us. If you don't participate, you don't share in the spoils. No one here gets a free ride," Steve sneered.

Above all, this was about sacrifice. Those who sacrificed would be the ones rewarded. If we lost a couple of cowards along the way, we lost a couple of cowards.

It only meant more for us.

"We have two urgent tasks ahead. One is education. The people in the tower must understand their vulnerability. Soon, I will personally brief the messengers who will set forth at first light. They will head to the tower and spread our message. *They will show the holes!*

"By the time the tower erupts in revolt, our mission here will be complete and we will be on to our main goal: breaking free. By that point, the guards will be too overwhelmed to stop us. The tower will run interference for our escape."

Steve straightened as two strangers approached, one smaller than the other. Three quick flashes of the larger one's flashlight indicated their allegiance. *News from the front.*

"Second, we must immediately and urgently begin construction of the ladder with the limbs that have been collected. It is the linchpin of our success. Without the ladder, we are guaranteed to fail!"

Steve assessed the two rapidly approaching shadows through narrowed eyes, "The raid will happen at first light, in a three-pronged attack. A-Team will use the ladder to ram the fence, freeing B-Team to ascend to the second floor walkway where they'll hit the restaurants above. A-Team will retreat with the ladder, to safety, while C-Team hits Del Sol, hard. *It's a two-front war, men. As above, so below.* A-Team will remain on standby until the mission is complete."

Steve paused, eyeing each of his supporters in turn. Several still remained skeptical.

"The fallout is certain to be chaos but out of that chaos, order will follow. Guards will crumble, falling like dominos. They'll drop their weapons at the first whiff of trouble."

"DJ!"

Steve flipped his light on the smaller one and stumbled. *Spike!*

He anxiously flipped his light to the larger visitor, expecting Sarah. It wasn't.

"The Camp has fallen, sir. Refugees are swarming the clearing!"

The escort extended a fist over his head in solidarity, then turned and raced back to his watch down the trail.

Pete ran to his father and they hugged as the group applauded.

"Where's Sarah?" Steve asked.

Pete's eyes were fierce, "If she's not here, they got her, DJ. Sarah's gone."

Pete looked out, over the gathering.

"The *terrorists*?!" Steve turned to the horrified faces of those assembled.

"I don't know, DJ. But the guards sealed the hole and our whole suite. And the Andrews have been arrested!"

"*I knew it!*"

"He was in our room, DJ! *Showing the hole.*"

"*What did I tell you?*" Steve growled to his followers, "That's a man who won't roll over. And they've got him. We've each got to be twice as strong! Twice as vigilant!"

The venom was back, "We'll need intelligence. *Where is he being held?* Beaten guards may be in a mood to talk if we offer them safe passage out of this mess!"

"DJ! It's bad, real bad. I've been in the camp. The employees are in real trouble down there, DJ. Real trouble. The hostages said so!"

Steve nodded to his commandos, his face scrunched in punctuation.

He turned back to Pete, whispering, "Maria came?"

"No, why, DJ?"

Steve couldn't continue. He smelled *food*. "Another failure!" he huffed loudly. "The infrastructure's crumbled!"

"It's bad, DJ. Something's gonna happen, people are really angry. The whole park is open and refugees are coming this way!"

"Let's spread the word, men, rouse the defenses!"

Distant shouting was already clouding the air.

"I've got this, DJ!" Pete nervously pulled the sweaty, folded paper from inside his pants. Steve grabbed it.

"Where'd you get this?"

Steve found himself staring at the hand-drawn sketches dated only a few short hours ago. *WANTED* stood out, just above the time, in quick dark strokes. There was no indication of its authenticity.

Pete wanted to spill the whole story, how he had stopped someone from poisoning the river and how he was a hero. How he had just eaten a huge meal and how Candy had kissed him on the lips and her boobs had brushed his arm. But he couldn't. He was sworn to secrecy and they had kept his medal to make sure.

He looked out at the expectant faces...

"A guard slipped it to me, DJ. He told me to give it to you! I *swear!*"

Steve shoved the paper towards the group who was rising to meet him.

"Look!" he screamed, *"The face of the enemy! Now let's get to work!"*

Revolution was certainly at hand.

Andrews, Steve thought. *This one's for Jimmy.*

"Come on, Spikers, let's go find your mom. Without Sarah, she'll be sick."

Hidden deep in the wetlands, Steve and Barb were devouring the meal Pete had brought for them under the guise of going to relieve themselves. There was no way Steve was sharing any of it. His son had brought it for *them*—*el capitán*—not a bunch of namby-pamby strangers.

I didn't care where my son had obtained his intelligence. It had done the trick, solidifying people's trust in their leader before the difficult storm ahead. His food had added energy at a critical moment. In the years to come, Spike's contribution could be remembered as the tipping point from which victory had been secured. And Spike?

An absolute hero.

Steve finished off the last bit of grilled steak and vegetables and fell back on the soft earth in a daze, after drowning the meal in the few gulps of purified water that Pete had brought with him.

In the distance, along the river's edge, they could make out the searchlights of the emergency team. The team had set out to match the faces of those guarding the river to Pete's paper. If there was any question, shirts would have to be raised.

"Wake me in two hours," Steve mumbled, exhaustion already overtaking him.

"DJ, you can't! Not now! It's just beginning!"

But Steve could not longer fight the darkness. This would be the biggest day of their lives, that was certain, and he needed to be as fresh as possible. Steve let himself go.

A tenth-of-a-second could literally be the difference between life and death.

Knowledge is spreading. The endgame is nearing. And inside is where the answers lie.

"Inside is where the answers lie," Steve mumbled.

Barb joined him on the dirt, with Sarah's backpack a pillow. She had wanted to keep watch, to let her remarkable son get some well-earned rest, but Pete wouldn't allow it. He knew he wasn't staying, and he didn't want any additional guilt involved.

Soon, Barb too was drifting off, despite Sarah's capture. She would dedicate herself solely to finding Sarah upon waking. But right now, like this, she knew she was useless.

Flashlight beams continued to dance in the distance while Peter watched the upside-down reflections of bonfires in the dome overhead.

He felt confident Sarah had been arrested along with the Andrews. The man on the walkway had definitely said *both*, not *all*, but there was simply nowhere else she could be.

Unless...

Unless the terrorists had taken her, surreptitiously, via the hole. That could explain why it was sealed—if the guards really cared.

It didn't matter. With his dad needed elsewhere, it was going to be up to Peter to find her. And he'd have to go inside. His dad was right: no matter what, that's where the secrets were.

It would all be over soon, Pete knew. It had to be. And now was time to act.

Pete leaned back, listening to his parents' increasingly regular breathing. Soon he too was fading, fading into the netherworld of dreams.

Images flooded his exhausted consciousness as worlds swept over him, phosphorescent lands of lost battles he'd waged against electronic demons. Mystical passageways, castles, wastelands and tree cities he had negotiated in stealth, with an agenda. An agenda others wanted stopped.

Pete's eyes flicked open.

He bolted up, shook himself awake.

Yes. He just had to find the Easter Egg.

Pete Beyers would *hack DisasterLand.*

Lean and mean, Pete had left Sarah's backpack under his mom's sleeping head. Wherever he was going, the weight would only slow him down.

It was still well before sunrise when Pete cautiously made his way back to the swimming hole. Sensing the lookouts atop the spring, Pete flipped off his light and carefully slipped off the trail and into the reedy river bank to think.

The security team had rotated shifts—or at least his contacts were gone—and he didn't want trouble. He certainly didn't want to be sent back but he also didn't want to be caught attempting an unauthorized crossing.

He had already stolen a look at the team constructing the ladder, leaving him confident for the future both in terms of his own ability to remain unseen and in the promise of the ladder itself. Even from a distance, it appeared a marvel of rough hewn craftsmanship, a harkening back to times Pete didn't know still existed. At over twenty feet long and growing, it would serve them well. His dad would be proud.

He desperately wanted to participate in the offensive which left him only a couple of hours for his own lone mission. A couple of hours to get out of the park, into the atrium, back to the tower and down. *Inside.*

But just getting across the atrium seemed an impossible task. If worse came to worse, he'd have to pull rank. His problems would begin well before that, however.

On the beach, the mob continued to grow. Word of the secret falls had spread. With the militia effectively denying the refugees passage across the river, tensions seemed to be rising fast.

His dad was right. Things couldn't last. There simply wasn't enough for everyone.

Pete would play it cool. He emerged from the reeds and flipped on his light to illuminate his own face as he approached the closest militia member.

"Yo," Pete called, and the guy turned, swinging his light into Pete's eyes, blinding him.

"It's me, Pete Beyers. I'm on an errand for my dad, *Commandante* Steve. I gotta cross the river dude."

The flashlight's glare dropped away. "Go on, kid."

On the bank, Pete stripped to his underwear and wrapped his tracksuit tightly into a ball. He slipped into the crisp, dark waters, clothes above him in his outstretched hands. He waded across quickly, tracked by the lights of nearby *comrades.*

Pete emerged from the river into the shadows of the opposite bank, downstream from the beach. The lights quickly cut behind him to conceal the sentinel's positions.

He dressed, then hurriedly picked his way to the beach, past the heated arguments and active prayer circles and on up to the trail. Families were huddled together at the forest edge, sleeping.

Pete approached the final militia outpost at the trailhead.

"Yo," Pete said.

"You're cool," the leader said. "Password back is *d-day.*"

"*D-day?*"

"Quiet kid, unless you want a riot on your hands."

"Gotcha bro."

Pete hurried on, into the dark, fragrant forest.

Hurrying on along the familiar main trail back to the atrium with legs protesting, Pete's worst fears were confirmed: increasingly, homeless families were clogging the sides of the trail and impeding his progress. Surely, by daybreak, passage would be difficult if not impossible. At the very least, he would be watched.

It was time to consider his next move. There was the ruined village, he knew, and the bomb craters. Some of the foundations had surely been damaged and probably lay completely unexplored. Even if the bombs had been carefully controlled, there would be unintended consequences. And maybe a way inside.

It was a shortcut he'd have to consider. There was no way he could make it back up to nineteen—that was clear—so at the very least he'd have to find a sympathetic family lower in the tower who would allow him to open a hole. *Was that even possible?*

And how would he cross the atrium?

He wished himself back inside *Ghost*, invisible and able to fly.

There was also the fire-damaged restaurant on the atrium's periphery. But again, how to get past the guards?

His mind whirred away with social engineering scenarios, attempts to construct useful arguments to gain him passage.

Topping the hill, Pete paused to lean against the skeleton of a ransacked bench, the wood long ago gathered for fires—or weapons. He would catch his breath and assess his next move.

While most of DisasterLand tried to sleep, Pete felt solid, *energized*, as if the sleeping bodies around him were renewing his own.

If *Ghost* was working, he realized, it meant surveillance was happening—or could be happening, with generators—no matter what Falco had said. Which meant that someone could be *allowing* him to continue.

What if DisasterLand *knew*? What if someone, somewhere, was *letting him do this*?

What if they knew he was their best hope against the terrorists?!

Maybe they had *allowed* the fence to come down to free *him*!

The guards may not matter at all, Pete realized. *There's a whole other layer, a surveillance master computer, ticking away in the background, unseen by the terrorists, sealed off in a secure area.*

Its commander may or may not be Falco. But, Peter imagined, this master computer liked him.

A warm glow of invincibility seemed to spread out around him as he understood: ways to succeed were hidden all around him. He just had to be brave.

"*Peter!*"

He spun. "*Sarah?*"

There she was, slogging up the hill!

"I looked everywhere for you!" Sarah said, dropping the duffle bags heavily onto the trail.

"Me too! I thought the terrorists got you!"

Pete hurried to her and they hugged. Sarah squeezed him.

"Careful, Spanks. I'm touching cloth. I gotta lose some dirt!"

Sarah slapped him.

This was his way of greeting her? She didn't understand boys and hoped she never would. If that happened, she thought, it meant that something was terribly wrong.

"Where's mom and dad?"

"Sleeping in the wetlands."

"You *left* them?"

"I'm going inside, DJ. For the answer."

"I'll go with you."

"Really?" Pete stared into her eyes. She meant it.

"OK," Pete said. "*Wicked.*"

Now he had a team. *Team Beyers.*

Sarah wasn't Zander, that's for sure, but she was another set of eyes, another set of ears. Most importantly, she was on his side. Zander would only try to steal his thunder.

Now he would tend to more pressing matters.

"OK, let's roll Spanks. But I'm serious. Where's the closest bathroom?"

"You don't want to Peter, really. I've been in three of them. They're horrible. People are really mad."

"Really?"

"You should go in the woods."

"It's number two, Spanks."

"Bury it."

Pete's eyes dropped. "OK, DJ. Wait right here by this bench."

Scurrying into the woods with his light, Pete carefully edged down the gentle slope. He placed himself as far from the trails as possible in every direction and dug himself a little hole in the damp earth with a stick. He squatted.

Pete saw himself as a Kentucky Derby thoroughbred before the race, losing all unnecessary weight: the true sign of a champion. And it was there, crouched precipitously with weight properly dispensed with, that Pete had his breakthrough.

Ahead of him was the largest tree he had seen in the park. And the trunk, it seemed, was *hollow.*

Pete pulled the small trapdoor shut over his head, enclosing them in inky darkness. A firm click resonated through the cramped space and his heart dropped. Panicking, Pete tried to push the door back up—without success.

They were locked inside.

Below, Sarah flipped on her light, illuminating the way for Peter as he cautiously descended the ladder. It dropped down through a tight passage which opened out almost twenty feet below, into a large room.

Pete had retrieved Sarah from the trail, excitedly dragging her into the woods without explanation and proceeding with a fierce determination that she had never seen. Not surprisingly, she was worried.

But when her eyes had landed on the tree, she agreed something about it was not right. It was too big, the bloated gap in its hollow trunk too ancient. Then Pete had showed her the trapdoor, hidden under a thin layer of debris.

They had dropped one bag then the other, and when there had been no reaction Sarah had cautiously followed.

Now, standing safely at the foot of the ladder, they breathlessly assessed the space around them. It was deserted. An overhead light was off and there was no switch anywhere that either of them could see.

"Holy shit Spanks," Pete finally whispered.

"Yeah."

Sarah hadn't moved much beyond that herself.

"You heard that hunh? The trapdoor? It's locked."

Sarah nodded, "I guess we keep going."

The ladder had dropped them into a comfortable but compact oddly-shaped room with a utilitarian concrete floor. Several couches and tables were scattered throughout as if they'd been left in a hurry.

Pete swallowed. "I bet this is for the actors, DJ!"

The room was shaped like a piece of pie with its tip removed. Three of the walls had doors but all were closed—one on the tip and two on the sides. The outer wall had no door and seemed to possibly match the dome above in terms of curvature.

Was the whole park hollow underneath? Or even all of DisasterLand?

Their lights searched the fourth wall and another light shot back. Startled, they froze, but it was only the reflection from a mirror. Pete stepped closer, with Sarah following. They peered at themselves, instantly wishing they hadn't.

Next to the mirror, a large DisasterLand safety notice was hung:

Think and Act!

It was only the first of dozens they would see throughout the labyrinth:

Emergency: hit location beeper—
Aid in 60 seconds!

DL Works for YOU!

Pete removed the poster from the wall and rolled it up carefully. Sarah stared. "eBay, Spanks. If I can smuggle some of these out I'll be *cakin'*."

Scattered on one of the tables was a small script, a set of actors' sides. Certain lines and cues had been highlighted.

It was from *Monday. Days ago.*

Creeped out, Sarah gently put her finger to mouth. They listened, hearts thumping, minds racing, for what seemed an eternity. But there was nothing. No sound at all.

She squeezed Pete's hand and he wiped his forehead. They were both dripping with sweat. It was *hot.*

No lights, no AC. And no-*body.*

Pete picked up the sides and slowly began to flip through them, heart still pounding.

"What's it say?" Sarah whispered.

"DJ, this isn't what happened at all!" Pete's eyes rose to meet her hers and she had to look away. He handed her the scenes. "It's all about the fashionistas!"

Her eyes teared. "I'm..." she started, but stopped herself. She wanted to say she was scared but it seemed stupid. *Of course* she was. And he was too. They had to move beyond it.

Peter stepped towards the door in the room's tip and held his breath, trying the handle. It turned. He gently cracked it open but Sarah interrupted.

"Wait... I can't carry these bags anymore, Peter."

"Then let's ditch the weight."

"But it's all we have. Mom and dad will..."

"It's just *stuff* Spanks! We'll buy more!"

"It's mom's jewelry and everything..."

"OK, we'll put what we can in our pockets. Come on!"

Sarah nodded, silently. They raided the bags, finally stashing what they couldn't pocket under a prominent couch. Pete scattered the cushions on the floor to mark their secret.

"OK, lights out," Pete whispered, and they did, in unison.

"Remember, there's no hurry," Pete continued. "We take our time. We know where we are at all times. *We don't get lost.*"

Sarah agreed. "Patience."

"And if we go down, we go down together."

They hit fists and Peter opened the door. Darkness confronted them and they slipped out to wait in silence while their eyes adjusted.

Unable to stand it any longer, Sarah finally flipped on her light. They were in a wide, curved hallway, and across from them, in exactly the same place, stood an identical door. To either side of them, the hallway circled around out of sight. Identical doors were spaced across from each other, as far as they could see.

It was now clear to them that they were in the green rooms, the actor's staging areas, and that these were deserted. Utterly and completely deserted. Dead, silent, and spooky.

"This place should be hoppin', yo."

Sarah nodded, gravely. "So what are we looking for?" she whispered.

"Anything. A sign. If there's lights on, we know there's electricity. If we hear people working, we know this is all fake. That it's part of the show."

"I hope we find one. A sign."

"Me too."

Pete stepped across the hallway, trying the handle of the opposite door. It turned. Pete threw the door open, shining his light inside.

They stepped cautiously into a very large circular room, an office or a command center. Desks lined the walls, directors chairs were tipped over. There was a water dispenser, even a shelf of snacks—but all had been ransacked. The hook to a fire extinguisher hung empty on the wall.

Headsets and radios had been discarded, the batteries dead. More sides were scattered about, all from Monday. Frustrated, Pete stuck his finger confidently in an electrical outlet. Nothing.

Sarah jumped back, yelping. Just in front of her lay a small pool of dried blood.

Pete began to examine the desks, the drawers, and soon he whispered excitedly to Sarah—he had found a small bottle of water.

Together, they finished it off but it did little to quell their thirst. Finding nothing more, they reluctantly retreated back out, into the hallway.

"Let's leave something here Spanks, so we don't get lost. It's really weird here. It all looks the same."

"OK," she breathed. She hurried back in and grabbed a set of sides.

They started around the hallway, shoes squeaking softly on the concrete as the sweat dripped from their soaked bodies. Identical sets of doors endlessly surrounded them, appearing ominous—not gateways to freedom, but rather barricades guarding dark secrets. Each, they discovered, was discreetly labeled with a letter and a number.

They continued circling around, and before they returned to the discarded sides they came to another hallway, leading out away from the command center. Wider and longer, it literally seemed to stretch away into infinity.

"The fountain," Sarah said. "I bet it leads to the fountain."

"Ladies and Gentlemen, Steve Beyers, tonight's *American Hero!*"

Theme music swelled and the studio audience roared.

Steve gave them an appreciative thumbs-up and a wink as he appeared from behind the curtain and slowly made his way across the stage. The cut over his eye had been stitched, a thin white strip of surgical tape the only remaining evidence of his now-famous struggle.

Barb had tried to shield him from the media, but it had proven impossible. His exclusive appearance was set to break all records. Advertisers were wetting themselves and thirty-second slots were going at twice the Superbowl rates.

Yet Steve wasn't nervous. He was in the eye of the hurricane.

Steve hiked up his shiny new DisasterLand track pants and took his place next to the prime-time host. Robotic cameras silently tracked in for close-ups.

"Welcome to the show, Mr. Beyers."

"Call me Steve."

"Look, everyone on the planet knows the story, Steve—at least everyone who matters—so let's cut to the chase. Tell us, how bad did it really get in there?"

Steve woke, shaking off the morning chill. Over the mountains in the East the sky was lightening, imperceptibly.

Why hadn't Pete woken him up?

Steve suddenly leapt to his feet, heart racing.

"Pete's gone!" Steve gasped. *"Spike!"* he called. *"Spike!"*

Barb rolled over, groggily, "Humm?"

"Honey, I told Pete to wake me in two hours and *he's gone.*"

"I..."

"I'm late Barb, Jesus I'm late for the offensive!"

Steve hurled himself towards the trail and disappeared, leaving Barb completely alone.

"Let's go boys!" he screamed, arriving in the wetlands shaken and panting. His comrades were staring out of the dome, the ladder resting on the ground between them, "My son's gone! I've looked everywhere. But it's time. *It's time boys!*"

Silently, one man pointed into the sky behind him. Steve turned.

The first faint glimmers of sunlight had revealed a large black helicopter hovering ominously in the sky over DisasterLand, motionless except for the silent pulse of its massive blades.

Steve eyed the copter with a paralyzing mix of wonder and suspicion, of hope and ultimately of fear. He turned to examine the frozen faces of the men around him, their eyes vibrating with what seemed like animal terror.

It was a military 'copter, that much was clear. But what the hell was it doing here? *What was its significance?* The tone was undeniably menacing, rescue surely an early-morning fantasy.

"Identify: Friend or Foe!" someone shouted.

"Easy boys. Easy... let's take this slow," Steve growled.

It was top of the ninth, Steve told the studio audience. *And we were standing on the precipice between salvation and destruction.*

It was there. Unbelievably, startlingly, devastatingly *right there.* One hundred yards from the dome and directly in front of them, the 'copter was frozen, hovering a few dozen feet off the desert. Sand was being kicked up, scrub tossed about.

Within the 'copter's darkly tinted bubble, Steve could make out goggled faces, the occupants insect-like.

Lenses, cameras, everywhere. Watching them. Watching *him*.

At the edge of the dome, Steve's small group and the powerful machine faced off.

Suddenly, it was all clear: even in the dim light, the movements of Steve's team had been as obvious to the 'copter's night-vision technology as they were at high noon—if not more so. The 'copter had watched everything, had observed all their plans for as long as it had wished.

But what did it mean?

"*The President!*" someone screamed.

"What?"

"In the 'copter! *The President!*"

Caught without his binoculars, Steve cursed his lack of foresight. He could make no clear call.

But *The President?*

"Yes! *He's there!*" others cried.

And Steve broke out in an icy sweat.

The 'copter began rising. It circled the park once, almost lackadaisically, then soared up towards the main atrium and disappeared from sight, leaving a void of infinite depth in its wake.

Steve and his men reeled from the complex and bitter cocktail of awe, terror and self-importance.

What the hell was going on here?

Then, from the Great Lawn, a wall of naked, raw screams of such incendiary force that everyone and everything was smothered. DisasterLand's twin domes had suddenly become terrifying echo-chambers of fear, of berserk desperation, of mindless hope. A wave of adrenalin crashed over DisasterLand like the concussion from a bomb.

Steve eyed the ladder resting uselessly at their feet, admiring the solid craftsmanship and the raw freedom it represented. It had been perfect. Yet from inside the 'copter, Steve's men must have looked like stone-age primitives with their farcical wooden tool.

The helicopter's effect on their emotional landscape had been profoundly destabilizing. His men had been left at sea.

The seconds pounded by.

In the distance, the screaming had only increased in volume. *The masses were waking.* Steve imagined anxious guests rushing out from every suite, every corner of the atrium, every crevasse of the park to get a glimpse of the awe-inspiring visitor.

The pre-dawn haze within Steve's mind was burning off with the extremity of the moment and a terrible realization was made: *their plans were wasted*.

The hours of planning, of preparation... gone in a flash. They had been minutes away from the attack, just waiting for the final word from their forward scout.

And now?

They would never reach the second floor, let alone make it to Del Sol. Their path was clogged, coagulated, gummed-up. With the atrium filled, Steve's men would never have a chance. It was mob rule.

Steve's stomach kicked up and his blood went sour. He spun and violently vomited onto the dry dirt. It was the undigested remains of the meal hours ago, and it frightened him. His body had simply ceased to function.

"Hey Beyers, what is that—*fajitas?*"

I had lost valuable nutrients. Worse yet, I had blown the trust of my men. It was the worst possible thing I could have done. I had to act quickly.

"A gift!" Steve said, whisking the chunks off his chin with his sleeve. "From my wife!"

His men looked on angrily. But froze.

A chant had arisen from the atrium, a chant of such heartbreaking desperation that many of Steve's men were frozen helplessly in place.

"*Help—us!—Help—us!—Help—us!*"

The atrium was now surely packed, the Great Lawn and the walkways filled. The voices of hundreds, in unison, were shaking the building to its emotional foundation.

"Men," Steve said, turning and meeting their eyes. "We have one chance. We've got to break the glass while the 'copter's still here. Whatever is happening, we will be free. We'll stand a chance. Our fates will be up to us."

"Give us twenty, Beyers. We need time to collect our families."

Families.

Steve staggered, remembering he had left Barb under their tree in a near-catatonic state. *Left her.* Just ran away, leaving her to search for his son and daughter alone. *For his own missing children.*

If he couldn't take care of his family, how the hell was he expecting to take care of the men now surrounding him? And *their* families?

Of them all, he needed the most time, time to search for his children. It could cost them their lives, but there was no alternative.

"We'll stow the ladder, boys. Return in thirty," he said, taking a deep breath. "Gather your families, your friends, your belongings. Stock up on water and what you'll need to survive in the desert. Let the men at the river know what's happening. We'll all go together, we'll share what we've got. We're making a break, boys, but in the meantime we keep the river at all costs. If we lose the river, we lose everything."

"We're gonna make it Steve," one of the men said.

"Of course we will, son. Of course we will."

Steve was staring at the ground, lost in thought, the men around him anticipating the gravity of his upcoming summary, "We're going to pull the ripcord boys and see where we land. If any of you have family in the tower you better get them out any way you can. Anything could happen here, boys, anything."

The men somberly hid the ladder by the dome's edge and hurried away to collect their families while Steve started down the trail back to Barb. He imagined her there, with Peter and Sarah, all awaiting his return. They'd be packed, raring to go, ready to face whatever challenges were to come.

But he knew it was a fantasy. In fact, he'd be lucky if Barb was there at all. She had probably given up on him long ago.

His mind spiraled down viciously as his mental house of cards collapsed. In his insanity, in his stupidity, he had sacrificed his family's safety for... *for what?*

Elektra stared through bleary eyes at the helicopter's live feed, pensively sipping her double cappuccino. Dressed in her DisasterLand tracksuit and Expos hat, she was enjoying a treat she allowed herself on special occasions or when absolutely necessary.

This was both.

On the monitors above, the first rays of the sun had struck the atrium, illuminating the guests' poignant cries for aid with a stark texture that raised the composition to the level of art. A supreme satisfaction spread over her, warming her as if by the sun itself.

She turned to the security team behind her and shared a wink.

Throughout the night a subtle but profound change had occurred on the bridge, with the theatrical replaced by the practical. The dreamers had given way to the pragmatists, firmly grounded in the business of danger.

The writers, the effects crews, hair and make-up—all were gone and more. They would no longer be of any help here, those whose services were still required had spread out to all corners, on call for the show's finale.

The stage had literally been set, the script had hit perpetual motion and the final culmination was now inevitable. It was just a matter of when.

In their place, DisasterLand's security and safety elites had set up shop on the mount's couches, now in constant radio contact with their assistants hidden on the floor. Techs had assembled the necessary mobile infrastructure around them, with laptops, radios and additional monitors spread across the coffee tables. The laptops were highlighting the latest updates to the guest database, cross-indexed with the guests' full criminal records obtained prior to entrance.

Hot guests, those highest at risk for causing real harm either because of their performance during the week or from earlier flags in their outside record, had been singled out and were now being targeted for live surveillance—courtesy of the opening night's dust which still allowed tracking of almost every guest even though the signals had weakened considerably.

Dedicated cameras would follow these guests through to the script's resolution, both for safety and, obviously, for entertainment. Anything could happen after all, and serious trouble could be only moments away. Then again, so could laughs. Or tears.

If necessary, reinforcement guards were staged all along the periphery of the atrium, unseen inside the security center and darkened bars and restaurants where the Feed and radio traffic was keeping them updated. Developments would be minute-by-minute from here on out and guest safety was paramount. Seconds counted.

Additionally, teams of guards were surreptitiously sweeping the crowd with metal detectors and offending objects were being confiscated as necessary.

Elektra, meanwhile, would be piloting the plot's trajectory, ensuring it moved ahead at a clip that both maintained tension and also the safety and security of the guests. At least, as much as was possible.

To that end, the three breakaway teams descending the interior tower and the Beyers' kids already well into the labyrinth were also being monitored live. One of the four seemed destined to succeed, and though nothing was guaranteed and nothing could be taken for granted, it did bode well.

Elektra took another long sip of her coffee and rubbed her eyes. An uneasiness was growing inside of her.

She felt a hand on her shoulder. It squeezed.

"How are you holding up?"

It was Shae.

"Something doesn't feel right."

"That's called letting go."

Elektra laughed. Shae was right, in a way. From here on out, she had very little control over specifics. The important shots would be called largely by the guests themselves and from those around her.

"Everything's going too well, Shae. It's scaring the hell out of me."

"Have faith, Elektra. We're professionals now. These things happen."

He flashed a smile and returned to his security team, while Elektra called for a wide surveillance panorama of the entire guest space.

Footage from the many re-opened cafés showed most of them deserted, yet only an hour ago they had been well beyond capacity with overwhelmed families.

The first had been opened last night on eleven by agent provocateurs, operatives for DisasterLand, but according to plan copy-cat guests had reopened their own on almost every floor, forming perfect release valves for families lost in the eddies. In essence, they were islands to re-enforce community and they had worked marvelously—taking a little bit of the edge off the guests' collective anguish while buying a bit of time and reducing the threat.

One last master touch from the psychologists.

Elektra called for a return to the 'copter's feed. They were getting close-ups now, frightened families cowering in dazed and hopeful disbelief.

Guests were buying it hook, line and sinker and the 'copter's gleeful pilot was rubbing it in their awed faces. Elektra smiled. Shae was right—she would try to enjoy it while she could.

Tomorrow would undoubtedly be melancholy, Friday mornings after a show always were. The inevitable loss of the edge, the responsibility, the living in the moment that the live show produced resulted in a tremendous sense of displacement, even loss. At that point they were all adrenalin junkies without a fix and things tended to get tense. After this show they'd have to wait over a month for next one, making the whole thing even more extreme.

Yes, she would enjoy it while she could.

Just after dawn, Barb placed the second pill back in the lip-gloss tube. She had decided to save it for later, just in case the first didn't cut it. It almost never did, but she always played it conservatively with medication.

She took a quick sip of water to remove the oddly bitter taste. Barb couldn't believe her luck, finding two aspirin in Sarah's backpack. She had ransacked the pack desperately in the bleak hope she would find something, anything. And she did.

Now that's Karma, Barb told herself.

But by the time Steve arrived thirty minutes later, Barb was convinced that she was dying. Literally. And, to Steve, she looked like it: hyper-ventilating, face flushed, her pupils dilated and her eyes bulging.

Steve was desperately worried and wanted to find a doctor but Barb wouldn't let him leave her side. The 'copter's arrival had nearly finished her off psychologically and she wasn't losing him again. Especially now.

The pain in Steve's heart was overwhelming and he wanted to end it all. All of this stupidity, this pain he was causing his family, and all in the name of doing good. What an absolute colossal fool he was.

Yes, he thought, *if Barb dies I'll go right after her. The kids will be fine. They'll have their pick of four lovely grandparents.*

Yet looking down again at Barb's disturbed face, he decided that he had to leave her to find help. He couldn't let her die, couldn't orphan the kids. He was being a stupid, sentimental idiot.

Barb took a big breath, staring at Steve. "Always frowning," she said, and lay back.

Then, remarkably, she began giggling. Uncontrollably.

Steve stared at her in shock.

"*Oh... my... God...*" she giggled.

Steve ducked in, closer. He took her hand. "Honey, what's going on? What's wrong?"

She shook her head, now red-faced, and continued giggling... Eventually, Barb managed to wipe the tears from her eyes with her free hand and giggle even harder.

"What's so funny?" Steve asked.

"Slippery," she asserted, giggling.

"Slippery?" he took her hand. Grimaced.

Barb cracked up.

Several long minutes passed as she struggled to regain her composure. Every time she looked at Steve his scowl seemed ever-more intense and ever-more ridiculous.

"Barb, please," he said, finally. "Stop laughing or I'm leaving!"

"I'm... sorry... honey. I just..." She faded away. Then giggled. She tried to swallow the giggles back, her free hand flapping in the air like an injured wing.

"You just... what?!"

"I just... feel... really weird. Funny," Barb giggled. "I feel... *funny*."

At this, Barb broke into waves of rippling, unstoppable laughter.

Steve eyed her curiously. Despite the obvious levity, she seemed in a vague state of discomfort.

"Should I take you to the Camp?" he asked. *Had she had a stroke?*

Barb struggled to collect herself, then lost herself in the dome's infinite geometry above. Finding herself again, she slowly pawed her way into a sitting position.

"Wow..." She placed her legs into half-lotus, breathed deeply for several long, extended minutes. "I don't think that was aspirin..." she said, finally.

"What do you mean?" Steve turned, his mind racing. "Are you out of your mind?"

"Yes. Yes, exactly."

Steve stared.

"I think it's some sort of drug," Barb said.

"Oh Lord..."

His head was spinning. A *DRUG*? From *where*?

She continued, under her breath, "You know, there's another one..."

Barb reached back, motioning to Sarah's backpack. Steve carefully removed the remaining pill from the tube and flipped it over, revealing a tiny, perfectly-formed dolphin.

"It's a dolphin," Steve said.

"A dolphin? What's that mean?"

"Well, I don't think Eli Lilly puts dolphins on their aspirin."

"It's a drug."

"It's a drug."

Steve stood. "I'll go get some help. You wait here."

She grabbed his leg. "No, don't go." She caught herself. "I mean... It's OK. I think I'm OK."

He stared down at her.

"As long as I know what's happening... I was just... scared."

Steve reluctantly sat back down and Barb unwound herself. A long silence crept over them.

Barb quietly resumed, "Yes. A drug. And I want you to take the other one."

Steve stared at her, stunned speechless. "Honey, we've got real problems here. We're under attack. You know people are saying the President is here?"

"The President of what?"

"*Of what?* Of the United States!"

"*The President?*" Barb exploded into laughter. "You're so gullible. You'll believe anything."

"Honey, this is *serious*..."

"You're going to work yourself into a heart-attack, Steve. You're not twenty-five anymore you know."

Steve recoiled. Barb took his hand and continued, almost in a whisper. "Please honey. I know it's strange. But I want company. I want you to do this for *me*. I can't have you staring at me."

"I won't stare at you... but..."

"I'm sure it's that Ecstasy stuff, honey. That those raver-kids take."

"You mean like *your daughter*."

"*Our* daughter. And let's leave her out of this right now."

Steve sulked hotly, fury coursing through his blood. He felt like a cartoon image of himself, complete with smoke coming out the top of his head.

Barb giggled and slowly got to her knees. "Everything is getting really colorful, honey. It's just shining. And I've got so much energy. I just want to *move*."

Steve hadn't taken a drug since his early twenties, and even then wasn't so sure he enjoyed it. But he did know—*for sure*—that he had outgrown it long ago. There was no doubt about that. Just the thought was making his brain spin.

"I feel so light... God, this is so nice."

Steve looked up at her, her eyes wide under the growing morning sun.

"You're always scowling, Steve. Grrr... boo-hoo."

Steve scowled.

"You've become such a party-pooper, Steve. Seriously. What happened? We used to have *fun* together."

Barb turned away and started for the river, unsteadily.

"Barb, wait."

Very, very suddenly and very, very completely Steve realized what a monumental jackass he'd been over this week and the last week and the month before that and the month before that and on and on and on...

His heart felt like it was cracking open.

"I'm sorry Barb," he called. "Wait. *Please*."

She turned back to face him. Quietly, he stood and continued. "I'm sorry, honey. For everything."

He stared at the tiny white pill in his trembling fingers. He prayed for whatever it was to be nice to him.

"I owe you," Steve said. And popped the pill.

Barb tripped on the run back to him, knocking them both to the ground in a heap.

The Andrews set an unsteady foot on the second floor of the atrium as nonsensical rumors swirled. Something, it seemed, about the President but they couldn't be sure. Hooded and shackled, they were part of twenty-three detainees that had just been released from their cells by DisasterLand security.

Jim had decided during a weak moment in the early morning that he'd play dumb. He'd shut up, do whatever they wanted. He'd play the game, mainly because he didn't need another hooded night in solitary, away from his wife. The Andrews' had each spent the night in complete isolation with no food, little water and only a hole in the floor for a toilet.

Terrible noises had echoed through his cell, raw shrieks of pain and the stomach-churning sounds of sickness. The smells were so intense as to wake him from his troubled sleep. At the end of a long week, Jim felt his very sanity beginning to crack.

Then, during his darkest moments, the guards had simply unlocked the door and marched him out. No explanation, no accusation nor apology. Only silence. He wasn't even aware it was morning.

Armed guards now took the reigns in front of the security center and without a word led the group single-file to the nearby stairs to begin their descent towards the park.

Jim was already having second thoughts.

Aftershocks of the 'copters appearance were continuing to reverberate throughout the riotous atrium. Having spent the night without sharing so much as a single word, the experience was profoundly overwhelming to all, even hooded.

The mood felt foreign, dark and anxious. It was clearly not the scene the Andrews had left the night before, a scene of martial law on the floor, and the guards, however tentatively, in control. This was a scene of toxic chaos, dangerously brewing.

"Where are you taking us!" Jim demanded, but received no answer until roughly twenty-five minutes later when first the shackles, then the hoods were finally removed by yet another set of guards.

They were inside a small holding tent located at the northeast corner of the park's periphery. Bordering the forest, it had been the refugee camp's processing center before the growing storm of protest had forced a retreat.

Now, it was being used as a decompression zone for shell-shocked guests under extensive armed guard. There was a small cooler of fresh water and the detainees fought for a few drops each.

Jim stepped away from the scrum to stand at the entrance, looking past the guards to get a glimpse of their own suite, so far above. Though guests stood almost shoulder-to-shoulder across the tower's walkways, he could still clearly make it out.

He shifted his gaze only slightly, over to what remained of the Beyers' door. *Was that their couch?* Regardless, it left no doubt to the ultimate message and a rush of anger flooded his senses.

Where were they?

When the hoods came off, Jim had somehow expected to be reunited with his brother-in-arms. Yet the Beyers were nowhere to be found.

Down the entire height of the tower the stairs were filled to overflowing, with the crush of people waiting to descend continuing to grow by the minute. It couldn't continue.

Soon, the atrium guards holding back the torrent would be overrun.

Jim's eyes followed the long lines of guests howling from the walkways and he spit. He wasn't in the best of moods. He was tired, hungry and his back hurt from the concrete floor. He wanted his bed back and he wanted a hot meal. From the looks of things, however, he would get neither for quite some time.

Jim could accept the night's treatment, however barbaric and misguided. But to put his wife through the same hell had gone too far. They had lost his respect.

"I don't like this Jenny," he whispered, ducking away from the entrance. "They wanted us out of the way. To cool us down or something. Something's going on. Something big."

Again without a word, the detainees were searched one by one and released from the tent into the park—without choice. Jim swallowed his fury and they negotiated the crowds, falling back from the park's periphery where conflict still continued to brew. The conditions were deteriorating—one visit to the overflowing porta-potties had told them that.

Then, without warning, the military 'copter swooped down from the tower and over the atrium. The reprise appearance was confronted by a round of fierce yet hopeful howls.

Jim's eyes narrowed. "UH-60, Jen. The Black Hawk."

"What the hell's it doing here?" she asked.

"Second time it's come," said a neighbor who shared the rest of the story. "Forty-five minutes ago it was circling the entire atrium."

It suddenly made sense. *The President.* These were high-level negotiations of desperate urgency.

Was the end near? *The President?*

Or had everyone become delusional?

"So what's it doing back?" Jim asked.

"Means the talks are over," another guest yelled. "If you ask me."

"You think they're picking up the President?" asked a third.

"With the CEO!" another growled.

"Or they're taking away the terrorists!" offered another. "Safe passage to Indonesia guaranteed, maybe a national park set up or something. Probably cost DisasterLand nothing. And it's good PR," the guest continued. "Green's in you know."

All eyes remained focused on the 'copter as it eased into another sweep. The yells grew in intensity, then faded as it disappeared once more.

Breathless minutes ticked by silently until chants began to grow, emotions coalescing around the copter's intolerable absence. "We want the truth!" the guests in the tower cried. And those in the park immediately echoed, *"We want the truth!"*

Jim stared, a curious look spreading over his face and Jenny began to worry. She would maintain silence, her long-time policy in dealing with stress and Jim out on a tether.

"Have you actually seen a terrorist lately, honey?"

Jenny shook her head.

"They got one last night. Poisoning the river," said another guest. "But the two at the fountain escaped."

"You saw him?"

The guest nodded.

"So there's one injured, one captured. Out of at least five. And whoever was in that SUV."

"Yeah, I guess that's right."

"I gotta tell you, man, I'm fucking sick of this," Jim said. "I haven't seen a real terrorist do shit for days. And we're supposed to be under attack? The only ones I've been attacked by are guards!"

Jim stared at those around him, turning the insight over and over in his mind. Yes, he knew, there was definitely something... odd about that.

He turned back to the atrium, to the masses, to the guards, to the anxious chants taking hold through the atrium. Moments later, Jim's chest bellowed and Jenny hid her eyes.

"We want the *terrorists!*" he roared. "We want the *terrorists!*"

Instantly, everyone within the sound of his voice turned to stare. With one eye peeking out, Jenny swore she could see their faces brighten as one by one they joined him.

"*We want the terrorists!*" they screamed.

Soon, the chant was rocking the atrium, all the way up the walkways.

"*We—want—the—terrorists!*"

Two years worth of emotional constipation burst through the opened dam within Steve's mind in a raging torrent. Not surprisingly, it was messy.

He was being pummeled with nerve-busting waves of paranoia and self-doubt, which dropped him, immobilized and cowering, just inside a small grove of trees. The river was gurgling somewhere in the distance.

Every feeling of insecurity—of anger, of being cornered, slighted, overlooked—all descended on him all at once.

They'd have to grab the ladder. They'd have to break the glass. They had no choice anymore. But who, exactly, were *they*?

His children were gone.

He had cast them off to the winds, stupidly. *Criminally.*

Steve pushed this thought out of his mind and a chasm of discomfort, a terrifying void of unrest, roared up to meet him. His recent life of anger—each incident, each frustration, each slight—was being replayed before his heart, each time his gut feeling as if he had been kicked.

He was swirling through the sea of hellish negativity that his daily life had become. Thoughts of Happinol disgraced him.

He was lost, out of control, with navigation malfunctioning.

Barb had planted herself not far away, determined to ride this thing out until the end. She took a deep breath and wiped her brow.

When it had started to come on, Steve had bolted for the woods, full speed. Barb had chased after him, frantically, having an extremely difficult time, her balance not

421

what it should be.

Fortunately he had stopped, finding refuge in the underbrush out of the view of basically anyone but the most adventurous guests, more of which she expected they'd see at any moment.

He hadn't even noticed when she had approached. And he hadn't moved an inch since.

Barb lay back against a tree and started stretching her body in various ways. The night spent on the ground, even though only a few short hours, had nonetheless proven moderately injurious to both her inner and outer organs.

She gasped, a remarkable insight gracing her consciousness. She made a mental note to remember, then promptly forgot what it was. Then, as if discovering it for the very first time, it hit her again: this was one of the most amazing experiences ever.

She caught a glimpse of Steve out of the corner of her eye—cross-legged, bent over, his head in his hands.

Her heart went out to him. It *was* fitting though, wasn't it?

She knew better than to try to help him out of it. It was all coming back to her now, a long-lost skill learned in her youth: the care of a tripper stuck in the weeds. Just let them ride it through, keep them safe.

It all was for the best in the end.

She couldn't believe it. Here they were, on Ecstasy, inside the world's most famous theme park, *while under attack*. It was too much. Just too much.

She felt good though. Really good. If not the downright best she'd felt. Ever.

She had been condensed into her essence, 100% Pure Barb, or the personality that was Barb. No additives, nothing artificial.

At her best. At her most joyful, most harmonious, most glowing. And now there *was* no other Barb. This was the only her. She had found it, she would keep it, and it would be with her forever.

She had been distilled, extracted, then re-infused into her body.

She was sparkling.

With these revelations she rose, light as a feather, again wanting to move, wanting to be in her body. To work it, to stretch it.

Sitting here, aching, simply wasn't cutting it. She needed to *move*. She needed music. She wanted to be an animal.

She began rocking, simply. The motion spread, rising through each vertebrae.

She felt each individual ray of the sun strike her neck through the mottled trees. She wanted to greet them, wanted to introduce herself, to let the sun know that everything was OK. She had finally received the message, sir, loud and clear. Thank you very much.

Barb laughed. She was thirsty.

"Steve?"

He grunted.

"You thirsty?"

He vomited, suddenly, hugely and then lay back on the grass heavily. He moaned. *There went the rest.*

Barb hurried over to him. "Are you OK?"

Steve assessed himself, attempted to breathe deeply. He wanted to be honest. Barb waited patiently.

"Yeah. I feel great," he finally said.

"You do?"

"Yes. Why?"

"No reason."

Barb took his hand.

"I feel amazing, Barb. I've been such a fool."

"What do you mean?"

"Everything, Barb. I've just been..."

She squeezed.

"It's hard... to talk."

"Then don't."

"No... I have something to say." He took a deep breath. Forced himself to his shoulders. "I just... I think I got lost."

"It's OK, I found you."

"No, not *now*." She realized he looked 10 years younger. She wondered if she did too.

As Steve struggled to compose his next sentence, Barb realized she very well could have just discovered the world's most enjoyable facial.

She imagined herself on TV, selling home-shopping Ecstasy facials. What a different world we'd live in, she realized. She shuddered, as if an electric current had passed through her.

What a different world.

Remarkably, this realization hurt her. Hurt her *physically*, to realize how life could be. How it *should* be. And then how it really was.

She saw it, she felt it, so easily, so clearly. And she vowed never to lose it, this feeling of hope. She would keep it in her heart. Always.

Steve continued, "for... forever. I've just been fucked up. I've been... I don't know."

"It's OK honey."

She hugged him.

Steve's men stood around the splintered ladder in disbelief, their families circling aimlessly.

They had returned, family by family, to find the sole means of their escape had been destroyed. It would be difficult—if not impossible—to rebuild.

And Steve Beyers was gone.

Gone.

"We're supposed to find something, Spanks. And once we find it, they'll unlock the way out. It's called an Easter Egg."

Screams were filtering through from above, growing in intensity with each passing moment. Images of torture, poisonings and explosions consuming their parents brutalized the kids' minds.

Yet the labyrinth was still silent, still dark and they were still alone. Worse yet, Pete's flashlight had died, leaving only Sarah's left and it was rapidly weakening. She shut it off, enclosing them in darkness.

"Did the Andrews go inside the hole?" asked Peter.

"No, but he showed it to everyone he could find. And the guards arrested him."

"Yeah, I figured that."

"You did?"

"I got there just after it happened."

"I knew it! Oh Peter, I was under mom and dad's bed!"

"You were? I called!"

"I thought I heard you but I didn't know... I was so scared. They sealed me in you know."

"The guards? What did you do?"

"I broke out with the couch."

Pete laughed, "Sweet, Spanks. That's *so wicked!*"

They were resting in the deep darkness, trying to keep their minds off the sounds of destruction above.

The wide hallway had indeed led to the center of the atrium, to a sort of empty command center, circling what had to be the fountain's water supply.

From there, the atrium's labyrinth had proven to be laid out just like the park's, only with more, and larger, rooms in two separate rings divided by hallways like the spokes of a wheel. They had searched them all, twenty or more of these rooms in two concentric circles. Each room had one or sometimes even two trapdoors, all locked, and Peter and Sarah had determinedly worked their way through every one. All of the doors they had found were open except for ones at the farthest ends of the outside rooms. They decided these must have led to some sort of storage spaces, probably for props.

Every room had been evacuated in what seemed like a hurry. But where had everyone gone? If the employees were all dead, like the hostage had said, *where were the bodies?*

It had been hours since their descent and their hopes of making it out were beginning to fade. Despite their extensive search, they had found no more water and no food. They were trapped, and things didn't look good.

Worse, once their motion had ceased, they realized how absolutely exhausted they were.

The constant up and down the ladders had taken a toll on Pete's body—his legs were cramping and his back felt stiff, like after the longest neighborhood football game in the world with all the big-kids playing.

Hundreds of pairs of feet were thudding distantly overhead while the piercing screams soon morphed into distinct and seemingly frantic pleas for help. Infectious, bone-chilling screams of fear and despair triggered images of families burning alive, of bone-crushing walls falling on flaming victims, of the horrors of lung-searing suffocation. Every form of macabre death was vibrantly alive in their minds, every scream a window into the utterer's soul.

They listened for explosions, for gunfire. For anything. Dread had begun to consume them.

Sarah tucked into a fetal position and Pete put his hand on her shoulder. She was sobbing now, channeling their pent-up emotions out and away as the kids lay in the darkness.

"What's going on?"

"I don't know," Pete answered, collecting himself. He had thought he too might cave, but one of them had to remain strong and no matter what it would have to be him. That's the way it was. That's what a man did.

Sarah heaved and Pete heaved with her, each sob forcing Pete to clarify his thinking.

They needed to acknowledge reality. Their light was failing. They were alone and they were trapped. There was no sign of anyone and there was no electricity, no food, no water. The signs strongly pointed to the fact that their father was right: they were under attack.

"This is horrible Pete, we're trapped and we're alone. I'm sure the terrorists are just watching us, laughing at us, like scientists watching rats in a maze," she sobbed. "They're going to kill us, Pete. I know it!"

She lost it completely, letting herself go. Sobs racked her body. "We're going to *die!*" she whimpered.

"Easy Spanks, you're gonna waste all that water."

She kicked him and he patted her damp shoulder in apology.

Pete pictured his dad, right now, rallying the troops tenaciously against the terrorists, or the guards, or whoever. Fighting for what's right. The image gave him strength, and he breathed, deeply.

"I think we're OK, Sarah. I think we're OK," he repeated. Something still didn't seem right to him.

She sniffed. "What about the people up there? About mom and dad?"

"They're fighting and we are too. We have to keep going."

There was no choice. They were trapped and they had to find a way out. Now. Not in a few hours. *Now.*

They'd have to go back towards the park, where they had come in, where their parents were. They hadn't examined those rooms at all. And they didn't want to exit here in the atrium anyway, not if it was as bad as it sounded.

Yes. They had to get away from the atrium.

Then it hit him: they'd been going in the wrong direction all along! Surely there was another level, *below this*, and the further they went away from the atrium, the better. *That's where everyone had gone.*

"Spanks, we've been looking in the wrong place! We're way out in the atrium. We don't want to go up here anyway. Not now, not in the middle of this!"

Sarah wiped her nose, crawled back up to lean against a wall.

Pete had caught his second wind. "Look, we go back to the park. And we don't just look up, we look *down*. That's were the answers are, Spanks. Think about it! There's probably tons more levels down there. And one of them will have exits. It *has to*."

Pete stood, smoothed his jeans. They stuck disgustingly to his legs. He wondered if he was in denial.

"Someone could be watching us, Spanks, you're right. But it's not terrorists, it's movie producers. If anything, we're stars!"

Sarah stared through grainy eyes, fighting to believe him. *Needing* to believe him. Color gradually returned to her face and she smiled, choking back another round of tears. "Really? You think so?"

"I don't know." Pete stood and pulled her up, grimacing. "But maybe."

The paranoia had lifted and with it the fear, all vanished, all in the instant of Steve getting sick. Every thought he couldn't stomach, every feeling, every undigested experience had shot out of his body like a projectile.

The storm had passed, the clouds had parted and clarity was immediately found. From that moment on, Steve knew the score. It was as if a giant boulder had been thrown off from around his neck, from where it had been tied, weighing him down, strangling him, for as long as he could remember.

Steve straightened. His back cracked.

Fuck the guards, fuck the terrorists, fuck the guests, fuck everyone he silently announced. *Fuck you!* he told the studio audience.

He was simply, effectively, as of now going to remove himself and his family from the equation. And screw the whole stinking place.

He wasn't going to live in fear anymore, and most of all wasn't going to *induce* it. He was going to get his family back together and they would decide what to do, *together*.

He would act from a place of strength, not weakness, both here and at home, in far away Kansas. If they ever got back there.

Fuck you wizard, Steve thought. *Wonderful wizard of DisasterLand.*

Barb greeted the new Steve warmly and broke the news: with the remarkable amount of material having been ejected from Steve's stomach, they couldn't stay.

They'd retreat to the farthest, most secluded point they could find—one with a view of the falls, where they would await their children.

She took his hand and together the found the trail.

But after a few steps it was unmistakable: something was happening. The previously deserted trails were now stamped with fresh footprints, the sounds of yelling not far away. Barb clinched Steve's hand and pulled him just a little more quickly. They couldn't get involved. Not now.

Nearing the dome's very edge, the yells grew louder. Soon, the tall reeds began to give way and in the clearing up ahead a dozen anxious families seemed to be agitating around a core group. Barb tugged Steve away, back into the reeds, roughly towards river and the falls, but not before Steve realized what was happening.

"Those are my boys!" he said, staring.

His eyes narrowed. "Where's the ladder? What time is it?"

"I have no idea."

"Jesus, Barb. I forgot all about it! They're breaking the glass! *They're going to escape!*"

"We're not going anywhere without the kids, Steve. Don't be ridiculous."

Barb tugged him away, forcefully, back into the remote depths of the wetlands before they were discovered. There, plunging cautiously through the reeds, they came across a small but inviting pool of water. They were as far from anyone and anything as they were going to get. And they were completely hidden from view.

It was a good thing. The calls had started to come.

"BEYERS! *BEYERS!*"

Steve turned to Barb, whispering. "Something happened Barb. Something's not right. They should be long gone."

Suddenly, Steve was overcome with laughter. Smiling, Barb placed her hand over his mouth.

"What's wrong?" she asked.

"I just can't believe this... any of this... It just seems so... amazing. So improbable."

Barb smiled. She had been wondering how their morning would have gone if she hadn't taken the pill. What else would have happened? What else *could* have happened?

Thank God, Barb thought, remembering her first words. *Karma.*

"I think so too. I think we're OK, Steve."

She quietly lowered herself into the cool water and leaned back until she was floating, her feet gently breaking the surface. She relished the sun's warmth on her skin.

Steve removed his shirt and gently followed her in. It was three or four feet deep, perfect for standing. He shut his eyes.

He was sure he could feel new mental pathways being forged, or at least widened, like the widening of a traffic way. The sun felt good, reassuring, and it seemed to be soldering the hole in the pit of his stomach.

No, he hadn't been himself this morning. Or for ages.

It was the stakes. The stakes were too high.

More money, more success, more security. Better schools for the kids, a safer car for his wife, better insurance, better computers and better networks with better firewalls.

Better pharmaceuticals and better surgeries to make people better and better and smarter and smarter and hotter and smelling like roses, with better and better advertising to convince them they needed it. All that. And more.

More and more and more and more, requiring more and more money, more and more time and more and more work. Better and better and better and better but Steve felt worse and worse and worse and worse.

It was out of control.

Steve used to be so laid back, so casual. Teflon-man. And it had all worked out just fine. But the stakes had snuck up on him. They had caught him where he wasn't looking: the 21st century.

Now here he was, passed over for a promotion he had worked his life for. This was it.

He was on vacation and it was telling him something. This was all telling him something—that he needed to be happy.

Steve had to make himself happy.

Quality of life isn't in what you do or how much you make, it's in the quality of your days, your hours, your minutes and your seconds.

But with Sarah's college costs coming in at tens of thousands a year, and Pete's right around the corner, he couldn't just escape to a desert island and write the great American screenplay. Or even the great American sentence.

He *was* trapped. And he *did* have to keep his job. Not for him but for his kids. For the promise of promise in their lives. Things were getting harder and harder economically and the days of easy money were gone. Kids needed any edge-up they could get. He'd have to sacrifice. They'd both have to sacrifice.

Steve opened is eyes and glanced over at Barb, floating, fingers tapping out a jazzy beat on her chest, a thin smile on her face.

They were worth it though. The kids were worth it.

It hit him, clearly: Pete had gone after his sister and they were OK. They were just fine. They would all be just fine.

Tears landing in the water around his waist, for a surreal second Steve thought it was raining.

The dark stench of violence was suffocating the atrium. The inconceivable had happened: the fountain had been poisoned.

Not invisibly poisoned, but poisoned in the terrible, sadistic way of terror, leaving a psychopathic sign towards DisasterLand's ghastly future.

The fountain was spewing blood.

The terrorists had struck at the worst possible time with uncanny precision and the guards had failed. Failed, simply and dramatically, to protect even the most obvious of targets. The implication was not lost on the besieged guests.

In the moment when the atrium floor was completely clear, when guests were quarantined to the park and tower and locked-down by guards, with many more guards even *surrounding the fountain*, the terrorists had struck effortlessly as if in sick response to the guests' own demands.

We're still here, the awful message was. *Thanks for asking*.

And in an instant, the tiny amount of fresh water remaining to safeguard the atrium and tower was gone. From now on, little could be done to stop fires in the tower from spreading and guests in the tower knew it. It was the worst possible development and the reaction had been swift and precise.

Increasingly desperate rumors of bombs planted inside the tower had been smoldering all morning long and exploratory holes had been made throughout. The results were shocking: the terrorists' infiltration could no longer be kept a secret.

As a result, to those now confined to the tower, the terrorist's dark plans seemed all too clear—the tower was primed to burn in a terrible homage to 9/11.

It was an intolerably dangerous situation and the fountain's destruction had triggered the inevitable: the betrayed stormed the atrium in fury and guards at the foot of the tower were rapidly overrun.

Meanwhile, the blood—glistening, bright, vibrant and vile—continued to flow unstoppably from the fountain, spilling out into the village ruins. Weaker guests, forced too close by the panicked crowds, soon emerged splashed in the grisly fluid.

The atrium was soon clogged in a sea of chaos.

DisasterLand itself appeared wounded, perhaps fatally.

Jim and Jenny eyed the rabid faces of the onrushing guests as they reached the park's fence. Their progress halted, they threatened anyone caught in their sights with blind panic.

This wasn't what Jim had meant.

Cries went up demanding entry into the already-filled park. Caught in the middle, guards were beginning to abandon their posts, leaving the park's defense to those quarantined guests who were the most passionate about maintaining their privilege. Tree limbs were being passed to those at the front of the crowd nearest the fence and wielded by the strongest. But even to them, their chances of holding the park now seemed slim in the face of the sheer numbers of guests fleeing the doomed tower.

Jim looked down to Jenny's grave face and they knew: it was only a matter of time before the entire park became a bloody warzone. And very soon, there would be no fresh water left at all. Somehow, they knew, the river would be polluted.

Clint arrived on the scene astride an EMS cart, appealing desperately for calm through a bullhorn as EMS peace-keepers fanned out through the population armed with sedatives.

To Jim and Jenny, still standing at the rattling Kevlar fence, it seemed clear: a new age of swift and horrible violence was about to take hold.

It was now about self-preservation. And it was going to get very, very ugly.

The atrium was descending into anarchy.

Barb was lying on the small strip of dirt at the pool's edge, her body to the sun, soaking up its rays with glee. Damn the skin-cancer zealots!

Could someone please turn down the volume?

The atrium now felt closer than ever, and she wondered if it was some sort of an acoustical trick. Yet something indeed seemed to be happening and it was starting to scare her.

Barb struggled to push it out of her mind. She wasn't playing *that game* anymore. She would focus her consciousness on her higher mind, not on the animal mind that DisasterLand worshipped.

More shouting—closer. *The river? The dome?*

She imaged the river overrun, the water poisoned. Barb eyed her empty water bottle resting nearby and suddenly the weight of their predicament was threatening. She forced it away.

Barb looked up at her husband. Their eyes met. And they saw each other as they hadn't for twenty years.

With a little fanciful obfuscation, this could be Africa, the reddish dirt and the thick, almost alien sunshine. Steve could almost smell the pungent air.

Yes, he was a lucky guy. He had known that, but it had taken *all this* to make him remember. Steve was suddenly crying again, this time at the beauty of Barb's presence and all she represented in his life.

Barb sat up and extended her hand.

In the day-to-day battles, he had simply been blown off-course. But he was back. The north star was directly over the bow and it was full steam ahead.

Nothing was proof of this more than his absurd—*grotesque!*—reaction to DisasterLand's challenge.

Butterfly terrorists?

He had lost his mind. That was the Happinol talking.

It was simply bizarre.

It was almost as if he had wanted to believe in the attack. *Needed* to believe in it. Needed to take *action*.

In so much of his life, he realized, he had so little control anymore. It was as if the temperature had constantly been rising and he, the frog, had nearly been boiled without knowing.

The studio audience was back, and Steve had a few words for them.

I'm vowing, and I'm repeating it to all of you now to keep me honest, that not one day will pass without me appreciating the beauty of my life and the people around me, even if they fuck up or piss me off.

And I will never take for granted the virtues of a shared history, of a long life lived well with my favorite people on the planet. The experiences, transformations and discoveries of a lifetime need to be treasured and honored each and every day as a living reminder of where we have come from and where we are going. A weight, but not a burden and not something to run away from.

This history is what makes us human.

A chill went down Steve's spine and he shook. The timeless essence of the desert, like the African Savannah, had always threatened him with its radical, unchanging persistence. Yet now, in this bizarre mood, this vibrating crystal orb of a mood, he somehow understood it. He could allow himself to dissolve into it. And it was comforting.

Steve rubbed his jaw. He had been clenching it intensely. It ached.

Advertising. It was putting food on his family's table, educating his children at expensive private universities, and offering exclusive vacations to out-of-the way places. But it was the work of the devil.

Pimping vulnerability and threat, pimping illness if not downright creating it—all while offering the illusion of immediate and painless solutions with very little side-effects, and all patented for the next 25 years, thank you very much.

He pulled himself out of the water, unsteadily, and sat down next to his wife. He lay his hands on her shoulders and began massaging.

"We construct our own reality. We create our own vacation," Steve whispered.

"Profound. Just add drugs and you're the Dalai Lama!"

He frowned but Barb giggled, softening Steve ever so slightly.

"Seriously," Steve continued, "If we want to be victims, hiding in our room, we can do that. If we want to do fear, to feel fear, to create it to spread it, we can do that too. But if we want to be strong, we can be strong."

"Ah, but that takes more work."

"It's worth it."

"I agree."

"Then let's be strong."

Barb smiled. To her, Steve's hands felt warm and electrified as if a current was passing between them.

Love, she thought. I can *feel love.*

And she meant it.

Peter picked up the paper as if it was a three-thousand-year-old sacred Egyptian papyrus. But it wasn't. It was a fax.

His hands were shaking and sweat dripped from his brow, threatening the precious fibers. It had been luck.

They were inside another green room, one earlier left unexplored under the park. The paper had spilled out from behind a desk and Pete knew instantly it had been hidden, deliberately. He chided himself for thinking their clue would just be out in the open, laying around where any loser could find it.

Covering almost every inch of the park's labyrinth, they had found nothing—no clues, no signs, no way out. More and more they had been searching in the dark, careful not to permanently lose their remaining light source.

They had grown more and more desperate but they had refused to stop, refused to give in.

Pete and Sarah had taken to flinging the desks and chairs as much out of anger as any real plan. Pete hoped for another trapdoor, another secret chamber. They just wanted *out*.

Terrifying noises had echoed through the dark hallways under the atrium but under the park itself nearly all noise was muzzled by the earth overhead. This, they found, was even more disturbing.

Their savior had been two small bags of potato chips crammed into a desk drawer in another room. Pete had reluctantly let Sarah have almost all of both bags since she hadn't eaten in days. Sarah had snarfed them, much more quickly than she would have liked.

Now, slightly refreshed, they had struck gold.

Sarah flipped on her fading flashlight, handing it to Peter. She stuck her head over his shoulder.

Pete stared at the footprint across the back, carefully straightening out the creases against his stomach. *Signs of authenticity*.

He flipped it over, their lives changing in an instant.

There, crudely, was the last thing they wanted to see.

The images were contrasty, the resolution low, a bad copy of a bad copy that had been into and out of multiple fax machines. But the images were unmistakable. It had been sent to DisasterLand just after midnight Wednesday morning from CNN/New York. It was dated the day before.

Three simple video frames, time code along the bottom of each. The first was of a butterfly, unmistakably a Pimpernel, squashed into the dirt of a jungle road in the center of a truck's tire tread. The second shocking frame was from seconds later: flames were engulfing the fragile body. The final image was from less than twenty seconds after that: a small, butterfly-shaped pile of ashes, blowing away in the wind.

All in all, almost thirty seconds, butterfly-to-ash. Thirty seconds that would shake the world.

The extinction of the Pimpernel.

"Don't you see what this is?" Sarah was hysterical. "We have to do something! We have to get this to someone!"

"No, DJ, this is what we're supposed to find! This is the golden ticket to open the door!"

Sarah was sobbing. "No! You don't understand! This is it, it's all over! The terrorists must have known they can do anything they want and they are, just listen! *People are dying, Peter!*"

Distant hallways were echoing with faint, brutal thuds and haunting wails.

"The world's going to end tomorrow anyway!" she yelled.

Sarah continued, desperately, "Haven't you been paying attention!? *This whole thing is real.*"

"No! Watch, DJ!" he yelled.

Sarah stood, motionless, as Peter raced to the nearest ladder. His legs screamed. If he had to go up another one, he thought, he wouldn't make it.

Pete rocketed straight up to the trapdoor, preparing to fling it wide open, triumphantly. Grabbing the handle, he pushed—and crashed into it painfully. Tears came to his eyes with the crack to his head.

Behind him, Sarah dropped to the ground, sobbing.

Pete's temper flared and he yelled. "No way! No more of that! We gotta be tough. You know dad's up there fighting. Rallying the troops. We gotta help! We gotta break through!"

Only feet above his head, Pete now heard the frantic yells of terrified guests.

It sounded like they were being burned alive.

The moment came in the middle of her meditation, distinct and crippling, when Barb realized that the experience she thought would last forever was ending. *She was coming down.*

Her new, higher self had begun to retreat, she wasn't that pure crystal of soul anymore. She was becoming diluted, materially corrupted. Like Lucifer, Barb was literally being tossed from heaven.

Below her lay devastation. Not only and most immediately at DisasterLand, but even more disturbingly of the tyranny of everyday life.

It hadn't been enlightenment, at least the way she imagined it, but the Ecstasy *had* created sort of mental paradise. A powerful clarified centeredness that combined with the absolute bliss of simply being alive, of being on this planet living and breathing with the joy of creation around her, at one with all of life.

After many dreadful moments, Barb realized she was foolishly, desperately trying to psychologically grasp it, to hold on for dear life. She knew there was nothing to stop it.

Barb surrendered. Instead, she would focus on preserving it in her memory, saving it as a place she could return to whenever she needed a refresher.

With immense longing, she waved goodbye to her pure self as it disappeared over the psychological horizon.

She knew Steve would soon follow.

The sound of automatic weapons fire rang out from the atrium, adding a new and unwanted texture to the days' razor-sharp emotional landscape.

Steve shot up. "That was gunfire, Barb."

She nodded, obliviously.

A thought had occurred to her, a much more important thought than whatever nonsense Steve was occupied with.

It was a plan. A plan to hold her pure essence. It was a beacon of light, one final moment of clarity shining in front of her. It was the answer and she was rapidly sifting through the implications. It was simple: *more Ecstasy.*

Could they get more Ecstasy?

It was problematic, but Barb's swift mind had traced a solution. They needed to find Sarah. *Immediately.*

"Barb, didn't your hear that?!"

Steve was on his feet, chasing himself in circles.

Barb realized the pressure she had been sensing, the force upon her which she had been avoiding at all costs, was indeed the growing tension and the exponential increase of people inside the park. She could feel their presence, their weight, their fear.

With terrible speed it had become clear: there was no point. What they had managed to avoid for several hours had become unavoidable. It had come to them.

The gunfire resumed and Barb sat up. It was impossible to ignore.

"We've got to find the kids, Steve."

"Yes!"

"Where?"

"We check the falls. There's no way they got out of the park."

"I'm not sure if I..."

Steve grabbed her. Hand in hand and weaving unsteadily, they hurried along the wetland trails. Bursts of gunfire from the atrium were growing more frequent and threatening and the tension was becoming unbearable. As Barb and Steve approached the falls, their hearts dropped.

Hundreds of people stood before them, hungry, dirty and fiercely passionate. Steve's men were trying to hold the river but it had become impossible. Fights were breaking out.

Someone was yelling, in the distance, "They're coming!"

And Steve knew. *The park fence had been breached.* The tower had cleared and guests had stormed the park.

The morning's negotiations must have failed. The tower could blow at any moment. The endgame had arrived.

And the whole time he had been on drugs.

Yet Steve's men remained shoulder to shoulder along the river, a desperate human shield bracing for the worst. But not even 24 hours after securing it, they were about to be overrun.

Anarchy was spreading before their eyes as more and more guests were pushing through into the clearing. From the atrium, an almost constant barrage of gunfire.

"There's no time for the kids Barb. We're breaking out. With the ladder. We've got to save ourselves, and others with us."

Barb stared at the barbarians in front of her.

"*No!* I will not..."

Steve grabbed her, shook. "No argument. This is real, Barb. We're in trouble. They're fine. Listen to me, they're fine. Please believe that."

Barb rolled her lip between her teeth as her eyes teared. The lip began to bleed. He hugged her, tightly.

"I'm sorry Barb. I'm sorry. I want you to pray for our children with all your best yoga powers and whatever else you got in there."

She nodded, silently.

"BEYERS!"

Steve turned.

"Where the hell were you Beyers? You're a wanted man!"

The man was angrily waving a limb.

"Hey, wait," Steve said, nervously stumbling, "I've been with my wife—she was sick. Our kids are gone."

The man frowned, dropping the limb, "You don't know?"

"You guys didn't break out?"

"The ladder's been destroyed! We've been trying to make a replacement but the fools have burned all the best wood purifying water and we can't find any more rope!"

"Destroyed?"

"We're trapped, man, we're fucking trapped!"

"Oh God."

Steve grabbed Barb's hand.

"Holy shit Spanks!"

Dazed and dripping wet, the kids stood on the cliff's narrow ledge overlooking the swimming hole.

They had tried every door under the park searching for a way out. Finding none and having already tried each of the trapdoors overhead, they panicked, frantically retrying each one more and more hastily, operating blindly out of fear. That's when the breakthrough came.

They had tried it before, but this time the trapdoor had magically opened into another vertical passage, this one shorter and wider, which led up to yet another trapdoor, identical to the first.

Holding his breath, Pete had opened it too, and exhaustedly hauled himself up into a damp cave. Sarah followed, and they filled their lungs with the fresh, vibrant air.

One side of the cave was open, masked by a cascade of water. The trapdoor, once shut, was invisible beneath their feet.

Pete had understood immediately: they were inside the falls. He stuck the fax inside his empty DisasterLand water bottle and they ducked confidently through the crisp falling water and out onto the cliff.

Word spread quickly amongst the sea of scruffy, wild-eyed guests below and the masses raised their eyes in shock. Many faces remained splattered with traces of blood.

Still flush with their first taste of freedom, the kids perversely found themselves longing for the cool quiet of the dark labyrinth below. Nothing the kids had imagined had prepared them for this.

The swimming hole was a tense cauldron of fear and desperation. They scanned the ruin for any sign of their parents.

"Bey-*yers!*" Pete yelled. "*Deeee-Jaaayyyyyy!*"

"Don't say anything Peter! Not yet!"

"Yeah, let's jam Spanks! This shit's creepin' me out yo!"

They scurried up and over the cliff, past the crowded spring and landing back on the wetlands trail. There was still no sign of their parents, no sign of Pete's sympathetic contacts as they approached the mobbed riverbank to cross.

It was unrecognizable. The river was now clearly the front line of a rapidly escalating conflict, with angry guests lining both banks, facing off across the tense divide. It was clear: one way or another, the river was about to fall.

"No way kids!" a man snarled, and others moved to prevent their access.

"Sorry bro! National security!"

Squirting through the angry wall of men, Pete raised the bottle above his head and leapt in, followed immediately by his sister.

"Hey! *HEY!*" men on both sides screamed viciously, "*OUT OF THE WATER KIDS!*"

"Swim Pete!"

Sarah took off with the current, soon reaching their bath hideaway out of sight amongst the forested cover. She climbed out onto the bank to help her exhausted brother.

"You OK?"

"I'm beat, Spanks."

"Just a few more minutes, we gotta get somewhere safe!"

Hearing the approaching search party, Pete took the lead and the kids slipped ahead through the trees.

Legs burning, stomachs growling and heads pounding, the kids emerged out into a Great Lawn which now appeared as if a plague of Kevlar-eating grasshoppers had descended. All barricades had been leveled and blood stained the grass a sickening red. It was a gruesome scene of horror, straight from the landscape of nightmares. It was *prehistoric*.

"Look Peter! The fountain!"

There, in the center of the atrium, stood the blood-soaked structure. The ring of guards had long ago retreated into the crowd and it was now the only open place in the atrium, the only place from which the children could be seen as guests continued to flee the panic-drenched tower.

Pete nodded.

Many long minutes later they were ascending its sticky base for the extra height, smeared in the essence of life used to such brutal effect. Climbing up almost thirty feet to the fountain's shaky tip, they looked out onto the ghastly masses surrounding them and scanned for familiar faces.

In front of them, the tide of anonymous guests spilling into the park was slowing. Above them, the tower was eerily deserted.

The children had aged years in days, their innocence distorted and now unrecognizable. They had clearly been through something unspeakable, the mysterious gleam in their eyes long ago snuffed out.

Startled looks greeted them, mistrust spreading like a disease.

Sarah shrieked.

Waving at them from the far junction of the two domes, under the largest structural supports at the park's edge, were the Andrews. From an almost impossible distance, Jim flashed a thumbs-up.

Ruthlessly negotiating the battlefield throngs to come to their aid while the kids carefully descended, the couple reached the fountain in a matter of minutes.

"The Pimpernel!" the kids screamed together, "It's *combusted!*"

Peter jumped back down onto the village street and handed Jim the fax while Jenny took Sarah in her arms.

Jim's face dropped.

This was it. This was the piece of paper that could change the face of history. It was all clear now. *They had to get out at any cost.*

The Andrews had been waiting in the safest point of all for the shakedown they knew was soon to come. But that tactic would no longer suffice.

At Jim's silent confirmation of the fax's validity, Sarah collapsed onto the bloody cobblestones in tears, more out of profound exhaustion than any true sadness. Jenny squatted next to her.

"Where's your dad?" Jim asked.

"I dunno," Pete answered. "But he's protecting the river with his troops. Mom's prolly with him."

"That's no place for a lady. You deserted them?"

"We snuck downstairs into the places where the actors go," Pete said, fighting to spit out the words. "Into these trapdoors. There's all these offices and hallways and stuff."

He was hyperventilating, "And there were no lights and no one down there at all. Just some scripts. From *Monday.*"

"And that paper!" Sarah sobbed.

"It's real. It's got CNN's fax number!" Pete yelled as Jenny rubbed Sarah's shoulders.

"It's all over isn't it? Nelly's gonna return to end the world! *Tomorrow!*"

"I don't know son..."

Pete bent down, removing the soggy employee poster from around his leg. "Look!"

He held it up and the Andrews could only stare. Other guests were now circling them like sharks, in awe.

Jim patted Pete on the back and looked to his wife. She turned away.

Jim returned his gaze to the blood-soaked wasteland surrounding them. For those still in the atrium, the realization was catching fire: they were too late. The park was approaching capacity. They wouldn't make it to the river.

They were trapped and if the tower went up they were doomed. Their threatened faces chilled Jim to the bone.

No one in their right mind would create this, he knew. *This has gone too far. It's all too terribly real.*

They stood in grave silence, islands in the rushing whitewater.

"You ready son?" Jim asked, joining Peter atop the fountain's base.

Pete nodded.

"Hold it up kid!" Jim yelled, and Pete was astride his back in seconds. He did as he was told, waving the paper for all to see.

Jim summoned all of his strength, letting loose a weighty bellow, "Three images! Three images which explain why we are still here and why so little attention is being paid to our welfare! Three images discovered by the brave little soldiers here, soldiers of freedom, showing the terrorists have nothing to live for and every reason to destroy us! Three images which show we're trapped on a ship of fools!

"Our future is in our hands and our hands only! We must take action! We must take action *now! We must escape!*"

Guests were crushing in for a closer look, forcing Jenny and Sarah up next to the men for safety. Pete lowered the fax just out of reach of the crowd's jumping hands while Jim fought to hold his balance amidst the surging masses.

"The Pimpernel!" Pete yelled, "It's *combusted! The last one is gone!*"

Jim launched into the final stretch with all his strength, "We have one day left, folks. *One day!* DisasterLand has known this for 24 hours. What have they done? Nothing! *The executives have just escaped on the 'copter!* They've left us here to die! To die like the Pimpernel!"

Word was rocketing across the atrium, stoking the frothing mob.

"We must break out! In case of emergency we must *break the glass!"*

Then, from nowhere, a man, bursting through the crowd towards Jim. Black bandanna across his nose and mouth, his dark, beedie eyes flashed as Jim was struck.

Pete fell forward, into the crowd. Jenny screamed as Jim fell backwards, landing in the fountain's shallow pool of blood while the man raced away, melting invisibly back into the crowd. The paper was gone.

Sarah and Jenny huddled over their men, weeping, as guards appeared from nowhere to surround them.

"You'll never take us!" Jim yelled in fury. "No one will let you!"

POP POP.

Two crystal-clear shots rang out, branding the moment in time and shattering the guests' frightened spirits.

Stone-cold silence followed.

It was the thunder of an approaching avalanche.

The thief was dead.

Murdered in cold blood by a guard only feet away.

The match had been tossed onto the gasoline and the fire now raged. The paper had disappeared.

"We want *the fax*! *We want THE FAX!*"

Teams of guards had again surrounded the fountain and began clearing the guests back. Reinforcements were attempting to battle through the crowd but guests were holding them off. Territory was not being conceded. The balance was starting to turn.

Word of the fax's existence blazed throughout the information-starved park like a wind-whipped wildfire. Chants were demanding an official appearance. Guards on the periphery were being chased from the floor, hunted by the frenzied masses.

Children were cowering, terrified, trapped in the crush of people. Families were breaking. Howls of heart-wrenching desperation were ringing out, the naked sound of limits being reached, of comprehension being crushed, of complete and utter abandonment to the primal forces of life and death.

DisasterLand was being torn apart.

And then terribly, unthinkably, the metaphor became literal as a deafening explosion tore through the center of the atrium.

Long, silent moments passed until the smoke once again began to clear.

It was more horrific than anyone had dared imagine. The fountain had again been hit and a tidal wave of blood had showered the atrium—the floor, the dome's glass and several stories of walkways had been stained. Nauseated guests shrieked, their blood-drenched bodies instinctively writhing in psychological agony. The once-beautiful fountain was now only a massive tangle of twisted metal.

Jenny reeled, retching and spitting. Like so many others, she had inhaled the unspeakable.

The wretchedly biological smells of a warzone again filled DisasterLand, with severed body parts discovered underfoot by many unlucky souls.

Thudding now echoed through the dome, a terrible noise of awesome power—guests were pounding the glass, throwing themselves at it in profound desperation, trying to break free of the devastation all around them. Fence posts were being used as rams. It was fight-or-flight.

Weak and overwhelmed guests were simply dropping and praying for an end to the carnage they knew was to come. The solid mass of people had reached frenetic paralysis.

The hold-outs left in the tower were now panicking, realizing their deadly mistake. Some managed to jump, caught by the subtle nets beneath each floor. Others were restrained by family members or neighbors.

Jim pulled his wife and the kids back across the remains of the village, fighting the crushing crowd back to the point where the two enormous domes met. Around them, the glass continued to resonate with guests' blows.

Pete and Sarah were screaming to be let go, to be let free to return to the park, to take their chances in finding their parents. But the Andrews wouldn't let them.

Then, suddenly, from the far side of the atrium, a shower of screams. Desperate, exhausted screams of terrible resignation, of utter abandonment.

Three terrorists appeared on the second floor walkway, backs to the atrium, naked except for massive, stunningly precise Nelly tattoos spanning their richly-muscled backs and many, many pounds of plastic explosives around their waists.

Their arms were linked in brotherhood. They spun in unison to address the crowd.

"Humanity has failed! Tomorrow the world burns! *You are the pilot light!*" they called, allowing the now-silent guests time to comprehend their terrible future.

"This tower is coming down!" they finished, pointing viciously to the helpless guests still stranded above them.

Blood-curdling screams echoed through the complex in response.

"Face the dome!" Jim screamed. "Face outside!"

Jim dropped, sheltering his wife and the kids in front of him. The dome around them rattled furiously, reflections dancing as the glass shook.

"We're OK," Jim yelled. "These supports will be the last thing standing. Remember that!" He grabbed the blankets from their D-PAKs and hurriedly layered them over their prone bodies. Their heads remained clear, focused behind them. Other families were dropping, all down the dome's periphery.

The masses were fighting their way into the park with renewed strength, intensifying the crush. Then, suddenly, into the space the fleeing guests had left, a lone man stepped into the void. One man, a small man, heavily bandaged and unrecognizable, hobbled out from the darkness of Good Health.

"RED ADMIRAL!"

His arm shot up in a fist, a breathtaking replay of his own defiance days earlier. He produced a small, semi-automatic weapon.

And the atrium froze.

He fired three times above him, rapid-fire, exploding each terrorist's chest in turn. One by one they fell to the walkway floor, against a background of stark, piercing silence.

Seconds later, before the cowed witnesses, each one of the bodies burst into flame and rapidly reduced to ash.

The terrorists had *combusted*.

Awe prevented so much as a breath by any witness. The explosives, remarkably, lay unignited.

Red Admiral spun, silently, to face the crowd.

Slowly, deliberately, he turned the gun on himself, screaming, "We have failed you Nelly! Humanity has failed you!"

He fired, his body dropping lifelessly to the atrium floor.

Seconds later in a massive puff of smoke, a giant iridescent butterfly was born in his place, its translucent wings shimmering tenuously in the sunlight.

Gently at first, with what approached frailty, the luminescent butterfly began to ascend, twirling up and up towards the center of the dome. Its beauty was indescribable, its being transcendent as it found its majestic strength.

As the butterfly swirled into the golden afternoon light, a marvelous coloring was revealed to all across the back of its magnificent wingspan of several feet: an enormous peace symbol.

Shocked guests were sobbing now, openly, its beauty alone reconstructing their shattered hearts.

The butterfly continued, floating up gently, almost playfully, until it had reached the very top of the dome.

It paused, fluttering. And disappeared in a puff of smoke.

Seconds crawled by as the atrium settled.

It was all over.

"Me tinks iz tihme tah pahty mon! Put dah past ina box an' nevah fahget! Open yah heahrt tah luv 'n dah fu-tah!"

MagicD's voice rang out through the atrium and an ecstatic roar went up, unmatched during all of the previous week.

It was the roar of relief, of a long-lost friend unexpectedly reappearing at the perfect moment. It was the roar of God, parting the sea. It was the roar of MagicD.

He appeared on the walkway in his Hawaiian shirt and lei, dancing without a care in the world, dancing as if he had never stopped.

An impossibly refreshing rain was falling from the support girders of the domes, invisible and scented with the essence of hope, blending with the guests' flowing tears below.

It was all over.

Guests were dropping to the bloody floor, paralyzed in rapture as the crushing emotional weight of the past few days was suddenly lifted.

The sounds of sobbing, hugging and kissing filled the dome as strangers clung to strangers. They were one that moment—one mind, one heart and one blood. They were family.

A feeling of supreme humanity, of supreme humility, had erupted in their hearts, radiating warmth, joy and ultimately, love.

It was all over.

The five terrorists sprinted out from a nearby suite to surround MagicD on the walkway: Monarch, Red Admiral and White Admiral, joined by their two rank-and-file comrades who removed their masks to triumphant roars of appreciation. They bowed.

The exhilaration continued as stunned guests drank in the overwhelming confirmation: *it - was - all - over!*

The murdered thief in black appeared with the guard who shot him, followed in turn by the employee hostages and finally the eight waving fashionistas.

Deafening cheering, impregnated with absolute and pure bliss, echoed across the atrium while surf music blasted out. The terrorists kicked enormous beach balls onto the rejuvenated, jubilant partyers.

Dazed guests continued to stumble out of the park, arm in arm through the gentle rain, while family, friends, strangers and guards danced together in delirium. All were cleansed by the rich, energizing shower as the blood and the filth was washed from their bodies and their souls, down the atrium's hidden drains.

They had passed through hell and together, they were now experiencing purification.

"It's Over!" the InfoTron blinked, in lurid, phosphorescent delight.

"And - that - is - a - *WRAP!*"

Champagne showered the mount in sweet and jubilant ecstasy. They'd done it again. *They had rocked it.*

Elektra slipped off her headphones, running a hand through her sopping wet hair as Alexi took prompt control of DisasterLand's coming rehabilitation.

All over the bridge remaining non-essential departments had begun shutting down in preparation for the humanitarian aid operations to come. Security and EMS crews were already moving in to take control of the mount, while the psychological teams were doubling their staff presence. Their work would be monitored by the production understudies while the leads remained on call.

The creative and story departments, along with A-list actors and production people—were free to begin their celebrations. And as of now, many had. In minutes, crew members would be invading the bridge for the traditional glass of decompression bubbly before hitting DmZ full-on for the celebrations proper. A quick drink, or ten, was almost essential to tame the rivers of adrenalin resulting from the show's dangerous climax and cumulative lack of sleep.

Plastic flutes were passed around and Shae took the microphone to lead a poignant traditional after-show toast, with the audio broadcast throughout the staff offices.

"This one goes out to Jimmy," Shae said, "and to you, to everyone here at

DisasterLand who has given it your all this show. It's been a tough one in many ways, but also the most satisfying one for me and I hope for you. I look forward to seeing you all on Sunday at the final dailies session, the memorial, and certainly at the party. *TO JIMMY!*"

A roar erupted throughout DisasterLand's staff, unmatched in their passionate history. It was a roar of satisfaction but also of relief—one of the most complicated shows had gracefully ended without further incident.

Overhead, the images from the atrium were forming a stunning backdrop for the crew's revelry. The specially-formulated rain continued to fall and guests were clearly making the most of it.

Providing total refreshment as well as total cleansing, the rain was infused with a special aromatherapeutic blend of essential oils, many of which were also powerful antibiotic and antifungal agents. These oils weren't just run-of-the-mill stuff, they were complex, centuries-old healing essences to restore and rejuvenate the spirit, specially blended by an Amazonian witchdoctor Jens had personally sought-out for the commission.

Elektra dropped into the sticky leather couch next to Greg, happily taking a refill from Shae as Karen, the beaming lead writer, arrived with her team. Colin and the ADs wouldn't be far behind, nor would Molly and her assistants. Dozens of others would filter in within the next half-hour, and hugs would be shared by all.

"Masterfully conducted, E," Shae said. "Virtuoso performance. To you."

They toasted.

"And to all of you," Elektra replied, "Who make my job easy. Beautiful script, Karen."

"Thanks. We'll have to do a rerun!"

"Indeed we will. It's a keeper," Shae agreed as glasses were repeatedly raised. "Continual refinement."

"MoDi was brilliant," Elektra said, toasting the writers. "And Special Ops rocked."

"I particularly liked the rumor of the CEO being dead," Shae said. "That was a nice touch."

"Nothing personal, Shae," Karen smiled.

"No, of course not," he winked.

"My traditional Friday night cocktail party will be on tomorrow night, for whoever is interested," announced Elektra. "I hope all of you have the strength to make it."

Plates of hors d'oeuvres arrived and the crew munched in reflective silence as the minutes ticked by, captivated by the guests' continuing revelry on the atrium floor above. After such intensely-prolonged connections, silence to all was indeed golden.

Molly soon arrived as did the team of ADs, all focused on the beauty splashed across the monitors above them. In very significant, very real ways, these were lessons to all of them and nothing was taken lightly.

The guests' faces were once again telling a thousand stories, stories destined to submerge below the surface upon their departure, but which certainly would never be forgotten. The video and audio teams were busy capturing it all.

Elektra sat back, in disbelief that the show was over, that the first year of their existence was coming to a close, that they had somehow survived the loss of their first actor.

Most of all, though, she felt contentment, a distinct pleasure that she had found so much joy in a terrorist plot.

Maybe, just maybe, they were growing on her.

"You missed the best part, DJs!"

Pete had leapt up before anyone else had seen Barb and Steve spilling out from the park with other stunned guests.

"The terrorists *combusted*," he yelled, "and the injured one turned into a butterfly and disappeared! Then they came *back*! *They were actors!*"

Sarah and the Andrews remained sprawled against the glass dome, where they had stayed, numb, throughout the celebrations.

Teary-eyed smiles were shared as Barb and Steve hurried towards the exhausted group. They were overwhelmed, still slightly buzzing from the day's remarkable journey.

A joyful reunion ensued, one of dozens already taking place and dozens more to come all over DisasterLand. After the show's curtain call, EMS lost persons workers had immediately fanned out over DisasterLand in search of separated souls, all in constant radio contact.

"Don't worry," Steve said, quietly, mussing Pete's hair. "I don't mind so much. What about you, Barb?"

Barb's oddly silent reaction, her overwhelmed tears of joy and relief, culminated in a confused, nervous round of laughter by all. Sarah thought they both looked kind of funny.

Steve hugged Jenny one more time and gave Jim another big bear hug.

"Guess we're fools," Steve admitted.

Jim laughed his agreement, "Better to live like fools than die wise-men!"

Steve returned the laughter heartily, joined by Barb and the kids.

Their laughter grew and grew, feeding back on itself, bubbling the tension and fear up and out of their systems. As it stretched on and on, they relished it, the tears continuing to fall.

"What happened to you guys?" Barb finally asked, wiping her cheeks with her sleeve.

Jenny rolled her eyes, deflecting the question, "It's a long story... and we've got plenty of time."

Barb hugged her once again, "That's right, Jenny. We have got plenty of time. Two whole days."

She pulled away, taking Jenny's hand. The tears resumed as she glanced at her children, then returned to the Andrews. "Thank you both so much... I don't even... we're just absolutely..."

"It's what you would have done for us, Barb. Nothing more, nothing less," Jim said.

Steve was beaming stupidly at the kids and a truly horrible thought lodged its way into Sarah's consciousness. She tried to force it out, but couldn't.

"That's right, Jim. Absolutely right. And we'll gladly repay the favor. Anytime," Steve said.

"That's a deal, Beyers."

Jenny tugged his sleeve and Jim smiled, "Look, we're beat..."

"Rough night last night," Jenny interrupted with a resigned smile.

"... we'll leave you guys alone to give you time to catch up. Think we'll have a look around before we crash somewhere for the evening. Stop by the suite tomorrow. We need to exchange some numbers."

"That we do," Steve agreed, and the Andrews bid farewell. They soon disappeared into the crowd, in the direction of the tower.

When Barb turned to wave goodbye Sarah had noticed the backpack around Barb's shoulders. Her heart plummeted.

Her parents' remarkable change of attitude, of *personality*, was undeniable. *But...*

Finally, with enormous discomfort she inquired meekly, "Are you guys OK? You look sort of... weird."

"Yeah, your eyes are all buggin' DJs," Pete said.

"Really? That's strange," Barb replied.

"Well, interesting you mention it, we had sort of a funny day," Steve said.

Sarah planted her gaze at her feet to offset her free falling stomach.

"Funny how DJ?"

"Oh, I suppose you could say we spent the day a little out of our minds."

Sarah stumbled. Her skin was crawling, her brain melting. Steve and Barb stared at her, witnessing the grotesque contortions of her young, exhausted face.

She mumbled, "You guys ate my pills?"

"*Pills?*" Pete was hopping up and down, an instinctive visceral reaction to the cognitive electrical storm raging through his mind and completely debilitating any advanced motor skills. Fortunately, it was temporary.

"You mean drugs, DJs?" he finally gasped, "You guys is trippin'?!"

Sarah pleaded for combustion.

Two hours later, the rain stopped, the euphoria waned and the party crashed. Hard.

MagicD took a well-earned triumphant bow as the music climaxed and bid a peaceful evening to the ocean of numbed guests below. One final roar went up as he too disappeared in a puff of smoke.

A warm floral wind was blowing through DisasterLand, cleansing the air of fear and drying off the purified guests.

DL:HumanAid workers had been setting up huge tents all along the atrium's periphery. Rows and rows of cots and blankets had been placed inside and some particularly exhausted guests were already laying down for the evening.

EMS workers were hurriedly distributing DL:Break_Fast picnic meals to ravenous guests. Designed for maximum refreshment from a minimal amount of food to prevent shock to the system, guests were tearing into them with gusto.

Sanitation crews were already swarming the vacated areas to begin the long work at hand.

The Beyers looked at the cots longingly, but the stimulation of the still-buzzing atrium was merely providing distraction from their overwhelming exhaustion. They simply needed quiet.

They took their meals, complete with two large energy drinks each, and retreated to the park, through the dark, muddy trails, across the deserted river in silence and finally past the very same spot where Barb and Steve had spent much of the day. To their surprise, it still retained some of its heightened glow, even in the evening.

The family sat down on the dirt at the edge of the smaller dome, the motionless desert spreading out before them. DisasterLand's shadow had already crept well out into the desert and the last traces of sunlight were rapidly disappearing from the sky above.

Periodically, the Beyers could hear sparse applause ringing out from the atrium behind them. DTV's roving camera crews had continued grabbing images of the shell-shocked reunited families and rapturous dancers all evening.

"So yes, to answer your question, Sarah, we did take your pills," Barb said as they wrapped up their meal. "I thought they were aspirin. But they were Ecstasy, right?"

Sarah nodded, choking.

"I hesitate to say this, honey, but we actually enjoyed it," Steve said.

The family was comfortably isolated with only diehard families remaining in the park, away from the atrium's portable shelters and fresh bathrooms. Now that digestion had commenced, their overloaded brains were fading. And with it, inhibitions.

Reflected in the dome overhead, they could see the reassuring glow from the InfoTron, so lacking in previous nights.

"You did?" Pete and Sarah were stunned.

"That is not an endorsement. We need to have a very serious talk about this. All of us," Barb said and Steve agreed. "But we're feeling very open at this moment and we're being honest."

Sarah was beside herself—it sounded like she wouldn't spend her freshman year in juvie after all.

"In fact," Barb continued, "we're looking forward to doing it again."

Steve whipped his gaze onto her.

"Or I am," she added, cautiously.

No juvie. In fact *Sarah'd be dealing to the 'rents.* But before her mind got too carried away with the possibilities of being in New York with Katie and wondering who else in Kansas needed some good shit, Sarah cut herself off. *Bad thoughts.*

She cleared her throat, "You know it's never as good as the first time."

Disappointment flashed across Barb's tired face and she was quick to dismiss, "Well, you know, that's what they always say about sex and it's not true."

Pete cringed.

"Well here it is. Promise," she said, too confident for her parents' taste, and Sarah realized it. "I mean, it's still good... but it's never the same," she finished, hurriedly. "At least, you know, that's what I was told."

Pete pinched himself to make sure he was with the right family. It was almost like aliens had stolen their souls and implanted hippies in their place.

A thoughtful silence descended and the family made themselves comfortable on what little grass was around. Pete couldn't figure out why they were way over here, on the dirt, but he wasn't complaining. His legs were stiffening and he wasn't about to move.

"I think that stuff saved my life," Steve admitted, quietly, reflectively.

"What do you mean?" Barb asked.

"Well, hearing you kids' stories... I think... I would have cracked if I had been caught in what happened today. The panic, the poisoning of the fountain, the shooting. That horrible bomb. I just would have *cracked.*"

Barb lifted her head and eyed her husband, just able to make out the outlines of his face in the rapidly deepening shadows. She took his hand.

"See, DisasterLand *does* give you what you need."

Steve chuckled.

Silence resumed and their breathing slowed. Their eyes soon shut.

Straining, Steve could just make out the cool desert wind blowing outside. He felt it reaching out to comfort him, thanking him for what he had done. Steve longed for it to fill his lungs, for it to become a part of himself.

Pete began with only a whisper,

> *"I don't wanna write this down,*
> *I wanna tell you how I feel right now."*

His voice faded, then gradually gained strength,

> *"I don't wanna take no time to write this down,*
> *I want to tell you how I feel right now..."*

He paused again, then his voice rapidly rebuilt steam:

> *"Tomorrow may never come,*
> *For you Umi,*
> *Life is not promised.*
> *Tomorrow may never show up,*

447

For you Umi,
This life is not promised..."

Then, the chorus,

"My Umi said shine your light on the world,
Shine your light for the world to see.
My Abi said shine your light on the world,
Shine your light for the world to see."

His hands began tapping out a gentle beat on his knees, and swaying, he continued,

"I put my heart and soul into this song,
I hope you feel me,
From where I am to wherever you are.
I mean that sincerely...
I ain't no perfect man,
I'm tryin to do the best I can,
With what it is I have..."

"For Umi,
Life is not promised,
Tomorrow may never appear...
You better hold this very moment,
Very close to you.
Don't be afraid, to let it shine."

Pete relaxed his hands, let the moment gently die out... but then resumed, even more strongly,

"Umi said shine your light on the world,
Shine your light for the world to see...
My dreamers said shine your light on the world,
Shine your light for the world to see...
...don't be afraid. Just let it shine."

"Sometimes I get discouraged,
I look around and, things are so weak,
People are so weak,
Sometimes I feel like crying."

"Sometimes my heart gets heavy,
Sometimes I just want to leave and fly away,

Sometimes I don't know what to do with myself,
Passion takes over me,
I feel like a man,
Going insane,
Losing my brain,
Trying to maintain,
Doing my thang…"

Steve laughed and Pete reprised the chorus. Sarah picked it up without a moment's hesitation, followed by Steve and then Barb, warm tears sliding down her face.

"My Umi says, shine your light on the world,
Shine your light for the world to see…"

They repeated it many times, until time itself faded away.

Their eyes opened, together, to find the area around them dark and silent, yet glowing, magically transfused with their words.

Barb was the first who could speak. "That's incredible. Did you just make that up?" asked Barb.

"No, it's Mos Def."

"Is that a Star Wars character?"

"No, mom, he's a hip-hop star. And an actor."

"I want a copy. I'm going to play it for my yoga class."

"I'll give you the Zero 7 remix. You'll dig it. It's bootlegged."

"Neat!"

"Don't do it, mom. That's bad for your Karma!" Sarah laughed.

The Beyers each lay back onto the bare earth, stretching their sore limbs, their exhausted minds at sea in bliss with the knowledge that *the long, dark night* was finally over.

The Beyers woke with the sun, howling like trapped wolves while they struggled to their feet.

After shaking off the disorienting fog from their first uninterrupted sleep for days, the tranquility of the park—and further on the atrium—truly began to sink in.

There would be no further pain, disfigurement or torture. It was time to heal.

They were free.

Yet each wanted nothing but an enormous meal, their own room and their own clean bed. They didn't care what shape their suite was in, what they'd have to do to make it inhabitable. They'd take it.

It was time to return.

Struggling for balance amidst the bracing river, every molecule of the Beyers' abused bodies screamed with life. Yet Pete and Sarah had to be helped halfway across, their legs proving unsteady in the rushing waters.

The muddy trails were deserted, though the unbroken mix of footprints, discarded belongings and occasional patch of blood proved testament to the realities of their previous week. In the crisp morning light, each step bore new revelations of the guests' desperation in their darkest hour. Already the past few days seemed difficult to comprehend, if not impossible.

Around them, the glistening forest was silent.

The family continued their slow, reflective journey out from the forest and onto the Great Lawn, fighting for each small step together until they encountered the improbable smells of coffee and frying bacon.

Steve howled for joy as the crippling pain of their limbs was overwhelmed by the pure longing in their stomachs. They bravely pushed on towards the atrium.

DL:HumanAid temporary feeding tents had been constructed around the mangled fountain, away from the tower and park. The lines for emergency food distribution were already long and wound through the surprisingly clean, fragrant village.

Amidst the stark beauty of the surreal wreckage, Steve told his faithful audience, *I felt as if I was inside a twisted, post-modern art installation. And maybe I was...*

He helped the kids to the end of the nearest line, hugging a couple of key members in his militia along the way. They shared awkward laughs, awkward yet proud, proud that they had resisted, even if it all now seemed slightly ridiculous.

While the family waited in silence, Steve realized they were getting more than the average amount of friendly nods. Still slightly disoriented, Steve couldn't tell why, wondering if it was the closeness of DisasterLand and the joy in people's hearts or if there was more to it than that. After the long week, almost all of the guests seemed recognizable in some way.

Arriving at the heart of the DL:HumanAid tent, they ordered the specialty of the house—four double DisasterBurritos. Stuffed with free-range eggs, artisan smoked bacon and a hint of real maple syrup—and pumped up with selected neutraceuticals—the colossal breakfast burrito was an entire meal wrapped in a giant fluffy, blueberry pancake. The kids stumbled ahead to find seats at the folding tables nearby as Barb collected coffees, juices and vitamins.

The meal was a blur as they disappeared into taste, blocking out any other possible sensory reception. Together, they had been sucked into a splendid black hole of food.

Steve was the first to crash out of his stupor, managing to return their plates and refresh his coffee before wrangling the family towards the tower.

The Beyers had caught the tail end of breakfast and the atrium had already emptied out considerably, many of the guests obviously sharing the same longing for solitary recuperation.

Approaching the stairs, they were surprised to find them deserted—until the most wonderful vision presented itself, a reward of glorious perfection.

It was the gleam of a lone elevator, ascending.

Barb's head dropped into her hands, tears of joy dampening her cheeks.

Pete patted her gently on the back.

"That's OK, DJ, you can walk if you want. We'll just meet you there."

The Beyers' replacement front door slid open as they approached and they paused to share a surprised yet uncertain glance. Steve took a deep breath and plunged in. He froze.

Their suite had been rebuilt, almost completely returned to its original utilitarian luster except for the crude patch over the hole in their wall. The furniture had been reset, the carpet shampooed and their beds had been made. The rooms were spotless.

An enormous bouquet of fresh flowers brightened the kitchen table and scented the suite.

Their laundry bag was sitting at the end of the entryway, the laundry inside folded into a neat, compact pile. On either side sat the still-packed duffle bags that Sarah and Peter had abandoned below.

The family stood paralyzed at their entrance as the impossible extent of their own filth now starkly revealed itself. Barb removed a small note attached to the bag and wiped yet another tear from her eye. It was a coupon, a final request for laundry, to be done for free and returned before departure on Sunday morning.

Steve smiled, "It's probably an EPA requirement. OK everyone, hopefully this will be the last time."

The family chuckled as they stripped, placing their clothes in the emptied bag. Barb hurried to the kitchen to sniff the bouquet with delight.

Pete and Steve went to examine the hole in the wall with Sarah, the Kevlar netting still secured tightly in place. Sarah longed to tell the story of her time under the bed, of Jim's heroics and ensuing arrest, but she simply didn't have the energy. It would have to wait.

"No one will be getting through that anytime soon," Steve observed.

"No one needs to, DJ," Pete pointed out.

Seeing the extent of the hole, Barb couldn't restrain herself, "Jesus, Steve, we're gonna get billed you know. *What in the world were you thinking?*"

"Twenty-five G's surely covers this type of thing, honey. And if not we'll badmouth them in the press."

Barb made her way to the bathroom, head shaking.

The trio turned their attention to the refrigerator and discovered it too had been restocked with a gourmet picnic lunch for four, including plenty of bottled waters.

Steve smiled. A little note from Maria was taped to a six-pack next to it.

> *Mister Beyers, here is your beer.*
> *I am sorry it took so long.*
> ❤ *Maria.*

Buried within the pile of fresh linens, Barb had discovered a stash of candles and a family-sized box of DL:Recovery herbal bath salts.

After the family had showered to remove the worst of the grime, she put both to good use to create a peaceful sanctuary overlooking the desert valley. A touch of contemplative jazz fit the mood perfectly.

Together, the family eased themselves into the fragrant, medicinal waters and drifted off into their own private reflections.

It had all truly begun to sink in.

Steve had shaved, somewhat reluctantly, bidding a private farewell to his image as guerilla savior. Yet now, within the entire family, his return to clean-cut normalcy was creating a profound disconnect, resurrecting powerful memories of their banal suburban existence and their arrival at DisasterLand burdened by now-forgotten worries.

They were already struggling to maintain their positive, newly-minted identities of import.

And soon, they would be returning home.

Around the table in DisasterLand's twenty-second floor conference room, the weight of Jimmy's death had returned to haunt the enervated air. DisasterLand's elite had gathered for the final morning dailies session which would officially conclude the show.

After a late lunch, they would fan out to their respective departments and share the wisdom, the praise as well as the criticism. Depending on further obligations, some lucky non-essentials would begin their vacations as early as this evening.

It would be a long day, pregnant with the loss of immediacy and forward direction both for cast and crew. Thoughts turned with difficulty from the future to the past, and all were tackling their adrenalin hang-over with whatever would get them by.

Far below them, the village ruins were being prepared for the show's last major production. A few tireless guests were still circulating to and from the falls, but by and large the guests had retreated to the comfort and isolation of their own private suites.

This day was the hardest. Tomorrow, while undergoing a sort of creative whip-lash, the department heads would begin breaking down the new show and a sense of renewed anticipation would spur them on.

The new show, Elektra realized. *The new script.*

Whatever happened to the new script? They *were* breaking it down, weren't they?

Surely they weren't about to leave for vacation without some idea of what would happen on their return?

The HDTV screen went dark, concluding a replay of Shae's earlier video conference with the board, who had reiterated their support and praise for such clear-headedness in the moments following Jimmy's fall. They had also acknowledged the astounding success of the past year while mysteriously hinting that something large might lay in their immediate future.

"Welcome, everyone," Shae said, returning his double cappuccino to the table. "And congratulations. We've done it."

A brief round of self-congratulatory applause was shared by all.

"I want to put Jimmy's fall aside for the rest of today. We will have our time to grieve, to reflect, to share our appreciation for his accomplishments together when Jimmy's parents arrive tomorrow.

"We've each been over that scene many times and in many ways, and we all know what we did and didn't do. We don't need to do it again collectively. As always, the scene will appear in the final intranet debriefing and anyone can share comments, reflections or lessons learned at any time. Now, let's begin. Elektra, take us through the entrances."

"Thanks, Shae. Back from the beach, folks. Vacation hasn't started yet, we're still at work here."

She tapped a few keys on her laptop and video began to roll on the screen behind her.

"Twenty-five hero families, two big hits. Several smaller successes and one surprise—Jim Andrews. I'll bring in the production notes in a moment, but I want to bring your attention to something our admissions staff did during the suite allocation which profoundly affected the story's outcome—at the last minute and with our approval, they switched the Andrews to a much higher floor.

"In many ways, this strategic stroke of genius paved the way for the show's success."

Steve awoke from a vast womb of deep sleep, still enveloped in thick darkness.

It had been the deepest sleep imaginable and rising, he struggled to place himself fully in context. He had been lost in an ocean of nirvana, with no awareness of the troubles of this world.

DisasterLand.

Next to him, Barb remained curled up, motionless, her breathing heavy and post-disaster facial mask dried and caked to her like concrete.

Bath.

If Steve did nothing else during his remaining time but sit in the hot tub tube-fed, that would be just fine.

He noticed the curtains had been pulled, eliminating any ambient moonlight. The door on the opposite side of the room seemed closed as well.

It was surely Saturday morning, early, or even Sunday morning Rumplestiltzkin-style. He couldn't be sure.

Steve experimentally tested his newly shaved skin, relieved it had stayed that way. It was probably Saturday.

Steve leaned up, across Barb, to check the clock. Eight.

Eight? It didn't make sense.

"What time is it?" Barb asked, groggily.

"Eight."

"Where's the sun?"

"I don't know. I think the clock has stopped."

"Digital clocks don't stop, honey. Ugh..." Barb had noticed the mask but was asleep again before she could take action.

Steve carefully made his way through the darkness to the toilet, into which he peed triumphantly just like it was all supposed to be. He thought he'd check on the kids.

Eyes adjusted, Steve snuck out of the bedroom, through the living room and on into the hallway, where he heard warm, uplifting music coming from the atrium. The dark suite suddenly felt like a morgue to him, his family's sleep absolute.

He stepped towards their door and it slid open. Steve shielded his eyes from the glare.

"DJ, look!"

The kids were on the walkway, sitting at the railing.

"What day is it?" Steve asked, recoiling from the floodlight atrium. The suddenly stimulus was almost painful.

"Friday, dad. It's Friday night. *Are you ready to rumble?*"

Friday, Steve confirmed, *eight p.m.* Ten hours of sleep flashing by in a moment. "I'm ready to slumber, kids. When did you wake up?"

"An hour or so ago, when the music started. Seriously, are you guys ready?"

"Ready for what?"

Steve shuffled over to join them. The elevator was busy shuttling people down and the floor was taking on an air of giddy anticipation.

Suspended down the south side of the dome to their right, just below the InfoTron where all could watch, was the largest video wall Steve had ever seen. Over five stories high and spanning well over three times the width of the massive InfoTron, the wall was featuring a country music show. The InfoTron, Steve noticed, had remained dark.

"No, DJ, look below!"

Steve lowered his gaze, confronted by yet another profoundly remarkable scene. A huge stage had been built and Nest, the country band, was in full swing. A few brave souls were on the floor, line-dancing while the growing crowd cheered them on. *The show was live!*

But that wasn't it. That wasn't the main thing.

Towering over the band, a massive wooden effigy was being constructed on stage.

It was a giant, four story butterfly-Buddha.

It was Nelly.

The atrium dimmed and a hush fell over the capacity crowd assembled on the floor. Everyone who was able—and many even who weren't—had arrived for the celebration. As if from far off, the DisasterLand theme gained strength, growing to its triumphant finale as the ground beneath the guests quaked.

The video wall had been lowered in front of Nelly's effigy and a sea of bloody refugees graced the screen. Images of rich, if disturbing, beauty, the refugees stared at the camera above them in terror and anticipation. Some had managed to construct signs, raising them with exhausted grimaces. *Help us!*, they silently screamed.

A collective gasp swept through the crowd as the shot pulled back and up, dramatically revealing the dome's roof below. The long, agonizing shot of yesterday morning's primal human desperation had been filmed by the Black Hawk.

"We want the *terrorists!*" a voice commanded, blasting over the magnificent sound system in vivid clarity, "*We want the terrorists!*"

The Beyers stood in disbelief. Jim's image followed in tight close-up, his animal determination fierce, his clenched fist waving overhead.

The audience joined in once again to share a moment the Beyers couldn't place: "*We want the terrorists!*" the atrium chanted in unison, "*We want the terrorists!*"

Cheering broke out as Jim's image faded to black.

Moments later the atrium burst into the hellish colors of a fiery inferno as the first massive explosion of the opening attack erupted across the screen. An apocalyptic drum 'n bass soundtrack tore out of the speakers, laid down live by the shadow of a DJ onstage, assaulting the atrium's post-traumatic crowd.

The images progressed rapidly and powerfully through a montage of the opening disaster, a complete mini-narrative including graphic play-by-play footage not seen earlier in the week, all intercut with on-the-scene eyewitness accounts. It was a time long gone, an almost inconceivably vast psychological distance, and only now did the startled guests begin to realize the true extent of what they had just experienced. Many cried out in remembrance, in pain, and some, even, in awe.

For the Beyers, their proximity to Sunday morning's events rekindled all of the incendiary emotions with startling immediacy as they relived each crushing moment. Like dying suns they were trapped in the gravity of a immense singularity, with the narrative accelerating dreadfully and inexorably towards the death of the two young honeymooners. When that terrible moment arrived, their psyches screaming for mercy, the images slowed, froze, and a spotlight hit the stage.

There, the same two young actors stood holding hands, faces tanned and shining. They kissed and raised their arms above their heads for a lush, theatrical bow. Ecstatic cheering echoed throughout the atrium as the audience shared the Beyers' profound relief. From then on, as victim after victim appeared onstage seemingly resurrected, the guests were whipped into an ever-more delirious frenzy.

"U-S-A! U-S-A!," roared from the speakers as the spotlight faded, joined by those in the atrium, "*U-S-A!*"

Powerful scenes of the attack's aftermath appeared: exhausted firefighters covered in dust, bent over with heads in hands; immobilized guests staring shocked into space; EMS crews working feverishly over downed bodies; strangers comforting strangers, iron-clad bonds being forged.

Disaster to disaster, bookended by misery, pregnant moments of magic were gradually illuminated, treasures most would have missed while lost in their own overwhelmed lives: small, wondrous gems of humanity that would live on forever in each guest's heart.

Carts were working the live audience, offering water, juice, tea and snacks for needed refreshment as the images moved on to Sunday evening's candle-lit vigil, featuring the beauty and grace of the teary-eyed hopeful.

A mood of heartbreaking purity was resurrected amongst those now on the atrium floor, and many in the crowd grasped hands in remembrance of their shared support. The atriums of now and then rejoiced together in song.

Onscreen, little girls were crying while families sported homemade peace signs and T-shirts. Above them in the tower other families shared food in impromptu walkway picnics following the aftermath of Good Food's ransacking. Somber speeches remembered the injured while images migrated to the exterior windows of Good Health featuring the living memorial to those injured during the opening attack.

Inside the hospital itself, scenes of uplifting togetherness played out as the injured and their families gathered together for strength and support. Board games, playing cards and family stories were rekindled as the stricken families bonded with and between themselves. Many families were holding hands as they eloquently shared their feelings of renewed love with DTV.

Sunday evening faded, replaced by an intermission of a rich, nocturnal time-lapse of the devastated village's stabilization and the hunt for the fashionistas within the sleeping tower. Lights swept by in staggering velocity as the guards attacked on multiple fronts while welders below worked to repair the flooring.

At dawn's first light the tension faded with the scenes.

The timeless charm of Friday night's quaint, pristine village faded in as guests arrived to begin their vacation. Hearts slowed as a bittersweet nostalgia, a rediscovered innocence, overtook the audience.

Vignettes of Friday night's street-life appeared, with well-dressed, glowing families shopping and enjoying the numerous street cafés, all drunk on near-mystical wonder. Picnickers lined the Great Lawn and Frisbees were tossed, but the sequence lingered on the little details of the village itself, details many had already forgotten. All served as poignant reminders of the beauty which had so dramatically been exterminated.

Introductory interviews from the previous weekend appeared throughout. Families bashfully introduced themselves, many of whom would reappear later as unwitting players in the disasters' powerful drama. Some would be heroes, others tragic victims.

Destinies were interwoven in a lavish emotional tapestry of reminiscence, resilience and rebirth.

Every family had been given a small, silent pager and the Beyers' now lit up, requesting their presence onstage. The family nervously excused themselves into the makeshift aisle through the center of the electrified audience. Onscreen, Tuesday evening was approaching and the family was certain of what was to come: Steve and Jim's rescue mission. The beginning of the end.

The audience was already nearing their emotional-saturation point, individual release often coming in intense and profoundly violent emotional purges. DisasterLand's entire team of psychologists were working the audience, at times pulling the most troubled guests aside for a private session.

Compared to the Sunday morning attack, images of Monday night's offensive had taken on a much more severe, undeniably dark and shocking tone, because of what followed but also because much of the attack had never appeared on DTV. Most guests were seeing the entirety of the assault for the first time, through well-placed camera angles in which the attack's choreographed brilliance was viscerally evident. The attack had built gradually, even poetically, from the opening smoke bomb to Jimmy's horrific fall, each heartbreaking moment a long and brutal journey. It had been innocence lost.

While the last moments of Jimmy's fall slowed to a halt and froze in time, carefully edited to avoid the actual landing, the spotlight had returned and Lhasa made another proud curtain-call. Appearing without his bandages for the first time and sporting an ear-to-ear grin, he received an overwhelming round of joyful, if surprised, applause as the spotlight faded.

He had, of course, been fully briefed about the truth. And he had understood the importance of his mission, the importance of the façade. For him, it only added to the poignancy of the moment.

Sarah's blood-curdling screams had followed immediately, blistering the audience's saturated ears. Horrified sympathetic howls rang out as the story of Sarah's fall was replayed from multiple angles and at numerous speeds. Pete had looked wide-eyed at his dad while Sarah shut her eyes and covered her ears. Barb fought for air.

"Holy cow, Spanks..." was all Pete could whisper.

Yet the atrium's tension, expertly constructed from the moment of the elevator's freeze through Sarah's desperate slip and fall, had been magnificently released with her final scream of joy. Sarah's shining face followed, super-sized during her post-fall interview, safely in her father's arms and the glow of DTV's portable video lights. Barb, feeling betrayed by her husband and daughter's silence, scowled in shocked and furious disbelief. It was a powerful and almost unknown episode in the guest's minds, leaving the vulnerable audience stunned.

At it concluded, an unmatched round of applause arose, not only for Sarah and Steve, but for DisasterLand's supreme construction and design which had planned for the occurrence. The guests now understood they had literally abandoned themselves into the arms of a master when they had entered one week ago.

The Beyers were reunited with the Andrews stage-side, joined by the L.A. waiter and his attorney wife, the victims. All were expertly placed in the shadows onstage by harried production assistants.

Over their heads the kidnapping and rescue played out, with the first shots ever of the appalling conditions faced by all the kidnapping victims. From Steve and

Jim's initial reaction to the dramatic turn-of-events leaving the couple handcuffed amongst the graffiti-splashed refuse at the mercy of DisasterLand's security force, the monumental episode was dissected for the rapturous audience.

Footage followed of the kidnapped man in Good Health after his check-up and a meal of rations, his wife by his side, where he praised and thanked his liberators.

The spotlight returned and the three families appeared for their triumphant reunion, sharing a teary-eyed hug for the live cameras. A poignant moment none would soon forget, culminating in a replay of the young woman's televised speech laying out the terrorists' demands. In front of the roaring masses, the attorney was presented with a prize for her performance under pressure. Her husband looked on jealousy.

The spotlight cut and the families returned to the audience while Wednesday morning dawned with another round of applause for the faith-based escorts who had taken control of the atrium crossings.

Amidst the ever-deepening insecurity, guests of faith throughout the park had reached for the light: some had opened their suites as impromptu places of worship where all could pray for safety and guidance.

Primitive sketches of the terrorists had been made into Old West wanted posters and stuck on doors throughout the tower.

Prayer circles had sprung up from the wetlands to the tower and everywhere in between, yet the darkness remained close to the surface: a young student with a *Save the Rainforest* T-shirt was shouted-down and beaten at the clearing, his attackers subdued by guards. Later in the morning, terrified Asian families were forced to produce homemade graphic *No Butterfly* T-shirts for their own safety.

The live audience riotously cursed intolerance.

As Wednesday progressed it had become clear to everyone in the audience, including Barb, that unseen and merciless cameras had captured significant parts of the week in graphic detail, and each guest in their own way was becoming increasingly wary of what could be shown. An undercurrent of edgy expectation and even dread had begun to circulate in the audience. For every brave soul there were many cowards, and as the days progressed each guest's true nature had been laid bare for all to see.

The audience's psychological temperature was rising now, exponentially, as the day of reckoning neared.

Following Jim's remarkable announcement and resulting arrest, the dramatic chaos of Wednesday evening and night was elegantly portrayed as fears grew of the undeniable infiltration and supreme power of the terrorists. In the dark shell of the wounded tower, word quickly spread. For the first time, guests were viscerally experiencing the fragility inherent in the tower's massive height.

In the park, Steve's men too had taken action and cameras had somehow captured it all.

Watching his own determined self on-screen as the night's action progressed, Steve felt little connection to the man he saw. The bravery, the quick insight, the undying passion seemed vastly removed from his ordinary self which had already begun to rematerialize.

Yet as proud as the scenes made him, he was simultaneously horrified at his crazed, mountain-man survivalist appearance, and deeply thankful for DisasterLand's secrecy. He imagined the fallout from the images being leaked to his boss.

Steve reeled. *His boss.*

Get Us In!

Steve's stomach dropped. It was the first time he'd really thought of life after DisasterLand, and perhaps the strength of his reaction was attributable both to the dismay of returning to his ordinary life as well as the sure knowledge that he'd failed on his mission.

But it was undeniable: he *had* failed. Worse than failed, he'd never really tried. And Monday morning was sure to be unpleasant.

Peter too was upset, his contribution to White Admiral's arrest utterly ignored. With overwhelming poignancy he fully realized what it meant to be a secret agent.

Thursday morning neared and Steve and Barb grew increasingly jittery, with Pete and Sarah following in sympathy, wondering if the couple would be outed as druggies. Steve's pager vibrated again and the family nervously returned to the stage.

Post-copter, a camouflaged SWAT team destroyed the ladder Steve's men had worked so hard to construct, thwarting the only viable attempt to break out of DisasterLand. And with that, the final confrontation was sealed.

As expectation rose, night-vision shots from inside the bowels of the tower appeared, where three separate teams of high-tech, low-resource spelunkers had carefully and silently descended the terrorists' lines ledge by ledge, story by story, crawlspace by crawlspace, using supplies the terrorists themselves had stashed. They methodically probed for weaknesses, checked for bombs and looked desperately for clues and confirmation.

Meanwhile, also in night-vision, Peter and Sarah were shown entering the tree's trunk. Once below in the labyrinth, their odyssey progressed through room after room, door after door, until Sarah's breakdown revealed their utter desperation.

"Told you we were stars!" Pete whispered proudly to Sarah while their adventure played out for all to see. The family had once again taken the stage in darkness, proudly next to the Andrews.

The tower's spelunkers reached the labyrinth just as Peter and Sarah began trashing rooms, leading to their discovery of the fax. The kids were shown examining the paper with horror, by flashlight.

The spotlight hit the stage and a deafening roar overtook the families. Pete raised his fist in triumph, followed by Sarah, as pride radiated from all of their faces.

Onscreen, the kids leapt out of the waterfall and raced for the fountain with remarkable determination.

Calls of "We want the fax! *We want THE FAX!*" shook the atrium as the magnificent final climax was presented, slow-motion and image by image, to the rapt audience. Barb, Steve and everyone who had been trapped the park were seeing the magical outcome for the very first time. To them, the beauty seemed impossible.

The terrorists' powerful final show of force, Lhasa's dramatic appearance and the butterflies' stunning final message, all had been meticulously and gorgeously captured.

Yet in many hearts the triumphant resolution was already tinged with the loss of treasured times gone by, with the knowledge that their once-in-a-lifetime DisasterLand experience was rapidly coming to an end.

The denouement of post-liberation misty-eyed family reunions followed, some the most compelling images of the entire evening. Simple joy and relief were shared by all, on-screen and live, within the atrium.

"I hope I never forget this feeling," a guest told DTV. "I won't always be a refugee, but I'll always understand what the word means."

The video cut. And seconds passed.

The spotlight fell on MagicD, who stood with his arms outstretched to the two families remaining onstage.

The Beyers and the Andrews, for their bravery, determination and strength under fire, were awarded the first special medals of sacrifice. In addition, Peter's hero medal was returned, with special whispered congratulations by MagicD.

The real reason for Peter's medal wasn't stated, only Pete and the other *Ghosts* knew for sure, but to him, this mystique somehow made it even more special.

Injured guests followed, escorted one by one to MagicD, each individually paraded across the stage with assistance as needed, with an accompanying video montage showing their finest moments. Wholesome rounds of applause were shared as each received a special medal of sacrifice.

The EMS workers were next, then the doctors and nurses and the DL:FireMen who appeared to an incredible display of love, support, and chants of *"Heroes! Heroes!"* from the audience.

Every single family then followed in the order of their entrance, each receiving a special medal for survival while highlights of their adventure graced the screen.

Then it was time for the terrorists to make one final appearance, one last marvelous curtain-call, once again taking a much-deserved bow as the spotlight faded.

As the DisasterLand theme built to another bruising climax, the spotlights returned, spinning over the atrium and dancing across the glass in furious glory, giving flight to the audience's dramatic expectations. The lights quickly refined their scope, flashing over the length and breadth of the ruined tower and dramatically swooping across the walkways. There, lining the third and fourth floors, were the uniformed guards.

"Tanks tah dah mon who mahke dis plahce sahfe! Tanks tah our poh-*leece*! DisastahLand luvs an' tanks yah all!"

Lightning boxes flashed as the audience cheered the appreciative men and women who formed the security staff. The guards bowed in unison to receive their due, and as they stood the lights dramatically cut, leaving the guests roaring for more.

A familiar guitar chord ripped through the atrium.

"Yo, yo DisasterLand you ready for *some 'ah 'dis?!*"

The video wall rose to reveal Smaug in full frontal assault, the Nelly effigy towering mightily behind them. Delirium pierced the exhausted masses as multicolored lights showered the atrium.

"This one goes out to a couple of special kids, Sarah and Pete Beyers, who did us all a big favor! We're gonna need you guys back up here! *Fo'real!*" Neil called as *Smaug* launched suddenly and ruthlessly into the fury of *All is One*.

Pete jumped onstage to high-five MagicD, flipping signs to the dancing masses before launching into his own white-boy hip-hop efforts.

Sarah followed, sporting her new T-shirt:

I f*cked Smaug
and rocked
this killer T

The crowd roared as MagicD joined her in his inimitable style for a marvelous reprise of their entry dance.

Nelly's effigy burned brightly, with flames licking a full eight stories above the atrium floor. It had been lit by Lhasa, who whispered a few words to Jimmy as the fire took hold.

The audience watched silently, in reverence and in prayer, as the fire's glow danced across their faces and warmed their hearts.

Way above amidst the disco lights of DmZ, DisasterLand's elite were mixing with the remaining bands and other VIPs, with all lost in revelry. As intense as the party was below, above it was abandon.

Yet as the fire took hold the party paused for a moment of silence, with each and every one of the staff taking the time to echo Lhasa's thoughts while giving thanks for another spectacular adventure.

They had done it again.

Sarah, Neil, Katie and Peter were relaxing in the secret clearing after the show, one of the very few places in the park that had remained relatively untouched. The atrium had long-ago quieted down, most guests having returned to their suites for much needed rest.

Sarah and Katie had their feet dangling in the river's crisp water.

"I got some good shots of you dancing onstage," Katie said. "I'll make sure you're in the final cut."

"Cool. What's it for again?"

"It's a documentary of the tour we're doing, our lifestyle, everything. It's like a reality documentary."

"Where'd you get the money?"

"Well, the label gave us a little bit but it wasn't enough... so that's why I'm selling the E."

"*Really?*"

"Don't tell anyone. So did you ever take it?"

"Not..."

"Don't worry. It's good. Clean. I wouldn't sell anything we haven't tried."

"Actually our parents took it."

"Your *parents!*"

"By accident."

"No!"

"And they loved it."

"You're kidding!" Katie's eyes flashed to Neil. He didn't buy it.

"No, I'm serious. They want to do it again," Sarah added.

Neil laughed in disbelief, "*Swweeeeeet!*"

"I can get you more when you come to New York."

Sarah lowered her eyes, "That'd be cool. Maybe."

"You don't do it a lot, do you? You've got to be careful you know."

"I am."

"There's lots of things you take during and after, did you know that?"

"Like what?"

"5-HTP, things like that. To replenish the serotonin. If you take it too much it'll screw up your personality."

"I didn't know that..."

"Girl, what do they teach you in the Midwest?"

Nada, Sarah thought. "It's just different there, you know."

"Yeah, we know..." they laughed.

"Not *bad*. I mean, I still like it."

"It's going to be a shock, New York."

Sarah nodded silently.

"Hey," Pete interrupted. "If I write some rhymes can I send 'em to you guys?" Pete asked.

"Sure, man," Neil said. "We'll take a look."

"You won't steal 'em or nothin'?"

"Of course not."

"You sure?"

"You sister will keep us in line."

"Cool. If you like 'em can I record 'em with you?"

"Maybe."

"And make the beats?"

Neil shrugged, laughing.

"That'd be *a'ight*," Pete said.

A long, comfortable silence enveloped them.

"So I'll call you guys when I get settled, OK?" Sarah finally said, her eyes tearing, "We really should be heading back."

"Yeah, we've got an early flight too."

Pete watched as Sarah kissed Neil and finally Katie goodbye. Pete high-fived them both.

"Spanks," he said later, on their way across the atrium, "that chick's got a sweet milkshake, yo."

Sarah laughed, "Yeah, I guess she does."

Pete's eyes narrowed.

"Last chance to be a star, *Monsieur Beyers*. We were in the neighborhood and..."

Steve blinked, attempting to focus his tired eyes which effectively continued their protest.

"Hi, Juliet," he began at last, "Thanks for dropping by and seeing us."

"Oh I'm sorry, *Monsieur Beyers*. Did we wake you?"

"No... but..."

"Are the kids here?"

"No," Steve laughed.

"*Perfectionner!*"

Barb appeared in her nightgown, yawning in the hallway behind her husband while Juliet introduced her camera crew.

"No, Juliet, you see... I'm afraid we... we can't. We're just too damned tired," Steve finished, shrugging.

"A long few days, *no?*" She stared, assessing their faces in turn. "OK, tomorrow then?"

Steve shook his head.

"OK... I see. Well, it was nice to meet you then *Monsieur Beyers*. Hope the ladies enjoy their gifts... Have fun in Kansas *mes amours*. Lots of sex, *no?* Like rabbits? And be safe from tornadoes, *oui?*"

She pecked the cheeks of Barb and Steve while her crew scurried off to their next house call.

The Beyers returned to their bed and their snuggle, where they had been enjoying the night in silence, cozy and half-asleep. With the kids still downstairs and Steve lost in his own thoughts, Barb was still distinctly failing to get used to the idea of living without *the feeling*, without *the self* that she had discovered—*rediscovered?*—with the Ecstasy.

"Honey," Barb asked, breaking the silence which lay over them like a warm blanket.

"Hunh?" Steve replied, groggily.

"Juliet distinctly said *girls*. And *presents*."

"Yes, I heard that too..."

"Any particular... reason for that?"

"Well..." Steve chuckled softly, avoiding her eyes, "It's funny you heard that."

Steve considered the implications, most of which were beyond comprehension in his nocturnal haze. In the end, he figured this was as good a time as any to get the small, curious episode of the previous weekend off his back.

"Yes, sweetie. I guess there is..." he continued.

Barb inched in.

"See, the other night when I bought your gift I... um... I sort of bought one for Sarah too."

"*You what?*" Barb sat up.

He met her eyes for a split second, long enough to flash a smile of dazed nonchalance, "Just like the one I bought you as a matter of fact."

Barb's jaw dropped but Steve didn't notice—his eyes had already shut.

"Matching?" she asked.

"Identical."

"Um..." Barb lay back and the seconds passed. "So that's how Juliet knew her," she continued. "When we ran into her in the..."

"Yeah..." Steve interrupted. "Well, kind of a funny thing happened and..." he said, voice fading.

He didn't go on and Barb wasn't sure she needed the details. Her eyes soon retreated to their window, looking out over the desert to the moonlit mountains in the distance.

"I guess it's a nice one," she whispered. "Why not start off with the best instead of working your way up the hard way, like I did?"

She curled up next to him.

"Kids today are just spoiled rotten."

SATURDAY

A knock came to the Beyers' door but no one stirred.

"*Meester Beyers*, wakey-wakey, breakfast breakfast!" Maria called.

She ducked in and quickly unloaded her cart onto the kitchen table before sneaking back out of the suite, unable even to pause. She had work to do. It was already after 10.

The family stumbled in moments later, their internal clocks devastated. By their own reckoning, Pete and Sarah hadn't returned home until after five and even Steve and Barb, who left just after Nelly's ashes were ceremoniously scattered over the atrium from a small hot-air balloon, arrived after two.

Following their full breakfast, the family settled heavily into the couch where they were determined to stay for the remainder of the lazy morning. Scanning the day's schedule with satisfaction it was clear: DTV's programming had obviously been geared for this inevitability.

Gone Together would be starting soon, and repeats of many of the live concerts including Smaug's first were available on-demand throughout the day. Meanwhile, on other channels more unseen footage would be featured: more interviews, more recaps and more subtle drama from days past. The day's programming would build to a special extended highlights show rerun in the evening.

But once was enough for the Beyers and they flipped off the television and broke out the board games. Occasionally during particularly tense moments or breaks between games, the family made trips out to the walkway, to get some fresh air or just to stretch their aching muscles.

While Pete and Steve were on the walkway and Barb was in the kitchen preparing some snacks for the next round, Sarah had flipped on the DTV:Music channel just in time to catch a Smaug promo.

It was the whole band acoustic in the clearing, and probably, Sarah realized, shot by Katie: "We're Smaug and you survived DisasterLand!" they called before breaking into laughter.

She knew they were gone, already on their way back to New York City where she'd join them in a few weeks. Sarah smiled to herself, realizing she now had something to look forward to besides school. She had *friends* there, a personal connection within the vast faceless metropolis. Though it was scary, she couldn't wait to begin her new life. Now more than ever.

Outside, Pete was tucked against the rail with legs dangling through, pretending he was in jail. Steve was casually pacing behind him, watching the proceedings on the atrium floor below.

DarkRoast had reopened, with chairs and tables placed around the maimed fountain which had been barricaded off for safety. Hard-core caffeine-starved socialites were taking in the afternoon sun.

Other families were lazily investigating the atrium, observing the construction of another network of tents around those for DL:HumanAid. Soon Steve knew, shops would be reopening in these new, temporary locations, just in time for their departure. In a way, he'd been right.

Crews had worked all night to clean and manicure the Great Lawn for the guests' use and some of the more adventurous had taken their breakfasts down for a picnic, choosing to remain long after.

Yet most families, it seemed, were perfectly happy to stay in their suites, to recover their strength, to process what had just happened and the melancholy realization that it was all truly over—and, worse, that it never would be again.

It was shocking, but in just a little over twenty-four hours, they would all be scattered to the winds, flying out of Vegas and back to their homes.

Back to real life, jobs and bills... and Monday morning with Dick.

Steve's thoughts were interrupted by the arrival of a familiar large man at their front door. Their masseuse.

Barb had ordered massages for the whole family. She didn't think they'd mind. And they didn't.

The Disasterati's panties were suddenly in a twist.

What had been scheduled as a traditional story breakdown had taken on an air of the unexpected with the message scrolling across the twenty-second floor conference room's sole HDTV:

LEAKS WILL BE TRACED AND PUNISHED

Everyone in the room know the score, knew it would be insane to risk one of the greatest jobs on the planet to speak to a reporter out of line, knew it would be practically suicidal to e-mail a snatched photo. DisasterLand was air-tight press-wise and united in keeping it that way—it was, after all, in their own best interest. But the stakes were high enough that a reminder obviously seemed justified.

Rumor quickly consumed the arriving staff and imaginations went wild. Many soon anticipated an announcement rivaling Shae's monumental oration which had invoked the park into existence—and Elektra may have been partially responsible.

To her the build up, the secrecy, Jude's enthusiasm, were now all startlingly obvious. In retrospect and without the pressures of a live script, it was ridiculously easy for her to see.

New, Jude had said. And new it would surely be.

Once all had taken their seats, the warning faded as did the room's lights—replaced by, of all things, a piece of poetry:

> *"Some say the world will end in fire*
> *Some say in ice.*
> *From what I've tasted of desire*
> *I hold with those who favor fire.*
> *But if it had to perish twice,*
> *I think I know enough of hate*
> *To say that for destruction ice*
> *Is also great*
> *And would suffice."*
>
> *– Robert Frost*

It too faded and frantic whispers rapidly spread.

Greg and Shae entered the dark room unseen and made their way silently to the darkly-fogged windows overlooking the atrium. When the lights went up, they stood, smiling broadly, giving a quick wink to Jude who remained stoic, hands crossed on the table.

A palpable sense of revolution overtook the room, of the significance of this time and place in the company's history. Everyone instantly felt the rush and the hairs on Elektra's arms suddenly stood on end.

Shae looked over his intimate audience, connected with each of them in turn. All had been at DisasterLand from the beginning, and in many ways each script session had the poignancy of a family reunion. Yet this one was clearly different.

"Friends," Shae said, finally breaking the silence, "today we are announcing the first new story in DisasterLand's young history."

All hearts stopped, leaving the room hanging in an unimaginably delicate tension. A shiver of anticipation slithered through the room. The temperature was suddenly rising fast.

The monitor flicked back on, revealing an image which no one in the room would ever forget.

"Avahlanche!" called MagicD, at full-out yell from just inside the doorway, his cry shattering the tension like glass. "Hah-li-dahy Speh-cial!"

Onscreen, an impossible computer-generated image of DisasterLand remade: multiple levels of snow-covered platforms were suspended from the dome, creating a compelling, almost Cubist, alpine landscape. Delicate netting, rope ladders, and makeshift bridges linked each platform and the tower itself.

DisasterLand had become three-dimensional, while present landmarks of the main floor—the village, its shops and fountain—had all been removed.

"The next eighteen months are going to immortalize this company," Shae said, quietly, as the room once again went silent. "It's a revolution within the revolution. In a little over a year, we're doubling the disasters."

He paused, for effect. He didn't need to.

"We can't rest on our laurels until disaster parks are a dime-a-dozen. We do them all, every disaster there is. And we do them *best*."

Eyes flitted about the room, stunned expressions were shared.

"This is *Shock and Awe*," Shae continued, his eyes hardening. "This is *capitalist chemotherapy*. Massive, uncontained growth to eliminate all competition before it has a chance to form.

"The pace of change in this world is rapid. There are other entertainment companies out there, folks—this is no big surprise—that have a lot more capital than we do. One decision by them to compete and everything's in play.

"We're a small shop of artisans, of dreamers. We're the passionate fools who believe in doing things right. But the public needs to be convinced that there is a right way to do disasters—and we need to be the ones to show them."

Shae paused with a long sip of water.

"The danger: some company opens up a shop to compete with us. They pay people half as much, don't do the proper safety tests, hire crazy kids just out of school and charge families ten grand for a week. OK?"

He paused, once again. "And they kill someone. A family goes there and one of them ends up dead. Do you think it'll affect just them? No. We'll take a hit too. You know how the media works."

Shae was gaining traction.

"We created this industry overnight. And it's our responsibility to guard it from the riff-raff. We have to make sure that doesn't happen. And the only way is expansion. We get very big, very, very fast. Grow or die, man. *Grow or die*."

Elektra was the first to speak. "The board has been busy."

"Real busy," Shae said. "And this is only half of it. But it's the only half you're going to get right now."

"The first four scripts next season," Greg began, "are all *Avalanche*."

The fire was in his eyes.

"As you can see, most of the largest dome will be transformed into a series of interconnected platforms, with many hosting specialty shops and offering rope ladders to ascend or descend. Each will also be fully prepared to unleash White Death upon those below. Underneath each of these platforms are snow-making machines of incredible capacity. Tens of thousands of pounds of snow will drop in all and DisasterLand will be chilled to a temperature of 28°F for most of the ten days.

"Bring your parka," Shae smiled.

"The park will be effectively cut off from the main dome by an enormous ice wall, sculpted out of glass, limiting damage to the park's effectiveness as a bioremediation device as well as its usefulness to the guests as a place of recuperation. It will continue to be available on a limited basis as a sanctuary, in ways similar to the current refugee center."

Greg let the frenzy subside slightly, then continued as the too-clean image dissolved to something, impossibly, even more beautiful. The dome had been transformed into a giant frozen snowball, with shadows moving inside.

And this wasn't a computer-generated image. This was *real*.

Shae resumed, "To make this happen, Greg and I have been working with a black-ops development team inside a secret specially-built Las Vegas warehouse for the past eighteen months."

The image dissolved to a night shot. Within the giant multi-leveled snowball, dim lights lit up the tunnels and passageways which were clearly visible. It was a complex, glowing snow maze—a remarkable, livable, ice sculpture. It was an ant-hive, and it was beautiful, almost delicate. Like a giant snow globe.

"And for the last two months," Greg continued, "we've been running one week safety runs with test-groups who were paid millions in hush money by mean lawyers and men with guns. We are ready. The technology and the stories have been fully developed and our insurers have just signed off."

"What was the result of the tests?" someone called.

Shae chuckled, "What do you think? We scared the shit out of the guinea pigs. And they've never been wrong!"

Laughter launched the tears which streamed down Elektra's face, and she wasn't the only one. She had, after all, a vague idea this was coming. But the whole thing was more beautiful, more satisfying, than she ever could have imagined. It somehow harkened back to the snowy, Midwestern winters of her youth, and the boys' meticulous construction of snow forts—except on an infinitely more vast scale.

"These images are from Day 8," Greg continued, "This is the successful culmination, the goal. This is survival. This is the buildup before the quick weekend thaw."

They were preaching now, to the converted. The snowball glowed a surreal blue, the sun outside was barely visible.

"A fine mesh barrier will be inserted just inside of the dome to cut the sun's direct light and restrict heat loss. On cue each of these platforms will drop 3 feet of snow in one minute and a foot every three minutes thereafter, trapping everything underneath. It will be an emergency. Anyone caught out will be trapped. Guaranteed."

Greg paused as slow-motion images of the avalanche cycled through the horror.

"For those inside their rooms, they will be trapped by blowing snow. They can stay, but the odds are that they will need to dig out eventually, if for no other reason than food. This forms the hive-effect as these passageways are joined.

"One foot will then fall every hour through the rest of the script. The atrium then becomes solid with tunnels and makeshift restaurants all around, some designed for the periphery to allow them to be illuminated by ice windows only a few inches thick.

"Safety. Heat sensors will allow us to locate guests and alert us when a guests' core temperature drops below threshold and hypothermia begins. EMS crews will be provided with 'hot suits' allowing them to literally melt a path through the snow in the case of extreme emergencies."

The images dissolved again, to the inside of one of the tunnels. A family of four was frantically trying to dig out a trapped daughter.

"You'll notice the gear," Shae added, "Sponsorships were the easiest to secure yet, with most of the top outdoor specialists aboard.

"But our greatest breakthrough has been the cameras. Built to withstand Arctic conditions, our tiny wireless cameras are the size of a 2-inch long ball-point pen and can be placed and maintained anywhere throughout the impromptu mazes by the camera team. In short, visual surveillance and image scavenging is easier than ever."

Elektra was imagining the fun they were going to have... it would be terrifying, a new script with new problems and new solutions, but it would surely be the thrill of a lifetime, for everyone.

"As you can see," Shae summarized, "this proves the staggering adaptability of DisasterLand's shell. Knut Boettels' original design has blossomed in ways we could only hope for, and we now know it can literally be transformed into anything. DisasterLand is limited only by the power of our imaginations. DisasterLand, indeed, is infinite."

Elektra was alone, lost in the forest approach to the falls. Publicized by the Beyers and now clearly marked, the waterfall was the guest's big destination today and judging by the crowds, every family at DisasterLand was paying a visit.

Making a solo lunchtime trip wasn't the smartest thing Elektra had ever done, but today it was necessary. She had tried the roof and though happy for a cigarette and some fresh air, it left her feeling even less settled than before. She had taken a deep breath and visited the less-traveled South side of the park, even crossing the *Bridge of Sighs*, but it still left her feeling oddly disconnected. What she needed was life, and today there was only one place for it.

She managed to secure a nice, sun-lit spot on the beach just in from the forest. If she was lucky, no one would even notice her. She had found a pair of Clint's shoes in her closet and placed them next to her with a spare towel, hopefully fending off suitors like garlic to Vampires.

The sound of jubilant kids and the tiny safety radios now mass-tuned to DisasterLand's music channel, the sight of bare flesh and the smell of sunscreen was all nearly enough to convince herself that in some ways, her vacation had already started.

Relieved, Elektra rolled up her sleeves, lay back and shut her eyes. Her head was swimming and she let herself drift away on the falls' white noise.

For the first time she had real trouble refocusing her mind on the next show. It was too big, the scale of change too much for her wrap her mind around.

Too much had happened this week, way too much, and she needed time to process it all. Unfortunately, right now when decisions had to be made, she didn't have that time.

She had a bad feeling that next week's silent meditation would have to be augmented with a small portable fax machine.

Avalanche was vast and dramatically all-encompassing in the sense that anything could truly happen. In many ways it was a blank slate, the least structured of any story thus far which would dramatically heighten both the stakes in general as well as their reliance on the guests for dramatic content. Whatever happened, it would be a seat-of-the-pants ride, and right now that was the last thing she could contemplate.

The guests would arrive at the mountain village with a gentle snow falling and an inch or so on the ground. Bonfires would line the atrium's periphery, where stories could be told and friendships struck up. A large frozen lake would replace the village and ice skates would be provided.

Saturday and Sunday would be a winter wonderland, with shopping and home cooking for the families. For the more adventurous, games would be staged on the platforms above the village to lure families higher and higher at greater and greater risk. This was a determinedly physical script in many ways, and the opening days were meant to test each family's mettle—the games had been carefully crafted to require a whole family's participation. The greater each family's success, the more danger they placed themselves in, the more confidence the crew would have in them.

The disaster itself had been pushed to Monday, to give both the guests and the crew time to settle in to the new physical and mental space. Mini-disasters, like the past show's blackout, had been scheduled to test real-world reaction time and make alterations as necessary. Elektra knew she was staring down the barrel of long hours.

Frightening, yes, but also thrilling.

She reminded herself of her firm belief that was good to keep pushing the bounds, to creatively never rest. After all, this was the one reason she never saw herself leaving for greener pastures—there simply weren't any greener pastures.

Elektra opened her eyes and checked her watch, pleased to find she still had a good twenty minutes before she had to start back to the conference room.

Part of this whole reaction was a sort of claustrophobia, she knew, and it seemed to be growing stronger every show. She was tied to DisasterLand like an infant to its mother, and taking an extended break simply wasn't possible. Yet the stakes increased relentlessly.

Fortunately, her travel agent had been on the ball, and their reservations had been confirmed that morning. She was set to depart Vegas late Monday afternoon, for New York. Two nights there to hit the old haunts with friends, then she'd meet Molly at JFK for the hop to the islands.

Elektra relaxed back down. *Who knows.* The important thing was on Wednesday night, she'd be in the Caribbean with Molly.

Then a month break, while DisasterLand was remade, and back for the month of rehearsals. Then four Avalanche scripts back-to-back, to fine-tune them. Shae was confident in the timing and Elektra had no choice but to trust him.

Plenty remained to be done before Monday, however.

The afternoon would be spent completing the breakdown in broad strokes, then dinner, with an after-dinner casting meeting with Greg, Shae and Jude, freshly back from Vegas last night. Word was his sessions had gone marvelously and three exceptional stand-outs were arriving Monday morning for screen tests.

In the meantime, he had brought video of each round for their scrutiny: a traditional casting session, then a visit to a local gym where the actors had tackled the state's largest rock-climbing wall for a specially-rigged late-night group improvisation.

Elektra was wondering if she'd have the energy on Monday to make a competent decision.

Then again it all boiled down to instinct. Didn't it?

She opened up the tiny bottle of wild rose essential oil she'd brought for the occasion and dabbed one drop just under her nose. She shut her eyes one last time, leaned back into the sun and cleared all thoughts from her mind.

She let herself drift deeper on the sounds of the river's powerful current...

Soon, an image appeared in her mind, an image which surprised her, but she never lost focus: it was the entire earth slowly spinning, suspended within DisasterLand's magnificent glass dome.

Pregnant with the slightest whiff of threat, she nonetheless found it reassuring. She let the image go when it was ready, allowing it to dissolve back into the darkness from whence it came.

Elektra sat up.

Rubbing her eyes, she drank in the beach, the falls and the guests around her. Their eyes were clear, their smiles bright. Their hugs seemed a little tighter, their kisses held just a moment longer.

Maybe, just maybe, they could reach everyone.
Maybe they could teach all who had forgotten what was really important.

The Beyers had spent a marvelously rejuvenative afternoon lost in massages and

473

hot tubbing that left their sore bodies remolded and reinvigorated. Not surprisingly, it ended in unconsciousness until a pounding on their door jolted Peter up off the couch.

He found the door, groggily.

"Yo, big dude. Your old man around?"

"They're sleeping."

"Come on Beyers get off your ass!" Jim Andrews yelled, "We may never see each other again! Meet us downstairs at *Margarita Mortal* in 30!"

He winked at Pete, slapping his shoulder. "You doing alright kid?"

Peter nodded.

Thirty minutes later, Steve and Barb were right on time, if a little dazed. They entered the restaurant like rock stars, to slurred chants ringing out from the bar.

"*We want the terrorists! We want the terrorists!*"

"Thought that meant you were here!" Jim said, standing for another round of hugs as the Beyers arrived at their table.

Two one-gallon margaritas sat on the table, each half empty.

"Quite a reception," Steve observed.

"Happens everywhere we go now," Jim said, tipping his ball cap to the appreciative crowd.

"Luckily we don't go anywhere!" added Jenny.

"You're gonna need a couple of these," Jim said as the waitress arrived. "At *least.*"

Barb saved margaritas for special occasions and this certainly qualified—to say it had been a long week was indeed an understatement.

"We'll do it," Steve agreed. "Top shelf."

"On the house," the waitress smiled. "Here's a couple of menus. Take your time, we ain't goin' nowhere."

"Hey, thanks for coming out guys," Jim said as the waitress hurried over to the bar. "We were getting' cabin fever."

"Glad you dragged us out of bed, we needed something like this. We're well into the last 24 hours and it'd be a shame sleep our way through. I sure can't believe we leave tomorrow afternoon."

"Flew by didn't it?"

"Guess it did…"

The waitress returned lugging two paint cans.

"Hey, we'll take a trough of nachos while you're at it," Steve said as she sloshed the margaritas onto the table in front of them. "Otherwise we'll be in trouble."

"Don't worry, cops are on speed dial," the waitress winked, and slid over to the next table.

The Beyers slurped happily.

"You've got a lot to be proud of, Beyers," Jim said.

Steve shrugged as Barb squeezed his leg, "We both do."

"I have to admit, I wasn't sure about you at first… going for that coffee in your robe.

But you must have sensed something, you were right on there. It was a statement. *Come and get me,* you were saying. And it worked."

Steve felt Barb's gaze. "Well…"

"I need to thank you both again for taking care of Pete and Sarah on Thursday…" Barb interrupted. "If that would have been…"

"We already told you, it was nothing," Jenny replied. "They're really something, you know."

"They're a handful."

"Brave," Jim added. "Take after their father."

Steve laughed, "Should I be concerned? Actually, I've never even thought about it. But thank you."

The nachos arrived in a three-foot long trough, true to the name. Enough for eight.

"You call me if you need anything else," the waitress said. "There's a convenience charge for being carried out of here. Just letting you know."

They dug in.

"You know we never saw the falls?" Jim said, almost embarrassed.

"Really?"

"Strange isn't it? We're going to take a little walk after this."

"You have to. You know how to get there?" Barb asked.

"They've got signs up now. Can't miss it."

"Doesn't surprise me."

"This place *is* really something," Jenny said.

"As high as our expectations were," Steve said. "It exceeded them. It's been quite a shock for us!"

"That's right, you won the trip," Jim remembered. "Saved yourself 25 G's."

"A miracle. Or fate or something, I don't know."

Barb interrupted, "I'm not sure if you ever told us what you do?"

"Real Estate. We're in Phoenix."

"You both?"

"Family business. Double-teaming instead of two-timing," Jenny said.

"You guys ever need any desert property, you let us know," Jim added.

"It's still growing down there?"

"You wouldn't believe it."

"It seems kind of odd, doesn't it? I mean, it's a *desert.*"

"It's got another few years of growth, then the bottom's going to fall out."

"Really?"

"Sure. You're right. There's no future. Huge water problems down the pike. Climate change, the whole deal."

"But doesn't that bother you?"

"Why should it?"

"I mean… you're selling people something…"

"They want desert. We sell them desert."

"And what will the two of you do then?"

"We've got property in Hawaii. We're going to build in the next year or two."

"Hawaii?"

"I'm a Navy man, Beyers. I need the ocean. Fifteen years in the desert has been enough. Jenny's mother and father both passed on these last couple of years so we've got no strong connections there anymore."

The ocean... the mountains... the desert. Kansas was beautiful, tremendously beautiful, but in an understated way. The older he got, Steve felt a growing need for the breathtaking.

He picked up the conversation, "May I ask you why you two came here? Seems like most of the families here have kids."

"We're not the type for kids. We've got horses, chickens and our share of cats and dogs back at the ranch. We were after something new, Beyers. It's that simple," Jim answered. "We're thrill-seekers."

Jenny added, "We're people people. This is a trend, and knowing trends helps our business. We made some good contacts too."

"Before the shit hit the fan of course," Jim quickly added.

231

Steve and Barb returned to the suite to find Sarah behind a camera with Pete enthusiastically reiterating how undeniably famous they were.

While the adults were out, Maria had dropped off a tiny digital video camera and several blank tapes, explaining the purpose which the kids enthusiastically embraced. Given to every family on the last night, the cameras were a way for them to capture the story of their trip safely and securely, while it was still as fresh as possible. It was a way for families to debrief and bond one final time before returning to real life.

Maria would pick everything back up the next morning, including the tapes which would become part of their family archive at DisasterLand. In 10 years, they could write and have the tapes released at no charge, though public and for-profit broadcast would remain prohibited. DisasterLand would make one copy for themselves and release the masters to the family.

Pete handed his dad the release form Maria had left, which was just a reminder of what they had signed before entering. In exchange for using the tapes and camera, they agreed to indemnify DL of all of liability, financial or otherwise, for illegal acts committed by them while on the premises. Steve cringed. They also agreed to only film the interior of their suite. Tapes containing footage of the atrium or park would not be returned.

The kids had just started their second tape of four, completing a full reenactment of their descent and the recovery of the fax which had proven the adventure's coup de grâce. They played highlights for their parents while Sarah grabbed the last of the bottled waters from the fridge.

Lubricated by two gallons of margaritas each, their parents were enthusiastic to join them. Everything progressed smoothly, in fact hilariously, until they hit Tuesday night and Sarah's fall. The lightness in their hearts faded as the wounds from the almost unthinkable event were reopened. The camera was turned off.

"I'm glad you didn't tell me," Barb had decided. "And to be honest, I wish I didn't know now. Sometimes secrets are good, I think. And this is a secret I would have been happy for you to keep."

"Any other secrets people?" Peter asked, eyeing his sister. No one 'fessed up.

Barb continued, wiping away a stray tear, "Weren't you scared of dying, honey?"

"It happened too fast, mom..."

"I suppose that's lucky."

"I guess. Yeah, maybe you're right," Sarah considered. "But you know what? I'm not really scared of dying. Or being dead I mean. I'm more scared of dying slowly on the inside."

Steve and Barb exchanged thinly-veiled glances of alarm.

"You know," Sarah continued, "I mean, look around. Everyone's eyes, they're just lifeless. They walk around like zombies, go through the motions, but there's nothing there. You know what I mean? They're living on the outside, but they're dead on the inside."

Steve gave a short, silent chuckle. "Yeah, I think I understand. And I think I was halfway there. Or *more*. But I've been rescued."

"So how does that happen?" Sarah wondered, "How do people forget they're alive? I mean, it's their *one life*."

"Like you said, honey, it happens little by little—second by second, minute by minute, day by day. And pretty soon, you've just forgotten. You've just sort of moved on."

Sarah was quiet.

"So tell me, dad," she finally asked, "I mean, does it hurt?"

Maria and Carla, her roommate, were lying on their bunk bed in pajamas, counting their final tips from the week. Parties were raging throughout the FunHouse but that wasn't their style—and why they had become roommates almost six months ago.

Gone Forever was repeating on DTV but they had the sound down. By now they both knew the film by heart and rolled their eyes at each syrupy moment.

It was Maria's tradition to save all her counting until the end, but Carla counted each night before she deposited the cash into the split safety deposit box that was built into the room. Carla had finished her totals long ago.

As each twenty flashed by, Maria got more and more excited. It was going to be a record for her. More importantly, she would be able to bring enough back to Guatemala to complete the renovations on her father's home.

In just a few days she would hand-deliver the money. Monday afternoon she'd catch the staff bus to Vegas to meet her cousin Filippé, then Thursday morning she'd fly to Houston and then on to Guatemala City. She would have nearly one month before she had to be back for training and to prep her floor for the next show.

Maria recounted the last of her take to make sure, then split the wad neatly in two and rubber-banded each for safekeeping. She hurried over to the deposit box and used the combination lock to open her side.

"How'd you do?" Carla asked.

"Thirty-six hundred and change," Maria said.

"That's your best, right?"

"*Sí*. Very good. And *jou?*"

"Almost forty-one."

"¡*Impresionante*! Another record, *no?*"

"The best ever. But I think forty-seven is still the all-time record for a runner. As of last show."

"Still very good."

"Five hundred of that came from one family. That's the secret: one family of frightened big spenders."

The girls giggled. Maria removed her journal and relocked her box. After the count, it was her tradition to take the notes she'd quickly scrawled on the shuttle home each night and transcribe them into a journal she kept specifically for this purpose. This reliving of each day was the highlight for her, forming the closure of every show. She wasn't sure what she'd do with the journal, but at the very least it was something for a lonely old lady to reflect on one day.

But starting tomorrow, once again she would only look forward.

"I have exciting news, Carla."

"Really?"

Maria sat down on the edge of her bed. Carla sat up.

"David stopped me in the office. Next show I am going to get narrative training!"

"You're kidding!"

"They will tell me the... *specifics*... tomorrow during the meeting. I guess nineteen is a *hot zone* next show."

Maria wondered if the wine incident had helped bring her to someone's attention, but she would probably never know—and it didn't really matter. The thing was, she was moving forward.

If the narrative training went well, she'd remain on her floor for the show. And if that went well, there was always the chance for a bit part as a *real actor*.

To her, coming from the cloud forests of a muddy town a morning's ride from Santiago de Atitlán, it felt like a dream.

Filippé had fought for the U.S. Army in the first Gulf War and now had his green card, working on the military desert training ground nearby. Two years ago, Maria had joined him in the United States as his wife—not his real wife of course—giving her an opportunity for citizenship.

Filippé had a girlfriend, Gabriela, from Las Vegas whose parents were Mexican, from Chiapas. When DisasterLand opened, Gabriela landed a job as a cook and found Maria an interview as a maid. They had roomed together, but six months ago Gabriela moved back in with Filippé.

Maria had impressed and after a runner cracked during the third show Maria had been called in to test. After a substantial battery of psychological tests and complex improvisations to test her ability to react in differing emergencies and conquer the language barrier, remarkably, Maria had been promoted to back-up runner, then, only three shows later, to full runner.

Now she was about to receive narrative training!

"Did you hear about the new uniforms?" Carla asked.

"No," Maria said, after a moment.

"Yeah, a couple of the girls were talking about them today. I guess they heard we're getting new wardrobes and everything for the next show."

"Wow..."

Maria had heard rumors too, rumors that the next script was going to be very special. Tomorrow's staff meetings were scheduled for much longer than usual as well.

DisasterLand never stayed still.

"Maria?"

"What?"

"Let's go to DmZ."

"DmZ—the *VIP bar*?"

"Not tonight, remember? Come on, let's go. We'll dress up and drink cocktails. It might be our last chance *ever*!"

"Really?"

"Sure. Who knows."

Maria smiled. "OK, we do it!"

"The shuttle leaves in 10."

SUNDAY

Steve and Barb were packing their bags in silence, individual thoughts miles away. Kansas City, their jobs, friends, their *real lives*... all oddly felt like the distant past. They had moved on, their lives and responsibilities seemed firmly *here*, *now*.

Barb thumbed through the laundry and removed her sun dress from the pile, examining it carefully. It was spotless. But while she continued to marvel, the dress transformed strangely in front of her. She did a double-take, yet it was true: what she had thought to be flowers were actually tiny little explosions.

Explosions. For the second time in as many hours, tears returned. Merely holding the dress she'd worn exactly one week ago was propelling her back to the beginning of... the *what?*

The *hell?* The *pain?*

Life's Greatest Adventure, she sniffed, wiping the tears from her eyes. There was some truth to that. It was, for now at least and despite Friday night's celebration, beyond words. And quickly coming to an end.

Maria had dropped off their final load of laundry and shared hugs with best-wishes for the future. She had left four T-shirts which proclaimed simply,

I Survived DisasterLand

Pete had seen the rip-offs on eBay and had nearly wet himself when he saw the holographic tags of authenticity. He begged for more but Maria had refused.

"One for each person. All I have," Maria giggled.

"Yo, if someone doesn't want theirs, bring it back here!"

"Everyone wants."

Peter and Sarah finished their packing and joined their parents in the bedroom,

480

staring out at the famous valley one final time.

"DJs, I wanna get a dog and call him Pooch," Pete said.

"What made you think of that?" Barb asked.

Their dog Bob, Bob Barker, a loyal Collie, had passed away over a year ago and they hadn't yet been able to think of replacing him.

"I was just wishin' we had something to look forward to when we got home, you know? Someone waiting there for us."

Steve paused, "You know, Spike, let's think about that. It's probably about time."

"Smoke it, DJ! Or we could call it Sarah and pretend she never left!"

"Or we could call it Pete and send it to school to raise his GPA!"

Steve didn't even hear the bickering. He had gone back to his packing, lost in the dread of the inevitable meeting with Dick tomorrow morning.

What would he say? What had Steve accomplished?

Nothing. Steve had fluffed it one hundred percent, and didn't even have an excuse. It was time for some creative thinking on the flight home.

Another knock and the Andrews stepped in, wanting to continue the DisasterLand tradition and trade signatures on the T-shirts.

Afterwards, the families tearfully moved out onto the walkway where they stood together, staring at the madness winding down below as the makeshift stores' final sales were coming to a close. More and more families were awaiting their departure at the white doors on every floor.

They were ending the trip the way it had begun.

"Falls were great, Beyers. We went back this morning."

"Yeah, really something, hunh?"

"Well worth fighting for!" Jim said, slapping Steve painfully on the back.

"I just can't believe we didn't find them earlier," Jenny said. "So beautiful. We got there just after sunrise."

"That's the best time," Steve said.

"Next time," Jim added with a wink and a laugh.

"Next time," Steve agreed, almost wistfully.

The stage below had long-ago been dismantled but Smaug still haunted Sarah's thoughts. She couldn't stop thinking about Katie and Neil, missing them like they were good friends, somehow even more than her friends at home. They seemed... adult or something, *sophisticated.* She hoped she'd be sophisticated too once she moved to New York.

A ring interrupted the family's chit-chat and after a few confused moments Steve realized it was the phone inside their suite.

Steve apologized and hurried inside, sharing one final hug with the Andrews who were booked on an early bus to the airport.

"Hello?" Steve answered, out of breath.

"Steve Beyers?" the voice confirmed.

"Yes..."

"Del Sol here, sir. We've got a table confirmed for you in one hour."

"You do?"

Barb stuck her head inquisitively into the suite, and Steve mouthed the question. Barb denied responsibility.

"I'm sorry, but we didn't make..."

"Our invitation, sir. On the house."

"*On the house?* But our flight..."

"Don't worry about that, sir. We look forward to seeing you soon."

"Thank you," Steve said, carefully replacing the phone. He scratched his head in wonder.

On the house?

Elektra tossed her suitcase back into the closet, frustrated. Packing was way too much to think about, just now. Way, way too much. She just didn't have the energy.

Between now and her frantic escape to McCarran, every minute had been blocked out. *Every friggin' minute.*

Yesterday's script breakdown had gone long, with all sorts of side-debates and ego-posturing accompanying what had been a surprisingly antagonistic meeting with territorial battles at every turn. Most of today would be spent hurriedly patching up loose ends before tomorrow's casting session. Then there was Jimmy's memorial.

She had just been reviewing Jude's casting tapes again in light of *Avalanche* and yesterday's meeting, but under these stifling conditions of profound sleep-deprivation and lack of time, she hadn't felt particularly insightful.

Her brain was about to throw in the towel.

In many ways she was angry at Shae for keeping this story a secret, yet she knew it had been the right choice. With this weight on her shoulders during the show, this distraction, she truly might not have made it through.

But now they were in a pinch, casting-wise. They needed a couple of superheroes but the specifics remained elusive, at least for her. And under these conditions, her trusted subconscious wouldn't have time to work.

Bottom-line: she'd fly to New York with nothing but a toothbrush and the clothes on her back. If she felt like it, she'd pick up a couple of things there, in New York. If not, then... not.

Who the hell would care?

Where they were headed they wouldn't need any clothes. *That was the whole flippin' point.*

Right now, she'd make a nice chamomile tea instead.

Her phone rang. Molly.

"What's up?"

"Have I got some news for you," Molly giggled. "I've cracked the mystery!"

"Mystery?"

"The cameraman, remember? Your shower? *The video?* I can put you in touch with someone who knows."

"You're joking."

"I'm not. She wouldn't talk to me, but she says she'll talk to you. Only you. In person. Today."

"No shit... *she?*"

"So whaddaya gonna do?"

In the midst of everything else, Elektra was being asked to meet with a pervert. Or at least the friend or acquaintance of a pervert.

"Look, Mol, I can't."

"*Are you serious?* I've just cracked the code, girl!"

"Not now. Not today. Can it wait?"

"I don't know. She might get cold feet."

"Well, find out. The water's up to my nose here. But the good news is I'm going to make it through airport security in record time."

The Beyers decided to spend the intervening time below, on the atrium floor. DTV Promos had been hyping the final sales all morning and the Beyers' resistance had slowly been worn down. They would investigate.

In the end, being amongst the last die-hard shoppers to swarm the tents might just raise their deflated spirits as would coming across some nice gifts for friends. Already, the idea of another brunch at Del Sol, inexplicably without charge, was a significant step in the right direction.

The family had donned their new T-shirts and headed for the elevators, pausing to wait on the landing outside Café Dansant which had formally reopened despite the ruined state of its interior.

Through what remained of the windows, the elderly couple waved them in. They were eating muffins.

"You folks have a good time?" Mildred asked.

"I suppose we did," Steve answered. "In a way."

"You were something to watch," the elderly gentleman said.

"Especially your fall, honey," Mildred added. "You were lucky."

Sarah nodded.

"How do feel now?"

"OK," said Sarah.

"No injuries?"

Sarah shook her head.

"That's wonderful. What about you others, must be something to see that."

"I just saw it for the first time Friday night," said Barb. "They hadn't even *told me*."

"And how do you feel?"

Barb was taken aback by the questions, but their interest seemed genuine and after Thursday's... *lessons*... she felt the need for honesty, if not true openness.

"I think I understand. I mean, at first I was angry, you know, shocked, but I... I don't know... I think I would have been a wreck if they had told me that night. I'm just so glad she's OK." Barb laid her arm across Sarah's shoulder.

"Of course..." agreed Mildred. "You've got some family there. You two can be very proud of 'em."

"Hey, you were sure right about the butterfly backpack," Pete said.

"We're right about a lot of things," the gentleman answered.

"I gotta ask you folks again if you don't mind," Steve said, "forgive me, but I still don't see you guys fitting the target demographic."

"We're staff psychologists," the gentleman said, wiping the corners of his mouth with his napkin. "For DisasterLand. Just making sure everyone's OK if you know what I mean."

"So I guess you had some inside information," Steve said.

"You could say that," the gentleman replied. "Or you could say inside *disinformation* which might be more accurate."

His eyes gleamed.

"Well thanks for taking the time to visit with us. You've just had your exit interview," Mildred confirmed. "And you've passed."

Steve shook his head. "This place is really something."

"You don't know the half of it, my friend," the gentleman laughed.

They shook hands warmly and the Beyers returned to the elevator.

Tiring of their image as cult celebrities, the Beyers had second thoughts about appearing in public. But once on the floor, all reservations had quickly disappeared as the full panoply of human emotion again spread out before them.

They hurried past the tents still overflowing with bargain-hunters and on to DarkRoast for a quick coffee. There, last goodbyes were being said over cappuccinos and e-mail addresses exchanged by the young and old.

Barb noticed Zander and his family in the distance. She pointed them out to Pete.

"He's a sore loser mom."

Pete turned away, but Zander's family was already approaching. His dad was forcing him by the looks of it.

"Good Morning, I'm Jerry Bentley and this is Latisha," he said, to Steve.

The families exchanged hugs.

"Good to meet you properly," Jerry said. "The other night we..."

"Don't worry about it," Barb said, "I'm sorry I..."

"Don't worry about that either."

"What happens in DisasterLand stays in DisasterLand," Latisha laughed.

"So how long have you been dating?" Barb asked innocently.

"We just met," Latisha said, smiling proudly.

"Here? *Really?*" Barb feigned surprise. Zander and Pete couldn't understand why.

"Happens all the time."

"That's fantastic!"

"We're going to be seeing lots of each other," Jerry said. "We're only a few hours drive away. I'm in Atlanta and she's in Savannah."

"It was meant to be."

Jerry's eyes grew distant. "My wife died last year in a car accident... it's been so good for me to be here, to begin to socialize again. I was hoping to meet someone like Latisha. And it happened!"

"This is a wonderful place, isn't it?"

"It's just so nice to be able to talk to your neighbors and not have to worry... everyone's been screened, you've got something to talk about. I just wish there was a real place like this. I'd move here in an instant."

"I'd join you," Steve laughed. "I think."

The parents looked over to their kids who seemed to have made up. Pete was squirming around, acting out his descent into the labyrinth.

"Maybe they can see each other outside of DisasterLand?" Barb ventured.

"Why not? We could arrange something... that would be fun."

"Pete tells me you're a dentist?"

"Oral surgeon actually."

"I'm sorry we didn't get to spend more time together," offered Steve.

"Don't worry, I had my hands full."

"You sure did!" Latisha responded, giving Jerry the eye.

"Hey, would you folks sign our T-shirts?" Barb asked.

"Only if you'll sign ours."

Passing the world-class stainless-steel refrigerators in their *I Survived DisasterLand* T-shirts, Steve gave Barb an awkward, slightly bemused shrug.

Del Sol had been almost completely deserted, but the Maître d' promptly escorted the Beyers through the kitchen to a private dining room in back.

They were seated at the round, antique hardwood table without menus and Steve began to grow more formally concerned.

"Your waiter will be with you momentarily," the Maitre 'd said, a twinkle in his eye. "Enjoy your meal."

The door shut behind him and the family waited in silence. The room continued the rustic feel of the main dining space, taken to the next level. Lush oil paintings of the Mediterranean landscape hung on the walls, contrasting with the dark simplicity that otherwise surrounded them. Yet even the simplicity, they realized, was somehow extravagant. Barb and Steve exchanged brief, frantic glances.

"What are we doing here, Steve?"

"Don't ask me! They just called and said we had a reservation."

"For the private dining room?"

"I don't know, honey. They probably feel bad for last weekend, you know, seating us next to those two kids. The whole thing happening right in front of us. *I would.*"

"You're aware there's an empty seat at this table, aren't you."

"Of course I am, honey, I'm not stu..."

The door swung open and their waiter entered, breaking the tension. It was the same gentlemen from the previous weekend and Steve winked at Barb knowingly.

Impressively having brought Bloody Marys for Steve and Barb and orange juice for the kids, the waiter re-introduced himself with a smile. A fixed menu would be offered, but after hearing it Pete wasn't impressed.

"I want a triple DisasterBurrito," he said.

"Don't be a trouble-maker, Peter," Barb chided. "We are their guests."

The waiter was staring into the distance, deep in thought. Finally, he stated with certainty, "I don't believe a triple is physically possible..."

Pete scowled.

"But I could bring you two doubles, sir."

"Yo, you in my head, man!"

"*Peter!*"

"Anything else?"

There wasn't.

Fifteen minutes later the meal arrived, more than any had dared wish for. It was a sumptuous feast fit for royalty, not a family of bourgeois Midwestern suburbanites. Amazonian tropical fruit salad, cremé brúlee brioche French toast, Italian white truffle scrambled eggs, hand-cured mesquite artisan slab bacon. As a tip of the cap to Latin culture, they also included two cactus ratatouille crêpes.

Steve speculated during breaks of near orgasmic reverie that they had been seated in back because of their pedestrian clothing. Barb took exception, arguing they represented DisasterLand's heart and soul and the salt of the earth.

Pete agreed, insisting they were *keepin' it real,* "This is *the people* talkin', DJs!" he said, arms out, hands motioning back to him.

Once again, they had stuffed themselves into a daze and Steve was the first to recover as the massive table was being cleared.

"If I'm going to stay conscious for the trip back, I'm gonna need a latte," Steve informed their waiter.

"Two," Barb said.

"Hot chocolate, bro," Pete said and Sarah doubled it.

"Of course," the waiter said, efficiently disappearing.

Steve checked his watch, grimly. "We gotta chug these folks or we're gonna be late. The bus leaves in twenty-five minutes."

"I can't believe this is it," Sarah said.

"Two more weeks and you'll be in a new home," Barb said, choking back emotion.

"Really worked well, didn't it," Steve said. "The timing of all this I mean."

The waiter returned with their drinks and hurried out quickly. The Beyers settled uneasily in to their steaming wonders, but with no mention of how to politely leave and with the necessity of their departure growing increasingly more urgent, they were unable to fully appreciate the drinks' perfection. The lavish room began to feel strangely like a white-collar prison cell.

But just as they'd finished and Steve was preparing an exploratory trip into the hallway, the door opened and the family turned expectantly. However, it wasn't their waiter.

It was a man in his early 30's with a large smile and a tailored funky suit, familiar to them through television interviews and business magazine features. He confidently shut the door behind him.

Steve flashed a look to Barb and stood, reflexively. The rest of the family followed.

"The Beyers! *Live!*" he exclaimed and clapped his hands enthusiastically.

Shae gave Barb and Sarah a peck on the cheek and offered his hand to Steve.

"Pleasure to meet all of you. I'm Shae Gibbons, the ship's captain. Yo dude!" he said to Peter and they high-fived.

He motioned the Beyers back to their seats. "Please..."

Barb eyed Steve, concerned, and he agreed, "Mr. Gibbons, I... well, unfortunately we've got to catch the bus in a few minutes. Our flight..."

Shae brushed Steve's concerns aside as he took his own seat, "Don't worry about that. I've got a limo waiting for you after we finish."

"Oh," Steve said. "Oh... well, OK."

Something was telling him most guests didn't get to meet the CEO in a private dining room at Del Sol with a limo waiting.

"A real limo, dude? Like black and tinted and stretch and everything?" Pete asked.

"Just like that, Spike. Is that OK? No more DisasterBurritos though, I'm afraid."

"That's OK I'm stuffed. This place is the coolest!"

"So DisasterLand is your creation, Mr. Gibbons?" Barb asked.

"*Shae.* Yes, I'm the CEO and founder. This was all my idea."

"Incredible. It's a pleasure to meet you, sir. You've got a remarkable thing going here. But I'm sure you're aware," Steve said.

"I've got an idea, yes."

"You're so young!" Barb laughed.

"I've been fortunate in life so far," Shae said, knocking the rustic table. "In that

I've been the given the opportunity to begin my mission."

Shae looked around the empty table. "Can I get you anything? Dessert?"

"We just had a wonderful meal, thanks," stated Barb.

"Then let's get down to business. There's a reason I've brought you here, as perhaps you've imagined. Mr. Beyers, I'm sure you're aware you've got an exceptional family."

Steve was stunned, "Well, I suppose Barb and I try..."

"In an age of timidity, of fear, you're an exception. You've got heart, you've got *passion*."

Steve was growing embarrassed.

"Yes, well, sorry about the whole... you know, the whole taking over DisasterLand thing."

Shae laughed, "It's all part of the trip, Mr. Beyers."

"*Steve.*"

"Steve... And it makes our job so much easier."

"What do you mean?" asked Barb.

"We can't just write people like you, Barb. We can only write situations for our guests and then hope."

Shae paused, looking each of them in the eye.

"Fortunately, each show some very special people come forward and enrich the whole experience for everyone. But it's never been a whole family with that *special something*. We've just never had one family influence a show so strongly."

Steve glanced at Barb, unsure of where this was headed. Shae sensed that, and smiled.

"My question is, what are you doing in a month?"

All eyes landed on Steve.

"I don't understand," he finally admitted.

"You're revolutionaries, Steve. You inspire, you *change*. We like that. Come to DisasterLand, be a force for change."

Pete gurgled in blissful amazement. Barb scowled at him.

"We're not revolutionaries," Steve chuckled, "What do we know about revolution?"

"Doesn't matter what you *know*. It's in your heart Beyers. You're a born leader of men."

Steve examined his speechless family.

"I was looking over the releases you submitted," Shae continued, "Tell me, Persistent, what do they do?"

Persistent!

"Medical advertising, both direct to consumer and direct to provider. Largely pharmaceutical. *In fact...*"

"And you're heading up the creatives?"

"One team."

"And it's killing you."

"I..." Steve felt Barb's glance, "Yes, I... well, last Thursday I sort of decided I'd start examining a career change."

"Well, there you go. Careful what you wish for."

Steve had started to argue but it was ridiculous... it was clear, crystal clear. The something that he'd been missing in his life, the flame that had been snuffed out was *passion*. It was *heart*. And Shae was right. DisasterLand had rekindled the flame.

"You mean you want to hire us? *All of us?*"

Shae nodded.

"Right now?"

"Yes."

"But you must have people queuing up for miles to work at this place."

"In a word: you're *proven*." Shae sank back into his dark leather seat. "We've got the best HR department, the best casting team in the world—but even they can't predict on-the-job performance. We lose a couple people every show—they just can't take it. They crack. The pressure, the intensity, the level of commitment. This kind of thing you can't tell by a resumé or an interview. But we know *you*—each one of you," Shae said, pausing, meeting their eyes. "Each one of you made things happen. You don't quit. You don't crumble. You're fighters."

"If you saw us two weeks ago..." Steve said.

Shae laughed. "Exactly. That's my whole point. Americans are *ossified*. We're mentally trapped in the 50's, in denial of the times we're living in. DisasterLand blows this out of the water. We provide an *American initiation*. It worked for you and it works for almost everyone, though for some it's more painful than others of course."

Steve turned to his family, "So what do you guys say?"

"All of us? The kids and all? Spike's just 14 you know," Barb said.

"They're naturals."

"What about school?"

"We've got a whole staff of full-time tutors."

Barb shook her head, slowly. "I don't think I can go through that again," she said, finally. "I really don't."

"Then you can work in our spa."

Barb's eyes grew as Shae continued, "Or if you want to tutor, we could always use you there. Or both."

Steve realized the practical implications, "But Sarah's going to Columbia in two weeks. She's..."

"The economics don't make sense, Beyers. She's going to drop 35G's a year instead of making it? For what? Anyone can go to college at any time."

Shae turned to Sarah, "You want to be a journalist?"

She nodded.

"Well we've got DTV, right here. We've got the daily paper. But personally, I'd like to see you act."

Steve stared. Shae was serious. *Totally serious.*

"Let's talk numbers," Steve said. "I mean, generally."

"Big."

"Big numbers?"

"Big ones."

"Big to you or big to me?"

"Both."

Steve leaned back, dazed.

Shae continued, "We provide housing in our village—the kids will live with other actors in the under-21 wing, you'll live in the professional wing."

"No stairs, right?" Barb asked.

Shae laughed, "Only if you want. But you'll have a similar view. Think of your stay on nineteen as an honor. Floors are assigned based on medical histories. It meant you're in great shape."

"It was beautiful," Barb said, her family agreeing.

"I can show you an apartment now if you'd like. I can't show you anything else, not until you sign, but I can show you the housing."

Once again, Steve found himself unable to speak.

"Well, I guess we might as well just take a look," Barb said, meekly, and the kids cheered.

"Then follow me!"

Shae rose and led the way to the door. Reaching it, he turned.

"You're a revolutionary, Beyers. If you stay on, you'll be known only as Ché."

Elektra and Molly were strolling across the atrium floor towards the theater, a profound serenity warming their beings at last. Minutes ago, Elektra had fogged her windows, ceremonially closing the show.

In just over 24 hours, they would be gone.

The last of the guests had departed roughly ninety minutes earlier and Shae was currently bidding the VIPs a memorable goodbye at DmZ. Elektra had popped in earlier to exchange autographs with the appreciative entertainers, this time staying well past her traditional one cocktail to unwind. It always amazed her who they managed to entertain—and how profoundly each had been affected.

Afternoon shadows were creeping over the village's ruined architecture, seductive in its disfigured beauty. In its midst, crews were constructing a small stage, sound system and multiple wet bars for the memorial and staff party to come.

A chill tickled Elektra's spine—within the ashes of the atrium lay the promise of a new show. The crew had finally put aside differences and come together, finishing the script's breakdown with the air of competitive competition that had marked their best work. It had been a profound relief.

Sanitation teams were silently swarming the entirety of DisasterLand, from the tower down to the atrium, with separate skilled DL:GreenTeams tackling damage to the park. Multi-disciplined workers were trailing them to swiftly begin the ruin's deconstruction.

In a few short days the tower would be remade, and *Avalanche*'s alpine village would begin to take form. Elektra had been told that crews from the top-secret construction warehouse had already begun to arrive, and were currently unloading the enormous platforms under wraps in the employees' parking lot in preparation for rigging.

Filtering into the theater in the lingering emotional twilight, a mood of somber satisfaction permeated DisasterLand's staff.

Elektra saw Clint limping in on his crutches and called out to him. She excused herself and hurried over. As best he could, Clint gave her one of his famous bear hugs and she gladly accepted it.

"Look," she said emotionally, "I'm sorry about everything."

"Don't worry about it, E. Seriously. I understand. The one thing this place doesn't do is relationships."

"You're right about that..."

She fidgeted awkwardly, concerned they would become a spectacle.

Clint leaned in, "Hey, thanks again for tipping me to Carlos."

"See? It does pay to sleep with the top."

"That's what got me in the mess in the first place," he laughed.

Got YOU in the mess?, Elektra thought, but ignored the remark. They were, after all, being watched.

"Well, look, great job, OK? Really fantastic. I'm proud of you," she said.

"Thanks, E. So where you headed for vacation?"

"Island hopping in the Caribbean. You?"

"Back to North Carolina to see the family and do some serious fishin' with my buds."

"Well have a great time, I'll see you next month."

"Yeah, see you."

"Catch a big one for me."

"Hey, E," he said, hobbling closer, "can you put in a good word for me in casting? I'll be OK in a few weeks and I don't want to..."

"Clint, man, you're so far above that..." Elektra said. *But it never hurts.* "Of course I will, sweetie. As best I can."

They shared another hug and Clint hobbled off to take his featured place onstage to sustained applause.

While he waved a crutch in acknowledgement, Elektra took up her own traditional place with Molly, in the front row.

The atmosphere electrified as Shae took the stage. His energy, his glow, was infectious, feeding back with the masses at his feet.

Pride washed over him like a warm tide and he felt overwhelmingly at one with the universe. He was perfectly configured, right place, right time. He was in his element and he would do whatever it took to stay there.

"Happy Birthday, DisasterLand!" he cried, and somehow the roar increased in volume. Elektra held her ears.

Two large video walls over Shae's head showed the assembled FunHouse troops howling from their separate locations.

"A bit premature, but sounds good, doesn't it?" Shae said, once the applause had died down. "Actually, we're close. Closer than I ever dared imagine. I mean that. Friends, today is all about future. But before we tackle the future we must pay homage to the present... and the past."

His eyes were glistening, and he motioned Jimmy's parents onstage. Jimmy's smiling face appeared on the screens behind him and before Shae could continue he was drowned out with applause. Applause which went on for several minutes as Jimmy's highlights reel was replayed, leaving everyone in both the FunHouse and theater in tears. Jimmy's second-generation Japanese-American parents stood waving, politely, welcoming the unexpectedly authentic outpouring of love.

After the reel's end, Shae intervened and managed to quiet the room.

"After this, we will have a short, formal memorial to Jimmy Ono, who touched us all with his bravery and spirit. Please join us. Jimmy will be buried tomorrow afternoon in Oregon, and there is more information available from the office if you're planning to attend.

"One thing I do want to acknowledge here, once and for all, are the truly amazing reactions of all of you who were on during those first few terrible moments. You were each truly grace under pressure, and for that I thank you all. This ship could have gone down in those moments, we were lurching, but instead we emerged, each of us, stronger."

Jimmy's parents quietly retook their seats below as Jimmy's picture faded out.

"Now," Shae said, "From the past to the future. I need to introduce the actor who stepped in under a great deal of pressure to perform absolutely flawlessly. Friends, Lhasa Lapsong!"

Lhasa took the stage with a smile, the tears still lingering in his eyes. Shae passed him the microphone and Lhasa took a moment to compose himself.

Onscreen, his final scene played—Red Admiral stumbling out of Good Health dramatically, pulling the gun and shooting the three terrorists on the walkway above, then finally turned it on himself.

"Thursday night," Lhasa began, "Shae took me to dinner. I thought it was a nice gesture, meant to thank me for filling in at the last moment. I expected him to tell me that Jimmy was expected to return next show, and that he probably wouldn't need me for a while, if ever."

The room was silent.

"That's when he told me the truth about Jimmy."

Lhasa was staring out into space, above the heads of those crowded into the theater. "I'm glad you guys didn't tell me right away, I don't know how I would have reacted. I don't know if I could have kept my composure. But I have to take a moment to say how awkward it is for me, how odd it is to be hired under these circumstances. But I will do the best I can, and in each of my actions I will pay tribute to Jimmy, who was undoubtedly a master of his craft. Since the show ended, I've had the chance to review much of his career here at DisasterLand, and I have no trouble using those words to describe Jimmy's work. Thank you all, and I look forward to this journey we are all on together."

Lhasa bowed toward Jimmy's parents, finally allowing himself to scan the appreciative audience, recognizing many already-familiar faces.

"This place is very special, you all know that. I thought I knew how special before I came, but I didn't. Because I *couldn't*.

"And *that* is the magic of this place: no one does. I didn't, you didn't and the guests certainly don't. The guests have seen the news, they've heard the rumors and they've even watched the DVD. But they don't know," he said. "They *can't know*. And neither could I. Because this place is simply *beyond belief*."

He paused, letting the words sink in, allowing the profound appreciation he felt to be shared with all.

"I knew I wanted to make a difference in people's lives and in the world we're in, that's not easy," he continued. "In fact, sometimes the world seems designed to alienate people, to splinter families and to ensure individual hope slips away.

"But that is the real magic of DisasterLand: despite the odds, it *does* work. It *does* heal. I have seen that to a degree I never could have imagined."

A roar of applause echoed throughout the theater and from the FunHouse.

"What I've experienced this week has touched me profoundly. The power of this place is undeniable, the journeys our guests have undertaken unimaginable.

"DisasterLand accomplishes the impossible so utterly convincingly as to make it the everyday. But you know this: you've seen the faces. You've seen lives transformed firsthand."

Lhasa collected himself, switching gears in summary.

"No one ever forgets their first time, and it has been a pleasure to witness each and every one of you doing what you do best. This show was truly a joy to experience and be a part of, and I look forward to many, many more. I am excited to be joining you on this journey, and I thank Shae and all of you for the opportunity to be a part of it. Most of all, I will never forget Jimmy."

The theater rose to their feet to join the raucous yells from the FunHouse as Lhasa handed the microphone to Shae who discreetly wiped away a tear.

"I'm just glad they don't drug test," Steve whispered.

"Shae was very good-sported about that..." Barb quietly concurred.

Steve was glowing, stuffed full of pride, a delicious breakfast and the prospect of imminent personal satisfaction and far greater wealth.

In less than twenty-four hours, he would tell his boss and the entire advertising industry to very literally *fuck off*. There could be no greater joy.

The Beyers were tucked away in the limo with DisasterLand's sparkling twin domes fading into the distance behind them as they ascended the pass.

Li'l J had been there to see them off, dressed in a Lakers tracksuit and ball cap, and Barb had cried as they had said their goodbyes—despite the still unbelievable news that they would be back.

It just didn't seem real.

And Li'l J couldn't have been happier.

They passed the security center and it was obvious the damage wasn't nearly as extensive as it had appeared from the tower. It had been flattened, yes, but somehow just beforehand, or perhaps even during the blast itself, the vital core had been sunk beneath the ground. Already it had been raised, and the center seemed, for the most part, as good as new.

The mood in the limo was electric, the knowledge they'd soon return still swirling in their minds and heightening their senses. Their lives were about to change, profoundly.

For their departure Shae had offered the employee entrance but Steve refused, believing it more important to bring the entire journey full-circle. They would exit as guests. And as they had made their way through the glowing universe to exit, Steve had paused so they could bring those first moments back.

The crowds, the happy honeymooners in front of them, the dance of MagicD, but also the worries of his job, his marriage and his mental condition.

It had only been a week but truly seemed a lifetime ago. A different lifetime, or even someone else's. This alone had convinced him they were now on the right track. He had found himself again, after a long absence, and DisasterLand had made it happen.

Now he would help others. In just over two weeks, they would be back for training.

"I'm going to start doing yoga, Barb."

She stared.

"I don't believe you."

"No, this is a commitment. My body's falling apart honey, my mind. I lost control there for a while. There was no one at the wheel. And I'm not letting that happen again."

It sure beats the Happinol, he thought.

Barb hugged him. "I think that's the best thing you've ever said to me. Other than whatever that Swahili thing was that got us hitched."

"Don't repeat that in front of the kids, honey."

"Are you guys gonna get all lovey like you used to, DJs?"

Sarah kicked her brother. Barb and Steve cuddled in reply.

"No more DJ, Spike. From now on, I'm Ché. You heard the man."

"Then I," Pete said, arms outstretched, "am *Chéito!*"

The DisasterLand sign passed silently above them and Barb understood.

It was keeping watch. It was guarding their safety.

And she trusted it.

494

D-i-s-a-s-t-e-r-L-a-n-d®

JOHN NIERNBERGER is a graduate of New York University's Tisch School of the Arts and has worked in almost all aspects of film production and post-production in New York, Kansas City and Los Angeles for over 10 years. He produced and directed the short film *Petrol Mart* and also wrote, produced and directed the experimental narrative short *The Happy Guy*.

John was the first content manager for Chris Blackwell's pioneering and Webby-award winning website sputnik7.com, where he supervised video encoding and production. Previously, he produced the Publishers' Spotlight section of the Bowker website bookwire.com for two years.

He has written for *PW Daily*, *Publishers Weekly* and *Res* magazine. This is his first novel.

www.ingramcontent.com/pod-product-compliance
Lightning Source LLC
Chambersburg PA
CBHW030752260626
47169CB00001B/17